OXFORD WORLD'S CLASSICS

CRIME AND PUNISHMENT

FYODOR MIKHAILOVICH DOSTOEVSKY was born in Moscow in 1821, the second in a family of seven children. His mother died of tuberculosis in 1837, and his father, a generally disliked army physician, died in apparently suspicious circumstances on his estate two years later. In 1843 he left the College of Military Engineering in St Petersburg and devoted himself to writing. *Poor Folk* (1846) met with great success from the literary critics of the day. In 1849 he was imprisoned and sentenced to death on account of his involvement with a group of utopian socialists, the Petrashevsky circle. The sentence was commuted at the last moment to penal servitude and exile, but the experience, described in *Memoirs from the House of the Dead* (1861–2), radically altered his political and personal ideology. In 1857, while still in exile, he married his first wife, Maria Dmitrievna Isaeva, returning to St Petersburg in 1859. In the early 1860s he founded two new literary journals, *Time* and *The Epoch*, and proved himself to be a brilliant journalist. He travelled in Europe, which served to strengthen his anti-European sentiment. Both his wife and his much-loved brother, Mikhail, died in 1864, the same year in which *Notes from the Underground* was published; *Crime and Punishment* and *The Gambler* followed in 1866, and in 1867 he married his stenographer, Anna Snitkina, who managed to bring an element of stability into his frenetic life. His other major novels, *The Idiot* (1868), *Devils* (1871), and *The Brothers Karamazov* (1880) met with varying degrees of success. In 1880 he was hailed as a saint, prophet, and genius by the audience to whom he delivered an address at the unveiling of the Pushkin memorial. He died seven months later in 1881; at the funeral thirty thousand people accompanied his coffin and his death was mourned throughout Russia.

NICOLAS PASTERNAK SLATER is the translator of several works by Boris Pasternak, including *Family Correspondence 1921–1960* (2010) and *Doctor Zhivago* (appearing 2019). He has also published translations of stories by Lermontov, Pushkin, Tolstoy and Chekhov.

SARAH J. YOUNG is Associate Professor of Russian at the School of Slavonic and East European Studies, University College London. She has written extensively on Dostoevsky.

OXFORD WORLD'S CLASSICS

*For over 100 years Oxford World's Classics have brought
readers closer to the world's great literature. Now with over 700
titles—from the 4,000-year-old myths of Mesopotamia to the
twentieth century's greatest novels—the series makes available
lesser-known as well as celebrated writing.*

*The pocket-sized hardbacks of the early years contained
introductions by Virginia Woolf, T. S. Eliot, Graham Greene,
and other literary figures which enriched the experience of reading.
Today the series is recognized for its fine scholarship and
reliability in texts that span world literature, drama and poetry,
religion, philosophy, and politics. Each edition includes perceptive
commentary and essential background information to meet the
changing needs of readers.*

OXFORD WORLD'S CLASSICS

FYODOR DOSTOEVSKY

Crime and Punishment

Translated by
NICOLAS PASTERNAK SLATER

With an Introduction and Notes by
SARAH J. YOUNG

OXFORD
UNIVERSITY PRESS

OXFORD
UNIVERSITY PRESS

Great Clarendon Street, Oxford, OX2 6DP,
United Kingdom

Oxford University Press is a department of the University of Oxford.
It furthers the University's objective of excellence in research, scholarship,
and education by publishing worldwide. Oxford is a registered trade mark of
Oxford University Press in the UK and in certain other countries

Translation © Nicolas Pasternak Slater 2017
Editorial material © Sarah J. Young 2017

The moral rights of the authors have been asserted

First published 2017
First published as an Oxford World's Classics paperback 2019

Impression: 1

Published in the United States of America by Oxford University Press
198 Madison Avenue, New York, NY 10016, United States of America

British Library Cataloguing in Publication Data

Data available

Library of Congress Cataloging in Publication Data

Data available

ISBN 978-0-19-870971-8

Printed and bound in Great Britain by
Clays Ltd, Elcograf S.p.A.

CONTENTS

CRIME AND PUNISHMENT

INTRODUCTION

Readers who do not wish to know details of the plot may prefer to read this Introduction as an Afterword.

A HUNDRED AND FIFTY years after its first publication, *Crime and Punishment* continues to fascinate readers. It was the first of Fyodor Mikhailovich Dostoevsky's long novels to feature not only profound debate on the most pressing philosophical and spiritual questions of the day, but also a murder plot and a level of intrigue and tension associated more commonly with popular fiction than high literature. It established the author's reputation as both a philosophical and a psychological novelist, generated huge levels of debate about contemporary Russian society and ideology, and exerted a degree of influence on subsequent Russian culture that is perhaps comparable only to the position of Shakespeare within British culture. From its role as an inspiration for Andrey Bely's 1913 modernist masterpiece *Petersburg*, to its absurdist rewriting in Daniil Kharms's short story 'The Old Woman' (1939) and its postmodern transformation in Viktor Pelevin's novel *Chapayev and Void* (1996, also translated as *The Clay Machine Gun*), Raskolnikov's story has become a ubiquitous part of St Petersburg lore. Visitors to the city can follow in the anti-hero's footsteps with guided tours of *Crime and Punishment*'s locations, taking in the plaque on the tenement where he lived and graffiti pointing out the moneylender's flat. Dostoevsky Day, celebrated in the city on the first Saturday in July with exhibitions, street theatre, and processions, coincides not with the author's anniversaries, but the novel's opening. *Crime and Punishment* is a permanent fixture on lists of the world's greatest novels, and has inspired almost forty film and television adaptations in over a dozen languages, as well as countless theatre productions. There are graphic novel and manga versions, even Raskolnikov transformed into a superhero. And although a whydunnit rather than a whodunnit, it has influenced the portrayal of numerous fictional detectives, most famously American TV's Columbo.

Why does this story of an impoverished student who commits murder in the grip of an idea, the wily detective who pursues him, the saintly prostitute who wants to save him, and the sinister libertine who encourages him to embrace his dark side, speak to so many cultures, and continue to resonate so strongly today? One of the reasons is that Raskolnikov's psychic and family drama, followed in compellingly

claustrophobic detail by a narrator who remains very close to the protagonist, turns a supposedly cold-blooded killer into a sympathetic hero.
He may wish to be a Napoleon, capable of overstepping all obstacles on
his way to greatness (the Russian word for 'crime', *prestuplenie*, is closely
connected to the verb 'to transgress', *perestupit´*), but the love he inspires
in those around him, and his own spontaneous acts of compassion and
generosity towards others, reveal the conflicting sides of his nature
that he is unable to reconcile. This psychological exploration of
a murderer—by an author whose own prison experience gave him the
opportunity to study killers of all types at close quarters—depicts all
the temptations and horrors of crime, the fear of being caught and the
urge to confess. It reveals the oppression, despair, and disgust of lives
lived in poverty, the profound necessity of changing that world, but also
the danger of rationalistic, utilitarian thinking that replaces human
beings with abstractions. Few literary works can match its power and
urgency, or its sympathy for 'the insulted and humiliated', as Dostoevsky
called Petersburg's poor in a novel of 1861. Even as they destroy their
families and peer into the abyss, the murderer Raskolnikov and the
drunkard Marmeladov still have the possibility of redemption. In his
first work to incorporate consistently the religious questions that
reflected the author's growing faith, love, not Napoleonic grandeur, is
the great transformative force.

Dostoevsky's Life

Dostoevsky's biography was as dramatic as the plots of his novels. Born
in Moscow in 1821, Fyodor was the second son of an army doctor, Mikhail
Andreevich, who practised at the Mariinsky hospital for the poor.
Hailing from a family of clergymen, Mikhail had been raised to the
nobility through his state service,[1] but the family remained impoverished
despite his professional ability and social pretensions. Family finances
were further damaged by the purchase of a small estate near Moscow
that failed to yield a decent income, exacerbating Mikhail Andreevich's
naturally irritable temperament. By contrast Dostoevsky's mother,
Maria Fyodorovna, who took charge of the estate whilst her husband
remained in Moscow to work, gained a reputation as a humane and
compassionate landowner. Both parents were devoted to their children's

---

[1] The clergy was a distinct social estate in imperial Russia, with generally hereditary
membership. Hereditary nobility was at the time bestowed on public servants who
reached the eighth grade in the Table of Ranks. See Note on the Table of Ranks, p. xxvi.

education, instilling in them a love of European and Russian literature as well as a solid religious upbringing. Both the religious dimension of Dostoevsky's novels and his use of Gothic features and melodramatic plots can be traced back to his childhood reading. However, when it came to formal education and planning his children's future careers, Mikhail Andreevich favoured the military he had chosen himself, and sent his two eldest sons to Petersburg to study at the Academy of Military Engineers in 1837. Their mother died shortly before their departure, and their father two years later. Rumours long circulated to the effect that he had been murdered by his serfs in revenge for his brutal treatment, and this version of events is repeated in numerous critical and biographical works.[2] It now seems likely that he in fact died of a stroke, but Dostoevsky himself appears to have believed the rumours and felt his own measure of responsibility for the supposed crime.[3]

In 1843 Dostoevsky graduated from the Engineers' school and began work as an officer in the Petersburg military planning department, but his interest in literature was already apparent. He soon resigned his commission, and published his first work, a translation of Honoré de Balzac's novel *Eugénie Grandet*. He gained access to literary circles through his friend from schooldays Dmitry Grigorovich, soon to become a prominent author in his own right, and met the influential literary critic Vissarion Belinsky and the radical publisher and poet Nikolay Nekrasov. Their praise for Dostoevsky's first original fictional work, the epistolary novel *Poor Folk*, guaranteed its success on its first appearance in 1846. His fortunes were soon reversed, however, when Belinsky attacked his 'fantastic' story *The Double*, published in the same year. Both these and his other early works conform to the social critiques of Petersburg life that were popular at the time, but also begin to develop Dostoevsky's trademarks: the hero's self-consciousness and need for affirmation from others, depictions of mental and emotional disturbance, and the split personality.

During this period Dostoevsky became involved in a philosophical discussion circle, named after its founder, Mikhail Petrashevsky, where radical and socialist ideas were debated. In April 1849 Dostoevsky was arrested along with other members of the circle for seditious activity,

[2] Notably, it was the basis of Sigmund Freud's analysis of *The Brothers Karamazov*; Freud saw Dostoevsky's epilepsy as having its origins in his own desire to murder his father. See 'Dostoevsky and Parricide', in Sigmund Freud, *Art and Literature*, ed. Albert Dickson, trans. James Strachey (London: Penguin, 1990), 437–60.

[3] See Joseph Frank, *Dostoevsky: The Seeds of Revolt, 1821–1849* (Princeton: Princeton University Press, 1976), 379–92.

and in December of that year the men were convicted and sentenced to death. The first three to be executed were already tied to the scaffold on Semionovsky Square in St Petersburg—Dostoevsky was in the second group—when a messenger rode up to commute their sentences to penal servitude in Siberia. Dostoevsky served four years of hard labour in the Omsk penal fortress, living alongside some of Russia's most violent criminals from amongst the peasantry. This experience, like his near-execution, unsurprisingly had a lasting influence on his outlook. It led gradually to what he described as the rebirth of his religious faith. He described himself in a famous letter of 1854 to the widow of one of the Decembrist revolutionaries as 'a child of the age, a child of unbelief and doubt', but admitted that nevertheless he would 'rather remain with Christ than with the truth'.[4] Following completion of his sentence, he was exiled to Semipalatinsk in what is now Kazakhstan as a common soldier. He was recommissioned as an officer in 1857, and married a local widow, Maria Isaeva, although the marriage was never happy. In the same year, he was diagnosed with epilepsy. He resumed his writing career, and in 1859 was able to publish two new short works, the humorous *Uncle's Dream* and *The Village of Stepanchikovo*. Permitted to return to European Russia, he soon threw himself back into literary life in Petersburg, founding a journal, *Time*, with his brother Mikhail, and publishing a fictionalized account of his imprisonment, *Memoirs from the House of the Dead*, which re-established his name after his prolonged absence from the literary scene.

In the early 1860s Dostoevsky's life became increasingly chaotic. An affair with Apollinaria Suslova, later a model for his heroines Polina in *The Gambler* and Nastasia Filippovna in *The Idiot*, was conducted mainly on visits to Europe, where he also developed a passion for gambling. The journal he was running—relaunched as *The Epoch* after trouble with the censorship—fell into financial difficulties, and ultimately folded early in 1865. The year 1864 saw the deaths of both his wife and elder brother; the former left a recalcitrant teenaged son to support, the latter debts for which Dostoevsky assumed responsibility. The same year also marked a turning point in Dostoevsky's literary career. His novella *Notes from Underground* for the first time featured the ideological dimension that became the key component of his mature novelistic voice. Its polemic with the new generation of radicals inspired by socialist and utilitarian ideas, and the figure of the

---

[4] Letter to N. D. Fonvizina, in F. M. Dostoevskii, *Polnoe sobranie sochinenii v tridtsati tomakh* (Moscow and Leningrad: Nauka, 1972–90), xxviii/1. 176.

proto-existentialist anti-hero, are the features with which Dostoevsky became so associated. He further developed both aspects in *Crime and Punishment*, and combined them with the insights he gained into the criminal mind whilst serving his prison sentence. The novel was published in serial form in the prominent journal the *Russian Messenger* in 1866, where it appeared to great acclaim alongside Tolstoy's *War and Peace* (which was serialized from 1865 to 1869), attracting an estimated 500 new subscribers to the periodical.[5]

Dostoevsky never had the private income that many of his contemporaries in the literary world enjoyed. He was instead entirely dependent on the money he earned from his writing and publishing endeavours, and his severe financial problems, exacerbated by his gambling and the family debts he took on, meant that he was routinely offered worse terms for his novels than his independently wealthy rivals Tolstoy and Turgenev. Such chaotic circumstances, which were particularly acute whilst he was working on *Crime and Punishment*, led him to accept a potentially disastrous contract with an unscrupulous publisher, F. T. Stellovsky. According to its terms, if he did not produce a new novel by the end of October 1866, he would lose all the rights to his work, both past and future. With less than a month left to the deadline and the book not yet begun, Dostoevsky employed a young stenographer, Anna Snitkina, who helped him complete *The Gambler* just in time. In the process they fell in love, and married in February 1867, but were forced to leave Petersburg soon after because of his debts. For almost four years they led a nomadic and troubled existence in Europe. Dostoevsky wrote *The Idiot* there, and began work on *Devils*, but they were impoverished by his gambling, dogged by his poor health, and suffered the death of their first child, Sonia. Returning to Petersburg in 1871, and living a gradually more stable life due to his wife's astute management of their affairs, Dostoevsky completed *Devils* and *The Adolescent* (also translated as *A Raw Youth* and *An Accidental Family*). In between his novels, he began to publish his *Writer's Diary*, a monthly compendium of frequently provocative essays on contemporary Russian life, politics, and culture that reflect his growing conservatism and often virulent religious nationalism. It also includes some of his best short stories: 'The Dream of a Ridiculous Man', 'Bobok', and 'The Meek Girl'. His health worsened, and he was diagnosed with pulmonary

[5] William Mills Todd III, 'Dostoevskii as a Professional Writer', in William J. Leatherbarrow (ed.), *The Cambridge Companion to Dostoevskii* (Cambridge: Cambridge University Press, 2002), 83.

emphysema in addition to his increasingly severe epilepsy. In 1879, when serialization of his final novel *The Karamazov Brothers* had just begun, his 3-year-old son Aliosha died following an epileptic seizure. Dostoevsky himself died in Petersburg of a pulmonary haemorrhage shortly after completing *The Karamazov Brothers*, in January 1881.

St Petersburg: Literary and Social Contexts

In his later years, Dostoevsky increasingly spent time outside St Petersburg, but as an author he is closely associated with the city. The role of *Crime and Punishment* in establishing that connection cannot be overstated. Operating on the level of both literary myth and concrete social context, the acute impact of Russia's imperial capital on Raskolnikov's psyche exemplifies the notion of the 'Petersburg text'.[6] The literary image of Petersburg was by this time already well established, most famously in the works of Alexander Pushkin and Nikolay Gogol. The story of the founding of the city by Peter the Great has become a literary legend thanks to Pushkin's *The Bronze Horseman*. This 1833 narrative poem vividly depicts Peter commanding the building of Russia's new, Western-facing capital, and its subsequent construction on the bones of slaves on the inhospitable banks of the Gulf of Finland, leaving it with a notoriously bad climate and vulnerability to flooding. Like several of Gogol's stories, Pushkin's poem features the 'little man' oppressed and driven insane by Petersburg's inhuman bureaucracy. The close association of the city with insanity and death engenders a hallucinatory dimension that causes Étienne Falconet's statue of Peter the Great to come to life in Pushkin's poem, a nose to detach itself and assume an identity of its own in Gogol's 'The Nose' (1835–6), and a socially inept civil servant's doppelgänger to appear in Dostoevsky's *The Double*. As Svidrigailov says to Raskolnikov, 'There aren't many places where the human soul is subject to so many gloomy, violent, and strange influences as here in Petersburg' (p. 413).

Petersburg as a locus of both oppression and the fantastic is often associated with the fogs, floods, and blizzards that assail the city in late autumn and winter. *Crime and Punishment* depicts the city's weather at its opposite extreme: an intense heatwave that would have been

---

[6] V. N. Toporov, *Peterburgskii tekst russkoi literatury* (St Petersburg: Iskusstvo SPb, 2003). On the 'Petersburg' theme in *Crime and Punishment*, see Valentina Vetlovskaia, 'Dostoevsky and Pushkin: Petersburg Motifs in *Crime and Punishment*', in Sarah Young and Lesley Milne (eds.), *Dostoevsky on the Threshold of Other Worlds* (Ilkeston: Bramcote Press, 2006), 21–39.

particularly oppressive in the wretched conditions of the poorest and most overcrowded district of the city, around the Haymarket Square and the Ekaterininsky (now Griboyedov) Canal, where the novel is set.[7] Dostoevsky's temporal location of the novel's action precisely reflects recorded weather conditions in Petersburg in early July 1865, the year in which the author began work on it.[8] The novel's geography is equally exact: not only are street names given, but in most cases specific buildings are indicated either through precise descriptions and directions in the narrative itself, or through identification by Anna Dostoevskaya, who recorded the prototypes her husband showed her.[9] We see Petersburg through Raskolnikov's eyes as he haunts the area close to his tiny garret—on Stolyarny Lane, where Dostoevsky himself lived at the time—and absorbs its febrile atmosphere, mentally mapping the city (he counts the number of steps from his own building to the pawnbroker's flat), and daydreaming about a Haussmann-style reconstruction of the centre.[10]

The use of real locations embeds the novel and its hero's perspective in the city, so that it becomes a part of his consciousness. But it also emphasizes the real-life social context as a significant dimension of the novel. Following the emancipation of the serfs in 1861 and the large-scale migration to urban centres that it sparked, the rapid growth of Petersburg exacerbated already high levels of deprivation and overcrowding, particularly around the Haymarket. Alcohol abuse and prostitution gave this area its reputation as the city's squalid underbelly: the sixteen buildings on Stolyarny Lane housed eighteen drinking dens at the time, and brothels and dosshouses filled the streets around the Haymarket itself. In the novel, Raskolnikov's regular encounters with drunks and prostitutes on the streets indicate the prominent place they hold in the hero's perception; they fall within our field of vision because he cannot help but notice them. The question acquires an individual dimension in the form of the Marmeladov family, when Raskolnikov makes the acquaintance of the alcoholic ex-civil servant Semion

[7] On the conditions of this part of the city in the mid-nineteenth century, see James H. Bater, *St Petersburg: Industrialization and Change* (London: Edward Arnold, 1976), 166–77.

[8] B. N. Tikhomirov, *'Lazar! Griadi Von'. Roman F. M. Dostoevskogo 'Prestuplenie i nakazanie' v sovremennom prochtenii: Kniga-kommentarii* (St Petersburg: Serebriannyi vek, 2005), 45–6.

[9] N. P. Antsiferov, *'Nepostizhimyi Gorod ...'* (Leningrad: Lenizdat, 1991), 222–3. The topography of the novel is explored at 'Mapping St Petersburg: Experiments in Literary Cartography', http://www.mappingpetersburg.org/site/?page_id=494.

[10] See Adele Lindenmeyr, 'Raskolnikov's City and the Napoleonic Plan', *Slavic Review*, 35/1 (1976), 37–47.

Zakharovich Marmeladov in a tavern, learning that his wife Katerina Ivanovna is dying of tuberculosis and the family's destitution has driven his daughter Sonia into prostitution. Indeed, Dostoevsky's earliest plan for the novel, before he developed the character of Raskolnikov, the murder plot, or its ideological dimension, focused specifically on 'the present question of drunkenness [. . . in] all its ramifications, especially the picture of a family and the bringing up of children in these circumstances'.[11] This plot moves into the background in the published version, but the poverty to which it relates continues to play a central role. Beyond the penury and social problems he witnesses around him, and his own experience of hardship—seldom having enough to eat, being forced to give up his studies, and not even having sufficiently decent clothes to earn money by giving lessons—Raskolnikov also equates Sonia's position with his sister Dunia's decision to marry for money for the sake of her family. The Marmeladovs represent a level of destitution his own family might easily reach, and the limited choices available to prevent that happening.

Motives for Murder: The Ideological Context

The acute awareness the Marmeladov family gives him of the precariousness of existence underlies one of Raskolnikov's apparent motives for the murder of Aliona Ivanovna. Developed in his mind before the beginning of the novel, but given fresh urgency in the run-up to the crime through his encounter with Marmeladov and the letter from his mother outlining his sister's marriage plans, the idea of murdering the pawnbroker in order to steal her wealth promises to kill two birds with one stone. It would not only eliminate a parasite who sucks the blood of the poor, but also provide a means to relieve poverty—his own and others'. At the expense of one small act of evil, great good could be achieved. Both the altruism of desiring to act for the benefit of society and the reasoning Raskolnikov uses to calculate that benefit derive from the utilitarian thinking adopted by the young radicals known as 'nihilists', who were influenced by the writer and critic Nikolay Chernyshevsky's concept of 'rational egoism'. Equating the good with the pleasurable, this theory viewed humans as physiological beings unhindered by the dualistic impulses of a soul or spirit, and capable of rationally identifying and acting upon their own self-interest, which inevitably coincides

---

[11] Letter to A. A. Kraevskii, June 1865, in Dostoevskii, *Polnoe sobranie sochinenii*, xxviii/2. 127.

with the wider benefit of society. Dostoevsky's narrator in *Notes from Underground* challenges this idea on the basis that humans are as much irrational as they are rational beings, and will even act against their own self-interest to prove they have freedom and individuality. *Crime and Punishment* revisits the question in a different form: the ideology of utilitarian calculation and the greater good, which reduces ethics to a simple matter of arithmetic, is used here to justify murder.

Dostoevsky makes the connection explicit in a letter of September 1865 to his future publisher Mikhail Katkov, editor of the journal *Russian Messenger*. He describes *Crime and Punishment* as 'the psychological account of a crime', in which 'a young man, a student suspended from the university, [. . .] living in extreme poverty, from giddiness, from weak understanding, succumbing to certain "unfinished" ideas floating around in the air, decided to escape his wretched position in a single stroke. He decided to kill an old woman, the widow of a Titular Councillor, who lent money for interest.'[12] The notion of ideas 'in the air' is emphasized in the novel when Raskolnikov discovers that he is far from the only one to contemplate such plans. When he overhears a student and an officer discussing the very same moneylender in a tavern he is astounded by the similarity of their thoughts to his own:

A hundred, a thousand good deeds could have been done, and enterprises set up or put to rights, on the old woman's money—which is all going to be wasted on a monastery! Hundreds, perhaps thousands of human beings could be given a start; dozens of families saved from beggary, decay, ruin, vice, venereal disease; and all with her money. If you killed her and took her money, and used it to devote yourself to serving all humanity and the common good: what do you think, wouldn't those thousands of good deeds wipe out that one tiny little crime? One life for thousands of lives, rescued from corruption and decay! One death, in exchange for thousands of lives—it's simple arithmetic! Anyway, what does the life of that consumptive, stupid, wicked old crone count for, when it's weighed in the balance? No more than the life of a louse, a cockroach—even less, because the old woman's actually harmful. (pp. 59–60)

Emphasizing the ease with which such utilitarian thinking can devalue human life despite its apparent root in compassion, the incident also normalizes Raskolnikov's idea within his own mind. Encountering it by chance in another's words enables him to characterize it merely as one of those 'commonplace everyday arguments such as he'd often heard before', so that he is not forced to face the reality of planning to murder in cold blood.

---

[12] Dostoevskii, *Polnoe sobranie sochinenii*, xxviii/2. 136.

At the same time, the coincidence of the conversation affirms his thinking, endowing it with an almost prophetic significance: 'why had it happened at this precise time, for him to hear this particular conversation and these particular thoughts, when his own mind had only just conceived... *precisely those same thoughts?*' The student Raskolnikov overhears, and by extension Raskolnikov himself (as he has just had '*precisely those same thoughts*'), assume the murder will enable a level of altruism that borders on the miraculous, helping 'hundreds, perhaps thousands of human beings'. The extent of the imagined benefits seems even more improbable when we consider the sums actually mentioned: Raskolnikov envisages stealing 3,000 roubles, but succeeds in taking only 317 roubles and 60 kopeks, and fails to find the 'fifteen hundred roubles in cash, not to mention banknotes' in the moneylender's dresser (p. 135). Compared to the 10,000 roubles Svidrigailov offers to Dunia, or the debt of 70,000 roubles the former's wife Marfa Petrovna paid off when they married, these are relatively trivial amounts. To do the type and number of good deeds envisaged would require a superhuman effort, even a superhuman personality.

The exaggerated sense of what may be achieved with the limited spoils from killing a low-level moneylender therefore suggests a degree of self-aggrandizement underlying this purportedly humanitarian venture. This exposes the connection of his supposed altruism to another, overtly anti-human, version of Raskolnikov's motivation: to test the theory that he is a 'great man', a Napoleon to whom laws do not apply and everything is permitted, regardless of the human cost. Critics have often viewed Raskolnikov's charitable and Napoleonic motives as contradictory, revealing the split in his personality indicated by his name (which means 'schism').[13] But they can also be seen as two sides of the same coin, not least because they prove to spring from the same source: 'commonplace everyday arguments'. Raskolnikov tells Sonia, 'I worked out an idea, for the first time in my life, which nobody had ever thought of before me! Nobody!' (p. 370). Yet this claim to be original has already been subverted; as the detective Porfiry Petrovich comments in response to Raskolnikov's article, which advances the argument that one-tenth of humanity is extraordinary and beyond the law, 'which of us Russians doesn't regard himself as a Napoleon these days?' (p. 235). The ironies surrounding Raskolnikov's attempt to prove his superiority pile up. Would a Napoleon be content to have his plan affirmed

---

[13] See e.g. Konstantin Mochulsky, *Dostoevsky: His Life and Work*, trans. Michael A. Minihan (Princeton: Princeton University Press, 1967), 282–3.

by a conversation overheard in a pub? Would a Napoleon need a charitable alibi for his actions? Whether he aims to achieve greatness through extraordinary deeds for the sake of others, or for himself alone, Raskolnikov's attempt to create his own identity is undone intellectually as much by the unremarkable and inconsistent nature of his ideas as by any incompatibility between them.

The Divided Self

The different emphases in the justifications Raskolnikov advances for the murder of the old woman suggest not just a lack of resolution, but also an overdetermination of his motives that only partially covers up their moral and intellectual insufficiency. They also indicate the growing tensions within his psyche, as conflicting external pressures augment his contradictory inner impulses. Before he commits the crime, he is placed in an untenable position by his mother's letter. Casting him as the perfect son and brother for whom any sacrifice is worthwhile, her words also reveal her misgivings about her potential son-in-law's character and behaviour, to imply that such a good son would never permit his sister to make the sacrifice she is planning.[14] The murder has indeed been interpreted as an attempt not to help his family but to free himself of the emotional burden placed on him by his mother through the proxy of his debt to the moneylender.[15] As Dostoevsky's exploration of motivation moves into the hero's unconscious, the horrific dream of the horse being beaten to death reveals the depth of Raskolnikov's inner conflict, and its connection to his own family. Raskolnikov as a small child in the dream is full of compassion and tries to protect the horse (connected here with Lizaveta, his second victim, through the refrain of their 'gentle eyes'). But he is also Mikolka, the frenzied peasant bludgeoning the horse and pronouncing his own morality, as Raskolnikov will also claim to do (the words Mikolka repeatedly screams, 'My property', in Russian are *Moe dobro*, literally 'My good'; as in English, *dobro* has both ethical and possessive meanings). The false confession to the murders by another Mikolka, the house painter and schismatic (*raskolnik*) later reinforces this connection. Meanwhile Raskolnikov's

---

[14] Malcolm V. Jones, *Dostoyevsky After Bakhtin: Readings in Dostoyevsky's Fantastic Realism* (Cambridge: Cambridge University Press, 1990), 79–82.

[15] W. D. Snodgrass, 'Crime for Punishment: The Tenor of Part One', *Hudson Review*, 13 (1960), 202–53 (at 219); Edward Wasiolek, 'Raskol´nikov's Motives: Love and Murder', *American Imago*, 31/3 (1974), 252–69.

father—absent from the rest of the novel—exhorts Rodia not to get involved, but his failure to intervene instead forces his son to take on all roles, however incompatible.

Raskolnikov's representation within the dream as both defender and attacker is replicated elsewhere in the novel. He acts with spontaneous compassion and generosity to protect the young girl from the predator who is about to assault her in the scene just before this dream, and he offers financial assistance to the Marmeladov family after Sonia's father's fatal accident. But he just as quickly switches into reverse, leaving the girl to her fate and instantly regretting the money he has given the Marmeladovs. He acts in just as contradictory a manner in relation to the murder itself. Waking from his dream, he is horrified at the idea that he might kill in this way:

I always knew I could never make myself do it, so why have I been tormenting myself all this while? Even yesterday, yesterday when I went to do that... *rehearsal*, I knew perfectly well then that I couldn't manage it. So now what? Why have I been in doubt even up to now? Yesterday, when I was going downstairs, I myself said it was loathsome, wicked, vile, vile... the very thought of it made me sick, filled me with horror, even when I was *awake*... (p. 54)

Returning to the city from the islands, he 'renounces' this dream. But immediately afterwards, as he walks through the Haymarket and learns when Lizaveta will be away from the old woman's flat, his mind changes again.

The lack of emotional and mental stability Raskolnikov exhibits is exacerbated by a strong sense of fatalism. The coincidence of overhearing Lizaveta is significant less for what she says than because Raskolnikov himself ascribes meaning and causality to chance events. As with the conversation he overhears in the pub that affirms his supposedly altruistic intent, he views the information Lizaveta supplies as providing not so much an opportunity for the crime as a portent of it: 'he was always superstitiously struck by one fact which, though not a particularly unusual one, seemed in a way to have foreshadowed his fate' (p. 55). But this recourse to fate suggests that far from being a great man shaping his own destiny, he actually views himself as being at the mercy of forces beyond his control.

Raskolnikov's fatalism would appear to offer him a means of absolving himself of responsibility for his actions, but it in fact does nothing to rescue him from the workings of his conscience after the crime. From his fever and his failure to do anything with the proceeds of his crime, to his sudden desire to confess to the police clerk Zametov in the

Crystal Palace tavern and his growing isolation and inability to speak to his family, everything points to his increasing sense of guilt, however little he is able to admit to any remorse. And if he is troubled subconsciously by his crimes, then the uncertainty of his situation haunts him on a conscious level, a factor exploited by Porfiry Petrovich. Raskolnikov's inability to see into the detective's mind is contrasted with Porfiry's apparent omniscience: the latter, disconcertingly, seems to know exactly what is going on even before the two meet. This not only contributes to Raskolnikov's doubts and sense of his own inability to control events, but also leads him to seek contact with others who offer a different dynamic and the possibility of resolution that Porfiry deliberately withholds.

Doubles

In his *Writer's Diary* for 1877 Dostoevsky wrote that he had 'never expressed anything in [his] writing more serious than [the] idea' that he introduced in *The Double*, his—at the time—unsuccessful 1846 novella about a lowly government official whose social isolation and mental instability lead to him being confronted by a doppelgänger who represents everything he wants to be but cannot.[16] Dostoevsky abandoned attempts to revise the work substantially in the 1860s (an edition with minor revisions was published in 1866, and it is this version that we generally read today), and he never revisited the figure of the doppelgänger in the fantastical form of its earliest incarnation. Yet the idea of human duality remained a crucial component of his fictional world, and he continued to regard the double as a 'supremely important social type'.[17] Critics have concurred, long viewing 'doubling' as a fundamental key to interpreting the interrelations of Dostoevsky's characters.[18] No longer residing in the realm of the unreal, doubles in Dostoevsky's later fiction are instead embodied characters whose psychic connections with the hero reveal the conflicting and irrational aspects of his personality.

In the case of Raskolnikov, the two relationships he develops in the second half of the novel, with Marmeladov's daughter, the prostitute Sonia, and Svidrigailov, the depraved gentleman whose unwelcome advances

---

[16] Fyodor Dostoyevsky, *A Writer's Diary*, trans. Kenneth Lantz (London: Quartet, 1995), ii. 1134. [17] Dostoevskii, *Polnoe sobranie sochinenii*, xxviii/1. 340.

[18] See Dmitri Chizhevsky, 'The Theme of the Double in Dostoevsky', in Rene Wellek (ed.), *Dostoevsky: A Collection of Critical Essays* (Englewood Cliffs, NJ: Prentice Hall, 1962), 112–29, and Roger B. Anderson, *Dostoevsky: Myths of Duality* (Gainsville: University of Florida Press, 1986).

compromised Raskolnikov's sister, reflect the contradictory impulses and underlying divisions within his character. On one level, they represent the options he faces following his crime: repentance and absolution, or acceptance of all the moral consequences of the ideology of 'everything is permitted'. But Sonia and Svidrigailov's connection to each other, the similar roles they play in Raskolnikov's psychic drama, and the extremes they symbolize, indicate that they are also more than this. They appear in the action of the novel at almost the same point. Sonia has briefly been seen at her father's deathbed, but it is only when she visits Raskolnikov to invite him to the funeral that her role within the hero's story is established. In the same chapter, Svidrigailov follows her home and discovers that they live in neighbouring flats in the same building. This circumstance subsequently enables Svidrigailov to eavesdrop on Raskolnikov's conversations with Sonia, giving him the opportunity to insert himself into events and offer his own solution to Raskolnikov's dilemma.

Beyond their parallel roles in the plot, Sonia and Svidrigailov also share ambiguous status as characters. Both have an air of unreality about them. Svidrigailov's direct contact with Raskolnikov begins when he seems to emerge from the latter's dream at the end of Part Three. Later, the uncanny aspect of his physical appearance is emphasized:

It was an odd face, almost like a mask—part pale, part pink, with ruddy crimson lips, a light-coloured beard, and fair hair that was still quite thick. His eyes were somehow too blue, and their look somehow too heavy and unmoving. There was something terribly unattractive about that handsome face, so extraordinarily young for his years. (p. 414)

Svidrigailov's face here seems unsettlingly inhuman, almost vampiric. The hints of the undead continue with his admission that he sees the ghosts of his late wife and of a servant he supposedly killed, suggesting that this character is himself close to the afterlife he envisages, of a dirty bathhouse full of spiders. He even argues that the sicker a person becomes, 'the more contact he has with the other world' (p. 255). Sonia, meanwhile, borders on being a fantasy. She represents a degree of innocence that reminds us how close to childhood she is, a strong and mature religious sensibility, a transgression that puts her on the same footing as Raskolnikov, and the voluntary acceptance of suffering that shows him his possible future path. In other words, Sonia's traits, however improbable when combined in one character, correspond precisely to the needs of Raskolnikov's conscience. This suggests that both characters function as constructs of his mind, externalizing his contradictory impulses. Indeed, Raskolnikov identifies both Sonia's and Svidrigailov's significance to him long before he meets either, from the very first reference to them: in Marmeladov's drunken monologue of Part One Chapter II (Sonia) and in the letter he receives from his mother in the following chapter (Svidrigailov). Thus although they have an independent, embodied existence beyond Raskolnikov's purview, they are also his own projection of the images first presented to him. In the case of Sonia in particular, Raskolnikov appropriates her as the symbol of redemptive suffering that Marmeladov propounds,[19] and she continues to play this role for most of the novel because we seldom see beyond Raskolnikov's view of her.

'Realism in a Higher Sense'

The ability of these two typically extreme Dostoevskian characters to maintain an embodied existence within the bounds of the novel, at the same time as originating in a verbal image presented to Raskolnikov and then developed by his divided mind, indicates the extent to which the author departs from the conventional realism of the day. Petersburg realia certainly crowds into the novel, and certain aspects of the plot, mainly relating to the Marmeladov family, contain strong echoes of the 'Natural School' poetics of critical realism popular in the 1840s. But the elements of everyday life we see are filtered through Raskolnikov's perception, indicating that Dostoevsky's focus is less on the supposedly objective depiction of reality than on the subjective experience of his characters. That transcends the physical world in various ways: through altered states of consciousness such as dreams, hallucinations, and epileptic auras, and through access to eternal planes of existence beyond death. While critics have come to use the term 'fantastic realism' to denote this aspect of his fiction, Dostoevsky described it as 'realism in a higher sense', a means of depicting 'all the depths of the human soul'.[20] By that he perceived a move beyond psychology to encompass the spiritual dimension that plays an increasingly prominent role in his post-Siberian novels.

In *Crime and Punishment*, it is primarily through the figure of Sonia that the religious aspect of the novel is channelled. Conscious of her own sin, her belief in divine justice gives her hope that her family

---

[19] Elizabeth Blake, 'Sonya, Silent No More: A Response to the Woman Question in Dostoevsky's "Crime and Punishment"', *Slavic and East European Journal*, 50/2 (2006), 252–71 (at 255).   [20] Dostoevskii, *Polnoe sobranie sochinenii*, xxvii. 65.

will be rescued from destitution, and it is to this that Raskolnikov, on the verge of despair even before he commits the crime, is attracted. Impelled to seek her out by his own guilty conscience and desire for redemption, he taunts her with the possibility that God might not exist as much to try to convince himself as her; if there is no God, then his calculation that led to murder might be correct. But in doing so, Raskolnikov also opens himself up to Sonia's faith. It is he who asks her to read the story of the raising of Lazarus from John's Gospel, in what has always been one of the novel's most controversial scenes. He is reminded of the story when Porfiry asks him whether he believes in it, and with the reawakening of his religious sensibility through his contact with Sonia, Raskolnikov recognizes that he is as much in need of the arbitrary miracle it represents as she is.

Sonia's faith is also significant because of the connection it creates with Lizaveta, Aliona Ivanovna's half-sister and Raskolnikov's second victim. The Bible from which Sonia reads belonged to Lizaveta—they used to read it together—and she now wears Lizaveta's simple wooden cross; it is clear that this meek, defenceless figure, about whom we know so little before she dies, was also a woman of faith. Her murder thus becomes unjustifiable in any terms, and this is why Raskolnikov persistently forgets about it: he is only able to think of the crime he planned, and the rationalizations he invented in order to execute it. Sonia's very presence, as well as her friendship with Lizaveta, undermines his justifications by confronting Raskolnikov with his second crime. This is, moreover, the only recognition Lizaveta's death receives, as even Porfiry, who equally wants Raskolnikov to confess and face his punishment, tends to refer solely to the first murder. The detective's psychologizing approach may leave Raskolnikov anxious and uncertain, but he still presents the crime in Raskolnikov's own terms. For that reason he proves unable to make the murderer rethink what he has done in the way that Sonia ultimately may.

That process begins only in the novel's Epilogue. Even when he confesses the fact of his crime first to Sonia and then to the police, Raskolnikov remains unrepentant and unable to accept he has done anything wrong, viewing his actions rather as an error of calculation. In the prison camp in Siberia, away from the oppressive and unnatural atmosphere of St Petersburg, his perspective gradually changes. The catalyst for Raskolnikov's transformation appears to be his nightmare of the pestilence that sweeps across Europe and sends people mad, as if possessed, whilst convincing them of the superiority of their own reason, which leads to wars and the destruction of almost all human life. The connection of this apocalyptic vision with Raskolnikov's own 'infection' with ideas is clear. Yet if the dream acts as a revelation to him, it is Sonia's constant presence, and the love she inspires amongst the other convicts—while he is despised as a nobleman and an atheist—that brings him unconsciously to the point where he is open to mental and spiritual transformation, and is finally ready to open the Bible she has given him.

The reappearance of Sonia's Bible in the closing moments of the novel roots this scene in Dostoevsky's own prison experience and the 'rebirth of his convictions' that began there. Reference to the banks of the River Irtysh tells us that Raskolnikov is imprisoned in Omsk, as was the author. The description of the New Testament Sonia gives to Raskolnikov, and from which she previously read the story of the Raising of Lazarus, matches that of Dostoevsky's own copy, given to him in Tobolsk on his way to serve his sentence by Natalia Fonvizina, the widow of one of the Decembrist revolutionaries. The only book he was permitted in prison, this Bible became one of Dostoevsky's most treasured possessions, which remained with him for the rest of his life and became the foundation for his own religious faith.

Such an autobiographical connection ought to endow the Epilogue with great authenticity. However, for many readers, the opposite is the case, as Raskolnikov's putative conversion hits a false note that appears to derive from the author's personal convictions rather than his artistic sensibilities. Konstantin Mochulsky may be more extreme than most critics in describing it as a 'pious lie', but many find it clumsy or implausible, concluding that the novel should have ended with Raskolnikov's confession.[21] Yet however problematic the Epilogue may appear, it is important to recognize the centrality of questions of faith within Dostoevsky's novelistic world. Indeed, in Russia since the collapse of the Soviet Union, scholarship has focused increasingly on the Orthodox Christian basis of Dostoevsky's work. Much of that research has proved invaluable, for example in its identification of Dostoevsky's use of biblical subtexts, but it can also result in a narrow view that equates his fiction with the more strident views expressed in his later journalism, and posits the author as a religious dogmatist, his novels as worthy tracts. For many readers, neither epithet fully accounts for the tumultuous world he depicts, in which doubt and the outright rejection of faith are often in the ascendancy. Questions about ethical and

[21] Mochulsky, *Dostoevsky*, 312; Edward Wasiolek, *Dostoevsky: The Major Fiction* (Cambridge, MA: MIT Press, 1964), 84.

spiritual life are part of what the scholar Mikhail Bakhtin identified in his seminal study _Problems of Dostoevsky's Poetics_ as the dialogue of Dostoevsky's characters and ideas. That dialogue continues throughout his novels, but is never finalized, and no world view emerges unambiguously triumphant. Even if Dostoevsky as a person believed in the necessity of a spiritual life, as an artist he created his characters as self-conscious carriers of their own ideas rather than vehicles for the author's beliefs. Thus the religious dimension participates in the dialogue and often represents the ideal, but it never fully overcomes other voices.

The emergence in the Epilogue of _Crime and Punishment_ of a faith restored is an affirmation of Sonia's religious world view, which seems to confirm the view of Dostoevsky as an Orthodox writer. Yet even if her Christian meekness and love have proven more viable than Raskolnikov's flawed will to power, his transformation remains in the realms of potential. He may now entertain the possibility of overcoming his pride and suffering, and recovering the compassion that we have glimpsed throughout the novel, but he still does not open her Bible. As the narrator widens the perspective to encompass the future 'story of the gradual renewal of a man, of his gradual rebirth, his gradual transition from one world to another' (p. 486), the removal of Raskolnikov's conversion from the pages of the novel renders it uncertain, for any 'new tale' remains unwritten and unfixed. Moreover, the reference to 'some great exploit in the future' that he will have to undergo as the price for this new life, alludes once more to his past striving for greatness, which may yet reassert itself in some way. For all the Epilogue's change of tone, therefore, it retains a sense of open-endedness that prevents it asserting any single truth. And that, rather than its perceived problematic nature, may be why critics continue to argue about it 150 years after it was written.

NOTE ON THE TRANSLATION

THE translator's task, ideally, is to produce a version that a modern reader will find fluent, natural, and stylish, while remaining faithful to the author's original text. Since such an ideal is generally unattainable when translating a literary work, a compromise has to be found. This is not a one-off choice: it has to be made afresh every step of the way, and the nature of the compromise will shift and fluctuate with the shifts in the author's language. Dostoevsky's style is sometimes strained, sometimes rough, and a purist could find many faults in it; but it is always direct and powerful.

I have tried to keep to an easily readable English style that doesn't smack too much of translation. In the dialogue, in particular, I have favoured colloquial English expressions over close adherence to the Russian ones: my guiding principle was 'What would this character actually have said (in English) at this point?' At the same time, it was important to keep to colloquial expressions with something of a neutral flavour, not too redolent of twenty-first-century London. The reader will judge how far I have succeeded.

The rendering of Russian names is always a problem. There are rules of transliteration from Russian, adopted with good reason by academic experts, which I have not followed, as they often produce awkward-looking English equivalents inappropriate in a story for the non-specialist reader. I have tried in each case to produce a name that bothers the English reader as little as possible (not always easy, with names like Lebeziatnikov or Svidrigailov). My ad hoc approach can lead to minor inconsistencies in the handling of certain Russian letters and combinations of letters, but for these I make no apology. Where a name (especially a place name) is generally familiar to educated English-speaking readers, I have stuck to the usual English spelling. The form of abbreviated place names (such as V——— Prospekt) has been standardized.

NOTE ON THE TABLE OF RANKS

THE Table of Ranks was introduced in 1722 by Peter the Great as part of his efforts to modernize Russia by establishing a European-style bureaucracy, encouraging state service, and weakening the power of the hereditary nobility. Each civil service rank had military and court equivalents, and (in theory at least) promotion through the ranks was open to all. Hereditary nobility was originally bestowed at the eighth grade, but this was raised in the 1840s and again in the 1850s; when *Crime and Punishment* was set, a civil servant would need to reach the fourth grade to gain hereditary nobility, and a military officer the sixth grade. The Table of Ranks was abolished in 1917 after the Bolshevik Revolution.

Civil Service rank	Military ranks[1]
1. Chancellor	Field-Marshal/General-Admiral
2. Actual Privy Councillor[2]	General/Admiral
3. Privy Councillor	Lieutenant General/Vice Admiral
4. Actual State Councillor	Major General/Rear Admiral
5. State Councillor	Brigadier/Captain Commodore
6. Collegiate Councillor	Colonel/Captain 1st rank
7. Court Councillor	Lieutenant Colonel/Captain 2nd rank
8. Collegiate Assessor	Major/Captain 3rd rank
9. Titular Councillor	Captain/Lieutenant
10. Collegiate Secretary	Staff-Captain/Midshipman
11. Naval Secretary	——
12. District Secretary	Lieutenant
13. Provincial Registrar	Sub-Lieutenant
14. Collegiate Registrar	Ensign

[1] Basic army ranks are given, followed by navy variants as appropriate. Ranks and their titles varied in different branches of the armed forces and were subject to numerous changes in the eighteenth and nineteenth centuries.

[2] The Russian term *deistvitel'nyi* can be translated as 'actual', 'real', 'true', or 'active' (but not 'acting' in the English sense of gaining rank or holding a position temporarily).

SELECT BIBLIOGRAPHY

Biographical Works

Bird, Robert, *Fyodor Dostoevsky* (London: Reaktion, 2012).

Dostoevskaya, A. G., *Dostoevsky: Reminiscences*, ed. and trans. Beatrice Stillman (London: Wildwood House, 1976).

Frank, Joseph, *Dostoevsky: The Seeds of Revolt, 1821–1849* (Princeton: Princeton University Press, 1976).

Frank, Joseph, *Dostoevsky: The Years of Ordeal, 1850–1859* (Princeton: Princeton University Press, 1983).

Frank, Joseph, *Dostoevsky: The Stir of Liberation, 1860–1865* (Princeton: Princeton University Press, 1986).

Frank, Joseph, *Dostoevsky: The Miraculous Years, 1865–1871* (Princeton: Princeton University Press, 1995).

Frank, Joseph, *Dostoevsky: The Mantle of the Prophet, 1871–1881* (Princeton: Princeton University Press, 2002).

Frank, Joseph, *Dostoevsky: A Writer in His Time*, ed. Mary Petrusewicz (Princeton: Princeton University Press, 2010).

Grossman, Leonid, *Dostoevsky: A Biography*, trans. Mary Mackler (London: Allen Lane, 1974).

Lowe, David A., ed., *Fyodor Dostoevsky: Complete Letters*, 5 vols. (Ann Arbor: Ardis, 1991).

Mochulsky, Konstantin, *Dostoevsky: His Life and Work*, trans. Michael A. Minihan (Princeton: Princeton University Press, 1967).

General Studies and Collections of Essays

Apollonio, Carol, *Dostoevsky's Secrets: Reading Against the Grain* (Evanston, IL: Northwestern University Press, 2009).

Bakhtin, Mikhail, *Problems of Dostoevsky's Poetics*, trans. Caryl Emerson (Minneapolis: University of Minnesota Press, 1984).

Catteau, Jacques, *Dostoyevsky and the Process of Literary Creation*, trans. A. Littlewood (Cambridge: Cambridge University Press, 1989).

Cassedy, Steven, *Dostoevsky's Religion* (Stanford, CA: Stanford University Press, 2005).

Fanger, Donald, *Dostoevsky and Romantic Realism: A Study of Dostoevsky in Relation to Balzac, Dickens, and Gogol* (2nd edn., Evanston, IL: Northwestern University Press, 1998).

Holquist, Michael, *Dostoevsky and the Novel* (Princeton: Princeton University Press, 1977).

Hudspith, Sarah, *Dostoevsky and the Idea of Russianness* (London: BASEES Routledge, 2003).

Jackson, Robert Louis, *The Art of Dostoevsky: Deliriums and Nocturnes* (Princeton: Princeton University Press, 1981).

Jones, Malcolm V., *Dostoyevsky After Bakhtin: Readings in Dostoyevsky's Fantastic Realism* (Cambridge: Cambridge University Press, 1990).

Jones, Malcolm V., *Dostoevsky and the Dynamics of Religious Experience* (London: Anthem, 2005).

Jones, Malcolm V., and Garth Terry (eds.), *New Essays on Dostoyevsky* (Cambridge: Cambridge University Press, 1983).

Knapp, Liza, *The Annihilation of Inertia: Dostoevsky and Metaphysics* (Evanston, IL: Northwestern University Press, 1996).

Lantz, Kenneth, *The Dostoevsky Encyclopedia* (Westport, CN: Greenwood, 2004).

Leatherbarrow, William J. (ed.), *The Cambridge Companion to Dostoevskii* (Cambridge: Cambridge University Press, 2002).

Leatherbarrow, William J., *A Devil's Vaudeville: The Demonic in Dostoevsky's Major Fiction* (Evanston, IL: Northwestern University Press, 2005).

Martinsen, Deborah, and Olga Maiorova (eds.), *Dostoevsky in Context* (Cambridge: Cambridge University Press, 2016).

Miller, Robin Feuer, *Dostoevsky's Unfinished Journey* (New Haven: Yale University Press, 2007).

Murav, Harriet, *Holy Foolishness: Dostoevsky's Novels & the Poetics of Cultural Critique* (Stanford, CA: Stanford University Press, 1992).

Offord, Derek, 'Dostoyevsky and Chernyshevsky', *Slavonic and East European Review*, 57/4 (1979), 509–30.

Pattison, George, and Diane O. Thompson (eds.), *Dostoevsky and the Christian Tradition* (Cambridge: Cambridge University Press, 2001).

Peace, Richard, *Dostoyevsky: An Examination of the Major Novels* (Cambridge: Cambridge University Press, 1971).

Scanlan, James P., *Dostoevsky the Thinker* (Ithaca, NY: Cornell University Press, 2002).

Schur, Anna, *Wages of Evil: Dostoevsky and Punishment* (Evanston, IL: Northwestern University Press, 2013).

Williams, Rowan, *Dostoevsky: Language, Faith and Fiction* (Waco: Baylor University Press, 2008).

Young, Sarah J., and Lesley Milne (eds.), *Dostoevsky on the Threshold of Other Worlds: Essays in Honour of Malcolm V. Jones* (Ilkeston: Bramcote Press, 2006).

Crime and Punishment: *Sources and Secondary Readings*

Blake, Elizabeth, 'Sonya, Silent No More: A Response to the Woman Question in Dostoevsky's "Crime and Punishment"', *Slavic and East European Journal*, 50/2 (2006), 252–71.

Bloom, Harold (ed.), *Dostoevsky's 'Crime and Punishment'* (New York: Chelsea House, 1998).

Bloom, Harold (ed.), *Raskolnikov and Svidrigailov* (Broomall, PA: Chelsea House, 2004).

Cox, Gary, *'Crime and Punishment': A Mind to Murder* (Boston: Twayne, 1990).

Dostoyevsky, F. M., *The Notebooks for 'Crime and Punishment'*, ed. and trans. Edward Wasiolek (Chicago: University of Chicago Press, 1967).

Jackson, Robert Louis (ed.), *Twentieth Century Interpretations of 'Crime and Punishment': A Collection of Critical Essays* (Englewood Cliffs, NJ: Prentice Hall, 1974).

Johnson, Leslie A., *The Experience of Time in 'Crime and Punishment'* (Columbus, OH: Slavica, 1985).

Kliger, Ilya, 'Shapes of History and the Enigmatic Hero in Dostoevsky: The Case of *Crime and Punishment*', *Comparative Literature*, 62/3 (2010), 228–45.

Klioutchkine, Konstantine, 'The Rise of *Crime and Punishment* from the Air of the Media', *Slavic Review*, 61/1 (2002), 88–108.

Leatherbarrow, W. J., 'The Aesthetic Louse: Ethics and Aesthetics in Dostoevsky's *Prestuplenie i nakazanie*', *Modern Language Review*, 71/4 (1976), 857–66.

Lindenmeyr, Adele, 'Raskolnikov's City and the Napoleonic Plan', *Slavic Review*, 35/1 (1976), 37–47 (also available in Richard Peace (ed.), *Fyodor Dostoevsky's 'Crime and Punishment': A Casebook* (Oxford: Oxford University Press, 2006), 37–49).

Nuttall, A. D., *'Crime and Punishment': Murder as a Philosophic Experiment* (Edinburgh: Sussex University Press, 1978).

Offord, Derek, 'The Causes of Crime and the Meaning of Law: *Crime and Punishment* and Contemporary Radical Thought', in Jones and Terry (eds.), *New Essays on Dostoevsky*, 41–65.

Peace, Richard (ed.), *Fyodor Dostoevsky's 'Crime and Punishment': A Casebook* (Oxford: Oxford University Press, 2006).

Rice, James L., 'Raskol′nikov and Tsar Gorox', *Slavic and East European Journal*, 25/3 (1981), 38–53.

Rosenshield, Gary, *'Crime and Punishment': The Techniques of the Omniscient Author* (Lisse: De Ridder, 1978).

Historical and Cultural Contexts

Abbott, Robert J., 'Crime, Police, and Society in St Petersburg, Russia, 1866–1878', *The Historian*, 40/1 (1977), 70–84.

Barran, Thomas, *Russia Reads Rousseau, 1762–1825* (Evanston, IL: Northwestern University Press, 2002).

Bater, James H., St *Petersburg: Industrialization and Change* (London: Edward Arnold, 1976).

Beer, Daniel, *The House of the Dead: Siberian Exile Under the Tsars* (London: Allen Lane, 2016).

Bernstein, Lauric, *Sonia's Daughters: Prostitutes and Their Regulation in Imperial Russia* (Berkeley and Los Angeles: University of California Press, 1995).

Brower, Daniel R., *Training the Nihilists: Education and Radicalism in Tsarist Russia* (Ithaca, NY: Cornell University Press, 1975).

Brower, Daniel R., *The Russian City between Tradition and Modernity, 1850–1900* (Berkeley and Los Angeles: University of California Press, 1990).

Buckler, Julie A., *Mapping St Petersburg: Imperial Text and Cityshape* (Princeton: Princeton University Press, 2005).

Engel, Barbara Alpern, 'St Petersburg Prostitutes in the Late Nineteenth Century: A Personal and Social Profile', *Russian Review*, 48/1 (1989), 21–44.

Frierson, Cathy A., *All Russia Is Burning!: A Cultural History of Fire and Arson in Late Imperial Russia* (Seattle: University of Washington Press, 2002).

Hosking, Geoffrey A., *Russia: People and Empire, 1552–1917* (London: HarperCollins, 1997).

Lincoln, W. Bruce, *The Great Reforms: Autocracy, Bureaucracy, and the Politics of Change in Imperial Russia* (DeKalb: North Illinois University Press, 1990).

McReynolds, Louise, *Murder Most Russian: True Crime and Punishment in Late Imperial Russia* (Ithaca, NY: Cornell University Press, 2013).

Meyer, Priscilla, *How the Russians Read the French: Lermontov, Dostoevsky, Tolstoy* (Madison: University of Wisconsin Press, 2008).

Nekrasov, Nikolai (ed.), *Petersburg: The Physiology of a City*, trans. Thomas Gaiton Marullo (Evanston, IL: Northwestern University Press, 2009).

Smith, Alison K., *For the Common Good and Their Own Well-Being: Social Estates in Imperial Russia* (New York: Oxford University Press, 2014).

Steinberg, Mark D., *Petersburg Fin de Siècle* (New Haven: Yale University Press, 2011).

A CHRONOLOGY OF FYODOR DOSTOEVSKY

1821   (30 October) Birth in Moscow of Fyodor Mikhailovich Dostoevsky, the second son of Mikhail Andreevich Dostoevsky, an army doctor working at the Mariinsky hospital for the poor, and Maria Fyodorovna Dostoevskaya.

1825   Death of Tsar Alexander I and succession of Nicholas I. Suppression of the Decembrist uprising, hanging of the five ringleaders, and imprisonment and Siberian exile of many more.

1825–32   Publication of Alexander Pushkin's *Evgeny Onegin*.

1826   Death of writer and historian Nikolay Karamzin, author of *History of the Russian State* and the sentimental short story 'Poor Liza'.

1828   Birth of Leo Tolstoy.

1836   Piotr Chaadaev's 'First Philosophical Letter' published in the journal *The Telescope*.

1837   Death of Dostoevsky's mother of tuberculosis. Travels to St Petersburg with his older brother Mikhail and enrols in the Academy of Military Engineers.
Death of Alexander Pushkin from wounds suffered in a duel.

1838–40   Publication of Mikhail Lermontov's *A Hero of Our Time*.

1839   Death of Dostoevsky's father, probably from a stroke. Rumours persist that he was murdered by his serfs.

1841   Death of Mikhail Lermontov in a duel.

1842   Publication of part I of Nikolay Gogol's *Dead Souls*, and his story 'The Overcoat'.

1843   Graduates from the Academy of Military Engineers and works briefly in the military planning department. Publication of his first work, a translation of Balzac's novel *Eugénie Grandet*.

1845   Publication of Nikolay Nekrasov's anthology *Petersburg: The Physiology of a City*.

1846   Publication to great acclaim of Dostoevsky's first original work, *Poor Folk*, in Nekrasov's almanac *The Petersburg Collection*. *The Double* appears, to universally critical reviews.

1847   Publication of Alexander Herzen's novel *Who is to Blame?*.

1848   Death of the influential literary critic Vissarion Belinsky.

1849   Publication of *Netochka Nezvanova*. Arrested with the Petrashevsky
        circle for seditious political activities. Sentenced to death and on
        22 December subjected to a mock execution with other members of the
        Petrashevsky circle before the sentences are commuted to hard labour.

1850–4 Serves a sentence of four years of hard labour in prison in Omsk.

1851   Opening of the Crystal Palace for the Great Exhibition, London.

1852   Publication of Ivan Turgenev's *Sketches from a Hunter's Album*. Death
        of Nikolay Gogol.

1852–6 Publication of Tolstoy's semi-autobiographical trilogy *Childhood*,
        Boyhood, and *Youth*.

1853–6 The Crimean War.

1854   Released from prison and sent into exile and military service in
        Semipalatinsk.

1855   Death of Nicholas I and succession of Alexander II. Publication of
        Tolstoy's *Sevastopol Sketches*.

1857   Marries Maria Isaeva, a local widow.
        Alexander Herzen begins publication of the radical newspaper *The
        Bell* in London.

1859   Permitted to return to European Russia. Publishes *Uncle's Dream*
        and *The Village of Stepanchikovo*.
        Publication of Ivan Goncharov's novel *Oblomov*.

1860   Returns to St Petersburg.
        Birth of Anton Chekhov. Radical critic and publisher Nikolay
        Chernyshevsky publishes his influential essay on 'rational egoism',
        'The Anthropological Principle in Philosophy'.

1861   Emancipation of the serfs.
        With his brother Mikhail sets up the journal *Time*. Publishes his
        novel *The Insulted and Injured* and the fictionalized account of his
        imprisonment, *Memoirs from the House of the Dead*.

1862   Takes his first trip to Europe, including an eight-day visit to London.
        Publication of Turgenev's *Fathers and Sons*.

1862–3 Begins an affair with 21-year-old Apollinaria Suslova.

1863   Publication of *Winter Notes on Summer Impressions*. *Time* is relaunched
        as *The Epoch* after trouble with the censorship. Travels to Paris to
        meet Apollinaria Suslova.
        Nikolay Chernyshevsky's novel *What is to be Done?* published in the
        radical journal *The Contemporary*.

1864   Publishes *Notes from Underground*. Death of his wife and his brother
        Mikhail.

1865   Publishes the satirical story 'The Crocodile'. Financial problems force the closure of *The Epoch*.

1865–9 Serial publication of Tolstoy's *War and Peace* in the journal *Russian Messenger*.

1866   Serial publication of *Crime and Punishment* in the *Russian Messenger*. Meets Anna Snitkina, a stenographer who helps him to write *The Gambler* in twenty-six days to fulfil an impending contract undertaken with an unscrupulous publisher.

First attempted assassination of the Tsar, by student and revolutionary Dmitry Karakozov.

1867   Marries Anna Snitkina. They leave for Europe to escape his debts.

1868–9 Serial publication of *The Idiot* in *Russian Messenger*.

1868   Birth of the Dostoevskys' first child, Sofia. She dies, aged 3 months, of pneumonia.

1869   Birth of the couple's second daughter Liubov.

1870   Death of Alexander Herzen.

1871   Returns to Russia with his family and settles in St Petersburg. Anna gives birth to their first son Fyodor.

1871–2 Serial publication of *Devils* (also known as *Demons* and *The Possessed*).

1873   Begins writing and publication of his *Writer's Diary* in the journal *The Citizen*.

1874–5 Serial publication of *The Adolescent* (also known as *An Accidental Family*).

1875   Birth of the Dostoevskys' second son Alexei (Aliosha).

1876   Buys a summer house in Staraya Rusa, near Novgorod. Tsar Alexander II asks the author to educate his sons.

1876–7 Returns to work on his *Writer's Diary*.

1877   Serial publication of Tolstoy's *Anna Karenina*.

1878   Death of Nikolay Nekrasov.

1879   Death of Dostoevsky's son Aliosha following an epileptic seizure.

1880   Serial publication of *The Brothers Karamazov*. Delivers his famous speech at the unveiling of the Pushkin monument in Moscow.

1881   (28 January) Death of Dostoevsky in St Petersburg from a pulmonary haemorrhage.

(1 March) Assassination of Alexander II.

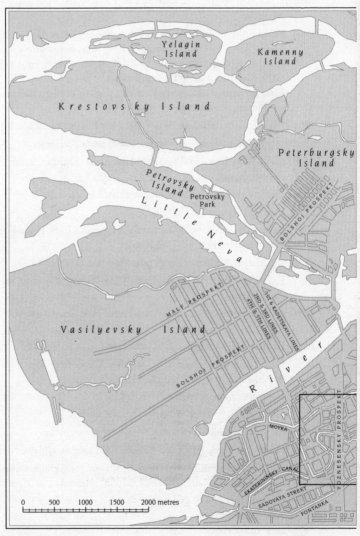

Map of St Petersburg

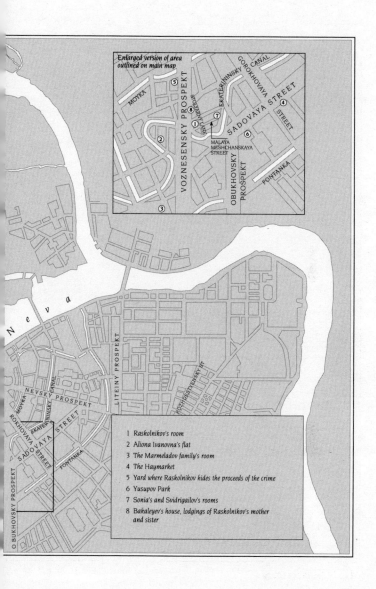

Enlarged version of area outlined on main map

GOROKHOVAYA CANAL
EKATERININSKY
VOZNESENSKY PROSPEKT
MOYKA
SADOVAYA STREET
STREET
MALAYA MESHCHANSKAYA STREET
OBUKHOVSKY PROSPEKT
FONTANKA

N e v a

LITEINY PROSPEKT
NEVSKY PROSPEKT
ROZHDESTVENSKY ST
MOYKA
EKATERININSKY CANAL
ROKHOVAYA
SADOVAYA STREET
FONTANKA
O BUKHOVSKY PROSPEKT

1 Raskolnikov's room
2 Aliona Ivanovna's flat
3 The Marmeladov family's room
4 The Haymarket
5 Yard where Raskolnikov hides the proceeds of the crime
6 Yusupov Park
7 Sonia's and Svidrigailov's rooms
8 Bakaleyev's house, lodgings of Raskolnikov's mother and sister

CRIME AND PUNISHMENT

PART ONE

CHAPTER I

ONE evening in early July, during a spell of exceptionally hot weather,* a young man came out of the garret he rented from the tenants of a flat in S—— Lane, went downstairs to the street and set off, slowly and rather uncertainly, towards K——n Bridge.*

He managed to avoid meeting his landlady on the stairs. His garret, more like a cupboard than a room, was just under the roof of the five-storey house. The landlady from whom he rented this garret, with service and one meal a day, lived in a separate flat on the floor below, and every time he went downstairs to the street he had to go past her kitchen, whose door was almost always open onto the stairway. And every time the young man passed this door, he was overcome by an uncomfortable, cowardly feeling which made him grimace with shame. He was hopelessly in debt to his landlady and afraid of meeting her.

Not that he really was so timid and cowardly; quite the reverse. But recently he had been in a tense, irritable frame of mind, almost like hypochondria. He had retreated so deeply into himself, withdrawn so completely from everyone else, that he not only feared meeting his landlady—he feared meeting anybody. He was crushed by his poverty; yet lately even his impoverished condition had ceased to weigh him down. He had completely given up managing, or wishing to manage, his day-to-day affairs. He wasn't actually afraid of any landlady, whatever she might be plotting against him. But stopping on the stairway to listen to all sorts of rubbish, everyday stuff that was none of his business, all that pestering about the rent, and threats, and complaints, and having to prevaricate and apologize and tell lies—no, better slip away downstairs like a cat, and make his escape unseen.

On this occasion, in fact, his terror of meeting his landlady and creditor surprised even himself, once he was out in the street.

'What a deed I'm planning, and yet I'm letting pointless little things terrify me!' he thought with a strange smile. 'Yes... a man is capable of anything, and yet he lets it all pass him by, out of pure cowardice... that's axiomatic... I wonder what people are most afraid of? Taking a fresh step, saying something new, that's what scares them most... Anyway, I'm chattering on too much. That's why I never get anything done—I'm too busy chattering. Actually, you could put it the other way round: the reason I chatter is that I don't do anything. It's over this past month that I've learnt to chatter, spending whole days on end lying on my bed in that corner and thinking about... Jack and the Beanstalk.* And why am I going there now, anyway? Am I really capable of *that*? Is *that* really serious? It's not in the least serious. I'm just letting my imagination run away with me—it's all a game! Yes, I suppose it's all a game!'

The heat outside was unbearably sultry; the streets were full of jostling crowds, there was whitewash everywhere, and scaffolding, and bricks, and dust, and that special summer stench that every inhabitant of Petersburg knows so well, if he isn't able to rent a dacha out of town.* All this at once assailed the young man's already shattered nerves. And the unbearable stink from the drinking dens, especially common in that part of town,* and the drunks he met at every step, although this was a working day, completed the revolting and depressing picture. An expression of profound disgust flashed across the young man's delicate features. He was, incidentally, remarkably good-looking, with fine dark eyes and dark auburn hair, above average height, slim and well proportioned. But soon he fell into deep thought, or rather into an absent state of mind, and walked ahead without either noticing or wishing to notice his surroundings. Now and again he muttered something under his breath—being in the habit, as he now realized, of talking to himself. At this point he was also aware that his thoughts were becoming confused, and that he was very weak, having eaten almost nothing for two days.

He was so shabbily dressed that many people, even if used to it, would have felt ashamed to go out in daylight in such rags—although in a district like this nothing one wore could have surprised anyone. The proximity of the Haymarket,* the profusion of establishments of a certain kind, and the large numbers of factory workers and tradesmen among the population packed into these streets and alleyways of central St Petersburg, made up such a kaleidoscope of odd characters that there could be no call for surprise no matter whom you met. But this young man had stored up so much anger and contempt, that—for all his sometimes youthful sensitivity—he wasn't in the least embarrassed by his rags in the street. It would be a different matter if he met anyone he knew, or any of his old classmates—and he didn't like meeting them. But just at this point a drunk was carried past him on a huge cart, drawn by a giant carthorse, heaven knows why or where to, and this drunk as he passed suddenly yelled out at him, 'Hey you, German hat!' pointing at him and giving a full-throated roar. At this the young man suddenly froze and made a convulsive grab at his hat. It was a tall, round one from Zimmermann's,* but completely worn out, brown with age, full of holes and stains, missing its brim, and knocked crooked to one side in the most grotesque way. Yet it wasn't embarrassment but an entirely different feeling, more like terror, that now seized hold of the young man.

'I knew it!' he muttered in confusion. 'Just as I thought! That's the worst thing that could happen! All it takes is a piece of stupidity, some trivial detail, to wreck the whole plan! Yes, the hat's too striking... It's ridiculous, that's what makes it stand out... With my rags, I need to wear a flat cap, any old pancake will do, not this monstrosity. Nobody wears hats like this, they'd notice it a mile off, and remember it... That's the worst thing, they'll remember it later on, and there's your incriminating evidence. I have to make myself as inconspicuous as I can... Trivial things, it's trivial things that matter most! Little details like this always spoil everything...'

He didn't have far to go; in fact he knew how many paces it was from the gates of his house—just seven hundred and thirty. Once, in an abstracted mood, he had counted them. At that point he hadn't yet started believing in those dreams of his—he would just tease his imagination with their repellent yet tempting audacity. But now, a month later, he had already begun to see things differently; and for all his sarcastic monologues about how powerless and indecisive he was, he had some-how, despite himself, got used to regarding this 'repulsive' fantasy as a real project, though still without believing in it. He was actually on his way now to carry out a *rehearsal* of this project, and he grew more and more agitated with every step he took.

He approached the house with a sinking heart, trembling with nerves. It was an enormous building, one side facing onto the canal and another onto —— Street.* The whole building was divided into tiny apartments, inhabited by all sorts of small tradespeople—tailors, lock-smiths, cooks, Germans with various occupations, girls selling them-selves, minor clerks and the like. People were hurrying in and out of its two gates and across the two courtyards. Three or four yardkeepers* were on duty here. The young man was very pleased not to meet any of them, and at once slipped unseen through the right-hand gate and up the stairs. It was a back stairway, dark and narrow, but he knew all about that, he had already sized it up, and the whole situation suited him. In darkness like this, even prying eyes were no threat. 'If I'm this scared right now, what would it be like if I ever found myself actually doing *the thing*?' That was his thought as he reached the fourth floor. Here he was obstructed by some retired soldiers acting as porters, carrying furniture out of one of the flats. He already knew that this flat was occupied by a German clerk and his family. 'That means that the German's moving out; so for a while the only flat still occupied on the fourth floor, up these particular stairs and on this landing, will be the old woman's. That's good... just in case...' he thought again, as he rang the bell of the old woman's flat. The bell gave a feeble clink, as though it were made of tin instead of brass. In buildings like these, the flats almost always have that sort of bell. He had forgotten the sound of it, and now its particular clink suddenly reminded him very vividly of something. He shuddered—his nerves were far too shaken today. After a few moments the door opened a tiny crack. Through that crack, the occupant peered at her visitor with evident suspicion. Nothing could be seen but her little eyes glinting in the dark. But once she saw several people on the landing, she took courage and opened the door wider. The young man stepped over the threshold into a dark entrance-hall, with a partition hiding a tiny kitchen. The old woman faced him silently, with a questioning look. She was a tiny, dried-up little old crone of around sixty, with sharp, evil-looking eyes and a short pointed nose. She was bareheaded, and her tow-coloured hair with its few streaks of grey was thickly greased. Her long neck, scrawny as a chicken's leg, was adorned with a piece of flannel rag, and despite the heat she wore a short fur jacket, tattered and yellowed with age, dangling off her shoulders. The little old woman kept coughing and grunting. The young man must have looked at her in some special way, because the suspicious look suddenly flashed in her eyes again.

'Raskolnikov,* I'm a student, I came to see you a month ago,' the young man muttered hastily, making a half-bow as he remembered to try to be more polite.

'I remember you coming, mister, I remember very well,' the old woman answered sharply, still not moving her questioning eyes from his face.

'Well, then... I'm here again, for the same sort of thing...' Raskolnikov went on in some confusion, taken aback by the old woman's suspicion. 'Still, perhaps she's always like this, and I just didn't notice last time,' he thought uneasily.

The old woman stood silently for a moment, as if in doubt; then she stepped aside and pointed to the inner door, saying 'Through there, mister,' as she let him pass.

The young man stepped into a small room with yellowed wallpaper, a few geraniums, and net curtains over the windows. At the moment it was brightly lit by the setting sun. 'So *then* the sun'll be shining just like this!' was the thought that sprang unbidden to Raskolnikov's mind, as he quickly scanned the contents of the room to fix the layout in his memory. But there was nothing particular here. The furniture, all very old and made of yellow wood, consisted of a divan with a high curved wooden back, and an oval table in front of it; between the windows there was a dressing table with a mirror, chairs stood by the walls, and there were two or three minuscule pictures in yellowing frames depicting young German ladies with birds in their hands. Nothing else. In one corner a lamp was burning before a small icon. Everything was very clean. The furniture and floors were highly polished and shining. 'That's Lizaveta's work,' thought the young man. There wasn't a speck of dust to be seen in the whole flat. 'It's cruel old widows who keep everything this clean,' Raskolnikov went on to himself, looking inquisitively at the muslin curtain over the doorway into the second, tiny room where the old woman had her bed and chest of drawers. He had never managed to see into that room. Those two rooms made up the whole flat.

'What can I do for you?' asked the little old woman dourly, coming into the room and again standing right in front of him, staring into his face.

'I've brought something to pawn. Here it is.' And he brought out of his pocket an old flat silver watch. On the back of the case was an engraving of a globe. The chain was steel.

'But your time's up for the last pledge. The month ran out two days ago.'

'I'll pay you the interest for another month, please be patient.'

'That's up to me, mister, whether I'm patient or just sell your thing right away.'

'How much can you give me for the watch, Aliona Ivanovna?'

'It's nothing but rubbish, what you bring me, mister. I don't suppose it's worth a thing. Last time I gave you two little rouble notes for your ring, but if you wanted to buy it new from a jeweller you could have got it for one and a half.'

'Let me have four roubles, I'll pay it back, it was my father's watch. I'll be getting some money soon.'

'One and a half roubles, interest in advance, if you want.'

'One and a half!' the young man cried out.

'Up to you.' And the old woman handed him back the watch. The young man took it, so angry that he would have walked out on the spot; but he quickly thought better of it, remembering that he had nowhere to go and that he had come with something else in mind.

'Let's have it!' he said rudely.

The old woman felt in her pocket for her keys and went through the curtains into the next room. The young man, left alone in the middle of the room, listened attentively to figure out what was happening. He could hear her opening her chest of drawers. 'That must be the top drawer,' he decided. 'So she keeps the keys in her right-hand pocket... All in a single bundle, on a steel ring... And one of those keys is bigger than all the rest, three times bigger, with a notched bit to it—obviously that's not the key to the drawers... So there must be something else, some casket or strongbox... Now that's interesting. Strongboxes always have keys like that... But how despicable all this is...'

The old woman returned. 'Here we are, mister. If it's ten kopeks a month for one rouble, then for a rouble and a half it'll be fifteen kopeks; one month in advance. And for your other two roubles, at the same rate, you owe me twenty kopeks in advance. So all that comes to thirty-five. That means you get one rouble fifteen kopeks now, all told, for your watch. Here you are.'

'What! So now it's only one rouble fifteen?'

'That's right.'

The young man didn't argue and took the money. He looked at the old woman and was in no hurry to leave, as if he wanted to say or do something more, but was himself uncertain just what that was.

'Aliona Ivanovna, I might bring you something else in a day or two... silver... a cigarette case... when I get it back from my friend...' He faltered and stopped.

'Well, we'll talk about it then, mister.'

'Goodbye... Are you all by yourself, here at home? Your sister not here?' he asked, as casually as he could, going out to the hall.

'What's your business with her, mister?'

'Oh, nothing special. I just asked. You're so... Goodbye, Aliona Ivanovna.'

Raskolnikov left, thoroughly discomposed. And his confusion got worse and worse. On his way downstairs, he actually stopped several times, as if suddenly struck by a thought. And when he eventually reached the street, he burst out:

'Oh God! How repulsive this all is! And am I really, really... No, that's all nonsense, it's ridiculous,' he said firmly. 'How could I even think of such a monstrous thing? What infamy I'm capable of! The thing is—it's dirty, revolting, foul, foul! And there I was, for a whole month...'

But neither words nor outbursts could do justice to his inner turmoil. The feeling of utter disgust that had begun to oppress and torment him earlier, even when he was on his way to the old woman, had now grown so sharp and powerful that he didn't know where to hide from his anguish. He walked along the pavement like a drunken man, not seeing the passers-by, bumping into them, and only came to himself in the next street. Looking around him, he found that he was close to a drinking den,* with steps leading down from the street to the basement. Just at that moment two drunks came out and mounted the stairs to the street, propping each other up and swearing. On the spur of the moment, Raskolnikov went straight down the steps. He had never been in a drinking den before, but just now his head was spinning and he was tormented by a burning thirst. He felt he needed a cold beer, particularly as he ascribed his sudden weakness to hunger.

He sat down in a dark, dirty corner by a sticky little table and ordered some beer. He drank down the first glass greedily. He felt better at once, and now he could think more clearly. 'That's all nonsense,' he said hopefully. 'I didn't need to get so anxious! It was just physical weakness. All it takes is one glass of beer and a piece of dry toast—and there you are, your mind is stronger straight away, your thoughts are clearer, you know what it is you want. Pah, how petty it all is!...' Despite his exclamation of scorn, he was looking cheerful now, as if he had suddenly shaken off some terrible burden, and he cast a friendly glance at the other customers. Yet even at that moment he had a faint premonition that all these optimistic feelings were themselves no more than the expression of a pathological state.

Not many people were left in the place now. The two drunks he had met coming up the stairs had been followed by a party of four or five men with a wench and an accordion.* The place was quiet and half-empty now; the only people left were one slightly tipsy man who could have been a shopkeeper,* sitting over his beer, and his companion, a big fat man with a grey beard, wearing a short Siberian kaftan, who was the worse for vodka and had fallen asleep on his bench; but from time to time, seemingly in his sleep, he would suddenly start snapping his fingers, stretching out his arms, and jerking the upper half of his body up and down, without getting up. All the while he was humming some nonsense or other, trying to recall the words of a song, such as:

> All year long I loved my wife,
> A-a-all year lo-o-ong I lo-o-oved my wife...

Or he would suddenly wake up and start:

> Off I went down Scrivener's Row*
> And found that girl I used to know...

But there was no one to share his happiness. His companion watched all these outbursts in silence, looking hostile and troubled. There was another man there too, who looked as if he might have been a retired clerk. He was sitting a little apart, his bottle in front of him, taking an occasional sip and looking around. He, too, seemed rather agitated.

CHAPTER II

RASKOLNIKOV wasn't used to crowds, and as we said, he had lately been avoiding company of any kind. Yet now something drove him to seek human fellowship. Something new seemed to be happening within him, giving him a kind of thirst for other people. A whole month of intense anguish and morose agitation had so tired him that he longed to spend at least a moment breathing the air of a different world, any world whatever; and despite all the squalor of his surroundings, he was happy now to spend time in the drinking den.

The landlord was in another room, but kept coming back down the steps into the main saloon from somewhere else—the first parts of him to appear being his showy polished boots with their broad red tops. He was wearing a long tunic and a fearfully greasy black satin waistcoat, but no tie; his whole face looked as if it had been oiled, like an iron padlock. There was a youth of about fourteen behind the bar, and a younger lad was there to wait on the customers. On the bar were sliced gherkins, rusks of black bread, and chunks of fish, and all of it smelt very bad. The atmosphere was so stuffy that sitting there was almost unbearable, and everything was so thick with vodka fumes that just breathing the air for five minutes would probably have been enough to get you drunk.

There are some encounters, even with people you don't know at all, which arouse your interest from the very first glance, quite immediately and suddenly, before a word has been spoken. That was just the impression made on Raskolnikov by a customer sitting some way away, who looked like a retired clerk. Later on, our young man was often to remember this first impression, and he even attributed it to a presentiment. Of course he kept glancing at this clerk, and that was partly because the man was staring fixedly across at him, evidently wanting to strike up a conversation. As for everyone else in the drinking den, including the host—the clerk viewed them all with familiarity and even boredom, yet at the same time with a hint of supercilious disdain, as if they were so far beneath him in rank and education that he could have nothing to say to them. He was a man past fifty, of average height and stocky build, with greying hair and a big bald patch; his face was yellow, greenish even, and bloated with constant drunkenness. Beneath his swollen eyelids there shone a lively pair of tiny, reddish, slitty eyes. But there was something very odd about him: he had a look that shone almost with enthusiasm, even good sense and intelligence—yet there seemed to be a glint of madness too.

He was wearing a tattered and torn old frock-coat missing its buttons; one button was somehow still holding on by a thread, and he had used that one to fasten his coat, evidently to preserve decency. A crumpled, bespattered, and soiled shirt-front protruded from his nankeen waistcoat. His face had once been shaved like an office clerk's, but that was some time ago, and now it was covered in thick grey stubble. His mannerisms, too, had something solid and civil-servant-like about them. But he was restless, ruffling his hair and sometimes resting his head miserably on both hands, propping his ragged elbows on the wet and sticky tabletop. At last he looked straight at Raskolnikov and said in a loud, firm voice:

'Might I make so bold, my good sir, to address a few decorous words to you? For although you make no show of distinction, yet my experience tells me that you are an educated man and unused to alcoholic beverages. I myself have always respected education when allied to sincere feeling; furthermore, I am a Titular Councillor.* Marmeladov, that is my name, Titular Councillor. Might I ask whether you have been in the Service?'

'No, I'm studying,' replied the young man, rather taken aback both by the other's very flowery speech and by his abrupt and forward mode of address. And although he had previously been overcome by a longing for human contact of any kind whatever, he now, at the very first word actually addressed to him, suddenly experienced his usual feeling of disagreeable irritation and revulsion towards any stranger who intruded, or merely threatened to intrude, on his personal world.

'Then you're a student, or an ex-student!' cried the clerk. 'Just as I thought! Experience, my dear sir, experience, on more than one occasion!' And he laid his finger to his forehead in self-congratulation. 'You used to be a student, or attended some learned institution. But allow me...'—and he got up, teetering unsteadily, picked up his bottle and glass, and sat down by the young man, a little to one side of him. Although tipsy, he talked glibly and fluently, only occasionally losing the thread and stumbling in his speech. He seized on Raskolnikov almost greedily, as if he too had not spoken to anyone for a whole month.

'My dear sir,' he began, almost majestically, 'poverty is not a vice, that is true. It is even truer, as I also know, that drunkenness is no virtue. But beggary, my dear sir, beggary—that is a vice. In poverty the nobility of your innate sentiments is still preserved, but never in beggary, not by anyone. In beggary, you are not even driven out with staves—you are swept out with a broom, from all human society, to humiliate you even more; and that is justice, because in beggary I am the first to wish to humiliate myself. And that's what leads to the drinking den! My dear sir, a month ago my wife was thrashed by Mr Lebeziatnikov, and yet my wife is not the same as me! Do you understand me, sir? Allow me to ask you another question, just so, out of pure curiosity—have you ever had occasion to spend the night on the Neva, on a hay barge?'

'No, I never have,' replied Raskolnikov. 'Why do you ask?'

'Well, I've just come from there, and that makes five nights in a row.'

He filled his glass, drank it down and began brooding. And it was true that wisps of hay could be seen sticking to his clothing here and there, even in his hair. It was very likely that he had neither undressed nor washed for five days on end. His hands, in particular, were dirty, greasy, and red, with blackened nails.

His conversation seemed to have caught most people's attention, of an idle kind. The boys behind the bar sniggered. The landlord seemed to have come down from upstairs purposely to listen to the 'joker'; he sat down nonchalantly at a distance, yawning self-importantly. Marmeladov was evidently well known here. Indeed, he had probably acquired his fondness for flowery speech through his habit of indulging in frequent conversations over vodka with all sorts of strangers. With some drunkards, this habit grows to be a necessity, especially if they are harshly treated at home. In the company of other drinkers, it seems to make them strive to justify themselves, and even, if possible, to earn some respect.

'Hey, joker!' called out the host. 'Why don't you do some work? If you're a clerk, why aren't you at the office?'

'Why am I not at the office, my dear sir?' answered Marmeladov, addressing himself exclusively to Raskolnikov as though it was he who had posed the question. 'Why am I not at the office? Does not my heart ache at my abject and pointless existence? When, a month ago, Mr Lebeziatnikov personally administered a thrashing to my wife, while I lay there drunk, did it not make me suffer? Let me ask you, young man, has it ever happened to you... hmm... well, say, to beg hopelessly for a loan?'

'Yes, it has happened... but what do you mean, hopelessly?'

'I mean altogether hopelessly, knowing perfectly well that nothing can come of it. Supposing you know in advance, beyond any doubt, that this particular person, this benevolent and most worthy citizen, will not let you have any money on any account—for why should he, may I ask? He knows perfectly well that I'll never pay him back. Out of compassion? But Mr Lebeziatnikov, who keeps up with modern ideas, was explaining the other day that in our time, compassion is actually proscribed by science, and that's already the way of things in England, where they have political economy.* Why, I ask you, should he let you have any money? And there you are, knowing in advance that he won't give you any, and nevertheless you set off...'

'What's the point of going?' broke in Raskolnikov.

'But if there's no one to go to, nowhere else to turn! Surely it must be so, surely everyone has to have somewhere to turn! For there comes a time when you simply have to turn somewhere! When my only daughter first went out on the streets with her yellow ticket,* I went too (for my daughter is on a yellow ticket, sir)'—he added in parentheses, looking at the young man rather uneasily—'but never mind that, my dear sir, never mind!' he added hurriedly, seemingly quite composed, while both boys behind the counter snorted with laughter and even the host grinned. 'Never mind that, sir! I am not offended by these wagging heads, for all is known already and all secrets revealed; and I look upon this not with scorn, but with humility. So be it, so be it! "Behold the man!" Excuse me, young man, could you... but no, I must express myself more strongly and strikingly: not *could you*, but *dare you*, looking upon me at this time, positively assert that I am not a swine?'

The young man answered not a word.

'Well, sir,' the orator continued, waiting composedly and now with even greater dignity for the sniggering in the room to subside, 'well, sir, I may be a swine, but she is a lady! I bear the form of a beast, but Katerina Ivanovna, my spouse, is a person of culture and by birth the daughter of a staff officer. I acknowledge that I am a scoundrel, but she has an exalted soul, she is filled with sentiments that have been ennobled by her upbringing. Yet at the same time... Oh, if she would take pity on me! My dear sir, my dear sir, every man needs, does he not, but a single place where even he can be pitied! But Katerina Ivanovna, though a magnanimous lady, is unjust... And although I myself understand that when she pulls me by the hair, it is but the compassion in her heart that makes her do it (for I repeat to you, without shame, young man, that she does pull me by the hair)', he added with redoubled dignity, hearing more tittering; 'but my God, if she could but once... but no, no! All this is but wasted breath, not worthy, not worthy to be mentioned! For that which I longed for has been given me, more than once, and more than once have I received pity, but... such is my character, I am a beast by nature!'

'I'll say,' yawned the landlord.

Marmeladov thumped his fist hard against the table.

'Such is my character! Do you know, do you know, my dear sir, that I even drank away her stockings? Not her boots—that would at least have borne some semblance of normality—but her stockings, I drank away her stockings! And I drank away her mohair scarf too, which she had as a gift before we married, it was her own, not mine. And the corner we live in is cold,* and this winter she caught a chill and started coughing, and now she's spitting blood. We have three small children, and Katerina Ivanovna works from morning till night, scrubbing and washing and bathing the children, for she has been used to cleanliness ever since her childhood, she has a delicate chest and is susceptible to consumption; and I feel this. How could I not feel it? And the more I drink, the more I feel it. That's why I drink—to find emotion and compassion in drinking. It's not joy I seek, only grief... I drink because I wish to suffer more!' And he leaned his head on the table in a gesture of despair.

'Young man,' he went on, raising his head again, 'I can read in your face some kind of heartache. I read it when you entered, and that was why I addressed you straight away. For I am relating the history of my life to you, not in order to expose my shame to these idlers here, who know it all anyway—I do so because I seek to find a sensitive and educated person. Let me tell you, therefore, that my spouse was educated in a high-class provincial institute for daughters of the gentry, and when she left it she danced the shawl dance* before the Governor and other personages, for which she received a gold medal and a certificate of merit. The medal... well, that medal was sold... a long time ago... um... but the certificate of merit is still kept in her trunk, and she showed it to our landlady quite recently. For although she is engaged in the most unremitting conflict with our landlady, she did wish to show off to somebody, anybody, to whom she could speak of her happy days of long ago. Nor do I condemn her, nor do I condemn her, for that is the last of the memories left to her, everything else has gone up in smoke! Oh yes, she is a hot-blooded lady, proud and unbending. She will wash the floor with her own hands, and live on black bread, but she will not tolerate disrespect. That was why she would not put up with Mr Lebeziatnikov's rudeness, and when Mr Lebeziatnikov beat her for that, it was not so much the beating as her own injured feelings that caused her to take to her bed. I took her as a widow, with her three children, each one smaller than the last. Her first husband was an infantry officer whom she married for love, and she ran away from home with him. She was passionately in love with her husband, but he took up cards, ended up in court, and that was how he died. By the end he used to beat her, and although she paid him back, of which I have reliable written proof, yet even now she remembers him with tears in her eyes, and holds up his example as a reproach to me, and I'm glad she does, yes, glad that—even if only in her imagination—she sees herself as having once been happy... And after he died she was left alone with three little children, in a far-off and savage district where I too found myself at the time; she was left in such abject poverty that I, though I have seen all kinds of adventures in my time, find it impossible to describe. All her family had cast her off. And how proud she was, unbelievably proud... And then it was, my dear sir, then it was, that I, a widower myself, with a fourteen-year-old daughter by my first wife, offered her my hand, for I could not bear the sight of her suffering. So you can judge for yourself how sunk in misery she was, an educated, well-bred woman from a good family, to have agreed to marry me! But she married me! Weeping, and sobbing, and wringing her hands, she married me! Because she had nowhere to turn. Can you understand, can you understand, my dear sir, what it means to have nowhere else to turn? No! You cannot yet understand that... And for a whole year long I fulfilled my obligations, honourably and religiously, and never touched this stuff (prodding the bottle with a finger), for I do have feelings. But even this did not serve; for I lost my position, and that not through any fault of my own, but because of staffing changes; and then I did touch it!... It must be a year and a half ago now that we eventually found ourselves, after much wandering and many disasters, in this splendid capital city adorned with numerous monuments. And here I obtained a post... obtained it and lost it again. Do you understand, sir? And I lost it through my own fault, for my weakness caught up with me... And now we live in a little corner at our landlady's, Amalia Fedorovna Lippewechsel, and how we stay alive and how we pay her I do not know. There are many other people living there as well as us... a real bear-garden, utterly disgusting... um, yes... And by this time my daughter had grown up, my daughter from my first marriage, and what she suffered, my little daughter, from her stepmother while she grew up—I'll say nothing about that. For although Katerina Ivanovna is filled with generous sentiments, yet she is a hot-tempered and irritable lady, with a sharp tongue... Yes indeed, sir! Well, no use talking about that. As you can imagine, Sonia has had no education. Some four years ago, I did try teaching her some geography and world history; but as I myself was none too knowledgeable in those matters, and had no suitable textbooks, for any books that we had... hm!... well, we don't have them any longer, those books; and that was the end of all her education. We finished up on Cyrus of Persia.* And after that, when she was grown up, she read a number of books of a romantic kind, and quite recently she read a certain book which she obtained through Mr Lebeziatnikov—Lewes's *Physiology*,* do you happen to know it?—and was most interested in it, and even read portions of it to us. That was the end of her education. And now, my dear sir, I should like to ask you a personal question. Can a poor but honest young girl, in your opinion, earn much by honest labour? She cannot even make fifteen kopeks a day, sir, if she is honest and possesses no special talents—not even if she works without ceasing. And even so, State Councillor Klopstock, Ivan Ivanovich—have you happened to hear of him?—has so far not only failed to pay her for making him half a dozen Holland shirts,* but drove her ignominiously away, stamping his feet and calling her bad names, on the pretext that the shirt collars were the wrong size and set in crooked. And there were the children, going hungry... And Katerina Ivanovna, walking up and down the room wringing her hands, with the red patches coming out on her cheeks—which always occurs in that disease—and telling her "Look at you, you bloodsucker, living in our home, eating and drinking and keeping yourself warm"—though how could she be eating and drinking when even the little ones never saw a crust for three days on end!—I was lying there at the time... well, never mind that!—I was lying there tipsy, and I heard my Sonia answer (she's so meek, with such a soft little voice... she's fair-haired, and her face is always pale and thin), and she said "What do you mean, Katerina Ivanovna, do I really have to come to that?" For Darya Frantsevna, an evil-minded woman well known to the police, had already been three times to see our landlady and make propositions. "What of it?" replies Katerina Ivanovna with a mocking laugh. "What are you so keen to protect? Some treasure, indeed!" But don't blame her, don't blame her, my dear sir, don't blame her! She was not in her right mind when she said that, her nerves were shattered, and she was sick, and the children crying because they had nothing to eat; and she said it more by way of an insult than meaning what she said. For Katerina Ivanovna is like that; if the children are crying, even if it's from hunger, she'll set about beating them at once. And so some time after five, I saw Sonia get up, put on her headscarf and cloak, and leave the apartment, and she came back after eight. In she came and went straight over to Katerina Ivanovna, and silently laid down thirty roubles on the table in front of her. And not a word did she say, she didn't even look at her, she just picked up our big green drap-de-dames* shawl—we have a big green shawl in our flat, made of drap-de-dames—and covered her head and face with it, and lay down on her bed with her face to the wall, with her little shoulders and body shaking, on and on... And I was still lying there, just as before, sir... And then I saw, young man, I saw Katerina Ivanovna go over to Sonechka's bed, without a word, and she stayed the whole evening kneeling at her feet, kissing her feet, and she wouldn't get up, and then the two of them fell asleep together like that, in each other's arms... the two of them... the two of them... yes, sir... while I... lay there tipsy, sir.'

Marmeladov stopped speaking, as though his voice had failed him. Then he hurriedly filled his glass, drank it down, and cleared his throat.

'Since that time, my good sir,' he went on after a brief silence, 'since that time, following a certain adverse occurrence and denunciation by some malicious persons—aided and abetted especially by Darya Frantsevna, on the grounds that we had failed to show her proper respect—since that time, my daughter Sofia Semionovna has been obliged to take a yellow ticket, which means that she can no longer go on living with us. For even our landlady Amalia Fedorovna would not allow that—though she herself had previously encouraged Darya Frantsevna—and Mr Lebeziatnikov too... hm... It was over Sonia that he had that business with Katerina Ivanovna. Before that he had been making up to Sonia himself, but now he was suddenly all full of himself, "How can I," says he, "such a cultured man as I am, share a flat with a creature like that?" But Katerina Ivanovna wouldn't have it, she stood up for Sonia... and that was how it happened... And now Sonechka mostly comes to see us after nightfall, and comforts Katerina Ivanovna, and gives her all she can afford... She lives with Kapernaumov the tailor,* she rents a place from him; Kapernaumov is lame and has a speech defect, and all his numerous family have speech defects. And his wife, she has a speech defect as well... They all live in one room, and Sonia has her own room, behind a partition... Hm, yes... Most impoverished people, they are, all with speech defects... yes... Well, I rose the next morning, and putting on my rags, I lifted up my arms to heaven, and set off to see his Excellency Ivan Afanasievich. Do you happen to know his Excellency Ivan Afanasievich?... No? Well, that's a saintly man you don't know. He is wax... wax before the face of the Lord; even as the wax melteth!... He was good enough to listen to the whole, and even shed tears over it. "Well," says he, "well, Marmeladov, you have already let me down once... I'll take you on a second time, on my own personal responsibility"—those were his very words—"just remember that; and now you may go." I kissed the dust beneath his feet, in my thoughts that is, for he would never have permitted it literally, being a high official and a man of modern and enlightened political ideas. So I returned home, and when I announced that I had gained employment again and would be receiving a salary, my God, what a thing that was!'

Marmeladov stopped again, in intense agitation. At this point a large crowd of revellers came in off the street, already drunk; and by the entrance someone struck up a tune on a hired hurdy-gurdy, and the cracked childish voice of a seven-year-old started singing 'My Little Farmstead'.* There was a lot of noise. The landlord and waiters were busy with the new arrivals. Marmeladov, taking no notice of them, went on with his story. The drink had evidently got to him, but the drunker he became, the more talkative he was. The recollection of his recent success in getting a job seemed to have cheered him up, and given a sort of radiance to his face. Raskolnikov listened attentively.

'All this, my dear sir, occurred five weeks ago. Yes... No sooner had the two of them, Katerina Ivanovna and little Sonechka, heard the news than, Oh Lord, it was as if I had been transported to the Kingdom of Heaven. Before that, all I heard was "Lie on the floor there, you—like a dumb animal!"—nothing but insults. But now they would tiptoe round me and hush the children—"Semion Zakharich has been working, he's tired and resting, sshhh!" They made coffee for me before I went to work, even made scalded cream for me! They began buying real cream, do you hear? And wherever did they find the money to get me a decent uniform, eleven roubles fifty kopeks—I'll never know! Boots, and calico shirt fronts—splendid ones—and a proper uniform, and they got it all together in magnificent style, all for eleven and a half roubles. When I got home from work the first day, what did I find—Katerina Ivanovna had cooked a two-course meal, soup and a dish of salt beef with horseradish—we'd never had such a thing in our lives. And she has nothing to wear... I mean no dresses whatsoever, sir; and yet now she was all dressed up for going out, and not just any old thing, no, she knows how to make whatever she wants, out of nothing: a new hairdo, and some kind of clean collar, and cuffs, and suddenly she's a completely different person, younger and prettier than before. Little Sonechka, my darling girl, also helped with money—but she says, "for the time being it's awkward for me to come here too often, unless I come after nightfall perhaps, so that nobody sees me." Do you hear that? Do you hear? When I went for a sleep after dinner, what do you think? Katerina Ivanovna just couldn't wait; it was only a week earlier that she'd had a terminal quarrel with our landlady Amalia Fedorovna, and yet now she invited her round for a cup of coffee. They sat over it for two hours, whispering together: "Semion Zakharich is in work now, and receiving a salary, and he's been to see his Excellency, and his Excellency came out in person and told everyone else to wait, and took Semion Zakharich by the arm and showed him into his office in front of all the others." Do you hear that? Do you hear? "Of course I remember your merits, Semion Zakharich, says he, and although you used to be subject to that irresponsible weakness, yet since you now give me your word, and since things have been difficult here without you (do you hear that? do you hear it?), so I now put my trust, says he, in your word of honour." I mean, she had gone and made all that up out of her own head, not in a frivolous way, but just so as to do me honour, sir! No, sir, she believes it all, she gets comfort from her own words, I swear to God she does! And I do not condemn that, no, I do not condemn it!... And six days ago, when I received my first wages—twenty-three roubles forty kopeks—and brought it all home to her, she called me her little treasure: "What a little treasure you are!" says she. In private, you understand? Well, you might think, I'm no beauty, and what sort of a husband am I for her? But no, she pinched my cheek—"What a little treasure you are!" says she.'

Marmeladov stopped, and seemed on the point of smiling, but suddenly his chin trembled. However, he controlled himself. This tavern, his debauched appearance, his five nights on hay barges, and his vodka bottle, alongside his morbid affection for his wife and family, all this had thrown his listener. Raskolnikov listened intently to him, sick at heart. He was annoyed with himself for coming here.

'My dear sir, O my dear sir!' cried Marmeladov, pulling himself together. 'O my dear sir, you may find all this ridiculous, as the others do; perhaps I am only bothering you with all these pathetic details of my home life; but I do not find them ridiculous! For I am capable of feeling it all... All the rest of that heavenly day in my life, and all that evening, I spent in blissful dreams—about how I would arrange everything, and get clothes for the children, and give my wife a quiet life, and rescue my one and only daughter from dishonour and return her to the bosom of her family... And much, much more. All that was right and proper, sir. Well then, my dear sir' (and Marmeladov gave a sudden shudder, raised his head, and stared straight at his listener), 'well, sir, and on the very next day, after all these dreams (that'll be just five days ago now), towards evening, I went slyly and surreptitiously, even as a thief in the night, and stole the key to Katerina Ivanovna's chest, and took all that remained of the wages I had brought—I don't remember any longer how much was left—and now look at me! It's all gone! Away from home for five days, and they're all searching for me, and that's the end of my job, and my uniform is lying in a drinking den by the Egyptian Bridge,* I got these clothes in exchange... and that's the end of everything!'

Marmeladov struck his fist on his forehead, gritted his teeth, closed his eyes, and leaned his elbow heavily on the table. But a minute later his expression suddenly changed; affecting an air of slyness and studied impertinence, he looked over at Raskolnikov, tittered and said:

'And today I've been to see Sonia, to ask for some money for a pick-me-up... Heh-heh-heh!'

'Don't tell me she gave you any?' cried one of the new arrivals, bursting into a loud guffaw.

'This very bottle was bought with her money,' announced Marmeladov, addressing himself exclusively to Raskolnikov. 'Thirty kopeks she brought out for me, with her own hands, the last money she had, all of it, I saw it with my own eyes... She didn't say anything, just looked at me silently... That doesn't happen on this earth, but up there... they grieve over us, and weep for us, but do not reproach us—no, they do not reproach us! And that's even more painful, even more painful, sir—when they don't reproach us!... Thirty kopeks, yes sir. And yet she herself needs the money, doesn't she? What do you think, my very dear sir? I mean, she has to stay neat and clean now. Cleanliness like that, you know, special cleanliness, costs money. You understand? Do you understand? Well, and buying lipstick and so on, you can't do without that; and starched petticoats, and those boots, really fetching ones, so you can show off your foot when you have to cross a puddle. Do you understand, sir, do you understand what all that elegance costs? Well, and so there am I, her very own father, taking those thirty kopeks off her to cure my hangover! And I drink them all up! And now I've drunk them all!... So who could ever pity someone like me? Eh? Are you sorry for me now, sir, or not? Tell me—sorry or not? Heh-heh-heh!'

He made to top up his glass, but there was nothing left. The bottle was empty.

'Why should anyone be sorry for you?' the landlord called out, happening to pass by them.

People laughed, and some even swore at Marmeladov. The laughter and oaths came both from those who had heard him and those who hadn't, who laughed merely at the sight of this retired clerk.

'Pity! Why should I be pitied!?' Marmeladov suddenly moaned, rising from his seat with his arm outstretched before him, appearing positively inspired, as if all he had been waiting for was those words. 'Why pity me, you ask? Yes! There is nothing to pity me for! I ought to be crucified, crucified on a cross, not pitied! But crucify him, O thou Judge, and when Thou hast crucified him, pity him! And I myself shall come to Thee to be crucified, for I thirst not after joy but after grief and tears! Do you, shopkeeper, imagine that this bottle of yours has brought me pleasure? It was grief, grief that I sought at the bottom of it, grief and tears, and I have tasted them, and received them; but we shall be pitied by Him who pitied us all, and understood all people and all things, He alone, He who is our Judge.* And He shall come on that day and shall ask: "Where is that daughter who sacrificed herself for a cruel and consumptive stepmother, and for the little children of another? Where is that daughter who took pity on her earthly father, a disgraceful drunkard, and was not overcome with horror at his bestial conduct?" And He shall say: "Come unto me! I have already forgiven thee once... forgiven thee once... And even now thy manifold sins shall be forgiven thee, for thou hast loved much..." And He shall forgive my Sonia, He shall forgive her, I know that He shall... Just now, when I went to see her, I felt it in my heart! And He shall judge all, and forgive them, the good and the evil, the wise and the humble... And when He shall have done judging them all, then shall He speak unto us also, saying: "Come forward, even ye too! Come forward, ye drunken ones, come forward ye feeble ones, come forward ye shameful ones!" And we shall all come forward, without shame, and shall stand before Him. And He shall say: "Swine that ye are! Ye are made in the image of a beast, and bear his mark; yet come unto me, even ye also!" And the wise shall speak, and the upright shall speak, and shall say: "Lord, why receivest Thou even these?" And He shall say: "Even these do I receive, O ye wise ones and ye upright ones, forasmuch as not one of them did think himself worthy of it..." And He shall stretch forth his hands to us, and we shall fall at His feet... and shall weep... and shall understand all! Then shall we understand all!... and all shall understand... and Katerina Ivanovna... even she shall understand... Thy Kingdom come, O Lord!'

And he sank back on the bench, weak and exhausted, looking at no one, as if he had forgotten his surroundings and was deep in thought. His words had created an impression—for a moment the place was in silence, but soon the laughter and jibes rang out again.

'What a speech!'

'What a lot of rubbish!'

'Pen-pusher!'

And so on and so forth.

'Let us go, sir,' said Marmeladov suddenly, raising his head and turning to Raskolnikov. 'Would you take me... to Kozel's house, to the courtyard. It's time to... go to Katerina Ivanovna.'

Raskolnikov had long been wanting to leave, and he had himself thought of helping Marmeladov, who turned out to be far weaker on his legs than in his speech, and leaned heavily on the young man. They had some two or three hundred yards to go.* As they came nearer to his home, the drunkard became increasingly prey to embarrassment and fear.

'It's not Katerina Ivanovna I'm afraid of now,' he muttered anxiously. 'And I'm not afraid that she'll start pulling my hair. What does my hair matter?... Bother my hair! That's just what I'm saying! Actually it's better if she starts pulling it—that's not what I'm afraid of... It's her eyes I'm afraid of... yes... her eyes... And I'm afraid of the red patches on her cheeks... and afraid of her breathing... Have you seen how people breathe, when they have that disease... and their feelings are stirred up? And I'm afraid of the children crying, too... Because if Sonia hasn't brought food for them, then... I don't know! I just don't know! But I'm not afraid of being beaten... Let me tell you, sir, that beatings of that sort are not only not painful for me, I actually enjoy them... For that is something I myself cannot do without. It's better that way. Let her beat me, and feel better for it... it's better that way. Well, here's the house. Kozel's house. He's a locksmith, German, a rich man. Take me in!'

They went in from the courtyard and walked up to the fourth floor. The higher they climbed up the staircase, the darker it became. It was almost eleven o'clock by now, and although there is no real nightfall in Petersburg at this time of year,* the top of the staircase was very dark.

Right at the top of the house, the little smoke-blackened door at the head of the stairs was ajar. A candle stub lit up a wretched little room about ten yards long; the whole of it could be seen from the landing. Everything inside was scattered about in disorder, with a lot of ragged children's clothing. A sheet full of holes hung over the far corner, no doubt hiding a bed. In the room there was nothing but a pair of chairs and a sofa covered with torn oilcloth, with an old deal kitchen table, unpainted and uncovered, standing in front of it. On the edge of the table stood the guttering stump of a tallow candle in an iron candle-stick. It appeared that the Marmeladovs had a room to themselves, not just a corner; but theirs was a through room. The door to the rest of the rooms, or cupboards, that made up Amalia Lippewechsel's flat was ajar, and noisy shouting and laughter could be heard coming from it. People seemed to be playing cards and drinking tea. From time to time you could hear snatches of the crudest talk.

Raskolnikov recognized Katerina Ivanovna at once. She was quite a tall and graceful woman, thin and dreadfully wasted, still with a fine head of dark auburn hair, and she really did have hectic red patches on her cheeks. She was pacing up and down the little room, pressing her hands against her breast. Her breath came in broken gasps through her parched lips. There was a feverish glitter in her eyes, but her look was firm and steady. Her tense consumptive gaze, lit up by the last flickers of the dying candle that shimmered on her face, was most upsetting to see. Raskolnikov reckoned she must be about thirty years old, and indeed she was a most unsuitable wife for Marmeladov. She did not hear or notice the two when they came in; she seemed to be in a sort of stupor, deaf and blind to everything. The atmosphere was stuffy, but she had not opened the window; a foul smell rose up from the stairway, but the door to the landing had not been closed; billows of tobacco smoke blew in from the inner rooms through the open door, making her cough, but she did not close that door either. The youngest girl, aged about six, was sitting hunched up on the floor asleep, her face hidden in the sofa. A boy, a year older than her, was trembling and crying in the corner; no doubt he had just been beaten. The oldest girl, some nine years old, tall and matchstick-thin, stood by her little brother in the corner. She was wearing nothing but a thin and very tattered shift, with an ancient drap-de-dames cape flung over her bare shoulders; the cape must have been made for her two years ago, for now it didn't even reach her knees. She had laid her long arm, thin as a dried-out stick, around the boy's neck and seemed to be comforting him, whispering some-thing to him and doing all she could to stop him whimpering again; at the same time she was anxiously watching her mother with her big, big dark eyes, which seemed even bigger in her emaciated and fearful little face. Without entering the room, Marmeladov got down on his knees right in the doorway, and pushed Raskolnikov in ahead of him. At the sight of this strange man, the woman stopped distractedly in front of him, seeming to come to her senses for a moment and ask herself—what was this man doing here? But she must have immediately concluded that he was going through to the other rooms, since this was a through room. At this realization she paid him no further attention, but went over to the entrance door to close it; and suddenly cried out when she saw her husband kneeling on the threshold.

'Aaah!' she screamed in fury, 'you're back! Criminal! Monster!... And where's the money? What have you got in your pockets? Show me! And your clothes are wrong! Where are your clothes? Where's the money? Tell me!'

And she hurled herself on him to search his pockets. Marmeladov instantly stretched out his arms to both sides, docilely and obediently, to allow her to search him. He had not a single kopek on him.

'But where's the money?' she cried. 'Oh God, don't say he's drunk it all! There were twelve silver roubles left in the chest!...' And suddenly, in a burst of fury, she seized him by the hair and dragged him into the room. Marmeladov helped her along, crawling submissively behind her.

'And I am enjoying this! There's no pain for me here, but en-joyment, my ve-ry dear sir!' he shouted, as he was shaken about by his hair and once even banged his forehead on the floor. The girl sleeping on the floor awoke and burst into tears. The boy in the corner could bear it no longer, and, trembling, cried out and flung himself into his sister's arms in a paroxysm of sheer terror. The older girl was shaking like a leaf.

'He's drunk it away! He's drunk it all, all of it!' cried the poor woman in despair. 'And he hasn't got his clothes! They're starving, they're starving!' she cried, wringing her hands and gesturing at the children. 'Oh, my accursed life! And you, aren't you ashamed?' she added, suddenly turning on Raskolnikov. 'Coming here straight from the tavern! Have you been drinking with him? Yes, you've been drinking with him too! Get out!'

The young man hurried away without a word. At the same time the inner door was flung wide open and a number of inquisitive people peered in, craning their impertinent heads in their skullcaps, laughing, and smoking cigarettes and pipes. You could make out shapes in dressing gowns that dangled wide open, or wearing barely decent summer clothes, and some had playing cards in their hands. They laughed with particular gusto when Marmeladov, as he was dragged along by his hair, shouted that he was enjoying this. They even began advancing into the room, at which point a furious yell rang out: it came from Amalia Lippewechsel herself, forcing herself through to sort everyone out in her own way, terrifying the poor woman for the hundredth time by swearing at her and ordering her to clear out of the flat by next morning. On his way out, Raskolnikov managed to shove his hand in his pocket and pull out all the small change he had from the rouble he had spent in the drinking den. He laid it unobtrusively on the windowsill. Then, on his way downstairs, he had a thought, and almost decided to turn back.

'Stupid of me to do that!' he thought. 'They've got Sonia, and I need the money myself.' But realizing that it was too late to take the money back, and that he would never have taken it even if he could, he shrugged and turned back towards his own flat. 'After all, Sonia does need lipstick,' he went on with a bitter smile as he walked down the street. 'Cleanliness of that kind costs money. Hm! And Sonechka herself may go bankrupt today, because it's always a risk, hunting that golden beast... gold-digging... so here they all are, and tomorrow they might all have nothing whatever to eat, but for my money. Well, good for Sonia! What a well they've managed to dig for themselves! And they're making a living from it! Yes, making a living! And they've got used to it. They wept a bit, and then got used to it. We humans can get used to anything, villains that we are!'

He paused in thought.

'Well, but if I was wrong,' he suddenly exclaimed, 'if human beings really aren't *villains*, all of them, the whole human race I mean, then it means that everything else is just second-hand ideas, nothing but bogeys to frighten us, and there are no boundaries, and that's just how it ought to be!'

CHAPTER III

IT was already late when he awoke next day, after a restless night. He felt no stronger for his sleep, and woke feeling queasy, irritable, and bad-tempered. He looked with loathing around his little room. It was a tiny cell about six paces long, and its dusty yellow wallpaper, peeling off the walls, gave it an abject appearance. It was so low that even a moderately tall person would have been uncomfortable, constantly feeling in danger of knocking his head against the ceiling. The furniture was no better than the room—there were three old chairs, in poor repair, and a painted table in the corner with a number of books and notebooks on it. The dust lay thick enough on them to show that they hadn't been touched for a long time. And finally, there was a large rickety sofa occupying almost the whole length of one wall and half the width of the room itself. It had once been covered with chintz, of which nothing but rags remained now; it served as Raskolnikov's bed. He would often sleep on it just as he was, without undressing, and with no sheet over him, covering himself with his ancient student's overcoat* and with a single little pillow under his head. All his linen, both clean and soiled, was shoved under the pillow to raise it higher. In front of the sofa stood a little table.

It would have been hard for Raskolnikov to sink lower or neglect himself more, but in his present mood that actually suited him. He had utterly cut himself off from everyone, as a tortoise withdraws into its shell; even the sight of the maid who was supposed to serve him, and occasionally looked into his room, made him cross and twitchy. Obsessional people, who focus excessively on one particular thing, are like that. As long as two weeks ago, his landlady had stopped supplying him with food, and so far he had not got around to going down to have it out with her, although he was doing without his dinners. Nastasia, the landlady's cook and only servant, was rather glad at the lodger's state of mind; she had quite given up tidying and sweeping his room, only occasionally running a broom over it, perhaps once a week. It was she who had woken him now.

'Get up, what are you sleeping for?' she cried at him. 'It's past nine. I've brought you some tea—d'you want a cup? You must be starving.'

The lodger opened his eyes, shuddered, and recognized Nastasia.

'Was it the landlady sent the tea up?' he asked, raising himself slowly and painfully on the sofa.

'The landlady? Some hope!'

She placed her own cracked teapot in front of him, with most of the tea already drunk, and handed him two yellow sugar-lumps.

'Look, Nastasia, here you are,' he said, groping in his pocket (for he had slept fully clothed) and extracting a handful of coppers. 'Run down and buy me some bread. And get me a bit of sausage at the butcher's, the cheapest sort.'

'I'll get you your bread right away, but wouldn't you like some cabbage soup instead of the sausage? It's good soup, I made it yesterday. I saved some for you yesterday, but you came in so late. It's nice soup.'

When the soup had arrived and he had begun drinking it, Nastasia sat down beside him on the sofa and started chatting to him. She was a peasant woman from the country, and a very garrulous one.

'Praskovia Pavlovna wants to complain to the police about you,' she said.

He scowled.

'The police? What does she want?'

'You're not paying her and you won't leave. It's obvious what she wants.'

'Oh hell, that's all I needed,' he muttered through clenched teeth. 'No... I can't cope with that right now. What a fool she is,' he added aloud. 'I'll go and see her today and talk it over.'

'A fool she may be, and I'm another; but what about you, clever clogs, lying there like a sack of potatoes, and nobody sees anything of you? You used to say you were going out and giving lessons to children; so why don't you do anything these days?'

'I do,' replied Raskolnikov sullenly and unwillingly.

'What do you do?'

'Work.'

'What sort of work?'

'Thinking,' he answered after a pause, in a serious voice.

Nastasia shook with mirth. She was easily moved to laughter, chuckling silently, quivering and shaking all over, until she felt queasy.

'Thought up a lot of money, then, have you?' she finally managed to bring out.

'Can't teach children when I've no boots. Anyway, to hell with them.'

'You shouldn't bite the hand that feeds you.'

'Children only earn you coppers. What can you do with a few coppers?' Raskolnikov went on reluctantly, as if answering his own thoughts.

'And you'd rather have a fortune straight away?'

He gave her a strange look.

'Yes, a whole fortune,' he replied firmly after a short silence.

'You go easy—you're frightening me. All that's very scary. So do I go for your bread or not?'

'Please yourself.'

'Oh, I nearly forgot! A letter came for you yesterday, while you were out.'

'A letter! For me! Whoever from?'

'I don't know who from. I gave the postman three kopeks of my own money. Are you going to pay me back, then?'

'Just bring it here, for God's sake! Bring it here!' cried Raskolnikov in great agitation. 'Oh Lord!'

In a minute the letter was brought. Just as he thought—it was from his mother, in R—— Province.* He turned pale as he took it. He had had no letters for ages; but now there was something else too, that suddenly gripped his heart.

'Nastasia, go away, for heaven's sake. Here are your three kopeks, but for heaven's sake get out, quick!'

The letter trembled in his hands. He didn't want to open it while she was there—he wanted to be left *alone* with it. When Nastasia had gone out, he quickly lifted the letter to his lips and kissed it. Then he gazed long and hard at the writing of the address, that fine, sloping handwriting of his mother's that he knew and loved—his mother who had once taught him to read and write. He put off opening it, as if he were afraid of something. Finally he broke the seal. It was a long, closely written letter occupying two sheets. Both big pages of letter paper were covered in tiny writing.

'My dear Rodia,' wrote his mother,

'It's over two months now since I last had a chat with you by letter. It's been hard on me too, and I've spent a few sleepless nights thinking about it. But I dare say you won't blame me for my silence, which I couldn't help. You know how much I love you—you're all we have, Dunia and I, you're our whole world—all our hope and trust is in you. What didn't I suffer when I found out that you'd left the university months before, because you had nothing to live on, and that your lessons and other earnings had stopped! What could I do to help you, on my pension of a hundred and twenty roubles a year? As you know, the fifteen roubles I sent you four months ago were borrowed from our local merchant Afanasi Ivanovich Vakhrushin, on the security of that same pension. He's a kind man who used to be your father's friend. But once I'd given him the right to draw my pension instead of me, I had to wait till the debt was repaid, and that's only just happened now, so I haven't been able to send you anything all this time. But now, thank God, I believe I can send you some more; and actually we can be quite pleased with our good fortune at the moment, which I can't wait to tell you about. And first of all, would you believe, dearest Rodia, that your sister has already been living with me for a month and a half, and we're never going to be apart again. Praise the Lord, her torments are over, but I'll tell you everything in order, so that you know how everything has been and everything that we have been keeping from you until now. When you wrote to me two months ago that you had heard from someone that Dunia was having to put up with a lot of rudeness at the Svidrigailovs' house, and asked me to tell you exactly what was going on—what could I have answered you at the time? If I'd told you the whole truth, you'd probably have thrown everything up and come to us, even if you had to walk all the way: for I know what you're like and how strongly you feel things, and you never would have let your sister be mistreated. I was quite desperate myself—but what could I do? I didn't know the whole truth then myself. But the main problem was that Dunechka, who had started working for them as a governess last year, had taken an advance of a whole hundred roubles, which was to be deducted in instalments from her monthly wages; so she couldn't leave her post till she had repaid the debt. She had borrowed that sum (I can tell you all about it now, my most precious Rodia) mainly so as to send you the sixty roubles you needed so badly at the time, and which you had from us last year. We told you that the money had come from Dunechka's earlier savings, but that wasn't true, and now I can tell you the whole truth, because by God's providence everything has suddenly changed for the better, and I want you to know how much Dunia loves you and what a generous heart she has. It's true that Mr Svidrigailov treated her very rudely at the beginning, talking disrespectfully to her in various ways, and making fun of her at table... But I don't want to go into all those unpleasant details, upsetting you for nothing, when it's all over now. So in short, and in spite of the fact that Mr Svidrigailov's wife Marfa Petrovna and everyone in the house treated her kindly and politely, Dunechka had a very hard time there, especially when Mr Svidrigailov, like the old soldier he is, found himself under the influence of Bacchus. But what happened next? Just imagine—that madman had nursed a passion for Dunia for a long time, but tried to hide the fact by treating her rudely and mocking her. Perhaps he felt ashamed and horrified at himself, a man of his age and father of a family, for cherishing such irresponsible hopes, and maybe that made him feel hostile to Dunia in spite of himself. Or maybe he hoped to hide the truth from everyone else by being rude to her and making fun of her. But in the end he couldn't control himself and had the effrontery to make Dunia a blatant and revolting proposition, promising her all kinds of bribes and even offering to throw everything up and run away to a different village with her, or more likely take her abroad. You can imagine what she went through! She couldn't leave her job straight away, not only because of the money she owed but also out of consideration for Marfa Petrovna, who might have come to suspect something, so that Dunia would have set off a family quarrel. And it would have been a great scandal for Dunechka as well—it couldn't have gone off quietly. And there were a lot of other reasons too, which meant that Dunia could never have hoped to escape from that dreadful household before another six weeks had passed. Of course, you know Dunia, you know how intelligent and strong-minded she is. Dunechka is capable of putting up with a great deal, and even in the very worst situations she finds enough generosity of heart so as not to weaken. She didn't even write to me about all that, not wanting to upset me, although we were always exchanging news. But it all ended unexpectedly. Marfa Petrovna accidentally overheard her husband pleading with Dunechka in the garden, and misinterpreted it all, accusing her of everything and thinking she was responsible for it. They had a terrible scene, right there in the garden: Marfa Petrovna even hit Dunia, refused to listen to anything, and spent a whole hour yelling at her; finally she gave orders for Dunia to be sent straight back to me in town, on an ordinary farm-cart, with all her belongings flung into it, linen, dresses, everything higgledy-piggledy, nothing packed up or folded. And just then a downpour started, and Dunia, insulted and shamed, had to ride a whole seventeen versts* with that peasant, in his open cart. Now just think—what could I have written to you in a letter, in answer to yours, which I had received two months ago? What could I have written about? I was in despair myself; I didn't dare tell you the truth, because you would have been so miserable, upset, and indignant—and anyway, what could you have done? You might have come to grief yourself—and besides, Dunechka wouldn't let me tell you. But filling a letter with trivialities and writing about just anything, when I was suffering such anguish—that was more than I could stand. For a whole month it was the talk of the town, and it got to such a pitch that Dunia and I couldn't go to church any more because of all the contemptuous looks and whispers—indeed, things were said aloud too, in our presence. All our friends dropped us, they even stopped bowing to us in the street, and I heard for a fact that some shop assistants and clerks were planning to insult us in a horrible way, by smearing our gates with pitch, so that our landlord began demanding that we should leave the flat. It was Marfa Petrovna who was behind all that—she had succeeded in slandering Dunia and blackening her reputation in every household. She knows everyone here, and all that month she kept coming over to town, and since she's a bit of a chatterbox and loves telling people her family stories, and particularly loves complaining about her husband to all and sundry, which isn't nice at all, she very quickly spread the whole story not only all round the town but over the whole district. It made me ill, but Dunechka was tougher than me, and if only you had seen how she herself stood up to everything, and comforted me and cheered me up! She's an angel! But by God's mercy, our trials came to an end: Mr Svidrigailov came to his senses and repented, and— probably out of pity for Dunia –presented Marfa Petrovna with full and incontrovertible proof of Dunechka's complete innocence, in the shape of a letter which Dunia had found herself obliged to write and hand to him, even before Marfa Petrovna came upon them in the garden, refusing any further private conversations and secret assignations, which he had been insisting on, and this letter had remained in Mr Svidrigailov's hands after Dunechka's departure. In that letter she had reproached him most angrily and indignantly for his improper behaviour towards Marfa Petrovna, reminding him that he was a father and a family man, and finally, how revolting it was of him to torment and cause misery to an already unhappy and defenceless young girl. In a word, my dearest Rodia, her letter was so dignified and so moving that I sobbed when I read it, and even now I can't read it without bursting into tears. And what is more, the servants eventually gave an account of the event which absolved Dunia from blame—they had seen and understood far more than Mr Svidrigailov imagined—which is invariably what happens. Marfa Petrovna was quite astonished, "crushed all over again" as she confessed to us, but utterly convinced of Dunechka's innocence, and on the very next day, which was a Sunday, she went straight to the cathedral, got down on her knees and prayed in tears to the Mother of God to give her the strength to bear this new trial and to do her duty. Then she came straight from the cathedral to us, not stopping anywhere on the way, and told us everything, and wept bitterly; and repenting with all her heart she embraced Dunechka and implored her to forgive her. And that same morning she went straight from our house to visit all the houses in town to testify again to Dunechka's innocence and explain, in tears, how noble her sentiments and behaviour had been. And that wasn't all—she showed everyone Dunechka's own handwritten letter to Mr Svidrigailov, and read it aloud to them, and even let people take copies of it (which I think was going too far). So she found herself having to spend several days on end visiting everyone in the town, in turn, because some people were offended that others had been given preference over them, so queues built up, and in every house she was expected in advance, and everyone knew that on such and such a day Marfa Petrovna would be reading that letter in a particular house, and at every reading people would come along even after they had already heard the letter read several times, in their own homes and then their friends' homes, one after the other. In my opinion, much of this, a very great deal of this, was going too far; but that's Marfa Petrovna's character. At least she completely succeeded in restoring Dunechka's honour, and all the ignominy of the whole business fell as an indelible disgrace upon her husband, the chief culprit, so that I even feel sorry

for him, crazy man, he's been too severely punished. Straight away
Dunia began getting invitations to give lessons in people's homes, but
she turned them down. And generally everyone started to treat her with
special respect. All that was particularly helpful in bringing about the
unexpected event which has now, as we may say, transformed our whole
destiny. Let me tell you, dear Rodia, that Dunia has received a proposal
of marriage and has already given her consent, which I want to tell you
about at once. And although this has all been settled without your
advice, I am sure you won't hold it against either me or your sister, since
you can see for yourself that we couldn't have waited and put off replying until we heard from you. And in any case you couldn't have judged
things properly without being here. This is how it all happened. He is
called Piotr Petrovich Luzhin and is already a Court Councillor, and
a distant relative of Marfa Petrovna, who helped in many ways to promote the match. He began by expressing a wish, through her, to make
our acquaintance, and was very properly received by us, and had coffee,
and on the very next day he sent a letter in which he made a very courteous proposal and requested an early and definite reply. He is an active
and busy man, and is now in a hurry to get to Petersburg, so every
minute is precious to him. Of course we were very taken aback at first,
since everything had happened too suddenly and unexpectedly. We
spent that whole day thinking about it and discussing it. He's a reliable
man, well-to-do, he has two positions and has already accumulated
some capital. Of course, he is forty-five years old, but he is quite pleas-
ant-looking and could still be attractive to women, and in any case he is
a very solid, decent person, only a little bit gloomy and rather haughty.
But that may only be a first impression. And let me warn you, my dear
Rodia, when you meet him in Petersburg, which you will do very soon,
don't judge him too hastily and impulsively, as you tend to do, if you
find anything in him that you don't like at first sight. I'm saying this
just in case, although I'm sure that he will make a good impression on
you. And in any case, if you want to get to know someone, you have
to take things gradually and cautiously if you're not to get them wrong
and become prejudiced, which would be very difficult to put right and
smooth over later on. And Piotr Petrovich is, or at least seems in many
ways to be, a most estimable person. At his first visit, he told us he was
a man of positive views, but that, as he put it, he shares many of the
"convictions of our younger generations",* and is against all forms of
prejudice. And he said a lot of other things too, because he seems to be
a little bit vain and very fond of being listened to, but of course that's not
much of a shortcoming. I didn't understand a lot myself, of course, but

Dunia explained that although he may not have all that much education, he's an intelligent man and seems to be a kind one too. You know your sister's character, Rodia. She's a firm, sensible, patient, and generous-hearted girl, though she has an impulsive heart, as I know very well. Of course there's no particular love either on her side or his, but Dunia, besides being an intelligent girl, is as good as an angel, and she'll make it her duty to keep her husband happy, and he in his turn will no doubt do the same for her, which so far we have no great reason to doubt, although it must be admitted that the whole business has happened very quickly. And besides, he is a very hard-headed man, and of course he'll see for himself that the happier he makes Dunechka, the more certain he'll be of his own happiness in marriage. And as for any quirks of his character, any old habits of his or even certain differences in their views (which you can't avoid even in the happiest marriages)—on that score, Dunechka herself has said to me that she'll put her trust in herself, that there's no need to worry about this, and that she can put up with a great deal so long as their future relationship is fair and honest. Even I, for example, found him rather abrupt at first; but of course that may be because he is a man who knows his own mind, which there is no doubt he does. For instance, at his second visit, when he had already had Dunia's consent, he mentioned during our conversation that even before meeting Dunia, he had resolved to choose a girl who was honest but had no dowry, and certainly one who had already experienced misfortune; because, he explained, a husband should not be indebted to his wife in any way, and it was much better if she saw him as her benefactor. I must add that he expressed himself rather more gently and kindly than I have just done, because I've forgotten the actual words he used, I only remember the sense of them, and what's more he didn't mean to say it, it probably just slipped out in the heat of the conversation, and he actually tried to put it right and soften it afterwards, but even so it struck me as rather harsh, as I said to Dunia later. But Dunia answered me quite crossly, saying that "words weren't deeds", and of course she's right. Before making up her mind, Dunechka spent a sleepless night, and thinking that I was asleep she got up from her bed and spent the whole night pacing up and down the room, and eventually knelt in front of the icon and prayed fervently for a long time, and then in the morning she told me she had made up her mind.

'I've already said that Piotr Petrovich is setting off for Petersburg now. He has got important business there, he wants to set up a law office in the city. He has been handling all sorts of actions and lawsuits for a long time, and just recently he won an important case. And another reason he has to go to Petersburg is that he has a big case before the Senate.* And so, my dearest Rodia, he could be most useful to you too, in all kinds of ways, and Dunia and I have already decided that you can definitely start out on your career right from this very day, and regard your future as clear and settled. Oh, if only that could come true! That would be so good for you, we would have to look on it as no less than a blessing on us from the Almighty himself. It's all that Dunia dreams of. We've already been bold enough to say a few words on the subject to Piotr Petrovich. He replied cautiously, saying that as he cannot of course do without a secretary, it's obviously better to pay a salary to a relative than some outsider, provided that the relative shows himself capable of fulfilling his duties (as if you could ever be incapable!), but at the same time he wondered whether your studies at the university would leave you enough time to work in his office. That was all that was said at the time, but Dunia now thinks of nothing else. She has been in an absolute fever for the past few days, and has dreamed up a whole plan for you to end up eventually as Piotr Petrovich's associate and even his partner in litigation, particularly as you're in the law faculty yourself. And Rodia, I absolutely agree with her and share all her plans and hopes, which seem perfectly realistic to me; and in spite of Piotr Petrovich's evasiveness at present, which is entirely understandable (because he doesn't yet know you), Dunia is firmly convinced that she will have enough influence with her future husband to manage the whole thing; she's quite certain of that. Of course we took care not to let slip a word to Piotr Petrovich about any of these future dreams of ours, and particularly not about you becoming his partner. He is a very hard-headed man and would probably take it quite amiss, thinking that it was all nothing but pipe dreams. And in the same way neither I nor Dunia have yet breathed a word to him about our firm hope that he will help us to support you financially while you're at university; the reason we haven't mentioned it is that, firstly, it will happen of its own accord in due course, and he will probably make the offer himself without anything more being said (for how could he refuse Dunechka that?), and even more so because you yourself can become his right-hand man in the office and receive that kind of support not as a favour, but in the form of your properly earned salary. That's what Dunechka wants to bring about, and I quite agree with her. And secondly, the other reason why we said nothing to him is that I particularly wanted you to be on an equal footing with him when we all meet together soon. When Dunia was talking enthusiastically to him about you, he answered that he would have to take a proper look at a person for himself, whoever it was, before judging him, and that when he makes your acquaintance he looks forward to forming his own opinion of you. Do you know what, my darling Rodia—it seems to me, for certain reasons (which actually have nothing to do with Piotr Petrovich, but are just my own personal whims, perhaps simply because I'm an old woman and feel that way)—it seems to me that I would perhaps do better to live by myself after their marriage, as I do now, and not together with them. I'm perfectly certain that he will be honourable and delicate enough to invite me himself, and ask me not to be parted from my daughter again, and if he hasn't said so up till now, it's simply because this is an obvious assumption; but I shall refuse. I have observed on a number of occasions during my life that husbands aren't all that keen on their mothers-in-law, and I not only don't want to be any sort of burden to anyone, but I myself would like to be entirely independent, so long as I have a crust of bread of my own, and such children as you and Dunechka. If possible I shall get a home near the two of you, because, Rodia, I've kept the best bit till the end of my letter. Let me tell you, my dearest treasure, that all three of us may perhaps, very soon, meet together and hold each other in our arms again, after a three-year separation! It has been *definitely* decided that Dunia and I are going to Petersburg, I don't know exactly when, but at all events very very soon, perhaps even next week. It all depends on Piotr Petrovich's arrangements; as soon as he has sounded matters out in Petersburg, he's going to let us know. What he wants, for various reasons, is to have the wedding fixed as soon as possible, and even to have it before the coming fast, or if that's too soon to be practical then immediately after Assumption.* Oh, how happy shall I be to clasp you to my heart! Dunia is all excited at the joyful prospect of seeing you, and once said for a joke that she would have married Piotr Petrovich just for that alone. What an angel she is! She won't add anything to this letter for you, but just asked me to say that she has such a lot to talk to you about, so much that she can't even take up a pen right now, because one can't write anything in just a few lines, one only gets upset; but she told me to hug you tightly and send you endless kisses. But although we may perhaps be meeting very soon, I shall still send you some money in the next few days, as much as ever I can. Now that everyone has heard that Dunechka is to marry Piotr Petrovich, my credit has suddenly improved, and I know for a fact that Afanasy Ivanovich will be willing to lend me as much as seventy-five roubles against my pension, so I may perhaps send you twenty-five or even thirty roubles. I would send even more, but I'm worried about our travelling expenses; and although Piotr Petrovich has been kind enough to cover part of the cost of our move to the capital, and himself offered to have our luggage and the large trunk delivered at his own expense (through someone or other that he knows), we still have to get ourselves to Petersburg, and you can't just turn up there without a kopek, just for the first few days. Anyway, Dunia and I have worked it all out in detail, and it turns out that the journey won't cost all that much. From us to the railway is only ninety versts, and we've already made an arrangement with a peasant driver we know, just in case; and then Dunechka and I will be perfectly happy travelling third class. So perhaps I'll manage to send you not twenty-five roubles, but probably thirty. But enough of all this—I've covered the whole of two sheets, and there's no more room; that's all our story; and what a lot of things have happened! And now, my most precious Rodia, I embrace you until we meet soon again, and send you a mother's blessing. Love your sister Dunia, Rodia; love her as she loves you, and know that she loves you endlessly, more than her own self. She is an angel, and you, Rodia, you are all we have, all our hope and trust is in you. So long as you're happy, we'll be happy too. Do you pray to God, Rodia, as you used to, and do you believe in the goodness of our Creator and Redeemer? I dread in my heart that you may have fallen prey to the new fashion for unbelief—have you? If you have, I pray for you. Remember, my love, how when you were a child, and your father was still alive, you used to lisp your prayers as I held you on my knees, and how happy we all were then! Farewell, or rather—till we meet again! I hug you ever so tightly and kiss you endlessly.

Yours till the grave
Pulkheria Raskolnikova'

Right from the start, as he read this letter, Raskolnikov's face was almost constantly wet with tears; but when he came to the end his face was pale and twisted, and a grim, angry, malignant smile snaked over his lips. He rested his head on his threadbare, grimy pillow, and for a long time he thought and thought. His heart was pounding, his thoughts were racing. Eventually he felt stifled and cramped in this tiny little yellow garret, no bigger than a cupboard or a portmanteau. His eyes and his thoughts longed for the open air. He grabbed hold of his hat and went out, no longer dreading to meet anyone on the stairs—he had forgotten all about that. He made for Vasilievsky Island, along V——Prospekt,* as if hurrying there for some purpose; but as was his usual habit, he walked without noticing where he was going, muttering and even talking aloud to himself, to the great astonishment of passers-by. Many took him to be drunk.

CHAPTER IV

READING his mother's letter had been excruciating. But as for its main, central point, he had not a moment's doubt, even as he read it. The essential issue was decided in his mind, and settled once and for all. 'This marriage shall never happen, so long as I'm alive, and to hell with Mister Luzhin!'

'The whole thing's obvious,' he muttered to himself with a sneer, feeling a vicious sense of triumph at the anticipated success of his decision. 'No, Mamasha, no, Dunia, you won't hoodwink me!... And they're even apologizing for not asking my advice, but settling the thing without me! Of course they would! They think it's too late to break it off now; we'll see if it's too late or not! And what a brilliant excuse: "He's such a businesslike man, Piotr Petrovich, such a businesslike man that there's no way he can get married except on the mail-coach, practically on the railway!" No, Dunechka, I see it all, I know what *a lot* you want to tell me; and I know what it was you were thinking about all night, pacing up and down the room, and what you were praying about to Our Lady of Kazan* who stands in Mamasha's bedroom. It's a hard climb, up to Golgotha.* Hm... So, it's firmly decided then: you, Avdotya Romanovna, are consenting to marry a businesslike and sensible man, a man who has his own capital (who *already* has his own capital— that sounds more solid and impressive), who has two jobs, and shares the convictions of our younger generations (as Mamasha writes), and *seems to be* kind, as Dunechka herself remarks. That *seems to be* is most priceless of all! And this same Dunechka is going to marry this same *seems to be*! Priceless! Priceless!

'And it's a curious thing—why did Mamasha write about "our younger generations"? Was it just to illustrate his character, or did she have something else in mind too—to get me to approve of Mr Luzhin? You sly creatures! And another thing it would be interesting to find out—how open were they with each other, that day and that night, and ever since? Were they straight in everything they said to one another, or did they both realize that they were feeling and thinking the same things, so there was no point in voicing them openly and letting it all out to no purpose? That was probably how it happened, more or less.

You can see from the letter that Mama found him *rather* harsh, and then Mama innocently went and told Dunia her impressions. And of course Dunia got angry and "answered crossly". Well, wouldn't she! Who wouldn't lose their temper, when the whole business is understood, with no need for naïve questions, and it's been decided, so there's no use talking about it. And what's all this that she writes to me—"Love Dunia, Rodia, she loves you more than her own self"? Isn't she being tormented by pangs of conscience herself, because she's agreed to sacrifice her daughter for the sake of her son? "You're our hope, you're everything for us!" Oh, Mamasha!'—He was seething with mounting fury, and had he come upon Mr Luzhin at that moment, he would probably have murdered him.

'Hm, that's true,' he went on, chasing after the whirlwind that stormed through his head. 'It's true that you have to approach a person "gradually and cautiously" if you want to get to know him; but Mister Luzhin is easy to read. The most important thing is that he's "a businesslike man, and *seems to be* a kind one"—and look, no joke, he's having their luggage sent on, he'll have the big trunk delivered at his own expense! Now isn't that kind! While the two of them, the *bride* and her mother, have hired a peasant with his cart, covered with bast matting (oh yes, I've travelled in those)! Never mind! It's only ninety versts, "and then we'll be perfectly happy travelling third class", for a thousand versts or so. And very sensible, you have to cut your coat according to your cloth; but you, Mister Luzhin, what about you? This is your bride, after all... And you couldn't have known that her mother was borrowing money against her future pension to pay for their trip, could you? Naturally, this would be your normal commercial practice, a mutually profitable enterprise on an equal footing, with expenses equally shared—food fifty-fifty, but buy your own tobacco, as the saying goes. But even then, this businesslike man of theirs has cheated a bit—their baggage will cost less than their fares, in fact it'll probably go free. Why can't they both see that—or don't they want to see it? And they're happy about it all! Happy! And this is only the start, remember—the real treats are yet to come! And what's important here isn't the stinginess, or the avarice—it's the *tone* of it all. That'll be the tone once they're married; this is a foretaste... And what's Mama up to, squandering her money? What'll she have left when she turns up in Petersburg? Three silver roubles, or two "little rouble notes", as that... old woman... says, hm! How does she propose to live in Petersburg after that? Somehow she's already worked out that she and Dunia won't be able to live together after the wedding, not even at the start—hasn't she? That charming man has probably "accidentally let slip" something of the sort, made his intentions known, even if Mama emphatically dismisses anything like that—"I'll refuse on my own account", says she. So what's she counting on—the hundred and twenty roubles from her pension, minus what she owes to Afanasy Ivanovich? She knits winter shawls and embroiders cuffs, and ruins her old eyes doing it—but those shawls only bring in twenty roubles a year on top of her hundred and twenty, I know that perfectly well. So they must be relying on Mister Luzhin's sense of honour—"he'll offer his help without being asked, he'll be pressing it on us". Some hope! And that's always the way with these beautiful souls straight out of Schiller*—they dress someone up in peacock feathers, right up to the last minute, they look for the best instead of the worst, right up to the last minute, and even if they suspect that the medal has a reverse side, they'll never breathe a word of the truth to themselves till it's too late, the very thought of it makes them cringe, they push the truth away with both hands, until the very moment when the man they've dressed up in false colours comes and personally thumbs his nose at them. And I wonder whether Mister Luzhin has any decorations; I'll bet anything that he has an Anna in his buttonhole,* and wears it when he dines out with contractors and merchants. And he'll probably wear it for his wedding too! Oh well, to hell with him!...

'No, forget about Mama, never mind her, that's just how she is—but what about Dunia then? Dunechka, my darling, I know you! You were all of twenty years old when we last saw each other, and I've understood your character. There's Mama writing "Dunechka can put up with a great deal". That I knew, my dear. I knew that, all of two and a half years ago, and I've been thinking about it for the last two and a half years, just about the fact that "Dunechka can put up with a great deal". If she could put up with Mr Svidrigailov, and all that that involved, it certainly shows that she can put up with a great deal. And now they've decided, Mama and she, that she can even put up with Mister Luzhin, as he expounds his theory about the advantages of wives rescued from poverty to marry husbands who are their benefactors—and expounds it practically at their first meeting. All right, let's suppose that he did "let it slip", although he's a rational person (so perhaps he didn't "let it slip" at all, but fully intended to make it clear from the start); but what about Dunia then? Dunia can see through that man, but that's the man she has to live with. She'd live on black bread and water, but she wouldn't sell her soul, she wouldn't sacrifice her moral freedom for the sake of comfort—she wouldn't sacrifice it for the whole of Schleswig-Holstein,* never mind Mister Luzhin. No, Dunia wasn't like that when

I knew her—and of course she won't have changed now! There's no denying it, the Svidrigailovs were hard to bear! It's hard to spend your whole life traipsing round the provinces as a governess earning two hundred roubles a year, but I know that she'd sooner toil on a plantation with the negroes, or slave away for a German landowner on the Baltic like a Latvian peasant, rather than pollute her soul and her moral feelings by binding herself to a man she doesn't respect, and who means nothing to her—for evermore, and for nothing but her own personal gain! And even if Mister Luzhin was made of solid gold or purest diamond, even then she'd never consent to become Mister Luzhin's legal concubine! So why's she consenting now? What's the solution? It's perfectly clear—she won't sell herself for her own gain, or her own comfort, or even to save her life—but for someone else, yes, she'll sell herself! For someone dear to her, someone she adores! That's the secret of the whole business—she'll sell herself for her brother, and her mother! Oh yes, if we have to, we can even suppress our moral sense; our freedom, our peace of mind, even our conscience—all of it, we'll carry it all down to the marketplace. And that's the end of her life! So long as those whom we love so dearly are happy. And not only that—we'll dream up our own casuistry, we'll learn from the Jesuits,* and for a time we'll even reassure ourselves, we'll persuade ourselves that this has to be done, it really has to be done, in a good cause. That's just how we are, and it's all as clear as daylight—clear that it's all about Rodion Romanovich Raskolnikov, none other, he's the one at centre stage. After all, this could bring him happiness, keep him at university, make him a partner in the firm, transform his whole life; indeed, he'll probably be a rich man later on, distinguished and respected, perhaps even famous before he dies! And Mother? But this is all about Rodia, her precious Rodia, her firstborn! How could one not sacrifice even such a daughter for the sake of such a firstborn son? Oh, you dear, prejudiced hearts! No, I don't suppose we'd even refuse Sonechka's destiny! Sonechka, Sonechka Marmeladova, the eternal Sonechka, as long as the world endures! But have you weighed up your sacrifice, both of you, all the sacrifice you're making? Have you? Are you equal to it? Is it worthwhile? Is it sensible? Do you know, Dunechka, that Sonechka's fate is in no way worse than yours with Mister Luzhin? "There can be no love here", writes Mama. But supposing that there not only can't be love, there can be no respect either; supposing, on the contrary, that there's revulsion, contempt, loathing—what then? And in that case it turns out that once again, "cleanliness has to be maintained". Aren't I right? Do you understand, do you realize what such cleanliness means? Do you realize that Luzhin's cleanliness is no different from Sonechka's, or perhaps even worse, even nastier and fouler, because you, Dunechka, can still look forward to plenty of comfort, while for the other one it's a simple question of starving to death! "It costs a lot, Dunechka, that sort of cleanliness!" And if you find out later on that you can't stand it, will you repent? How much grief and sadness, curses and tears, all in secret—how much? Because you're not a Marfa Petrovna, are you? And what'll happen to Mama then? She's tormented with anxiety already; but what'll happen then, when she sees it all clearly? And what'll happen to me?... I mean, what did you actually take me for? I don't want your sacrifice, Dunechka! I don't want it, Mama! It'll never happen while I'm alive, never, never! I won't accept it!'

He suddenly broke off and stood still.

'It'll never happen? And what'll you do to stop it happening? Forbid it? What right do you have? What can you promise them, you yourself, to buy yourself that right? To devote your whole life, your whole future, to them, *once you've finished your studies and got a job*? Yes, we've heard that story before, but that's part two—what about now? It's now that you've got to do something, don't you understand? And what are you up to right now? Stealing from them, that's what. All the money they have comes from the hundred-rouble pension and a secured loan from Messrs Svidrigailov! How are you going to protect them from those Svidrigailovs, and from Afanasy Ivanovich Vakhrushin—you future millionaire, you Zeus who holds their fate in your hands? Will you do that in ten years' time? But in ten years your mother will have gone blind from knitting shawls, and probably from her tears too; she'll be wasted away with fasting; and what about your sister? Just work it out—what's going to happen to your sister in ten years' time, or during those same ten years? Can't you see?'

So he tormented himself, fretting himself with these questions and even quite enjoying it. Of course all these were not new questions that had suddenly occurred to him; they were old, familiar heartaches. They had begun gnawing at him a long time ago, and his heart was worn out with them. The anguish he now suffered was born in him ages ago; it had grown and accumulated, and now it had ripened and condensed and taken on the form of a terrible, monstrous, fantastic question which had worn out his heart and soul, insistently demanding an answer. And now his mother's letter had burst on him like a thunderbolt. It was clear that this was no time for mental agony or passive suffering, or mere reflection on how insoluble the questions were. He had to do something, right now, as quickly as he could. He must make up his mind, decide on something, anything—or else...

'Or else give up my life altogether!' he suddenly cried out in a frenzy. 'Meekly submit to my fate, as it is now, once and for all, and stifle all that's in me, and give up any right to act, or live, or love!'

'Can you understand, can you understand, my dear sir, what it means to have nowhere else to turn?'—all at once he remembered Marmeladov's question the day before. 'Surely everyone has to have somewhere to turn...'

And suddenly he gave a shudder. Another thought, again from the previous day, had flashed through his mind. But it wasn't the sudden thought that had made him shudder. For he had known, he'd had a *premonition*, that it couldn't fail to 'flash through his mind', and he'd been expecting it. Nor had this thought only come to him yesterday. But the difference was this: a month ago, and even yesterday, it had only been a dream; whereas now... now it no longer appeared to him as a dream, but in some new, ominous, altogether unfamiliar form; and he had suddenly sensed this himself. There was a pounding in his head, and everything went black.

He hurriedly looked round, searching for something. He wanted to sit down, and was looking for a bench. He was now walking along K—— Boulevard,* and could make out a bench some hundred yards ahead. He hurried on as fast as he could; but on the way a small incident occurred which absorbed all his attention for several minutes.

As he looked at the bench, he observed a woman walking some twenty yards ahead of him. At first he took no notice of her, just as he had noticed nothing that had passed before his eyes so far. It often happened that he would walk, perhaps on his way home, and then would remember nothing of the route he had taken. That was how he usually behaved. But there was something so strange about the woman ahead of him, something so striking from the very first glance, that she gradually caught his attention, first against his will and almost to his annoyance, but then more and more insistently. He suddenly wanted to make out what it was that was so strange about her. Firstly, the woman—seemingly a very young girl—was walking bareheaded in the blazing heat, with no parasol or gloves, and waving her arms about in a peculiar way. She was in a thin silk dress, but she wore it very oddly, somehow; it was almost unbuttoned, and the back of the waist, at the very top of the skirt, was torn, with a whole flap of fabric dangling loose. She had a small scarf flung over her bare neck, but it was rather crooked and lopsided. And to complete the picture, the girl was walking unsteadily, stumbling and staggering from side to side. Eventually this encounter absorbed all Raskolnikov's attention. He caught up with the girl just as they came level with the bench, but when she reached it she just sank down onto it, at one end, leaning her head against the backrest; she closed her eyes, looking utterly exhausted. He looked closely at her and saw at once that she was quite drunk. It was a strange and shocking sight. He even wondered if he could be mistaken. He saw before him a very youthful little face, sixteen or maybe even just fifteen years old—small, fair-haired, pretty, but quite flushed and puffy-looking. The girl seemed barely aware of herself; she had crossed one leg over the other, exposing much more than she should, and to all appearances had no idea that she was in the street.

Raskolnikov didn't sit down, but didn't want to leave; he stood before her in puzzlement. The boulevard was always half deserted, and now, at one in the afternoon on this blazing hot day, there was almost nobody about. And yet, some fifteen yards away to one side, a gentleman had stopped by the roadside, and evidently would have very much liked to come up to the girl as well, for some purpose of his own. He, too, had probably noticed her from a distance and hurried after her, but Raskolnikov had forestalled him. He was looking malevolently at Raskolnikov, while trying not to show it, and impatiently awaiting his turn once this annoying ragamuffin took himself off. His intentions were clear. The gentleman was some thirty years old, plump and thick-set, with a pink-and-white complexion, rosy lips, a little moustache, and very modishly dressed. Raskolnikov was overcome with fury; he suddenly longed to insult this sleek dandy. He left the girl for a minute and walked up to the gentleman.

'Hey, you, sir—Svidrigailov!* What do you want here?' he shouted, clenching his fists and laughing through angry, foam-flecked lips.

'What's the meaning of this?' asked the man sternly, frowning in haughty astonishment.

'Get away from here, that's what!'

'How dare you, you lout!...'

And he raised his cane. Raskolnikov hurled himself at him, fists flying, oblivious of the fact that this thickset gentleman could have dealt with two of him. But at this point someone seized him firmly from behind, and a policeman stood between them.

'That's enough of that, gentlemen, no fighting in a public place. What do you want? Who are you?' he said, turning sternly to Raskolnikov and eyeing his rags.

Raskolnikov looked closely at him. He had an honest soldierly face, with a grey moustache and side whiskers, and looked sensible.

'You're just the man I want,' he cried, seizing hold of his arm. 'I'm Raskolnikov, ex-student... You may as well know that too,' he added to the other gentleman. 'But you, come with me, please, I want to show you something.'

And he pulled the policeman by the arm towards the bench.

'Here, look at her, totally drunk, she was just walking along the boulevard: no saying what sort of girl she is, but she doesn't look like a professional. Most likely someone got her drunk and seduced her... her first time... see what I mean? And then just packed her off into the street. Look at how her dress is torn, look how she's got it on: someone must have dressed her, she didn't dress herself, someone who didn't know how to do it, some man. That's obvious. And now have a look over there: that dandy I was just going to fight with, I don't know who he is, never seen him before; but he'd noticed her on the street too, just now, saw she was drunk and not in her right senses, and now he's desperate to come along and pick her up—since she's in such a state—and take her off somewhere. That's got to be how it is, believe me, there's no mistaking it. I saw him myself, watching her and following her, only I got in his way, and now he's just waiting for me to go away. There he is, just walked off a bit, standing there, pretending to roll a cigarette... How can we keep her out of his clutches? How can we get her home? Have a think!'

The policeman saw and understood everything at once. The fat gentleman—that was obvious, of course. But there was the girl too. The policeman bent over her to take a closer look, with sincere pity on his face.

'Oh, what a shame!' he said, shaking his head. 'She's no more than a child. Led astray, that's for sure. Listen, lady,' he said aloud to her, 'where do you live?' The girl opened her tired, drowsy eyes, looked dully at the men questioning her, and waved them away.

'Listen,' said Raskolnikov, 'here you are.' He felt in his pocket, succeeded in finding twenty kopeks and brought them out. 'Here, hire a cab and get the man to take her home. If only we knew her address!'

'Miss! Hey, miss,' the policeman began again, taking the money. 'I'm just going to call you a cab, and I'll see you home myself. Where do we go, eh? Where's your home?'

'Get off! Leave me alone!...' the girl mumbled, waving him away again.

'Oh dear, oh dear, that's not good! Oh, what a shame, young miss, what a disgrace!' He shook his head again, with disapproval, pity, and indignation. 'Well, here's a problem!' he said to Raskolnikov, and instantly sized him up again from head to foot. This was another odd creature—dressed in such rags, and handing out money!

'Did you find her far from here?' he asked.

'I tell you—she was walking in front of me, staggering along, right here on the boulevard. The moment she got to the bench, she just collapsed onto it.'

'Oh Lord, what's the world coming to! What a shame! Such a young thing, and already drunk! She's been taken in, that's for certain. And her dress is all torn... What vice there is nowadays!... I expect she's from a good family, fallen on hard times... There are lots like that these days. She looks nicely brought up, almost a young lady...'—and again he bent over her.

Perhaps he too had young daughters like her—'like young ladies, nicely brought up', acting well bred and aping the new fashions...

'The main thing', said Raskolnikov anxiously, 'is not to let that villain get her! Just think how he'll abuse her! It's clear as daylight what he wants. Look at the villain there, he's not moving from the spot!'

Raskolnikov was speaking loudly and pointing directly at the man, who heard him and was on the point of getting angry again. But he thought better of it and contented himself with a contemptuous look. Then he slowly walked some ten paces further off, and stopped again.

'Well, we can stop him getting her,' replied the police officer thoughtfully. 'If only she'd tell us where to take her—otherwise... Young lady! Young lady!' he repeated, bending over her.

She suddenly opened her eyes wide, looked attentively at him as if something had dawned on her, then got up from the bench and walked back in the direction from which she had come.

'Phoo, disgusting men, won't leave us alone!' she muttered, waving them away again with her hand. She was walking fast, but staggering as badly as ever. The dandy followed her, keeping to the opposite pavement and not taking his eyes off her.

'Never you mind, sir, I won't let him,' said the whiskered policeman, setting off after them. 'Oh my, what terrible vice these days!'

At that moment something seemed to sting Raskolnikov; in an instant his feelings were turned on their head.

'Hey, you! Listen!' he shouted to the whiskered policeman. The man turned round.

'Stop! What's the point? Leave it! Let him have his fun!' he cried, pointing at the dandy. 'What's it to you?'

The policeman stared at him uncomprehendingly. Raskolnikov laughed.

'E-eh!' sighed the policeman, waving him away and walking on behind the dandy and the girl. He probably took Raskolnikov for a lunatic, or worse.

'He's gone off with my twenty kopeks,' said Raskolnikov viciously when he was alone. 'Let's hope he takes some more off the other man, and lets the girl go off with him, and that'll be an end of it... Whatever came over me to get involved? Should I be the one to help? And do I have the right to help? Let the two of them eat each other alive—what's it to me? And how dared I give away those twenty kopeks—were they mine to give?'

Despite these strange words, he felt very downcast. He sat down on the empty bench, thinking confused thoughts... At that moment he felt too gloomy to think about anything at all. He would have liked to sink into oblivion, forget everything, then wake up and start afresh.

'Poor girl!' he said, looking at the empty corner of the bench. 'She'll come to herself, cry a bit, and then her mother will find out... First she'll knock her about, and then she'll give her a proper thrashing, to hurt her and shame her—and she'll probably send her away. And even if she doesn't send her away, the Darya Frantsevnas will sniff her out, and then my girl will start sneaking out of doors in secret, going off this way and that... And that'll lead straight to the hospital (that's always the way with these girls who live with very honest mothers, and run wild on the sly); and then—then hospital again... and vodka... and taverns... and another hospital... and in two or three years she's a wreck, still only eighteen or nineteen years old... Haven't I seen girls like that? And how did they get that way? Just like this, that's how... Ugh! Well, let her! That's how things have to be, so they say. Such and such a percentage, they say, has to go that way each year... go some-where... to the devil, no doubt, so the rest can stay clean and be left in peace. Percentage! What wonderful words they have, don't they! So reassuring, so scientific. Percentage, they say, and that means there's nothing to worry about. But if they used a different word... well then, perhaps it might be more upsetting... And supposing Dunechka her-self somehow ends up in that percentage? Or if not that one, then another one?'

'And where am I going?' he suddenly thought. 'How odd. There was something I went out to do. As soon as I'd read the letter, I went straight out... I was going to Vasilievsky Island to see Razumikhin, that's what it was... I remember now. But what for? And why did I sud-denly have the idea, right now, of going to see Razumikhin? That's very strange.'

He was astonished at himself. Razumikhin was one of his old class-mates at university. The strange thing was that when Raskolnikov was at university he had had almost no friends, avoided everybody, visited no one and hated being visited. And everyone soon gave up on him. He somehow took no part in general gatherings, or conversations, or amusements, or anything else. He studied hard, he drove himself, and people respected him for that, but no one liked him. He was very poor, but haughty and proud and uncommunicative, as if he were nursing some secret. Some of his companions suspected him of looking down on them as if they were children; as if he had outstripped them all in maturity, knowledge and opinions, and regarded their own opinions and interests as beneath him.

And yet, for some reason, he'd grown close to Razumikhin, or if not close, he was at least more open and communicative with him. As a matter of fact it was impossible to have any other sort of relationship with Razumikhin, who was an unusually cheerful, open-hearted young man, good-natured to the point of simplicity. But that simplicity con-cealed depth and dignity; the best of his companions understood that, and everyone liked him. He was far from stupid, though sometimes a little naïve. His appearance was characteristic—tall, slim, always ill-shaven, with black hair. He was sometimes rowdy, and had the reputa-tion of being very strong. On one night out with friends, he had knocked down a policeman over six feet tall, with a single blow. He could drink a place dry, but was capable of not drinking at all; he sometimes got up to unforgivable pranks, but was capable of behaving impeccably. Another remarkable thing about Razumikhin was that he was never put off by failure, nor ever apparently oppressed by adversity. He could set up house on a roof if he had to, and put up with desperate hunger and extreme cold. He was very poor, but kept himself entirely by his own efforts, earning money from all kinds of work. He knew endless ways of earning money. Once he had left his room unheated for a whole win-ter, insisting that it was actually pleasanter because he slept better in the cold. Just now he'd had to drop out of university, but not for long; he was doing all he could to put his affairs straight as quickly as he could so as to get back to his studies. Raskolnikov hadn't been to see him for about four months, while Razumikhin didn't even know where Raskolnikov lived. On one occasion some two months ago they had almost run into one another in the street, but Raskolnikov had turned aside and actually crossed the road so as not to be noticed; and although Razumikhin did notice him, he walked straight past, not wishing to upset his *friend*.

CHAPTER V

'TRUE enough, not so long ago I meant to ask Razumikhin for work—
get him to find me some lessons or something like that...' recalled
Raskolnikov, 'but how can he help me right now? I suppose he could get
me some lessons; I suppose he'll even share his last kopek with me, if
he has a kopek; so I could actually buy myself some boots, and get my
suit mended, so that I could go out to give lessons... hmm... Well, and
after that? What can I do with a few coppers? Is that what I need now?
No, really, it was ridiculous to set out for Razumikhin's.'

The question of why he had set off for Razumikhin's at this point
bothered him even more than he realized. Anxiously he tried to find some
ominous significance for himself in this seemingly quite ordinary act.

'Can I really have wanted to put the whole business right, just through
Razumikhin—did I see Razumikhin as the solution to everything?' he
wondered in astonishment.

He pondered, rubbing his brow, and after long thought, very strangely
and half-accidentally, suddenly and almost spontaneously, a most
extraordinary idea occurred to him.

'Hmm... to Razumikhin's,' he said suddenly and perfectly calmly, as
though it was a firm decision. 'I'll go to Razumikhin's, of course I will...
but—not right now... I'll go and see him... the next day, after *that*,
when *that's* done with and everything is new and different...'

Suddenly he realized what he was thinking.

'After *that*,' he cried, starting up from his seat, 'but will *that* ever
happen? Can it be, is it really going to happen?'

And he hurried away from the bench, almost at a run; he almost
turned back homewards, but suddenly found the idea of going home
quite unbearable. It was there, in the corner of his room, in that same
terrible cupboard, that all *that* had been coming to a head for over
a month; so he just followed his nose.

His nervous tremor had grown to a feverish chill; despite the heat, he
was starting to feel cold. With something of an effort he began, almost
unconsciously and under a sort of inner compulsion, to peer closely at
everything he came across, as if searching hard for something to distract his thoughts; but he couldn't manage it, and kept falling into
a reverie. And then, when he jerked his head up again and looked about
him, he immediately forgot what he'd just been thinking about, and
even where he was going. In this way he walked right across Vasilievsky
Island and emerged on the Little Neva, where he crossed the bridge
and turned towards the Islands.* His tired eyes, grown used to the city's

dust, the whitewash, and the enormous buildings that hemmed him in and pressed down on him, were refreshed by the greenery and cool air. Here it wasn't stuffy, there were no bad smells, no drinking dens. But soon these pleasant new sensations gave way to morbid and vexatious ones. Sometimes he would stop in front of a painted dacha surrounded by greenery, look over the fence and see smartly dressed women far away, and children running round the garden. He was particularly attracted by the flowers, and spent a long time looking at them. And he passed luxurious carriages, and ladies and gentlemen on horseback; he would follow them with a curious look, and forget about them even before they disappeared from view. Once he stopped still and counted out his money; he turned out to have about thirty kopeks. 'Twenty to the policeman, three for Nastasia for the letter—so yesterday I must have given the Marmeladovs about forty-seven or fifty,' he thought, calculating it out for some reason; but soon he even forgot why he had taken the money out of his pocket. He thought about it again when he passed a cookshop, a sort of eating house, and felt hungry. Going in, he drank a glass of vodka and ate a pie filled with something or other, which he finished off in the street. It was a long time since he had last drunk vodka, and it affected him at once, though he had only had one glass. His legs were suddenly heavy, and he began to feel very sleepy. He turned to go home, but once he reached Petrovsky Island he stopped in utter exhaustion and turned off the road into the bushes, where he sank down onto the grass and immediately fell asleep.

In morbid states, dreams often appear unusually real and vivid, and extraordinarily lifelike. Sometimes the vision is a monstrous one, but its entire nature and context are so plausible, its details so subtle, unexpected, and artistically so true to the whole picture, that the dreamer could never have invented them in his waking state, not even if he were a Pushkin or a Turgenev.* Such dreams, such morbid dreams, linger in the memory, and work powerfully on the dreamer's already disordered, agitated mind.

Raskolnikov had a horrible dream. He dreamed of his childhood, in the little town where they lived. He's seven years old, and one holiday evening he's walking out in the country with his father. It's a grey day, the heat is stifling, the scenery exactly as he remembers it, except that in his memory it's far less detailed than it now appears in his dream. The little town lies spread out before him as though on the palm of his hand—not a willow tree to be seen. Somewhere far in the distance, right on the horizon, lies the dark shadow of a little wood. A few yards beyond the last of the town allotments stands a tavern, a large tavern, which had always awakened uncomfortable feelings and even fear in him, whenever he passed it on a walk with his father. There always used to be such a crowd there, yelling and laughing and swearing, and singing in such ugly, rough voices, and often brawling. Around that tavern, people's faces were always so drunk and frightening... When he passed them, he would press tightly against his father's side, trembling all over. The road by the tavern, the village path, was always dusty, and the dust was always so black. The road went winding on, and about three hundred yards away it curved to the right, around the graveyard. In the middle of the graveyard there stood a stone church with a green dome; once or twice a year he would go to a service there with his father and mother, when requiem masses were held for his grandmother who had died long ago, and whom he had never known. They would always bring with them a rice pudding wrapped in a napkin, on a white dish; the sugary rice had raisins pressed into it in the shape of a cross.* He loved that church with its ancient icons, most of them unmounted, and the old priest with his doddering head. Beside his grandmother's grave and the slab that covered it there was another little grave for his younger brother, who had died at six months and whom he had never known either, and couldn't remember. But he had been told that he had a little brother, and every time he went to the graveyard he crossed himself religiously and respectfully over the little grave, knelt down before it, and kissed it.

And here he is, dreaming that he's walking with his father along the road to the graveyard, and they're passing the tavern. He's holding his father's hand and looking round fearfully at the tavern. One particular circumstance attracts his attention: on this occasion there seems to be some sort of celebration, there's a crowd of townswomen and peasant women in their best clothes, with their husbands and all sorts of riff-raff. Everyone is drunk, everyone is singing, and by the tavern entrance a cart is waiting. But it's a strange cart, one of those big ones to which they harness heavy draught horses for transporting provisions and liquor barrels. He's always liked watching these enormous draught horses with their long manes and thick legs, walking steadily and placidly along, effortlessly drawing a mountain of stuff behind them as though it were even easier with a cart than without one. But now, very strangely, the great big cart has a skinny little roan farm-nag harnessed to it, one of those horses that he's often seen straining to pull a cart piled high with firewood or hay, particularly if the cart gets bogged down in the mud or caught in a rut; and the peasants always lash those horses so hard and so painfully with their whips, sometimes even about their mouth or eyes, and he feels so sorry, so sorry whenever he sees them that he almost cries;* and his mother always takes him away from the window. But now all of a sudden there's a lot of noise, people are pouring out of the tavern, yelling and singing, with their balalaikas—great peasant men, blind drunk, in their red-and-blue tunics with heavy jackets over their shoulders. 'Get in, everybody get in!' cries one young man with a bull neck and a fleshy face, as red as a carrot. 'I'm taking you all home, everybody get in!' But straight away laughter breaks out, with shouts of:

'Is that nag supposed to carry us?'

'Are you crazy, Mikolka—putting that little mare to your great cart?'

'Boys, that little roan must be all of twenty years old!'

'Get in, I'm taking everybody home!' cries Mikolka again, springing up onto the cart to lead the way. He takes up the reins and stands upright at the front. 'The bay's just gone off with Matvey,' he shouts from the cart, 'and this old mare, boys, she's just breaking my heart— I've half a mind to put an end to her, eating and doing no work. Get in, I say! I'll make her gallop! She's going to gallop!' And he picks up the whip, relishing the prospect of lashing his little roan.

'Well go on then, get in!' they laugh in the crowd. 'She'll go at a gallop, d'you hear?'

'Don't suppose she's galloped these last ten years.'

'Yes she will!'

'Let her have it, boys! Out with your whips, everybody!'

'That's the way! Let her have it!'

Everybody clambers up onto Mikolka's cart, roaring with laughter and cracking jokes. About six men get on, and there's room for more. They take a woman up with them, a fat red-faced peasant woman dressed in bright red and wearing a beaded headdress and fur-lined shoes; she's cracking nuts and giggling. People in the crowd are laughing too—you couldn't help laughing at the sight of that miserable little mare, setting off to drag all that load at a gallop! Straight away, two lads on the cart pick up a whip each, to help Mikolka. He cries 'Giddy-up!' and the nag jerks forward with all her might, but it's all she can do to take a few steps, never mind gallop; all she can do is shuffle her legs this way and that, gasping and shrinking under the blows rattling down on her like hail from the three whips. The laughter redoubles from the cart and the crowd around, but Mikolka is annoyed, and furiously lashes the little horse again and again, as though he really imagines she's going to gallop.

'Let me up too, boys!' cries a young man in the crowd, attracted by the goings-on.

'Get in! Everybody get in!' roars Mikolka. 'She'll take you all! I'll flog her to death!' And he's whipping and whipping her, so enraged he can't think what else to beat her with.

'Papochka, Papochka!' cries the boy to his father. 'Papochka, what are they doing? Papochka, they're hitting the poor little horsey!'

'Come away, come away!' replies his father. 'They're drunk, they're fooling around like silly idiots. Come along, don't look!' And he wants to lead him away, but the boy breaks free, and almost out of his mind he rushes over to the horse. But the poor little horse is in a bad way by now. It pants, stops still, tugs forward again, and almost falls.

'Flog her to death!' yells Mikolka. 'It's come to that! I'll do her in!'

'What are you up to? You're no Christian, you lunatic!' cries an old man in the crowd.

'Did anyone ever see such a little horse pull a great load like that!' adds another.

'You'll be the death of her!' cries a third.

'Hands off! My property! I'll do what I like! Come on up, more of you! Everybody up! I'll have her gallop, see if I don't!'

There's a sudden roar of laughter that drowns everything. The little mare, worn out with all the whipping, lashes out feebly with her hoofs. Even the old man can't hold back a grin. No wonder—a broken-down little mare like that, and kicking!

Two youths from the crowd get hold of a couple of whips and run over to the little horse to whip her on the flanks, one on each side.

'Get her on the mouth, on the eyes, get her on her eyes!' yells Mikolka.

'Let's have a song, boys!' calls someone on the cart, and all the passengers take him up. Everybody joins in a riotous song, jangling a tambourine and whistling the refrains. The woman carries on cracking nuts and giggling.

And the little boy runs up to the horse, runs in front of her, and sees her being whipped across her eyes, her actual eyes! He's crying. His heart is breaking, his tears are streaming down. One of the men with whips catches him across the face; he feels nothing, he wrings his hands, shouts, rushes over to the grey-haired old man with his grey beard who's shaking his head in disapproval. A woman takes him by the hand and wants to lead him away, but he breaks free and runs back to the little horse. She's at her last gasp by now, but she starts kicking again.

'Blast you to hell!' yells Mikolka in a blind rage. He tosses his whip aside, bends down to the floor of the cart, and pulls out a long, thick wooden shaft. Holding it by the end with both hands, he flourishes it with all his strength over the little roan horse.

'He's going to smash her!' cry the people around.

'He's going to kill her!'

'My property!' shouts Mikolka, and brings the shaft crashing down with full force. There's a heavy thud.

'Whip her, keep on whipping her! Don't stop!' cry voices from the crowd.

And Mikolka brandishes the shaft a second time, and a second blow crashes down full tilt on the poor nag's back. Her hind legs buckle under her, but she pulls herself up and tugs, tugs this way and that with the very last of her strength, trying to get away. But six whips are raining blows on her from every side, the shaft rises and falls a third time, and then a fourth, with a steady swing. Mikolka is in a frenzy of rage that he can't kill her at one blow.

'She's a tough one!' they shout.

'This time she'll go down for sure, lads, and that'll be it!' cries one enthusiast from the crowd.

'Get an axe to her! Finish her off!' cries another.

'Blast you to hell! Stand clear!' shrieks Mikolka in a fury, dropping the shaft, bending down to the cart floor again and dragging out an iron crowbar. 'Watch out!' And taking a great swing he brings it crashing down onto his poor little horse. The blow falls, the little mare staggers, sinks down, tries to pull herself up again, but the crowbar swings and crashes down onto her back once more, and she falls to the ground as if all four legs had been cut from under her.

'Finish her!' shouts Mikolka, leaping off the cart in a blind rage. Several lads, all flushed and drunk, seize hold of anything they can see—whips, sticks, the wooden shaft—and run over to the little dying mare. Mikolka stands beside her and starts beating her pointlessly on the back with his crowbar. The nag stretches out her head, heaves a heavy sigh and dies.

'Done for her!' they cry from the crowd.

'Well, why wouldn't she gallop!'

'My property!' cries Mikolka, holding the crowbar. His eyes are bloodshot. He stands there looking sorry that there's nothing left to beat.

'You're no Christian, anyone can see that!' By now there are many voices from the crowd shouting this.

But the poor little boy is beside himself. With a scream he bursts through the crowd to the little roan mare, he's hugging her dead and

bleeding muzzle, and kissing her, kissing her on her eyes and her lips...
Then he suddenly leaps up and hurls himself at Mikolka in a frenzy,
fists flying. At that moment his father, who has been searching for him
for some time, finally lifts him up and carries him out of the crowd.

'Come along, come along!' he says. 'We're going home.'

'Papochka! What did they... kill... the poor horsey for?' he sobs,
his breath choking so that the words burst in a scream from his
panting chest.

'They're drunk, they're playing the fool, it's none of our business.
Come along!' says his father. The boy flings both arms around his
father, but his chest is bursting, bursting. He wants to take a breath, he
wants to scream—and he wakes up.

He awoke covered in sweat; his hair was damp. He got up, panting
with horror.

'Thank God that was only a dream!' he said, sitting down under
a tree and breathing heavily. 'But what's up? I'm not getting a fever, am
I? What a foul dream!'

His body ached all over; his mind was dark and confused. Leaning
his elbows on his knees, he rested his head in both hands.

'My God!' he exclaimed. 'Am I really, really going to take an axe and
start beating her on the head, and split her skull open... and slip on her
warm, sticky blood, and break open the lock, and steal, and tremble—
and hide, all covered in blood... with the axe... Oh my God, is that
really true?'

He was trembling like a leaf as he spoke.

'What am I thinking of?' he went on, sitting up again with a sense of
profound astonishment. 'I always knew I could never make myself do
it, so why have I been tormenting myself all this while? Even yesterday,
yesterday when I went to do that... *rehearsal*, I knew perfectly well then
that I couldn't manage it. So now what? Why have I been in doubt even
up to now? Yesterday, when I was going downstairs, I myself said it was
loathsome, wicked, vile, vile... the very thought of it made me sick,
filled me with horror, even when I was *awake*...'

'No, I can't do it, I can't do it! Supposing, even supposing there was
no doubt about all my calculations, supposing everything that I've
decided during this month was as clear as daylight, as conclusive as
arithmetic. Lord! Even then I won't make up my mind to it! I can't do
it, I can't do it! So why do I even now...'

He rose to his feet, looked around in surprise as if wondering at the
fact that he had got here, and walked off to T—— Bridge.* He was pale,
his eyes were burning, all his limbs were shattered, but suddenly he

seemed to breathe easier. He felt that he had already cast off the terrible burden that had so long oppressed him, and all at once his soul felt light and peaceful. 'Lord!' he prayed, 'show me my path; and I renounce this accursed... dream of mine!'

As he crossed the bridge, he gazed quietly and serenely down at the Neva and the bright red sun in a bright sunset. Despite his weakness, he actually felt no fatigue—it was as if an abscess on his heart that had been festering all the past month had suddenly burst. Freedom, freedom! He was free at last from all the magic spells, the sorcery, the enchantment, the obsession!

Later on, whenever he thought back to this time and all that happened to him during these days, recalling it minute by minute, he was always superstitiously struck by one fact which, though not a particularly unusual one, seemed in a way to have foreshadowed his fate.

It was this. He could never understand or explain why, tired and worn out as he was, when the best thing for him would have been to take the shortest and most direct way straight back home, he had instead returned through the Haymarket which was quite out of his way. It wasn't a long detour, but clearly a quite unnecessary one. Of course it had happened to him dozens of times to go home without remembering the streets he walked along. But why, he always asked himself later, had this crucial, decisive, and yet utterly fortuitous meeting on the Haymarket (where he had no reason to go at all) taken place just at this very hour and minute of his life, when he was in this particular mood, and when the circumstances were just right for the meeting to have the most decisive and terminal effect on his whole life? As if it had been purposely lying in wait for him!

It was about nine o'clock when he crossed the Haymarket. All the traders at their tables, barrows, shops, or stalls were shutting up shop, taking down and packing up their wares, and—like their customers—going home. Crowds of costermongers, rag-and-bone-men and the like, had gathered beside the food stalls at street level, or in the foul, stinking courtyards of the Haymarket houses, or—most of them—by the drinking dens. Raskolnikov used to seek out those particular places, and all the little alleys around them, when he wandered aimlessly out onto the streets. Here his rags didn't attract supercilious glances, and he could walk about looking just as he pleased without scandalizing anyone.

Right on the corner of K—— Alley* a townsman and his wife had set up two stalls selling thread, laces, cotton handkerchiefs, and the like. They, too, were getting ready to go home, but had stopped to talk to a friend who had just turned up. This friend was Lizaveta Ivanovna, or simply Lizaveta as everyone called her, the younger sister of that same old Aliona Ivanovna, Collegiate Registrar's widow and money-lender, whom Raskolnikov had gone to see yesterday in order to pawn his watch and carry out his *rehearsal*. He had long known all about this Lizaveta, and even she knew him a little. She was a tall, gangling girl, quiet and timid, almost simple-minded; she was thirty-five years old and the complete slave of her sister, for whom she worked night and day, trembling with fear of her and even suffering beatings from her. She was standing beside the stallholder and his wife, carrying her bundle and listening carefully and doubtfully to what they said. They were explaining something to her very heatedly. When Raskolnikov suddenly caught sight of her, he was seized with a strange feeling, a sort of profound astonishment, although there was nothing astonishing about this meeting.

'Lizaveta Ivanovna, you ought to make up your own mind about that,' said the stallholder loudly. 'Come round tomorrow after six. The others'll be coming too.'

'Tomorrow?' asked Lizaveta slowly and thoughtfully, as if undecided.

'Hasn't that Aliona Ivanovna got you scared, then!' gabbled the stallholder's wife, a high-spirited little woman. 'Just look at you—no better than a little child. And she's no blood sister of yours either, just a stepsister, and see how she's got you under her thumb!'

'Just you don't say anything to Aliona Ivanovna this time,' her husband interrupted. 'That's my advice. Just come round to us without asking anyone. It'll be worth your while. Your sister herself will see the sense of it later on.'

'Shall I come then?'

'After six tomorrow; and one of that lot'll be there too; and then you can make up your own mind.'

'And we'll light the samovar,' added his wife.

'All right, I'll come,' decided Lizaveta, still in some doubt. And she slowly got ready to leave.

Raskolnikov had walked past by this time, and heard no more. He passed them silently and unobtrusively, trying not to utter a word. His initial astonishment had slowly given place to horror, and a chill seemed to run down his spine. He had just discovered, suddenly and quite unexpectedly, that tomorrow, at precisely seven in the evening, Lizaveta, the old woman's sister and sole companion, would be away from home; in other words, at precisely seven in the evening the old woman *would be at home alone*.

He was only a few steps from his lodging. He entered it like a condemned man. He did not reason, he was quite incapable of reasoning, but all at once he felt with his whole being that he no longer possessed any freedom of thought or will, and that everything had suddenly been finally decided.

Even if, having formed his plan, he had had to wait for a suitable opportunity for years on end—even then he could never have relied with any certainty on finding a better way of ensuring its success than the one now suddenly presented to him. It would have been difficult under any circumstances to find out for certain, more accurately and with less risk, a day in advance, without any hazardous enquiries or investigations, that on the following day, at such and such a time, such and such an old woman, against whose life an attempt was planned, would be at home all on her own.

CHAPTER VI

LATER on, Raskolnikov happened to find out why the stallholder and his wife had invited Lizaveta to visit them. The reason was a perfectly ordinary one with nothing very special about it. A family who had come to live in Petersburg and fallen on hard times were selling their possessions—clothing and suchlike, all women's things. Since they couldn't have got much for them at the market, they were looking for a dealer, and this was something Lizaveta did. She sold goods on commission, going round to see clients, of whom she had a great many, because she was very honest and always named her best price. Once she had named it, she stuck to it. Generally she spoke little, for as we have said, she was so meek and timid...

But Raskolnikov had grown superstitious of late. Long afterwards, he still retained traces of this superstition, which proved almost impossible to shake off. For ever afterwards, he felt there had been something strange and mysterious in this whole affair, something like the presence of extraordinary influences and coincidences. Only the previous winter, a student called Pokorev whom he knew, who was leaving for Kharkov, had happened to give him the address of old Aliona Ivanovna in the course of some conversation or other, in case he should ever want to pawn anything. It was a long time before he went to see her, because he was still giving lessons and somehow managing to get by. But about a month and a half ago he had remembered her address, because he had two items worth pawning—his father's old silver watch and a little gold ring with three red stones of some sort, which his sister had given him as a keepsake when they parted. He decided to pawn the ring. Once he had traced the old woman, and even before finding out anything particular about her, as soon as he first set eyes on her, he was overcome by an insurmountable loathing for her. He took the two 'little rouble notes' she had given him, and on his way home he entered a scruffy little tavern and ordered tea. He sat down, deep in thought. A strange idea was tapping at his brain, like a chick breaking out of its egg; and he found the thought very, very absorbing.

At the next table, almost by his side, a student was sitting, someone whom he didn't know at all and never recalled seeing; he was sitting with a young officer. They had played a game of billiards and then begun drinking tea. Suddenly he heard the student telling the officer about Aliona Ivanovna the moneylender, widow of a Collegiate Registrar, and giving him her address. This had struck Raskolnikov as rather odd—he had just come from there, and here was someone talking about her. Of course it was just a coincidence, but a moment ago he'd been unable to shake off a very unusual impression, and here was somebody apparently out to help him—for the student had started telling his friend all sorts of details about Aliona Ivanovna.

'She's good,' he said, 'you'll always get money from her. Rich as a Jew, she could pay out five thousand roubles on the spot, but she's not above taking a pledge worth a single rouble. A lot of us have been round there. But she's a terrible harpy.'

And he began describing how spiteful she was, and so strict that if you were a single day late redeeming your pledge, it would have gone. She lent four times less than the thing was worth, and took five or even seven per cent each month; and so forth. The student had let his tongue run away with him, and had gone on to mention that the old woman had a sister, Lizaveta, whom she used to beat all the time, though she herself was such an ugly little creature; and she kept Lizaveta in downright slavery like a little child, though Lizaveta stood at least five foot ten.

'What a phenomenon!' the student had exclaimed, bursting out laughing.

Then they had started talking about Lizaveta. The student seemed to be describing her with particular relish, laughing continually; the officer, meanwhile, had listened with great interest, and asked the student to send Lizaveta round to him to mend his underwear. Raskolnikov hadn't missed a single word of all this, and found out everything. Lizaveta was the old woman's younger sister, a stepsister from a different mother, and she was already thirty-five years old. She worked day and night for her sister, served as her cook and laundress, and also sewed clothes for sale; she even went out scrubbing floors, and gave all her earnings to her sister. She didn't dare accept a single commission or take on any work without the old woman's permission. And yet the old woman had already made her will, as Lizaveta herself knew, and under that will she didn't inherit a single kopek, nothing but the furniture, the chairs, and so forth. All the money was to go to a monastery in N——— Province,* for masses to be said in perpetuity for the old woman's soul. Lizaveta was a lower-class woman, an uneducated spinster, very tall and ungainly, with long legs and splay feet, always in worn-out goatskin boots. She kept herself very clean. But the main thing that astonished and amused the student was the fact that Lizaveta was constantly falling pregnant...

'But didn't you say she was a hideous monster?' asked the officer.

'Well, she's sort of swarthy, looks like a soldier in disguise—but she's not at all a monster, you know. She has such a kind face and eyes. Very kind. And the proof is that lots of men fancy her. She's so quiet and meek, never answers back, she's got an agreeable nature—she'll agree to anything. And she's got a really nice smile.'

'Fancy her yourself then, do you?' laughed the officer.

'Because she's so odd. No, listen to me. I should like to kill that damned old woman and rob her, and I promise you I wouldn't have the slightest qualm about it,' the student said heatedly.

The officer had laughed again, but Raskolnikov had shuddered. How strange this was!

'Listen, I want to ask you a serious question,' said the student in some excitement. 'I was joking just now, of course, but look here: on the one hand, here's this stupid, pointless, worthless, evil, sick old crone, whom nobody wants, in fact she does harm to everybody, she herself has no idea what she's alive for, and tomorrow she'll die in any case. Do you see? Do you see?'

'All right then, I see,' replied the officer, looking closely at his excited friend.

'Let me go on. On the other hand, there are fresh, young, vigorous people perishing needlessly for lack of support, thousands of them, all over the place! A hundred, a thousand good deeds could have been done, and enterprises set up or put to rights, on the old woman's money—which is all going to be wasted on a monastery! Hundreds, perhaps thousands of human beings could be given a start; dozens of families saved from beggary, decay, ruin, vice, venereal disease; and all with her money. If you killed her and took her money, and used it to devote yourself to serving all humanity and the common good: what do you think, wouldn't those thousands of good deeds wipe out that one tiny little crime? One life for thousands of lives, rescued from corruption and decay! One death, in exchange for thousands of lives—it's simple arithmetic!* Anyway, what does the life of that consumptive, stupid, wicked old crone count for, when it's weighed in the balance? No more than the life of a louse, a cockroach—even less, because the old woman's actually harmful. She's eating away at another person's life: the other day she bit Lizaveta's finger out of pure spite, and they almost had to cut it off!'

'Of course, she doesn't deserve to live,' remarked the officer; 'but that's just nature.'

'But look, man, nature needs to be put right and directed—otherwise we'd all be drowning in superstition. If that wasn't done, there could never have been a single great man. People talk about "duty" and "conscience"—and I've no objection to duty or conscience—but what do we mean by them? Wait, let me ask you another question. Listen!'

'No, you wait, I'm going to ask you a question myself. Listen!'

'Go on then!'

'Well, here you are talking and holding forth—but just tell me, are *you yourself* going to kill that old woman or not?'

'Of course not! I'm simply talking about justice... It's not about me at all.'

'Well, what I say is, if you can't make up your mind to do it yourself, then justice doesn't come into it! Come on, let's have another game!'

Raskolnikov was in a highly agitated state. Of course all that was just the way young people thought and talked, commonplace everyday arguments such as he'd often heard before, if differently expressed and touching on other topics. But why had it happened at this precise time, for him to hear this particular conversation and these particular thoughts, when his own mind had only just conceived... *precisely those same thoughts*? And why had it happened just at that time, when he had just left the old woman with the germ of his idea in his head, that he had come upon people talking about that same old woman?... This coincidence had never ceased to strike him as strange. The trivial tavern conversation had a profound influence on him as matters developed further; as though they really had been somehow predestined and foreshadowed.

And now, returning home from the Haymarket, he sank down on the divan and sat there for an hour without moving. Meanwhile it grew dark; he had no candle, and in any case it never occurred to him to light one. Afterwards he could never remember whether or not he had been thinking about anything at this point. Finally he felt his feverish chills returning, and he recalled with delight that he could lie down on the same divan. Soon he fell into a heavy slumber, which pressed down on him like a lead weight.

He slept an unusually long time, without dreaming. When Nastasia came into his room at ten the following morning, she barely managed to shake him awake. She had brought him some tea and bread. It was leftover tea again, and again in her own teapot.

'Look at him sleeping!' she cried indignantly. 'He's always asleep!'

He sat up with an effort. His head ached. He tried to stand up, turned round in his garret, and sank back onto the divan.

'Off to sleep again!' cried Nastasia. 'Are you ill, or what?'

He didn't reply.

'Well, do you want the tea, then?'

'Later,' he replied with an effort, shutting his eyes once more and turning away to the wall. Nastasia stood over him.

'Perhaps you really are ill,' she said, turning and leaving the room.

She came back again at two o'clock with some soup. He was lying as before, and the tea hadn't been touched. Nastasia was quite offended, and shook him angrily.

'Why d'you keep sleeping?' she exclaimed, looking at him with disgust. He raised himself and sat up, but said nothing, just stared at the floor.

'You ill, or not?' asked Nastasia, and once again received no answer.

'You ought to go out, at least,' she said after a silence. 'Get a bit of air on your face. Are you going to eat this, then?'

'Later,' he said faintly. 'Get out!' And he waved her away.

She stood still a little longer, with a pitying look; then she went out.

A few minutes later he raised his eyes and took a long look at the tea and the soup. Then he picked up the bread and a spoon, and began to eat.

He ate only a little, mechanically and without appetite—not more than three or four spoonfuls. His headache was a bit better. When he had eaten he stretched himself out on the divan again, but now he couldn't sleep; he lay motionless, face down, burying his head in the pillow. He kept seeing visions, and always very strange ones. Mostly he imagined being somewhere in Africa, in Egypt, by an oasis.—The caravan is resting, the camels lying quietly, there's a circle of palm trees around them, and everyone is eating their midday meal. He himself keeps drinking water, straight from a brook that flows and gurgles along just beside him. And it's so cool, and the beautiful, beautiful water, so blue and cold, is flowing over the brightly coloured stones and the clean sand with its specks of shining gold...

Suddenly he distinctly heard a clock striking. He roused himself with a start, lifted his head, looked out of the window, realized the time, and leapt straight to his feet, with all his wits about him, as if someone had dragged him up off the divan. He tiptoed to the door, opened it quietly and listened for sounds from downstairs. His heart was pounding hard. But all was quiet on the stairs; everyone seemed to be asleep... He found it weird and extraordinary that he could have slept in such a stupor ever since the previous day, without getting anything done or making anything ready... And by now that clock could have been striking six... Suddenly his drowsy stupor gave way to a strange state of feverish, confused, frantic haste. Not that there was much to prepare. He concentrated as hard as he could, to get everything clear in his mind, without overlooking anything. But his heart was pounding, thumping so hard that it was difficult to breathe. First of all he had to make a loop and sew it into his overcoat—a matter of only a minute. He felt under his pillow, and amongst the underclothes shoved underneath it he found an old, unwashed, completely disintegrating shirt. He tore a strip off this rag, a couple of inches wide and a foot or so long, and folded it in two. Then he took off his broad summer coat, made of some thick, tough cotton material (the only outer garment he possessed), and set about stitching the two ends of the fabric strip to the inside of the coat, under the left armpit. His hands shook as he sewed, but he managed to do it so that nothing was visible on the outside when he put the coat on again. The needle and thread had been got ready a long time ago, and wrapped in a sheet of paper in the table drawer. This loop was a clever invention of his own: it was meant for the axe. He could never have carried an axe in his hands as he walked along the street; and if he had kept it hidden under his coat, he would still have had to hold it in place with one hand, which would have attracted attention. As it was, with the loop, all he had to do was hang the axe blade in it, and there it would hang quietly all the way, inside the coat and under his arm. With his hand in the side pocket of the coat, he could keep hold of the tip of the axe handle to stop it swinging. And since the coat was a very wide one, a real sack, one could never have seen from the outside that his hand was holding on to something inside it. This loop, too, was something he had invented at least two weeks earlier.

When he had finished, he slid his fingers into the narrow crevice between the bottom of his 'Turkish' divan and the floor, felt around near the left-hand end and pulled out the *pledge* he had prepared and hidden there a long time ago. This pledge wasn't actually a pledge at all—it was nothing more than a little wooden board, planed smooth, no bigger and no thicker than a silver cigarette case. He had happened to find this bit of board on one of his walks, in a courtyard where there was a workshop in one of the outbuildings. Later on he had added a smooth, thin iron plate (probably an offcut from something) which he had found on the street the same day. Laying the board against the iron plate (which was a little smaller), he tied them tightly together with a thread, lengthwise and crosswise. Then he wrapped them up elegantly in a smart white paper packet, which he tied—again crosswise—with a length of thin tape, producing a knot which would be very complicated to unravel. This was in order to distract the old woman's attention for a while, as she struggled with the packet, and thus give him a little time. He had added the iron plate as a makeweight, so that the old woman shouldn't guess, at least for a moment, that the 'item' was made of wood. All these things he had so far kept under the divan. But no sooner had he got the pledge out than he heard a shout in the courtyard:

'It's long past six!'

'Long past! My God!'

He ran over to the door, listened, grabbed his hat and started down his thirteen steps, as silently and stealthily as a cat. He still had to manage the most important task—stealing the axe from the kitchen. The decision to use an axe had been taken long ago. He did also own a folding garden knife, but he didn't trust either the knife or—even less—his own strength; so he had finally decided on the axe. We should point out here one particular feature of all the final decisions he had so far taken in this affair. They all had one strange point in common. The more final a decision became, the more hideous and absurd it immediately appeared even to his own eyes. Despite all his agonizing inner struggles, throughout all this time, he had never for a single moment been able to believe that his plans were feasible.

And even if everything had been finally planned and decided, down to the very last detail, with no doubts whatsoever remaining—even then, he would probably have given up the whole idea as too absurd, too monstrous and impossible. But there were still countless unsolved problems and doubts. As for the question of where to get hold of an axe—that was a trivial detail that didn't worry him in the slightest, because nothing could have been easier. The fact was that Nastasia was always leaving the house, especially in the evenings. Either she would drop in on the neighbours, or go out to the shop; and she always left the door open. That was the landlady's only quarrel with her. So all he had to do was slip quietly into the kitchen when the time came, take the axe, and then, an hour later—when it was all over—go in and put it back. Naturally some problems remained. He might, for instance, return after an hour to replace the axe, and there would be Nastasia, back home again. In that case, of course, he'd have to walk past the door and wait for her to go out again. But supposing she noticed meanwhile that the axe was missing, and started hunting for it, and raised an outcry? That would arouse suspicion at once, or at least give grounds for it.

But he gave no thought whatsoever to all those details—he hadn't the time. He was thinking about the main issue, putting off the details until he had *convinced himself of everything*. And this last seemed absolutely impossible. That, at least, was how it seemed to him. He could never imagine, for instance, that there would be a time when he would stop thinking, get up, and—just go there... Even his recent *rehearsal* (going to take a thorough look at the place) was something he had only meant to *try*, but not really carry it through at all—it was just 'come on, why not just go and try it out, what's the point of just dreaming!' And he hadn't been able to bear it, he had given up and run away, livid with anger at himself. At the same time, one would have thought that his whole analysis of the question, his solution to the moral problem, was a settled matter; his casuistry had been sharpened to a razor's edge, and he himself could no longer find any conscious objections. But in the last analysis he simply didn't trust himself; he was searching, obstinately, slavishly, for objections of one sort or another, groping around for them as if someone were forcing him and dragging him along. And then this last day, which had started so unexpectedly and then resolved everything in one go, had affected him in an almost entirely mechanical way. It was as if someone had taken him by the hand and pulled him along, irresistibly, blindly, with supernatural strength, allowing no objections. As if a flap of his clothing had become caught in the wheels of a machine, and now he was being dragged into it.

In the beginning—a long time ago—there had been one question that interested him. Why are almost all crimes so easily detected and solved, and why do almost all criminals leave such obvious clues? Little by little, he had reached all sorts of curious conclusions. In his view, the main reason lay not in the material impossibility of concealing a crime, but in the criminal himself. At the moment of committing a crime, the criminal himself—almost any criminal—suffers a sort of collapse of his will and reason, which give place to an extraordinary degree of childish thoughtlessness—and this at the precise moment when rational judgement and caution are most essential. And he became convinced that this clouding of the criminal's judgement and collapse of his will come upon him like an illness, gradually progressing and reaching their peak shortly before the crime is committed. They continue unchanged through the moment of the crime itself and for some time after, depending on the individual. Then they pass off like any other illness. As for the question of whether the illness itself gives rise to the crime, or whether the crime, through its special nature, is somehow always accompanied by a sort of illness—that was a question he didn't yet feel able to answer.

Having come to these conclusions, he had decided that in his own personal case, no such morbid upsets could occur. He would keep an inexorable hold on his rational judgement and his will, throughout the execution of his plan—for the single reason that what he had planned was 'not a crime'. We pass over in silence the whole process of reasoning that led him to this conclusion, for we have already run too far ahead... Let us merely add that the practical, purely material difficulties lying in his way played only a very secondary role in his thinking. 'All I need do is keep control of them, with all my will and reason, and they'll all be overcome in due course, when I come to understand all the ins and outs of the affair, down to the finest details...' But the business did not get under way. Less than anything did he believe in his final decisions, and when the hour struck everything turned out not at all as planned, but rather fortuitously, and indeed almost unexpectedly.

One utterly trivial detail completely threw him, even before he reached the foot of the stairs. Coming level with his landlady's kitchen, whose door as usual was wide open, he gave a cautious sidelong glance inside to spy out the situation. With Nastasia away, was the landlady herself inside, and if not, were the doors to her own room properly shut, so that she couldn't suddenly look out just as he was going in for the axe? But what was his astonishment on suddenly seeing that not only was Nastasia herself at home this time, in her own kitchen—but she was actually busy taking linen out of a basket and hanging it out on the line! When she caught sight of him she stopped hanging out the clothes, turned towards him, and watched him walk past. He looked away and went on as though unaware of her. But all was lost—he didn't have the axe! It was a terrible blow.

'And why did I decide that she'd be out, just at this point?' he thought on his way out of the gate. 'Why, why was I certain of that?' He felt crushed, even somehow humiliated. He could have laughed spitefully at himself... He was seething with dull, animal rage.

He stopped in the gateway to think. To go out into the street, just like that, for show, and walk around, was more than he could bear. To go back home was even worse. 'And what a chance I've missed, for ever!' he muttered, standing irresolutely in the gateway, right in front of the porter's dark little room, which was also standing open. Suddenly he gave a start. Inside the porter's cubbyhole, a couple of steps away, something glinted at him from under a bench on the right... He looked all round—nobody! On tiptoe he walked up to the porter's room, descended two steps, and in a faint voice called the porter. 'There you are, he's not at home! Though he must be close by somewhere, probably in the yard, since the door's wide open.' He flung himself at the axe (for it was an axe), pulled it out from under the bench where it lay between two logs; and straight away, before coming out, hung it in the loop, and shoved both hands in his pockets. Then he came out of the porter's room. No one had noticed him! 'If that wasn't clever of me, then it was the devil's work!' he thought, with an odd smirk. He was extraordinarily cheered by this lucky chance.

He walked on slowly and sedately, without hurrying, so as not to arouse suspicion. He didn't look much at any passers-by, in fact he tried not to look anyone in the face, but to remain as inconspicuous as possible. At this point he remembered his hat. 'My God! And the day before yesterday I had some money—but I forgot to change the hat for a cap!' He uttered a heartfelt curse.

Happening to glance with half an eye into a shop, he saw the wall clock already showing ten past seven. He had to hurry, but at the same time he had to make a detour so as to approach the house from the other side.

Previously, when picturing all this to himself, he had sometimes thought that he would be very frightened. But he wasn't very frightened at the moment, in fact not frightened at all. His mind at this moment was occupied with completely irrelevant thoughts; but they didn't stay with him for long. As he passed Yusupov Park, he briefly became very interested in the design of the tall fountains there, and thought how well they could have cooled the air in all the squares. Bit by bit he persuaded himself that if the Summer Gardens could be extended to occupy the whole of the Field of Mars and even join up with the Mikhailovsky Palace Gardens,* that would be an excellent and valuable thing for the city. And now he suddenly wondered why it was that in all great cities, people chose—not out of bare necessity, but through some sort of special inclination—to settle and live in those particular parts of the city where there were no gardens, no fountains, just dirt and smells and squalor of every kind. And now he recalled his own walks in the Haymarket, and came to himself for a moment. 'What nonsense!' he thought. 'No, better not think about anything at all!'

'I suppose a man being led to his execution will fix his mind on every object he encounters on his way.'* This thought flashed through his mind—but just flashed like lightning; he himself quickly extinguished it... But here he was, quite close, and here was the house, and here was the gateway. Somewhere a clock chimed once. 'What's that, can it be half past seven already? Impossible, it must be fast!'

At the gate, his luck was in and everything went well once more. Indeed, almost as if by design, a huge cart full of hay drove in through the gate at that same moment, just in front of him, completely hiding him from view as he walked through. As soon as the cart emerged into the courtyard, he instantly slipped off to the right. On the far side of the cart, several voices could be heard shouting and arguing, but no one noticed him and nobody met him on their way out. Many of the windows looking out onto the courtyard were open at the time, but he hadn't the strength to look up. The staircase to the woman's flat was close by, just to the right of the gateway. And already he was on the stairs...

He got his breath back and pressed his hand to his pounding heart. He felt for the axe and adjusted it in its loop, and then started climbing the stairs, cautiously and silently, listening at every step. The stairway was quite empty at that moment, and all the doors off it were shut. He met no one. True, there was an empty flat on the second floor, and its door was wide open, with painters working inside, but they didn't even spare him a glance. He stood still, thought for a moment, and went on. 'Of course, it would have been better if they hadn't been here at all; but... there are two more floors to go.'

And here was the fourth floor, and here was the door, and here was the flat opposite, the empty one. On the third floor, the flat directly below the old woman's appeared to be empty too; the visiting card tacked to the door had been removed. They've left!... He was gasping. Just for an instant, a thought passed through his mind—'why not just go away?' But he gave himself no reply; he started listening to the old woman's flat. Deathly silence. Then once more he listened down the staircase, long and attentively... He looked around one last time, pulled himself together, straightened his clothing, and once again checked the axe in its loop. 'Aren't I pale... very pale?' he wondered. 'Aren't I in a terribly nervous state? She's mistrustful... Shouldn't I wait a little longer... until my heart stops thumping?'

But his heart wouldn't stop. Indeed, as if on purpose, it was thumping harder, and harder, and harder... He couldn't bear it any more. Slowly he stretched out his hand to the bell and rang it. Half a minute later he rang again, louder.

No answer. There was no point ringing for nothing, and that would have made no sense to him. Of course the old woman was at home, but she was suspicious and on her own. He knew something of her habits... Once more he pressed his ear against the door. Could his sensations have become so acute (which was hard to believe), or were the sounds really so clear—at all events, he could suddenly distinguish something like the cautious touch of a hand by the lock, and something like the rustle of clothing against the door itself. Someone was standing furtively by the very latch, listening just as he was listening here on the outside, holding her breath in there and, he thought, pressing her own ear against the door...

He purposely made a movement and muttered something more audibly, so as not to suggest in any way that he was hiding. Then he rang a third time, but quietly, firmly, with no sign of impatience. When he recalled all this later, so clearly and plainly—for this moment was stamped in his memory for ever—he couldn't imagine where he had found so much cunning; particularly as his mind seemed to keep clouding over, while he was almost completely unaware of his body... A moment later he heard the door being unbolted.

CHAPTER VII

JUST like last time, the door opened a tiny crack, and once again there were two sharp, suspicious eyes peering at him out of the darkness. At this point Raskolnikov lost his head and almost committed a major error.

Fearing that the old woman would be frightened at the two of them being alone, and not trusting that the sight of him would reassure her, he took hold of the door and pulled it towards him, in case the old woman took it into her head to lock herself in again. At this, she didn't pull the door back again, but nor did she let go of the handle, so that he almost dragged both her and the door out onto the landing together. Realizing that she was barring the doorway and not letting him in, he advanced straight towards her. She sprang back in a fright, was about to say something, but seemed unable to speak, and just stared at him open-eyed.

'Good day, Aliona Ivanovna,' he began, as casually as he could. But his voice didn't obey him, stuttering and trembling. 'I've... brought you... something... why don't we move over here... to the light...' And stepping away from her, he walked straight into the room uninvited. The old woman hurried after him, and found her speech.

'Good Lord! What do you want?... Who are you? What's your business?'

'But Aliona Ivanovna... you know me... Raskolnikov... here, I've brought something to pawn, I promised you the other day I would.' And he held out his pledge.

The old woman glanced briefly at the pledge, but immediately stared back at her uninvited guest, looking him straight in the eyes, intently, malevolently and suspiciously. A minute or so passed in silence. He even seemed to see a sort of mockery in her eyes, as though she had already guessed everything. He could feel himself losing his nerve, almost becoming afraid—so afraid that if she were to look at him like that, without saying a word, for another half-minute, he would have run away.

'What are you looking at me like that for, as if you didn't recognize me?' he burst out suddenly, angry in his turn. 'Take it if you want it; if you don't, I'll go elsewhere, I've no time to waste.'

He'd never meant to say anything of the sort—it just suddenly came out.

The old woman recollected herself, evidently reassured by her visitor's resolute tone.

'No need to be so cross all of a sudden, mister. What is it?' she asked, looking at the pledge.

'A silver cigarette case—I told you about it last time.'

She held out her hand.

'Why are you all pale like that? And your hands are shaking! Have you come from the bathhouse or something?'

'Fever,' he replied abruptly. 'You can't help getting pale... if you've nothing to eat,' he added, barely getting the words out. His strength was failing him once again. But his reply seemed plausible, and the old woman took the packet.

'What's this?' she asked, eyeing Raskolnikov attentively once more, and weighing the pledge in her hand.

'A... something... a cigarette case... silver one... take a look.'

'Well, I don't know, it doesn't feel like silver... Goodness, how you've wrapped it up!'

She was trying to untie the string, turning to the light from the window (all her windows were locked shut, in spite of the stifling heat). For a few seconds she walked right away from him and turned her back on him. He unbuttoned his coat and got the axe free of its loop, but still didn't take it out; he was just holding it in his right hand, under the coat. His hands were terribly weak—he could feel them getting more and more numb and stiff every moment. He was afraid of losing his grip and dropping the axe—and suddenly his head seemed to spin.

'What on earth has he tied it all up for like this!' the old woman cried out in annoyance, and turned towards him.

There was not a moment to be lost. He pulled the axe right out, brandished it in both hands, scarcely feeling a thing, and without using any force, almost mechanically, he let the butt end of it fall on her head. His strength seemed to have deserted him. But as soon as the axe fell, strength returned to him again.

The old woman was bareheaded, as always. Her pale wispy hair, just turning grey, was thickly greased as usual, plaited into a rat's tail and fastened with a broken horn comb which stuck out above the nape of her neck. She was so short that the blow fell right on the crown of her head. She cried out, but very faintly, and suddenly sank to the floor, just managing to raise both hands to her head. One hand still held the 'pledge'. Now he struck her again, and yet again, with all his strength, each time with the butt end of the axe and each time on the crown of her head. Her blood poured out as if from an overturned glass, and her body toppled over on its back. He stepped out of the way to let it fall, and immediately bent down to her face. She was already dead. Her eyes bulged as if they would start from their sockets; her forehead and face were puckered and contorted in spasm.

He laid the axe on the floor beside the dead woman and put his hand straight in her pocket, trying not to smear himself with her still flowing blood—that same right-hand pocket from which she had taken her keys last time. By now he had his wits about him, there was no more clouding of his mind or dizziness, but his hands still shook. He recalled later on that he had actually been very attentive, very careful, and kept trying not to get blood on himself... He got the keys out straight away; as before, they were all in a single bunch, on a single steel ring. He ran straight into the bedroom with them. It was a very small room, with an enormous case of icons. Against another wall was a large bed, very clean, with a padded silk patchwork quilt. By the third wall was the chest of drawers. Strangely enough, as soon as he started trying the keys in the chest of drawers, as soon as he heard the keys chinking, a sort of shudder passed through his body. He suddenly longed to give up and run away. That only lasted an instant—it was too late to leave. He even sneered at himself; but then he was forcibly struck by a different thought. He suddenly imagined that the old woman might actually still be alive, and might come to her senses. Leaving behind the keys and the chest of drawers, he ran back to the body, grabbed the axe and brandished it in the air; but he didn't bring it down. There was no question about it—she was dead. Bending over her and looking closer, he could clearly see that her skull was shattered, and even slightly lopsided. He almost felt it with his fingers, but snatched his hand back—all was clear enough without touching her. A big pool of blood had collected meanwhile. Suddenly he noticed a cord round her neck, and tugged at it; but the cord was tough and wouldn't come off. And it was sodden with blood too. He tried to pull it out from under her clothing, but it was stuck, there was something in the way. Impatiently he raised the axe again, to chop at the cord from above, even as it lay on the body; but his courage failed him, and he spent a laborious two minutes, getting his hands and the axe covered with blood, cutting away at the cord without letting it touch the body, and getting it free. As he had expected—there was a purse on it. There were two crosses, one of cypress wood and one of brass, and a little enamelled saint, and next to them hung a small greasy chamois-leather purse with a steel frame and clasp. The purse was stuffed full; Raskolnikov shoved it into his pocket without looking at it, dropped the crosses onto the old woman's breast, and ran back into the bedroom, this time taking the axe with him.

In frantic haste he snatched up the keys and again set about trying them. But somehow nothing worked, the keys wouldn't go into the locks. Not that his hands were shaking particularly hard—he just kept making mistakes. He might see, for instance, that a key wasn't the right one, but still he would persist in pushing it into the lock. Suddenly he recalled that the big key with the toothed bit, which hung with the other, small ones, must belong not to the chest of drawers (he had realized this last time too), but to some sort of strongbox, and that it might be in there that everything was hidden. He gave up the chest of drawers and felt under the bed, knowing that old women generally put their strongboxes under their beds. And so it was—there was a solid-looking round-lidded chest about thirty inches long, studded with steel and covered in morocco leather. The toothed key fitted perfectly and opened it. Inside, under a white sheet, was a little rabbit-fur coat with a red lining; beneath it a silk dress, then a shawl, and right at the bottom there seemed to be nothing but rags. At first he was about to wipe his bloodstained hands on the red lining—'it's red, the blood won't show up so much on red,' he almost decided, but suddenly realized what he was doing. 'My God! Am I going out of my mind?' he thought in alarm.

As soon as he shifted the rags, a gold watch slid out from under the fur jacket. Hastily he began turning everything over; and indeed, there among the rags were all sorts of gold objects—all of them probably pledges, redeemed or not: bracelets, chains, earrings, pins, and the like. Some were in jewel boxes, others just wrapped in newspaper, but all done up tidily and carefully, in double layers, and tied up with tape. Wasting no time, he started filling his trouser pockets and coat pockets with them, all indiscriminately, without unwrapping any packets or opening the boxes. But he didn't have time to pick up much...

Suddenly he heard the sound of footsteps in the room where the old woman was lying. He stopped and froze like a dead man. But all was quiet—he must have imagined it. Then he clearly heard a sudden weak cry, or perhaps a faint moan, abruptly cut short. And another deathly silence, lasting a minute or two. He waited, crouching by the trunk and scarcely breathing, but then suddenly leapt up, seized the axe, and ran out of the bedroom.

In the middle of the room stood Lizaveta, holding a big bundle in her arms and staring in petrified horror at her dead sister. She was white as a sheet, and seemingly had no strength to cry out. When she saw him burst out of the bedroom, she began to tremble like a leaf, her body shivered and her whole face twitched. She raised an arm and opened her mouth, but no scream came out. Then she backed slowly away from him into a corner, staring him straight in the face and still not uttering a cry, as if she had no breath left to do so. He ran at her, still holding the axe; her lips worked as pitifully as a small child's when something frightens it, and it stares fixedly at the terrifying object and is on the point of crying out. And so simple-minded was this pathetic Lizaveta, so thoroughly browbeaten and intimidated, that she didn't even raise an arm to protect her face, though that would have been the most vital and natural gesture at that moment, with the axe raised straight above it. She barely lifted her free left arm, not bringing it up anywhere near her face, and slowly stretched it out in front of her towards him, as if to ward him off. The blow fell right on her skull, blade downwards, instantly splitting the whole of her upper forehead, almost as far back as the crown of her head. She fell like a stone. Raskolnikov completely lost his head, grabbed her bundle, threw it down again, and ran to the entrance.

He was becoming more and more panic-stricken, particularly after this second and entirely unexpected murder. He wanted to get away as quickly as he could. Indeed, if he had at that moment been capable of clearer vision and rational thought; if he could only have realized all the difficulty of his position and all the despair, hideousness, and absurdity of it; if he could have seen what complications he would have to cope with, and what deeds of savagery he might yet have to commit, before getting out of this mess and finding his way home—then he would very likely have let everything go and gone straight off to give himself up; and that not even out of fear for himself, but purely out of horror and revulsion at what he had done. Revulsion, in particular, was rising and growing within him with every minute that passed. Not for anything in the world could he now have gone to the chest, or even into that room.

But gradually he was succumbing to a kind of distraction, even pensiveness; at times he seemed to forget himself, or rather to forget the most important things while clinging to trivial details. But happening to look into the kitchen, and noticing a bucket half full of water on the bench, he did think to wash his hands and the axe. His hands were sticky and covered in blood. He lowered the axe blade straight into the water, took a piece of soap from a cracked saucer on the windowsill, and started to wash his hands in the bucket. When he had done, he lifted out the axe, washed the iron blade, and spent a long time, three minutes or so, washing the wooden handle where it was stained with blood. He even attacked the blood with soap. Then he wiped everything with the linen hanging on the line that stretched across the kitchen, and took a long time carefully examining the axe by the window. There were no traces left, though the wood was still damp. He carefully replaced the axe in its loop under his coat. Then he inspected his coat, trousers, and boots, so far as the dim light in the kitchen allowed. On the outside, there seemed at first sight to be nothing visible, except for some stains on his boots. He moistened a rag and wiped his boots. However, he knew that he wasn't seeing very well, and that there might still be something quite eye-catching that he hadn't noticed. Standing in the middle of the room, he stopped to think. A dark and agonizing thought was taking shape within him—the thought that he was out of his mind, and that he was at that moment incapable of reasoning or protecting himself, and that all this might not at all be what he should have been doing. 'My God! I must get away! I must get away!' he muttered, and rushed into the hallway. But here there awaited him a new horror, one that he had of course never envisaged.

He stood and stared and couldn't believe his eyes. The door—the outer door, from the hallway to the stairs, the very one at which he had rung the bell and walked in, a short while ago—was standing open, a whole hand's breadth; not locked, not even latched, for the whole time, all that time! The old woman hadn't locked up after him, perhaps as a precaution. But good God! He had seen Lizaveta after that! And how could he, how could he not have guessed that she must have come in from somewhere! It hadn't been through the wall, after all.

He ran to the door and locked it.

'But no, that's not right either! I must get out, must get out...'

He unlocked the door and opened it, and stood listening down the stairs.

He listened for a long time. Somewhere far below, probably in the gateway, two loud, shrill voices were shouting, swearing and quarrelling. 'What's up?' he wondered, and went on patiently waiting. Suddenly everything went quiet, as though the voices had been cut off. The men had parted. He was about to go back in, when the entrance door of the flat just below opened noisily and someone started going downstairs, humming some sort of tune. 'What a noise everybody makes!' was his fleeting thought. He closed the door behind him again and waited some more. Finally all was quiet, not a soul was to be heard. He was just about to step onto the stairs when he suddenly heard more footsteps.

These footsteps sounded very far down, right at the bottom of the staircase, but he later remembered very clearly and distinctly that at the very first sound of them, he immediately suspected for some reason that they were coming precisely *here*, to the fourth floor, to the old woman's flat. Why? Was it the sounds themselves that were so peculiar and significant? The steps were heavy, even, and unhurried. Now *he* had passed the first floor, now he had come higher still; his steps were getting louder and louder! Raskolnikov could hear the man's heavy breathing as he climbed. Now he had started up the third flight... He's coming here! And suddenly Raskolnikov felt himself turned to stone, as in one of those dreams where someone is chasing you, coming close behind you, wanting to kill you, and you're rooted to the spot and can't even move your hands.

And eventually, when the visitor had already started mounting up to the fourth floor, Raskolnikov suddenly pulled himself together and just had time to slip swiftly and adroitly back from the landing into the flat, closing the door behind him. Then he grasped the bolt and quietly, inaudibly, slipped it into its socket. Instinct helped him here. When that was done, he came and stood right next to the door, holding his breath. The unwanted visitor had reached the door too. Now they were standing right against one another, just like him and the old woman a short while ago, when there was nothing but the door between them, and he had stood listening.

The visitor drew several deep breaths. 'Big and fat, I expect,' thought Raskolnikov, holding the axe tightly. Everything felt just like a dream. The visitor took hold of the little bell and rang it hard.

As soon as the little bell gave its metallic clink, Raskolnikov suddenly had the feeling that someone in the room had moved. Indeed, he listened keenly for a few seconds. The stranger rang again, waited some more, and suddenly fell to rattling the door handle impatiently, as hard as he could. Raskolnikov watched in horror as the bolt handle shook up and down in its socket, and waited in numb terror for it to come out. It really seemed as if that might happen, so vigorously was it being shaken. He thought of holding the bolt in place with his hand—but then *the other one* might guess. His head seemed to be starting to spin again. 'I'm going to fall down!' he thought; but the stranger spoke, and Raskolnikov at once recollected himself.

'What are they all up to in there, fast asleep—or has someone strangled them all? Damn you all!' the visitor roared in a booming voice. 'Hey, Aliona Ivanovna, you old witch! Lizaveta Ivanovna, my raving beauty! Open up! Ooh, damn you both, are they asleep or what?'

And once again he tugged furiously at the bell, ten times in succession, with all his strength. Obviously an important person who knew his way around here.

At that very moment there was the sound of other steps, light and hurried ones, on the stairway nearby. Someone else was approaching, whom Raskolnikov hadn't heard at first.

'Is there really nobody there?' cried the newcomer in a loud and cheerful voice, addressing the first visitor who was still tugging at the bell. 'Hello, Koch!'

'Must be quite young, to judge by his voice,' thought Raskolnikov suddenly.

'Heaven knows. I've almost broken the door down,' replied Koch. 'And how do you come to know me?'

'Well there you are! It was only the day before yesterday I took three frames in a row off you at billiards, at Gambrinus!'*

'A-a-ah...'

'So aren't they here? That's odd. In fact it's quite ridiculous. Where would the old woman go? I've got business with her.'

'I've got business with her myself, my friend.'

'Well, what can I do? Go back home again. Huh! And there was I thinking I'd get some money off her!' exclaimed the young man.

'Of course we have to go back home—but why make an appointment with me? She named the time herself. Getting here is out of my way. And where the devil would she be wandering off to, I'd like to know? She sits in here, day in day out, the old witch, grousing about her bad legs, and now she's suddenly out on the town!'

'Shouldn't we ask the porter?'

'Ask him what?'

'Where she's gone and when she'll be back.'

'Hm... damn it... ask him... But she never goes anywhere...' And he tugged at the latch once more. 'Damn her, nothing for it, we'll have to go.'

'Stop!' cried the young man suddenly. 'Look—did you see how the door moves when you pull at it?'

'So?'

'So that means it's not locked, it's bolted! Do you hear the bar rattling?'

'Well?'

'Don't you get it? That means there's someone at home. If they'd all gone out, they would have locked it from the outside with the key, not bolted it from inside. But here—can you hear the bolt rattling? Bolting yourself in from the inside means you have to be at home, see? So that means they're at home, but they're not opening up!'

'Well! True enough!' Koch cried out in surprise. 'So what are they up to in there?' And he started savagely yanking at the door.

'Stop!' cried the young man again. 'Stop tugging at it! There must be something wrong here... you rang the bell, and pulled the door, and they aren't opening it; so either they've both fainted, or...'

'Or what?'

'Look here. Let's go and fetch the porter, he can wake them himself.'

'Right!' And they both started downstairs.

'Wait! You stay here, and I'll run down for the porter.'

'Why should I wait here?'

'Just in case...'

'I suppose you're right...'

'Well, I'm training to be an examining magistrate.* There's obviously, ob-vi-ous-ly, something wrong here!' the young man cried out excitedly, and ran off down the stairs.

Koch remained behind. He gave another light touch to the bell, which tinkled once. Then he started gently moving the door handle, lifting it towards him and lowering it again, seemingly considering and observing it so as to convince himself once more that the door was held only by its bolt. Then he bent down, puffing, and tried to look through the keyhole; but the key was sticking out of the hole on the inside, so he could see nothing.

Raskolnikov stood, clutching the axe in his hand. He seemed to be in a sort of delirium. He was even preparing to fight with the men when they came back. When they were knocking at the door and discussing what to do, he had several times had the sudden thought of calling it all off straight away, and shouting out to them from behind the door. At times he had felt like swearing at them or taunting them, while they tried in vain to open the door. 'If only they were quick about it!' he thought.

'But—blast him!...'

Time was passing, a minute had gone, and another, and nobody came. Koch moved restlessly about.

'Blast it all!' he burst out impatiently, abandoned his vigil, and hurried off downstairs, his boots clattering down the steps. The sound of his footsteps died away.

'Oh Lord, what should I do now?'

Raskolnikov unbolted the door and opened it slightly. There was nothing to be heard. And suddenly, without even thinking, he came out of the flat, shut the door behind him as tightly as he could, and started downstairs.

He had already gone down three flights when he suddenly heard loud noises below. Where could he go? There was nowhere to hide. He almost ran back upstairs, back to the flat.

'Hey, you devil, you fiend! Stop him!'

With a yell, someone burst out of one of the flats below, and ran—or rather tumbled—down the stairs, shouting at the top of his voice:

'Mitka! Mitka! Mitka! Mitka! Mitka! Damn your eyes!'

The shouting ended with a shriek. The last sounds came from the courtyard, and then it all fell quiet. But at the same moment a number of people started noisily climbing the stairs, talking fast and loudly. There were three or four of them, and he could make out the young man's resonant voice. 'That's them!' he thought.

In utter desperation he walked straight towards them—come what may. If they stop him, all's lost; if they let him pass, all's still lost, they'll remember him. They were just about to meet—only a single flight separated them—when suddenly salvation appeared. Just a few steps down, on the right, was an empty flat with the door wide open, the same second-floor flat where the workmen had been painting; but just now, providentially, they were gone. It was probably they who had just rushed out, with all that shouting. The floors had been newly painted, and in the middle of the floor was a tub and a cracked earthenware pot with some paint and a brush. In an instant he had slipped through the open door and hidden behind the wall—and only just in time, for the men were now on the very landing. Then they turned and went on up towards the fourth floor, talking loudly. He waited, tiptoed out, and ran downstairs.

Nobody on the staircase! Nor in the gateway. He quickly walked through it and turned left along the street.

He knew very well—perfectly well—that at this moment those men were already inside the flat; that they had been very surprised to find it unlocked, when it had been locked a few minutes earlier; that they were already looking at the bodies, and that no more than a minute could pass before they guessed, and then realized for certain, that the murderer had just been there and had managed to hide somewhere, or slip past them and escape. They'd probably realize, too, that he had been lurking in the empty flat while they were making their way upstairs. And meanwhile he couldn't possibly risk hurrying too fast, although the nearest turning was some hundred paces ahead of him. 'Shouldn't I slip into a gateway and wait on a staircase somewhere? No, hopeless! Shouldn't I get rid of the axe somewhere? Or take a cab? Hopeless! Hopeless!'

Here was an alleyway at last. More dead than alive, he turned in to it. Here he was halfway safe already, and he realized that: he would be looking less suspicious, and there were lots of people scurrying this way and that, he could mingle with them and vanish like a grain of sand. But all these trials had so sapped his strength that he could barely move. Sweat was pouring off him, his neck was dripping wet. 'Been putting it away, haven't you!' someone called out to him as he emerged on the canal side.

His wits were scattered now, and the further he went the worse it became. But later on he remembered that as he came out by the canal he had suddenly taken fright, because there were fewer people here and he was more conspicuous, and he almost turned back into the alley. Although he could barely hold himself upright, he managed to take a roundabout route and come home from a different direction altogether.

With his wits still wandering, he walked in through the gateway of his house. At the very least, he had got to the stairs. And not till then did he remember the axe. He still faced the crucial problem of how to replace it, as inconspicuously as possible. Of course he was too far gone by now to realize that it might have been much better not to put it back where he had found it at all, but to dump it later on in someone else's courtyard.

But it all ended well. The door to the porter's room was shut but not locked, so the most likely thing was that he was at home. But Raskolnikov had so completely lost his powers of reasoning that he walked straight up to the porter's door and opened it. If the porter had asked him what he wanted, he might have simply handed him the axe. But the porter was out again, and he managed to put the axe in its place under the bench, even laying the plank back on top of it. And he met no one, not a single soul, as he made his way back to his own room. His landlady's door was locked. Once inside, he flung himself down on the divan just as he was. He didn't sleep, but lay in a stupor. If anyone had walked into his room just then, he would have sprung up at once and cried out. Scraps and fragments of thoughts were swirling around in his head, but try as he might, he couldn't catch hold of a single one.

PART TWO

CHAPTER I

HE lay like that for a very long while. From time to time he seemed to wake up, and then he would realize that it was far into the night; but it never occurred to him to get up. At last he realized that it was broad daylight. He was lying face down on the divan, still dazed from his recent stupor. A strident clamour of hideous, frantic shrieks reached him from the street—but these were just the same sounds that he would hear beneath his window between two and three every morning. It was these sounds that had woken him now. 'Ah! So the drunks are already coming out of the taverns,' he thought, 'it's gone two o'clock,'—and he suddenly sprang up as if someone had tugged him up off the divan. 'What! Gone two already!' He sat back down on the divan—and then he remembered everything. Suddenly, in an instant, he remembered it all!

In that first moment he thought he was going out of his mind. He was seized with a dreadful sense of cold—but that was partly caused by the fever which had come upon him a long time back, while he slept. Now he was suddenly overcome with the shakes, which almost rattled his teeth loose, and all his limbs trembled. He opened the door and listened—everyone in the house was fast asleep. He looked in astonishment down at himself and around him at everything in the room, and couldn't make out how on earth he could have come in last night without locking his door on the hook, and flung himself down on the divan without undressing and even without taking off his hat, which had rolled off his head and was now lying beside him on the floor, next to his pillow. 'If anyone had come in, what would they have thought? That I was drunk, but...' He ran over to the window. There was enough light to see by, and he quickly began looking himself over from head to foot, and inspecting all his clothing. Were there any traces to be seen? But he couldn't go on like this—and all shivering with his chill, he started to undress and examine his clothing inside and out. He turned everything over and over, looking at every last thread and rag; then, not trusting himself, he repeated the whole examination three times over. But there seemed to be nothing, so far as he could see, no traces at all, except for the frayed bottoms of his trouser legs where the threads hung down, and thick drops of congealed blood had stuck to them. He took a big clasp knife and cut off the frayed ends. Apart from that there seemed to be nothing. Suddenly he remembered that the purse and all the things he had taken out of the old woman's trunk were still in his pockets! He hadn't yet had the sense to get them out and hide them! He hadn't even remembered them just now, when he was looking over his clothes! What was wrong with him? He immediately hurried to take them out and fling them onto the table. When he had got everything out and even turned out his pockets to be sure that there was nothing still left there, he carried the whole pile of things to the corner of the room. Here, right in the corner, the wallpaper had peeled away at the bottom and hung in tatters. Instantly he set about pushing everything into the hole under the paper. 'In it goes! All of it, out of sight, and the purse too!' he thought with relief, straightening up and staring blankly into the corner, where the hole gaped even wider than before. Suddenly he gave a shudder of horror. 'My God!' he whispered in desperation. 'What's come over me? Call that hidden? Is that any way to hide things?'

He hadn't been expecting to take any objects: he thought he would only find money, and that was why he hadn't prepared a hiding place in advance. 'But now—what am I so happy about now?' he thought. 'Is that any way to hide stuff? Honestly, I'm losing my mind!' He sat down exhausted on the divan, and at once was again overcome by uncontrollable shivering. Mechanically he pulled on the winter coat lying on a chair nearby, which he once used to wear as a student; it was a warm one, though by now worn and tattered. Covering himself up in it, he was instantly overcome by drowsiness and delirium. He fell unconscious.

No more than five minutes later he sprang up again, and at once in a fury rushed over to his clothes. 'How could I have gone back to sleep again, with nothing done! And there it is, there it is—I still haven't taken off the loop under my armpit! I'd forgotten—forgotten such a vital thing! What a damning piece of evidence!' He ripped off the loop and began quickly tearing it to shreds, which he shoved among his linen under the pillow. 'Some bits of torn canvas won't ever arouse suspicion—no, I don't think so, I don't think so!' he repeated, standing in the middle of the room; and with a painful effort of concentration he once again began looking around him, at the floor and everywhere, in case he'd forgotten anything else. He was becoming agonizingly tormented by the conviction that everything, even his memory, even the simple faculty of thought, was deserting him. 'Can it really have started already, is this really the beginning of my punishment? Yes, yes, that's exactly what it is!' And indeed, the scraps of frayed material he had cut off his trousers were scattered about the floor in the middle of the room, ready to be found by the first comer! 'What on earth is wrong with me?' he cried out again in utter bewilderment.

At this point a strange thought occurred to him. Perhaps all his clothing was bloodstained; perhaps there were a great many spots, but he just couldn't see them or wasn't noticing them, because his powers of observation were weakened, shattered... his mind was clouded... Suddenly he remembered that there had been blood on the purse as well. 'So there! That means there must be blood in the pocket too, because I shoved the purse in my pocket while it was still wet!' In an instant he had turned out the pocket, and sure enough, there were traces, stains on the lining. 'So I haven't entirely lost my wits, then, I've still got my reason and my memory, if I was able to realize that and work it out on my own!' he thought triumphantly, heaving a profound sigh of relief. 'It was just weakness from my fever, a moment's delirium.' And he ripped out the whole lining of the left trouser pocket. At that moment a sunbeam fell on his left boot. There seemed to be some traces on the sock where it stuck out of the boot. He kicked off the boot. 'Yes, bloodstains, sure enough! The whole toe of the sock is soaked in blood.' He must have carelessly trodden in the pool of blood at the time... 'So what can I do about all this now? Where can I hide this sock, those trouser ends, that pocket lining?'

He scooped up everything in his hand and stood in the middle of the room. 'In the fireplace? But that's the first place they'll look. Burn it all? But what with? I don't even have any matches. No, better go out somewhere and throw everything away. Yes! Better throw it away!' he repeated, sitting back down on the divan. 'Straight away, this very minute, wasting no time!... 'But instead of that, his head sank back down onto the pillow, an unbearable icy chill came over him, and once again he covered himself with the overcoat. And for a long time, several hours on end, he kept having sudden impulses: 'I must do it right now, stop putting it off, go out somewhere and throw the whole lot away, get rid of it, just do it, do it!' And several times he struggled up from the divan and tried to get up, but couldn't manage it. He was finally woken by a loud knock at the door.

'Come on, open up, are you alive or aren't you? He's still fast asleep!' shouted Nastasia, banging on the door with her fist. 'He lies there sleeping day in day out, like a dog! A dog, that's what he is! Open up, come on. It's past ten.'

'Perhaps he's not at home at all!' said a male voice.

'Oho! That's the porter's voice... What does he want?'

He sprang up and sat down on the divan. His heart was beating so hard that it hurt.

'So who put the hook on then?' objected Nastasia. 'Look at that, he's started locking himself in! Is he afraid someone'll steal him away? Open up, you crazy man, wake up!'

'What do they want? Why's the porter here? They know everything. Do I resist or open up? To hell with it!'

He raised himself, bent forward, and took the hook off the door. His whole room was so small that he could unhook the door without leaving his bed.

And there they were, the porter and Nastasia.

Nastasia looked him over in an odd way. He himself cast a challenging, desperate look at the porter, who silently handed him a sheet of grey paper, folded in two and sealed with bottle wax.

'A note, from the office,' he said, giving him the paper.

'What office?'

'The police, they want to see you, you're to go to the office. It's obvious what office.'

'The police!... What for?'

'How do I know? They want you, so you go there.' He looked attentively at Raskolnikov, cast an eye around the room, and turned to leave.

'Are you really ill?' asked Nastasia, without taking her eyes off him. The porter also looked back for a moment. 'You've been in a fever since yesterday,' she added.

He made no reply, holding the paper in his hands without breaking the seal.

'Don't you get up,' Nastasia went on, feeling sorry for him as she saw him lowering his feet from the divan. 'If you're ill, don't go—it'll keep. What's that in your hands?'

He looked down. His right hand was holding the cut pieces of his trouser legs, the sock, and the shreds of the torn-out pocket lining. He had been asleep with them like that. Later on, reflecting on all this, he remembered that even when he had half awoken in a fever, he had been clenching his fist tightly around all this, and had fallen asleep again that way.

'Look at the rags he's picked up, and he's been sleeping with them as if he had a treasure there!' And Nastasia burst out in her neurotic, hysterical laugh. Instantly he shoved everything under his overcoat and stared intently at her. Although incapable of much rational thought just then, he had the feeling that he'd be treated rather differently if they were coming to take him away.

'But... the police?'

'Could you drink some tea? D'you want some? I'll bring it—there's some left...'

'No... I'll go. I'll go in a minute,' he stammered, getting to his feet.

'Get away! You won't even get downstairs, will you?'

'I'll go...'

'Just as you like.'

She followed the porter out of the room. He immediately rushed over to the light and inspected his sock and the frayed threads. 'There are stains, but they're not too noticeable; they're all dirty and rubbed and discoloured. Anyone who didn't know would never notice. So Nastasia couldn't have spotted anything from a distance, thank God!' And with trembling hands he broke the seal on the paper and began reading it. He spent a long time reading it before he eventually understood. It was a routine summons from the district police office ordering him to appear that day at half past nine in the office of the district superintendent.

'Whatever can it mean? I've never had any business of my own with the police! And why today of all days?' he thought in a torment of doubt. 'Oh Lord, if only it was over!' He almost fell to his knees in prayer, but burst out laughing—not at his prayer, but at himself. Hurriedly he began dressing. 'If I'm done for, I'm done for, who cares! I have to put on the sock!' he suddenly thought. 'It'll get even dirtier in the dust, and the traces will vanish.' But as soon as he had put it on, he tore it straight off again with horror and revulsion. Having pulled it off, he realized that he didn't have another one, so he picked it up and put it on again—and laughed once more. 'All this is just convention, it's all relative, all meaningless,' he thought for an instant, with no more than a corner of his mind, while his whole body trembled. 'There, I've put it on! I ended up putting it on!' But his laughter at once gave way to despair. 'No, I can't take it...' he thought. His legs were shaking. 'From terror,' he muttered to himself. His head was spinning and aching from his fever. 'It's a trick! They want to lead me on, and suddenly catch me out,' he went on to himself as he stepped out onto the staircase. 'The trouble is, I'm almost delirious... I might do something stupid...'

On the staircase he recalled that he had left all those things in the hole under the wallpaper—'and now they'll come and do a search while I'm out', he thought, and stopped. But suddenly he was overcome by such a feeling of despair, and of what one might call cynical self-destructiveness, that he just shrugged his shoulders and went on. 'If only it was all over quickly!'

Out on the street it was unbearably hot again. Oh for a single drop of rain, in all these days! The same dust, brick-and-plaster dust, the same stench from the shops and taverns, the same drunks passing every moment, Finnish pedlars, broken-down cabs. The glaring sun dazzled his eyes, making it painful to look and causing his head to spin—the usual sensations of someone with a fever who suddenly emerges out of doors on a bright sunny day.

When he reached the corner of *yesterday's street*, he glanced down it in a torment of anxiety, looked at *that house*—and immediately looked away again.

'If they ask me, perhaps I'll simply tell them,' he thought to himself as he walked to the police office.

The office was only about a quarter of a verst from his lodging. It had just moved to new premises on the fourth floor of a new building.* He had once, at some point, briefly visited the old office, but that was a long time ago. As he walked in through the gateway he saw a staircase on the right, and a peasant coming downstairs holding a booklet. 'So that must be a yard porter; so the office must be up there,' he thought, and set off upstairs on the off-chance. He didn't want to ask anyone anything.

'I'll go in, fall on my knees, and tell them everything...' he thought as he reached the fourth floor.

The staircase was steep and narrow, and wet with slops. All the kitchens of all the flats on all four floors opened onto the staircase, and stood open almost all day long, making it unbearably stuffy. There were yard porters going up and down the stairs carrying books under their arms, and policemen, and visitors of all kinds and both sexes. The office door was wide open too. He went in and stopped in the anteroom. A number of peasants or the like were standing around waiting. This room, too, was overpoweringly stuffy, with the acrid smell of rancid oil from the fresh wet paint in all the rooms. He waited a little, but then decided to go on into the next room. All the rooms were tiny and low-ceilinged. His fearful impatience drove him further and further in. No one paid any attention to him. In the second room some clerks were sitting and writing, dressed scarcely better than him. They all looked very odd. He asked one of them for help.

'What do you want?'

He showed the summons from the police office.

'Are you a student?' the man asked, glancing at the paper.

'Yes—an ex-student.'

The clerk looked him over without the slightest curiosity. He was an extremely dishevelled man with the look of a fixed idea in his eyes.

'I'll never find out anything from this one—he doesn't care about anything,' thought Raskolnikov.

'Go through there, to the head clerk,' said the man and pointed his finger towards the last room.

Raskolnikov entered the room—the fourth in line. It was narrow and cram-full of people, somewhat better dressed than in the other rooms. Two of the visitors were ladies. One of them, poorly dressed in mourning clothes, was sitting at a table in front of the head clerk and writing something to his dictation. The other was a very plump and showy woman with a blotchy crimson-red complexion, very flamboyantly dressed, with a brooch the size of a saucer on her breast. She was standing to one side, apparently waiting for something. Raskolnikov pushed his summons over to the chief clerk, who glanced at it, told him to wait, and went on attending to the lady in mourning.

Raskolnikov breathed more easily. 'It can't be that!' Gradually his spirits recovered. He tried his hardest to pluck up courage and gather his wits.

'All it would take is some piece of stupidity, the slightest bit of carelessness, and I could give myself away! Hmm... I wish there was some air in here,' he added. 'It's stifling. My head's spinning even worse than before... and my mind too...'

He felt that everything inside him was in a terrible state of confusion, and he was afraid of losing control of himself. He tried to concentrate on something, think about something completely irrelevant, but utterly failed. However, the head clerk interested him greatly—he kept trying to guess something from the man's face, trying to read him. He was a very young man, about twenty-two years old, with a dark complexion and mobile features. He looked older than his age, and was modishly dressed, like a dandy. His pomaded hair was brushed forward from a back parting. He wore a great many rings on his scrubbed white fingers, and gold chains on his waistcoat. Speaking to a foreigner who was in the room, he even said a few words in quite good French.

'Luisa Ivanovna, do take a seat,' he said in passing to the overdressed crimson-faced lady who was still standing there, as though she dared not sit down of her own accord, though a chair stood beside her.

'*Ich danke*,' she replied, quietly taking a seat with a rustling of silks. Her pale blue dress with its white lace border ballooned out from the chair, occupying almost half the room. There was a sudden waft of perfume. But the lady seemed embarrassed at taking up half the room and smelling so strongly of perfume; and though her smile was at once timid and impudent, she was clearly uneasy.

Eventually the lady in mourning had done, and began getting up. Suddenly an officer strode noisily into the room, with a most dashing air and an odd jerky swagger of his shoulders. He tossed his cockaded cap onto the table and seated himself in an armchair. The overdressed lady started up as soon as she saw him, and began curtseying apparently with great delight, but the officer paid her not the slightest attention. She no longer dared to sit down again in his presence. He was a lieutenant, the district police inspector's assistant.* He wore a sandy-coloured moustache that stuck out horizontally on both sides of his face, and his features were particularly delicate, though they expressed nothing much beyond a certain insolence. He cast a sidelong, somewhat indignant glance at Raskolnikov—whose clothes were really excessively shabby, and yet whose bearing, though humble, had a dignity that belied his dress. Without meaning to, Raskolnikov had eyed him too long and hard, and the officer had actually taken offence.

'What do you want?' he shouted, probably astonished that this ragamuffin had made no attempt to shrink from the lightning that flashed from his eyes.

'I was summoned... by a letter...' Raskolnikov just managed to reply.

'It's about the demand for money from him, from this *student*,' the head clerk hastened to explain, tearing himself away from his papers. 'Here you are, sir!'—and he tossed a book over to Raskolnikov, pointing out the place. 'Read that!'

'Money? What money?' wondered Raskolnikov. 'But... that means, it can't possibly be *that*.' And he gave a shiver of joy. He was suddenly overcome with a terrific, unspeakable sense of relief. The whole burden had fallen from his shoulders.

'And what time did the letter order you to appear, my good sir?' cried the lieutenant, getting more and more outraged for some reason. 'You're told to appear at nine, and now it's past eleven!'

'They only brought me the letter a quarter of an hour ago,' replied Raskolnikov, speaking loudly over his shoulder. He too had suddenly become angry, to his own surprise, and was even finding some pleasure in the fact. 'You ought to be glad that I've come at all, ill and feverish as I am!'

'Don't you dare shout!'

'I'm not shouting, I'm talking very calmly, it's you that's shouting at me. I'm a student, and I won't be shouted at.'

The assistant inspector flared up so violently that for a minute he was unable to speak; all that came out was spluttering. Then he leapt to his feet.

'Just—you—hold—your—tongue! You're in a Government office. None of your impertinence, sir!'

'And you're in a Government office too,' exclaimed Raskolnikov, 'and you're not just shouting, you're smoking a cigarette, so you're insulting us all.' Raskolnikov found an inexpressible pleasure in saying all this.

The head clerk was watching them with a smile. The hot-tempered lieutenant was visibly nonplussed.

'That's nothing to do with you, sir!' he eventually shouted, in an unnaturally loud voice. 'And be good enough to give your response as you're required to do. Show him, Alexander Grigorievich. There's a complaint against you! Not paying up what you owe! What a fine fellow we have here!'

But Raskolnikov had stopped paying him any attention. He eagerly seized the paper, searching for a clue to the mystery. He read it over and then read it again, but couldn't make it out.

'What's all this?' he asked the head clerk.

'It's a demand for repayment of a promissory note—a writ. You either have to pay it off, including all expenses, penalties, and so on, or you have to respond in writing, stating when you can pay and meanwhile undertaking not to leave St Petersburg until the debt is paid, and not to sell or conceal your belongings. And the lender has the option of selling off your belongings or commencing legal proceedings against you.'

'But I... I don't owe anyone anything!'

'That's not our concern. We've received an application for recovery of an overdue and legally protested promissory note for one hundred and fifteen roubles, delivered by you nine months ago to the widow of Collegiate Assessor Zarnitsyn, and assigned in payment by the widow Zarnitsyna to Court Councillor Chebarov. And you are now invited to submit your reply.'

'But she's my landlady!'

'So what if she's your landlady?'

The head clerk was watching him with a smile of pitying condescension, and also a certain air of triumph, as one might watch a raw recruit coming under fire for the first time—'Well, and how does it feel now?' But what did he care any longer about the promissory note, or about the writ! Did all that merit the slightest anxiety, the slightest attention even? He was standing, reading, listening, answering, even asking questions of his own, but doing it all mechanically. A triumphant sense of self-preservation, of salvation from a threat hanging over him—that was what filled his whole being right now; with no thoughts of the future, no analysis, no guesses or surmises about what might happen, no doubts, no questions. It was a moment of complete, spontaneous, purely animal joy. But at that very moment something like a tempest of thunder and lightning erupted in the office. The lieutenant, still smarting from the disrespect he had endured, burning with fury and evidently intent on salvaging his injured pride, pounced savagely upon the poor 'elegant lady' who had been staring at him ever since he came in, with the silliest smile on her face.

'As for you, you baggage,' he suddenly shouted at the top of his voice (the lady in mourning had already left), 'what was going on at your place last night? Eh? Disorderly behaviour, outrageous carryings-on, disgracing the whole street again! More brawling and drunkenness! Just asking to be locked up, you are. I've told you ten times over, I've warned you, if there's an eleventh time, you're for it! And now you're at it again, you shameless harridan, you!'

The paper slipped from Raskolnikov's hand as he stared wild-eyed at the elegant lady who was being so roundly abused. But he soon realized what was going on, and began to be amused at the whole scene. He listened with enjoyment, tempted to laugh and laugh and laugh... All his nerves were on edge.

'Ilya Petrovich!' began the head clerk anxiously, but stopped to wait for a better moment. Experience had taught him that there was no way of restraining the incandescent lieutenant without physically taking hold of him.

As for the elegant lady, she had indeed started trembling when the thunder and lightning burst out; but strangely enough, the more insults she received and the worse they were, the friendlier her expression became, and the more charming the smile she directed at the terrifying lieutenant. She shuffled her feet and curtseyed again and again, waiting impatiently until she too could get a word in. Eventually she managed it.

'No noise and fighting in my place is being, *Herr Kapitän*,'—the words tumbled out like peas rattling onto the floor, all with a strong German accent, though she spoke voluble Russian. 'And nothing, nothing *Skandal*, only they come drunken, and I tell you all this, *Herr Kapitän*, and it none my fault... I keeping respectable house, *Herr Kapitän*, and respectable visitors, *Herr Kapitän*, and always, always, I don't want no *Skandal*. And he quite drunken coming, and then he ordering more three pottles, and then he is lifting one feets and start play pianoforte with feets, and that is quite not nice in respectable house, and he quite breaking the pianoforte, and this he has no manners at all, and I telling him. And he taking pottle and start push all people from back with pottle. And then quickly I call porter and Karl coming, and he taking Karl and punch him on eye, and Henriette he also punch on eye, and me five times he hitting on cheek. And all this quite bad manners in respectable house, *Herr Kapitän*, and I shouting. And he opening window on canal and stand in window, like small pig he screaming; and this is disgrace. And how is possible stand in window on street, like small pig shouting; this is disgrace. Pfui-pfui-pfui! And Karl behind him he hold his coat, he pulling him from window, and now, this true, *Herr Kapitän*, he tearing him *seinen Rock*. And so he shouting *man muss ihm* fifteen roubles to pay. And I myself, *Herr Kapitän*, pay him *seinen Rock* five roubles. And this is dishonourable guest, *Herr Kapitän*, and he making great *Skandal*! I make one great Satire *gedruckt* against you, he saying, because I can write about you in all newspapers.'

'So he's a writer, then?'

'Yes, *Herr Kapitän*, and what for dishonourable guest is this, *Herr Kapitän*, when in the respectable house...'

'All right, all right! That'll do! I've told you over and over again, I've told you...'

'Ilya Petrovich!' said the head clerk once more, in a meaningful voice. The lieutenant glanced quickly at him, and the head clerk gave a little nod.

'So there you are, most respected *Lavisa* Ivanovna, this is my final word to you, this is absolutely the last time,' went on the lieutenant. 'If there's ever one more scandal in your respectable house, I'll send you yourself off to the lockup, as they call it in polite circles. D'you hear? So an author, a writer, took five roubles off you for his coat, in a "respectable house", did he? They're all the same, these writers!'— and he shot a scornful glance at Raskolnikov. 'Day before yesterday there was another scene in a tavern—the man had eaten his lunch, but didn't feel like paying; "I'll write a satire against you for this!" says he. And another one, on a steamship, last week, grossly insulted a State Councillor's family, his wife and daughter—respectable people. And the other day one of those men was bodily thrown out of a pastry cook's shop. That's what they're all like, these writers, men of letters, students, loud-mouths—phoo! As for you, get out! I'll be round to your place one of these days, and then you look out! D'you hear?'

Luisa Ivanovna hastily began curtseying in all directions with an ingratiating smile, gradually backing towards the door as she did so; but when she reached the doorway she ran backwards into an impressive-looking officer with a fresh, open countenance and a most splendid pair of luxuriant blond side-whiskers. This was the district inspector, Nikodim Fomich himself. Luisa Ivanovna hastened to curtsey again, almost down to the ground, and skipped out of the office with tiny mincing steps.

'More crashing and banging, more thunder and lightning, hurricanes and whirlwinds!' said Nikodim Fomich to Ilya Petrovich, in an affable and friendly voice. 'Upsetting your heart again, boiling over again! I could hear you all the way from the stairs.'

'What of it!' drawled Ilya Petrovich with well-bred negligence (or rather he said something like 'Whaat aaahve it!') And he carried a sheaf of papers to another table, swinging his shoulders elegantly with every step, one leg forward, one shoulder forward with it. 'Look here sir, just take a look at this. This Mr Author here, this student that is to say, or rather this ex-student, doesn't pay what he owes, he's been handing out promissory notes, won't keep his flat clean, there are everlasting complaints against him, and he's had the gall to complain that I lit up a little cigarette in front of his honour! Behaves disgracefully himself, but just cast an eye over the gentleman, sir: here he is, looking his very best for you right now, sir!'

'Poverty is no sin, my old friend; but never mind that! We all know you're made of gunpowder, you won't stand for any disrespect. You probably took offence at something he said,' he went on, turning to Raskolnikov with a friendly air, 'and then you couldn't stop yourself—but there was no need for that, he's the fi-i-inest fellow in the world, I promise you—but he's gunpowder! Gunpowder! He'll flare up, boil over, burn up—and it's all over! Finished! And all that's left is a heart of gold! Even back in his regiment, they used to call him Lieutenant Gunpowder...'

'And what a r-r-regiment that was!' cried Ilya Petrovich, very content to be so pleasantly teased, but still acting sulky.

Raskolnikov suddenly felt the urge to say something particularly friendly to everyone there.

'Excuse me, Captain,' he began very nonchalantly, turning suddenly to Nikodim Fomich, 'but try to put yourself in my place... I'm happy to apologize if I've done anything wrong. I'm a poor, sick student, crushed' (that was the word he used—'crushed') 'by poverty. An ex-student, because at the moment I'm unable to maintain myself, but I shall be

getting some money... I have a mother and sister in —— Province,*
they'll send me some, and I'll... pay. My landlady's a kind woman, but
she was so furious when I lost the lessons I was giving and couldn't pay
her for over three months that she won't even send me up my meals
now... And I haven't the slightest idea what this bill is! Here she is
demanding money against this promissory note, but how on earth can
I pay her, I ask you?'

'Well, that's nothing to do with us...' the head clerk began again.

'Allow me, allow me, I entirely agree with you, but please let me explain
too,' interrupted Raskolnikov, addressing not the head clerk but Nikodim
Fomich again, while trying his hardest to include Ilya Petrovich as well,
though the latter obstinately pretended to be hunting through some
papers, and contemptuously avoided taking any notice of Raskolnikov.
'Let me explain my side of it too—I've been living in her house for
about three years, ever since I arrived from the provinces, and earlier
on... earlier on... well, why shouldn't I admit it myself? At the very
beginning, I gave her a promise that I'd marry her daughter, a verbal
promise, quite freely given... She was a girl... well, I did fancy her...
although I wasn't actually in love... well, in a word, I was young, and
I mean to say, my landlady used to allow me a lot of credit, and the life
I led sometimes... I was very thoughtless...'

'Nobody's asking you for all these intimate details, my good sir,
and we've no time for them,' Ilya Petrovich interrupted rudely and
triumphantly; but Raskolnikov stopped him and continued hotly—though
he was suddenly finding it very difficult to speak.

'But allow me, do allow me to tell you everything... how it all was...
my own side of it... although you don't need all that, I agree—but that
girl died of typhus a year ago, and I stayed on as a lodger, as before, and
the landlady, when she moved to her present flat, told me... told me in
a friendly way... that she had absolute confidence in me and all that...
but wouldn't I agree to give her that promissory note for a hundred
and fifteen roubles, which was all she reckoned I owed her. Listen, she
actually said that as soon as I gave her that note, she'd grant me all the
credit I needed, as she had done before, and she herself would never,
never—those were her very words—she'd never use that paper, until
I paid her back myself. And now that I've lost my lessons and I've nothing to eat, she hands it over for recovery... What am I supposed to say?'

'All these moving details are nothing to do with us, my dear sir,'
Ilya Petrovich interrupted sharply. 'You're obliged to respond and give
an undertaking, but as for your deciding to be in love and all that tragic
stuff, that doesn't concern us in the least.'

'Well, you know... that's a bit hard...' muttered Nikodim Fomich, sitting down at the desk and also beginning to sign papers. He was feeling a bit ashamed.

'Go on, write,' said the head clerk to Raskolnikov.

'Write what?' Raskolnikov retorted very rudely.

'I'll dictate to you.'

Raskolnikov had the impression that the head clerk had grown more offhand and contemptuous with him after his confession, but strange to say, he himself suddenly felt utterly indifferent to anybody's opinion. That change had taken place all at once, in a single instant. If he could have given it any thought, of course, he might have been surprised at how he had been addressing everyone a minute earlier, and actually forcing his feelings upon them. Where had all those feelings come from? Indeed, if the whole room were now suddenly to become filled with all his closest friends, instead of these policemen, even then he would probably not manage to find a single sincere word to say to them, so empty had his heart suddenly become. He was aware of a dark sense of endless, anguished loneliness and estrangement suddenly invading his soul. It was not the indignity of his heartfelt outpourings to Ilya Petrovich, nor the lieutenant's humiliating triumph over him, that had caused this sudden revulsion in his feelings. Oh, what did he care now about his own baseness, or all those ambitions, lieutenants, German ladies, demands for payment, police stations, and all the rest of it! Even if he'd been condemned to be burned that very minute, he still wouldn't have moved from the spot, probably not even paid any attention to his sentence. What was happening to him was something he had never experienced before, something suddenly new and unheard-of. Not that he understood it in his mind; but he could clearly feel, with the full force of his emotions, that he was no longer able to communicate with these people in the district police office—not only by way of the sentimental outpourings of a few minutes ago, but in any way whatsoever. If they had all been his own brothers and sisters, instead of district police lieutenants, there would still have been no point in communicating with them, no matter what was happening in his life. Never before this moment had he experienced such a strange and terrible sensation. And worst of all was the fact that this was more a sensation than an awareness of an idea; it was a direct feeling, the most agonizing feeling he had ever experienced in his life.

The head clerk started dictating the standard response in such cases, stating 'I am unable to pay, I undertake to pay on such and such a day (some time or other), I shall not leave the city, I shall not sell or give away my property,' and so forth.

'But you're not managing to write—the pen's dropping from your fingers,' remarked the head clerk, looking at Raskolnikov with curiosity. 'Are you ill?'

'Yes... my head's spinning... Go on!'

'That's it! Sign here.'

The head clerk took the paper and turned to attend to other people.

Raskolnikov handed back the pen, but instead of getting up and going, he leaned his elbows on the table and pressed both hands to his head. It felt as if someone was hammering a nail into the top of his skull. He suddenly had a strange idea—to get up now and go to Nikodim Fomich and tell him all about yesterday, down to the last detail, and then go with them to his flat and show them the things hidden in the corner, down the hole. The urge was so strong that he had actually risen from his seat to carry it out. 'Shouldn't I think it over, just for a minute?' he wondered. 'No, better not think, just get it off my chest!' But suddenly he stopped, and stood rooted to the spot. Nikodim Fomich was talking heatedly to Ilya Petrovich, and Raskolnikov could overhear his words:

'Absolutely impossible! They'll both be released. Firstly, it's full of contradictions. Just think—why fetch the porter, if they'd done it? To incriminate themselves? Or was that a cunning ploy? No, too cunning by half! And then, both porters and a housewife saw the student Pestryakov just as he was entering the gate; he was walking with three friends, and separated from them right by the gate, and he asked the porter about who lived there, while his friends were still with him. Well, would someone like that have been asking about the residents if he was planning to do that? And as for Koch, before going up to the old woman he'd spent half an hour with the silversmith downstairs, and it was just a quarter to eight when he left him to go upstairs to her flat. Just think about it...'

'But look at the contradiction in their story. They insist that they knocked at the door and it was locked, and yet three minutes later when they came up with the porter, it turned out that the door was open!'

'That's just it. The murderer must have been hiding there, with the door bolted shut; and they'd have been bound to catch him there if Koch hadn't been stupid enough to set off hunting for the porter himself. And he just seized that moment to get away downstairs and slip past them all. Koch swears by all that's holy, "If I'd stayed there," he says, "he'd have rushed out and murdered me with the axe!" He wants to lay on a Russian thanksgiving service, ha-ha!'

'And nobody saw the murderer?'

'How could they? That house is a Noah's ark,' remarked the head clerk, listening from his desk.

'It's quite obvious, quite obvious!' repeated Nikodim Fomich heatedly.

'No, it's not obvious at all,' insisted Ilya Petrovich.

Raskolnikov picked up his hat and walked to the door; but he never reached it...

When he came to his senses, he found himself sitting on a chair, with somebody supporting him on his right, while someone else was standing on his left holding a yellow glass filled with yellow water, and Nikodim Fomich was standing in front of him, staring at him. He got up from the chair.

'What's up? Are you ill?' asked Nikodim Fomich, quite sharply.

'When he was signing the paper, he could hardly hold the pen,' said the head clerk, going back to his place and picking up his papers again.

'Been ill long?' cried Ilya Petrovich from his own desk, where he too was leafing through some papers. He, too, had of course come to look at the sick man when he fainted, but had moved off as soon as he recovered consciousness.

'From yesterday,' muttered Raskolnikov in reply.

'Did you leave your house yesterday?'

'Yes.'

'Sick as you were?'

'Sick as I was.'

'What time?'

'Between seven and eight in the evening.'

'And where did you go, may I ask?'

'Along the street.'

'Crisp and clear.'

Raskolnikov was answering sharply and abruptly, standing white as a sheet, without lowering his burning black eyes under Ilya Petrovich's stare.

'He can hardly stand up, and you're...' began Nikodim Fomich.

'Ne-ver mind!' drawled Ilya Petrovich in a meaningful voice. Nikodim Fomich was about to add something more, but glancing at the head clerk who was also staring hard at him, he said nothing. Everyone suddenly fell silent—it was very strange.

'Well, sir, very well,' concluded Ilya Petrovich, 'don't let us keep you.'

Raskolnikov left. He could still make out the lively conversation that broke out once he had left the room, with the enquiring tones of Nikodim Fomich sounding loudest of all... Once he reached the street, he came fully to himself.

'A search, a search, they'll do a search right now!' he repeated to himself as he hurried home. 'The villains! They suspect me!' And his former terror returned, enfolding him from head to foot.

CHAPTER II

'But suppose they've already done a search? What if I find them right there when I get back?'

But here was his room. Nothing, nobody. No one had been in. Even Nastasia hadn't touched it. But, good God, how could he have left all those things in that hole just now?

He rushed to the corner, thrust his hand under the wallpaper and started pulling the objects out and filling his pockets with them. There were eight items in all: two little boxes containing earrings or something of the sort—he didn't look properly; and four small leather jewel-cases. One chain, simply wrapped in newspaper. And something else, also in newspaper—probably a medal...

He distributed the things in various pockets, in his coat or the remaining right-hand trouser pocket, trying to make it all inconspicuous. He picked up the purse with all the other things. Then he went out of the room, this time leaving the door wide open.

He walked fast and resolutely, and although he ached in every limb, he had his wits about him. He was afraid of being pursued; afraid that in half an hour, or even a quarter of an hour, orders would be given to follow him; so he had at all costs to hide every trace before that happened. He must sort everything out while he still had some strength left, and some power of reasoning. So where should he go?

It had all been settled long ago. 'Throw everything into the canal, so there'll be nothing to find, and there's an end of it.' That was what he had decided last night, while he was delirious, when—as he remembered—he had tried again and again to get up and go out: 'hurry, hurry, throw it all away'. But throwing everything away turned out to be very difficult.

He had been wandering along the bank of the Ekaterininsky Canal for half an hour now, perhaps longer, and had inspected several places where steps led down to the water. But there was no question of carrying out his plan here: either there were rafts moored right up against the steps, with washerwomen at work on them, or there were boats tied up; and everywhere there were crowds of people, and besides, everything could be seen from the canal banks, from every side, and he'd be noticed—it would be suspicious if a man deliberately went down the steps, stopped there, and threw something into the water. And supposing the jewel cases floated instead of sinking? Of course they would. Anyone would notice. And anyway everyone was staring at him as they passed by, looking him up and down as though they had nothing else to think about. 'Why should that be happening?—or perhaps it's my imagination,' he thought.

Eventually he had the idea that it might be better to go somewhere along the Neva River. There'd be fewer people about, and he'd be less visible, and anyway it would be more convenient, and—most important of all—he'd be further away from these parts. And suddenly he was astonished at the way he had just spent a whole half-hour wandering here, full of misery and dread, in these dangerous places, and hadn't managed to work this out earlier! And the only reason he had wasted a whole half-hour on this pointless activity was that this was what he'd decided on in his sleep, while he was delirious! He was becoming very distracted and forgetful, and he knew that. Now he really had to hurry!

He walked to the Neva by way of V—— Prospekt, but on the way he had another thought. 'Why go to the Neva? Why throw it all in the water? Wouldn't it be better to go somewhere very far away, perhaps back to the Islands, and find a deserted place there somewhere, in a wood, and bury it all there, under a bush—and make a note of a tree nearby?' And although he knew that he was incapable of thinking it all out, clearly and sensibly, at that moment, this new thought struck him as completely right.

But he was not destined to get to the Islands. Something else happened instead. Coming out of V—— Prospekt onto a square, he suddenly noticed to his left a passage leading to a yard entirely surrounded by blank walls.* Along the right-hand side of the passage, starting immediately inside the gate, was the rough, windowless back wall of a neighbouring four-storey house, extending far into the yard. On the left, parallel to the blank wall, and again starting just inside the gate, stood a wooden hoarding running about twenty paces into the yard and then bending round to the left. Here was a hidden area of fenced-off ground with all sorts of rubbish lying about. Further in, at the far end of the yard, the corner of a low, smoke-blackened stone shed could be seen projecting from behind the fence—evidently part of some workshop, probably a carriage repair shop or a locksmith's or something of the sort. The whole place, almost up to the gateway, was black with coal dust. 'This is where I ought to drop the stuff, and get away!' Raskolnikov thought suddenly.

Seeing no one in the yard, he walked in through the gate and at once noticed, right by the entrance, a trench dug in the ground below the hoarding, the kind of thing often provided for factory hands, trades-men, cab drivers, and the like; and chalked up on the hoarding directly above it was the usual witticism in such places: 'Standing Hear Stricly Forbiden.' This was lucky, if only because nobody would get suspicious at seeing him walk in and stop here. 'This is where I ought to dump everything, all in a heap somewhere, and get away!'

Looking about him one last time, he had already shoved his hand into his pocket when he suddenly noticed a great block of uncut stone weighing perhaps forty pounds, standing right against the outer wall, in the gap between the gate and the trench which was less than a yard across. It was leaning directly against the street wall. Beyond the wall was the street, with a pavement along which passers-by could be heard hurrying this way and that; there were always a lot of people about here. And yet behind the gates no one could see him, unless someone were to walk in from the street—which as a matter of fact might quite easily happen, so he had to be quick.

He bent down over the stone, gripped the top of it firmly in both hands, pulled with all his might and toppled it. Underneath it was a small depression. He immediately threw in all the contents of his pockets. The purse lay on top of the pile, and there was still some room left. Then he grabbed hold of the stone again, and with a single effort rolled it back up. It fitted perfectly in its old position, except that it seemed to stand a little, just a very little higher. He scraped some earth together and pressed it against the edge. Now there was nothing to be seen.

He walked out and set off for the square. Once again he was over-come for a moment by a sense of extreme, almost unbearable happi-ness, just as he had been in the police office earlier on. 'No traces left! And who could possibly think of looking underneath that stone? It could have stood there ever since the house was built, and might stay there just as long again. And supposing they do find it: who'd think of me? It's all done! No evidence left!' And he burst out laughing. Yes, and later on he would remember that he had laughed a thin, nervous, inaudible laugh, a long laugh, one that went on and on as he walked across the square. But when he entered K—— Boulevard, where he had encountered that girl two days ago, his laughter suddenly stopped. Other thoughts crept into his head. And he suddenly thought how profoundly repugnant he would find it to walk past that bench where he had sat and pondered the other day, after the girl had gone, and how much he would hate to meet that whiskered policeman to whom he had given twenty kopeks. 'Blast him!'

He walked on, looking about him with a distracted, ill-tempered air. All his thoughts were now centred on a single crucial point; and he himself felt that this was indeed the crucial point, and that now, right now, he had come face to face with this crucial point, for the first time in two months.

'Oh, to hell with all of it!' he suddenly thought, in a fit of uncontrollable fury. 'So it's started, well then, it's started, and to hell with it all and with my new life! Lord, how absurd it all is!... And what a lot of lying and grovelling I've done today! How I cringed and sucked up to that revolting Ilya Petrovich back then! But that's all rubbish too. To hell with the lot of them, and to hell with my fawning and cringing! That's not the point, not the point at all!'

Suddenly he stopped still. A new and quite unexpected question, and an extremely simple one, had suddenly confused him and filled him with bitter amazement. 'If this whole business was really done consciously, and not just as a piece of idiocy—if you really had a firm and definite purpose in mind—then how is it that you never even looked inside the purse, you still don't know how much you got, or what you went through all those torments for, when you deliberately did such a vicious, wicked, contemptible thing? Just now you were even wanting to throw it into the water, that purse, and all the other things you never even looked at. So what about all that?'

Yes, that was true—that was how it was. True, he had known all this before, it wasn't a new question for him at all; and when, last night, he had resolved to throw everything into the water, that had been decided without the slightest doubt or hesitation, just so, as if that was how it had to be, and anything else was unthinkable... Yes, he knew all that, and remembered it all; in fact it had almost been settled yesterday, at the very moment when he was leaning over the chest and pulling out the jewel cases... That was how it had been, really!

'That's because I'm very ill,' he concluded gloomily at last. 'I've worn myself out and exhausted myself, and I don't know what I'm doing. Yesterday, and the day before, and all this time, I've been tormenting myself... I'll get better, and... I'll stop tormenting myself... But supposing I never do get better? Oh God, I'm so sick of it all!...'

He was walking on without stopping. He desperately wanted to find some distraction, but he had no idea what to do, what to attempt. With every minute that passed, a new and irresistible feeling took an ever firmer hold on him—a boundless, almost physical revulsion towards everything he saw and everything around him, a stubborn, angry sense of loathing. Everyone he met repelled him—their faces, their walk, their movements. He would actually have spat at anyone, perhaps even bitten anyone who spoke to him.

He suddenly halted when he emerged onto the bank of the Little Neva, on Vasilievsky Island, next to the bridge. 'This is where he lives, in that house,' he thought. 'What's all this, have I really come to Razumikhin's of my own accord? It's the same story as last time... But it's a very curious business all the same—have I come here of my own accord, or just walked and found myself here? Never mind—I said to myself... the day before yesterday... that I'd come and see him on the next day after that. So I will! It's not as if I couldn't do it!'

He went upstairs to Razumikhin's flat on the fifth floor.

Razumikhin was at home, in his little garret. He was working, writing something, and he let Raskolnikov in himself. They hadn't seen each other for some four months. Razumikhin was sitting wrapped in a dressing gown that was all rags and tatters, with slippers on his bare feet; he was dishevelled, unshaven, and unwashed. There was a look of astonishment on his face.

'What's up?' he cried out, looking his friend up and down. Then he stopped and gave a whistle.

'As bad as that, is it? But you're so natty, my friend, you put us all in the shade!' he added, staring at Raskolnikov's rags. 'Do sit down, I dare say you're tired.' And when his friend sank down onto the oilcloth-covered Turkish divan, which was in a worse state even than his own, Razumikhin suddenly realized that his visitor was ill.

'But you're seriously ill, you know that?' He tried to feel Raskolnikov's pulse, but the other pulled his hand away.

'Don't!' he said. 'I've come... Look here, I've got no lessons to give... I was going to... well, actually I don't need any lessons.'

'You know what? You're raving!' remarked Razumikhin, staring intently at him.

'No, I'm not raving,' said Raskolnikov, getting up from the divan. On his way up to Razumikhin's flat, he hadn't reflected that he was going to find himself face to face with him. But now, in a single instant, he could feel and see that the last thing he wanted at this moment was to find himself face to face with anyone in the whole world. All his bile rose up in him. He almost choked with fury at himself for having so much as crossed Razumikhin's threshold.

'Goodbye!' he said abruptly, and walked to the door.

'Stop, wait a minute, you odd fish!'

'Don't!' repeated Raskolnikov, pulling his hand away again.

'So what the devil did you come here for, then? Have you gone crazy? You're being... almost insulting. I shan't let you go like this.'

'Well then, listen. I came to you because you're the only person I know who could help me... to start... because you're kinder than all of them, I mean more sensible, and you can judge... But now I see that I don't need anything, d'you hear, anything at all... I don't need anyone's help or sympathy... I myself... on my own... Oh, enough of all that! I wish everyone would leave me alone!'

'Just stop a minute, you chimney sweep! You're raving mad! I mean, you can do as you like for all I care. Look: I don't have any lessons either, and don't give a toss; but there's a bookseller in the flea market,* called Kheruvimov, and he's a lesson himself in a way. I wouldn't swap him now for five lessons in a merchant's house. He does a bit of publishing, and brings out little books on natural science, and they sell like anything! The titles alone are a treasure! There you were, always calling me stupid—but I promise you, old man, there are people stupider than me! And now he's gone in for modern ideas; of course he hasn't a clue himself, but I encourage him, naturally. Take these two-and-a-half sheets of German text—if you ask me it's the stupidest sort of humbug, I mean it's all about whether a woman is a human being or not.* And of course it proves triumphantly that she's human. Kheruvimov is bringing it out as a contribution to the Woman question, and I'm translating it. He'll blow up those two-and-a-half sheets to six, we'll add a magnificent title page on a half-sheet, and sell the book for half a rouble. And it'll sell! He pays me six roubles a sheet, so I'll be paid fifteen roubles for all that, and I've had six roubles in advance. When that's done, we're going to start translating something about whales, and then we've picked out some really boring gossip from Part Two of the *Confessions*, we'll be translating that—someone or other has told Kheruvimov that Rousseau is a sort of Radishchev.* And of course I don't contradict him—what do I care? So, would you like to translate the second sheet of "Is Woman Human?"? Take the text with you now, if you like, and some pens and paper—it's all on the firm—and you can have three roubles. Since I've been paid in advance for the whole translation, both the first and second sheets, that means you get three roubles for your bit. And when you've finished the sheet, you get another three roubles. And another thing—don't imagine that this is some sort of favour I'm doing you. Quite the opposite—as soon as you came in, I reckoned straight away that you could be useful to me. Firstly, I'm not good at spelling, and secondly my German is sometimes quite *schwach*,* so that I make up a lot of it as I go along, and my only comfort is that I'm probably improving it. Though who knows, perhaps I'm not making it better but actually worse... Do you want it or not?'

Raskolnikov silently picked up the sheets of the German article, took three roubles, and went out without a word. Razumikhin gazed after him in amazement. But no sooner had he got to the First Line* when he suddenly turned round, went back upstairs to Razumikhin's flat, laid the sheets of German and the three roubles on the table, and walked out again without a word.

'You must be raving mad!' roared Razumikhin, losing his temper at last. 'What's this farce you're playing at? Even I can't understand you. What did you come here for then, damn it?'

'I don't want... any translations,' muttered Raskolnikov, already on his way downstairs.

'Then what the hell do you want?' Razumikhin yelled down at him. Raskolnikov carried on down without replying.

'Hey, you! Where do you live?'

No reply.

'Well go to blazes then!...'

But Raskolnikov was already on his way out to the street. On Nikolaevsky Bridge* he was forced to come fully to his senses again, because of a most unpleasant episode. He received a sharp cut with a whip on his back from a carriage driver because he had almost walked right in front of his horses, despite three or four warning shouts from the driver. The lash of the whip so enraged him that, leaping sideways to the parapet (for some reason he had been walking in the very middle of the roadway, meant for riders and not walkers), he ground and snapped his teeth with fury. Naturally enough, laughter erupted around him.

'Quite right too!'

'Must be some sort of crook.'

'You know the sort, they pretend to be drunk and fall under the horses' hooves on purpose, and then you're held responsible.'

'That's what they do for a living, my dear fellow. That's what they do.'

But even as he stood by the parapet, staring after the vanishing carriage in futile rage and rubbing his back, he suddenly felt someone press a coin into his hand. He looked and saw an elderly woman from the merchant class, in a kerchief and goatskin shoes, with a young girl—probably her daughter—wearing a little hat and carrying a green parasol. 'Take it, my dear, in Christ's name.' He took the money, and they walked on. It was a twenty-kopek piece. By his clothing and general appearance they could well have taken him for a beggar, someone who really solicited small change on the streets; and he probably owed the gift of a whole twenty-kopek piece to the whiplash he had received, which had probably made them sorry for him.

He clenched the coin in his hand, walked on a dozen paces, and turned towards the Neva, facing the palace. There was not the smallest cloud in the sky, and the water was almost blue, which so rarely happens on the Neva. The cathedral dome,* which nowhere shows up better than when viewed from this spot on the bridge, twenty paces short of the chapel, was simply glowing, and through the clear air he could easily make out every detail of its ornamentation. The pain from the whip had eased, and Raskolnikov had forgotten about it. There was just one troubling but quite vague thought that preoccupied him now, to the exclusion of all else. He was standing there, gazing long and hard into the distance; this place was a particularly familiar one to him. When attending the university, he would usually stop at this precise spot, particularly on his way home; this might have happened as many as a hundred times. He would stare hard at this truly magnificent prospect, and almost every time he would wonder at one particular, indistinct, and puzzling impression. He always felt an inexplicable breath of cold air on him as he stood before this magnificent prospect; for him, the imposing spectacle was permeated by a deaf and mute spirit.* He wondered every time at the mysterious, sombre impression he experienced, and—not trusting himself—would put off trying to explain it. And suddenly now he sharply recalled the questions and problems that had troubled him in the past, and felt that it was no accident that they had come to his mind again. The very fact that he had stopped at the same spot where he always used to, struck him as peculiar and bizarre—as though he could really imagine himself capable of thinking the same thoughts as before, and being interested in the same questions and images now, as those that had preoccupied him... such a short time ago. It seemed almost absurd—yet at the same time it gave him a painful tightness in his chest. All this past life of his, all his past thoughts, and past preoccupations, and past ideas, and past impressions, and this whole view, and he himself, and all of it, all of it—he seemed to see it all somewhere far below him, down in the depths, somewhere out of sight down there. He felt as if he was flying up and away, and everything was vanishing before his eyes... He made an involuntary movement with his arm, and suddenly became aware of the twenty-kopek piece clutched in his fist. He opened his hand, stared hard at the money, drew his arm back, and flung the coin into the water; then he turned and set off homeward. He felt that he had in that moment cut himself off from everyone and everything, as though with scissors.

It was evening by the time he reached home; so he must have been out for about six hours in all. How he had got there—of that he had no recollection at all. He undressed, shivering like an overdriven horse, lay down on the divan, pulled his coat over himself, and instantly fell asleep.

It was quite dark when he was recalled to his senses by a frightful shriek. God, what a shriek it was! Never in his life had he heard such an unearthly noise, such a howling, wailing, grinding, weeping, such blows and curses. He could never have imagined such ferocity and rage. He raised himself up in horror and sat on his couch in a torment of dread. The fighting, bellowing, and swearing only got louder and louder. And suddenly, to his utter astonishment, he could make out the voice of his landlady. She was howling, screeching, wailing, words tumbling out of her so fast that nothing could be made out—she was imploring something—of course, imploring people to stop beating her, because she was being mercilessly thrashed on the stairs. The voice of the man who was beating her had become so terrible in his frenzy of rage that it was almost no more than snorting, but he too was saying something, just as rapidly and indistinctly, falling over his words in his haste. Suddenly Raskolnikov began to tremble like a leaf—he had recognized the voice. It was Ilya Petrovich. So Ilya Petrovich was here, and was beating the landlady! He was kicking her, banging her head against the stairs, you could hear that quite clearly from the sounds, from her screams, from the blows! What was going on—had the world turned upside down, then? You could hear all the people on all the floors, up and down the staircase, crowding together, you could hear their voices, their exclamations, hear them running upstairs, knocking on doors, slamming doors, running hither and thither in a body. 'But what's it for, what's it for? and how is it possible?' he repeated, seriously thinking that he had gone quite mad. But no, he could hear it only too clearly! And that meant that in a minute they'd be coming into his own room, 'because... it must all be about that... about yesterday... Oh God!' He thought of fastening his door on the hook, but couldn't raise his arm—and what good would it do anyway! Icy terror gripped his heart, agonizing and numbing... But at last all this hullabaloo which had gone on for a full ten minutes was beginning to quieten down. The landlady was groaning and gasping, Ilya Petrovich was still threatening and cursing... Finally he too seemed to have fallen silent, you couldn't hear him any longer—'Can he really have left? Lord!' Yes, and now the landlady was going away too, still groaning and weeping... that was her door slamming... And now the people were leaving the staircase and going to their own flats, exclaiming and arguing and calling out to one another, raising their voices to a shout, then dropping them to a whisper. There must have been a great many of them, almost everyone in the house had joined in. 'But God, how could all that have happened? And why, why had that man been here?'

Raskolnikov sank back onto the divan, all his strength gone, but he could no longer close his eyes. He lay there for about half an hour, suffering an unbearable sense of boundless horror such as he had never before experienced. Then suddenly his room was flooded with bright light. Nastasia had come in with a candle and a plate of soup. She looked closely at him, and when she saw that he wasn't asleep, she stood the candle on the table and began laying out what she had brought—bread, salt, a plate and spoon.

'I don't suppose you've eaten anything since yesterday. Wandering around all day, with a high fever on you too.'

'Nastasia... what were they beating the landlady for?'

She stared at him.

'Who was beating the landlady?'

'Just now... half an hour ago. Ilya Petrovich, the assistant superintendent. On the stairs... What was he beating her up for like that? And why was he here?'

Nastasia looked him up and down in silence, frowning. She gazed at him for a long time. Her stare made him feel most uncomfortable, it even frightened him.

'Nastasia, why don't you say anything?' he finally asked, in a timid, weak voice.

'That's blood,' she said quietly at last, as though speaking to herself.

'Blood!... What blood?...' he gabbled, turning pale and recoiling towards the wall. Nastasia went on looking silently at him.

'Nobody was beating the landlady,' she said in a firm, decisive voice. He stared at her, scarcely breathing.

'I heard it myself... I wasn't asleep... I was sitting up,' he went on, even more fearfully. 'I listened to it for a long time... The assistant superintendent was here... Everybody ran out onto the stairs, from all the flats...'

'Nobody came here. That's the blood crying out in you. When the blood can't get out, and starts curdling in your liver, that's when you begin seeing things... So are you going to eat anything, then?'

He didn't reply. Nastasia was still standing over him, staring fixedly at him and not going away.

'Get me something to drink... Nastasyushka, dear.'

She went off downstairs and returned a couple of minutes later with a white earthenware mug of water; but he knew nothing of what happened next. All he knew was that he took a single gulp of cold water and spilt the mug over his chest. Then he fell unconscious.

CHAPTER III

BUT in fact he wasn't completely unconscious throughout his illness. He was running a high fever, half-comatose and delirious; but later on he remembered a great deal. Sometimes it seemed to him that crowds of people had gathered round him and wanted to seize him and carry him off somewhere; they argued and quarrelled about him a lot. Or else he would suddenly find himself alone in his room, and everyone else was scared of him and had gone away, but just occasionally they would open the door a crack and look at him, threatening him and hatching plots about him, and laughing and mocking at him. He often remembered seeing Nastasia nearby. And he could make out another person, someone whom he seemed to know very well—but quite who it was, he could never work out, and this upset him and even reduced him to tears. Sometimes he imagined he had been lying here for a whole month; at other times, it was all on a single day. But *that—that* was something he had completely forgotten; though he constantly kept remembering that he had forgotten something which he mustn't forget. He racked his brains and tormented himself trying to remember it, and groaned and got into rages or fell into horrible, unbearable terrors. Then he would drag himself out of bed and try to run away, but there was always someone stopping him by force, and then he would fall helplessly unconscious again. Eventually he came to himself again.

That happened one morning, at ten o'clock. At that hour of the morning on fine days the sun always cast a long bright streak of light over his right-hand wall, lighting up the corner by the door. At his bedside Nastasia was standing with someone else who was inspecting him very curiously: someone whom he didn't know at all. He was a young man with a little beard, wearing a kaftan and looking like a factory foreman. The landlady was peering in through the half-open door. Raskolnikov raised himself.

'Who's this, Nastasia?' he asked, pointing to the young man.

'Look at that—he's come round!' said she.

'So he has,' replied the visitor. Once she saw that he had come round, the landlady who had been peering through the doorway shut the door at once and vanished. She had always been very shy, dreading conversations and explanations. She was about forty, stocky and plump, with dark eyebrows and eyes, really quite good-looking, with the good nature of a fat and lazy woman. But she really was excessively shy.

'So who... are you?' Raskolnikov went on, turning to the man himself. But at that moment the door was flung open again and in came Razumikhin, stooping a little because of his height.

'What a ship's cabin!' he exclaimed as he came in. 'I've been bumping my head everywhere. Call this a lodging! So have you come round, old man? I just heard from Pashenka.'

'Just come round,' said Nastasia.

'Just come round,' repeated the stranger with a smile.

'And who would you be, sir?' asked Razumikhin, turning suddenly to him. 'Let me explain that I'm Vrazumikhin, see; not Razumikhin,* as everybody calls me, but Vrazumikhin, gentleman and student, and this is my friend. So who are you, sir?'

'I'm the head clerk in our office, that's Shelopaev the merchant's office, sir, and I'm here on business, sir.'

'Be so good as to sit down on that chair,' said Razumikhin, sitting down on another one across the table. 'You did very well to wake up, my friend,' he went on to Raskolnikov. 'You've scarcely eaten or drunk anything for over three days. They did give you spoonfuls of tea, though. I brought Zosimov to see you twice. Remember Zosimov? He examined you thoroughly and said straight away that it was nothing much—just something wrong in your head. Some sort of nervous attack, due to bad rations, he said, because they weren't giving you enough beer or horseradish, that's what made you ill, but it's all right, it'll pass and you'll be fine. He's a good chap, is Zosimov. Turned into a first-class doctor. Well then, sir, I won't hold you up,' he went on to the head clerk, 'would you like to explain what you want? Look here, Rodia, this is the second time someone's come from that office, only the first time it wasn't him but someone else, and we explained things to that other fellow. So who was it came here before you?'

'Well, that must have been the day before yesterday, sir, that's right. That'll have been Alexei Semionovich, he works in our office too, sir.'

'I dare say he'll have been more competent than you—what do you think?'

'Well yes, sir, he's a bit sounder than I am, that's true.'

'Well said! Go on, then.'

'Well, it's through Afanasy Ivanovich Vakhrushin, who I suppose you'll have heard of several times, sir, and at your Mama's request there's a money transfer to you through our office,' began the clerk, addressing Raskolnikov directly. 'In the event that you're now in a state of conscious, sir—I'm to deliver you thirty-five roubles, sir, seeing that Semion Semionovich was notified to that effect by Afanasy Ivanovich, as on previous occasions, at your good Mama's request. Do you happen to know him, sir?'

'Yes... I remember... Vakhrushin...' said Raskolnikov thoughtfully.

'Listen to that! He knows the merchant Vakhrushin!' exclaimed Razumikhin. 'How could he not be conscious? Actually, I see now that you're a sensible fellow too. Well, then! It's always a pleasure to listen to intelligent talk.'

'That's him himself, sir, Vakhrushin, Afanasy Ivanovich, and at your good Mama's request, on account of she had once remitted you money through him in the same manner, he didn't refuse this time either, and he notified Semion Semionovich as of that date to pay over thirty-five roubles to you, sir, in the hopes of better to come.'

' "In the hopes of better to come"—that's the best thing you've said; and "your good Mama" wasn't bad either. So what's your opinion—is he fully conscious, or not fully conscious, eh?'

'That's all right by me, sir—it's just for that little matter of a signature.'

'He'll manage to scribble something! So, do you have a receipt book, or what?'

'Yes, sir, a book, here it is.'

'Hand it over. All right, Rodia, get up. I'll hold you up, and you do him a "Raskolnikov", just take the pen—money's sweeter than honey to us, my boy!'

'No,' said Raskolnikov, pushing the pen away.

'No what?'

'I'm not going to sign.'

'But damn it, how can we manage without a signature?'

'I don't want... money...'

'So it's money you don't want, is it? You're talking nonsense, boy, and I'm a witness! Don't take any notice, please, that's just him... he's wandering again. Though he can be like that when he has his wits about him too... You're a sensible man, we'll guide him, I mean we'll simply guide his hand, and he'll sign. Let's get on with it...'

'Well, I could come back another time, sir.'

'No, no, why bother? You're a sensible man... Come on, Rodia, don't keep your visitor waiting... You can see he's waiting...' And he prepared in all seriousness to guide Raskolnikov's hand.

'Leave me alone, I'll do it myself...' said Raskolnikov, picking up the pen and signing the book. The clerk laid out the money and left.

'Bravo!... And now, my boy, do you want something to eat?'

'Yes,' replied Raskolnikov.

'Have you got any soup?'

'Yesterday's,' replied Nastasia, still standing there.

'With potato and rice?'

'Yes, potato and rice.'

'I know it by heart. Bring along the soup, and some tea too.'

'All right.'

Raskolnikov was observing everything with profound surprise and numb, unthinking fear. He resolved to say nothing, but wait and see what happened next. 'I don't think I'm delirious,' he thought, 'I think this is all really happening.'

Two minutes later Nastasia came back with the soup and announced that the tea would be coming shortly. The soup came with two spoons, two plates, and all the condiments—a salt cellar, a pepper shaker, mustard for the beef, and so forth—things that hadn't been seen here, set out like this, for a long time. And the tablecloth was clean.

'It wouldn't be a bad idea, Nastasyushka, if Praskovia Pavlovna ordered in a couple of bottles of beer. We'd love a drink.'

'Who d'you think you are, then?' muttered Nastasia, going off to obey her orders.

Raskolnikov continued looking about him with a tense, wild expression. Meanwhile Razumikhin came and sat by him on the divan, put his left arm round his friend's head as clumsily as a bear (though Raskolnikov could perfectly well have raised himself), and with his right hand carried a spoonful of soup to Raskolnikov's mouth, first blowing on it a few times so as not to scald him. But the soup was barely warm. Raskolnikov greedily swallowed a spoonful, then another and a third. But after feeding him a few spoonfuls, Razumikhin suddenly stopped and announced that before doing anything more they had to consult Zosimov.

Nastasia came in with two bottles of beer.

'Do you want some tea too?'

'Yes, please.'

'Hurry along with the tea then, Nastasia; as far as the tea goes, I think we can do without the faculty of medicine. But here's the beer!' and he moved back to his own chair, pulled up his plate of soup and some beef, and set to eating with as much gusto as if he hadn't touched food for three days.

'Rodia, my boy, I've been having my lunch here like this every day,' he mumbled as best he could through a mouth crammed full of beef.

'And it's all thanks to Pashenka, your little landlady, who's been plying me with food with the best will in the world. Well, naturally I don't insist on it, but I don't refuse either. And here's Nastasia with the tea. What a nimble creature she is! Nastenka, want some beer?'

'Oh, get along with you!'

'What about tea?'

'Don't mind if I do.'

'Pour it out, then. Wait, I'll pour it myself. You sit down at the table.'

He took charge straight away, poured out a cup and then a second one, left his meal and moved back to the divan. Once again he put his left arm round his patient's head, raised him up and started feeding him teaspoons of tea, again blowing constantly and very assiduously on it, as if this act of blowing represented the most important and life-saving part of the whole healing process. Raskolnikov said nothing and put up no resistance, although he felt quite strong enough to raise himself and sit up on the divan without anyone's help; and not only felt capable of controlling his hands sufficiently to hold a spoon or a cup—he thought he might even manage to walk. But a strange sort of almost animal cunning suddenly prompted him to hide his strength for the time being; to lie low, and if necessary even pretend that he wasn't quite in his right mind; and meanwhile to listen and work out what was going on here. But he couldn't control his revulsion: after swallowing a dozen spoonfuls of tea, he suddenly shook his head free, capriciously pushed the spoon away and collapsed back onto the pillow. He actually had proper pillows under his head now, down pillows with clean pillowslips; he saw that too, and took note of it.

'We must get Pashenka to send up some raspberry jam today, to make him a drink,' said Razumikhin, sitting back down on his chair and returning to his soup and beer.

'And where's she going to find raspberries for you?' asked Nastasia, balancing her saucer on five outstretched fingers while she sucked up her tea through a sugar lump.

'My dear girl, she'll find raspberries in a shop. You see, Rodia, there's been a great carry-on in your absence. When you ran away from me like an absolute villain without telling me where you lived, I suddenly got so furious, I decided to hunt you down and punish you. I set about it the same day. And I went to one place after another, asking everywhere about you. I'd forgotten about this present flat of yours; actually I could never have remembered it anyway, because I didn't know about it. But your last flat—all I could recall was that it was Kharlamov's house near the Five Corners.* So I hunted and hunted for this Kharlamov's house—and then it turned out not to be Kharlamov's house at all, but Buch's house. How one can muddle up sounds sometimes! So then I got angry. So angry that on the off-chance, I went to the address bureau next day, and just imagine, they found you for me in a couple of minutes. You're registered there.'*

'Registered!'

'Indeed you are; while a certain General Kobelev, they couldn't find him at all while I was there. Well, it's a long story. But as soon as I landed up here, I found out all about your doings, all of them, my friend, I know everything. This one saw me at it—I met with Nikodim Fomich, and they pointed out Ilya Petrovich to me, and I met the yard porter and Mr Zametov, Alexander Grigorievich, the head clerk in the local police office, and finally Pashenka, she was the crowning glory; Nastasia knows about that too...'

'Sweet-talked her, he did,' murmured Nastasia with a wicked grin.

'You should sweeten your tea yourself, Nastasia Nikiforovna!'

'Will you get lost!' Nastasia exclaimed, bursting into giggles. 'Anyway, my name's Petrova, not Nikiforova,' she added suddenly when she had stopped laughing.

'I'll treasure the fact, my lady. So there you are, my friend, not to waste words—at first I wanted to galvanize the whole place, to get rid of all the rotten ideas around here once and for all; but Pashenka won the day. I never imagined, old man, that she'd be such a... dear little thing, eh? What do you say?'

Raskolnikov said nothing, but went on staring at him full of alarm, never taking his eyes off him.

'Yes, absolutely so,' Razumikhin continued, not at all embarrassed by the silence, as though echoing Raskolnikov's reply. 'Just as she should be, in every way.'

'What a monster!' squealed Nastasia again. The whole conversation seemed to fill her with inexpressible delight.

'Your mistake, old man, was not to take things in hand right from the start. You shouldn't have handled her the way you did. I mean, she's what I'd call a most unusual character! Well, as for her character, I'll come to that... But how did you let things get to such a point that she dared to stop sending you up your food? Or that loan note, for instance? Had you gone crazy, to go signing loan notes? Or that engagement, when her daughter Natalia Egorovna was alive... I know all about it! Actually, I can see that's a delicate business and I'm an ass, please forgive me. But talking about being stupid—Praskovia Pavlovna, what do you think, she's not at all such a fool as one might think at first sight, eh?'

'Yes...' Raskolnikov muttered, averting his eyes but realizing that he'd do better to keep the conversation going.

'Isn't that right?' cried Razumikhin, evidently pleased to get an answer. 'But she's not clever either, is she? A quite, quite unusual character! I must say, I don't quite know what to think. I reckon she must be all of forty years old. She says she's thirty-six, and she's every right to say so. Actually, I swear, I mostly judge her on the intellectual level, metaphysically; we've got a sort of symbolism going between us, something like your algebra! I can't make it out! Anyway, that's all nonsense; but when she saw that you weren't a student any more, and weren't giving any lessons and had no decent clothes, and after that young lady died, since there was no reason for her to go on treating you as one of the family, she suddenly took fright. And then, when you locked yourself away in your room and gave up all your old ways, that was when she decided to throw you out. She'd been meaning to do that for a long time, but she didn't want to give up on the loan note. And you promised her yourself that your Mama would pay it off...'

'I wasn't being honest, saying that... My mother's practically a beggar herself... but I told a lie so that I'd be kept on in my flat and... and fed,' said Raskolnikov in a loud, clear voice.

'Yes, that was sensible of you. The whole trouble was that Mr Chebarov turned up here, a Court Councillor and businessman. Pashenka would never have thought of it without him, she's very timid—but the businessman wasn't timid at all, and the first thing he asked was, was there any hope of getting the money? And she said yes, because there's this Mama with a pension of a hundred and twenty-five roubles, who'll help her Rodenka out even if she has to go without food; and there's a sister who'd sell herself into slavery for her brother. So that's what he was counting on... What are you squirming about for? My friend, I've already found out every last detail of your life, thanks to your heart-to-heart talks with Pashenka when you were still one of the family; and now I'm telling you everything because I'm your friend... Well, that's how it is: the honest and sensitive person has a heart-to-heart talk, and the businessman listens, and takes it all in, and eventually eats him up. So then she handed over that little note, supposedly in payment to this Chebarov, and he formally protested it, quite shamelessly. When I found out, I felt like giving him what for, to clear my conscience, but by then I'd got on good terms with Pashenka, and I told her to call the whole thing off, all of it, and I promised that you'd pay her. So I stood bail for you, do you hear? We called Chebarov in, chucked him ten roubles, got the paper back, and now I have the honour to present it to you. She'll trust your word now. Here you are, take it, I've torn it the way you're supposed to.'

Razumikhin laid the loan note on the table. Raskolnikov glanced at it and turned his face to the wall without a word. Even Razumikhin felt uncomfortable.

'Look, old man, I can see I've made a fool of myself again,' he went on after a pause. 'I thought I'd entertain and amuse you with my chatter, but it looks as if I've only made you angry.'

'Was it you that I didn't recognize when I was hallucinating?' asked Raskolnikov after another pause, without turning his head.

'Yes, and you even got into rages with me, especially once when I brought Zametov with me.'

'Zametov?... The head clerk?... What for?' asked Raskolnikov, quickly turning round and fixing his eyes on Razumikhin.

'What's up with you?... Why are you all upset? He wanted to meet you; asked me himself, because we'd been talking a lot about you... How else could I have found out so much about you? He's a fine chap, a wonderful man... in his own way, of course. We're friends now, we see each other almost every day. I've moved to this district—didn't you know? Just moved. We've been to see *Lavisa* together a couple of times. You remember *Lavisa*? Luisa Ivanovna?'

'Did I say anything when I was raving?'

'You bet! You were right out of your mind.'

'What did I rave about?'

'Listen to him! What did you rave about? Whatever people do rave about... Well, my boy, let's not waste time, let's get down to business.'

He got up from his chair and grabbed his cap.

'What did I rave about?'

'Doesn't he go on! Not afraid that you let out some secret, are you? Don't worry, you didn't drop a word about the Countess.* Something about a bulldog, and earrings, and chains of some kind, and Krestovsky Island, and about some porter or other, and Nikodim Fomich, and Ilya Petrovich the assistant superintendent—you talked a lot about all that. And then you chose to take a great interest in your own sock, a very great interest! Hand it over, you moaned, and that was all you'd say. Zametov himself hunted for your socks in all the corners, and handed you that garbage with his very own hands, all washed in perfume as they were, and covered with rings. That was the only thing that calmed you, and then you lay for days on end holding on to that garbage, we couldn't tear it out of your hands. It must still be lying somewhere under your blanket. And then you begged for a fringe for your trousers, and so tearfully too! We were trying to make out what sort of fringe that could be, but we couldn't make any sense of it... Well, anyway, now to business! Here's thirty-five roubles; I'll take ten myself, and give you an account of the money in a couple of hours. And meanwhile I'll let Zosimov know, although he ought to have been here ages ago, since it's gone eleven. And you, Nastenka, keep coming back while I'm out, ask him if he wants a drink or anything... Meanwhile I'll go and tell Pashenka what she needs to know. Goodbye!'

'Pashenka, he calls her! Cheeky so-and-so! You...' Nastasia called out after him; then she opened the door and listened, but she couldn't contain her curiosity and ran downstairs herself. She was desperate to find out what he was talking about with the landlady down there; besides, it was clear that she was quite enchanted by Razumikhin.

No sooner was the door shut behind her than the sick man flung off his blanket and leapt up from his bed like a crazed man. He had been waiting with burning, convulsive impatience for them all to go away, so that he could set about things at once while they weren't there. But set about what? It seemed to have slipped his mind, as though on purpose to spite him. 'Oh Lord! Just tell me one thing: do they know about it all, or not yet? Supposing they do know, and they're just pretending, playing games with me while I lie here, and then they'll suddenly come in and tell me that they've known everything for ages and they were just stringing me along... What should I do now? There, it's gone, just to spite me—I've suddenly forgotten it, I had it a moment ago!'

He stood in the middle of the room, staring around him in agonized bewilderment. He went up to the door, opened it and listened—but that wasn't it. Suddenly, seeming to remember, he rushed to the corner where there was a hole in the wallpaper, and began examining everything, put his hand down the hole and groped about; but that wasn't it either. He went to the stove, opened it, and poked among the ashes. Pieces of the fringe off his trousers and scraps of the torn pocket were still lying there as he had left them earlier; so no one had looked in there! Now he remembered the sock that Razumikhin had just been talking about. True enough, the sock was lying on the divan, under the blanket, but so scuffed and soiled by now that Zametov couldn't possibly have noticed anything.

'Oh! Zametov!... The police office!... And what do they want me for? Where's the summons? Oh, no!... I've mixed it all up—it was back then that they summoned me. And I was looking at my sock then too, but now... now I've been ill. And what did Zametov come for? Why did

Razumikhin bring him here?' he muttered helplessly to himself as he sat back on the divan. 'What's going on? Am I still delirious, or is this real? Real, I think... Ah, I remember: I have to run away! Run away as quick as I can, I absolutely must, must run away! Yes... but where? And where are my clothes? No boots! They've taken them away! Hidden them! I see! Ah, here's my coat—they missed that! And money on the table, thank God! And here's the loan note too... I'll take the money, and go and rent another lodging, they'll never find me!... Yes, but the address bureau? So they'll find me! Razumikhin will. Better get right away... far away... to America, and to hell with them all! And take the loan note with me... it'll come in useful. What else shall I take? And they think I'm ill! They don't even know I can walk, heh-heh-heh!... I could see it in their eyes, they know everything! I just have to get downstairs. But supposing they've got guards, police guards waiting there? What's this, tea? Ah, and here's some beer left, half a bottle, and cold!'

He snatched up the bottle which still contained a whole glassful of beer, and knocked it back with relish, as though quenching a fire in his breast. In less than a minute the beer had gone to his head, while a mild, almost enjoyable shiver ran down his spine. He lay down and pulled the blanket over him. His thoughts, sick and incoherent as they were, became more and more confused, and soon he succumbed to a light, pleasant somnolence. With luxurious enjoyment he found a place for his head on the pillow, wrapped himself up tighter in the soft wadded quilt which had taken the place of his torn overcoat, sighed gently and fell into a deep, sound, restoring sleep.

He was woken by the sound of someone coming into the room. Opening his eyes, he saw Razumikhin, who had opened the door wide and was standing in the doorway, in two minds whether to come in or not. Raskolnikov quickly raised himself and looked at him as if straining to recall something.

'Ah, so you're not asleep: well, here I am! Nastasia, bring in the package!' Razumikhin shouted down the stairs. 'I'll just give you the account...'

'What time is it?' asked Raskolnikov, looking uneasily about him.

'You've had a fine sleep, my friend: it's evening outside, must be around six. You've slept over six hours...'

'Heavens! How could I!...'

'What of it? Good for you! Where are you rushing off to? Meeting a girlfriend? We've got all the time in the world. I've been waiting for you for three hours or so—I looked in a couple of times, but you were sleeping. I called on Zosimov twice, but they just said he wasn't at home. Never mind, he'll turn up!... And I've been about my own affairs too—I only moved across today, with all my things; my uncle helped me. I've got an uncle now, you know... Well, never mind all that, let's get down to business... Hand over the package, Nastenka. And now we'll... But how are you feeling, old boy?'

'I'm well! I'm not ill... Razumikhin, have you been here long?'

'I told you—I've been waiting three hours.'

'No, but before that?'

'Before what?'

'How long have you been coming here?'

'But I told you all about that earlier—don't you remember?'

Raskolnikov pondered. The events of earlier in the day seemed like a dream. He couldn't remember anything on his own, and looked at Razumikhin for help.

'Hm!' said Razumikhin. 'Forgotten! I did think this morning that you weren't quite... Now your sleep has put you right... You really do look much better. Well done! Now, to business. It'll all come back to you in a minute. Just look here, my dear boy.'

He began laying out the contents of his package, which was evidently of particular importance to him.

'This here, my friend, I can tell you, this was particularly close to my heart. Because we've got to turn you into a proper person. Let's begin from the top. See this cap?' he began, taking out quite a smart but very ordinary, cheap cap. 'Shall we try it on?'

'Later, afterwards,' said Raskolnikov, waving it peevishly aside.

'No, no, young Rodia, don't fight me, or it'll be too late—and I'll get no sleep tonight, because I bought it at a venture, I didn't know your size. Just right!' he exclaimed triumphantly when he had tried it on his friend; 'exactly the right size! Your headgear is the first and most important part of your outfit, it acts as a sort of introduction. My friend Tolstyakov has to take his lid off every time he goes into a public place where everyone else is standing around in hats and caps. They all think he's servile, but he's just ashamed of his bird's nest. Such a bashful fellow! Well now, Nastenka, here you have two items of headgear: this Palmerston (and he picked up Raskolnikov's crumpled round hat from the corner; no one knew why he called it a Palmerston*), or this jeweller's article? Put a price on it, Rodia, guess how much I paid for it? Nastasyushka?' he said, turning to her, seeing that Raskolnikov said nothing.

'I suppose you'll have paid twenty kopeks,' replied Nastasia.

'Twenty! You idiot!' he cried, quite offended. 'Even you would fetch more than that these days! Eighty, I paid, and that was because it was second-hand. But there's a deal: if you wear it out, they'll give you another one free next year, I swear to God! Well, and now for the United Pants of America, as we used to call them at school. Let me tell you—I'm proud of these trousers!' And he laid out before Raskolnikov a pair of grey summer trousers in a light woollen cloth. 'There's not a hole nor a stain, they're very decent for all they're second-hand; and a waistcoat to match, a plain one, as fashion dictates. Being second-hand is all the better, actually: they're softer and smoother... You see, Rodia, if you're to make a career in the world, I reckon you just have to go with the season. If you don't insist on asparagus in January, you'll save yourself a few roubles—and the same goes for this stuff. It's the summer season right now, and I've bought summer things. In autumn you'll need warmer fabrics in any case, so you'll have to throw these away... particularly as they'll all be no good by then, either because you'll be wanting more luxury, or the stuff will have fallen to pieces. Well, price them! How much do you reckon? Two roubles twenty-five! And remember, you get the same deal again—if you wear these out, next year you get replacements free of charge! That's the only way they trade at Fedyaev's shop—you pay once, and you're supplied for life, because you'd never go there again of your own accord. Well now, sir, on to the boots: what do you think of them? Of course you can see that they're worn, but they'll do you for a couple of months—because they're from abroad, and made up abroad. The English embassy secretary sold them at the flea market last week—he'd only worn them six days, but he badly needed the money. Price one rouble fifty. A bargain?'

'But they mightn't fit!' remarked Nastasia.

'Mightn't fit? What about this?'—and he pulled out of his pocket Raskolnikov's old boot, stiff and cracked, full of holes and coated all over with dried mud. 'I took my supplies with me, and they got the right size from this revolting object. The whole thing was done with loving care. And as for the linen, I sorted that out with your landlady. Firstly, here are three shirts, they're hemp but they've got fashionable fronts... Well, so there we are: eighty kopeks for the cap, two twenty-five for the rest of the clothes, making three roubles five; one fifty for the boots (because they're really very good), that makes four roubles fifty-five; and five roubles for all the linen, we got a wholesale price, so it all amounts to just nine roubles fifty-five kopeks. Forty-five kopeks change, all in copper fives, here you are, take it. And so, Rodia, you've got a complete outfit again, because I reckon your coat isn't just still serviceable, it even has a most distinguished air about it—that's what you get when you order your clothes from Scharmer!* As for socks and the rest of it, I leave that to you; we've still got twenty-five roubles over, and don't worry about the rent you owe Pashenka—as I told you, you've got absolutely unlimited credit. But now, my boy, let's change your linen, otherwise you might still have some infection clinging to your shirt...'

'Leave me alone! I don't want to!' Raskolnikov tried to brush him aside, having listened with disgust to the forced playfulness of Razumikhin's account of how he had bought the clothes.

'None of that, boy! What did I wear out my shoe leather for?' insisted Razumikhin. 'Nastasyushka, don't be bashful, give me a hand, that's the way!' And despite Raskolnikov's insistence, he managed to change his clothes. Then Raskolnikov slumped back on his pillow and said nothing for a minute or two.

'I'll never get rid of them!' he thought. 'Where did the money come from to buy all this?' he finally asked, staring at the wall.

'Money? There you go! It's your own money. That clerk was here this morning, with money from Vakhrushin—your Mama sent it. Had you forgotten that too?'

'I remember now,' said Raskolnikov, after brooding in long and morose silence. Razumikhin frowned and eyed him anxiously.

The door opened and a tall, thickset man came in; he seemed to Raskolnikov vaguely familiar.

'Zosimov! At last!' exclaimed Razumikhin, delighted.

CHAPTER IV

ZOSIMOV was tall and plump, with a pale, colourless, puffy face, clean-shaven, with straight straw-coloured hair and spectacles, and wearing a large gold ring on one tubby finger. He was twenty-seven. He wore a modish loose lightweight overcoat, pale summer trousers, and in fact everything about him was loose, modish, and brand new; his linen was irreproachable and his watch chain massive. His manner was languid, a mixture of listlessness and studied nonchalance; his self-importance, which he tried hard to hide, showed through every minute. Everyone who knew him found him ponderous, but agreed that he knew his job.

'I've been over to your place twice, old man... Look, he's come round!' cried Razumikhin.

'So I see, so I see. Well, how are we feeling now, eh?' said Zosimov, turning to Raskolnikov, staring hard at him and sitting down at the foot of the divan, where he immediately stretched himself out as far as the place allowed.

'Still down in the dumps,' Razumikhin went on. 'We've just changed his linen, and he was almost in tears.'

'That's understandable. You might have changed him later on, if he didn't want to... The pulse is splendid. Head still aching a bit, is it?'

'I'm fine, absolutely fine!' insisted Raskolnikov irritably, suddenly sitting up on the divan, his eyes flashing. But at once he fell back onto the pillow and turned over to the wall. Zosimov watched him closely.

'Very good, all in order,' he said languidly. 'Had anything to eat?'

He was given an account and asked what the patient could be given.

'You can give him anything you like... Soup, tea... No mushrooms or gherkins, of course, and he'd better not have beef either, and... well, what's the point of talking!...' He exchanged a glance with Razumikhin. 'No more medicine or anything; I'll take a look at him tomorrow... Perhaps today... well, yes...'

'Tomorrow evening I'll take him out!' declared Razumikhin. 'We'll go to Yusupov Park, and then look in at the Palais de Cristal.'*

'I wouldn't move him at all tomorrow evening; although perhaps... a little... well, we'll see.'

'What a shame! I'm having a house-warming party tonight, just round the corner—he might have come along. He could even have lain on a couch amongst us! But you'll be there?' Razumikhin asked Zosimov. 'Don't forget—you promised you'd come.'

'Very well—perhaps later. What have you laid on?'

'Oh, nothing really—tea, vodka, herring. There'll be a pie. Just a few friends.'

'Who, exactly?'

'They're all people from round here, mostly new friends, really—apart from my old uncle, and he's new here too: he only arrived in Petersburg yesterday, on some business of his own. We only meet once in five years.'

'What is he?'

'He's lived a humdrum life as a district postmaster... has a small pension, sixty-five years old, there's nothing to tell... But I'm fond of him, actually. Porfiry Petrovich will be there, he's the local examining magistrate—a lawyer. But you must know him...'

'Is he some sort of relative of yours too?'

'A very distant one. What are you scowling for? Just because you fell out with him once, does that mean you won't be coming now?'

'I couldn't care less about him.'

'All the better. Well, and then some students, a teacher, an official, a musician, an officer—Zametov...'

'Would you kindly tell me what you—or he—' and Zosimov nodded at Raskolnikov, 'can possibly have in common with someone like Zametov?'

'Oh, you grumpy lot! Principles!... you're driven by your principles as though they were clockwork springs, you daren't turn round of your own accord... To my way of thinking, he's a good man, and that's my principle, and I won't hear anything against him. Zametov is a wonderful person.'

'With sticky fingers.'

'So, he's got sticky fingers—I don't care! So what!' cried Razumikhin, suddenly affecting great irritation. 'Was I praising him for having sticky fingers? I simply said he was a good man in his way. If you examined everyone that closely, inside and out, how many good people would be left? I'm sure that I, with all my guts thrown in, wouldn't rate more than a single roasted onion—and then only if you were thrown in too!'

'That's not much. I'll give two for you myself.'

'And I'll only give one for you! Carry on wisecracking! Zametov's still a lad, I could pull his hair, but you have to win him over, not drive him away. If you drive a man away, you won't improve him, especially if he's just a lad. You have to be twice as careful with a lad. Oh, you progressive dimwits, you don't understand a thing! You don't respect others and you harm yourselves... And if you'd like to know, he and I have a common interest at the moment, as it happens.'

'Yes, I would like to know.'

'It's all about that same painter, I mean the house painter. We're going to get him released! Actually there's no problem any more. The thing's absolutely obvious. All we have to do is put a bit more pressure on.'

'What house painter?'

'What, didn't I tell you? Really? No, I just told you the beginning... it's about the murder of that old woman, the pawnbroker, the official's widow... well, now there's a house painter mixed up in it...'

'I'd heard about that murder before you told me, and as a matter of fact I'm interested in it... a bit... because of one thing... and I'd read about it in the newspapers. But now...'

'That Lizaveta, she was killed too!' Nastasia burst out, addressing Raskolnikov. She had stayed in the room the whole time, lurking by the door and listening.

'Lizaveta?' mumbled Raskolnikov, almost inaudibly.

'Yes, Lizaveta, who sold old clothes, didn't you know her? She used to visit downstairs here. She mended your shirt, too.'

Raskolnikov turned to the wall and contemplated the dirty yellow wallpaper with little white flowers; he picked out one odd-shaped white flower with some brown lines on it, and began examining it, counting the petals, looking at the scallopings on each petal and counting the little lines. His hands and feet felt numb, as if they didn't belong to him, but he made no attempt to move—he just went on looking at the flower.

'So what about the house painter?' asked Zosimov, interrupting Nastasia's chatter, which seemed to annoy him greatly.

'Well, they've marked him down as a murderer too!' Razumikhin went on heatedly.

'Any evidence?'

'Evidence my foot! Well, they've got him because of some evidence, but it isn't evidence at all, and that's what needs to be proved. It's exactly the same way they pulled in those others, whatever they're called... Koch and Pestryakov. Ugh! How stupidly they go about things, you're revolted even if it's nothing to do with you. Actually Pestryakov may be coming round to see me today. Incidentally, Rodia, you know about this story, it happened before your illness, just the day before you were in the police office and fell down in a faint while they were talking about it.'

Zosimov looked curiously at Raskolnikov, who made no move.

'You know what, Razumikhin?' remarked Zosimov, 'come to think of it—you're a great busybody, I must say.'

'Maybe so, but we'll get him out all the same!' cried Razumikhin, thumping his fist on the table. 'I mean, what's the most hurtful thing about it all? Not the fact that they're lying—one can always excuse lying, lying's a good thing because it leads you to the truth. No, the offensive thing is that they're lying and then treating their own lies with reverence! I have respect for Porfiry, but... Well, what was it that led them astray, right from the start? The door was locked, and then when they came back with the porter, it was unlocked. And that means that Koch and Pestryakov did the murder! That's their logic for you.'

'Don't get so heated up. They've just been detained—you can't... Incidentally, I've met that Koch: it turns out that he used to buy up unredeemed pledges from the old woman, didn't he?'

'Yes, some sort of swindler! He buys up loan notes too. A profiteer. To hell with him! But can you understand what it is I'm angry about? It's their antiquated, idiotic, hidebound routine. And right here, in just this one case, one could open up a whole new approach. Using nothing but psychological data, one could show the way to get onto the right track. "We have the facts!" they say. But facts aren't everything; at least half the secret lies in how you manage to deal with the facts!'

'And do you know how to deal with facts?'

'Well, you can't keep quiet when you can feel, you can sense, that you might be able to help, if only... Eh!... Do you know the details of the story?'

'I'm still waiting to hear about the house painter.'

'Yes, of course! Well, here's the story. Just two days after the murder, in the morning, while they were still fussing over Koch and Pestryakov— although the pair of them had proved every step they had taken, the truth was crying out to be heard—a most unexpected fact came out. There was a peasant called Dushkin, who owns a drinking shop opposite the house, he turned up at the police office with a pair of silver earrings in a jewel case, and he had a whole tale to tell. "He ran in to my place day before yesterday evening, just after eight or so,"—note the day and time!—"this workman Mikolay, a house painter, who'd been round to see me earlier that day, and he brought this here box with gold earrings and little stones, and asked me to lend him two roubles against them, and when I asked him where he got them, he said he'd picked them up off the pavement. I didn't ask him any more about that,"—this is Dushkin speaking—"but I got out a note for him, I mean a rouble, thinking that if I didn't take the stuff and lend him the money someone else would, there's no difference—he'll drink the money away, and it's better if I hold on to the stuff: safe bind, safe find; and if anything comes up, or if there's any talk about it, I'll hand it in." Well, naturally he dreamed all that up, he lies like a trooper, I know this Dushkin, he's a pawnbroker and a fence himself, and when he got that thirty roubles' worth of stuff off Mikolay, it wasn't to "hand it in" at all, but then he just took fright. Anyway, never mind about that; so listen, then Dushkin says: "And I've known that there peasant Mikolay Dementyev since we was kids, he's from the same province and district as me, Zaraysk, we both come from around Ryazan.* And though Mikolay's not a drunk, he does like a drop, and I knew he was working in that there same house, painting it, along with Mitry, and him and Mitry, they come from the same place. And once he'd got my note, he changed it right away, drank off two glasses at a go, took the change and left, and I didn't see Mitry with him just then. And next day I heard that Aliona Ivanovna and her sister Lizaveta Ivanovna was killed with an axe; now I used to know them, and I wondered what to do about them earrings, because I knew that the dead lady used to lend people money against their things. So I went to the house and began quietly finding out, treading carefully, and the very first thing I asked was, is Mikolay here? And Mitry told me that Mikolay had gone out on a bender, and come home drunk at daybreak, and didn't stop at home more than ten minutes but went out again, and Mitry never saw him again, and was finishing off the job on his own. Their job's on the same staircase as the murdered women, on the second floor. When I hear all that, I says nothing to no one" (this is Dushkin speaking), "but I nose out all I can about the murder and then I goes home, still wondering what to do. And this morning at eight"— so this is the third day, right?—"I see Mikolay coming in to my place, not sober but not all that drunk, he could understand what you said to him. He sat down on a bench and didn't say anything. And the only people in the shop just then were one stranger; and someone else asleep on a bench, a fellow I knew; and a couple of our lads. 'You seen Mitry?' I ask him. 'No,' says he, 'I haven't.'—'And have you been here?'—'Not since the day before yesterday,' he says. 'So where did you spend last night?'—'On the Sands, with Kolomna folk.'*—'And where did you get them earrings?' 'Found them on the pavement,' he says, avoiding my eye, looking as if he didn't expect me to believe him. 'Did you hear about all that happened, up that staircase, that same evening at the same time?'—'No,' says he, 'I didn't'—and he stands there listening to me, his eyes popping out, and all of a sudden he goes as white as chalk. There I am, telling him everything, and I see him grabbing his cap and getting up. I wanted to stop him, 'Wait a minute, Mikolay,' I says to him, 'won't you have a drink?' And I tips my boy the wink to hold the door fast, and I comes out from behind the bar, and he dashes away from me, out onto the street, and races off, disappears into an alleyway, and that's the last I see of him. So then I stops wondering what to do, because he's the culprit, right enough...' "

'I should say so!' said Zosimov.

'Wait! Wait for the end! So naturally everyone rushed off at top speed to find Mikolay; and they detained Dushkin and did a search. And Mitry as well; and they turned over the Kolomna folk too. And then, the day before yesterday, they bring in Mikolay himself; they got him near the —— toll gate,* at an inn. He'd pitched up there, taken off his silver cross, and asked for a glass of vodka in exchange. They let him have one. A few minutes later, a peasant woman went into the cowshed and peeped through a crack: he was in the barn next door, he'd tied his sash to a beam, made a noose, and he was standing on a block of wood and just about to slip the noose over his neck. The woman screamed her head off, and people came running, saying "So that's the sort of man you are!"—"Take me away", says he, "to such and such a police station, and I'll confess everything." Well, they took him off with all due ceremony and presented him to such and such a police station, in other words here. Then they asked him this and that, and who and how, and how old he was—"twenty-two" he says—and so on and so forth. When they asked "While you were working with Mitry, did you see anyone on the stairs, at such and such o'clock?", he says "Of course there may have been folk passing up and down, but not so as we'd notice." "And did you hear anything, any particular noise or anything?"—"No, we didn't hear anything special." "And did you know, Mikolay, on that particular day, that this widow and her sister had been murdered and robbed on such and such a day and time?" "I didn't know, I had no idea. The first I heard of it was from Afanasy Pavlich two days later, in his drink shop."—"So where did you get those earrings?"—"Found them on the pavement."—"Why didn't you turn up to work with Mitry next day?"—"Because I'd gone out drinking."—"Where did you go drinking?"—"This place and that."—"Why did you run away from Dushkin?"—"Because I got really scared."—"What were you scared of?"—"Being sent down by a court."—"How could you be afraid of that, if you thought you weren't guilty of anything?" Well, believe it or not, Zosimov, that question was put to him, in those precise terms, as I know for certain, I have reliable information. What do you think of that?'

'Well, but really though—there is incriminating evidence.'

'I'm not talking about the evidence now, I'm talking about the question of what they think they're about! Well, to hell with it!... So they pressed him and pressed him, and squeezed him and squeezed him, and finally he confessed: "It wasn't on the pavement I found it, but in the flat where Mitry and I were painting."—"And how did that happen?"—"How it happened, was that Mitry and I had been painting there all day, till eight o'clock, and we were just going to leave when Mitry took his paintbrush and smeared paint all over my face, and ran off, and I chased him. So I'm chasing him, and yelling my head off; and just as I come out of the staircase into the gateway, I run slap into the porter and those gentlemen, and how many gentlemen there were I don't know, but the porter swore at me, and the other porter swore at me too, and the porter's wife came out and she swore at us as well, and a gentleman was just coming in at the gate with a lady, and he swore at us too, because Mitka and I were lying across the gateway—I'd grabbed Mitka by his hair, and pulled him down, and I was thumping him, and Mitka had got hold of my hair while he was underneath me, and he was thumping me, but we weren't being vicious, it was all friendly, just having a bit of fun. And then Mitka got away and ran off down the street, and I went after him, but I couldn't catch him, so I came back to the flat on my own—'cause we were supposed to have tidied up. So I started clearing up, waiting for Mitry to come back. And in the entrance by the door, just behind a little wall, in the corner, I trod on this box. So I look and see, and it's all wrapped in paper. I got the paper off, and there were these tiny little hooks on the box, so I open the hooks, and there's earrings in the box...'

'Behind the doors? Lying behind the doors? Was it behind the doors?' cried Raskolnikov suddenly, raising himself slowly off the divan, propping himself on one arm and staring at Razumikhin with a look of confusion and terror.

'Yes... what is it? What's up with you? Why are you...?' said Razumikhin, getting up himself.

'Never mind!...' replied Raskolnikov almost inaudibly, subsiding onto his pillow and turning back to the wall. For a while nobody spoke.

'He must have dozed off, probably talking in his sleep,' Razumikhin said at last, looking questioningly at Zosimov; but he shook his head.

'Well, do go on,' said Zosimov, 'what happened next?'

'What happened next? As soon as he saw the earrings, straight away he forgot about the flat, and Mitka, and just grabbed his cap and ran off to Dushkin's, and as we know he got a rouble off him, lying to him that he'd found them on the pavement, and went straight off to drink. As for the murder, he repeats what he said before: "I didn't know, I had no idea, the first I heard of it was two days later."—"And why didn't you report it earlier?"—"I was scared."—"Why did you try to hang yourself?"—"From thinking about it."—"Thinking what?"—"That they'd send me down." Well, that's the whole story. So what do you think they deduced from all that?'

'No need to think, there's a trail there, not much of one but there is one. That's a fact. Not expecting them to let your house painter go free, are you?'

'But they've got him down as a murderer, straight off! They aren't in any doubt about it...'

'Not true—you're getting too worked up. What about the earrings? You must admit, if Nikolay got hold of earrings from the old woman's trunk, that very same day and hour—admit it, he must have got them from somewhere? That's no trifle, in that sort of investigation.'

'How did they get there? How did they get there?' cried Razumikhin, 'can't you see, Doctor—you're supposed to study mankind, you've more opportunities than anyone to learn about human nature—don't you see from his whole story what sort of a character this Nikolay is? Can't you really see, straight off, that the whole of the statement he gave when he was questioned is God's own truth? He got those earrings in precisely the way he said. Stepped on the box and picked it up!'

'God's own truth? When he confessed himself that he started by lying!'

'Listen to me. Listen carefully. The porter, and Koch, and Pestryakov, and the other porter, and the wife of the first porter, and a woman who was sitting in the porter's lodge with her at the time, and Court Councillor Kryukov who had got out of a cab at that precise moment and was walking in through the gate arm in arm with a lady—all of them, that's to say eight or ten witnesses, unanimously confirm that Nikolay was holding Dmitry on the ground, lying on top of him and thumping him, and Dmitry had got hold of his hair and was thumping him back. They were lying across the carriageway obstructing the entrance, and everyone was swearing at them, while they, "like little children" (the witnesses' very words), were lying one on top of the other, squealing, fighting, and giggling, both of them giggling their heads off, with the silliest expressions on their faces, and then rushed off into the street, one chasing the other, like little children. Do you hear? Now bear in mind: the bodies upstairs were still warm, d'you hear, warm—that's how they were found! If they'd done the murder, or just Nikolay on his own, and if they'd broken into the trunks and robbed them, or even just helped in a robbery—let me just put one question to you. Does that sort of state of mind, I mean squealing and giggling and having a childish fight in the gateway, does that go along with axes, and blood, and bestial cunning, and caution, and robbery? So they'd only just done the murders, no more than five or ten minutes back—because that's what the evidence shows, the bodies were still warm—and suddenly they leave the bodies, and leave the flat open, knowing that people had just gone up there, and they drop their stolen goods and tumble all over the road like little children, giggling and attracting everyone's attention, as ten witnesses all agree!'

'Yes, of course, it's strange! Naturally it's impossible, but...'

'No, my friend, no "buts"—if the earrings that turned up in Nikolay's hands on that same day and hour really constitute important factual evidence against him—although it's directly explained by his statement, so it's *disputed incriminating evidence*—then you surely have to take into account the facts in his favour, particularly as they're *indisputable* facts. But what do you think, knowing what our judicial system is like: will they accept, are they even capable of accepting such a fact—based on nothing but a psychological impossibility, nothing but a state of mind—as an incontrovertible fact which demolishes all substantive incriminating evidence of any sort whatsoever? No, they won't accept it, not for anything, because they'll say that they've found the box, and the man wanted to hang himself, "which he couldn't have done if he hadn't felt he was guilty"! That's the crucial question, and that's why I'm so worked up. Try to understand!'

'Yes, I can see you're worked up. Hold on, I forgot to ask: what's the proof that that box with the earrings really came from the old woman's trunk?'

'That's been proved,' replied Razumikhin with a frown, and with apparent reluctance. 'Koch recognized the article and named the depositor, and that man provided positive proof that it really was his.'

'That's bad. And another thing: did anyone see Nikolay when Koch and Pestryakov went upstairs, and can't that be proved in some way?'

'That's just the thing, no one did see him,' replied Razumikhin in some vexation. 'That's the worst of it: even Koch and Pestryakov didn't notice them when they went upstairs, though their evidence wouldn't mean much now anyway. "We saw that the flat was unlocked," they say, "and that there must have been people working there; but we didn't pay any attention to it when we went past, and we can't remember for certain whether there were workmen there at that moment or not."'

'Hmm. So the only evidence in his favour is that they were pummelling one another and laughing. That's strong evidence, I grant you, but... Let me ask you this now: how do you account for all the facts yourself? How do you explain the finding of the earrings, if the man really found them in the way he claims?'

'How do I explain it? What is there to explain? It's obvious! At least the line of enquiry they ought to follow is clear and proven, and it's the box itself that proves it. The real killer dropped those earrings. The killer was upstairs when Koch and Pestryakov knocked at the door, and he had the door bolted. Koch made the stupid mistake of going downstairs, and at that point the killer skipped out and ran off downstairs as well, since there was nothing else he could do. On the staircase, he hid from Koch, Pestryakov, and the porter by slipping into the empty flat, where he stood and waited behind the door while the porter and those others went upstairs. He waited until the footsteps died away, and then walked downstairs as cool as you please, just at the very moment when Dmitry and Nikolay had run out onto the street, and everyone had dispersed, and there was no one left in the gateway. Perhaps someone did see him, without noticing anything—there would have been plenty of people passing by. And that box, he dropped it out of his pocket while he was hiding behind the door, and didn't notice he'd dropped it because he had other things on his mind. But the box itself clearly proves that he was standing right there. That's all there is to it!'

'Brilliant! My friend, that's brilliant. Cleverer than anything!'

'Why so? What do you mean?'

'Because everything comes together so perfectly... and fits in so well... just like in a play.'

'Oh!' Razumikhin began, but at that moment the door opened and a new individual entered, a stranger to all those present.

CHAPTER V

THIS was a middle-aged gentleman, prim and self-important, with a cautious and irritable expression. He first paused in the doorway, looking around him with offensive and ill-disguised astonishment as if to say: 'Where on earth have I landed up?' He inspected Raskolnikov's narrow, low-ceilinged 'ship's cabin' suspiciously, putting on an air of being frightened and almost offended. With the same astonishment he turned to look at Raskolnikov himself, lying half-dressed, unkempt, and unwashed on his wretched dirty divan and staring fixedly back at him. Then, just as deliberately, he began examining the tousled, unshaven, and dishevelled figure of Razumikhin, who also stared straight back at him with an arrogant, questioning look, without moving from his place. The tense silence lasted a minute or so, after which, as was to be expected, there was a slight change of scenario. Evidently realizing, from various very clear indications, that his exaggerated sternness and pomposity would get him nowhere in this 'cabin', the new arrival softened slightly and spoke politely, though still severely, to Zosimov, articulating every syllable of his enquiry.

'Rodion Romanovich Raskolnikov, gentleman student or ex-student?'

Zosimov made a languid movement and might even have answered him, if Razumikhin (who had not been addressed at all) had not at once broken in:

'There he is, lying on the divan! What d'you want?'

The familiarity of that 'What d'you want?' utterly disconcerted the pompous gentleman. Indeed, he was on the point of turning towards Razumikhin, but managed to stop himself in time and hastily turned back to Zosimov.

'This is Raskolnikov!' drawled Zosimov, nodding at his patient. Then he yawned, opening his mouth particularly wide and holding it open for a particularly long time. Next he slowly reached into his waistcoat pocket, drew out an enormous bulging gold pocket-watch, opened it, looked at it, and just as slowly and languidly returned it to its place.

All this time Raskolnikov was lying on his back in silence, staring fixedly at the new arrival without a thought in his head. His face, which he had turned away from the curious flower on the wallpaper, was unusually pale and bore an expression of great suffering, as though he had just emerged from an excruciating operation or been delivered from torture. But his visitor was gradually arousing more and more of his attention, followed by perplexity, mistrust, and almost fear. When Zosimov pointed to him and said 'This is Raskolnikov', he quickly raised himself, almost springing to his feet, then sat down on his bed and said in an almost challenging tone, though in a weak and faltering voice: 'Yes. I'm Raskolnikov! What d'you want?'

The visitor looked attentively at him and pronounced in imposing tones:

'Piotr Petrovich Luzhin. I have every confidence that my name is not entirely unknown to you.'

Raskolnikov, who had been expecting something quite different, looked at him dully and thoughtfully without saying anything, as though he was hearing the name of Piotr Petrovich for the first time in his life.

'How is this? Have you really not heard anything about me before now?' asked Piotr Petrovich, looking uncomfortable.

Instead of replying, Raskolnikov slowly lowered himself onto his pillow, placed his hands behind his head and stared up at the ceiling. Luzhin seemed annoyed. Zosimov and Razumikhin looked him up and down with even greater curiosity, till eventually he became visibly embarrassed.

'I had supposed, indeed assumed,' he faltered, 'that the letter, posted over ten days, nay almost two weeks, ago...'

'Look here, what's the point of standing stuck there in the doorway?' Razumikhin suddenly interrupted him. 'If you need to explain something, take a seat. There's no room for you and Nastasia together over there. Nastasyushka, move aside and let him pass. Come along in, take this chair, over here! Squeeze through!'

He moved his chair away from the table, making a little space between the table and his knees, and waited in this rather awkward posture for the visitor to 'squeeze through' into the tiny space. The moment had been chosen in such a way that there could be no refusal, and the visitor clambered, stumbling in his haste, through the narrow gap. On reaching the chair he sat down and glared suspiciously at Razumikhin.

'Well, don't feel embarrassed,' Razumikhin blurted out. 'Rodia's been ill for the last five days, delirious for three of them, but now he's come to himself and even eaten a hearty meal. This is his doctor here, he's just been examining him, and I'm a friend of Rodia's, an ex-student myself, and now I'm looking after him. So never mind about us, don't be shy, just go ahead with whatever it is you've come for.'

'I thank you. But shall I not be incommoding your patient by my presence and conversation?' asked Piotr Petrovich, turning to Zosimov.

'N-no,' drawled Zosimov, 'you might even keep him amused.' And he gave another yawn.

'Oh, he's been in his right mind for ages, ever since this morning!' went on Razumikhin. His familiar mode of address had such an air of unaffected sincerity that Piotr Petrovich began to feel more confident— perhaps, too, because this insolent ragamuffin had introduced himself as a student.

'Your good Mama—' began Luzhin.

'Hm!' exclaimed Raskolnikov aloud. Luzhin cast him a questioning look.

'Never mind, I was just... Carry on.'

Luzhin shrugged his shoulders.

'Your good Mama, while I was still with them, began a letter to you. When I arrived here, I purposely allowed several days to pass before visiting you, so as to be absolutely certain that you were informed about everything. Yet now, to my surprise...'

'I know, I know!' said Raskolnikov suddenly, with great impatience and irritation. 'So it's you, is it? The bridegroom? Well, I know! That'll do!'

Piotr Petrovich was most offended, but said nothing. He was hurriedly trying to work out what all this could mean. The silence lasted a minute or so.

Meanwhile Raskolnikov, who had turned slightly towards Luzhin when he spoke to him, now began once more to stare at him with great curiosity, as if he hadn't yet had the time to get a good look at him, or as if he were now suddenly struck by something new about him. He even raised himself from the pillow for the purpose. And indeed, there was something especially striking about Piotr Petrovich's general appearance—something that could have justified the epithet of 'the bridegroom' which he had just so unceremoniously applied to him. For one thing it was quite clear, and even rather too obvious, that Piotr Petrovich had made a hasty effort to use his few days in Petersburg to get himself fitted out and smartened up in readiness for his bride; and this, of course, was something quite innocent and allowable. On this occasion, too, one might even have excused his rather over-complacent awareness of how smart he had made himself, seeing that Piotr Petrovich was here as the bridegroom. His whole costume was fresh from the tailor's, and everything was just right, except that it was all too new, and betrayed too blatantly the purpose he had in mind. Even his dashing new round hat bore witness to it: Piotr Petrovich was treating it with far too much respect, holding it too carefully in his hands. Even his splendid pair of lilac-coloured gloves, genuine Jouvins,* conveyed the same message, if only because he was not wearing them but holding them in his hand to show them off. He wore mostly light and youthful colours: a handsome pale-brown summer jacket, pale lightweight trousers and waistcoat, newly bought fine linen, a cravat of the finest cambric with pink stripes—and the best of it was that all this actually suited him. His face, very fresh and quite handsome, seemed younger than his forty-five years. His cheeks were agreeably shaded by dark mutton-chop whiskers, which grew attractively bushier next to his shiny clean-shaven chin. Even his hair, just faintly receding, had been combed and curled at the barber's, yet this had not made it seem in the least comic or silly, though this is what generally happens when a man sports curled hair, because it invariably makes him look like a German on his wedding day. If there really was anything unpleasing or unattractive about his reasonably good-looking and stolid appearance, it was due to something else. After his unceremonious inspection of Mr Luzhin, Raskolnikov gave a venomous smile, subsided onto his pillow and went back to staring at the ceiling.

But Mr Luzhin had taken himself in hand and apparently resolved to ignore this strange behaviour for the time being.

'I am most, most sorry to find you in such a situation,' he began, forcing himself to break the silence. 'Had I known of your indisposition, I should have come before this. But business, you know!... As a lawyer, moreover, I have a most important case to attend to in the Senate. To say nothing of those cares which you yourself will guess at. I am expecting your people, that is, your good Mama and your sister, at any moment.'

Raskolnikov stirred and seemed on the point of saying something: he was looking anxious. Piotr Petrovich stopped and waited, but as nothing followed he continued:

'At any moment. I have found them temporary lodgings...'

'Where?' asked Raskolnikov in a faint voice.

'Very close by, in Bakaleyev's house.'

'That's on Voznesensky Prospekt,'* interrupted Razumikhin. 'There are two floors let out as rooms. The merchant Yushin rents them out. I've been there.'

'Yes, that is so—rooms.'

'Revoltingly seedy—a dirty, smelly, disreputable place. Things have happened there. And God knows what sort of people live there!... I've been there in connection with some scandalous goings-on. But it's cheap.'

'Well, naturally I have not been able to accumulate so much information, being new here myself,' demurred Piotr Petrovich, somewhat nettled. 'But I have actually obtained two most, most clean little rooms, and as this is for a very short period... I have also located a real apartment, our future home that is,' he said, addressing Raskolnikov; 'and it is being decorated at the present time; meanwhile I myself am obliged to put up in rooms, very close by, at Madame Lippewechsel's, in the apartment of a young friend of mine, Andrei Semionich Lebeziatnikov. It was he who directed me to the Bakaleyev house.'

'Lebeziatnikov?' repeated Raskolnikov slowly, as if recalling something.

'Yes, Andrei Semionich Lebeziatnikov—he works at one of the Ministries. Do you happen to know him?'

'Yes... No...' replied Raskolnikov.

'I beg your pardon. It appeared to me from your question that you did. I was at one time his guardian... a very pleasant young man... and interested in everything... I enjoy meeting young people: you get to discover what's new.' Piotr Petrovich looked hopefully round the company.

'What do you mean by that?' asked Razumikhin.

'I mean it in the most serious sense, as it were, the most fundamental sense,' answered Piotr Petrovich, apparently pleased with the question. 'You see, it is ten years since I was last in Petersburg. All the new developments here, new reforms, new ideas—all that has reached us in the provinces too; but if you wish to see more clearly, to see everything, you have to be in Petersburg. And so, my thought was just this: that you will see and discover much more if you observe our younger generation. And I must say, I have been pleased...'

'Pleased with what, exactly?'

'That is a very broad question. I may be mistaken, but it appears to me that I find a clearer outlook, more of what one might call criticism, a more pragmatic approach...'

'That's true enough,' interjected Zosimov.

'Nonsense, that's not a pragmatic approach at all,' Razumikhin objected. 'That's a hard thing to acquire, and it doesn't come down to us from heaven above. We lost the knack of doing anything pragmatic almost two hundred years ago... Of course there are new ideas bubbling up, I grant you,' he said to Piotr Petrovich, 'and a longing for goodness, though it's a childish one; and you'll find honesty too, in spite of the hordes of swindlers who've descended on us from all sides. But there's still no pragmatic approach at all. Pragmatism wears smart boots.'

'I cannot agree with you,' responded Piotr Petrovich with evident relish. 'Of course people can get carried away and make mistakes, but you have to be tolerant of them—it all comes about through their enthusiasm for the matter in hand and the unfavourable circumstances surrounding it. And though not much may have been achieved, there has not been much time either. Not to mention the lack of resources. In my personal opinion, if I may say so, something has indeed been achieved; new and valuable ideas have been propagated, a number of new and valuable works have been published, in place of the old dreamy, romantic ones; literature is adopting a more mature outlook; many injurious prejudices have been rooted out and held up to ridicule... In a word, we have cut ourselves free from the past, once and for all, and in my view that is an important achievement.'

'Got it off by heart! Wants us to approve of him!' Raskolnikov suddenly announced.

'Pardon?' said Piotr Petrovich, who had not heard him. But he received no answer.

'That's all quite true,' Zosimov hastened to add.

'Is it not?' continued Piotr Petrovich, with a friendly look at Zosimov. 'You must agree', he went on, addressing Razumikhin, but now with a shade of triumph and superiority in his manner—he almost added 'young man'—'that there are advances, or what is nowadays termed progress, if only in the name of science and economic truth...'

'That's a cliché!'

'No, it is no cliché, sir! If I had always been told to "love thy neighbour", and I did so, what would be the result?' continued Piotr Petrovich, perhaps too hurriedly. 'The result would be that I would tear my cloak in two and share it with my neighbour, and each of us would be left half-naked, for as the Russian proverb says, "chase several hares at once and you'll catch none". But science tells us: "Love yourself above all, for everything on earth is founded on self-interest."* If you love yourself alone, you will manage your concerns properly, and your cloak will remain whole. And economic truth adds that the better that private concerns are managed in our society—the more whole cloaks there are, as it were—the firmer society's foundations become, and the more the common good is promoted. Hence by acquiring wealth exclusively for

myself alone, I thereby acquire it for all others too, and ensure that my
neighbour gets something more than a torn cloak; and this comes
about, not thanks to individual private bounties, but as a consequence
of universal progress. The idea is a simple one, but has, regrettably,
remained unrecognized for too long, overshadowed as it is by mis-
guided enthusiasms and dreamy idealism; though it would apparently
not take much intelligence to realize...'

'Forgive me, but I don't have much intelligence either,' interrupted
Razumikhin sharply. 'So let's stop this. What I started saying had
a point—but all this self-indulgent chatter, all these incessant, endless
commonplaces, the same thing over and over, it's all made me feel so sick
over the past three years that, honest to God, I blush to hear other
people talking that way, never mind myself. Of course you were in a hurry
to demonstrate your knowledge to us; that's quite pardonable and I don't
hold it against you. But all I wanted right now was to discover the sort
of person you are; because so many opportunists of all kinds have lately
latched on to the idea of the common good, and twisted everything
they got their hands on while pursuing their own ends, that the whole
idea has got thoroughly tainted. There, that's enough of that!'

'My dear sir,' began Mr Luzhin, bridling with a great show of
dignity, 'can you have been wishing to include me too, in these most
uncomplimentary terms, in...'

'Oh, please!... How could I?... Anyway, sir, enough of that!' interrupted Razumikhin, turning abruptly to Zosimov to carry on their earlier
conversation.

Piotr Petrovich had the sense to accept his explanation at once.
He had in any case decided to leave in a couple of minutes.

'I hope that the acquaintance we have formed here', he said to
Raskolnikov, 'will be further strengthened after your recovery, in view
of the circumstances of which you are aware... I particularly wish you
all good health...'

Raskolnikov didn't even turn his head. Piotr Petrovich made to get
up from his chair.

'So it was definitely a client of hers that did the murder!' said
Zosimov positively.

'A client, definitely!' agreed Razumikhin. 'Porfiry won't let on what
he's thinking, but he's questioning her clients.'

'Questioning her clients?' asked Raskolnikov in a loud voice.

'Yes—why?'

'Nothing.'

'Where does he find them?'

'Koch pointed out some of them; some had their names written on the wrapping of their pledges, and some turned up of their own accord when they heard the news...'

'What a clever, hardened villain he must be! How bold of him! How decisive!'

'That's just the point—it isn't!' interrupted Razumikhin. 'That's just what you're all getting wrong. What I say is that he's not clever, not experienced, and probably this was his first time! If you imagine it being planned by a clever villain, it doesn't make sense. But if you imagine someone inexperienced, then it's quite clear that there was just one lucky chance that saved him from disaster—and chance can do anything. I mean, perhaps he never foresaw any difficulties! And how does he set about it? He takes some things worth ten or twenty roubles apiece and fills his pockets with them, he burrows in the old woman's trunk, amongst all her rags, and all the while there's a box in the top drawer of her chest of drawers where they've found fifteen hundred roubles in cash, not to mention banknotes! He didn't even manage to rob her—all he managed to do was kill her! It was his first time, I'm telling you, his first time, and he lost his head! And it wasn't any planning on his part, it was pure luck that saved him!'

'You appear to be discussing the recent killing of the old woman, the official's widow,' interposed Piotr Petrovich, addressing Zosimov; he was already standing up and holding his hat and gloves, but wanted to dispense a few more words of wisdom before leaving. He appeared to be trying to make a good impression, and his vanity overcame his common sense.

'Yes, have you heard about it?'

'Naturally, being in the neighbourhood...'

'Do you know the details?'

'I could not say that. But there's a different thing that interests me here, what you might call the broader issue. I do not speak of the fact that crime among the lower classes has increased over the past five years or so; nor of the incessant robberies and arson attacks committed everywhere; the strangest thing for me is the fact that crime among the upper classes is increasing in the same way, in parallel as it were. So we hear of a former student robbing the mail on the highway; or of people in the topmost ranks of society forging banknotes; or of a whole gang of forgers in Moscow caught counterfeiting the latest issue of lottery tickets, and one of the ringleaders was a lecturer in world history; or of one of our embassy secretaries murdered abroad for some mysterious financial reason...* And now, if this old pawnbroker woman was killed by one

of her clients, that must have been someone from the upper classes—
for peasants do not pawn gold articles. So how are we to account for
what one might call such depravity among the civilized sections of our
society?'

'There have been a lot of economic changes...' responded Zosimov.

'How to account for it?' Razumikhin chimed in. 'You might account
for it by our excessively deep-rooted lack of pragmatism.'

'How do you mean, sir?'

'Well, what did that lecturer of yours in Moscow say when he was
asked why he forged the tickets? "Everyone's getting rich as best they
can, and I wanted to get rich too." I don't remember his exact words,
but the point was that he wanted money for nothing, double-quick, and
easy! People have got used to living with all found, to being led along in
leading strings, even having their food chewed up for them. And when
the great hour strikes, they all reveal what they stand for...'

'But what about morality? Or principles, so to speak?'

'What are you worrying about?' Raskolnikov unexpectedly interposed. 'It all falls in with your own theory!'

'What do you mean, my own theory?'

'If you take it to its logical conclusion, all that you were preaching
just now, then it turns out that you can cut people's throats...'

'How can you!' exclaimed Luzhin.

'No, that's not right,' opined Zosimov.

Raskolnikov had gone pale and was lying there breathing heavily, his
upper lip twitching.

'There is moderation in all things,' continued Luzhin haughtily.
'An economic idea does not amount to incitement to murder, and if we
only assume...'

'And is it true,' Raskolnikov suddenly interrupted him again, his
voice trembling with fury that covered an undertone of pleasure at
being insulting, 'is it true that you said to your betrothed bride... in that
same hour when you got her consent, that your greatest joy was... the
fact that she was a beggar... because there's a greater advantage in res-
cuing a wife from beggary, so that you can dominate over her afterwards... and cast your bounties in her teeth?...'

'My dear sir!' shouted Luzhin in furious annoyance, red-faced with
confusion. 'My dear sir—to twist my notion to such an extent! Pardon
me, but I have to tell you that the rumours that have reached you,
or rather have been conveyed to you, bear not the faintest vestige of
foundation, and I... suspect the person... in a word... this arrow... in
a word, your Mama... She had in any event struck me, for all her

otherwise excellent qualities, as someone of an excitable and romantic cast of mind... But I was nonetheless a thousand miles away from imagining that she could have misunderstood and misrepresented the matter in such a fantastically warped way... And finally... finally...'

'Do you know what?' cried Raskolnikov, raising himself from his pillow and glaring at him with piercing, glittering eyes. 'Do you know what?'

'What, sir?' Luzhin paused and waited with an offended, challenging expression. The silence lasted several seconds.

'This: that if you ever again... have the gall to say a single word... about my mother... I'll kick you downstairs, head over heels!'

'What's come over you?' cried Razumikhin.

'Aha, so that's how it is!' Luzhin went pale and bit his lip. 'Now listen to me, my good sir,' he began with deliberation, holding himself in check with all his might but still panting for breath, 'I have been aware of your hostility from the very first moment, but I have remained here on purpose in order to find out more. I could have excused a great deal in a sick man and a family member, but now... you... shall never, sir...'

'I'm not sick!' shouted Raskolnikov.

'So much the worse, sir!'

'Get the hell out of here!'

But Luzhin was already on his way out, leaving his speech unfinished; he clambered back between the table and chair, and this time Razumikhin stood up to let him pass. Without a glance at anybody, without even a nod to Zosimov who had been signalling to him for quite a while to leave the sick man alone, Luzhin went out, cautiously raising his hat to shoulder height as he stooped to pass through the door. The very curve of his back seemed to express the terrible insult he was carrying away with him.

'How can you talk like that? How can you?' said Razumikhin, shaking his head in bewilderment.

'Leave me alone, all of you! Leave me alone!' yelled Raskolnikov in a frenzy. 'Are you ever going to leave me alone, you torturers! I'm not afraid of you! I'm not afraid of anyone, anyone at all, any more! Get away from me! I want to be alone, alone, alone!'

'Let's go!' said Zosimov with a nod at Razumikhin.

'What do you mean? How can we leave him like this?'

'Come on!' repeated Zosimov insistently, and left the room. Razumikhin thought a moment and ran out after him.

'It could have got worse if we hadn't done as he said,' said Zosimov on the stairs. 'We mustn't infuriate him.'

'What's wrong with him?'

'If only we could give him some sort of a prod in the right direc-tion—that's what he needs! He'd got his strength back earlier on... You know, he's got something on his mind! Some sort of burden he can't shake off... That's what I'm really afraid of—it has to be that!'

'Well, it might be this gentleman, Piotr Petrovich. From what they said, he seems to be marrying Rodia's sister, and Rodia got a letter about that just before he fell ill.'

'Yes, he was the last person we needed right now. He may have spoiled everything. But did you notice that Rodia doesn't care about anything, he's got nothing to say about anything, except this one thing that drives him wild: that murder...'

'Yes, yes!' Razumikhin agreed. 'I certainly did notice. He's inter-ested in it, and scared by it. They frightened him about it on the very day he fell ill, in the assistant superintendent's office. He fell into a faint.'

'You tell me all about that tonight; and then I'll tell you something myself. I find him very, very interesting! I'll drop in to check on him in half an hour. But there won't be any inflammation...'

'Thank you! And meanwhile I'll wait with Pashenka, and get Nastasia to keep an eye on him for us...'

When his visitors had left, Raskolnikov looked miserably and impa-tiently at Nastasia, who was still lingering there.

'So will you have some tea now?' she asked.

'Later! I want to sleep! Leave me alone...'

He turned convulsively towards the wall, and Nastasia went out.

CHAPTER VI

BUT as soon as she was gone, he got up, put the hook on the door, undid the bundle of clothes that Razumikhin had brought with him and then bundled up again, and began to dress. Strangely enough, he had suddenly become perfectly calm—there was none of the half-crazed raving of earlier on, nor of the panic-stricken terror of recent days. This was the first minute of a strange state of sudden tranquility. His movements were crisp and precise, and reflected his firm purpose. 'Today, this very day!' he muttered to himself. He realized that he was still weak, but a powerful inner tension had brought him to a state of cool, unshakeable determination, and filled him with strength and con-fidence. However, he did hope that he wouldn't keel over in the street.

Once he was fully dressed in all his new clothes, he glanced at the money lying on the table, thought for a moment, and pocketed it. It amounted to twenty-five roubles. And he picked up all the copper five-kopek coins that Razumikhin had brought back, the change out of the ten roubles he had spent on clothes. Then he quietly unlatched the door, left the room, walked downstairs, and glanced in through the wide-open kitchen door. Nastasia was standing with her back to him, bending over and blowing on the coals in her mistress's samovar. She didn't hear him—and indeed, who could have supposed that he would go out? In another minute he was in the street.

It was around eight o'clock and the sun was setting. It was as sweltering hot as before, but he greedily breathed in this stinking, dusty, city-contaminated air. His head was almost spinning, and a sort of wild energy suddenly lit up his burning eyes and gaunt, sallow features. He didn't know where he was going, nor did he think about that. All he knew was that he had to finish with all *that* this very day, all at once, right now; that he could never go back home otherwise, because *he didn't want to live like this*. How could he finish with it? He had no idea, nor did he want to think about it. He drove the thought away, the thought that tormented him. The only thing he felt and knew was that everything had to change, one way or another, 'no matter how', he repeated to himself with desperate, unflinching certainty and determination.

From force of habit he followed the route of his previous walks, making straight for the Haymarket. Before he got there, he came upon a black-haired young organ grinder* standing in the roadway in front of a little general store. He was grinding out a very sentimental song, accompanying a girl of fifteen or so who stood before him on the pavement, dressed like a young lady, in a crinoline, a short mantle, gloves, and a straw hat with a flame-coloured feather. All her clothes were old and worn. She was singing her song in a coarse, quavering but quite attractive and powerful voice, in the hope of a couple of kopeks from the shopkeeper. Raskolnikov stopped among two or three other bystanders, listened to her singing, got out a five-kopek piece and handed it to her. She broke off her song abruptly, cutting it off on its most moving top note, and shouted sharply to the organ grinder 'That'll do!' Then they both trudged off to the next shop.

'Do you like listening to street-singing?' Raskolnikov suddenly asked one of the passers-by, a man standing by his side near the barrel organ. The man, who was getting on in years and looked like a flâneur, gave him a strange, startled look. 'I do,' went on Raskolnikov, looking as if he wasn't talking about street-singing at all. 'I like hearing someone singing to a barrel organ on a cold, dark, damp autumn evening—it has to be a damp one—when all the passers-by have pale, greenish, sickly faces; or better still, when there's wet snow falling, straight down, with no wind, you know? and the gaslight shining through it...'

'I don't know... Excuse me...' muttered the man, scared both by Raskolnikov's question and by his strange appearance; and he crossed to the other side of the street.

Raskolnikov walked straight on and came out onto the Haymarket at the very corner where the stallholder and his wife had been trading when they spoke with Lizaveta a few days before; but they weren't there now. Recognizing the place, he stopped and looked around, then turned to address a young fellow in a red shirt who stood yawning by the door of a corn chandler's.

'Isn't there a stallholder who trades on this corner, with his wife, eh?'

'All sorts of people do,' replied the man, staring disdainfully down at him.

'What's his name?'

'Whatever they christened him.'

'Aren't you from Zaraysk* too? What province?'

The young man gave Raskolnikov another look.

'What we have, your Highness, is not a province but a district; now my brother travelled the wide world, but I stayed home, so I wouldn't know, Sir. I humbly beg your Highness's gracious pardon.'

'Is that an eating house upstairs?'

'Yes, it's a tavern, and they've got billiards; and you'll find princesses* there too... Heigh-ho!'

Raskolnikov walked across the square. On the opposite corner stood a dense crowd of peasants. He pushed his way into the thick of them, looking at people's faces. For some reason he felt the urge to strike up conversations with all and sundry. But the peasants took no notice of him; they had gathered in groups, talking loudly among themselves. He stood for a while in thought, then walked off to the right along the pavement towards V——. Leaving the square behind him, he found himself in an alley...*

He had often come through this short alleyway, which took a bend on its way from the square towards Sadovaya Street. Recently he had often felt inclined to wander through all these places, when he was feeling sick of things—'to make everything even more sickening'. But now he entered the alleyway with nothing on his mind at all. Here was a large building, full of taverns and other eating and drinking places; women were constantly coming out of them, dressed for 'just dropping round to the neighbour's', bareheaded and with no coats over their dresses.

Here and there they had gathered in groups on the pavement, mostly in front of basement stairways where a couple of steps could bring them into all sorts of highly entertaining establishments. One of these places was reverberating with banging and shouting that filled the street; a guitar twanged, people were singing songs, and there was great merriment. A big crowd of women had gathered by the entrance, some sitting on the steps, some on the pavement, others standing and talking. A drunken soldier shambled along the roadway smoking a cigarette and swearing at the top of his voice; he seemed to be wanting to go in somewhere, but had forgotten where. One ragged tramp was swearing at another, and someone was lying across the road dead drunk. Raskolnikov stopped beside a crowd of women. They were conversing in hoarse voices; all were bareheaded, wearing cotton dresses and goatskin shoes. Some were over forty, others only seventeen or so; almost all had a black eye or two.

For some reason he was attracted by the singing and all the thumping and noise downstairs... He could hear the sounds of squeals and laughter, the strumming of a guitar, and a thin falsetto voice singing a jaunty air, while someone else was doing a frantic dance, beating out the time with his heels. He listened intently, gloomily, and thoughtfully, bending down on the pavement by the entrance and peering in curiously.

> 'Hey, you gorgeous soldier lad,
> Don't you hit me, I ain't bad,'

—quavered the singer's thin voice. Raskolnikov was desperate to hear the words of the song, as though that was the point of everything.

'Should I go in?' he wondered. 'They're laughing—they're drunk. Shouldn't I get drunk too?'

'Won't you come in, my nice gentleman?' asked one of the women, in quite a musical voice, not yet entirely coarsened. She was young and not actually hideous—the only one of the whole group.

'Look at you—what a beauty!' he replied, straightening up and looking at her.

She smiled, very pleased with the compliment.

'You're very good-looking yourself,' she said.

'Skinny, though!' remarked another woman in a deep voice. 'Just out of hospital, are you?'

'You'd think they were all army generals' daughters, but every one of them's got a snub nose!' broke in a tipsy peasant who had just come up, his coat unbuttoned and a sly grin on his face. 'Having fun, are we?'

'Now you're here, come along in!'

'So I will! A treat, you are!'

And he staggered down the steps.

Raskolnikov walked on.

'Listen, mister!' the girl called after him.

'What?'

She looked bashful.

'You're a nice gentleman, and I'd love to spend an hour with you any time, but right now I'm not brave enough. Just give me six kopeks for a drink, there's a charmer!'

Raskolnikov pulled out whatever came to hand—three fives.

'Oh what a lovely kind man you are!'

'What's your name, then?'

'Just ask for Duklida.'

'Whatever are you up to?' remarked one of the girls suddenly, shaking her head at Duklida. 'How can you have the brass to beg like that? Me, I'd sink into the ground from shame...'

Raskolnikov gave a curious look at the girl who had spoken. She was a pockmarked lass of about thirty, covered in bruises, with a swollen upper lip. She had delivered her opinion in a calm and serious voice.

'Where was it,' wondered Raskolnikov as he walked on, 'where was it that I read about someone who was condemned to death, and an hour before his execution he said, or thought, that if he was made to live on some great height, on a cliff, on a platform so narrow that there was just room for his two feet, with the abyss all around, the ocean below him, everlasting darkness, everlasting solitude, and everlasting storms—and he had to stay up there, standing on a foot of ground, for all his life, a thousand years, for all eternity—it would be better to live like that than die at once!* Just to live, live, and live! No matter how one lives—just to be alive!... How true that is! Lord, how true! Humankind are villains! And anyone who calls them villains for being like that is a villain himself,' he added after a minute.

He emerged onto another street. 'Aha! The "Crystal Palace"! Razumikhin was talking about the "Crystal Palace" not long ago. So what was it I was wanting? Yes, to read about it!... Zosimov said he'd read it in the paper...'

'Got the papers?' he asked, walking into a spacious and clean tavern consisting of several rooms, all fairly empty. Two or three customers were drinking tea, and in one of the further rooms a group of four or five people were drinking champagne. Raskolnikov had the impression that one of them was Zametov, although it was hard to be sure from a distance.

'Never mind if it is!' he thought.

'Vodka, sir?' asked the waiter.

'I'll have some tea. And bring me some newspapers, back numbers, over the last five days or so; I'll give you a tip.'

'Yes sir. Here's today's, sir. And a vodka as well, sir?'

The tea and back numbers turned up. Raskolnikov sat down and began searching. 'Izler—Izler—Aztecs—Aztecs—Izler—Bartola—Massimo—Aztecs—Izler...* damn it all! Ah, here's the latest: woman falls downstairs—merchant sets house on fire when drunk—fire on the Sands—fire on Peterburgskaya—another fire on Peterburgskaya—another fire on Peterburgskaya*—Izler—Izler—Izler—Izler—Massimo... Ah, here we are...'

He finally found the thing he was searching for, and began reading. The lines of print danced before his eyes, but he read to the end of the news item and began eagerly searching for later additions in the following issues. His hands trembled with nervous impatience as he turned the pages. Suddenly someone came and sat down at his table next to him. He glanced at him—it was Zametov, the same Zametov, looking the same as before, with his rings and chains, the parting in his pomaded black curls, wearing a natty waistcoat, a rather worn frock coat, and none too fresh linen. He was in a good mood, or at least smiling very cheerfully and good-humouredly. His dark face was flushed from the champagne he had drunk.

'What's all this? You here?' he began in astonishment, speaking as if they'd known each other all their lives. 'Razumikhin was telling me only yesterday that you were unconscious. Isn't that odd! And I've been round to your place...'

Raskolnikov had known that he would come over. He put the papers aside and turned to Zametov. He was smiling a mocking smile, and a shade of testy impatience now showed through it.

'I know you came,' he replied, 'I heard all about it. Hunting for my sock... You know what, Razumikhin is crazy about you, he says the two of you went to see Lavisa Ivanovna, that woman you were trying to wink to Lieutenant Gunpowder about, that time, and he kept not catching on, remember? How could he not have caught on—so obvious, wasn't it, eh?'

'And what a hothead he is!'

'Who, Gunpowder?'

'No, your friend. Razumikhin.'

'You live a fine life, Mr Zametov. Free entry to all the best places! Who was it standing you champagne just now?'

'Well, we... were having a drink. They kept pouring out more!'

'Just a perk! Everything comes your way!'—Raskolnikov laughed. 'Never mind, my fine lad, never mind!' he added, clapping Zametov on the shoulder. 'I didn't mean any harm—it was "all friendly, just having a bit of fun", as that workman told you when he was thumping Mitka back then, over that business of the old woman.'

'How d'you know that?'

'Aha, maybe I know more than you do yourself.'

'You're being very peculiar... You're probably still very ill. You should never have come out...'

'Do I strike you as peculiar then?'

'Yes. What are those newspapers you're reading?'

'Newspapers.'

'There's a lot about fires in them.'

'No, I'm not reading about fires.' Here he gave Zametov a mysterious look, and once again his lips twisted in a mocking smile. 'No, it's not fires,' he went on, winking at Zametov. 'Now admit it, my dear young man, aren't you desperate to know what I was reading about?'

'Not in the least; I just asked. Can't a fellow ask? Why do you keep on...?'

'Listen, you're an educated man, cultured, aren't you?'

'I finished sixth class at high school,' replied Zametov with dignity.

'Sixth! Well, well, my little cock sparrow! With your parting and your rings—a wealthy man! Phoo, what a pretty little lad!' And Raskolnikov burst out in a nervous laugh, right in Zametov's face. Zametov drew back, not exactly affronted but extremely astonished.

'Phew, how peculiar you are!' repeated Zametov in a very serious voice. 'It looks to me as if you're still delirious.'

'Delirious? Not at all, my little sparrow!... So I'm odd, am I? Well, and are you curious about me, then? Curious, eh?'

'Yes, I am.'

'What I was reading, perhaps? What I was searching for? I mean, look what a lot of papers I had them bring me! Suspicious, eh?'

'Well, so tell me then.'

'All ears, are we?'

'What d'you mean, ears?'

'I'll tell you what I mean about ears. Later. And meanwhile, my dear friend, I'll announce to you... no, I mean I'll "confess"... No, that's not right either. "I'll make a statement, and you take it down", that's what! So I'm making a statement that I was reading, I was interested in... I was looking... searching...' Raskolnikov screwed up his eyes and waited. 'And that was the reason I came here—looking for something about the killing of that old woman,' he brought out eventually, almost in a whisper, bringing his face right up to Zametov's. Zametov was staring straight back at him, without moving or drawing back. The strangest thing of all, Zametov thought later on, was that this silence lasted a full minute, and for the whole of that minute they went on staring at one another.

'Well so what, if you were reading that?' he suddenly cried out in impatient astonishment. 'What's it to me? What does it matter?'

'This is the very same old woman,' went on Raskolnikov, still in a whisper, not flinching at Zametov's outburst, 'the same one that you were all talking about in the police office when I fell in a faint. There now, d'you get it?'

'What do you mean? "Get" what?' said Zametov in a voice almost of alarm.

In an instant Raskolnikov's serious, impassive face was transformed, and suddenly he exploded in the same nervous giggle as a moment ago, as if he simply couldn't contain himself. And at that very instant he recalled with extraordinary clarity a certain moment in the recent past, when he had been standing behind a door, holding an axe, and the bolt was shaking up and down, and those men behind the door had been cursing and battering the door, and he had suddenly longed to call out to them, curse them back, stick out his tongue at them, mock them, and burst out laughing, and laugh and laugh and laugh!

'Either you're mad, or...' said Zametov, and stopped as if stunned by a thought that had suddenly taken shape in his mind.

'Or? Or what? What is it? Go on, say it!'

'Nothing!' replied Zametov angrily. 'It's all nonsense!'

Both men fell silent. After his sudden paroxysmal outburst of laughter, Raskolnikov had suddenly become thoughtful and melancholy. He leaned his elbows on the table and rested his head on one hand. He seemed to have forgotten Zametov altogether. The silence lasted quite a time.

'Why don't you drink your tea?' said Zametov. 'It'll get cold.'

'Eh? What? Tea?... All right...'—Raskolnikov took a gulp from his glass, put a piece of bread in his mouth, and then, glancing at Zametov, suddenly seemed to remember where he was, and pulled himself together. At the same time his face again took on its former mocking expression. He went on drinking his tea.

'There are lots of these swindlers about nowadays,' said Zametov. 'Just recently I was reading in the "Moscow News" that they'd caught a whole gang of forgers in Moscow. There were quite a number of them, counterfeiting banknotes.'

'Oh, that was ages ago! I read about it last month,' replied Raskolnikov calmly. 'So you reckon they're swindlers?' he added with a smirk.

'What else would you call them?'

'Them? They're just children, beginners, not swindlers! Four dozen people getting in on it together! It doesn't make sense! Three people would be too many, and even then each of them would have had to trust the others more than he trusted himself. Otherwise all it takes is for one to get drunk and blab, and they're done for! Beginners! Hiring unreliable stooges to change their banknotes in offices—how can you hand over a job like that to the first comer? Well, just suppose that even those beginners had got away with it, and each of them passed off a million or so—what then? What about the rest of their lives? Each one of them depending on all the others for the rest of their lives! Better hang yourself right away! They couldn't even get the notes changed properly. This man was changing one in an office, he got handed five thousand, and his hands shook. He counted up four bundles of a thousand, and then picked up the fifth without counting it, took it on trust, just so he could pocket the lot and get away fast. Well, and the people got suspicious. And the whole thing was blown, just because of one idiot. How can you go on like that?'

'Because his hands shook?' Zametov took him up. 'No, that can happen. Yes, I'm absolutely certain that can happen. Sometimes you just can't help it.'

'Can't help it?'

'And I suppose you'd hold out? Well, I wouldn't! Going through a terrible ordeal like that for a hundred-rouble pay-off! Going in with a forged note—and where?—into a bank, where they're all experts at that sort of thing. No, I'd go to pieces. Wouldn't you?'

All of a sudden Raskolnikov was terribly tempted to stick out his tongue again. Momentary shivers ran up his spine.

'I wouldn't do it like that,' he began in a faraway voice. 'This is how I'd set about changing the notes: I'd count over the first thousand, say four times, beginning at this end and then at that one, looking closely at every note, and then I'd start on the second thousand. I'd start counting it, get halfway through, and then pull out some fifty-rouble note or other, hold it up to the light, turn it over and hold it up again, checking to see if it was a fake. "I'm concerned", I'd say, "because a relation of mine was swindled out of twenty-five roubles this way the other day." And I'd tell the whole story. And then when I started counting the third thousand—no, I'm sorry, I'd probably have made a mistake in the second thousand, I'd have counted up the seventh hundred wrong, and got worried, and I'd drop the third thousand and go back to the second one—and go on like that through the whole five thousand. And when I finished, I'd take out a note from the fifth thousand, and another one from the second, and hold them up to the light again, and get all worried and say "would you change these, please?"—and I'd get the clerk into such a state that he just couldn't wait to get shot of me! And when I was all done, I'd go to the door and open it—and no, I'd come back again and ask about something, get something explained to me. That's how I'd do it!'

'My, what terrible things you're saying!' laughed Zametov. 'But all that's just talk—if you really did set about it, you'd be certain to mess things up. In my view, it's not just you and me—even a hardened, desperate person can't be sure of himself. Just for example—in our own district, that old woman got murdered. You'd think that was done by some desperate fellow, risking everything in broad daylight; only a miracle saved him. But his hands shook too. He didn't manage to rob her, he lost his nerve, that's obvious from all the facts.'

Raskolnikov seemed almost hurt.

'Obvious! But you go ahead and catch him now!' he cried, maliciously taunting Zametov.

'Well, they'll catch him all right.'

'Who will? You? You're going to catch him? You'll wear yourselves out trying. The main question for all of you is—is a man spending money or not? He had no money before, and now he's suddenly throwing his money about—so how could it be anyone else? But a child could prove you wrong if it wanted to!'

'That's the point, that's what they all do,' replied Zametov, 'commit a clever murder, risk their lives, and then make straight for the drinking den. It's their spending that gets them caught. They're not all as smart as you are. You wouldn't have gone off drinking, of course, would you?'

Raskolnikov frowned and looked hard at Zametov.

'You seem to have got a taste for this—and you'd like to know what I would have done?' he asked with some displeasure.

'Yes, I would,' replied Zametov. He seemed to be looking at Raskolnikov and talking far too seriously.

'Very much?'

'Yes, very much.'

'Very well. This is what I would have done,' began Raskolnikov, suddenly bringing his face right up to Zametov's again, staring straight into his eyes and once more speaking in a whisper, this time causing Zametov to start. 'This is what I would have done. I would have taken the money and the things, and when I left I wouldn't have gone into any building, I'd have gone straight to some derelict place where there was nothing but fences, and almost nobody about—some kitchen garden or something of the sort. I'd have scouted around the place in advance and found some kind of stone there, something weighing forty to sixty pounds, somewhere in a corner by a fence, a stone that might have been lying there ever since the house was built. I'd lift that stone—there would have to be a hollow under it—and I'd put all the things and the money into the hollow, and I'd put the stone back on top, just as it was lying before, and I'd press the earth down with my foot, and walk off. And then I wouldn't touch it for a year, or two years, or three—and now go and find your murderer! Vanished into thin air!'

'You're mad!' said Zametov, also in a whisper for some reason; and then he moved right away from Raskolnikov. The latter's eyes sparkled, he grew terribly pale and his upper lip twitched and trembled. He leaned right over to Zametov, as close as he could, and began silently moving his lips. This lasted about half a minute. He knew what he was doing, but couldn't stop himself. The terrible word trembled on his lips, as the latch on the door had trembled then. At any moment it could all have come out, he could have let the latch go, he could have spoken it aloud!

'And supposing it was me that killed the old woman and Lizaveta?' he suddenly said; and then remembered himself. Zametov gave him a wild look and grew as white as a sheet. His face twisted into a smile.

'But that's not possible, is it?' he said, almost inaudibly.

Raskolnikov gave him an angry look.

'Admit it—you believed me! Didn't you? You did!'

'Not at all! Now less than ever!' replied Zametov hastily.

'Got you at last! Got you, my little cock sparrow! That must mean you did believe it before, if you believe it "now less than ever"!'

'Not in the least!' cried Zametov, visibly confused. 'Were you scaring me like that just to get me to this point?'

'So you don't believe it? Then what did you talk about after I left the office that day? And why was Lieutenant Gunpowder quizzing me after I'd fainted? Hey, you!' he called out to the waiter, getting up and taking his cap, 'what do I owe?'

'Just thirty kopeks, sir,' replied the waiter as he ran up.

'And here's another twenty for you. Look what a lot of money!' he said to Zametov, stretching out his trembling hand full of banknotes. 'Red ones, blue ones, twenty-five roubles. Wherever from? And where did I get my new clothes? When you know that I didn't have a single kopek! I'm sure you've been questioning my landlady already... Well, that'll do! *Assez causé!** Till our next meeting... our very pleasant meeting!...

He left, trembling all over with a kind of wild, hysterical emotion, but one that contained an element of almost unendurable relish. Yet he was gloomy, and terribly tired. His face was distorted as if he had just suffered a stroke. His exhaustion was mounting fast. His energy came and went, aroused and summoned in a sudden burst at the onset of an irritant stimulus, and waning just as fast when the sensation faded.

When Zametov was left on his own, he went on sitting in the same place, deep in thought. Raskolnikov had unexpectedly overturned all his ideas about a particular point, and had now fixed his opinion once and for all.

'Ilya Petrovich is a blockhead!' he decided firmly.

Just as Raskolnikov opened the street door, he suddenly ran into Razumikhin in the doorway, on his way in. Neither had seen the other till the last moment, so that they almost crashed their heads together. They stood for a time looking each other up and down. Razumikhin was in a state of total amazement, but suddenly an ominous flash of fury, real fury showed in his eyes.

'So that's where you are!' he shouted at the top of his voice. 'Left your bed and ran away! And there was I, even searching for him under his bed! They were looking for you up in the attic! I almost thrashed Nastasia because of you... And this is where you are! Rodka, what does this mean? Tell me the whole truth! Confess! Do you hear?'

'What it means is that I'm sick to death of the lot of you, and I want to be alone,' replied Raskolnikov coolly.

'Alone? When you can't even walk, and your face is white as a sheet, and you're gasping for breath! Idiot!... What were you up to in the "Crystal Palace"? Tell me the truth, now!'

'Let me go!' said Raskolnikov, trying to pass. Razumikhin, quite beside himself at this, grabbed him hard by the shoulder.

'Let you go? How dare you tell me to let you go? Do you know what I'm going to do with you now? Pick you up in my arms, tie you up, carry you bodily to your home, and lock you up!'

'Listen, Razumikhin,' Raskolnikov began quietly and seemingly quite calmly. 'Can't you see that I don't want your charity? Why keep forcing your good deeds on people who... don't give a damn? People who really just can't bear them? What did you hunt me down for, when I first fell ill? For all you know, I might have been very glad to die! And today—didn't I manage to make it clear that you're tormenting me— that I'm sick of you! What's the point of going on torturing people? I swear to you that all this is seriously stopping me getting better, because it constantly gets on my nerves. After all, Zosimov left me just a while back so as not to irritate me! And you, too, for God's sake get off my back! What right have you to restrain me forcibly, anyway? Can't you see that I'm completely in my right mind now? Tell me, just tell me how I can get you to stop pestering me and doing me good deeds? Perhaps I'm ungrateful, perhaps I'm mean, but for God's sake leave me alone, everybody! Leave me alone! Leave me alone!'

He had started calmly, enjoying in advance all the venom he was about to pour out; but by the end he was beside himself, panting with fury as he had been with Luzhin earlier on.

Razumikhin stood and thought for a minute, and then let go of his hand.

'Well then, go to hell!' he said quietly, almost meditatively. 'Wait!' he suddenly roared when Raskolnikov was about to walk away. 'Listen to me. Let me tell you this: you're all, every last one of you, windbags and show-offs! The moment you find something to suffer about, you fuss over it like a hen with her egg! And even then you're poaching from other authors. You haven't a trace of independent life in you. You're all made of whale oil, with whey instead of blood! I don't trust a single one of you! All you care about, wherever you are, is making sure you don't look like human beings! Sto-o-op!' he cried with redoubled fury, noticing that Raskolnikov was once more trying to leave. 'Wait till I've finished! You know I've got a house-warming party today, there may be people there already, I left my uncle at home to let them in, I just dropped by there a minute ago. So now, if you weren't an idiot, a stupid idiot, a senseless idiot, a translation from some foreign language—you see, Rodia, you're a clever lad, I grant you, but you're an idiot!—so there you are, if you weren't an idiot you'd do better to come round to my place and spend the evening with us, instead of wearing your shoe leather out to no purpose. After all, you've come out anyway, so what would it matter? I'd draw up such a nice soft armchair for you, the landlady has one... A glass of tea, a bit of company... Or if you don't want that, you could lie down on my couch—you'd still be there amongst us... And Zosimov will be there too. So you'll come, won't you?'

'No.'

'Yes you will!' cried Razumikhin impatiently. 'How can you know? You can't answer for your own actions! And you don't understand a thing... I've done the same as you a thousand times, quarrelled with people—and then come running back... You feel ashamed of yourself—and want a bit of company again! So remember—Pochinkov's house, third floor...'

'If you go on like this, you'll be letting people beat you up, Mr Razumikhin, just for the pleasure of doing them a good turn.'

'Who? Me? I'd twist their nose off if they even thought of it! Pochinkov's house, number forty-seven, Babushkin's apartment...'

'I shan't come, Razumikhin!' And Raskolnikov turned and walked away.

'I'll bet you do!' Razumikhin shouted after him. 'Or else you're... or else I don't want to know you! Hey, wait a minute! Is Zametov there?'

'Yes.'

'Did you see him?'

'Yes.'

'And talk to him?'

'Yes.'

'What about? Oh well, blast you, don't tell me. Pochinkov's, forty-seven, Babushkin's, remember!'

Raskolnikov walked to Sadovaya Street and turned the corner. Razumikhin gazed after him thoughtfully. Eventually he shrugged, turned to go into the building, but stopped halfway down the steps.

'Damn it!' he went on, almost aloud, 'he talks sense, but it looks as if... But I'm an ass myself! Don't madmen talk sense too? And as far as I could see, that's just what Zosimov was afraid of!' He tapped his forehead. 'And what if... well, how can one let him go about on his own? He might even drown himself... Oh, I slipped up there! It won't do!' And he ran back after Raskolnikov, but there was no sign of him. He shrugged and hurried to the 'Crystal Palace' again, to question Zametov.

Raskolnikov walked straight to the —— Bridge,* stopped halfway across by the railing, leaned both elbows on it, and looked along the bridge. After parting with Razumikhin he had grown so weak that he had barely managed to drag himself here. He felt like sitting or lying down on the roadway somewhere. Leaning over the water, he was mechanically watching the last rosy glow of the sunset, gazing at a row of buildings as they grew darker in the gathering twilight; and at the distant little window of an attic somewhere on the left bank, which glowed as though on fire in the last rays of the sun that struck it just at that moment; and at the darkening waters of the canal—he seemed to be examining the water with close attention. Eventually he started seeing red circles before his eyes, the houses shimmered, and the passers-by, the embankments, the carriages, everything began to spin and dance around him. Suddenly he gave a start; it might have been this frightful, horrible sight that saved him from fainting. He sensed someone standing close by him on his right, and looked and saw a tall woman wearing a headscarf, with a long, yellow, sunken face and hollow red-rimmed eyes. She was looking straight at him, but evidently not seeing anything, nor distinguishing one person from another. Suddenly she leaned her right arm on the rail, raised her right leg and swung it over the barrier, then the left leg, and threw herself into the canal. The dirty water parted and covered its victim for a moment, but soon the drowning woman floated to the surface again and the current carried her away, face downwards, her head and legs in the water, her skirt ballooning above it like a pillow.

'She's drowned herself! Drowned herself!' cried dozens of voices. People came running, spectators crowded on both banks and on the bridge around Raskolnikov, pressing and jostling him from behind.

'Gracious, but that's our Afrosinyushka!' wailed a woman somewhere close by. 'Oh Lord, help her, someone! Oh, kind people, get her out!'

'Get a boat! A boat!' cried people in the crowd.

But there was no need for a boat any more. A policeman had run down the steps to the canal, thrown off his greatcoat and boots, and leapt into the water. There was no difficulty about it: the drowning woman was floating downstream a couple of yards from the foot of the steps. He took hold of her clothes in his right hand, while his left managed to grab the pole that his comrade stretched out to him, and the woman was pulled out at once. They laid her on the stone steps, where she soon came to herself, sat up and began sneezing and sniffing, aimlessly wiping her wet clothes with her hands. She said nothing.

'She's drunk herself silly, friends, drunk herself silly,' wailed the same female voice, close to Afrosinyushka by now. 'The other day she tried to hang herself, we cut her down. I'd just gone out to the shop, and left my little girl to look after her—and now look what she's done! She's a respectable woman, sirs, a neighbour of ours, second house from the end, right here...'

The crowd began to disperse; the policemen were still busy with the drowning woman, and someone called out something about the police office... Raskolnikov observed everything with a strange feeling of indifference and detachment. He began to feel repelled. 'No, it's filthy... that water... better not,' he muttered to himself. 'Nothing's going to happen,' he added, 'no point waiting. What's all that about the police office... And why isn't Zametov in his office? It opens after nine o'clock...' He turned away from the railings and looked around.

'Well, all right then! Why not?' he said firmly, walking away from the bridge in the direction of the police office. His heart was empty and numb. He didn't want to think about anything. Even his dejection had passed, and there was not a vestige of the energy he had felt when he left his house to 'finish with it all'! Nothing was left but total apathy.

'Anyway, that's one way out!' he thought, walking slowly and limply along the canal embankment. 'I'll put an end to it, because that's what I want... But is it a way out, really? Oh, never mind! I'll have my arm's-width of ground—ha–ha! But what an ending! Is it really the end? Shall I tell them or not? Oh... damn it! And how tired I am! If only I could lie down, or sit down somewhere, quickly! The most shameful thing is that it was all done so very stupidly. But I don't care about that either. Phoo, what nonsense comes into one's head...'

To get to the police office, he had to walk straight ahead and then take the second turning to the left; it was only a matter of a few yards. But when he reached the first turning he stopped and thought a moment, then turned into the alleyway and took a roundabout route passing along two other streets, perhaps for no reason at all, but perhaps to delay matters for another minute, to gain some time. He was walking along looking down at the ground. Suddenly he felt as if someone had whispered in his ear. He looked up and saw that he was standing by *that* house, right by the gateway. He hadn't been here, or passed by, since *that* evening.

Drawn on by an irresistible, incomprehensible desire, he entered the building, walked through the gateway, took the first entrance on the right and started up the familiar staircase towards the fourth floor. The steep, narrow staircase was very dark. He stopped on each landing and looked curiously around. On the first-floor landing, one of the window frames had been taken out: 'it wasn't like that then', he thought. And here was the second-floor flat where Nikolashka and Mitka had been working: 'locked, and the door newly painted; so it's up for rent'. And the third floor... and the fourth... 'Here!' He stopped in amazement: the door to the flat was wide open and there were people inside, he could hear voices. He hadn't expected that at all. He hesitated a little, then climbed the last few steps and entered the flat.

This was also being redecorated, and there were workmen there. This rather astonished him; for some reason he had been expecting to find everything just as he had left it then, perhaps even with the dead bodies lying on the floor as they had been. But now—bare walls, no furniture... how strange! He walked through to the window and sat down on the sill.

There were only two workmen there, both lads, one rather older, the other much younger. They were pasting up new white wallpaper with little lilac-coloured flowers in place of the old, worn, tattered yellow paper. For some reason Raskolnikov was terribly displeased by this—he looked with dislike at the new wallpaper as if sorry that everything was so changed.

The workmen had evidently worked late and were now hurriedly rolling up their paper and getting ready to go home. They barely noticed Raskolnikov's arrival. They were talking together, so Raskolnikov folded his arms and listened.

'So she comes to me, that one, in the morning,' said the older man to the younger, 'bright and early, all dressed up to the nines. "So what are you doing parading around here, showing off to me like that?"—"Tit Vasilyich," she says, "from now on I want to do everything you tell me." So that's how it was! In all her glad rags, too—just like a magazine!'

'And what's a magazine, uncle?' asked the younger one. 'Uncle' was evidently teaching him the trade.

'A magazine, my lad, it's got pictures in it, coloured ones, and they get sent to the tailors round here every Saturday, by post from foreign lands, to tell them how people have to dress themselves, men and women too. From drawings, I mean. The male sex mostly get their pictures done in long coats, but when you get to the females, boy, the fancy stuff they've got on, you could pay out all you've got and you'd never afford any of it!'

'What a lot of things they've got in this Petersburg town!' cried the young lad in delight. 'Aside from mum and dad, they've got everything!'

'Aside from that, my lad, you'll find everything,' confirmed the older man magisterially.

Raskolnikov got up and walked to the next room, where the trunk, the bed, and the chest of drawers had stood. Without its furniture, the room looked terribly small. The wallpaper hadn't been changed; in the corner there was a clear outline showing where the icon stand had been. He looked around and went back to his windowsill. The older workman looked suspiciously at him.

'What do you want here?' he asked suddenly.

Instead of answering, Raskolnikov stood up, went out to the landing, took hold of the bell and tugged it. The same little bell, the same tinny sound! He pulled it a second time, and a third, listening and remembering. He began to recall the old, excruciating, frightening, horrible feeling, ever more clearly and vividly; he winced with every pull at the bell, feeling more and more pleasure each time.

'What do you want? Who are you anyway?' cried the workman, coming out to him. Raskolnikov went back in to the flat.

'I want to rent this flat,' he said, 'so I'm looking round it.'

'They don't rent flats out at night. Anyway, you have to come with the porter.'

'The floor's been washed; is it going to be painted?' went on Raskolnikov. 'No blood there?'

'What blood?'

'An old woman was killed here, and her sister. There was a whole pool of it here.'

'What kind of a person are you?' cried the workman uneasily.

'Me?'

'Yes.'

'You'd like to know, would you?... Come along to the police, I'll tell you there.'

The workmen stared at him in amazement.

'We've got to go now, we're late. Come along, Alyoshka. Time to lock up,' said the older workman.

'Well then, let's go!' replied Raskolnikov indifferently, leading the way and walking slowly downstairs. 'Hey, porter!' he called when he reached the gateway.

A group of people stood by the street entrance, watching the passers-by: the two porters, a countrywoman, a tradesman in a long coat, and some others. Raskolnikov went straight up to them.

'What do you want?' demanded one of the porters.

'Have you been to the police office?'

'Just been there. Why?'

'Are the staff there?'

'Yes.'

'The assistant too?'

'He was there just now. What do you want?'

Raskolnikov made no reply but stood near the others, pondering.

'Came to look over the flat,' said the older workman, joining the group.

'What flat?'

'The one we're working in. "Why did they wash away the blood?" he wants to know. Says there was a murder done here, and he's come to take the flat. Then he starts ringing the bell, almost tore it off he did. And says, let's go to the police, I'll tell you all about it there. Couldn't shake him off.'

The porter frowned and stared at Raskolnikov in astonishment.

'So who are you anyway?' he cried, more threateningly.

'I am Rodion Romanovich Raskolnikov, former student, living in Shil's house, in a lane not far from here, flat fourteen. Ask the porter, he knows me...'

Raskolnikov spoke languidly and meditatively, without turning his head, but continuing to stare into the darkening street.

'But why did you go into the flat?'

'To have a look.'

'What's there to look at?'

'Why don't we take him off to the police?' broke in the man in the long coat, and shut his mouth.

Raskolnikov glanced back at him over his shoulder, took a good look, and then said just as calmly and languidly:

'Let's go!'

'Yes, take him down!' insisted the man, more confidently. 'What was he asking about *that* for, what's on his mind, eh?'

'Perhaps he's drunk, perhaps he isn't—God knows!' muttered the workman.

'What's it to do with you?' cried the porter again, getting really angry. 'What are you going on for?'

'Frightened to go to the police now, are you?' asked Raskolnikov mockingly.

'Who's frightened? What are you going on about?'

'A crook, that's what he is!' cried the woman.

'What's the good of talking to him?' shouted the second porter, a giant peasant with his coat hanging open and a bunch of keys in his belt. 'Get out!... A crook, right enough... Get out!'

And seizing Raskolnikov by the shoulder, he threw him out into the street. Raskolnikov almost tumbled head over heels, but saved himself, pulled himself upright, gave a silent look at all the bystanders, and walked on.

'A weird customer,' said the workman.

'People have got weird nowadays,' said the woman.

'Ought to have taken him to the police,' added the man in the coat.

'No need to get mixed up in that,' declared the huge porter. 'A crook, sure as fate! Asking for trouble, clear enough, but if you get mixed up in it, you'll never get out again... I know all about that!'

'So do I go there or not?' wondered Raskolnikov, stopping in the middle of the roadway at a crossroads and looking around as if expecting a decision from someone else. But no reply came; all was as silent and dead as the stones he trod on, dead for him, for him alone. Suddenly, in the gathering darkness, he made out a crowd in the distance, a couple of hundred steps away at the end of the street; people were talking and shouting... A carriage stood in the midst of the crowd. A flame flickered in the street. 'What's up?' thought Raskolnikov, turning to his right and making for the crowd. He seemed to be ready to clutch at anything, and smiled a cold smile at the thought, because he had taken a firm decision to go to the police, and he knew for certain that everything would soon be over.

CHAPTER VII

A GENTLEMAN'S carriage of great elegance, harnessed to a pair of sprightly greys, stood in the middle of the road. There was no one inside, and the coachman himself had come down from the box and was standing beside it, while someone held the horses by their bridles. A crowd of people was milling around, with policemen in front. One of them was holding a lighted lantern; he was bending down to throw light on something lying on the roadway next to the wheels. Everyone was talking, shouting, lamenting; the coachman seemed dazed, just repeating every now and then:

'How dreadful! Oh Lord, how dreadful!'

Raskolnikov pushed his way through as best he could, and at last saw the object of all this bustle and curiosity. Lying on the ground was a man whom the horses had just run over; he appeared to be unconscious. He was very shabbily dressed, though in 'respectable' clothes, and was covered in blood. Blood ran from his face and head; his face was crushed, lacerated, and disfigured. It was clear that he was gravely injured.

'Blessed saints!' lamented the coachman. 'What else could I have done? If I'd been racing the horses or I hadn't shouted at him—but I was driving slow and quiet. Everyone saw it, they'll all tell you the same. We all know a drunk can't even light a candle...* I saw him crossing the road, staggering, almost falling over—so I shouted out to him once, and then twice, and then three times, and reined in the horses—and he fell right under their hooves! Was it on purpose, or was he terribly drunk...? The horses are young ones, high-strung—they shied, and he cried out, and that made them worse... and then it happened.'

'That's just how it was!' someone backed him up from the crowd.

'Yes, he was shouting, that's the truth, three times he shouted out,' said another.

'Three times, that's right! Everyone heard him!' cried a third.

The coachman wasn't particularly upset or scared. Evidently the coach belonged to some rich and important person who was waiting somewhere for it to arrive; and the policemen were naturally doing all they could to enable this to happen. The injured man would have to be taken to the police and then to hospital. No one knew his name.

Meanwhile Raskolnikov had pushed his way through and bent down close to the victim. Suddenly a lantern threw a bright light on the man's face, and Raskolnikov recognized him.

'I know him! I know him!' he cried, getting right to the front. 'He's a clerk, a retired clerk, Titular Councillor, Marmeladov! He lives here, close by, in Kozel's house. A doctor, quick! I'll pay, here!' He pulled out some money from his pocket and showed it to a policeman. He was amazingly agitated.

The policemen were glad to know who the victim was. Raskolnikov gave his own name and address, and begged them as earnestly as if it had been his own father, to have the unconscious Marmeladov carried home.

'It's right here, three houses away,' he fussed. 'Kozel's house, a German, a rich man... He'll have been drunk, for sure, and trying to get home. I know him... He's a drinker... He's got a family there, a wife and children, he's got a daughter. Don't waste time taking him off to hospital—there'll be a doctor in the house, I'm sure! I'll pay, I'll pay!... At least he'll have his own people looking after him, they'll help him right away, otherwise he'll die before you can get him to hospital...'

He even managed to slip some money surreptitiously to the policeman. In any event, the whole business was clear and legal, and this way help was closer at hand. People were found to lift up and carry the injured man. Kozel's house was about thirty yards away. Raskolnikov walked behind, carefully supporting the man's head and guiding the others.

'This way, this way! You'll have to carry him upstairs with his head up, turn him around... that's it! I'll pay, I'll be very grateful!'

Katerina Ivanovna, as ever when she had a free minute, had just begun walking up and down her little room, from the window to the stove and back again, her arms tightly folded across her chest, talking to herself and coughing. She had recently started talking more and more to her eldest daughter, ten-year-old Polenka, who maybe still didn't understand much, but understood very well that her mother needed her. She would always follow her mother with her big, intelligent eyes, and spare no effort to pretend that she understood everything. On this occasion Polenka was undressing her little brother, who had been poorly all day, and getting him ready for bed. The boy was waiting for his shirt to be changed so that it could be washed that same night, and meanwhile sat silently on a chair with a serious expression on his face. He sat bolt upright, motionless, his little legs stretched out in front of him, feet pressed together, heels forward, toes apart. He was listening to what his Mama was saying to his sister, his lips pouting, eyes starting out of his head, without moving an inch, just as all good little boys are supposed to sit when they're being undressed for bed. A little girl even smaller than him, in abject rags, was standing by the screen waiting her turn.

The door to the stairway was open, to give what little relief could be had from the waves of tobacco smoke billowing in from the other rooms, forcing the poor consumptive woman to cough long and agonizingly. Katerina Ivanovna seemed to have grown even thinner over the past week, and the red spots on her cheeks burned even brighter than before.

'You wouldn't believe, Polenka,' she said, walking up and down the room, 'you couldn't even imagine how happy and prosperous we were when we lived at home with Papenka, and how that drunkard has ruined me and is going to ruin you all! Papasha was a State Councillor, almost a Governor; he only had one more step to take—everyone would drive up to our house and say "We all regard you as our Governor already, Ivan Mikhailich." When I... khhh! when I... khhh-khhh-khhh... Oh, curse this life!' she cried, bringing up the phlegm and clutching her chest, 'when I... oh, when I went to my last ball, at the Marshal's... Princess Bezzemelnaya—who gave me her blessing later on, when I married your Papa, Polia—she saw me and straight away asked "Isn't that the pretty young lady who did the shawl dance at the end of term?"... (That torn bit has got to be mended; you ought to get your needle and darn it straight away, as I taught you, otherwise... khhh! tomorrow... khhh-khhh-khhh! he'll tear it even worse)' she cried out over a fit of coughing. 'Prince Shchegolskoy, he was a Gentleman of the Bedchamber,* he'd only just arrived from Petersburg... he danced the mazurka with me,* and the very next day he wanted to drive to my house with a proposal of marriage; but I myself thanked him in the most flattering terms and said that my heart had long belonged to another. That other was your father, Polia. My Papenka was terribly cross... Is the water ready? All right, pass the shirt; and the stockings?... Lida,'—she turned to her younger daughter—'you can sleep without a nightshirt tonight, you'll manage somehow... and put your stockings there too... we'll wash them all in one go... Why doesn't that drunken tramp come home? He's worn his shirt out till it's more like some kind of dishrag, torn it to shreds... Better do it all together, and not wear myself out two nights running! Oh my God! Khhh-khhh-khhh-khhh! Not again! What's this?' she cried, looking at the crowd on the threshold and the people pushing their way into her room, carrying something. 'What's this? What are they carrying? God Almighty!'

'Where can we put him?' asked the policeman, looking around him, once the unconscious and bleeding figure of Marmeladov had been brought into the room.

'Onto the couch! Lay him straight down on the couch, with his head up here,' Raskolnikov directed.

'Run over in the street! Drunk!' called someone from the doorway.

Katerina Ivanovna stood there, pale and fighting for breath. The children were all terrified. Little Lidochka screamed and flung herself at Polenka, hugging her and trembling all over.

When Marmeladov had been laid down, Raskolnikov ran over to Katerina Ivanovna.

'In God's name, keep calm, don't be scared!' he gabbled at her. 'He was crossing the road, a carriage ran over him, don't worry, he'll come round, I had them bring him here... I came here once, remember... He'll come round! I'll pay!'

'Got what you wanted, at last!' shrieked Katerina Ivanovna in despair, and rushed over to her husband.

Raskolnikov soon realized that she was not one of those women who instantly fall into a swoon. Next moment there was a pillow under the unfortunate man's head—something no one else had thought of. Then Katerina Ivanovna set about undressing him, examined him, and busied herself about him without losing her head. She had forgotten all about herself, biting her trembling lips and choking back the screams that threatened to burst from her throat.

Raskolnikov meanwhile had persuaded someone to go for the doctor. It turned out that he lived two houses away.

'I've sent for the doctor,' he kept repeating to Katerina Ivanovna. 'Don't worry, I'll pay. Is there any water?... And pass me a napkin, a towel, anything, but quickly; we don't yet know how badly he's hurt... He's hurt, but he's not killed, you can be sure of that... We'll see what the doctor says.'

Katerina Ivanovna rushed over to the window, where a large earthenware basin full of water had been put out on a chair without a seat, in the corner, ready for the overnight wash of her husband's and children's clothes. This night-time wash was done by Katerina Ivanovna with her own hands, at least twice a week and sometimes more; for matters had come to such a pass that there were almost no changes of clothing in the home; each member of the family possessed just one of each item. Yet Katerina Ivanovna couldn't abide dirt, and preferred to torment herself beyond her strength at night, while everyone else was asleep, so that the wet clothes could dry out by morning on a line stretched across the room and she could let everyone put on clean linen, rather than have dirt in the house.

She tried to pick up the basin and carry it over to Raskolnikov, but almost fell over from its weight. Raskolnikov had meanwhile already found a towel, which he moistened in the water and began sponging off the blood that covered Marmeladov's face. Katerina Ivanovna stood beside him, struggling for breath, pressing her hands against her chest. She needed help herself. Raskolnikov was beginning to realize that it might have been a mistake to persuade the people to bring Marmeladov here. The policeman, too, was looking bewildered.

'Polia!' cried Katerina Ivanovna. 'Run over to Sonia, quickly. If you don't find her there, never mind, leave a message that her father's been run over and she's to come here straight away... as soon as she gets back. Hurry, Polia! Here, cover your head with this scarf!'

'Run your vewy fastest!' cried the boy all of a sudden from his chair, and then sat back, silent and upright as before, eyes popping, heels forward and toes apart.

Meantime the room had become so full of people that you couldn't have dropped an apple on the floor. The policemen had left, except for one who had stayed behind for a while and was trying to persuade the onlookers crowding in from the staircase to leave the room. But from the inner rooms of the flat, almost every one of Madame Lippewechsel's lodgers had trooped out, at first only filling the doorway but then flooding in a body right into the room. Katerina Ivanovna flew into a rage.

'You might at least let a man die in peace!' she yelled at the crowd. 'What sort of a show do you think you're gawping at? And smoking cigarettes! Khhh-khhh-khhh! Might as well have kept your hats on!... And there's one who actually has!... Get out! Have some respect for the dead!'

Her cough was choking her, but her fury had its effect. People even seemed a bit afraid of Katerina Ivanovna; one after another, the inhabitants of the building pushed their way out, full of that strange sense of inner satisfaction that always manifests itself, even among the victim's nearest and dearest, when someone is afflicted by a sudden catastrophe; a sensation that not a single one of us is proof against, however sincere our feelings of pity and sympathy.

Voices could be heard outside the door, however, talking of the hospital and saying how it wasn't right to cause such a disturbance for no reason.

'It's not right for a person to be dying!' shouted Katerina Ivanovna, and was just rushing over to open the door and let loose a storm, but in the doorway she ran into Madame Lippewechsel herself, who had just heard about the calamity and hurried along to sort everyone out. She was a very cantankerous and chaotic German.

'*Ach, mein Gott!*' she cried, flinging up her hands, 'your drunken husband horse trampling! Into hospital him! I am in charge here!'

'Amalia Ludwigovna! Kindly consider what you are saying,' began Katerina Ivanovna haughtily (she always spoke haughtily to her land-lady, so that the latter should 'remember her place', and even now she could not deny herself that pleasure). 'Amalia Ludwigovna...'

'I am already telling you one time before, you don't dare speak me Amali Ludwigovna, I am Amali-Ivan!'

'You are not Amali-Ivan, you are Amalia Ludwigovna, and as I am not one of your creeping toadies like Mr Lebeziatnikov, who is giggling out there behind the door' (and indeed laughter could be heard out-side, and a cry of 'They're at it again!'), 'I shall always call you Amalia Ludwigovna, and I have not the faintest idea why you have taken against that name. You can see for yourself what has happened to Semion Zakharovich—he is dying. Would you please lock that door at once and let no one in. Let him at least die in peace! Otherwise I can assure you that your behaviour will be made known tomorrow to the Governor General. The Prince knew me before I was married, and remembers Semion Zakharovich very well; he helped him on many occasions. Everyone knows that Semion Zakharovich had a great many friends and patrons, whom he himself gave up from a sense of honourable pride, being aware of his unfortunate weakness; but now' (pointing at Raskolnikov) 'we are being assisted by this generous-hearted young man of wealth and influence, whom Semion Zakharovich has known since his childhood. And you may be assured, Amalia Ludwigovna...'

All this was uttered at breakneck speed, getting faster and faster every moment; but a cough suddenly cut short Katerina Ivanovna's eloquence. At that moment the dying man regained consciousness and let out a groan, and she ran over to him. He opened his eyes, and with-out recognizing her or understanding where he was, he looked intently at Raskolnikov who was standing over him. The sick man was drawing deep, laboured and infrequent breaths; blood trickled from his lips, and there was perspiration on his brow. Not recognizing Raskolnikov, he began anxiously looking this way and that. Katerina Ivanovna watched him with a sad but stern expression, tears running from her eyes.

'My God! His whole chest is crushed! And all that blood, all that blood!' she said despairingly. 'We must take off all his outer clothes. Turn round a bit, Semion Zakharovich, if you can,' she cried.

Marmeladov recognized her.

'Get a priest!' he said hoarsely.

Katerina Ivanovna went over to the window, leaned her forehead against the frame and cried out in despair:

'Oh, this cursed life!'

'A priest!' repeated the dying man after another minute.

'Ye-e-e-ess, they're getting one!' Katerina Ivanovna shouted at him. He obeyed her shout and said no more. His eyes sought her out, with a timid, anguished look; she came back to his side and stood at the head of the bed. He became a little calmer, but not for long. Soon his eyes rested on little Lidochka, his favourite, who was standing in the corner trembling as though in a fit, and watching him with an astonished, childishly intense gaze.

'A... a...' he said, looking anxiously at her and trying to say something.

'What is it now?' cried Katerina Ivanovna.

'Barefoot! Little one... barefoot!' he mumbled, directing a half-crazed look at the little girl's bare feet.

'Shut up!' yelled Katerina Ivanovna angrily. 'You know perfectly well why she's barefoot!'

'Thank God, the doctor's here!' cried Raskolnikov, much relieved.

The doctor entered. He was a neatly dressed little old German gentleman who looked uncertainly around him and then went over to the patient. He took his pulse, carefully felt his head, and with Katerina Ivanovna's help unbuttoned the whole of the injured man's blood-sodden shirt and laid bare his chest. The whole chest was caved in, crushed and lacerated, and a number of ribs on the right were fractured. On the left, directly over the heart, there was a large, evil-looking yellowish-black patch where a hoof had dealt him a cruel blow. The doctor frowned. The policeman told him that a carriage wheel had caught and dragged him, turning him over and over, for some thirty yards along the roadway.

'It's surprising he ever came round at all,' whispered the doctor quietly to Raskolnikov.

'What do you think of him?' asked Raskolnikov.

'He'll die any minute.'

'Is there really no hope?'

'Not the slightest! He's at his last gasp... Besides, his head is very badly injured... Hmm. Well, we could let some blood... but... it won't help. In five or ten minutes he'll be dead, for certain.'

'Then better bleed him!'

'Very well... Though I warn you it won't be the slightest use.'

At that moment some other steps were heard, the crowd in the doorway moved apart, and a priest appeared in the entrance carrying the sacraments: a little grey-haired old man. He was followed by a policeman who had come in from the street. The doctor immediately made room for him and they exchanged meaning looks. Raskolnikov begged the doctor to wait just a little longer; the doctor shrugged and stayed.

Everyone stood back. The confession was soon over; the dying man probably understood little or nothing, and all he could bring out was indistinct broken noises. Katerina Ivanovna took little Lida, picked the boy off his chair, went off into the corner by the stove, knelt down and made the children kneel in front of her. The little girl did nothing but tremble; but the boy, on his bare knees, was rhythmically raising his little hand, crossing himself in full, and bowing down to the ground, knocking his forehead on the floor—something that appeared to give him particular satisfaction. Katerina Ivanovna was biting her lips and holding back her tears; she too was praying, intermittently adjusting the little boy's shirt; she had managed to cover the girl's bare shoulders with a headscarf she had pulled from the chest of drawers, without rising from her knees or interrupting her prayers. Meanwhile curious onlookers had again begun opening the doors from the inner rooms, while the crowd of spectators on the landing, the tenants from the whole staircase, grew denser and denser, though nobody ventured over the threshold. A single candle end lighted up the whole scene.

At that moment Polenka appeared in the doorway, briskly pushing her way through the crowd on her way back from fetching her sister. She came in, panting for breath after running so fast, took off her headscarf, looked round for her mother, went up to her and said: 'She's coming! I met her in the street!' Her mother pressed her down onto her knees by her side. And out from the crowd, silently and timidly, a girl edged forward; her sudden appearance in this room was a strange sight, in the midst of abject poverty, rags, death, and despair. She too was in rags; her clothing was cheap and gaudy, as befitted her trade, and was governed by the taste and principles that held sway in her particular world; its shameful purpose blatantly displayed. Sonia stood still in the doorway, not crossing the threshold; she looked around her in bewilderment, seemingly not taking anything in; forgetting about her fourth-hand brightly-coloured silk dress, so unseemly here with its ridiculously long train, and the enormous crinoline that blocked the whole doorway, and her light-coloured boots and little parasol which she was carrying though it served no purpose at night, and her absurd round straw hat with its bright flame-coloured plume. Under this rakishly tilted hat there peeped out a thin, pale, frightened little face, open-mouthed, with eyes frozen in horror. Sonia was a small, thin but quite attractive girl of eighteen, fair-haired and with splendid blue eyes. Out of breath with running, she stood staring at the bed and the priest.

Eventually some whispering in the crowd, some words that were spoken, penetrated to her; she cast down her eyes, stepped across the threshold, and stood inside the room, still right next to the door.

The confession and administration of the sacrament were over. Katerina Ivanovna went back to her husband's bedside. The priest withdrew, and on his way out of the room he turned to Katerina Ivanovna to say a few words of encouragement and comfort.

'So what am I to do with them?' she asked sharply and angrily, pointing at her little children.

'God is merciful. Trust in the help of the Most High.'

'Hah! Merciful, but not to us!'

'That's a sin, lady, a sin,' remarked the priest, shaking his head.

'And isn't this a sin?' exclaimed Katerina Ivanovna, pointing to the dying man.

'Those who were the unwitting cause of this may perhaps be willing to compensate you, at least for his lost earnings...'

'You don't understand!' cried Katerina Ivanovna crossly, dismissing his words with a gesture. 'What is there to compensate? He was drunk and fell under the horses' feet of his own accord! What earnings? He never brought in any earnings, all he brought was trouble. He drank away all our money, the drunkard! Stole our money and took it off to the tavern, squandered all their lives and mine on drink! And thank God he's dying! One less to pay for!'

'You should be forgiving him in his dying hour, lady, that's a sin, such feelings are a great sin!'

Katerina Ivanovna had been busying herself around the sick man— giving him water to drink, wiping the sweat and blood from his brow, straightening his pillows—and talking to the priest, just managing to address him from time to time in the midst of what she was doing. But now she almost hurled herself at him in fury.

'Hey, father! That's all words, nothing but words! Forgive him! If he hadn't got run over today, he'd have come home drunk, in his one and only shirt, and that all worn to shreds, and fallen down to sleep it off, while I'd have had my arms in water all night till daybreak, washing his rags and the children's, and then drying them by the window, and as soon as dawn broke I'd have sat down to mend them—and that's how I'd have spent the night!... So why go on about forgiveness? I'd forgiven him anyway!'

A terrible, racking cough interrupted her. She spat into a handkerchief and thrust it towards the priest for him to see, holding her other hand painfully to her chest. The handkerchief was covered in blood...

The priest bowed his head and said nothing.

Marmeladov, in his last agony, did not move his eyes from Katerina Ivanovna's face as she bent over him again. He was trying to say something to her; he had even begun to speak, straining to move his tongue and bringing out inarticulate words; but Katerina Ivanovna, realizing that he was trying to ask her forgiveness, at once shouted peremptorily:

'Sile-e-ence! Stop it!... I know what you're trying to say!' And the sick man fell silent; but at that same moment his wandering gaze fell on the door, and he saw Sonia...

He hadn't noticed her before: she had been standing in the shadows in a corner.

'Who's that? Who's that?' he suddenly asked in a thick, hoarse voice full of alarm, directing his horrified gaze to the door where his daughter was standing, and struggling to raise himself.

'Lie down! Lie do-o-own!' Katerina Ivanovna cried. But he made a superhuman effort and raised himself on his elbow. He stared wildly and fixedly at his daughter for a time, as if he didn't know her. And indeed, he had never before seen her dressed like this. Suddenly he recognized her, standing there crushed and humiliated, full of shame in her gaudy attire, meekly awaiting her turn to bid her dying father farewell. His face was filled with endless suffering.

'Sonia! Daughter! Forgive me!' he cried, and tried to stretch out his hand to her; but without its support he toppled over and crashed down off his couch, striking his face on the floor. People ran to lift him up, and laid him back on the couch, but he was already going. Sonia uttered a faint cry, ran up to hug him, and almost fainted as she held him. He died in her arms.

'He's got what he wanted!' cried Katerina Ivanovna when she saw her husband's dead body. 'And now what are we to do? How am I going to bury him? And what about them—how am I going to feed them tomorrow?'

Raskolnikov came over to her.

'Katerina Ivanovna,' he began, 'last week your late husband told me the whole story of his life, and everything that had happened... Please believe me, he spoke of you with great admiration and respect. Ever since that evening, when I heard how devoted he was to you all, and in particular how he respected and loved you, Katerina Ivanovna, in spite of his wretched weakness—ever since that evening we've been friends... So please allow me now... to repay some of my debt to my departed friend. Here are... twenty roubles, I believe; and if they can be of any help to you, then... I... in short, I'll come to see you—I'll definitely come round... I may actually come tomorrow... Goodbye!'

And he quickly left the room, hurriedly pushing his way through the crowd on the stairs; but among the crowd he suddenly ran into Nikodim Fomich, who had heard about the accident and had come to organize matters in person. The two had never met since the scene in the police office, but Nikodim Fomich recognized him instantly.

'Ah, it's you, is it?' he said to him.

'Died,' replied Raskolnikov. 'The doctor came, and the priest, it's all in order. Don't upset the poor woman too much, she's consumptive. Cheer her up, if you can manage it... You're a kind person, I know...' he added with a mocking smile, looking him straight in the eyes.

'But look at you, all soaked with blood,' remarked Nikodim Fomich, noticing by the light of the lantern that Raskolnikov had a number of fresh stains on his waistcoat.

'Yes, soaked... I'm covered in blood!' said Raskolnikov with a strange look. Then he smiled, nodded and went downstairs.

He went slowly and unhurriedly, in a fever again but without realizing it; he was suddenly overcome by a new, overwhelming awareness of the richness and power of life, flooding over him. It was such a feeling as a man condemned to death might have if he was suddenly told that he had been reprieved. Halfway down the stairs he was caught up by the priest on his way home; Raskolnikov silently made way for him to pass, and they exchanged wordless bows. But when he had almost reached the bottom of the stairs, he heard hurried steps behind him. Someone was running after him. It was Polenka, hurrying to catch him up and calling 'Hey! Mister!'

He turned back to her. She ran down the last steps and stopped right in front of him, on the step above. There was a dim light from the courtyard. Raskolnikov could make out the girl's thin but pretty face, smiling at him with a cheerful, childlike expression. She had come with a message, which she was evidently very pleased to deliver.

'I say, what's your name?... And where do you live?' she asked, panting with her haste.

He laid both hands on her shoulders and gazed at her with a kind of happiness. He was so glad to look at her—he had no idea why.

'Who sent you, then?'

'It was my sister Sonia that sent me,' replied the girl, smiling even more cheerfully.

'I knew it was your sister Sonia that sent you.'

'And my Mama sent me too. When my sister Sonia told me to go, Mama came up too and said "Run along quickly, Polenka!"'

'Do you love your sister Sonia?'

'I love her better than anyone!' announced Polenka with particular emphasis, and her smile suddenly became more serious.

'And will you love me too?'

Instead of an answer he saw the girl's little face and plump lips moving innocently towards him to give him a kiss. Suddenly her matchstick-thin arms were round his neck, her head leaned down against his shoulder, and she burst into quiet sobs, pressing her face harder and harder against him.

'Poor Papochka!' she said after a minute, lifting her tear-stained little face and wiping away the tears with her hands. 'Such terrible things keep happening now,' she went on unexpectedly, wearing that particularly serious expression that children try to put on when they want to talk 'like grown-ups'.

'And did your Papa love you?'

'He loved Lidochka best of all,' she went on very seriously, without smiling, talking in exactly the way grown-ups do; 'he loved her because she's little, and because she's sick too, and he'd always bring her a treat; and he taught us to read, and he taught me grammar and scripture,' she added solemnly, 'and Mama wouldn't say anything, but we know she liked that, and Papochka knew, and now Mamochka wants to teach me French, because it's time for me to be educated.'

'And do you know your prayers?'

'Of course we do! We've known them for ages. Now I'm big, I say my prayers to myself, but Kolia and Lidochka say them aloud with Mama; first they say the "Mother of God", and then another one: "Lord, forgive and bless our sister Sonia", and then "Lord, forgive and bless our old Papa", because our old Papa is dead, and this is our other one, but we pray for the old one too.'

'Polechka, I'm called Rodion; pray for me sometimes too, just say "and thy servant Rodion", that's all.'

'I'm going to pray for you for the rest of my life,' said the little girl passionately; and then she suddenly laughed again, rushed to him, and hugged him hard once more.

Raskolnikov told her his name and address, and promised faithfully to come back next day. The little girl left, absolutely entranced by him. It was after ten when he reached the street. Five minutes later he was standing on the bridge, just where the woman had thrown herself off earlier that day.

'That's enough!' he declared, solemnly and resolutely. 'Away with mirages, away with imaginary terrors, away with phantoms!... Life exists! Wasn't I alive just now? My life didn't die with that old woman!

God rest her soul, and that's enough of her, old lady, time to go to your rest! Now it's time for the reign of reason and light, and... and will, and strength... and now we'll see! Now we'll try our strength!' he added truculently, as if hurling defiance at some dark power. 'And there was I, about to settle for six feet of earth!'

'I'm very weak at present, but... I believe my illness has gone completely. I knew it would pass, when I went out just now. Come to think of it—Pochinkov's house is right near here. I simply must go to Razumikhin's, even if it isn't close by... let him win his bet! He can make fun of me—I don't mind, let him!... Strength, strength is what I need; you can't gain anything without strength; but it takes strength to win strength, that's something they don't know,' he added proudly and confidently, as he walked off the bridge, though he could barely move his legs.

His pride and self-confidence grew with every minute that passed; a mere minute later he was no longer the man he had been a minute before. But what had happened that was so very special, what had changed him so? He himself didn't know; as if clutching at a straw, he suddenly felt that he, too, 'was allowed to live, that life still went on, that his own life hadn't died with the old woman'. Perhaps he had leapt too hastily to this conclusion, but he gave no thought to that.

'But I did ask her to remember "thy servant Rodion" in her prayers,' flashed through his mind; 'well, that was... just in case!' he added, immediately laughing at his boyish joke. He was in excellent spirits.

He had no trouble finding Razumikhin. People already knew the new tenant at Pochinkov's, and the porter showed him the way at once. From halfway up the stairs, he could already hear the noise and lively babble of a large gathering. The door from the stairs was wide open, and exclamations and arguments could be heard. Razumikhin's room was quite big, and there were about fifteen guests there. Raskolnikov stopped in the hallway. Here, behind a partition, two of the landlady's serving girls were busying themselves over two large samovars, bottles, plates, and dishes with pies and snacks sent up from the landlady's kitchen. Raskolnikov asked for Razumikhin, who came running out in delight. It was obvious at first sight that he had drunk a very great deal; although he almost never got drunk, something of the sort was apparent on this occasion.

'Listen,' Raskolnikov said hurriedly, 'I've only come to tell you you've won your bet and that it's true that no one knows what might happen to him. But I can't come in—I'm so weak, I could fall down any minute. So hello and goodbye! Come and see me tomorrow...'

'Do you know what? I'll see you home! If you yourself are telling me how weak you are, then...'

'What about the guests? Who's that curly-headed man who just looked in here?'

'Him? Heaven knows! He must be a friend of my uncle's, unless he's just turned up of his own accord... I'll leave uncle with them; he's really invaluable—what a pity you can't meet him now. Oh well, bother the lot of them! They don't care about me now, and I need to get some fresh air myself. You turned up in the nick of time, my friend—another two minutes and I'd have got into a fight, I promise you! They talk such rubbish... You can't imagine how far people will go, with all the nonsense they talk! Well, of course you can imagine it. Don't we talk nonsense ourselves? Let them say whatever they like. Later on they'll talk sense... Sit down a minute, I'll fetch Zosimov.'

Zosimov pounced almost greedily upon Raskolnikov. It was obvious that he was particularly curious about something. Soon his expression cleared.

'Straight off home to bed,' he declared after examining his patient as best he could. 'And you ought to take a little something before you go to sleep. Will you? I made it up a little while back... a powder.'

'Two if you like,' replied Raskolnikov. And he swallowed the powder straight away.

'It's a very good thing that you're seeing him home,' remarked Zosimov to Razumikhin. 'We'll see how he is tomorrow, but he's not at all bad today: there's a great change from earlier on. One lives and learns...'

'Do you know what Zosimov whispered to me just now, just as we were leaving?' Razumikhin blurted out as soon as they were on the street. 'I'll tell you everything straight, my friend, because they're all fools. Zosimov told me to have a chat with you on the way home, and make you talk too, and then tell him what you said, because he's got it into his head... that you're... crazy, or almost. Just imagine! Firstly, you're three times cleverer than him, and secondly, if you're not crazy then you won't care a damn what nonsense he has in his head, and thirdly, that great lump of meat, who's a surgeon by trade, has become obsessed with mental disease; and in your case, it was your conversation with Zametov today that completely turned his head.'

'Did Zametov tell you all about it?'

'Yes, everything, and a good thing too. I've worked it all out now, and so has Zametov. Well, in a word, Rodia... the point is... I'm a little bit tipsy just now... But that doesn't matter... the point is that this idea... d'you understand me? It's been hatching in their heads... get me? That is, none of them dared say it aloud, because it's the wildest nonsense, and particularly when that painter was arrested, the whole thing was exploded and blown sky-high for good. But why are they such fools? I gave Zametov a bit of a hiding at the time—that's just between ourselves, brother, please don't even give a hint that you know; I can see he's a bit touchy; that happened at Lavisa's—but today, today everything's become clear. And it's mostly because of that Ilya Petrovich! He took advantage of your faint at the police office, but he was ashamed of that himself later on; I know...'

Raskolnikov was listening avidly. Razumikhin, in his cups, was blabbing it all out.

'The reason I fainted then was that it was stuffy and smelt of oil paint,' said Raskolnikov.

'No need to explain! And it wasn't just the paint: you'd been working up a fever for the last month, Zosimov says so himself! And how crushed that lad is now, you simply can't imagine! "I'm not worthy of his little finger!" he says. Meaning yours. He sometimes has kind impulses, you know. But the lesson you gave him today in the "Crystal Palace", that was the peak of perfection! I mean, you frightened him at first, you had him shaking in his shoes! You almost made him believe all that revolting nonsense all over again, and then suddenly you stuck your tongue out at him: "There, look at you, you fell for it!" Perfect! Now he's crushed and wiped out! You're brilliant, I swear you are—that's what they deserve. Oh, I wish I'd been there! He was so looking forward to meeting you just now; and Porfiry wants to as well...'

'Oh... Him, too... But why have they got me down as a lunatic?'

'Well, not a lunatic. Look, my friend, I think I've been saying too much... You see, what struck him then was that you were only interested in that one point. Now it's clear why you're interested; knowing all about it... and the way all that irritated you so much then, and got jumbled up with your illness... My friend, I'm a little bit drunk; but he's got some idea of his own, heaven knows what it is... I'm telling you, he's obsessed with mental illness. But you needn't give a damn about him...'

For half a minute or so, neither said anything.

'Listen, Razumikhin,' Raskolnikov began. 'I want to tell you straight out: I've just been to a dead man's home, a clerk who died... and I gave away all my money there... and what's more, I've just been kissed by a creature who, even if I had really killed someone, would have... well, in short, I saw another person there too... with a flame-coloured feather... but I'm getting mixed up, I'm very weak, give me your arm... here are the stairs...'

'What's up? What's wrong with you?' asked Razumikhin in alarm.

'My head's spinning a little, but that's not the point, the point is that I'm so sad, so sad! As if I was a woman... honestly! Look, what's that? Look! Look!'

'What?'

'Don't you see? The light in my room, see it? Through the crack...'

They had already reached the last flight of stairs, next to the landlady's door, and one could indeed see from below that a light was burning in Raskolnikov's little room.

'That's odd! Perhaps it's Nastasia,' remarked Razumikhin.

'She never comes up to my room at this hour, and anyway she'll have been asleep for hours, but... never mind! Goodnight!'

'What d'you mean? I'm seeing you home, let's go in together!'

'Yes, I know we'll go in together, but I want to shake hands with you here, and take my leave of you here. So give me your hand, and goodbye!'

'What's wrong with you, Rodia?'

'Nothing; let's go in, you'll be a witness...'

They started up the stairs, and it struck Razumikhin that Zosimov might have been right after all. 'Oh dear, I've upset him with all my chatter!' he muttered to himself. Suddenly, as they approached the door, they heard voices in the room.

'What's going on here?' cried Razumikhin.

Raskolnikov was the first to take hold of the latch, and opened the door wide: opened it and stood rooted to the spot.

His mother and sister were sitting on his divan. They had been waiting for him for an hour and a half. Why were they the last people in the world that he expected, or even thought about, in spite of the news he had received, and heard again this very day, that they had set off, they were on their way, they would soon arrive? For the past hour and a half they had been questioning Nastasia, who was still standing there in front of them and had already told them the whole story. They were out of their minds with dread when they were told that he had 'run away today', sick and (according to her story) undoubtedly delirious. 'Dear God, what's happened to him?' They were both in tears; both of them had suffered untold agonies during their hour and a half of waiting.

A cry of rapturous delight greeted Raskolnikov's arrival. They both ran over to embrace him. But he stood there like a dead man: an unbearable sudden realization had struck him like a thunderbolt. He couldn't even raise his arms to embrace them; he couldn't move them at all. His mother and sister were hugging him tightly in their arms, kissing him, laughing, crying... He took a step, staggered, and crashed to the floor in a dead faint.

Alarms, cries of horror, groans... Razumikhin, standing in the doorway, rushed in, seized the sick man in his powerful arms and in an instant had him laid down on the divan.

'It's nothing, it's nothing!' he cried to the mother and sister. 'It's a faint, it doesn't matter! Only just now the doctor was saying that he's much better, he's perfectly well! Get some water! There, now he's coming round, look, he's conscious again!...'

He grabbed Dunechka's hand, so hard that he almost wrenched it off, and bent her down to see: 'Look, he's conscious again.' Mother and sister looked at Razumikhin, as tenderly and gratefully as if he were Providence itself; they had already heard from Nastasia all that Razumikhin had done for Rodia throughout his illness—this 'capable young man', as Pulkheria Alexandrovna Raskolnikova had herself described him that very evening, in a heart-to-heart talk with Dunia.

PART THREE

CHAPTER I

RASKOLNIKOV raised himself and sat up on the divan.

He gestured feebly at Razumikhin to stem his flood of earnest but incoherent reassurances to his mother and sister, then took both women by the hand and gazed silently first at one and then the other. His mother was alarmed by his look, which was eloquent of profound emotion and suffering, but at the same time contained something fixed, almost insane. Pulkheria Alexandrovna burst into tears.

Avdotya Romanovna had turned pale; her hand trembled in her brother's grasp.

'Go away home... with him,' he said in a broken voice, pointing at Razumikhin; 'till tomorrow; tomorrow everything will... Have you been here long?'

'Since this evening, Rodia,' replied Pulkheria Alexandrovna. 'The train was terribly late. But Rodia, I shan't leave you now, not for anything! I'm going to spend the night here, next to...'

'Don't pester me!' he said with a gesture of annoyance.

'I'll stay with him!' cried Razumikhin. 'I shan't leave him for an instant; to hell with all my people back there, they can climb up the walls for all I care! My uncle's in charge there.'

'Oh, how can I thank you!' Pulkheria began, squeezing Razumikhin's hands again, but Raskolnikov interrupted her a second time.

'I can't stand it, I can't stand it!' he repeated testily. 'Don't pester me. That's enough, go away... I can't stand it!'

'Come along, Mamenka, let's just go outside for a minute,' whispered Dunia in alarm. 'We're upsetting him, you can see that.'

'Aren't I allowed to have a look at him then, after three whole years?' wept Pulkheria Alexandrovna.

'Wait!' he stopped them again. 'You keep interrupting me, and my thoughts get mixed up... Have you seen Luzhin?'

'No, Rodia, but he knows we've arrived. We've heard that Piotr Petrovich was kind enough to call on you today, Rodia,' Pulkheria Alexandrovna added rather timidly.

'Yes... kind enough... Dunia, I told Luzhin I'd throw him downstairs, and I sent him to the devil.'

'What do you mean, Rodia? I'm sure you... You can't mean...' began Pulkheria Alexandrovna in alarm; then she looked at Dunia and broke off.

Avdotya Romanovna was looking intently at her brother and waiting for him to go on. Nastasia had done her best to warn them about this quarrel, so far as she had understood it, and they had suffered agonies of bewilderment and suspense.

'Dunia,' went on Raskolnikov with an effort, 'I don't want this marriage to happen, so tomorrow, as soon as you see Luzhin, you're to break it off with him, so we never have to see or hear of him again.'

'My God!' cried Pulkheria Alexandrovna.

'Just think what you're saying, brother!' Avdotya Romanovna burst out heatedly, but at once controlled herself. 'Perhaps you're not up to it just now, you're tired,' she went on meekly.

'You mean I'm delirious? No. You're marrying Luzhin for my sake. But I won't accept the sacrifice. And so, please write a letter, by tomorrow morning, breaking it off. Show it to me in the morning, and have done with him!'

'I can't do that!' cried the girl, very hurt. 'What right have you...'

'Dunechka, you're in a state yourself, stop it! Leave it till tomorrow... Can't you see...?' cried her mother in alarm, running over to Dunia. 'Oh, we'd better leave!'

'Raving!' cried Razumikhin tipsily. 'Otherwise he'd never have dared! He'll have forgotten all that nonsense by tomorrow... Though he really did throw that man out today. That's perfectly true. And the man lost his temper... started speechifying, showing off his education, and then slunk away with his tail between his legs...'

'So it's really true?' lamented Pulkheria Alexandrovna.

'We'll see you tomorrow, brother,' said Dunia compassionately. 'Come along, Mamenka... Goodbye, Rodia!'

'Listen, sister,' he repeated to her as she was leaving, making a last effort, 'I'm not raving. This marriage is a villainous thing. I may be a villain myself, but you don't have to... one's enough... and even if I'm a villain, I couldn't call you sister if you did it. It's either me or Luzhin! Now go away...'

'You're out of your mind! Tyrant!' roared Razumikhin. But Raskolnikov said no more; perhaps he no longer had the strength to answer. He stretched himself out on the divan and turned to the wall in utter exhaustion. Avdotya Romanovna looked questioningly at Razumikhin, with a glint in her dark eyes; Razumikhin actually shuddered under her gaze. Pulkheria Alexandrovna stood thunderstruck.

'I can't possibly go away!' she whispered to Razumikhin in near-despair. 'I'll stay here, somewhere... please see Dunia home.'

'That'll ruin everything!' Razumikhin whispered back in a fury. 'Come out onto the stairs at least. Nastasia, give us some light! I swear to you,' he went on in a half-whisper when they were on the stairs, 'he almost knocked us out, the doctor and me, earlier on! Do you understand? The doctor himself! And the doctor gave in, so as not to irritate him, and went away, and I stayed downstairs to keep watch, but he got dressed and slipped out. And he'll get away again if you irritate him, for all that it's night-time, and do himself some harm...'

'Oh, what are you saying?'

'Anyway, Avdotya Romanovna can't possibly spend the night in a rented room without you! Just think where you are! That villain Piotr Petrovich might at least have found you a flat... Actually, you know, I'm a little bit drunk, that's why I... called him names; pay no attention...'

'But I'll talk to the landlady here,' insisted Pulkheria Alexandrovna, 'I'll beg her to find a corner for Dunia and me tonight. I can't leave him like this, I just can't!'

They were standing in the stairwell, on the landing by the landlady's own door. Nastasia was lighting the way from the bottom step. Razumikhin was in a state of extraordinary agitation. Half an hour ago, while seeing Raskolnikov home, he had indeed been over-talkative (and aware of it), but still perfectly wide awake and almost clear-headed, in spite of the enormous amount he had drunk that evening. But now he was in an almost exalted state, and at the same time it seemed as if all the drink he had swallowed had gone straight to his head once more, with redoubled strength. Standing there with the two ladies, he had seized each of them by the arm, and was remonstrating with them and arguing his case with astonishing frankness. It was probably to reinforce his arguments that he squeezed both their arms so hard, so painfully hard, as though in a vice, almost with every word that he spoke. And he seemed to be quite unashamedly devouring Avdotya Romanovna with his eyes. From time to time the pain would make them wrench their arms out of his enormous, bony paws, but he not only failed to notice that—he pressed them even more tightly to him. If they had commanded him to dive head first down the stairs as a favour to them, he would have obeyed at once, without hesitation or discussion. Pulkheria Alexandrovna, full of anxiety about her Rodia, did indeed feel that this young man was rather too eccentric, and was crushing her arm too hard and painfully, but since at the same time she regarded him as her Providence, she chose not to pay attention to all these strange details. And although

Avdotya Romanovna, no less anxious than her mother, was not a timid person, she still observed with amazement and almost with fear the looks she received from her brother's friend, looks that burned with a wild flame, and it was only her boundless trust, inspired by Nastasia's accounts of this strange man, that stopped her from trying to run away, taking her mother with her. Besides, she realized that it was probably too late for them to run away from him. And ten minutes later she had grown much calmer; Razumikhin had the knack of laying all his cards on the table in a few words, whatever his mood, so that people very quickly understood what sort of a man they were dealing with.

'You can't possibly stay with the landlady, and that's all absolute nonsense!' he insisted to Pulkheria Alexandrovna. 'You may be his mother, but if you stay you'll drive him out of his mind, and then goodness only knows what'll happen! Listen, this is what I'll do. Nastasia is going to sit with him for a while now, and I'll see the two of you home, because you mustn't go through these streets on your own; here in Petersburg, that sort of thing... Oh well, never mind!... And then I'll run straight back here from your place, and within fifteen minutes, on my word of honour, I'll report back to you how he's getting on, whether he's gone to sleep or not, and everything. And then, listen! Then I'll go straight from your place to my home—I've got guests there, they're all drunk—and pick up Zosimov, who's the doctor treating him, he's at my place now, not drunk—no, he's not drunk, that one, he's never drunk! And I'll drag him over to Rodia's and then come straight to you, so within the hour you'll have had two reports on him—one from the doctor, you see, the doctor himself—that's far better than anything I could tell you! And if things are bad, I swear I'll bring you back here myself, but if they're good, then you can go to bed. I'm going to spend the whole night here, in the passage, where he won't hear me; and I'll tell Zosimov to stay at the landlady's so that he's on the spot. Now who's going to be better for him just now, you or the doctor? Surely the doctor's more use, he must be. So off you go home! You can't possibly go to the landlady's now—I can, but you can't, she won't let you in, because... because she's stupid. She'll be jealous of me and Avdotya Romanovna, if you want to know; and of me and you too... but definitely of me and Avdotya Romanovna. She's a most, most peculiar character. Anyway, I'm an idiot myself... Never mind, forget it! Let's go! Will you trust me? Well, will you trust me or not?'

'Come on, Mamenka,' said Avdotya Romanovna. 'I'm sure he'll do as he's promised. He's already brought my brother back to life, and if it's true that the doctor will agree to spend the night here, what could be better?'

'There! You... you... understand me, because you're—an angel!' cried Razumikhin delightedly. 'Let's go! Nastasia! Straight upstairs and sit by him, with a candle; I'll be back in a quarter of an hour...'

Pulkheria Alexandrovna might not have been entirely convinced, but she offered no further resistance. Razumikhin took them both by the arm and dragged them downstairs. But she was still worried about him: 'he may be competent and kind, but is he capable of keeping his promise? Look at the state he's in!'

'Ah, I understand, you think that I'm all in a state!' Razumikhin broke into her train of thought, reading her mind as he strode along the pavement with his enormous steps, leaving the two ladies barely able to keep up with him—which he didn't notice. 'That's nonsense! I mean... I'm drunk as a lord, but that's not the point; it's not drink that's made me like this. It was seeing you two—that was what went straight to my head. But never mind about me! Take no notice; I'm getting it all wrong, I'm not worthy of you... I'm unworthy of you in the highest degree!... But when I've seen you home, I'll go straight to this canal right here, and pour a couple of buckets of water over my head, and that'll be it... If you only knew how much I love you both!... Don't laugh at me, and don't be cross!... You can be cross with everyone, but not me! I'm his friend, so I'm your friend too. That's what I want... I had a premonition of this... last year, there was a particular moment like that... Well, actually, I didn't have a premonition at all, because you've turned up here right out of the blue. And now I probably won't sleep a wink all night. That Zosimov was saying a while ago, he was afraid Rodia might go crazy... That's why we mustn't irritate him...'

'What are you saying!' cried Rodia's mother.

'Did the doctor himself really say that?' asked Avdotya Romanovna in alarm.

'Yes, he did, but it's not true, not true at all. He even gave him some sort of medicine, a powder, I saw it, but then you arrived... Oh dear!... You'd have done better to turn up tomorrow! It's a good thing we left. And now Zosimov will get back to you himself in an hour, and tell you all about it. Now that man, he isn't drunk! And I won't be drunk by then... Whatever was I doing, swilling it down like that? It was because they got me into an argument, damn them! And I'd sworn not to argue!... But they talk such rubbish! Almost got into a fight! I left my uncle in charge there... Well, would you believe it: they insist that one has to be totally impersonal, that's what they really admire! How to avoid being one's own self, how to be as little like oneself as possible! That's the height of progress for them. And if all that rubbish was even their own ideas, but no...'

'Listen,' Pulkheria Alexandrovna interrupted timidly; but that only spurred him on.

'So what do you think?' cried Razumikhin, raising his voice even more. 'D'you think I'm complaining because they're talking nonsense? Not at all! I like people talking nonsense. Talking nonsense is humanity's only privilege over the rest of creation. If you talk nonsense, you'll find your way to the truth! Talking nonsense is what makes me human. No one ever found his way to the truth without first getting things wrong fourteen times, or even a hundred and fourteen times, and that's a good thing in its way; the trouble is we're not even capable of getting things wrong with our own brains! You can talk nonsense to me, if it's nonsense of your own, and I'll kiss you for it. Talking nonsense of your own—that's almost better than talking someone else's truth; in the first case you're human, in the second you're nothing but a parrot! Truth won't go away, but life can get choked up; we've seen that happen. Well, what are we now? In science, progress, thought, invention, ideals, desires, liberalism, judgement, experience, and all, all, all, all, all of it, we're every one of us, without exception, still stuck in the first, pre-preparatory class of high school! We've got fond of living off other people's ideas, and now we're addicted to it! Isn't that right? Isn't it?' cried Razumikhin, shaking and squeezing both ladies' arms. 'Isn't that so?'

'Oh Lord, I don't know,' said poor Pulkheria Alexandrovna.

'Yes, yes... though I don't agree with everything you say,' added Avdotya Romanovna in a serious voice, and immediately cried out in pain, as Razumikhin crushed her arm again.

'Yes? Did you say yes? Well, after that, you're... you're...' he exclaimed in rapture, 'you're a fount of goodness, and purity, and judgement, and... perfection! Give me your hand, do... and you too, give me yours, I want to kiss your hands, right here and now, on my knees!'

And he fell on his knees right there on the pavement, which fortunately was deserted at the time.

'Please stop, please, what are you doing?' cried Pulkheria Alexandrovna, very distressed.

'Do get up, please!' said Dunia too, laughing and upset all at once.

'Never, until you've given me your hands! There, and that's enough, and now I'm up, and let's go! I'm a hopeless ass, I'm unworthy of you, and I'm drunk, and ashamed of myself... I'm not worthy to love you, but to bow down before you—that's the duty of anyone who isn't a brute beast! And so I did bow down... And now here are your rooms, and if nothing else, Rodion was right to turf your Piotr Petrovich out today! How dared he put you in rooms like these? It's a disgrace! Do you know what sort of people stay here? And you a bride to be! You are engaged to him, aren't you? Well let me tell you, this shows that your bridegroom is a villain!'

'Look here, Mr Razumikhin, you're forgetting yourself...' Pulkheria Alexandrovna began.

'Yes, yes, you're right, I was forgetting myself, I beg your pardon!' said Razumikhin, recollecting himself, 'but... but... you mustn't be cross with me for talking like that! Because I was speaking sincerely, not out of... hm! that would have been despicable of me; in short, not because I've fallen... hm! well, let's leave it there, never mind, I shan't explain why, I don't dare!... But we all realized as soon as he came in that he wasn't one of us. Not because he arrived straight from the barber's with his hair just curled, and not because he was desperate to show off how clever he was: but because he's a spy and a profiteer, he's a Jew and a clown, anyone can see that. D'you think he's clever? No, he's a fool, he's a fool! Well really, is he a match for you? Oh my Lord! Look, ladies,'— and he suddenly stopped on his way upstairs to their room, 'everyone at my place may be drunk, but they're all honest people, and although we talk a lot of rubbish—for I talk rubbish too—still, we'll talk our way through to the truth eventually, because we're on an honourable path; but Piotr Petrovich... he's not on an honourable path. I may have used hard words about all of them just now, but I do respect them all; even Zametov, though I don't respect him, I do like him, because he's— a puppy! And even that brute Zosimov, because—he's an honest man and knows his job... But that'll do, all's been said and forgiven. It is forgiven, isn't it? Well then, let's go. I know this passage, I've been here: right here, in number three, there was a scandal... So, where's your room? What number? Eight? Well then, lock yourselves in for the night, don't let anyone in. I'll be back in a quarter of an hour with news, and half an hour later I'll come back again with Zosimov, see if I don't! Goodbye, I must run!'

'My God, Dunechka, what's going to happen now?' asked Pulkheria Alexandrovna, turning anxiously and fearfully to her daughter.

'Keep calm, Mamenka,' replied Dunia, taking off her hat and cloak. 'God himself has sent this gentleman, even if he's come straight from some drunken revelry. We can trust him, I promise you. And all that he's done for my brother already...'

'Oh dear, Dunechka, heaven knows if he'll come back! And how could I have made up my mind to leave Rodia! I hadn't been expecting to find him like that, not at all! How stern he was, as if he wasn't glad to see us...'

Her eyes were wet with tears.

'No, that's not true, Mamenka. You didn't take a proper look at him, you were crying all the time. He's been terribly upset by this serious illness, that's all there is to it.'

'Oh dear, that illness! Whatever is going to happen to him? And the way he talked to you, Dunia!' the mother went on, looking timidly into her daughter's eyes to read her thoughts, and already half reassured by the fact that Dunia herself was standing up for Rodia, so she must have forgiven him. 'I'm sure he'll think better of it tomorrow,' she added, probing still further.

'Well I'm certain he'll say the same thing tomorrow... about that,' said Avdotya Romanovna, cutting her short; and of course that was the end of the matter, because this was a point that Pulkheria Alexandrovna was too frightened to speak of. Dunia went up to her mother and kissed her, and her mother silently gave her a hug. Then she sat down, full of anxiety, to await Razumikhin's return, and timidly watched her daughter who was now walking up and down the room with folded arms, thinking to herself, as she too waited. Avdotya Romanovna often had this habit of pacing the room from end to end, pondering deeply, and at such times her mother was always scared of breaking her train of thought.

Of course Razumikhin was being ridiculous with his sudden, drink-fuelled passion for Avdotya Romanovna; but quite apart from his present eccentric mood, many people might have forgiven him if they had seen Avdotya Romanovna just now, walking sadly and thoughtfully about the room with her arms folded. Avdotya Romanovna was remarkably attractive—tall, strikingly well-proportioned, strong and self-assured, and this showed in every gesture she made, without at all detracting from the gentleness and grace of her movements. In her features she resembled her brother, but she might actually have been called a beauty. Her hair was dark chestnut, a little lighter than her brother's; her eyes almost black, glittering, proud, and yet at times extraordinarily kind. She was pale, but it was no sickly pallor; her face had a fresh and healthy glow. Her mouth was rather small, with a fresh pink lower lip that projected forwards slightly, as did her chin too; this was the only irregularity in her beautiful face, but one that spoke of particular strength of character and even something like haughtiness. Her expression was generally serious and reflective rather than cheerful; but how well a smile suited that face, and how well her laughter became it too—happy, youthful, wholehearted laughter! It was no wonder that Razumikhin—tempestuous, open-hearted, straightforward, honest, strong as a fairy-tale hero, and tipsy, a man who had never come across anything of the sort, should have lost his head the moment he saw her. What was more, chance had decreed that he had his first sight of Dunia in that beautiful moment of love and joy at her reunion with her brother. Later on, when he saw her lower lip tremble with indignation at her brother's insolent, harsh, ungrateful commands, he could resist no longer.

The words he had drunkenly blurted out on the stairs that evening, claiming that Raskolnikov's eccentric landlady Praskovia Pavlovna would be jealous not only of him and Avdotya Romanovna, but even jealous of his relations with Pulkheria Alexandrovna herself—those words had actually been true. Despite the fact that Pulkheria Alexandrovna was all of forty-three years old, her face still retained traces of her former beauty, and she looked much younger than her age; this is almost always true of those women who, as they grow old, preserve their clarity of mind, the freshness of their impressions, and a pure and honest ardour of the heart. Let us add in passing that preserving all these qualities is the only way to avoid losing one's beauty even in old age. Her hair was already growing thin and grey, little radiating wrinkles had long ago appeared around her eyes, her cheeks were sunken and withered with grief and care; and yet her face was beautiful. It was a portrait of Dunechka's face in twenty years to come, save for the expression of that lower lip which in the mother's case did not project forwards. Pulkheria Alexandrovna was a sentimental woman, though not in a mawkish way; she was timid and yielding, but only up to a point; capable of yielding much, consenting to much, even if it went against her convictions; but there was always a bedrock of honesty, principle, and firm assurance which nothing would make her overstep.

Precisely twenty minutes after Razumikhin's departure there came two quiet, hasty knocks on the door. He was back.

'I shan't come in—no time!' he said hurriedly when the door was opened. 'He's sleeping like a log, soundly and peacefully, and with God's help he'll sleep ten hours without waking. Nastasia is with him—I told her not to leave till I came back. Now I'm going to get Zosimov over here, he can report back to you, and then you must go straight to bed; I can see you're absolutely exhausted.'

And off he ran down the corridor.

'What a capable and... devoted young man!' exclaimed Pulkheria Alexandrovna with profound relief.

'He seems to be an admirable character,' replied Avdotya Romanovna warmly, beginning to walk up and down the room once more.

Almost an hour later there were footsteps in the corridor and another knock at the door. Both women were expecting it, for by now they believed wholeheartedly in Razumikhin's promise; and indeed, he had managed to bring Zosimov over. Zosimov had instantly consented to abandon the party and come to look at Raskolnikov, but had been very unwilling to visit the ladies, and mistrustful of Razumikhin's drunken assurances. However, his self-esteem was immediately restored and he was even flattered to realize that he was being awaited like an oracle. He sat there for a full ten minutes and succeeded in thoroughly persuading and reassuring Pulkheria Alexandrovna. He talked with great sympathy, but with restraint and a sort of intense seriousness, exactly as a twenty-seven-year-old doctor at an important consultation should; he said not a word off the subject, and showed not the least inclination to enter into more private or personal relations with the two ladies. Having noticed as soon as he entered how radiantly beautiful Avdotya Romanovna was, he immediately tried to pay her no attention at all throughout his whole visit, addressing all his remarks to Pulkheria Alexandrovna alone. All this afforded him the greatest private satisfaction. Speaking of the patient, he said that at the present time he had found him in a most satisfactory condition. According to his observations, the patient's illness had a number of other, moral causes in addition to his poor material circumstances over the past few months. 'It is, so to speak, the product of many complex moral and material factors, alarms, fears, anxieties, certain ideas... and so forth.' Having noticed in passing that Avdotya Romanovna had begun listening particularly attentively, Zosimov expanded further on this topic. When Pulkheria Alexandrovna asked, timidly and anxiously, about 'possible suspicions of insanity', he replied with a calm, frank smile that his words had been exaggerated; that of course, the patient showed signs of a fixed idea of some kind, something suggestive of monomania—for he, Zosimov, was closely studying this exceptionally interesting branch of medicine—but that it must be remembered that the patient had been in a state of delirium almost until that very day, and... and of course, the arrival of his family would strengthen him, dispel his anxieties, and have a salutary effect—'so long as we can avoid any new severe shocks', he added meaningfully. Then he rose, bade them a dignified and cheerful farewell, and in return received blessings, heartfelt thanks, entreaties, and

even Avdotya Romanovna's hand, which she extended to him unasked
for him to shake; and he left, extremely pleased with his visit and even
more so with himself.

'We'll talk tomorrow. Go to bed now, straight away, you must!'
insisted Razumikhin as he left with Zosimov. 'Tomorrow I'll come and
report to you as early as I can.'

'Well, what an enchanting girl that Avdotya Romanovna is!' remarked
Zosimov, almost licking his lips, when they were both out on the street.

'Enchanting? Did you say enchanting?' roared Razumikhin, suddenly flinging himself on Zosimov and seizing him by the throat. 'If
you ever dare... Understand? Understand?' he shouted, shaking him by
the collar and pinning him against the wall. 'Do you hear?'

'Let go of me, you drunken devil!' said Zosimov, fighting him off;
once free of him, he looked intently at him and suddenly burst out
laughing. Razumikhin stood before him, arms dangling, sunk in profound and gloomy thought.

'Obviously, I'm an ass,' he said, looking black as thunder; 'but... so
are you.'

'Nothing of the sort, my boy. I'm not dreaming stupid dreams.'

They walked on in silence, and it was not till they were approaching
Raskolnikov's lodgings that Razumikhin, deeply troubled, broke the
silence.

'Listen,' he said to Zosimov. 'You're a good chap, but on top of all
your other bad qualities you're a womanizer, as I well know, and a dirty
one. You're a feeble, nervous wretch, you're capricious, you've spoiled
yourself rotten, you can't deny yourself anything—and that's what
I call dirty, because it leads you straight to the dirt. You've grown
so soft—I must tell you that the hardest thing for me to understand
is how you manage, with all that, to be a good and dedicated physician. Sleeps in a feather bed, does this doctor, and yet he'll get up
at night for a sick patient! In another three years' time you won't be
getting up for your patients any more... Well, to hell with that, it's
not the point; the point is this—tonight you're going to sleep in
the landlady's flat (I twisted her arm till she agreed), and I'll sleep
in the kitchen. Now there's an opportunity to get to know her better!
But it's not what you think! There's not a shadow of anything like
that...'

'I wasn't thinking anything!'

'That woman, my friend, is all modesty, reticence, shyness, uncom-
promising chastity, and yet with all that—such sighs, and as melting as wax! Preserve me from her, in the name of all the devils on

earth! A most fetching creature!... I'll pay you back, with my life if need be!'

Zosimov laughed even louder.

'Really carried away, aren't you! What would I want her for?'

'Honestly, it won't take much—all you need do is talk any nonsense you like to her, just sit down beside her and talk. And you're a doctor, too—start treating her for something. I swear you won't regret it. She's got a clavichord; you know I strum a bit; there's a song I play, a real Russian one: "I'll weep burning tears..." She likes real songs—well, it all started with singing; and you're a virtuoso on the pianoforte, a maestro, a Rubinstein...* I promise you won't regret it!'

'Why, have you made her promises of some kind? Signed a paper? Promised to marry her, even?'

'No, nothing, absolutely nothing of the kind! And she's not that sort at all; Chebarov tried that...'

'Well then, just drop her!'

'You can't just drop someone like that!'

'Why ever not?'

'You just can't, that's all! There's an element of attraction here.'

'Why ever did you lead her on?'

'I didn't lead her on at all, I might even have been led on myself, through my own stupidity; but she won't care in the slightest whether it's you or me, so long as someone sits by her side and sighs to her. This, brother... I can't explain it to you; this... well, you're good at mathematics, and you still work at it, I know... so, start telling her about integral calculus, I swear I'm not joking, I mean every word, she won't mind in the least: she'll gaze at you and sigh, and that'll go on for a year on end. As a matter of fact, I once talked to her for ages, two whole days, about the Prussian House of Lords (I mean, what could one talk to her about?), and all she did was sigh and glow. Only don't start talking about love—she's paralytically shy; but look as if you can't tear yourself away; well, and that's all you need. It's wonderfully cosy there, just like home—you can read, sit, lie down, write... You could even kiss her, if you go carefully...'

'But whatever would I want her for?'

'Oh, there's no way I can explain it to you! Look, the two of you suit each other perfectly! I'd been thinking about you before now... You know you'll end up like that! So what does it matter to you whether it's now or later? This is all about feather beds—and more than just feather beds! It's about attraction, the end of the world, an anchorage, a safe haven, the centre of the earth, the three fishes that hold up the world, the essence of pancakes, most delicious fish pies, the samovar at night-fall, gentle sighs and warm jackets and a warm stove to lie on—it's just like being dead, but at the same time you're alive, you've the best of both worlds! Well, brother, I've let my tongue run away with me, it's time to go to sleep! Listen, I sometimes wake in the night, so I'll go in and take a look at him. Only it doesn't matter, there's no need, all's well. Don't worry too much about him yourself; though if you like, you could go in to him once as well. But if you notice anything—delirium, say, or fever, or anything—wake me at once. Not that that could ever happen...'

CHAPTER II

RAZUMIKHIN woke before eight the following morning, serious and troubled. He suddenly found himself that morning confronted by a great many new and unexpected puzzles. Never before had he imagined waking up like this. He remembered everything that had occurred the previous day, down to the finest detail, and realized that something utterly new had happened to him; that he had never known anything of the kind before. At the same time he could clearly see that the dream that had fired his imagination was utterly unattainable—so unattainable that he had even grown ashamed of it; and very quickly he passed on to the other, more everyday cares and problems that awaited him after that 'thrice-accursed yesterday'.

His most dreadful recollection was of how 'mean and despicable' he had been that day, not only by being drunk, but also by taking advantage of a young girl's situation to abuse her fiancé to her face, out of a stupid impulse of jealousy, without knowing anything about their mutual relationship and commitments, and without even properly knowing the man himself. Anyway, what right did he have to judge him so hastily and recklessly? Who had appointed him their judge? And was it possible that such a being as Avdotya Romanovna would give herself to an unworthy man for money? So the man had to have some virtues. And the lodgings? But how could the man have known that they were lodgings of that sort? After all, he was getting an apartment ready... Ugh, how despicable all this was! And what sort of an explanation was it to say that he was drunk? A stupid excuse that disgraced him even more! *In vino veritas*; and the whole truth had come out: 'all the filth of his coarse and jealous heart had betrayed itself!' And was it in any way excusable for him, Razumikhin, to cherish such a dream? Who was he in comparison to a girl like her—he, the drunken brawler and braggart of last night! 'How cynical and absurd to set the two of them side by side!' Razumikhin blushed in despair at the thought, and suddenly, at that very moment, remembered all too clearly how he had told them last night, standing on the stairs, that the landlady would be jealous of him and Avdotya Romanovna... the thought was absolutely unbearable. With a swing of his arm he crashed his fist against the kitchen stove, injuring his hand and knocking out one of the bricks.

'Of course,' he muttered to himself after a minute, with a feeling of humiliation, 'of course, all that nastiness can't ever be covered up or smoothed over... so there's no point in even thinking about that; so I have to turn up in silence, and... carry out my obligations... in silence too, and... not ask for forgiveness, and not say anything, and... and of course, everything's lost now!'

Even so, as he dressed himself, he examined his suit more closely than usual. He did not possess another one, and even if he had, he might not have worn it—'I just wouldn't have put it on, on purpose.' But at all events, he mustn't continue to be a filthy, slovenly cynic; he had no right to hurt other people's feelings, particularly when those same other people needed his help and invited him to their home. He carefully brushed his clothes. His linen was always respectable—he was particularly clean and neat in that way.

He washed very thoroughly that morning—Nastasia found him some soap; he washed his hair, his neck, and especially his hands. But when it came to the question of whether he should shave his stubble or not (Praskovia Pavlovna possessed some excellent razors, which she had kept after the late Mr Zarnitsyn's death), that question was answered somewhat savagely in the negative. 'Let it stay as it is! Supposing they think that I only shaved in order to... well, they're bound to think that! No, not for anything in the world!'

But the main thing was, he was such a filthy, coarse type, with pot-house manners; and... even supposing he knew that he was a decent fellow too, at least to some extent... well, what was there to be proud of in being a decent fellow? Everyone ought to be a decent fellow, and better than that, and... and yet (he remembered) he himself had been involved in some dealings... not actually dishonest ones, but still!... And what designs he had had! Hmm... and compare all that with Avdotya Romanovna! 'Oh, damnation! So what! So I'll be a filthy, greasy, vodka-soaked type, and to hell with it! I'll be even worse still!...'

He was still busy talking to himself like this when Zosimov found him, after spending the night in Praskovia Pavlovna's parlour. He was on his way home, but first he had hurriedly looked in on his patient. Razumikhin reported that the patient was sleeping like a log. Zosimov gave orders not to disturb him until he woke of his own accord. He promised to come back after ten.

'So long as he's still at home,' he added. 'Confound the fellow! How can you treat someone if you can't even control him! Do you know whether *he*'s going to *them*, or are *they* coming here?'

'They'll be coming here, I think,' replied Razumikhin, understanding the question. 'And of course they'll be talking about family business. I'll go away. As a doctor, of course, you have more rights than me.'

'I'm not their confessor. I'll look in and go away again; I've plenty to do without them.'

'There's one thing that worries me,' interrupted Razumikhin with a frown. 'Last night when I was drunk, I let something slip to him as we talked on our way here, something stupid... about all kinds of... including that you were afraid that he might...have a tendency to madness...'

'You blabbed that to the ladies last night too.'

'I know, it was stupid of me! I ought to be whipped! But did you really have some definite idea of the kind?'

'No, nonsense—what definite idea could I have? You called him a monomaniac yourself, when you brought me to see him... And then last night we stirred things up even more, I mean you did, with your stories... about that painter; not a brilliant topic to talk about, when that may be just what's driven him mad! If I'd known exactly what went on in that office, and how some swine there... insulted him by suspecting him! Hmm... Then I wouldn't have allowed that sort of talk last night. These monomaniacs can turn a drop of water into an ocean, they see things in broad daylight that aren't there. As far as I can remember, when Zametov was telling me that story last night, I half-understood it. Anyway!—I know one case, a forty-year-old hypochondriac who couldn't bear being made fun of at the dinner table, day after day, by an eight-year-old boy—and he cut his throat! And here's our man all in rags, and an insolent police officer, and an illness just starting, and that sort of suspicion! A hypochondriac half out of his mind! With his incredible, crazy vanity! I mean, that might have been the whole trigger for his illness! Yes, well, damn it!... And that Zametov, too—he's a nice lad, but, hmm... he didn't need to talk about all that last night. A terrible blabbermouth!'

'But who did he tell? Just you and me?'

'And Porfiry.'

'Porfiry? So what?'

'By the way, do you have any influence with those two—his mother and sister? They ought to be a bit careful with him today...'

'They'll sort themselves out!' Razumikhin reluctantly replied.

'And why's he got it in for that Luzhin? The man's got money, she doesn't seem to mind him... and they haven't a penny, have they? Eh?'

'What are you quizzing me for?' cried Razumikhin irritably. 'How can I know if they have a penny or not? Ask them yourself—you might find out...'

'Phoo, how stupid you are sometimes! Still drunk from yesterday... Goodbye; give my thanks to your Praskovia Pavlovna for putting me up last night. She's shut herself in, I called good morning to her through the door but she didn't answer, though she'd been up since seven herself—they brought her the samovar along the passage from the kitchen... I wasn't even allowed a look at her...'

At nine o'clock precisely, Razumikhin turned up at the room at Bakaleyev's. Both the ladies had been waiting for him for ages, bursting with impatience. They had been up since seven or even earlier. He entered with a face as black as night, gave them an awkward bow which immediately made him angry—with himself, of course. But he had reckoned without the lady of the house: Pulkheria Alexandrovna flung herself at him, seized him by both hands and all but kissed them. He glanced fearfully at Avdotya Romanovna; but that haughty face, too, was so full of gratitude and friendship, such absolute and unlooked-for respect (instead of mocking looks and uncontrollable, ill-concealed contempt) that he would honestly have found it easier to be greeted with abuse—as it was, everything was too confusing. Luckily there was a ready-made topic of conversation to hand, and he seized it at once.

On hearing that her son 'hadn't woken yet', but that 'all was well', Pulkheria Alexandrovna announced that it was all for the best, because she 'very, very, very much needed to talk things over first'. That was followed by enquiries about tea, and an invitation to take it together; the ladies had not yet had any, waiting for Razumikhin to arrive. Avdotya Romanovna rang the bell, and a grubby ragamuffin answered it; he was told to bring some tea, and this was eventually served, but in such a disgracefully dirty way that the ladies were ashamed. Razumikhin was about to condemn the rooming house in forceful terms, but remembering Luzhin, he held his tongue, became embarrassed, and was much relieved when Pulkheria Alexandrovna's questions at last began pouring out in an endless torrent. His replies kept him talking for three-quarters of an hour, incessantly being interrupted and cross-questioned; he managed to convey all the principal and most essential facts that he knew about Rodion Romanovich's life during the past year, ending with a detailed account of his illness. Of course he left out a great deal that needed to be left out, including among other things the scene in the police office and all its consequences. His story was eagerly listened to; but when he thought he had come to the end and satisfied his audience, it turned out that as far as they were concerned he had scarcely begun.

'Tell me, do tell me, what do you think... oh dear, I'm sorry, I don't know your name yet?' began Pulkheria Alexandrovna hurriedly.

'Dmitry Prokofich.'

'Well then, Dmitry Prokofich, I should very, very much like to know... how he... how he generally views things—I mean to say, please understand me, how can I put it, what I mean is—what does he like, and what doesn't he like? Is he always as bad-tempered as this? What does he wish for, what are his dreams, so to speak, if I can put it that way? What is it that particularly influences him just now? In other words, I'd like...'

'Oh, Mamenka, how can he answer all those questions straight off like that?' put in Dunia.

'Oh Lord, I never, ever expected to see him like this, Dmitry Prokofich.'

'And that's very natural,' replied Dmitry Prokofich. 'I don't have a mother, but my uncle comes to see me every year, and almost every time he fails to recognize me, even by sight, though he's an intelligent man; and a lot of water has passed under the bridge during your three-year separation. What can I say to you? I've known Rodion for a year and a half; he's gloomy, sullen, haughty, and proud; and lately (or perhaps much longer than that) he's been a morbid hypochondriac. He's generous and kind-hearted. He hates letting his feelings show, and he'd sooner treat a person harshly than come out with what's on his mind. Sometimes, actually, he's not a hypochondriac at all, he's just cold and unfeeling, in an almost inhuman way—as if he had two personalities inside him, and he was switching between them. He can be terribly taciturn. He keeps saying he's got no time, or people are always getting in his way, and yet he lies there doing nothing. He doesn't laugh at you, but it's not because he's short of wit—it's as if he just didn't have time for that sort of triviality. He won't hear people out when they tell him things. He's never interested in what everyone around him is interested in. He has a dreadfully high opinion of himself, and to some extent I believe he's justified. Well, what else?... I think your arrival is going to be his absolute salvation.'

'Oh, please God it may!' cried Pulkheria Alexandrovna, very distressed by Razumikhin's opinion of her Rodia.

And now Razumikhin looked rather more boldly at Avdotya Romanovna. He had been glancing at her frequently during this conversation, but fleetingly, for an instant at a time, and looking away at once. Avdotya Romanovna had been alternating between sitting down by the table to listen carefully, and getting up to walk back and forth across the room, as was her habit, with folded arms and pursed lips; sometimes she would ask a question, without interrupting her walk; sometimes she would become thoughtful. She, too, had a habit of not hearing a person out when they spoke. She was wearing a lightweight dress of some dark material, with a transparent little white scarf tied round her neck. Razumikhin could immediately see many indications that the two women were very badly off. If Avdotya Romanovna had been arrayed like a queen, he probably wouldn't have been at all afraid of her; but as it was, perhaps just because she was so poorly dressed and he had observed how impoverished they were, his heart was filled with fear and he began to be nervous of every word and every gesture—which of course made it difficult for someone who in any case lacked self-confidence.

'You've told us a lot of interesting things about my brother's character, and... you told them impartially. That's good—I thought you were in awe of him,' remarked Avdotya Romanovna with a smile. 'And maybe it's true, too, that he needs a woman by him,' she added thoughtfully.

'I never said that; but perhaps you're right, only...'

'What?'

'He doesn't love anyone, does he? Perhaps he never will,' Razumikhin cut her off.

'You mean he isn't capable of loving anyone?'

'You know, Avdotya Romanovna, you're amazingly like your brother yourself—in every way!' he suddenly burst out, taking himself by surprise; but then he recalled what he had just been telling her about her brother, turned as red as a lobster, and became terribly confused. Avdotya couldn't help laughing at the sight of him.

'You could both be wrong about Rodia,' interposed Pulkheria Alexandrovna, rather piqued. 'I'm not talking about just now, Dunechka. What Piotr Petrovich writes in that letter... and what you and I had been supposing... perhaps that's all wrong; but you can't imagine, Dmitry Prokofich, how peculiar and—what can I say—how capricious he is. I never could rely on his character, even when he was only fifteen. I'm sure that he's capable even now of doing something that no one in the world would dream of doing... Well, only just think what happened a year and a half ago, when I was so astonished and shocked that it almost killed me, because he'd taken it into his head to marry that... what's her name... his landlady Zarnitsyna's daughter?'

'Do you know any of the details of that story?' asked Avdotya Romanovna.

'You'd have thought', Pulkheria Alexandrovna went on heatedly, 'he might have been held back by my tears, my entreaties, my illness, even my death from grief, perhaps, and our desperate poverty! But no, he would have walked over all the obstacles, as coolly as you please. Is it possible, is it truly possible that he doesn't love us?'

'He's never said anything to me about that story,' replied Razumikhin cautiously. 'But I did hear something from Mrs Zarnitsyna herself; though she's not a great talker either, and what I did hear was actually rather strange...'

'Why, what was it? What did you hear?' asked both women in unison.

'Well, nothing so very special, actually. All I heard was that the marriage, which had been firmly arranged and only didn't come about because the fiancée died, hadn't been at all to Mrs Zarnitsyna's liking... And besides, the bride wasn't particularly pretty, in fact she was rather ugly... and so sickly, and... and peculiar... well, I believe she did have some good qualities too. She simply must have had some good qualities, otherwise you couldn't have made head or tail of it... And she had no dowry—but he wouldn't have been expecting anything... The whole business is hard to judge.'

'I'm sure the girl was a worthy person,' commented Avdotya Romanovna briefly.

'God forgive me, I was glad to hear that she'd died, though I don't know which of them would have driven the other into their grave, he or she,' concluded Pulkheria Alexandrovna. Then she began, hesitantly and cautiously, with endless glances at Dunia which her daughter clearly found unwelcome, to question Razumikhin about the previous day's scene between Rodia and Luzhin. This scene had evidently upset her more than anything, and she was in fear and trembling over it. Razumikhin told the whole story over again, in detail, but this time he added his own view of it, explicitly accusing Raskolnikov of intentionally insulting Piotr Petrovich, and scarcely trying to excuse him on the grounds of illness.

'He'd thought of that before he became ill,' he added.

'That's what I thought myself,' said Pulkheria Alexandrovna, looking crushed. But she was most impressed by the fact that Razumikhin had this time spoken about Piotr Petrovich so discreetly, almost respectfully. Avdotya Romanovna was also struck by it.

'So what's your opinion of Piotr Petrovich?' Pulkheria Alexandrovna could not stop herself asking.

'As regards your daughter's future husband, I can't take any other view,' replied Razumikhin warmly and decisively. 'And I'm not just saying that to be boringly polite, but because... because... well, just because Avdotya Romanovna herself has freely consented to choose that man. And if I abused him as I did last night, that's because I was revoltingly drunk yesterday, and... mad besides: yes, mad, out of my mind, I'd completely lost my reason... and today I'm ashamed of myself!...' He blushed and stopped. Avdotya Romanovna coloured too, but did not break the silence. Since the conversation first touched on Luzhin she had not said a single word.

And Pulkheria Alexandrovna, without her support, was evidently in a state of indecision. Eventually she announced with some hesitation, constantly looking at her daughter, that there was one particular issue that particularly troubled her.

'You see, Dmitry Prokofich...' she began. 'I'll be absolutely frank with Dmitry Prokofich, shall I, Dunechka?'

'Naturally, Mamenka,' replied Avdotya Romanovna solemnly.

'It's like this,' she hurried on, as if this permission to voice her worries had lifted a heavy weight off her shoulders. 'This morning, very early, we got a note from Piotr Petrovich in answer to the message we sent to announce our arrival yesterday. You see, he was supposed to meet us, and he'd promised to do so, actually inside the station. Instead of that, some sort of lackey was sent to the station to meet us, with the address of these rooms and instructions to show us the way; and he brought a message from Piotr Petrovich to say that he would come to see us here this morning. And instead of that, this morning this note arrived from him...The best thing is if you read it yourself: there's a point in it that worries me very much... you'll see straight away what it is, and... give me your honest opinion, Dmitry Prokofich! You know Rodia's character better than anyone, and you can best advise us. I warn you, Dunechka has already made up her mind, straight away, but myself, I'm not sure yet what to do, and... and I kept waiting for you.'

Razumikhin opened the letter, dated the previous day, and read the following:

'Dear Madam, Pulkheria Alexandrovna,

'I have the honour to inform you that owing to unforeseen difficulties I was unable to meet you at the station platform, but sent a highly competent individual to do so in my stead. And I must also deny myself

the honour of meeting you tomorrow morning, owing to pressing
Senate business and in order not to intrude on a family reunion between
yourself and your son, and between Avdotya Romanovna and her
brother. However, I shall have the honour of visiting you and presenting my respects at your lodgings no later than tomorrow, at eight o'clock
in the evening precisely; venturing to add my earnest and, may I add,
categorical request that Rodion Romanovich should not be present at
our meeting together, since he yesterday subjected me to unheard-of,
insulting abuse during my visit to his sickbed; furthermore, I absolutely require to discuss one particular point in detail with you, so that
I may hear your own interpretation of it. I have the honour to inform
you in advance that if, contrary to my request, I encounter Rodion
Romanovich, I shall be obliged to withdraw immediately, and you will
then have no one to blame but yourself. I write this on the supposition
that since Rodion Romanovich, who appeared so sick when I visited
him, suddenly recovered within the space of two hours, it follows that
on leaving his lodgings, he will be capable of finding his way to you too.
I have been confirmed in this view by seeing with my own eyes, in the
apartment of a certain drunkard who was run over by some horses and
died in consequence, how your son yesterday handed over almost twenty-
five roubles, on the pretext of funeral expenses, to this man's daughter,
a young woman of notorious conduct; which greatly surprised me,
knowing how difficult you had found it to raise this sum. And hereupon
may I express my particular regard to your respected Avdotya Romanovna,
and beg you to accept the assurance of the devoted esteem of

Your humble servant
P. Luzhin.'

'What am I to do now, Dmitry Prokofich?' began Pulkheria
Alexandrovna, almost weeping. 'How can I ever ask Rodia not to come?
He was so insistent yesterday, demanding that the engagement with
Piotr Petrovich had to be broken off; and now we're being ordered not
to receive Rodia himself! And as soon as he finds out, he'll come along
on purpose, and... what'll happen then?'

'You must do what Avdotya Romanovna has decided,' replied
Razumikhin calmly and without hesitation.

'Oh, Lord! She says... she says heaven knows what, and she won't
explain why! She says that it'll be better, I mean, not that it'll be better,
but for some reason it's absolutely essential, so she says, for Rodia to
make a point of turning up at eight this evening, and that they absolutely have to meet... While as for me, I didn't even want to show him

the letter: I wanted to arrange things in secret, with your help, to make sure that he didn't come... because he's so hot-tempered... And I don't understand anything about that drunkard who's died, or who this daughter is, and how he could have given away the last of his money to her... money that...'

'...that cost you so dear to raise, Mamenka,' added Avdotya Romanovna.

'He wasn't himself yesterday,' said Razumikhin thoughtfully. 'If you only knew what he came out with in the tavern yesterday—though it was clever enough... hmm! He did tell me something about a dead man, and about some girl, when we were walking home yesterday, but I couldn't make head or tail of it... Well, actually, yesterday I myself was...'

'The best thing would be, Mamenka, for us to go to him ourselves, and I promise you, there we'll see straight away what's to be done. Anyway, it's time—good heavens! It's past ten!' she cried, looking at the splendid enamelled gold watch that hung round her neck on a delicate Venetian chain, terribly out of keeping with the rest of her costume. 'A present from the bridegroom,' thought Razumikhin.

'Oh dear, we must go! We must go, Dunechka, now!' fussed Pulkheria Alexandrovna in alarm. 'Or he'll think we're cross after yesterday, not coming till so late. Oh, dear Lord!'

As she spoke, she hurriedly flung a shawl round her shoulders and put on a little hat; Dunechka put on her things too. Her gloves were not only worn but actually torn, as Razumikhin noticed; and yet the obvious poverty of their dress actually conferred a special kind of dignity on the two ladies, as is always the case when people know how to wear poor clothes well. Razumikhin gazed at Dunechka with adoration, proud that he would be escorting her. 'That queen,' he thought to himself, 'who darned her own stockings in prison—at that moment, of course, she looked a real queen, even more so than at her most grandiose celebrations and processions.'*

'My God!' exclaimed Pulkheria Alexandrovna, 'did I ever think that I'd dread meeting my son, my dear, dear Rodia: but I'm dreading it now!... I'm frightened, Dmitry Prokofich!' she added, looking timidly at him.

'Don't be frightened, Mamenka,' said Dunia, giving her a kiss. 'It's best to trust him. I do.'

'Oh, my God! I trust him too, but I didn't sleep all night!' cried out the poor woman.

They went out onto the street.

'You know, Dunechka, as soon as I fell asleep for a bit in the early morning, I suddenly dreamed of Marfa Petrovna who died... she was all in white... she came up to me, took me by the hand, and she was shaking her head at me, so sternly, so sternly, as though she was blaming me for something... Is that a good sign? Oh my God, Dmitry Prokofich, you don't know yet—Marfa Petrovna is dead!'

'No, I didn't know; who's Marfa Petrovna?'

'Died suddenly! And just imagine...'

'Wait a bit, Mamenka,' interrupted Dunia, 'he doesn't yet know who Marfa Petrovna is.'

'Oh, don't you know? I thought you'd know it all by now. Forgive me, Dmitry Prokofich, I've just been out of my mind these last few days. Honestly, I look on you as our special Providence, so I was sure you'd know all about it. I regard you as one of my family... Don't be angry with me for saying that. Oh, my God, what's happened to your right hand? Did you knock it?'

'Yes, knocked it,' mumbled Razumikhin in delight.

'I sometimes speak too much, straight from my heart, and then Dunia puts me right... But good Lord, what a cupboard he lives in! I wonder if he's awake? And that woman, his landlady, does she call that a room? Listen, you said that he doesn't like saying what's on his mind, so perhaps he'll be fed up with me for my... weakness?... Won't you advise me, Dmitry Prokofich? How should I talk to him? You know, I'm going around like a lost soul.'

'Don't question him about things if you see him frowning. And particularly, don't ask him a lot about his health: he doesn't like it.'

'Ah, Dmitry Prokofich, how hard it is to be a mother! And now here's the staircase... What a dreadful staircase!'

'Mamasha, you're quite pale, do calm down, my darling,' said Dunia, caressing her. 'He ought to be happy to see you, and here you are tormenting yourself,' she added, her eyes flashing.

'Just a minute, I'll take a look first, and see if he's awake.'

The ladies quietly followed Razumikhin upstairs, and on reaching the landlady's door on the fourth floor they noticed that the door was open a little crack, and two lively black eyes were inspecting them out of the darkness. When their eyes met, the door suddenly slammed shut, with such a bang that Pulkheria Alexandrovna almost cried out in alarm.

CHAPTER III

'HE'S well, he's well!' Zosimov called out cheerfully as they came in. He had arrived some ten minutes earlier and was sitting on the same corner of the divan as last night. Raskolnikov was sitting at the opposite

end, fully dressed and even scrupulously washed and combed, something he hadn't done for a long time. The room filled up at once, but
Nastasia still managed to slip in behind the visitors and stayed to listen.

It was true, Raskolnikov was almost well, especially compared to the
day before, but he was very pale, abstracted, and sombre. He looked like
someone injured or suffering severe physical pain: his brows were
puckered, his lips compressed, his eyes feverish. He spoke little and
reluctantly, as though forcing himself to perform a duty; and his movements from time to time appeared rather restless.

All it needed was for him to have had his arm in a sling, or a gauze
dressing on his finger, and he would have looked just like a man with
a painful poisoned finger, or an injured hand, or something of the kind.

Even so, this pale and gloomy face seemed to light up for a moment
when his mother and sister came in; but that merely transformed his
expression of listless dejection into one of more concentrated torment.
The light in his face soon faded, but the torment remained, and Zosimov,
who had been watching and studying his patient with all the youthful
zeal of a doctor at the dawn of his career, was surprised to observe that
the arrival of his family brought out in him not gladness but a sort of
grim, hidden determination to endure an hour or two of torture that
could no longer be avoided. He then saw that almost every word of the
ensuing conversation seemed to touch a raw nerve of some sort in his
patient, and irritate it; yet at the same time he was surprised to see this
monomaniac of yesterday now able to control himself and hide his feelings, whereas yesterday he would have been goaded almost to a frenzy
by the slightest word.

'Yes, now I can see for myself that I'm almost well,' said Raskolnikov,
welcoming his mother and sister with a kiss which left Pulkheria
Alexandrovna beaming with joy. 'And I'm not saying that in *yesterday's
way*,' he added to Razumikhin with a friendly handshake.

'Well, I was quite surprised at him today,' began Zosimov, very glad
to see the new arrivals, because in just ten minutes he had managed to
lose the thread of his conversation with his patient. 'If things go on this
way, in three or four days he'll be quite his old self, I mean the way he
was a month ago, or two months... or even three, perhaps? All this goes
back a while, it's been brewing up... hasn't it? Admit it, now, perhaps it
was your fault too?' he went on, smiling tentatively as if still afraid of
somehow annoying him.

'That might well be,' replied Raskolnikov coldly.

'The reason I say that', went on Zosimov, getting a taste for this conversation, 'is that your complete cure now really depends on you alone.

Now that it's possible to talk to you at last, I'd like to persuade you to eliminate the original, as it were, root causes that brought about your morbid state; if you do, you'll recover, but if not, things will get even worse. What those original causes were, I don't know, but you must know them yourself. You're an intelligent man, and naturally you must have been observing yourself. It seems to me that the beginning of your disorder coincided in part with your dropping out of university. You mustn't go on without any occupation, so it seems to me that you could be greatly helped by working hard and setting yourself some firm goal.'

'Yes, yes, you're absolutely right... I'll go back to university now, as quick as I can, and then everything... will be just fine...'

Zosimov, who had started out dispensing his wise advice partly to impress the ladies, was naturally somewhat puzzled, on ending his speech and glancing at the man he was addressing, to observe a distinct expression of mockery on his face. However, that only lasted a moment. Pulkheria immediately began thanking Zosimov, particularly for visiting them at their lodgings the night before.

'What, did he even come and see you in the night?' asked Raskolnikov in apparent alarm. 'So you haven't slept after your journey either?'

'Oh, Rodia, all that was only up till two o'clock. Dunia and I never go to bed before two, even at home.'

'I don't know how to thank him either,' went on Raskolnikov, suddenly frowning and looking down. 'Quite apart from the matter of money—excuse my mentioning it,' he said to Zosimov, 'I don't actually know how I've come to deserve such special attention from you. I simply don't understand it... and... and I don't like it either, because I don't understand it, I tell you quite frankly.'

'Now don't get irritated,' said Zosimov with a forced laugh. 'Just see yourself as my first patient. We doctors, when we're just starting to practise, we love our first patients as though they were our own children; some of us almost fall in love with them. And I'm not oversupplied with patients myself.'

'Not to mention him there,' added Raskolnikov, pointing to Razumikhin; 'but he's had nothing from me either, except insults and trouble.'

'What nonsense you talk! Have you gone all sentimental today, or something?' cried Razumikhin.

Had he been more perceptive, he would have seen that there was no sentimental mood here at all, but almost the opposite. Avdotya Romanovna, however, did notice it, and watched her brother intently and anxiously.

'As for you, Mamenka, I don't even dare say anything,' he went on, as though reciting a lesson he had learned that morning. 'It was only today that I realized how you must have suffered here yesterday, waiting for me to come back.' Saying this, he suddenly held out his hand to his sister, with a silent smile. But this time, his smile showed genuine, unfeigned emotion. Dunia at once grasped his hand and pressed it warmly, full of happiness and gratitude. This was the first time he had addressed her after their disagreement the day before. Their mother's face lit up with joy and delight at the sight of this conclusive, wordless reconciliation between brother and sister.

'Now that's just what I love him for!' whispered Razumikhin, carried away as usual, as he swung himself round in his chair. 'What gestures he's capable of!'

'And how well he does it all!' thought his mother, 'what noble impulses he has, and how simply and delicately he's put an end to all that misunderstanding of yesterday with his sister—just by holding out his hand at that moment, and looking kindly at her... And how beautiful his eyes are, and how beautiful his whole face is!... He's even better-looking than Dunechka... But, good Lord, what clothes he's wearing, how appallingly he's dressed! That errand boy, Vasya, in Afanasy Ivanovich's shop, is better dressed!... And how I'd love to run to him now, and hug him, and... burst into tears—but I'm scared, I'm scared...oh Lord, he's so strange... There he is, talking kindly, but I'm scared! Whatever am I scared of?'

'Oh, Rodia, you wouldn't believe', she added, hastily responding to his last remark, 'how... unhappy Dunechka and I were yesterday! Now that it's all over and done with and we're all happy again, I can tell you. Just imagine, there we were, almost straight off the train, hurrying to get here and hug you, and that woman—ah, here she is! Hello, Nastasia!... She suddenly told us that you'd been in bed with a raging fever, and you'd just given your doctor the slip, delirious as you were, and secretly gone out, and people were searching for you. You wouldn't believe what we went through! I was just remembering the tragic end of Lieutenant Potanchikov, your father's friend, whom we knew—but you won't remember him, Rodia—he was in a raging fever too, and had run out just like you, and he'd fallen into a well in the courtyard, and they couldn't pull him out till next day. And of course we were imagining even more dreadful things. We were going to run out to look for Piotr Petrovich, to get him to help... because we were all alone, on our own,' she went on pitifully, and suddenly stopped short, remembering that talking about Piotr Petrovich was still quite dangerous, in spite of the fact that they were all 'perfectly happy again'.

'Yes, yes... all that's a great shame, of course...' muttered Raskolnikov in reply; but with such a distracted, almost inattentive air that Dunechka stared at him in amazement.

'Now then, what else did I want to say?' he went on, making an effort to remember. 'Yes: Mamenka, and you too, Dunechka, please don't think that I didn't want to come over to see you myself, but just waited for you to come here first.'

'What are you talking about, Rodia!' cried Pulkheria Alexandrovna, just as surprised.

'Is he just saying all this out of a sense of duty?' wondered Dunechka. 'Making his peace, and asking forgiveness, as if it was a religious service, or a lesson he'd learned by heart?'

'I'd just woken up and was on my way out, but I couldn't go because of my clothes: I'd forgotten to tell her... Nastasia... to wash out that blood... I've only just had time to get dressed.'

'Blood? What blood?' asked Pulkheria Alexandrovna in alarm.

'It was just... Don't worry. There was blood because yesterday, when I was wandering around, a bit delirious, I came upon someone who'd been run over... a clerk...'

'Delirious? But you're remembering everything,' Razumikhin interrupted him.

'That's true,' replied Raskolnikov, talking with especial care. 'I remember everything, down to the last detail, but if you asked me why I did something, or went somewhere, or said something—I couldn't rightly tell you.'

'That's a very well-known phenomenon,' interposed Zosimov. 'One performs one's actions very skilfully, brilliantly, and yet one's control over those actions, the motivation for them, is deranged and governed by a variety of morbid impressions. It's like a dream.'

'It's probably just as well that he almost regards me as out of my mind,' thought Raskolnikov.

'But perfectly healthy people can act in just the same way,' remarked Dunechka, looking anxiously at Zosimov.

'That's very true,' replied Zosimov. 'In that sense, indeed, all of us are, very frequently, almost like deranged people; but with a small difference, in that "sick" people are rather more deranged than we are; that distinction needs to be drawn. But an entirely harmonious personality almost doesn't exist, that's true; you might come across one among tens of thousands, perhaps among many hundreds of thousands, and even then that person will be a pretty poor specimen...'

When Zosimov incautiously dropped the word 'deranged', while prattling on about his favourite topic, everyone frowned. Raskolnikov sat deep in thought, apparently paying no attention, with a strange smile on his pale lips. He was still following his own train of thought.

'So what about that man who'd been run over?' Razumikhin hastily exclaimed. 'I interrupted you.'

'What?' said Raskolnikov, as if waking up. 'Yes... well, I got blood on me when I was helping to carry him into his flat... Incidentally, Mamenka, I did something unpardonable yesterday; I must really have been out of my mind. I gave away all the money you'd sent me... to his wife... for the funeral. She's a widow now, consumptive, a pathetic creature... three little orphans, starving... there's nothing in the house... and there's another daughter too... Perhaps you might have given them the money yourself, if you'd seen them... But I admit I had no right, particularly knowing how you'd got that money yourselves. If one wants to help, one has to have the right to do it, otherwise "*Crevez, chiens, si vous n'êtes pas contents!*" '* He laughed. 'Isn't that so, Dunia?'

'No, it isn't,' replied Dunia firmly.

'Bah! You yourself... you've got your own plans!...' he muttered, with a look almost of hatred, smiling a mocking smile. 'I should have thought... And why not, it does you credit; it's better for you... and then you'll come up against a line, and if you don't cross it you'll be unhappy, but if you do cross it—perhaps you'll be even unhappier... Anyway, that's all nonsense!' he added irritably, annoyed at letting himself get carried away. 'All I wanted to say, Mamenka, is that I'm asking your pardon,' he finished curtly and abruptly.

'That's enough, Rodia! I'm sure that everything you do is right!' said his mother happily.

'Don't be too sure,' he replied with a twisted smile. A silence fell. There was something strained about the whole exchange, the silence, the reconciliation, the forgiveness; everyone could feel it.

'It really seems as though they're all afraid of me,' thought Raskolnikov to himself, looking at his mother and sister under lowered brows. And indeed, the longer Pulkheria Alexandrovna remained silent, the more frightened she became.

'But I believe I did love them, when they weren't here,' was the thought that passed through his mind.

'Do you know, Rodia, Marfa Petrovna has died!' Pulkheria Alexandrovna suddenly exclaimed.

'Who's Marfa Petrovna?'

'Oh, for heaven's sake, Marfa Petrovna, Svidrigailov's wife! I wrote you such a lot about her.'

'A-a-ah, yes, I remember... So she's dead? Really?' He suddenly roused himself, as if waking from sleep. 'Did she really die? What of?'

'Just imagine, she died suddenly!' Pulkheria Alexandrovna hastily explained, encouraged by his curiosity. 'Just when I had sent off my letter to you that time, it was the very same day! Think of it—that dreadful man, I think he must have caused her death. They say he'd beaten her dreadfully!'

'Was that really how they lived?' he asked his sister.

'No, quite the opposite in fact. He was always very patient, and even courteous to her. There were many occasions when he was overly tolerant of her character, for the whole seven years... And then somehow he suddenly lost patience.'

'So he wasn't all that terrible, if he stuck it out for seven years? Dunechka, you seem to be standing up for him?'

'No, no, he was a dreadful man! I can't imagine anything worse,' replied Dunia, almost with a shudder. She frowned and fell into thought.

'It happened one morning,' Pulkheria Alexandrovna hurriedly continued. 'After that she had the horses harnessed straight away, so as to drive off to town straight after her meal, because when that sort of thing happened she would always go off to town; she made a good meal, they say...'

'What, after being beaten up?'

'Well, and she always had that... habit—as soon as she had eaten, she set off straight away for her bathe, so as not to be late for the drive... You see, she was having some sort of bathing cure: they've got a cold spring there, and she used to bathe in it every day, and as soon as she'd got into the water, she suddenly had a stroke!'

'No wonder!' exclaimed Zosimov.

'And had he beaten her badly?'

'Surely that's not the point,' replied Dunia.

'Hmm! And what's the sense of going on about this sort of rubbish, Mamenka?' asked Raskolnikov suddenly, almost without thinking, in tones of annoyance.

'Oh dear, my boy, I just didn't know what to talk about!' she burst out.

'Why, what is it—are you all afraid of me, or something?' he asked with a crooked smile.

'That's just it,' said Dunia, looking sternly straight at her brother. 'Mamenka, when she started up the stairs, was actually crossing herself in terror.'

A spasm twisted his face.

'Oh Dunia, what are you saying! Rodia, please don't be cross... What did you say that for, Dunia?' said Pulkheria Alexandrovna in embarrassment. 'But it's true that all the way here, in the railway carriage, I was dreaming of how we'd meet together, and tell each other everything... and I was so happy, I never noticed the journey! But what am I saying?—I'm happy now too... Dunia, you shouldn't have! Just seeing you, Rodia, makes me happy...'

'That'll do, Mamenka,' he muttered in confusion, squeezing her hand without looking at her. 'We'll have plenty of time to tell each other everything!'

As soon as he said that, he faltered and turned pale. A terrible sensation of a while ago had passed once again through his mind and cast a deathly chill. Once more he realized, with absolute clarity and conviction, that he had just told a dreadful lie: not only would he never again have the time to talk about everything with her; he could never, ever again, even *talk* about anything, with anyone at all. This agonizing realization was so powerful that for a moment he almost completely forgot himself. He stood up and made to leave the room, without a glance at anyone.

'What are you doing?' cried Razumikhin, seizing him by the arm.

He sat down again and looked around him in silence. Everyone was staring at him in astonishment.

'Why are you all being so boring?' he suddenly exclaimed, quite unexpectedly. 'Say something! What's the point of just sitting there like that? Come on, talk! Let's have a conversation... Here we all are together, sitting in silence... Well, somebody say something!'

'Thank God! I thought he was going the way he did yesterday,' said Pulkheria Alexandrovna, crossing herself.

'What is it, Rodia?' asked Avdotya Romanovna mistrustfully.

'Oh, nothing, I just remembered something,' he replied, and suddenly laughed.

'Well, if it was something, that's fine! Otherwise I myself was just thinking...' mumbled Zosimov, getting up. 'But I've got to go. I might drop by again... if you're in...'

He bowed and went out.

'What a wonderful person!' remarked Pulkheria Alexandrovna.

'Yes, wonderful, splendid, educated, intelligent...' Raskolnikov suddenly began, talking uncommonly fast and with an air of vivacity unusual for him. 'I don't remember where I came across him before my illness... I think I did meet him... And this one's a good man too!' he said, nodding at Razumikhin. 'Do you like him, Dunia?' he asked her suddenly, and inexplicably burst out laughing.

'Very much,' replied Dunia.

'Ugh, what a... pig you are!' said Razumikhin, red in the face with extreme embarrassment. He got up from his chair. Pulkheria Alexandrovna smiled slightly, while Raskolnikov guffawed loudly.

'Where are you off to?'

'I've got to... go as well.'

'You don't have to go at all, stay here! Zosimov's gone, so you think you have to go too. Don't!... What time is it? Is it twelve yet? What a pretty watch you have, Dunia! And why has everyone shut up again? I'm the only one who's talking!...'

'It was a present from Marfa Petrovna,' said Dunia.

'And very expensive too,' added Pulkheria Alexandrovna.

'Well, well! What a big one, almost too big for a lady.'

'I like them like that,' said Dunia.

'So it wasn't a gift from her fiancé,' thought Razumikhin, and for some unknown reason felt pleased at the fact.

'I thought it was a present from Luzhin,' remarked Raskolnikov.

'No, he hasn't given Dunechka anything yet.'

'A-ha! Remember, Mamenka, I was in love once, and wanted to get married,' he suddenly went on, looking at his mother. She was struck by the unexpected turn of the conversation, and by his tone of voice as he mentioned it.

'Oh yes, my dear, I know!'

Pulkheria Alexandrovna exchanged glances with Dunechka and Razumikhin.

'Hmm! Yes! So what can I tell you? I don't actually remember much. She was a sickly sort of girl,' he went on, once again becoming thoughtful and lowering his gaze. 'She was quite an invalid; she liked giving alms to beggars, and was always dreaming of becoming a nun, and once she burst into tears when she started telling me about that; yes, yes... I remember... I remember it very well. She was an ugly little thing... I really don't know what it was that attracted me to her; I think it was because she was always ill... If she'd been lame, or hunchbacked, I think I'd have loved her even more...' He smiled thoughtfully. 'So... it was a sort of spring fever...'

'No, that was more than a spring fever,' said Dunechka with conviction.

He looked closely and attentively at his sister, but either didn't hear what she was saying, or perhaps didn't even understand it. Then he got up, in deep thought, went over to his mother and gave her a kiss, returned to his place and sat down.

'You still love her!' exclaimed Pulkheria Alexandrovna, moved.

'Her, you mean? Now? Oh yes... you mean her! No. All that feels like a different world now... and it was so long ago. Anyway, everything around me seems not to be happening here at all...'

He looked closely at them.

'Even you... I feel as if I'm looking at you from a thousand miles away... And heaven only knows why we're talking about all this! And what's the point of asking me questions?' he added with annoyance; then he fell into a pensive silence again, biting his nails.

'What a nasty room you have, Rodia—it's like a coffin,' said Pulkheria Alexandrovna suddenly, breaking the strained silence. 'I'm convinced that half your gloomy mood is due to this room.'

'My room?' he replied absently. 'Yes, the room certainly helped... I've thought that too... But if you only knew, Mamenka, what a strange thing you've just said,' he suddenly added with an enigmatic smile.

A little more of this, and the whole of this company, this family he hadn't seen for three years, the familiar tone of their conversation despite their total inability to converse about anything whatever—all this would have become utterly intolerable for him. However, there was one question that couldn't be put off, that had to be settled this very day, one way or another; he had already decided that a while back, when he woke up. Now he was glad to turn to *business* as a way out of the situation.

'Look here, Dunia,' he began forthrightly and seriously. 'Of course I beg your pardon for what happened yesterday; but it's my duty to remind you once more that I won't change my mind about the most important point. It's either me or Luzhin. I may be a villain, but you mustn't be one too. It's either him or me. If you marry Luzhin, you'll cease to be my sister, straight away.'

'Rodia, Rodia! This is all just the same as yesterday!' cried Pulkheria Alexandrovna sorrowfully. 'And why keep calling yourself a villain? I can't bear it! And yesterday it was just the same...'

'Brother,' said Dunia firmly and no less forthrightly, 'you're making a mistake in all this. I thought about it last night, and I see what your mistake is. It's all because you seem to be assuming that I'm sacrificing myself to someone, for some reason. That isn't so at all. I'm simply marrying for my own sake, because my life is hard; at the same time, of course, I'll be glad if I manage to be useful to my family, but that's not the main reason why I'm determined to marry...'

'She's lying!' he thought to himself, biting his nails with rage. 'She's so proud! She can't admit she wants to be a do-gooder! Oh, what despicable characters! Even when they love you, it's as if they hated you... Oh, how I... hate them all!'

'So, in a word, I'm marrying Piotr Petrovich', continued Dunechka, 'because I'm choosing the lesser of two evils. I intend to fulfil honourably everything he expects of me; so I'm not deceiving him... Why did you smile just then?'

She reddened, and there was a flash of anger in her eyes.

'You'll fulfil everything?' he asked, with a venomous smile.

'Up to a point. From the start, the manner and form in which Piotr Petrovich courted me made it clear what he required. Perhaps, of course, he may have too high an opinion of himself; but I hope he has a high opinion of me too... Why are you laughing again?'

'And why are you blushing again? You're lying, sister, you're lying on purpose, out of nothing but feminine obstinacy, just to get your own way with me... You can't respect Luzhin; I've seen him and spoken to him. And so it follows that you're selling yourself to him for money, so you're committing a vile act, no matter what, and I'm glad that at least you're capable of blushing!'

'That's not true! I'm not lying!' cried Dunechka, losing all her composure. 'I shan't marry him unless I'm convinced that he values and respects me; and I shan't marry him unless I'm really sure I can respect him too. And I'm glad to say I can make sure of that for certain, this very day. And a marriage like this isn't a dishonourable act, as you call it! And even if you were right, even if I had truly resolved to act dishonourably, wouldn't it be pitilessly cruel of you to talk to me like that? How can you demand heroism from me which you yourself, perhaps, aren't capable of? That's tyranny, despotism! If I destroy anyone, it'll be myself alone... I haven't murdered anyone yet!... Why are you looking at me like that? Why have you gone so pale? Rodia, what's happened to you? Rodia, my darling!'

'Good God, he's going to faint! Look what you've done to him!' cried Pulkheria Alexandrovna.

'No, no... nonsense... I'm all right! Just a little dizzy. Not a faint... You keep going on about fainting!... Hmm! Yes... what was it I wanted to say? Oh yes: how are you going to convince yourself, this very day, that you can respect him and that he... values you, wasn't that how you put it? You said it would be today, didn't you? Or didn't I hear you right?'

'Mamenka, show my brother Piotr Petrovich's letter, please.'

With trembling hands, Pulkheria Alexandrovna gave him the letter. He took it with great interest, but before opening it he suddenly gave Dunechka a surprised look.

'Strange,' he pronounced slowly, as if suddenly struck by a new idea. 'What am I fussing about anyway? What's all the shouting about? Marry who you like!'

He seemed to be talking to himself, but he spoke the words aloud, and stared at his sister in seeming puzzlement for some time.

Eventually he opened the letter, still with a strange, surprised look; then he began reading it slowly and attentively, and read it through twice. Pulkheria Alexandrovna was particularly uneasy; and everyone was expecting something extraordinary.

'What surprises me', he began after some reflection, handing the letter back to his mother but addressing no one in particular, 'is that he's a businessman, a lawyer, and his conversation is so... pompous; and yet he writes such an illiterate letter.'

Everyone shifted in their seats; this wasn't at all what they expected.

'But they all write like that,' remarked Razumikhin abruptly.

'Have you read it, then?'

'Yes.'

'We showed it to him, Rodia, we... were asking his advice just now,' began Pulkheria Alexandrovna in some confusion.

'That's actually legal language,' interrupted Razumikhin; 'legal papers are still written like that to this day.'

'Legal? Yes, legal, just so, official language... Not very illiterate exactly, but not very literary either—it's official language!'

'Piotr Petrovich makes no secret of the fact that he didn't have an expensive education, in fact he prides himself on having made his own way,' remarked Avdotya Romanovna, rather hurt by her brother's new tone of voice.

'Well, and if he does pride himself on it, that's fair enough—I wouldn't deny him that. You, sister, seem offended because I only had that one frivolous comment to make about the letter; you think I picked on that trivial thing out of spite, on purpose to annoy you. On the contrary—it was the style of the letter that made me think of one especially relevant point. There's a particular expression there: "you will have no one to blame but yourself". That's stated very clearly and meaningfully; and then he threatens to walk out at once if I come. That threat of walking out is no less than a threat to abandon the two of you if you're disobedient; and abandon you right now, after summoning you to Petersburg. Now, what do you think? Could you feel just as offended at the expression Luzhin used, if he' (pointing at Razumikhin) 'had written it, or Zosimov, or any one of us?'

'N-no,' replied Dunechka, becoming more animated. 'I could see quite clearly that it was too naïvely expressed, and that he might just not be very good at expressing himself on paper... You were quite right, brother. I didn't even expect...'

'It's put in legal language, and there's no other way of writing legal language, so it came out coarser than he might have intended. But I have to disillusion you a bit: there's another phrase in that letter, a libel on me, and a pretty mean one. Yesterday I gave some money to a widow, ill with consumption and crushed by despair, not "on the pretext of funeral expenses", but actually for funeral expenses, and not into her daughter's hands—a young woman "of notorious conduct", as he writes (whom I met yesterday for the first time in my life)—but to the widow herself. In all this, I see an overhasty desire to blacken my name and stir up trouble between us. And once again it's put in legal language, which means that it all too obviously betrays his purpose, and with very naïve hastiness. He's an intelligent man, but intelligence alone isn't enough to make him act sensibly. It all adds up to the picture of a man who... I don't think values you very highly. I'm only saying so to warn you, because I sincerely wish you well...'

Dunechka said nothing to this; her decision was already taken, and she was only awaiting that evening.

'So what will you decide, Rodia?' asked Pulkheria Alexandrovna, even more troubled than before by this sudden, new, *businesslike* tone of his.

'What do you mean, "decide"?'

'Well, Piotr Petrovich writes that you're not to be with us this evening, and that he'll go away... if you come. So what will you... will you be there?'

'That, of course, isn't up to me. You yourself have to decide if you find Piotr Petrovich's stipulation offensive; and then Dunia must decide if she does. As for me, I'll do as you think best,' he added shortly.

'Dunechka has already decided, and I completely agree with her,' put in Pulkheria Alexandrovna hurriedly.

'I've decided to ask you, Rodia, please, please, to come and be with us without fail, at that meeting,' said Dunia. 'Will you come?'

'Yes, I'll come.'

'I'm asking you, too, to come at eight o'clock,' she said to Razumikhin. 'Mamenka, I'm inviting him as well.'

'And quite right too, Dunechka. Well,' added Pulkheria Alexandrovna, 'Let's do as you've decided. That's easier for me too: I don't like pretending and lying, let's have the whole truth out. And now Piotr Petrovich can be angry or not, just as he pleases!'

CHAPTER IV

AT that moment the door quietly opened and a young girl entered the room, looking timidly about her. Surprised and intrigued, everyone turned towards her. Raskolnikov didn't recognize her at once. It was Sofia Semionovna Marmeladova. He had seen her for the first time the day before, but at such a time, in such surroundings and dressed in such a way that his memory had retained the picture of quite a different person. Here, now, was a simply, even poorly dressed girl, still very young, almost a child, with a modest and respectable manner and a bright but rather frightened face. She was wearing a very simple house-dress, with an old, unfashionable hat on her head; but still carrying a parasol, as she had yesterday. When she saw to her surprise that the room was full of people, she was not so much embarrassed as disconcerted; she took fright, like a little child, and even made to leave the room again.

'Oh... it's you, is it?' said Raskolnikov, extremely surprised, and suddenly feeling embarrassed himself.

He recalled at once that his mother and sister already had some idea, from Luzhin's letter, of a girl of 'notorious conduct'. He had just been protesting against Luzhin's calumny, and mentioning that he had never met her before; and suddenly she herself walked in. He also remembered that he hadn't made the least protest at the expression 'notorious conduct'. All this flashed indistinctly through his mind. But when he looked more closely at her, he suddenly realized that this downtrodden creature was so completely downtrodden that he felt sorry for her. And when she made a move to escape in terror, something turned over within him.

'I wasn't expecting you at all,' he said hurriedly, holding her back with a look. 'Please, do sit down. I expect you've come from Katerina Ivanovna. Excuse me, don't sit there, come over here...'

When Sonia came in, Razumikhin, who had been sitting on one of Raskolnikov's three chairs very close to the door, stood up to let her in. Raskolnikov was at first going to show her to the place on the end of the divan where Zosimov had been sitting; but recalling that this divan was too *intimate*, since it served him as a bed, he hastily showed her to Razumikhin's chair.

'And you can sit here,' he said to Razumikhin, indicating Zosimov's place in the corner.

Sonia sat down, almost shaking with fright, and glanced timidly at the two ladies. She clearly couldn't believe that she was supposed to take a seat beside them. Realizing that this was so, she became so scared that she once again stood up and turned to Raskolnikov in extreme embarrassment.

'I... I... I just came by for a moment, I'm sorry to disturb you,' she stammered. 'I've come from Katerina Ivanovna, she had nobody else to send... Katerina Ivanovna told me I was to beg you ever so much to come to the funeral service, tomorrow morning... to the Mass... at the Mitrofanievsky cemetery,* and then at our place... her place... for refreshments... It'll be an honour for her... She said I was to ask you.'

Sonia faltered and stopped.

'I'll definitely try... definitely...' answered Raskolnikov, rising to his feet and also faltering without finishing what he wanted to say. 'Please, do sit down,' he added suddenly, 'I have to talk to you. Please—perhaps you're in a hurry, but do me a favour, give me two minutes of your time...'

And he drew up a chair. Sonia sat down again, and again cast a quick, timid, lost look at the two ladies; then dropped her gaze.

A flush covered Raskolnikov's pale face, and he seemed to shudder all over. His eyes burned.

'Mamenka,' he said in a firm, insistent voice. 'This is Sofia Semionovna Marmeladova, the daughter of that same unfortunate Mr Marmeladov who was crushed to death by horses before my own eyes yesterday: I've mentioned him to you before...'

Pulkheria Alexandrovna peered at Sonia through narrowed eyes. Despite all her confusion in the face of Rodia's insistent, challenging look, she was quite unable to deny herself that pleasure. Dunechka stared seriously and intently straight into the poor girl's face, examining her in some perplexity. On hearing herself introduced, Sonia was about to look up again, but became even more confused.

'I wanted to ask you,' Raskolnikov asked her quickly, 'how have things turned out for you today? Have you had any trouble?... from the police, for instance?'

'No, sir, everything passed all right. It was quite clear how he'd died, so they didn't bother us. It's only the other lodgers who are cross.'

'Why?'

'Because of the body being there so long... the weather's hot just now, there's a smell... so today they're taking him over to the cemetery, in time for vespers, he'll be there till tomorrow, in the chapel. Katerina Ivanovna didn't want it to start with, but now she can see for herself, it can't be helped...'

'So, today?'

'She asks you to do us the honour of coming to the funeral service in church tomorrow, and then to her place for the wake.'

'She's arranging a wake?'

'Yes, sir, just some cold refreshments. She said I was to thank you very kindly for helping us yesterday... without you, we couldn't have afforded a funeral.' Her lips and chin suddenly trembled, but she controlled herself with an effort, quickly looking down at the floor again.

Raskolnikov had been examining her closely during this exchange. Her little face was thin, very thin and pale, with rather irregular features, a bit pinched, with a pinched little nose and chin. She couldn't even have been called pretty, but her blue eyes were so bright, and when they livened up, her expression became so kind and simple-hearted that one was immediately charmed by her. And there was something else very characteristic about her face, and her whole person: although she was eighteen, she still looked like a little girl, much younger than her years, almost a child in fact; and this sometimes came out rather comically in her movements too.

'But how could Katerina Ivanovna manage with so little money, and even produce refreshments?' went on Raskolnikov insistently.

'Well, the coffin will be a simple one, sir... and everything will be simple and not expensive... I worked it all out with Katerina Ivanovna, and there'll be enough left to eat and drink something in his memory... and Katerina Ivanovna is very keen on that. We simply have to... it's a comfort for her... she's like that, you do understand...'

'I do, I do... of course... Why are you looking at my room like that? Here's Mamenka too, saying that the room's like a coffin.'

'You gave us all you had, yesterday!' Sonechka suddenly blurted out in a rapid, emphatic whisper, again looking firmly down at the floor. Her lips and chin trembled once more. She had been struck by Raskolnikov's impoverished surroundings for some time now, and her words burst out of their own accord. A silence followed. Dunechka's eyes brightened, and even Pulkheria Alexandrovna gave Sonia a friendly look.

'Rodia,' she said as she stood up, 'we'll be dining together, naturally. Dunechka, let's go... Rodia, you ought to go out and have a little walk, and then lie down and rest a bit; and after that come as quick as you can... But I'm afraid we've tired you out...'

'Yes, yes, I'll come,' he replied, getting up in a hurry. 'Though there's actually something I have to do...'

'Surely you won't be dining separately, will you?' cried Razumikhin, staring at Raskolnikov in amazement. 'What do you mean?'

'Yes, yes, I'll come, naturally, naturally... But could you stay behind a minute? Mamenka, you don't need him now, do you? Or am I taking him away from you?'

'Oh, no, no! But Dmitry Prokofich, you will come to dinner, won't you? Will you be so kind?'

'Do, please, come,' added Dunia.

Razumikhin bowed, beaming with pleasure. Everyone became terribly embarrassed for a moment.

'Goodbye, then, Rodia, I mean, see you soon; I hate saying "goodbye". Goodbye, Nastasia... oh dear, I said it again!...'

Pulkheria Alexandrovna was about to bow to Sonechka too, but somehow it didn't come out, and she hurriedly left the room.

But Avdotya Romanovna seemed to be waiting her turn, and as she followed her mother and walked past Sonia, she gave her an attentive, courteous, proper bow. Sonechka was flustered, made a sort of hasty, frightened bow, with a pained expression as though Avdotya Romanovna's polite attentions were a hurtful torment for her.

'Dunia, farewell then!' cried Raskolnikov from the doorway. 'Do give me your hand!'

'But I did—had you forgotten?' replied Dunia, turning awkwardly but affectionately towards him.

'Well, never mind—give it me again!'

And he squeezed her fingers tightly. Dunechka smiled at him, blushed, quickly pulled her hand away and followed her mother out, very happy herself for some reason.

'Well, this is wonderful!' he said to Sonia, returning to his room and looking cheerfully at her. 'God grant peace to the dead, but the living still have to live! Isn't that right? Isn't it? Surely it is!'

Sonia stared in wonderment at the sudden brightening of his face. He looked intently at her in silence for a while; everything her late father had told him about her suddenly rose up in his memory...

'Goodness me, Dunechka!' began Pulkheria Alexandrovna as soon as they were out on the street. 'I'm quite glad myself that we've left him—it's quite a relief. But did I ever imagine, yesterday in the railway carriage, that I'd ever be glad about that!'

'I keep telling you, Mamenka—he's still very ill. Really, can't you see that? Perhaps being anxious about us may have upset him too. We have to make allowances, and forgive a very, very great deal.'

'Well, you weren't making any allowances!' Pulkheria Alexandrovna instantly interrupted her, hotly and jealously. 'Do you know, Dunia, I was watching the two of you: you're the living image of him, not so much in your face as in your character. You're both melancholics, both moody and hot-blooded, both haughty, and both generous-hearted... I mean, it can't be that he's a selfish person, Dunechka, can it?... And when I think what's going to be happening in our place this evening, my heart really sinks!'

'Don't fret, Mamenka—what must be, will be.'

'But Dunechka! Just think of the situation we're in now! What if Piotr Petrovich breaks it off?' poor Pulkheria Alexandrovna blurted out incautiously.

'And what's he worth if he does?' retorted Dunechka scornfully.

'We did right, leaving him now,' Pulkheria Alexandrovna interrupted hastily. 'He needed to get away in a hurry. It'll do him good to have a walk and breathe some fresh air... it's terribly stuffy in there... though where would you find fresh air around here? Even in these streets, it's like being in a room with no windows. My God, what a town!... Look out, stand aside, they'll crush you, they're carrying something! That was a piano they were carrying, honestly... the way they jostle you... And I'm very scared of that girl too...'

'Which girl, Mamenka?'

'Why, that one, Sofia Semionovna, the one who was there just now...'

'Why on earth?'

'I've got a bad feeling about her, Dunia. Believe it or not, as soon as she came in, I thought straight away: here's what it's all about.'

'Nothing of the sort!' cried Dunia angrily. 'You and your forebodings, really, Mamasha! He's only known her since yesterday, and just now he didn't even recognize her when she came in.'

'Well, you'll see!... She bothers me—you'll soon see, you will! I was really frightened: there she was, looking and looking at me, with those eyes... I could hardly sit still on my chair, do you remember, when he began introducing her? And I think it's very odd, Piotr Petrovich writing those things about her, and then Rodia introduces her to us, even to you! So he must be fond of her!'

'Never you mind what he wrote! People were saying things about us as well, and writing them too: have you forgotten that? I'm certain that she's... a wonderful girl, and that it's all nonsense!'

'Please God she may be!'

'And Piotr Petrovich is a disgraceful scandalmonger,' Dunechka snapped suddenly.

Pulkheria Alexandrovna shrank into herself. Nothing more was said.

'Look here, this is what I want to talk about...' said Raskolnikov, drawing Razumikhin aside to the window.

'So I'll tell Katerina Ivanovna that you'll come,' said Sonia hurriedly, bowing her way out.

'Just a minute, Sofia Semionovna, we're not talking secrets, you're not in the way... I had something else to say to you... Look here,' he interrupted himself, suddenly turning back to Razumikhin. 'You know that man, don't you... what's his name?... Porfiry Petrovich?'

'I should say so! He's a relation. What about him?' Razumikhin added, in a burst of curiosity.

'Well, he's... that business... I mean, about the murder... you were saying yesterday... he's in charge of the case?'

'Yes... Well?' Razumikhin was staring open-eyed.

'He's been asking about her clients; well, I'd pawned some things with her too—just rubbishy stuff, but there was a ring of my sister's which she gave me as a keepsake when I moved here, and my father's silver watch. It's not worth more than five or six roubles all told, but I value it for its memories. So what am I to do now? I don't want the things to be lost, especially the watch. I was trembling just now in case my mother asked to see it, when we were talking about Dunechka's watch. It's the only thing of my father's that's survived. It would make her ill if it were lost. Women! So there you are, tell me what to do! I know I ought to let the police know. Or would it be better to tell Porfiry himself, eh? What do you think? I ought to do something quickly. You'll see, Mamenka will be asking about it even before we have dinner!'

'Certainly not the police—you absolutely must tell Porfiry!' cried Razumikhin in extraordinary excitement. 'Well, I'm delighted! Why wait—let's go straight away, it's just round the corner, and we're bound to find him in!'

'Very well then... let's go...'

'And he'll be very, very, very glad to make your acquaintance! I've told him a lot about you, at various times... I was talking to him only yesterday. Come on!... So you knew the old woman? Well, well!... This has all turned out splen–did–ly!... Oh, yes... Sofia Ivanovna...'

'Sofia Semionovna,' Raskolnikov corrected him. 'Sofia Semionovna, this is my friend Razumikhin, he's a good chap...'

'If you have to leave now...' began Sonia, without even looking at Razumikhin, and consequently becoming even more embarrassed.

'Yes, let's be off!' decided Raskolnikov. 'I'll come and see you this very day, Sofia Semionovna, but could you just tell me where you live?'

He was not exactly floundering in his speech, but affecting to be in a hurry and avoiding Sonia's eye. She told him her address, and blushed. They all left the room together.

'Don't you lock up?' asked Razumikhin as he followed them downstairs.

'Never! Though I've been meaning to buy a padlock for the last two years,' he added carelessly. 'How lucky people are if they've nothing to lock up, eh?' he laughed, turning to Sonia.

They stopped in the gateway.

'Are you turning right, Sofia Semionovna? Incidentally, how did you find me?' he asked, with an air of wanting to say something quite different to her. He kept wanting to look into her bright, gentle eyes, and not managing to.

'But you gave Polechka your address yesterday.'

'Polia? Oh yes... Polechka! She's... the little one... is she your sister? So I gave her my address, did I?'

'Do you mean you'd forgotten?'

'No... I remember...'

'But I'd heard about you before then, from my poor father, that time... Only I didn't know your name then, for he didn't know it himself... And today I came here... since I'd heard your name yesterday... and so today I asked, where does Mr Raskolnikov live?... I didn't know you were a lodger like me... So, goodbye... I'll tell Katerina Ivanovna...'

She was terribly glad to get away at last. She walked off, head down, hurrying along to get out of their sight as quickly as she could, to cover those twenty paces to the right turn outside in the street, and be alone at last, and then walk on, still hurrying, not looking at anybody, not noticing anything, just thinking, remembering, turning over every word that had been said and every circumstance of her visit. Never, never, had she felt anything like this. A whole new world had entered her soul, mysterious and shadowy. She suddenly recalled that Raskolnikov himself was meaning to visit her this same day, perhaps this very morning, perhaps this minute!

'Only not today, please not today!' she murmured, her heart sinking, as though imploring someone, like a frightened child. 'Oh Lord! Coming to me... to that room... he'll see... Oh Lord!'

And of course, at that moment she could not have noticed a certain gentleman, unknown to her, who was following carefully behind her, watching her every step. He had been following her from the moment she came out of the gateway. At that moment, when the three of them, Razumikhin, Raskolnikov and she, had stopped briefly on the pavement to talk, this passer-by had given a start as he walked by them, happening to hear Sonia say 'so today I asked, where does Mr Raskolnikov live?' He had thrown a quick but searching look at all three of them, but particularly at Raskolnikov, whom Sonia was addressing. Then he looked at the house, and made a mental note of it. All this had happened in a single instant, as he walked past them. Then this passer-by had walked on, trying not to attract attention, slowing his pace and apparently waiting for something. He was waiting for Sonia: he could see that the three were separating and that Sonia was about to go home, wherever that was.

'So where's her home? I've seen her somewhere before,' he thought, recalling Sonia's face... 'I must find out.'

When he reached the corner, he crossed the side street, looked round and saw that Sonia was already following him along the same road, without noticing anything. When she reached the turning, she too turned into the side street. Now he followed her along the opposite pavement, never taking his eyes off her. After some fifty steps, he crossed back to Sonia's side of the street, caught up with her and followed five paces behind her.

He was a man of about fifty, above average height and rather thick-set, with broad, sloping shoulders which gave him a rather stooping look. He was stylishly and comfortably dressed, and appeared to be a gentleman of some importance. He carried a handsome cane which he tapped on the pavement at every step; his gloves were fresh and clean. He had quite a pleasant, broad face with high cheekbones, and a fresh complexion—a rare sight in Petersburg. His hair was still very thick, fair with just a touch of grey, and he had a broad, thick, spade-shaped beard, even fairer than the hair on his head. His eyes were blue, with a cold, intent, meditative look. His lips were scarlet. All in all, he was a very well-preserved man who looked far younger than his years.

When Sonia emerged onto the canal bank, they found themselves side by side on the pavement. He looked at her and noted how perplexed and preoccupied she was. When she reached her house, she turned in to the gateway and he followed her, apparently somewhat surprised. On entering the yard she turned right, making for the corner with the staircase up to her flat.* 'Well!' muttered the stranger, and followed her upstairs. Only now did Sonia notice him. She went up to the third floor, turned along the gallery and rang the bell of number nine, where the words 'Kapernaumov Tailor' were marked in chalk on the door. 'Well!' repeated the stranger, surprised at this strange coincidence, and rang the bell of number eight next door. The two doors were half a dozen paces apart.

'So you live at Kapernaumov's!' he laughed, looking at Sonia. 'He was altering a waistcoat of mine yesterday. And I live here, next door to you, at Madame Resslich's, Gertruda Karlovna's. What a strange chance!'

Sonia looked at him closely.

'Neighbours!' he went on, in a particularly merry voice. 'I've only been in town two days myself. Well, well, goodbye for now.'

Sonia said nothing in reply; the door was opened for her, and she slipped in. For some reason she felt ashamed, and perhaps a bit shy.

On the way to Porfiry's house, Razumikhin was in a particularly animated mood.

'This is splendid, my boy,' he repeated several times. 'And I'm glad, so glad!'

'What on earth are you glad about?' wondered Raskolnikov.

'I never even knew you'd pawned things with the old woman. And... and... was it a long time ago? I mean, is it long since you were there?'

'What a naïve idiot he is!'

'When it was?...' Raskolnikov paused, thinking back. 'It was about three days before her death that I went to see her, I think. But I'm not on my way to redeem my things now,' he put in hastily, evincing particular concern about the things. 'In any case, all I've got is one silver rouble—thanks to my blasted delirium yesterday!'

He laid special stress on the word 'delirium'.

'Well, yes, yes, yes,' Razumikhin said hurriedly, though one couldn't tell what he was agreeing with. 'So that's why you were... a bit overcome that time... but do you know, even when you were delirious you kept talking about rings and chains and things!... Well, yes, yes... that's quite clear, it's all clear now.'

'So that's how it is! See how they've all latched on to that idea! I mean, here's a man who'd let himself be crucified for me, and yet he's very glad that *it's all clear* why I was talking about rings when I was raving! They've all got it fixed in their heads!...'

'Shall we find him in?' he asked aloud.

'Certainly, certainly,' replied Razumikhin quickly. 'He's a splendid chap, you'll see! A bit awkward—I mean, he's a society man too, but I meant awkward in a different sense. He's very, very bright, not stupid at all, but he does have his own way of looking at things... he's mistrustful, sceptical, cynical... he likes to mislead you, or rather make a fool of you... well, that's a well-tried technique... But he knows his job, he certainly does... There was one case last year, a murder, which he cleared up when the trail had practically gone cold. He's very, very, very keen to meet you!'

'But why so very keen?'

'I mean, it's not that... You see, in these last few days, when you had fallen ill, I found myself talking about you a great deal, on several occasions... Well, and he was listening... and when he discovered you'd been studying law, but your circumstances prevented you from finishing your course, he said "What a pity!" So I concluded... well, it was everything taken together, not just that single fact; and Zametov, yesterday... You see, Rodia, I said all sorts of things to you last night, when I was drunk, seeing you home... so I'm afraid, my dear fellow, you may have taken me too seriously, you see...'

'What do you mean? That everyone thinks I'm mad? Well, that could even be true.'

He smiled a strained smile.

'Yes... yes... I mean, no, damn it, no!... And everything I said then, about other things too, all that was nonsense, it was just drunken talk.'

'What are you apologizing for? I'm so bored with it all!' cried Raskolnikov with exaggerated annoyance—though in truth he was half putting it on.

'I know, I know, I understand. Believe me, I understand. I'm even ashamed to mention it.'

'So if you're ashamed, then don't!'

They both fell silent. Razumikhin was in a state of utter delight, and Raskolnikov was revolted by that. He was also alarmed by what Razumikhin had just been saying about Porfiry.

'I'll have to sing Lazarus* with this one too,' he thought, his face pale, his heart pounding. 'And do it naturally. The most natural thing would be not to show anything at all. Strictly nothing at all. No, *strictly* would be unnatural again... Oh well, we'll see how it turns out... we'll see... in a moment... Is it good or bad that I'm going? A moth deliberately flying to the candle flame. My heart's thumping, that's not good!'

'It's this grey house here,' said Razumikhin.

'The main thing is—does Porfiry know, or doesn't he, that I was in that witch's flat yesterday... asking about the blood? I have to find out at once, right from the start, as soon as I go in—I have to tell by his face; o-ther-wise... Even if it kills me, I'll find out!'

'D'you know what?' he suddenly said to Razumikhin, with a wicked smile, 'I've noticed, my boy, that you've been in a state of unusual excitement all day today. Haven't you?'

'What excitement? I'm not in any state of excitement!' Razumikhin protested hotly.

'No, my boy, it's quite obvious. When you were on that chair just then, you were sitting in a way you never normally do, right on the edge, and you kept twitching as if you had cramp. And leaping up from your chair for no reason. One minute you'd be looking cross, and then you'd put on a silly expression as sweet as sugar. And blushing, too—especially when they asked you to come to dinner, you blushed like anything.'

'I did nothing of the sort! Nonsense! What are you going on about?'

'Why keep wriggling out of it, like a schoolboy? Oh, the devil, he's blushing again!'

'What a swine you are, though!'

'What are you so embarrassed about? Romeo! You wait till I tell all this somewhere tonight, ha! ha! ha! That'll amuse my Mamenka... and someone else too...'

'But listen, listen, this is serious, this is... What next, damn it!' said Razumikhin, utterly disconcerted, and chilled with horror. 'What are you going to tell them? Look here, brother, I'm... Oh, you really are a swine!'

'Just like a rose in springtime! And how well it suits you, if you only knew: a six-foot Romeo! And how you've washed yourself clean today, scrubbed your nails too, didn't you? When did you ever do that? And my God, you've pomaded your hair! Bend down!'

'Swine!'

Raskolnikov laughed so hard, he seemed unable to restrain himself; and laughing together like this, they entered Porfiry Petrovich's flat. That was just what Raskolnikov needed: they could be heard from indoors, walking in, laughing together, and still laughing in the hallway.

'Not a word here, or I'll... brain you!' whispered Razumikhin in fury, seizing Raskolnikov by the shoulder.

CHAPTER V

RASKOLNIKOV was already on his way in. He entered with the air of a man doing his best to stop himself bursting out laughing. Following behind him, looking furious and thoroughly crushed, blushing as red as a peony, came Razumikhin, lanky, awkward, and covered in embarrassment. His face and whole bearing at that point were truly ridiculous, and fully deserved Raskolnikov's laughter. Raskolnikov himself, without having been introduced, bowed to his host, who was standing in the middle of the room and looking questioningly at them. Raskolnikov held out a hand and shook hands with the man, while still obviously making a huge effort to choke back his mirth and at least utter a word or two to introduce himself.

But no sooner had he put on a serious face and muttered something, than he suddenly, almost involuntarily, glanced back at Razumikhin and broke down. His suppressed laughter burst out all the more uncontrollably for having been held back until this moment. The extraordinary ferocity with which Razumikhin greeted this apparently sincere laughter made the whole scene appear unaffectedly good-humoured and— most importantly—natural. Razumikhin himself accidentally reinforced the impression.

'Damn it!' he roared, waving his arm about. He caught it on a little round wooden table with an empty tea glass on it, bringing everything crashing to the floor.

'No need to break up the furniture, gentlemen—you're costing the State money!'* cried Porfiry Petrovich cheerfully.

This was the scene: Raskolnikov was calming down from his merriment, forgetting his hand which was still grasping his host's; not wanting to go too far, he was waiting for the right moment to end all this as quickly and naturally as possible. Razumikhin, utterly discomfited after upsetting the little table and smashing the tea glass, glanced miserably at the shattered fragments, spat and turned abruptly away to the window, where he now stood with his back to the others, scowling ferociously and staring unseeingly out of the window. Porfiry Petrovich was laughing, quite happily, but it was evident that he needed explanations. By a chair in the corner stood Zametov, who had risen when the guests entered and was standing waiting to see what happened. He had parted his lips in a smile, but was observing the scene with astonishment and some perplexity, and looking at Raskolnikov with positive embarrassment. His unexpected presence gave Raskolnikov an unpleasant feeling.

'Here's something else to think about!' he said to himself.

'Please excuse us,' he began with a great show of embarrassment. 'Raskolnikov...'

'Not at all, delighted to meet you, sir, and how good of you to drop by like this... What's up, doesn't he even want to say hello?' Porfiry Petrovich went on, nodding towards Razumikhin.

'I honestly don't know why he's in such a rage with me. All I did was tell him on our way here that he looked like a Romeo, and... and proved it; I think that was all that happened.'

'Swine!' said Razumikhin, without turning round.

'So, he must have had very serious grounds for taking such offence over a single word,' laughed Porfiry.

'Oh, you... detective!... To hell with you all!' snapped Razumikhin, and then burst out laughing himself, looking as cheerful as if nothing had happened at all, and walking up to Porfiry Petrovich.

'That'll do! We're both fools. Now let's get down to business. This is my friend Rodion Romanovich Raskolnikov, who's heard a lot about you and wanted to meet you, and he's also got a bit of business with you. Hey! Zametov! How do you come to be here? Do you two know each other? Since when?'

'What's all this now?' thought Raskolnikov in alarm.

Zametov appeared somewhat disconcerted, but not greatly so.

'We met yesterday, at your own place,' he said easily.

'God saved me some trouble, then. Last week this man was begging me to find a way of introducing him to you, Porfiry, but now you've sniffed each other out without my help... Where d'you keep your tobacco?'

Porfiry Petrovich was casually dressed, in a dressing gown over very clean linen; his slippers were down at heel. He was a man of about thirty-five, below average height, stout and even paunchy; clean-shaven, with no moustache or side whiskers; he had a big, round head that bulged conspicuously at the back, and his hair was thick and close-cropped. His plump, round, rather snub-nosed face was greyish-yellow like a sick man's, but quite cheerful and with a hint of mockery. It could even have been a good-natured face, but for the expression in his eyes, which had a moist, watery gleam under almost white eyelashes that flickered as though he was winking at someone. The look in those eyes was strangely out of harmony with the rest of him; he had something of the figure of a peasant woman, yet his eyes gave him a more serious look than one might have expected at first sight.

As soon as he heard that his visitor had 'a bit of business' with him, he straight away invited him to sit down on the divan, seated himself at the other end and fixed his eyes on him, in the expectation of having the business explained on the spot. He wore an expression of intense, even excessively serious attention—the sort of expression that would be sure to disturb and disconcert you from the start. Particularly if you were speaking to a stranger; and even more so if what you needed to discuss struck you as far too trivial to deserve such unusually solemn attention. But Raskolnikov set out his business in brief and coherent terms, clearly and precisely, and was so pleased with himself that he even managed to take a proper look at Porfiry. Porfiry Petrovich never once took his eyes off him. Razumikhin, sitting opposite them at the same table, followed the explanations with restless impatience, constantly shifting his gaze from one to the other and back again in a quite unnecessary way.

'Idiot!' thought Raskolnikov to himself.

'You need to give a statement to the police,' replied Porfiry with the most businesslike expression, 'saying that having heard about such and such an occurrence, I mean about this murder, you now wish to inform the investigator in charge of the affair that such and such objects are your property and that you wish to redeem them... or that... Anyway, they'll write it for you.'

'But that's just the trouble—at this precise moment,' began Raskolnikov, trying his hardest to appear embarrassed, 'I'm not quite in funds... I'm not even in a position to find such a small amount... what I want to do now, you see, is just to state that those things belong to me, but that as soon as I have the money...'

'That doesn't matter,' replied Porfiry Petrovich, listening coolly to this talk of money. 'Or, if you like, you can write directly to me to the same effect, saying that having ascertained these facts and now given a statement about your property, you request...'

'Can I do that on plain paper?' Raskolnikov hastened to interrupt him, again returning to the money question.

'Oh, the very plainest!' And suddenly Porfiry Petrovich gave him a frankly mocking look, screwing up his eyes and seeming to wink at him. Actually Raskolnikov might just have imagined it, for it only lasted an instant. But there certainly had been something of the sort. Raskolnikov could have sworn that Porfiry had winked at him, heaven knows why.

'He knows!' The thought flashed like lightning through his mind.

'Forgive me for troubling you with such trivialities,' he went on, rather disconcerted. 'My things are only worth five roubles all told, but they're particularly precious to me as mementoes of the people who owned them; and I must say I was quite alarmed when I heard...'

'So that was why you got in such a panic yesterday, when I let it out to Zosimov that Porfiry was questioning the people who had left pledges!' put in Razumikhin, evidently on purpose.

This was quite intolerable. Raskolnikov couldn't stop himself glaring viciously at him out of his dark eyes. But he recollected himself straight away.

'You're making fun of me, aren't you, my boy?' he said, with well-feigned irritation. 'I know you probably think I'm making too much fuss over that stuff; but that doesn't make me either selfish or greedy, and as far as I'm concerned those two trivial items may not be rubbish at all. I told you a while back that the silver watch, though it's barely worth a few coppers, is the only thing my father left me. You can laugh at me, but'—and he suddenly turned to Porfiry—'my mother has come on a visit, and if she found out'—and he quickly turned back to Razumikhin, with a particular effort to make his voice tremble—'that the watch was lost, I swear to you, she'd be in despair! Women!'

'No, no! I didn't mean that at all! Quite the opposite!' cried Razumikhin in dismay.

'Was that all right? Was it natural? Didn't I overdo it?' Raskolnikov wondered anxiously. 'What did I say "Women!" for?'

'So your mother has come to see you, has she?' Porfiry enquired for some reason.

'Yes.'

'When did she get here?'

'Last night.'

Porfiry was silent, as if reflecting.

'Your things wouldn't ever be lost,' he went on, coolly and calmly. 'I've been expecting you here for some time.'

And as though he had said nothing in particular, he officiously set about finding an ashtray for Razumikhin, who was mercilessly scattering cigarette ash over the carpet. Raskolnikov started, but Porfiry appeared not to be looking at him, still concentrating instead on Razumikhin's cigarette.

'Wha-at? Expecting him? Why, did you know that he'd pawned things *there*?' cried Razumikhin.

Porfiry Petrovich addressed Raskolnikov directly. 'Both your things, the ring and the watch, were in *her* place, wrapped up in a single packet, with your name clearly marked in pencil together with the date when she got them from you.'

'How is it you're so observant?' Raskolnikov grinned awkwardly, making an effort to look Porfiry straight in the eyes. But he couldn't hold back from suddenly adding: 'I made that comment just now, because there must have been a great many clients pawning their things... so you'd have found it difficult to remember them all... And yet you remember each of them so distinctly, and... and...'

'Stupid! Feeble! Why did I add that?'

'Well, almost all of them are known by now, you were the only one not to have troubled to contact us,' replied Porfiry with a barely perceptible hint of mockery.

'I haven't been quite well.'

'Yes, I'd heard about that too. Actually, I heard that you'd been seriously upset about something. Aren't you looking a bit pale, even now?'

'I'm not in the least pale... on the contrary, I'm perfectly well!' snapped Raskolnikov rudely and venomously, suddenly changing his tone. Irrepressible fury was boiling up inside him. 'If I'm furious, I'll let something slip!' flashed through his mind again. 'But what are they tormenting me for?...'

'Not quite well!' Razumikhin put in. 'What nonsense! He was raving, out of his mind, right up to yesterday... Would you believe it, Porfiry, he could barely stand, and yet the moment Zosimov and I left him yesterday, he got up and sneaked away, and was out on the tiles somewhere till nearly midnight, though he was in a state of complete delirium, I tell you. Can you imagine that? Simply extraordinary!'

'*Complete delirium?* Really? Well I never!' said Porfiry, shaking his head like a peasant woman.

'Oh, what nonsense! Don't you believe him! Actually, I know you don't believe him anyway!' Raskolnikov blurted out, more angrily than he should. But Porfiry Petrovich seemed not to have heard his strange words.

'How could you have gone out, unless you were delirious?' Razumikhin asked heatedly. 'Why go out? What for?... And why go out in secret? Tell me, were you in your right mind just then? Now that you're out of danger, I can talk to you straight!'

'I was heartily sick of them yesterday,' said Raskolnikov, suddenly addressing Porfiry with an insolent, provocative smile. 'So I ran away from them to rent a flat, so that they shouldn't find me, and I took a whole heap of money with me. Mr Zametov here saw the money. So what do you say, Mr Zametov, was I in my right mind or was I delirious? Can you settle the argument?'

At that moment he could happily have strangled Zametov, so hateful did he find the other's silent look.

'I think you were talking very rationally, and cleverly too, but you were far too irritable,' replied Zametov drily.

'And today', put in Porfiry Petrovich, 'Nikodim Fomich was telling me that he'd met you yesterday, very late indeed, at the lodgings of a certain clerk who'd been knocked down by some horses...'

'And what about that clerk then!' Razumikhin took him up. 'Well, weren't you crazy at his place? Handing over the last of your money to his widow! All right, if you wanted to help, you could have given her fifteen, or even twenty, or just kept three roubles for yourself—but no, you tossed over the whole twenty-five!'

'So perhaps I'd found a treasure somewhere, that you don't know about! And that's why I was overcome with generosity yesterday... Here's Mr Zametov, he knows that I found a treasure!... Please excuse us', he said, turning to Porfiry with trembling lips, 'for taking up a whole half-hour of your time with this nonsensical argument. I dare say you've had enough of us, haven't you?'

'Not at all, my dear sir, not—at—all! If you only knew how much you interest me! It's fascinating, watching you and listening to you... and I confess, I'm so glad that you've finally had the goodness to come round and see me...'

'Well at least let's have some tea then! My throat's parched!' cried Razumikhin.

'An excellent idea! Perhaps you'll all join us. But wouldn't you like... something a little stronger, before your tea?'

'Get away with you!'

Porfiry Petrovich went out to order the tea.

Raskolnikov's thoughts were whirling about in his head like a hurricane. He was at the end of his tether.

'The main thing is that they aren't even hiding it, or trying to be polite! How is it that although you don't know me at all, you've been talking to Nikodim Fomich about me? That means they're not even trying to hide the fact that they're after me like a pack of hounds! Openly spitting in my face!' He was trembling with fury. 'Well then, knock me down if you like, but don't play cat-and-mouse with me. That's really rude, Porfiry Petrovich—and perhaps I won't put up with it!... I'll stand up and shove the whole truth in everybody's face, and then you'll see how I despise you!' He panted for breath. 'But what if I'm just imagining it? What if it's all a mirage, and I've got everything wrong, and I'm only getting angry because I'm naïve, and can't manage to keep up my shameful pretence? Perhaps it was all unintentional? All their words are quite ordinary, but there's something about them... One could always say all that, but still, there is something. Why did he say "in *her* place"? And why did Zametov add that I was talking "cleverly"? Why does he use that tone of voice? Yes... his tone... Razumikhin was sitting here too, so why didn't he see anything? That innocent fool never does see anything! My fever again!... Did Porfiry wink at me just then, or not? That's probably nonsense—why would he wink? Do they want to shatter my nerves, or are they teasing me? Either it's all an illusion, or *they know*!... Even Zametov is being brazen... Is he being brazen? He's changed his mind overnight. I had the feeling he would! He's acting quite at home here, though it's his first visit. Porfiry isn't treating him as a guest—he's sitting with his back to him. They've sniffed each other out! No question, they've sniffed each other out *because of me*! No question, they were talking about me before we arrived!... Do they know about the flat? If only it was all over quickly!... When I said that I'd run out yesterday to find myself a flat, he let it pass, he didn't pick it up... But that was clever of me, to mention looking for a flat: that'll come in useful! In delirium, so they say!... Ha! ha! ha! He knows all about yesterday evening! But he didn't know that my mother had arrived... So that witch even marked down the date with her pencil!... No, you're wrong, I shan't give myself away! There are no facts here, nothing but a mirage! No, let's have some facts from you! And the flat isn't a fact, it was delirium; I know what to say to them... Do they know about the flat, though? I shan't leave until I know! Why did I come here? And my being in a rage now, that's a fact too, I suppose. Phew, how short-tempered I am! But perhaps that's a good thing, if I'm playing the part of a sick man... He's probing me. Wants to get me confused. Why did I come?'

All this flashed through his head like lightning.

Porfiry Petrovich returned a moment later. He seemed to have suddenly become more jovial.

'Your party last night, my friend, has given me such a head... And I'm really not myself today at all,' he said to Razumikhin with a laugh, in quite a different tone of voice.

'So how was it? Interesting? I had to leave you yesterday just at the most interesting point. Who won?'

'No one, obviously. They had moved on to the eternal questions, and were soaring about in the clouds.'

'Just imagine, Rodia, what they got on to yesterday. Whether crime exists or not! I told you they'd talked themselves silly!'

'What's surprising about that? An ordinary social question,' replied Raskolnikov absently.

'That wasn't how the question was put,' remarked Porfiry.

'Not quite, that's true,' Razumikhin agreed hastily, becoming heated as usual. 'Look here, Rodion: listen to me and say what you think. I wish you would. I was going out of my mind with them last night, waiting for you to turn up: I told them you were coming... It all started with the socialist position, which we all know: crime is a protest against the abnormality of the social structure, that's all, nothing more, and no other explanation is admissible—none whatever!...'

'You've got that wrong!' cried Porfiry Petrovich, becoming visibly more animated, laughing every minute as he looked at Razumikhin, and making him even more excited.

'N-nothing else is admissible!' Razumikhin interrupted him heatedly,

'I'm not wrong!... I'll show you their pamphlets—it's all because people have been "corrupted by their environment",* nothing else! That's their favourite phrase! From which it follows that if society was properly organized, all crime would immediately disappear, since there would be nothing to protest about, and in an instant everyone would become law-abiding. They don't take nature into account, they've banished nature, nature isn't supposed to exist! They don't see humanity developing along a historical, *living* pathway to the end, where it eventually evolves of its own accord into the perfect society; they see a social system generated in some sort of mathematician's brain, which will instantly organize the whole of humanity and instantly make it righteous and virtuous, quicker than any living process, without any historical, living pathway!* That's why they dislike history so instinctively—"there's nothing there but infamy and stupidity"—and they explain everything on the basis of stupidity alone! That's why they dislike the *living* process of life: they don't want the *living soul*! The living soul will demand life; the living soul won't obey mechanical laws; the living soul is an object of suspicion; the living soul is retrograde! Their own scheme may have a whiff of carrion, it may be made of India rubber—but at least it's not alive, it has no will, it's slavish and won't rebel! And the result is, they've boiled it all down to how you lay the bricks and arrange the rooms and corridors in some phalanstery!* Very well, the phalanstery may be ready, but your human nature isn't ready for this phalanstery, it wants life, it hasn't yet accomplished its living process, it's too early for the graveyard! Logic alone won't bypass nature! Logic can envisage three possibilities—but there are a million of them! Cutting out all that million and reducing everything to the mere question of comfort! That's the easiest solution to the problem! Temptingly clearcut, and with no need to think! That's the main thing—no need to think! The whole mystery of life fitted onto two pages of print!'

'Look at him, off again, banging his drum! Grab him by the arms, someone!' laughed Porfiry. 'Just imagine,' he said, turning to Raskolnikov, 'that's how it was last night, all in the same room, six of them, and he'd filled them up with punch first. Can you imagine that? No, my friend, you've got it wrong: the "environment" accounts for a great deal in crime, I can assure you of that.'

'I know it does; but tell me this. A forty-year-old man violates a girl of ten*—was it the environment that drove him to it?'

'Well, in the strictest sense, yes, it was his environment,' remarked Porfiry with startling authority. 'His crime against the girl could very, very well be explained by the "environment".'

Razumikhin almost exploded with fury.

'All right then, would you like me to *deduce* to you', he bellowed, 'that the only reason you've got white eyelashes is that the tower of Ivan the Great is two hundred and fifty feet tall:* and I'll deduce it clearly and precisely, and progressively, and even with a liberal flavour? I could! Well, will you bet me?'

'Done! Let's hear him make the deduction!'

'Oh, damn him, he's just pretending!' cried Razumikhin, leaping up with a dismissive gesture. 'What's the point of talking to you? He's putting it all on, you don't know him yet, Rodion! Yesterday he was taking their side, just to make fools of us all. And what he was saying yesterday, my Lord! And they were pleased with him!... I mean, he could keep this sort of thing up for two weeks on end. Last year he was persuading us for some reason that he wanted to become a monk; he went on like that for two months! And recently he decided to convince us that he was marrying, and everything was ready for the wedding. He'd even had a new suit made. We were all congratulating him; but there was no bride, nor anything else—it was all a fantasy!'

'Wrong again! I'd had the suit made before. It was because of it that I had the idea of making fun of you all.'

'Are you really such a play-actor?' asked Raskolnikov carelessly.

'Did you think I wasn't? Wait a bit, I'll take you in as well—ha! ha! ha! No, look, I'll tell you the whole truth. All these questions about crime and the environment and little girls have just reminded me of an article you wrote—well, it's actually always interested me—"On Crime", or whatever you called it, I've forgotten the title. I had the pleasure of reading it two months ago in the *Periodical Review*.'

'An article by me? In the *Periodical Review*?' asked Raskolnikov in astonishment. 'I did write something six months ago, when I left the university—something about a particular book; but I submitted that article to the *Weekly Review*, not the *Periodical*.'

'And yet it came out in the *Periodical*.'

'But surely the *Weekly Review* closed down, that's why they didn't print it at the time...'

'That's true, but when it closed down, the *Weekly Review* merged with the *Periodical Review*, and that's why your little article appeared in the *Periodical Review* two months ago. Didn't you know?'

Raskolnikov had really not known anything about it.

'For goodness' sake, you could demand a fee for your article! What a character you are, really! Living such an isolated life that you don't even know things like that, which directly concern you. It's a fact, though.'

'Bravo, Rodka! I didn't know either!' cried Razumikhin. 'I'll run over to the reading room and ask for the issue! Two months ago? What date? Never mind, I'll find it anyway. What a thing! And he says nothing about it!'

'How did you find out that the article was by me? It's only signed with an initial.'

'That was by chance, and only a few days ago. It was through the editor—we know each other... I was most interested in it.'

'I remember that I was looking at the criminal's psychological state throughout the course of the crime.'

'Yes, and you maintain that the act of committing a crime is always accompanied by illness. That's very, very original, but... it wasn't actually that part of your little article that interested me. It was a particular idea that was slipped in at the end, but one that you unfortunately only hint at, without expressing it clearly... In brief, if you recollect, there was a suggestion that there exist in the world certain individuals who can... well, not that they can, but they have the full right to, commit all kinds of outrages and crimes, and that the law does not apply to them.'

Raskolnikov smiled wryly at this extreme and deliberate perversion of his idea.

'What? What's all this? The right to commit a crime? But not because they're "corrupted by their environment", surely?' enquired Razumikhin in some alarm.

'No, no, not quite that,' replied Porfiry. 'The whole point is that in his article, people are somehow all subdivided into "ordinary" and "extraordinary". Ordinary people have to live in obedience and have no right to break the law, because they're ordinary, you see. While the extraordinary people have the right to commit all kinds of crimes and break the law in all sorts of ways, simply because they're extraordinary.* That's your argument, I believe—unless I'm mistaken?'

'But how can that be? You can't possibly have written that!' muttered Razumikhin in bewilderment.

Raskolnikov smiled again. He had understood straight away what this was about, and what he was being pushed into admitting. He decided to take up the challenge.

'That's not quite what I said,' he began, simply and modestly. 'As a matter of fact, I admit it, you've stated it almost correctly; indeed, if you like, absolutely correctly...' (He almost enjoyed accepting that it was absolutely correct.) 'The only difference is that I don't at all insist that extraordinary people are necessarily bound to commit all sorts of outrages all the time, as you put it. In fact I don't think that such an article would have passed the censor. I merely suggested that an "extraordinary" person has the right—not the legal right, I mean, but the personal right, to allow his conscience to overstep... certain obstacles; and that only where the practical fulfilment of his idea (which might on occasion bring salvation for the whole human race) demands it. You were pleased to say that my article wasn't clear; I'm prepared to do my best to clarify it for you. I may not be wrong in believing that you'd like me to do that. Very well. In my view, if circumstances had been such that Kepler's and Newton's discoveries* could not have become known to the world, otherwise than through the sacrifice of the lives of one, or ten, or a hundred or more people who were impeding those men's discoveries or obstructing their work, then Newton would have had the right, indeed the duty... to *eliminate* those ten or a hundred people, in order to bring his discoveries to humanity at large. But it doesn't at all follow that Newton had the right to kill people right and left, just as he liked, or to go stealing from the market every day. Furthermore, I seem to remember that in my article I explored the idea that all the... well, let's say the lawgivers and leaders of men, in history, beginning from ancient times and going on by way of Lycurgus, Solon,* Mohammed, Napoleon, and so forth, were each and every one of them criminals, if only by virtue of the fact that in creating a new law they were ipso facto infringing an old one, held sacred by society and inherited from their forefathers; and of course these men didn't hold back from shedding blood, so long as the shedding of blood served their purpose (for all that the blood was often guiltless, and was nobly shed in defence of the ancient laws). Indeed, it's a remarkable fact that the majority of those benefactors and leaders of humanity were particularly bloodthirsty people. In a word, I deduce that all of them, not only the great ones but even those who ever so slightly diverged from the common run of humanity, I mean those who were just slightly capable of saying something new, must by their very nature be criminals—to a greater or lesser extent, of course. Without that, it would be difficult for them to stand out from the common herd; and of course they can't consent to remain within the herd, yet again by virtue of their own nature. So they're obliged not to accept things as they are. In short, you can see that up to this point there's nothing particularly new. It's been printed and read a thousand times over. As for my classification of people into ordinary and extraordinary, I grant that it's fairly arbitrary, but after all I'm not insisting on exact figures. I merely believe in my central idea, which is that people, according to a law of nature, are *generally* divided into two categories: a lower one (ordinary people), which represents a material that serves solely to reproduce its own likeness; and real men, those who possess the gift or talent of saying *something new* in their own milieu. There are, of course, infinite numbers of possible subdivisions; but the distinctive features of the two categories are fairly well marked. The first category, that is to say the material, in general terms, consists of people who by their nature are conservative, orderly, live obedient lives and enjoy being obedient. In my opinion they're actually compelled to obey because that's their destiny, and there's nothing in the least degrading for them in that. In the second category everyone breaks the law, they're all destroyers or inclined to be destructive, depending on their capabilities. The crimes committed by these people are of course relative and very varied; most of them seek, in a wide variety of situations, to destroy what exists in the name of something better. But if, for the sake of his ideas, such a man has to step over a corpse or wade through blood, then I think he may, subject to his own conscience, permit himself to wade through blood—depending of course on the nature and magnitude of his idea; note that. It's only in that sense that my article talks about such people's right to commit crimes. (Remember that our discussion started from the question of legality.) Anyway, there's no need to be too alarmed: the masses hardly ever recognize the rights of those people, they execute them and hang them (more or less), thereby quite properly fulfilling their conservative destiny; although in succeeding generations this same mass will stand its victims on a pedestal and render homage to them (more or less). The first category is always master of the present, while the second is master of the future. The first preserves the world and increases its numbers, the second moves it forward towards its goal. Both categories have an absolutely equal right to exist. In short, as I see it, everyone possesses equal rights, and—*vive la guerre éternelle!** Until the coming of the New Jerusalem,* naturally!'

'So you do believe in the New Jerusalem?'

'I do,' replied Raskolnikov firmly. As he spoke, he stared down at a particular spot on the carpet—as he had done throughout his long tirade.

'And... and do you believe in God too? Please forgive my curiosity.'

'I do,' repeated Raskolnikov, raising his eyes to look at Porfiry.

'And you believe in the raising of Lazarus?'*

'I... I do. Why are you asking me all this?'

'You believe it literally?'

'Yes, literally.'

'I see... I was just curious. Please forgive me. But may I ask—coming back to what you were saying just now—not all of them are executed; indeed, some of them...'

'Triumph in their own lifetimes? Oh yes, some achieve their aims during their lifetimes, and then...'

'Then they start executing other people?'

'If they need to; indeed, most of them do. So your remark is quite acute.'

'Thank you. But tell me this: how are we to distinguish these extraordinary people from the ordinary ones? Are there signs when they're born? What I mean is, we could do with more precision, so to speak, more objective clarity. Please excuse the natural anxiety of a practical, well-meaning man: couldn't there be some special clothing for them, shouldn't they wear something special, or be branded, or something?... You must admit that if there's a misunderstanding and someone from one category imagines that he belongs to the other, and sets about "eliminating all obstacles", as you so happily expressed it, then this...'

'Oh, that very frequently happens! That remark of yours was even more acute than your last...'

'Thank you.'

'You're welcome. But bear in mind that the mistake can only be made by people in the first category, the "ordinary" people (as I, perhaps inappropriately, named them). Despite their inborn tendency to obey, by some quirk of nature (which may be found even in cattle), a great many of them enjoy seeing themselves as leaders of men, "destroyers", with "something new" to say; and all this is quite sincere. At the same time, they very often overlook the truly *new* individuals among them, or even despise them as reactionaries with a humiliating approach to life. But I don't think there can be any particular danger here, and you've nothing to worry about, because they never go far. One might, of course, thrash them now and then, for the pleasure of it and to remind them of their place; but that's all. In fact there's no need to find someone to do that: they'll thrash themselves, because they're very well behaved; some will do each other the service, and others will do it to themselves with their own hands... And they impose all sorts of public acts of self-abasement in the process—it all turns out very pretty and very instructive. In short, you've no need to worry... that's a law of nature.'

'Well, you've reassured me a little, at least on that score; but here's another problem. Tell me, please, are there many of these people who have the right to cut other people's throats, these "extraordinary" men of yours? I mean, I'm happy to bow down to them, but you must agree—it's a bit frightening, isn't it, if there are lots and lots of them?'

'Oh, don't worry about that either,' went on Raskolnikov in the same tone of voice. 'Surprisingly few people are born who have new ideas, or are even just barely capable of saying something *new*; it's remarkable how rare they are. One thing is clear: the birth rates of people of all these categories and subdivisions must be very accurately and precisely determined by some law of nature. That law is at present, of course, still unknown to us; but I believe that it exists, and that it may in future be discovered.* The great mass of humanity, the "human material" I mean, only exists on this earth for one purpose: so that it can eventually, through some sort of effort, some hitherto hidden process, through the interbreeding of different tribes and races, bring painfully into the world perhaps one man in a thousand who has a spark of independence. Men with a greater degree of independence might appear, perhaps, once in ten thousand (I'm approximating, to make my point clearer). With even greater independence—once in a hundred thousand. Geniuses will be one among millions, and the greatest geniuses, the crowning glory of humanity, may occur once in many thousands of millions of human beings on the earth. Anyway, I haven't looked into the vat where all this is brewing. But there undoubtedly exists, there has to exist, a definite law for it; it can't be a matter of chance.'

'What on earth are you two up to—are you having a joke?' cried Razumikhin at last. 'Are you making fun of one another, or what? Sitting there and making game of each other! Are you serious, Rodia?'

Raskolnikov silently lifted his pallid, almost mournful face to look at him, but didn't reply. And Razumikhin felt the strange contrast between this sad, quiet face and Porfiry's undisguised, obtrusive, provocative, *ill-mannered* waspishness.

'Well, my friend,' Razumikhin went on, 'if you're really serious about it, then... Of course you're right to say that it isn't new, it looks like everything we've read and heard, a thousand times over. But what's truly *original* about it all—and really belongs to you alone, to my horror—is that you sanction the spilling of blood *in the name of conscience*; and so fanatically, too, if you'll excuse my saying so... So that's the main idea of your article, then. But this sanction of the spilling of blood *in the name of conscience* is... is more terrible, I think, than some official authorization to shed blood, in the name of the law...'

'Absolutely fair: it is more terrible,' agreed Porfiry.

'No, you must have got carried away somehow! There's some mistake. I'll read the article... You got carried away! You can't think like that... I'll read it.'

'All that isn't in the article, it's only hinted at,' said Raskolnikov.

'Yes, yes.' Porfiry couldn't sit still. 'I can almost understand now how you choose to regard crime; but... do please forgive me for going on at you (I know I'm imposing on you, I'm quite ashamed of myself!)—do you see: you set my mind quite at rest just now, about those mistaken cases where the categories get confused, but... I'm still concerned about all sorts of concrete cases. Supposing some man, or some youth, imagines that he's a Lycurgus or a Mohammed—of the future, of course—and so he sets about eliminating all the obstacles in his way... He has to embark on a distant campaign, so he says, and that takes money... and so he starts acquiring money for his campaign... see what I mean?'

Zametov in his corner suddenly snorted with laughter. Raskolnikov didn't even raise his eyes to him.

'I have to agree', he replied calmly, 'that there must indeed be such cases. Silly, vain people are especially likely to rise to the bait, particularly if they're young.'

'Yes, so you see. And what then?'

'What then?' smiled Raskolnikov. 'That's not my fault. That's how it is, and always will be. This man here' (he nodded towards Razumikhin) 'has just been saying that I allow the shedding of blood. Well, so what? Society is too well protected by sentences of exile, prisons, criminal investigators, labour camps—what's the worry? Go and catch your thief!'

'Very well, and if we catch him?'

'Serves him right.'

'You're logical, at least. Well, and what about his conscience?'

'Whatever business is that of yours?'

'Well, just to be humane.'

'If he has a conscience, let him suffer, if he acknowledges his fault. That'll be his punishment—over and above the labour camp.'

'What about the true geniuses?' asked Razumikhin with a frown. 'Those who are granted the right to cut people's throats: so they shouldn't have to suffer at all, even for the blood they shed?'

'Why use the word *should*? There's no question of permission or prohibition. Let the man suffer, if he's sorry for his victim... Suffering and pain are always obligatory for people of broad intellect and a deep heart. Truly great people, I think, must feel great sadness for the world,' he suddenly added in a pensive voice, out of keeping with the conversation that had gone before.

He raised his eyes, looked thoughtfully at them all, smiled, and picked up his cap. He was too tranquil, compared to his behaviour on entering, and he could feel that. Everyone rose.

'Well, gentlemen, you can scold me if you like, be angry with me if you like, but I can't resist,' began Porfiry Petrovich again. 'Let me ask just one little question (I know I'm imposing on you a great deal!), I just wanted to raise one little idea, just so as not to forget it...'

'Very well, tell us your little idea,' replied Raskolnikov, standing pale and serious before him and waiting for what was to come.

'Well, this is it... honestly, I don't know how best to put it... it's very frivolous... a psychological idea... Look here, when you were composing your little article—it's not possible, is it, that you yourself, heh–heh! that you didn't regard yourself, the least little bit, as another "extraordinary" individual, someone with "something new" to say—I mean in your own sense. That's so, isn't it?'

'That may well be,' replied Raskolnikov disdainfully. Razumikhin made a movement.

'But if that's the case, could you really have made up your mind—perhaps because of some problems and hardships in your own private life, or to help humanity as a whole—to overstep an obstacle?... I mean, let's say, by killing and robbing someone?'

And yet again he seemed to be winking his left eye at him, with a silent laugh—exactly as he had done a while back.

'Even supposing I had done so, I obviously wouldn't tell you,' responded Raskolnikov with haughty, challenging contempt.

'No, I'm just interested in the question to help me understand your article better, purely in a literary context...'

'Ugh, how obvious and insulting!' thought Raskolnikov in disgust.

'Allow me to point out', he replied drily, 'that I don't regard myself as a Mohammed or a Napoleon, or anyone else of that kind; and not being one of them, I can't give you a satisfactory explanation of how I would have acted.'

'Oh, come on—which of us Russians doesn't regard himself as a Napoleon these days?'* said Porfiry suddenly, with dreadful familiarity. Even his tone of voice bore something particularly blatant this time.

'Couldn't it have been some budding Napoleon who did for our Aliona Ivanovna with an axe last week?' Zametov suddenly barked from his corner.

Raskolnikov looked at Porfiry in silence, intently and firmly. Razumikhin frowned gloomily. Even before this, he had begun to have an uncomfortable feeling. He looked round angrily. A sombre silence fell. Raskolnikov turned to leave.

'Leaving already?' asked Porfiry politely, holding out his hand with excessive friendliness. 'I'm very, very glad to know you. And as for your application, don't worry at all. Just write, exactly as I said. Or best of all, come and see me there in person... in a day or two... perhaps tomorrow. I'll be there around eleven, I expect. We'll sort it all out... and have a chat... As one of the last people to go *there*, you may be able to tell us something...' he added with the most benevolent expression.

'You want to question me officially, with all the formalities?' asked Raskolnikov sharply.

'No, what for? There's no need for that at present. You misunderstand me. You see, I don't pass up an opportunity... and having talked to all the depositors... I've taken statements from some of them... and as you're the last of them... Ah yes, by the way!' he cried, suddenly very pleased about something, 'I've just remembered—how could I have forgotten it!...' He turned to Razumikhin. 'You know how you went on to me about that Nikolashka, that time... well, I know perfectly well myself,' he said, turning to Raskolnikov, 'I know the lad's innocent; but what can we do? And then we had to trouble that Mitka... the point is this: when you were on the stairs... let me just ask... that was between seven and eight, wasn't it?'

'That's right,' replied Raskolnikov, and immediately became unpleasantly aware that he needn't have said so.

'So, as you passed by on the stairs between seven and eight, didn't you notice, on the second floor, an open door to a flat—remember?— with two workmen inside, or one of them at least? They were painting in there, didn't you notice them? That's very, very important for them!...'

'House painters? No, I never saw any...' replied Raskolnikov slowly, as if searching his memory, straining every fibre of his being, tortured with anxiety as he tried to guess where exactly the trap had been set, and intent on not overlooking anything. 'No, I didn't see anything; I didn't even notice an open flat, actually... but on the fourth floor, now' (he had by now clearly seen the trap, and felt triumphant) 'I do remember that some official was moving out of his flat... opposite Aliona Ivanovna's... I do remember... I remember that clearly... some soldiers were carrying out a divan of some sort, and pressed me against the wall... but house painters—no, I don't remember any... and I don't think there was an open flat anywhere there either. No, there wasn't...'

'What are you talking about!' cried Razumikhin suddenly, as if recalling and realizing something. 'The house painters were working there on the day of the murder, but he'd been there three days earlier! What are you asking that for?'

'Oh bother, I've got it jumbled up!' exclaimed Porfiry, slapping himself on the forehead. 'The devil—I'm going out of my mind over this business!' he went on, turning to Raskolnikov almost apologetically. 'It's so important for us to discover whether anyone saw them, between seven and eight, in that flat, that I suddenly imagined that you yourself might be able to tell us... I was quite mixed up!'

'You ought to pay more attention,' remarked Razumikhin morosely.

His last words were spoken in the vestibule. Porfiry Petrovich walked them most politely right to the door. They both emerged into the street sullen and gloomy, and walked several steps without saying a word. Raskolnikov drew a deep breath...

CHAPTER VI

'I DON'T believe it! I can't believe it!' repeated Razumikhin in perplexity, trying his hardest to refute Raskolnikov's arguments. They were already approaching Bakaleyev's rooms, where Pulkheria Alexandrovna and Dunia had long been expecting them. Razumikhin kept stopping still, in the heat of the conversation, agitated and embarrassed because this was the first time they had openly talked about *that*.

'Don't believe it then!' replied Raskolnikov with a cold, careless smile. 'You, as usual, noticed nothing, but I was weighing up every word he spoke.'

'You're suspicious, that's why you weighed it up... Hmm... true, I agree with you, Porfiry's tone of voice was quite odd, and that scoundrel Zametov's even more so!... You're right, there was something about him—but why? Why?'

'He'd changed his mind overnight.'

'But no, quite the contrary! If they'd had that senseless idea, they'd have been doing their best to disguise it and hide their hand, so as to catch you out... But as it is—it's insolent and careless of them!'

'If they'd had any facts, I mean real facts, or even remotely plausible suspicions, then they'd certainly have tried to hide their game, in the hope of winning a bigger prize (and anyway they'd have searched my place ages ago!). But they've got no facts, not a single one, it's all fanciful and double-edged; and as soon as they have a fleeting idea, they try to catch me out by being offensive. Or maybe he was furious himself because he's got no facts, and he was so annoyed that he let it all come out. Or perhaps he has some plan... He seems to be a clever fellow... Perhaps he wanted to scare me by implying that he knows everything... There's some psychology in all this, my friend... Anyway, it's loathsome trying to explain it all. Drop it!'

'And it's insulting too! Insulting! I understand you! But... now we've begun talking openly about it (and that's good, I'm glad we have!)—I can tell you frankly: I noticed it a long time ago, this idea that they've had, all this time, of course only just the faintest hint, an insinuation; but why even insinuate? How dare they? What's hidden behind their suspicions? If you only knew how furious I've been! Just because some poor student, crushed by poverty and hypochondria, on the point of falling seriously ill with delirium, which perhaps he's already incubating (note that!), a suspicious, vain man with a sense of his own importance, who hasn't seen or spoken to a soul in six months, who's reduced to wearing rags and boots without soles—has to face a crew of police nobodies and suffer their taunts; and has an unexpected debt shoved at him, an overdue bill presented by Court Councillor Chebarov, and there's a stink of paint and it's thirty degrees Réaumur* and the air is stifling, and there's a crowd of people, with talk of the murder of someone he went to see yesterday, and all that on an empty stomach! Of course he's going to faint! And it's all built up on that, nothing but that! Damn it all! I can understand how maddening it all is; but if I were you, Rodka, I should just laugh in their faces; or better still, I'd spit in all their ugly faces, good and hard, and hit out a couple of dozen times in all directions, aiming my blows properly, as one should, and have done with it. Spit on them! Cheer up! Shame on you!'

'I must say he's put that very well,' thought Raskolnikov.

'Spit on them? And tomorrow I'm to be interrogated again!' he said bitterly. 'Am I really to start explaining things to them? As it is, I'm annoyed at letting myself down so far as to talk to Zametov in the bar yesterday...'

'Damn it! I'll go and see Porfiry myself! And I'll squeeze him, in a *cousinly* way, and get him to explain everything from start to finish! And as for Zametov...'

'At last he's got the point!' thought Raskolnikov.

'Wait!' cried Razumikhin, suddenly seizing him by the shoulder. 'Wait! You got it wrong! I've just realized: you got it wrong! How could that have been a trap? You said that his question about the workmen was a trap? Think about it: if you had done *that thing*, could you have slipped up and said you'd seen the flat being painted... and seen the workmen? No, you wouldn't have seen anything, even if you had! Whoever would give evidence against himself?'

'If I'd done *that thing*, I should most certainly have said that I'd seen the workmen and the flat,' replied Raskolnikov unwillingly, with evident distaste.

'But why ever give evidence against yourself?'

'Because it's only yokels and utter greenhorns who flatly deny everything outright, as soon as they're questioned. The moment you have someone who's educated and knows his way about, he'll always do his best to admit all the incidental facts that can't be denied; he'll just find different explanations for them, he'll produce his own special story which they aren't expecting, giving the facts quite a different slant, showing them in another light. Porfiry might have calculated that I'd certainly answer that way, saying that I'd seen the men, to make my story plausible, and then putting something in to explain it...'

'But then he'd have told you straight away that those two workmen couldn't possibly have been there two days earlier, so consequently you must have been there on the day of the murder, after seven o'clock. And he'd have caught you out on an irrelevant detail!'

'That's just what he was counting on: that I wouldn't realize until too late, and I'd hastily give him a plausible answer, forgetting that the workmen couldn't have been there two days earlier.'

'How could you ever forget that?'

'Nothing easier! It's just those very simple things that trip clever people up. The cleverer a man is, the less he expects to be tripped up by something simple. The cleverest people have to be caught out by the simplest things. Porfiry isn't at all as stupid as you think.'

'What a villain he is, then!'

Raskolnikov couldn't help laughing. But at once it struck him as odd that he had given this last explanation so readily and enthusiastically, whereas the whole conversation up till then had filled him with morose disgust, and he had evidently only been talking like that because he needed to, for a particular reason.

'I'm getting a taste for this, in a way!' he thought.

But almost at once he felt uneasy, as though struck by some unexpected and alarming thought. His uneasiness grew worse. They had just reached Bakaleyev's rooms.

'You go in by yourself,' said Raskolnikov suddenly. 'I'll be back in a minute.'

'Where are you off to? We're here now!'

'I have to go, I must; there's something I have to see to... I'll come in half an hour... Tell them.'

'You do as you like, but I'm coming with you!'

'So you want to torture me to death too!' cried Raskolnikov, with such bitter irritation, such despair in his eyes, that Razumikhin let his hands drop. He stood on the threshold for some time, gloomily watching Raskolnikov as he strode briskly away towards his lodging. Finally he gritted his teeth, clenched his fists, swore that he'd squeeze Porfiry dry like a lemon that very day, and went upstairs to reassure Pulkheria Alexandrovna, who was already anxious at their long absence.

By the time Raskolnikov reached his home, his brow was dripping with sweat and he was breathing heavily. He hurried upstairs and entered his unlocked room, immediately fastening the door with the hook. Fearfully, distractedly, he rushed to the corner of the room, to that same hole in the wallpaper where he had once hidden the things. Thrusting his hand inside, he spent several minutes meticulously feeling round the cavity, poking his fingers into every crevice and every fold of the wallpaper. Finding nothing, he stood up and drew a deep breath. Just now, on reaching the entrance to Bakaleyev's house, he had suddenly fancied that there might be some object, a chain or a stud or even a scrap of wrapping paper with some writing on it in the old woman's hand, which had escaped his notice and slipped into some crack from which it could later emerge in his presence, as unexpected and incontrovertible evidence against him.

He stood as if in deep thought, with a strange, humiliated, half-pointless smile hovering on his lips. Then he picked up his cap and quietly left the room, his head full of confused thoughts. Pensively he entered the gateway.

'There's the gentleman himself!' cried a loud voice. He raised his head.

The porter was standing by the door of his little room and pointing him out to a short man who appeared to be a tradesman; he was dressed in a long coat and waistcoat, so that from a distance he looked remarkably like a peasant woman. He wore a greasy cap on his bowed head, and his whole body seemed to stoop. His flabby, wrinkled face was that of a man over fifty. His small, watery eyes had a sullen, severe, discontented look.

Raskolnikov went up to the porter and asked: 'What is it?'

The tradesman gave him a sidelong look from under his lowered brows, and examined him carefully, intently, and unhurriedly. Then, without a word, he walked out from the gate into the street.

'What on earth!' cried Raskolnikov.

'There was this man asking if a student lived here, and he gave your name and said where you were lodging. And just then you came down, and I pointed you out, and off he went. Imagine that!'

The porter was rather puzzled himself, though not particularly so, and after a moment's reflection he turned and disappeared into his den.

Raskolnikov ran after the stranger and at once caught sight of him walking along the opposite side of the street, with the same even, unhurried gait as before, fixing his eyes on the ground and apparently pondering something. Raskolnikov soon caught up with him, but followed behind him for a while; at length he came up beside him and glanced sideways at the man's face. The stranger noticed him at once, looked him quickly up and down, but then dropped his gaze again. They continued like this for a minute or so, one beside the other, without saying a word.

'You were asking the porter... about me?' Raskolnikov said at last, in rather a low voice.

The other didn't reply, and didn't even look at him. There was a silence.

'Why ever did you... come to ask... and now you're saying nothing... what's all this about?' Raskolnikov spoke hesitantly, and somehow couldn't manage to get his words out clearly.

This time the stranger raised his eyes and gave him a sombre, inimical look.

'Murderer!' he suddenly pronounced, quietly but clearly and distinctly.

Raskolnikov was walking beside him. His legs suddenly felt terribly weak, a chill ran down his spine, and his heart seemed to stop for a moment; then it began hammering as though it had come loose. They walked like this for a hundred steps or so, side by side, without saying a word.

The stranger didn't look at him.

'What do you mean... what... who's a murderer?' muttered Raskolnikov barely audibly.

'*You are,*' said the other, even more distinctly and impressively, with a sort of smile of triumphant hatred, and once again stared straight into Raskolnikov's pallid face and lifeless eyes. Both men were just approaching a crossing. The stranger turned left and walked away without looking back. Raskolnikov remained where he was, following the man with his eyes for a long time. He saw him, now some fifty yards away, turn back and watch him still standing motionless at the same spot. It was impossible to be sure, but Raskolnikov had the impression that the man was once more smiling his smile of cold triumphant hatred.

Raskolnikov turned back, walking with slow, faltering steps. His knees were trembling, and he was shivering all over. He went upstairs to his little room, took off his cap, laid it on the table, and stood there motionless for some ten minutes. Then, with all his strength gone, he lay down on the divan and stretched out painfully, uttering a faint groan. His eyes were shut. So he lay for about half an hour.

He was not thinking about anything. Some thoughts, or tattered scraps of thoughts, passed through his head, fragmentary disconnected images—faces of people he had seen in his childhood, or met once in his life, people he would never have thought about; the bell tower of V—— church;* the billiard table at a particular inn, and some officer playing on it, the smell of cigars in a basement tobacco shop somewhere, a tavern, a back staircase, very dark, sodden with slops and littered with eggshells, and the ringing of Sunday bells penetrating from outside... The memories shifted and circled around him like a whirlwind. Some were good ones, and he would seize on them, but they faded away. Through all this, something inside him was oppressing him, though not badly. In fact sometimes it was good... His mild shivering still continued, and that, too, was almost good to feel.

He heard Razumikhin's hurried footsteps and his voice, and closed his eyes, pretending to be asleep. Razumikhin opened the door and stood for a time on the threshold, as if in thought. Then he advanced quietly into the room, and cautiously approached the divan. Nastasia was whispering:

'Let him be, let him have his sleep. He can eat later.'

'True enough,' replied Razumikhin.

They went out quietly and pulled the door to. Another half-hour passed. Raskolnikov opened his eyes and rolled over on his back, clasping his hands behind his head.

'Who is he? Who is that man, come up from underground? Where has he been, what has he seen? He saw it all, there's no doubt about that. So where was he standing then, watching? Why has he only just come up from under the floor? And how could he have seen—is that really possible? Hmm...' Raskolnikov thought, turning cold and giving a shudder. 'What about the jewel box that Nikolay found behind the door: could that be possible, too? Incriminating evidence? You overlook the tiniest detail, and there's your evidence, as big as an Egyptian pyramid! A fly flew past, and it saw me! Can that really be?'

Overcome with disgust, he could feel himself growing weak, physically weak.

'I should have known,' he thought with a bitter smile. 'How dared I, knowing myself, knowing in advance what I was like, take up an axe and cover myself in blood! I must have known in advance... Eh! and I surely did know in advance!' he whispered in despair.

Sometimes he paused at a particular thought:

'No, those men aren't made like this. A real *master*, someone who's allowed to do whatever he likes—he'll storm Toulon, massacre people in Paris, *forget* his army in Egypt, *squander* half a million men in a march on Moscow, and get off with a pun at Vilna.* And when he dies, that same man will have statues raised to him. So for him, *everything* is permitted.* No, men of that sort clearly aren't flesh and blood, they're bronze!'*

A sudden irrelevant thought almost made him laugh:

'Napoleon, the Pyramids, Waterloo—and a nasty skinny little clerk's wife, an old hag of a moneylender, with a red treasure chest under her bed—now how is even Porfiry Petrovich going to digest all that?... How could any of his kind?... Their aesthetic sense* wouldn't let them—is Napoleon going to go poking under an old woman's bed? Oh, what rubbish!'

At times he felt as if he was raving, and he would fall into a state of feverish exaltation.

'That old woman is nothing!' he thought in a momentary burst of excitement. 'In fact the old woman may have been a mistake—but it's not about her! She was just part of my illness... I wanted to step over the barrier as soon as I could... it wasn't a person that I killed, but a principle! Well, and I did kill the principle, but I didn't overstep anything, I'm still on this side of it... All I managed to do was kill. And I didn't even manage that, as it turns out... Principle? What was that little fool Razumikhin abusing the socialists for, a while ago? Hard-working people, tradespeople, working for the "common good"... No, I've only got one life, there'll never be another, and I don't want to wait for the "common good". I want to have a life myself, otherwise I'm better off not living at all. What then? I just didn't want to pass by a starving mother, clutching my rouble in my pocket, in the expectation of the "common good". "Here I am," I might say, "bringing my little brick to help construct the common good,* and thanks to that my heart is at peace." Ha! ha! Why did you let me go? I've only got one life, and I, too, want to... Oh, I'm nothing but an aesthetic louse,' he suddenly added in a burst of crazy laughter. 'Yes, I really am a louse,' he went on, holding on to the idea with malicious pleasure, delving into it, playing with it, amusing himself with it; 'if only because, firstly, I'm now arguing about being a louse; and secondly, because I've been pestering all-loving Providence for a whole month, calling on it to witness that it's not for my own whims and fancies that I'm undertaking this thing—that I have a magnificent and admirable goal in view—ha! ha! And thirdly, because I had resolved to observe absolute justice, by weight and measure,* when carrying out my design, and out of all lice I picked out the most useless one, and when I had killed her, I resolved to take from her just so much as I needed for my first step, no more and no less (so the remainder would actually have gone to a monastery, under the terms of her will, ha! ha!)... And that, that's what makes me an absolute louse,' he added, grinding his teeth, 'because it may be that I myself am even nastier and fouler than the louse I killed; and I *sensed in advance* that I'd tell myself that, but only *after* I'd killed her! Can anything compare with such a horror! Oh, what vulgarity! Oh, what infamy!... Oh, how I understand the "Prophet", mounted on his horse, armed with his scimitar! Allah commands, and let all creatures "tremble and obey"!* He's right, he's right, the "Prophet", to station a tr-r-remendous battery across some street and blast the innocent and guilty alike, without a word of explanation! Tremble and obey, all you creatures, and—*have no desires*, for that's not your business! Oh, never, never shall I forgive that old woman!'

His hair was moist with sweat, his twitching lips were parched, his gaze was fixed on the ceiling.

'My mother, my sister, how I used to love them! Why do I hate them now? Yes, I hate them, physically hate them, I can't bear them near me... A short while ago I came up to my mother and kissed her, I remember... Kissing her and thinking that if she were to find out... Should I have told her at that very moment? I'd have been capable of it... Hmm! *she* must be the same sort of person as me,' he added, forcing himself to think, as though fighting off the delirium about to engulf him. 'Oh, how I loathe that old woman now! I believe I'd kill her again, if she came back to life! Poor Lizaveta! Why did she have to turn up?... How strange, though, that I almost never think of her—as if I hadn't ever killed her!... Lizaveta! Sonia! Poor, meek creatures, with meek eyes... Dear ones!... Why don't they weep? Why don't they moan?... They give up everything... they look at you meekly and gently... Sonia! Sonia! Gentle Sonia!...'

He fell into a swoon. He found it strange that he couldn't remember how he had ended up in the street. It was late evening already. Dusk was falling, and the full moon shone brighter and brighter; but there was something particularly stifling about the air. There were crowds of people in the streets; tradesmen and employees making for their homes, others out for a walk; there was a smell of lime, dust, and stagnant water. Raskolnikov walked on, sad and anxious; he clearly remembered that he had left his home with some purpose in mind, that he had to do something, and quickly; but what it was, he had forgotten. Suddenly he stopped and noticed a man standing on the opposite pavement, beckoning to him. Raskolnikov crossed to his side of the road, but suddenly the man turned away and walked off, seemingly quite unconcerned, with his head lowered, not turning round nor giving any indication of having called him over. 'So did he call me or not?' wondered Raskolnikov; but he hurried after him. Before he had gone a dozen paces, he suddenly recognized the man—and took fright. It was the same stranger he had met earlier, in the same long coat, and bent forward as before. Raskolnikov followed him at a distance, his heart pounding. They turned in to an alleyway, but the stranger still didn't turn round. 'Does he know I'm following him?' wondered Raskolnikov. The stranger entered the gates of a large house. Raskolnikov hurried to the gates and looked in: would the man look round, would he call him again? And indeed, after passing right through the gateway and coming out into the yard, the man suddenly turned round and actually seemed to beckon him again. Raskolnikov immediately went through the gateway himself, but the man was no longer in the yard. So he must have just entered the first staircase. Raskolnikov ran after him. And true enough, he could hear someone's measured, unhurried footsteps two flights up. Strangely, this staircase seemed somehow familiar! There was the window on the first floor, with the moonlight penetrating, melancholy and mysterious, through the glass; and here was the second floor. Ah! This was the very same flat where the workmen had been painting... How had he failed to realize it at once? The sound of the footsteps of the man ahead ceased: 'so he must have stopped, or hidden somewhere'. And here was the third floor; ought he to go higher? And how quiet it all was—it was even frightening... But he went up. He was frightened and alarmed by the sound of his own steps. God, how dark it was! The man had most likely hidden himself in a corner somewhere. Ah! the door of the flat was wide open to the stairs: he hesitated for a moment, and went in. The hallway was dark and empty, as if everything had been taken away, and not a soul was there. Quietly, on tiptoe, he went through to the sitting room. The whole room was bathed in bright moonlight. Everything was as it had been—the chairs, the mirror, the yellow divan, the little pictures in their frames. The enormous, round, coppery-red moon was looking straight in at the windows. 'It's the moon making everything so quiet,' thought Raskolnikov; 'it must be asking a riddle now.' He stood and waited; waited a long time; and the quieter the moon became, the louder his heart pounded, so much that it hurt. And still this silence. Suddenly there was the sound of a crack, as though someone had snapped a wooden taper; then everything fell quiet again. A fly awoke, banged into a windowpane, and buzzed plaintively away. At that same moment, in the corner between a small cupboard and the window, he made out what looked like a woman's cloak hanging on the wall. 'Why's that coat here?' he wondered. 'It wasn't there before...' He crept closer and realized that someone must be hiding behind it. Cautiously he moved the coat aside and saw that there was a chair in the corner behind it, and sitting on the chair was the old woman, all huddled up and with her head bent forwards, so that he couldn't manage to see her face; but it was she. He stood over her. 'She's frightened!' he thought; stealthily he pulled the axe out of its loop, and struck the old woman on the crown of her head, once, and again. Yet strangely enough, she didn't budge when he struck her—almost as if she was made of wood. He took fright, bent closer and peered at her; but she, too, bent her head even further. Then he leaned right down to the floor and looked up at her; he took one look, and froze. The old woman was sitting there laughing—shaking with silent, inaudible laughter, trying her hardest to stop him hearing her. Suddenly he had the impression that the bedroom door had opened a fraction and there were people laughing and whispering in there too. He went wild, and began beating the old woman over the head with all his might; but with every blow of the axe, the laughter and whispering in the bedroom grew louder and clearer, while the old woman shook with mirth. He took to his heels, but the hallway was full of people now, every door on the staircase was wide open, and the landing, and the staircase going down, everywhere was full of people, one head after another, all looking at him—but all pressed back, silently waiting... His heart tightened, his legs seemed rooted to the spot, he couldn't move them... He tried to scream—and awoke.

He drew a deep breath; but it was strange that his dream seemed to be continuing: his door was wide open, and a complete stranger was standing in the doorway, staring intently at him.

Raskolnikov hadn't yet managed to open his eyes completely, and now he instantly shut them again. He was lying on his back, and remained motionless. 'Is this dream still going on, or not?' he thought, and furtively raised his eyelids a fraction to take a look. The stranger was still standing in the same place, still staring at him. Then he stepped cautiously over the threshold, shut the door carefully behind him, came up to the table, waited a minute or so—all this without taking his eyes off Raskolnikov—and gently, noiselessly, sat down on the chair beside the divan. He laid his hat beside him on the floor, and leaned with both hands on his cane, resting his chin on his hands. He was evidently prepared to wait a long time. As far as Raskolnikov could make out under his twitching eyelids, this was a man no longer young, stoutly built, with a thick, light-coloured, almost white beard...

Ten minutes or so passed. It was still light, but dusk was falling.

There was absolute silence in the room. Not a sound came from the staircase either. There was only a big fly, buzzing and bumping against the windowpane. Finally it became unbearable. Raskolnikov suddenly raised himself and sat up on the divan.

'So tell me, what do you want?'

'I knew perfectly well that you weren't asleep, just pretending,' the stranger replied oddly, with a cool laugh. 'Allow me to introduce myself: Arkady Ivanovich Svidrigailov.'

PART FOUR

CHAPTER I

'COULD this be my dream still going on?' wondered Raskolnikov again, peering warily and suspiciously at his unexpected guest.

'Svidrigailov? What rubbish! Impossible!' he eventually said aloud in bewilderment.

His guest seemed not in the least surprised at this exclamation.

'I've looked in on you for two reasons. First of all, I wanted to get to know you personally, because I've been hearing a lot of very curious and complimentary things about you, for quite a while; and secondly, I'm hoping you may not refuse to help me in a particular enterprise that directly affects the interests of your good sister Avdotya Romanovna. At the moment, because of some prejudice, she might not even permit me to come anywhere near her in person, without an introduction from you; but now, with your help, I reckon that...'

'You're out in your reckoning,' Raskolnikov interrupted him.

'I believe they only arrived yesterday, if you don't mind my asking?'

Raskolnikov did not reply.

'It was yesterday—I know it was. I myself only arrived the day before. Well, Rodion Romanovich, sir, this is what I'd like to say to you about all that. I don't in the least feel called upon to justify myself, but let me just ask—what was there in all that business that was so particularly criminal on my part, speaking without prejudice and with an open mind?'

Raskolnikov continued to look at him without speaking.

'Was it the fact that in my own home I persecuted a defenceless young girl, "insulting her with my vile proposals"—is that it? (I'm running ahead of you!) But you just have to accept that I'm a human being too, *et nihil humanum...** in short, that I too am capable of being attracted and falling in love (which is of course something that happens without our willing it)—and then everything explains itself in the most natural way. This is the whole question: am I a monster, or a victim myself? So, how am I a victim? Well, when I invited the object of my affections to run away with me to America or Switzerland, I may perhaps have been filled with the most honourable sentiments at the time, and actually hoped to achieve happiness for us both! After all, reason is passion's slave; in fact I was going to ruin myself even worse than her—you must see that!'

'That's not the point at all,' interrupted Raskolnikov in disgust. 'The simple fact is that you're a revolting person, whether you're right or wrong, and therefore people don't wish to know you, and want nothing to do with you; so be off with you!'

Svidrigailov suddenly burst out laughing.

'Well, you're... there's just no getting round you!' he said, with the most sincere-sounding laugh. 'I was planning to be a bit crafty, but it was no good—you've gone straight to the very point!'

'You're still trying to be crafty, right this minute.'

'And so what? So what?' repeated Svidrigailov, laughing heartily. 'That's just what's called *la bonne guerre*,* a most legitimate ruse!... Even so, you've got the better of me; one way or another, I say it again: there wouldn't have been any unpleasantness, but for what happened in the garden. Marfa Petrovna...'

'You did for Marfa Petrovna too, so they say?' Raskolnikov interrupted rudely.

'So you've heard about that too? Well, of course, you were bound to... Well, as far as that question of yours goes, I don't know what to say, though my own conscience is absolutely clear. I mean, don't imagine that I'd been afraid of anything of the kind: it was all done absolutely properly and correctly, and the autopsy showed apoplexy resulting from bathing immediately after a substantial dinner, including almost a whole bottle of wine; they couldn't have found anything different... No, sir, this is what I've been wondering to myself for some time, particularly on my way here, sitting in the railway carriage: didn't I contribute to this whole... unfortunate event, by some sort of moral stress or something of the kind? But I concluded that that could not possibly have been the case.'

Raskolnikov laughed.

'Why should you worry about that?'

'What are you laughing for? Just consider: I only ever hit her twice with my little riding-crop, it didn't even leave any marks... Please don't dismiss me as a cynic; I know very well how revolting that was of me, and all that; but I also know for a fact that Marfa Petrovna was very likely quite pleased that I got so... carried away, as it were. The whole business with your sister had been talked into the ground; Marfa Petrovna had been stuck at home for three whole days, with nothing to show for herself if she went to town; everyone was so bored with that letter of hers (you've heard about the reading of the letter, have you?).

And suddenly those two flicks of my crop, like a gift from heaven! The first thing she did was have the carriage made ready!... Not to mention the fact that women sometimes find it very, very pleasant to be insulted, however indignant they may seem. Such things happen with everybody—people in general are very, very fond of being insulted, have you ever noticed? But especially women. One might even say it's their only amusement.'

At one point Raskolnikov had been thinking of getting up and walking out, to put an end to this meeting. But he held back for a moment, partly out of curiosity and partly because of a sort of calculation.

'Do you enjoy fighting?' he asked absently.

'No, not particularly,' answered Svidrigailov calmly. 'Marfa Petrovna and I hardly ever fought. We lived very amicably, and she was always happy with me. In all our seven years, I only ever used the whip on her twice (not counting a third occasion, a very questionable one to say the least). The first time was two months after our wedding, just after we arrived in the countryside; and then there was this last time just recently. I'm sure you were thinking I was such a monster, a reactionary, a slave driver, weren't you? Heh-heh!... Incidentally, Rodion Romanovich, don't you remember, some years ago, in those days when misbehaviour used to be publicly censured, there was a nobleman (I forget his name) who was publicly disgraced everywhere, in all the papers, because he whipped some German woman in a railway carriage—remember that? And it was about then, in the same year, I believe, that there was the "disgraceful act of *The Century*"* (you know, the "Egyptian nights", the public reading, remember? Those dark eyes! Oh, where are they now, those golden days of our youth?). Anyway, here's what I think. That gentleman who whipped the German woman—I don't sympathize with him at all, because actually... what's the point of sympathizing? But at the same time I have to say, one sometimes comes across such provoking "Germans" that I doubt if there's a single progressive individual who could altogether answer for himself in such a situation. Nobody saw things in that light at the time, and yet that's the truly humane way to look at them, believe me!'

Having said that, Svidrigailov burst out laughing once more. Raskolnikov was in no doubt that this was a man who had firmly decided on something, and knew what he was about.

'I suppose you haven't spoken to anyone for a few days?' he asked.

'More or less. Why, are you surprised to find me such a cool individual?'

'No, what surprises me is that you're far too cool.'

'Because I haven't been offended by your rude questions? That's it, isn't it? But... what's there to be offended at? As you asked, so I answered,' he added, with an expression of surprising simplicity. 'After all, I'm not really particularly concerned about anything, I promise you,' he went on thoughtfully. 'Particularly now, I'm not busy with anything. Of course you're entitled to think I've got some ulterior motive for approaching you, particularly since I need to speak to your sister, as I told you myself. But I tell you frankly—I'm very bored! Particularly these last three days; so much so that I was actually glad to find you... Don't be angry, Rodion Romanovich, but for some reason I find you, too, extremely odd. Say what you like, but there's something about you, especially right now—I don't mean this minute, but now in general... All right, all right, I'll stop, don't scowl at me! I'm honestly not such a bear as you take me for.'

Raskolnikov cast him a sombre look.

'You might not be a bear at all,' he said. 'In fact I think you're probably a very well-bred man, or at least you can behave as one when you need to.'

'I'm not particularly interested in anyone's opinion of me,' replied Svidrigailov shortly and almost haughtily; 'so why shouldn't I be a bit of a vulgarian, when that's such a convenient outfit to wear in our climate, and... especially since I'm naturally inclined that way,' he added with another laugh.

'But I've heard that you've a lot of acquaintances here; you're what they call "a man with connections". So what do you want me for, if not for some purpose or other?'

'You're right, I do have friends here,' replied Svidrigailov, without answering the main question. 'I've come across some of them—after all, I've been hanging about here for over two days. Some people I recognize, and some I think recognize me. Of course I'm wearing decent clothes, and I'm not reckoned a poor man; the peasant reforms* didn't affect us, we own forests and water meadows, and the income from them carries on. But... I'm not going to see anyone; I was already fed up with them all. This is my third day here, and I haven't shown myself to anybody... And then, this town! Just look at what it's turned into, for heaven's sake! A town of office clerks and seminary students! There was a lot here that I didn't notice eight years or so ago, when I was knocking about here... My only hope now is anatomy, I swear to you!'

'What do you mean, anatomy?'

'And as for those clubs, those Dussauts, those *Pointes** of yours, or even just progress—I want no part of all that,' he went on, again ignoring the question. 'And what's the fun of being a card sharp again?'

'Did you use to be a card sharp, too?'

'What else could I do? There was a whole crowd of us, highly respect-able people, eight years ago or so; we did it to kill time; and we were all well-bred people, you know—we had poets, we had property owners too. In Russian society, you know, the most elegant manners are seen among people who've been thrashed—have you ever noticed that? It's living in the country that's brought me down. But I was on the point of being imprisoned for debt at the time—all because of a little Greek from Nezhin. And just then Marfa Petrovna turned up, haggled with him, and bought me off for thirty thousand pieces of silver (I owed seventy thousand altogether). So we got lawfully married, and she carted me straight off with her to the country, just like some treasure. She was five years older than me, and very much in love with me. For seven years I never left the country. And please note: all her life, she kept hold of that note for thirty thousand, made out to someone else, so that if ever I took it into my head to rebel, I'd have been caught in the trap straight away! And she'd have done it, too! Women see nothing incongruous in all that, you know.'

'And if there hadn't been that document, you'd have run off?'

'I don't know what to say. The document hardly bothered me. I didn't want to go anywhere, and Marfa Petrovna herself twice offered to take me abroad, when she saw how bored I was. But what would have been the point? I'd been abroad before, and always hated it. Not that... but there's dawn breaking, and there's the bay of Naples, and the sea, and you look at them and feel sad, somehow. The worst of it is that you're genuinely sad about something. No, your own country is better; at least you can blame someone else for everything here, and be in the right yourself! Perhaps I might go off on an expedition to the North Pole, because *j'ai le vin mauvais*,* and drinking doesn't agree with me, but apart from drinking there's nothing to do. I've tried. By the way, they say that Berg's going to make an ascent in a huge balloon in Yusupov Park on Sunday,* and he'll take passengers who pay their fare—is that right?'

'Why, would you go up?'

'Me? No... I just wondered...' mumbled Svidrigailov, whose thoughts seemed far away.

'What does he mean? He's not serious, is he?' wondered Raskolnikov.

'No, that document didn't bother me,' Svidrigailov continued pensively. 'It was my own decision not to leave the country. Anyway, it's a whole year now since Marfa Petrovna gave me the document back, on my name day, and gave me a considerable sum of money too. She had some capital, you see. "See how I trust you, Arkady Ivanovich"—she really said that. You don't believe she did? But you know, I'd become a proper gentleman out there in the country; everybody in the neighbourhood knew me. And I used to have books sent to me. Marfa Petrovna approved at first, but afterwards she was always afraid of my getting too bookish.'

'You seem to be missing Marfa Petrovna a great deal, aren't you?'

'Me? Perhaps. Yes, perhaps I am. Incidentally, do you believe in ghosts?'

'What ghosts?'

'Ordinary ghosts, of course!'

'Do you?'

'Well, not really, *pour vous plaire*... That is, I don't exactly mean "no".'

'You see them, do you?'

Svidrigailov gave him a peculiar look.

'Marfa Petrovna pays me a visit sometimes,' he said, twisting his mouth in an odd smile.

'What do you mean, pays you a visit?'

'Well, she's been three times. The first time I saw her was on the actual day of the funeral, an hour after we'd left the cemetery. That was the day before I left to come here. The second time was the day before yesterday, on the way here, at daybreak, at Malaya Vishera station;* and the third time was two hours ago, in the flat where I'm staying, in my room. I was alone then.'

'Awake?'

'Absolutely. I was awake all three times. She would come, talk for a minute, and go out of the door. She always left by the door. I even seemed to hear her going.'

'Why did I always think that something of the kind would be bound to happen with you!' said Raskolnikov suddenly, and immediately felt surprised at having said that. He was extremely agitated.

'Re-e-eally? You thought that?' asked Svidrigailov in surprise. 'Fancy that! Well, didn't I say that we two have something in common, eh?'

'You've never said that!' riposted Raskolnikov sharply and heatedly.

'Haven't I?'

'No!'

'I thought I had. Just now, when I came in and saw you lying there with your eyes shut, pretending to be asleep—straight away I said to myself, "He's the one!"'

'What do you mean, the one? What are you talking about?' cried Raskolnikov.

'What I mean? I don't really know what I mean...' muttered Svidrigailov candidly, seemingly confused.

For a minute or so neither spoke. Each stared at the other.

'This is all nonsense!' cried Raskolnikov angrily. 'What does she say to you when she appears?'

'She? Just imagine, she talks of the most trivial stuff. You wouldn't believe it—it always makes me cross. The first time she came in (I was tired, you know: that funeral service, and "rest in peace with the Saints", and then the prayers, and the meal—at last I was alone in my study, and I lit a cigar and started thinking). She came into the room, saying "Arkady Ivanovich, with all that going on, you've forgotten to wind the dining-room clock". And true enough, all those seven years I'd wound that clock myself, every week, and if I forgot she'd always remind me. Next day I was on my way here. And at dawn I got out at a station—I'd dozed off in the night and now I ached all over, my eyes wouldn't open—and I got myself some coffee. I looked up, and suddenly there was Marfa Petrovna sitting down beside me holding a pack of cards. "Wouldn't you like me to tell your fortune for the road, Arkady Ivanovich?" Now she was an expert fortune teller. And I'll never forgive myself for not letting her do it! I took fright and ran off; actually the station bell went at the same time. And now today, I'd just eaten a perfectly foul dinner from the cookshop, and I was sitting there smoking and feeling bloated, when suddenly Marfa Petrovna walks in again, all dressed up in a new green silk dress with a long train. "Good afternoon, Arkady Ivanovich! How do you like my dress? Aniska couldn't make one like this." (Aniska is a seamstress in our village, a former serf who went to Moscow to learn her trade; a fine young girl.) So she stands in front of me and turns this way and that. I had a look at the dress, and then looked her straight in the face. "What's come over you, Marfa Petrovna, going to all the trouble of coming to see me about such nonsense?"—"Oh, good Lord, man, I'm not even allowed to bother you now!" To needle her, I told her: "Marfa Petrovna, I want to get married." "That's just like you, Arkady Ivanovich; and it doesn't do you much credit, going off to get married when you've scarcely buried your wife. And if only you'd even chosen properly—but I know you, it won't do either her or you any good, all you'll do is make yourself a laughing stock for honest folk." And she turned and walked out, and her train seemed to rustle over the floor. What nonsense, eh?'

'I dare say this may all be lies, eh?' responded Raskolnikov.

'I hardly ever tell lies,' answered Svidrigailov thoughtfully, seeming not to have noticed how rude the question was.

'And before that, you'd never seen any ghosts?'

'N...no, I had, just once in my life, six years ago. I had a servant called Filka, and once, just after he'd been buried, I forgot and called out "Filka, my pipe!"—and he came in and went straight to the cabinet where I kept my pipes. I sat there and thought "he's come to get his revenge", because just before he died we'd had a serious quarrel. "How dare you come in here with a hole in your elbow!" I said. "Get out, you rascal!" He turned round and went out, and never came back. I didn't tell Marfa Petrovna about it at the time. I was going to have a funeral mass said for him, but I was too ashamed.'

'You should see a doctor.'

'You don't need to tell me that I'm unwell, though I really don't know what's wrong with me. I should think I'm probably five times healthier than you. I wasn't asking you whether or not you believed that ghosts appear to people. What I asked you was: do you believe that ghosts exist?'

'No, nothing would make me believe that!' cried Raskolnikov, almost angrily.

'What do people generally say?' muttered Svidrigailov, as if to himself, looking to one side with his head slightly bent. 'They say "you're ill, consequently what you're seeing is nothing but a delirious vision". But that's not strictly logical. I grant that ghosts only appear to sick people—but that merely proves that ghosts can only appear to sick people, not that they themselves don't exist.'

'Of course they don't exist!' insisted Raskolnikov irritably.

'Don't they? You think not?' Svidrigailov went on, taking a long look at him. 'But supposing we were to argue this way (please help me here): "Ghosts are, as it were, the scraps and shreds of other worlds, their first beginnings. A healthy person, naturally, has no need to see them, because a healthy person is the most earth-bound kind of person, and for the sake of completeness and order he is obliged to live a purely earth-bound life. But then, as soon as he falls ill, as soon as the normal terrestrial ordering of his body is impaired, the possibility of another world begins to show itself, and the sicker he becomes, the more contact he has with the other world, so that when this person actually dies, he crosses straight over into the other world." I've thought along those lines for a long time. If you believe in a life to come, you could believe this argument too.'

'I don't believe in a life to come,' said Raskolnikov.

Svidrigailov sat sunk in thought.

'But supposing there was nothing there but spiders, or something like that,' he said suddenly.

'The man's mad!' thought Raskolnikov.

'We always imagine eternity as an idea that can't be grasped, as something enormous, simply enormous. But why does it have to be enormous? Just suppose, instead of all that, it's nothing but a single little room, something like a village bathhouse, all grimy with soot, with spiders in all the corners—and that's eternity for you! You know, I sometimes find myself imagining it like that.'

'And you really, really can't imagine anything more just and comforting than that?' cried Raskolnikov in distress.

'More just? How can we know? Perhaps that's what justice is, and do you know, I'd have made it like that on purpose!' replied Svidrigailov with a vague smile.

A sudden chill gripped Raskolnikov at this horrible answer. Svidrigailov raised his head, stared intently at him and suddenly burst out laughing.

'No, but just think of this,' he cried out. 'Half an hour ago we'd never seen one another, we were supposed to be enemies, there was unfinished business between us; and now we've dropped that business, and look at the flights of fancy we're indulging in! Wasn't I right to say we were birds of a feather?'

'Do me a favour,' said Raskolnikov irritably. 'Would you kindly explain yourself as quickly as you can, and tell me why you've honoured me with this visit... and... and... I'm in a hurry, I've no time, I want to go out...'

'Certainly, certainly. Your sister Avdotya Romanovna is to marry Mr Piotr Petrovich Luzhin, isn't she?'

'Can't you manage to keep off anything to do with my sister, and not mention her name? I don't even understand how you dare pronounce her name in my presence, if you really are Svidrigailov!'

'But I only came here to talk about her—how can I avoid mentioning her?'

'Very well then, talk, but hurry up about it!'

'I'm sure that you've already formed your own opinion about this Mr Luzhin (a connection of mine through my wife), if you've seen him for as much as half an hour, or heard anything at all true and reliable about him. He's not a suitable match for Avdotya Romanovna. As I see it, Avdotya Romanovna is sacrificing herself here, in a very generous and ill-advised way, for... for her family. And it seemed to me, from all that I had heard about you, that you yourself would be very glad if this engagement could be broken off, without harming anyone's interests. Now that I know you personally, I'm quite certain of that.'

'That's very naïve of you. Excuse me, I meant to say—insolent of you,' said Raskolnikov.

'What you're saying is that I'm trying to further my own interests. Don't worry, Rodion Romanovich—if I had been acting out of self-ishness, I wouldn't ever have spoken so freely. I'm not a complete fool. But I'll tell you a strange psychological fact. Just now, when I was justifying my love for Avdotya Romanovna, I said that I was a victim myself. So let me tell you that I don't feel any love for her now, none at all; I even find that strange myself, since I really did feel something...'

'Born of idleness and depravity,' interrupted Raskolnikov.

'That is true, I am a depraved and idle person. But your sister does indeed have so many virtues that even I couldn't fail to be rather impressed by them. Still, all that was nonsense, as I can see for myself now.'

'How long ago did you realize that?'

'I began to see it some time ago, but I was finally convinced of it the day before yesterday, almost as soon as I arrived in Petersburg. In fact when I was in Moscow I still imagined that I was on my way here to try to win Avdotya Romanovna's hand and cut out Mr Luzhin.'

'Pardon my interrupting you, but do me a favour. Can't you cut short all this talk and come straight to the reason for your visit? I'm in a hurry, I have to leave this place...'

'With the greatest pleasure. Once I had arrived here, and then made up my mind to go on a certain... voyage, I needed to make some prelim-inary arrangements. My children are staying with their aunt; they're rich, and they don't need me. What sort of a father am I anyway! All I've kept for myself is what Marfa Petrovna gave me a year ago; that'll do for me. I'm sorry, now I'll come straight to the point. Before this voyage, which may actually happen, I want to deal with Mr Luzhin too. Not that I particularly detest him, but it was over him that I had my quarrel with Marfa Petrovna, when I discovered that she had cooked up this marriage. Now I'd like you to help me meet Avdotya Romanovna, meet her in your presence in fact, so that I can explain to her, first of all, that Mr Luzhin won't be the slightest good to her, in fact he'll probably do her actual harm. And then, after begging her pardon for all this recent unpleasantness, I'd like to ask her permission to give her ten

thousand roubles, to make up for the rupture with Mr Luzhin—
a rupture which I'm sure she herself wouldn't mind, if only she had
the chance.'

'But you're really, really mad!' cried Raskolnikov, not even angry so
much as astonished. 'How dare you talk like this?'

'I knew you'd start shouting. But firstly, though I'm not rich, those
ten thousand roubles are free for me to dispose of, I mean to say that
I don't need them at all. If Avdotya Romanovna doesn't accept them,
I'll probably spend them even more stupidly. That's the first thing.
Secondly: my conscience is absolutely clear; I'm offering the money
without any ulterior motive. You can believe me or not, but in time both
you and Avdotya Romanovna will see it's true. The whole point is that
I really did cause your respected sister a certain amount of trouble and
distress, and now I truly repent and wish with all my heart—not to buy
myself off, nor to pay for the unpleasantness, but simply to do her some
good, for after all I don't claim the privilege of doing nothing but harm.
If there was a millionth part of calculation in my offer, I shouldn't be
making it so openly; nor should I be offering her just ten thousand
roubles, when only five weeks ago I was offering her more. And what's
more, I may very, very soon be marrying a certain young lady, which is
enough on its own to dispel any suspicion that I have designs on Avdotya
Romanovna. And finally, let me add that if she marries Mr Luzhin,
Avdotya Romanovna will simply be accepting the same sum from a different quarter... Now don't be angry, Rodion Romanovich, just think
about it coolly and calmly.'

As he said this, Svidrigailov himself was extremely cool and calm.

'Please finish what you have to say,' said Raskolnikov. 'All I can say is,
you're being outrageously impertinent.'

'Not in the least. If that were so, everyone on this earth would be
obliged to do nothing but harm to others, and wouldn't have the right
to do a bit of good, all because of meaningless convention. That would
be absurd. Supposing I died, say, and left your sister that money in my
will, would she really still refuse to accept it?'

'Quite possibly she would.'

'No, she wouldn't. But anyway, if it's no, then no; so be it. Though
ten thousand is a fine thing when you need it. At all events, please pass
my message to Avdotya Romanovna.'

'No, I shan't.'

'In which case, Rodion Romanovich, I shall have to try to get a personal meeting with her, in other words to trouble her.'

'And if I do tell her, you won't try to meet her in person?'

'I honestly don't know what to say to you. I should very much like to see her once more.'

'You can forget that.'

'A pity. But you don't know me; we may come to know each other better.'

'You think we'll come to know each other better?'

'Why ever not?' said Svidrigailov with a smile, standing up and taking his hat. 'After all, I wasn't so keen on disturbing you, and on my way here I wasn't really counting on anything; though I had been very struck by your face this morning...'

'Where did you see me this morning?' asked Raskolnikov uneasily.

'I just happened to... I keep thinking there's something in you that's very like me... But don't worry, I don't make a nuisance of myself; I've got on with card sharps, and Prince Svirbey, my distant relative and a powerful man, didn't find me boring, and I managed to write something about Raphael's Madonna* in Madame Prilukova's album, and I lived seven years with Marfa Petrovna without a break, and in the old days I used to spend the night in Vyazemsky's house on the Haymarket,* and now I may go up with Berg in his balloon.'

'Oh, very well. Are you leaving on your journey soon, may I ask?'

'What journey?'

'Well, the "voyage" you mentioned... You said so yourself.'

' "Voyage"? Oh, yes!... That's true, I was telling you about a voyage... Well, that's a big question... If you only knew what you're asking me about!' he added, and suddenly uttered a short, loud laugh. 'Perhaps I may marry, instead of going on a voyage. They're trying to arrange a match for me.'

'Here?'

'Yes.'

'How did you find time for that?'

'But I really should like to see Avdotya Romanovna once more. I'm asking you seriously. Well, goodbye now... Oh, yes! I'd quite forgotten. Rodion Romanovich, please tell your sister that she's mentioned in Marfa Petrovna's will, with a bequest of three thousand roubles. That's definite. Marfa Petrovna made the arrangement a week before her death, and that was done in my presence. Avdotya Romanovna could even get that money in two or three weeks' time.'

'Are you telling the truth?'

'Yes, that's the truth. Please tell her. Well, sir, your servant. I'm lodging quite close by, you know.'

On his way out, Svidrigailov bumped into Razumikhin in the doorway.

CHAPTER II

IT was almost eight by now, and both of them were hurrying to Bakaleyev's so as to get there before Luzhin.

'So who was that, then?' asked Razumikhin as soon as they got outside.

'That was Svidrigailov, that landowner. My sister worked as a governess for them, and that's where she was molested. He tried to make love to her, so she had to leave—in fact she was ordered out by his wife Marfa Petrovna. Some time later this Marfa Petrovna apologized to Dunia, and now all of a sudden she's died. It was her we were talking about just now. I don't know why, but that man really frightens me. He came here straight after his wife's funeral. He's a very strange man, and he's plotting something... He seems to know something... We have to protect Dunia from him—that was what I wanted to tell you, do you hear me?'

'Protect her! What can he do to Avdotya Romanovna? Well, thanks for telling me, Rodia—we'll protect her, we certainly shall! Where does he live?'

'I don't know.'

'Why didn't you ask him? Oh, what a shame! Still, I can find out.'

'Did you see him?' asked Raskolnikov after a brief silence.

'Well yes, I did notice him—took a good look at him.'

'You really saw him? Saw him clearly?' persisted Raskolnikov.

'Oh yes, I remember him very well. I could pick him out of a thousand—I've a good memory for faces.'

For a while neither man spoke.

'M-m... all right, then...' mumbled Raskolnikov. 'Because otherwise, you know what?... It occurred to me... I keep thinking... all that could just have been my imagination.'

'What are you talking about? I don't really understand what you're saying.'

'Well, you all keep telling me I'm mad,' Raskolnikov went on, with a twisted smile. 'I just thought perhaps I really was mad, and I'd simply seen a ghost!'

'What on earth do you mean?'

'Well, who knows? Perhaps I really am crazy, and everything that's been happening these last few days—perhaps it's all just been my imagination...'

'Come on, Rodia! You're all upset again!... What was he saying to you, why did he come to see you?'

Raskolnikov made no reply, and Razumikhin thought for a minute or two.

'Well, listen to my story,' he began. 'I came round to see you, and you were asleep. Then it was dinner time, and then I went to see Porfiry. Zametov was still there. I was going to tell him, but it didn't come out right. I couldn't manage to say what I wanted. They don't seem to understand—don't seem able to understand—but that doesn't bother them in the least. I took Porfiry over to the window and started talking, but for some reason it didn't come out right that time either—he was avoiding my eye, and I was avoiding his. In the end I shook my fist in his face and told him, in a cousinly way, that I'd beat his brains out. He just looked at me. And I gave up and walked off, and that was it. All very stupid. I didn't say a word to Zametov. But you see—I was thinking I'd made a mess of everything, but then on my way downstairs I had a thought, it came to me in a flash: what on earth are you and I fussing about? If you were in any danger, or anything like that, well then, of course. But what do you care? This is all nothing to do with you, so to hell with them! We'll have our laugh at them later on, and if I were in your shoes I'd mystify them some more. Just think how ashamed they'll be later! Forget the whole thing—we can thrash them one day, but for now let's just have a laugh!'

'Yes, obviously!' replied Raskolnikov, thinking to himself, 'But what'll you be saying tomorrow?' Strangely enough, it had never yet occurred to him to wonder what Razumikhin would say when he found out. At the thought of this, Raskolnikov gazed intently at him. As for Razumikhin's present account of his visit to Porfiry, Raskolnikov wasn't really interested—so much had happened, so much had changed, since then!

In the corridor they ran into Luzhin. He had turned up at eight o'clock precisely, and was looking for the flat, so they all went there together, without looking at or acknowledging each other. The young men went in ahead, while Piotr Petrovich, for appearances' sake, lingered a moment in the corridor taking off his coat. Pulkheria Alexandrovna came out at once to meet him in the doorway. Dunia greeted her brother.

Piotr Petrovich came in and bowed to the ladies, quite affably but with redoubled self-importance. In point of fact he looked a little disconcerted, as if he hadn't quite collected his wits. Pulkheria Alexandrovna, who also seemed rather embarrassed, hastily seated everyone at the oval table where the samovar was simmering. Dunia and Luzhin sat facing one another at the two ends, while Razumikhin and

Raskolnikov sat opposite Pulkheria Alexandrovna—Razumikhin closer to Luzhin, and Raskolnikov next to his sister.

There was a moment's silence. Piotr Petrovich unhurriedly drew out a cambric handkerchief, wafting perfume about the room, and blew his nose with the air of a man who, despite his virtue, is somewhat wounded in his dignity, and firmly resolved to demand explanations. Out in the hallway he had already half-wondered whether he shouldn't keep his coat on and leave, thus administering a stern and impressive punishment to both ladies and letting them feel the whole reality of the situation. But he couldn't make up his mind to do that. This was a man, moreover, who disliked uncertainty, and at this point he needed to settle the question: if his orders had been so blatantly flouted, there must be something behind it, in which case it would be better to find everything out at once. There would always be time to punish them, and that would rest with him.

'I trust your journey was satisfactory?' he began in a formal tone, addressing Pulkheria Alexandrovna.

'Yes, thank God, Piotr Petrovich.'

'Very glad to hear it. And Avdotya Romanovna, not too tired either?'

'Well, I'm young and strong, I don't get tired, but it was very hard on Mamasha,' replied Dunechka.

'What can you do? Our national railways cover very long distances. Our "Mother Russia", as we call her, is a vast country... As for me, much though I wished to, I was unable to hasten to meet you. I trust, however, that you managed everything without undue trouble?'

'Oh, no, Piotr Petrovich. It was very upsetting,' Pulkheria Alexandrovna declared hurriedly and with particular emphasis. 'And if God himself, so it seemed, hadn't sent Dmitry Prokofich to us yesterday, we would have been absolutely lost. Here he is—Dmitry Prokofich Razumikhin,' she added, presenting him to Luzhin.

'Yes indeed, I had that pleasure... yesterday,' muttered Luzhin, casting an unfriendly sidelong glance at Razumikhin; then he frowned and said no more. Piotr Petrovich belonged to that class of people who appear particularly affable in company, and make a particular point of their affability, but who, when things are not going their way, instantly lose all their social skills and become more like sacks of flour than relaxed, sociable gentlemen. Everyone fell silent again—Raskolnikov remained stubbornly mute, Avdotya Romanovna didn't want to break the silence too soon, Razumikhin had nothing to say, and Pulkheria Alexandrovna began to feel anxious again.

'Marfa Petrovna is dead, had you heard?' she began, playing her best card.

'Yes, of course, I had heard, madam, I was informed as soon as it became known, and as a matter of fact I am here to inform you that Arkady Ivanovich Svidrigailov set off for Petersburg in a hurry, immediately after his wife's funeral. That, at least, is the most reliable information I have received.'

'Petersburg? Here?' asked Dunechka in alarm, exchanging glances with her mother.

'Precisely so, and naturally not without some plan in his mind, considering his sudden departure, and prior events in general.'

'God in heaven! Won't he leave Dunechka in peace, even here?' cried Pulkheria Alexandrovna.

'It seems to me that you have no particular cause for alarm—neither you, nor Avdotya Romanovna—provided, of course, that you yourselves do not wish to enter into any form of communication with him. As for myself, I am taking steps to discover where he is lodging at present...'

'Oh, Piotr Petrovich, you've no idea how you've scared me now!' Pulkheria Alexandrovna went on. 'I've only ever seen him twice, and I found him terrible, terrible! I'm sure he was responsible for poor Marfa Petrovna's death.'

'As to that, one cannot draw any definite conclusion. The information I have is precise. I don't dispute that he may perhaps have hastened the course of events, by the moral effect, so to speak, of his affronts to her; but as regards this individual's conduct, and his moral character in general, I agree with you. I don't know whether he is rich now, nor exactly how much Marfa Petrovna left him; I shall have information on that point in the very near future; but naturally, here in Petersburg, if he has anything at all in the way of financial resources, he will immediately return to his old ways. He is the most corrupt, most depraved and vicious individual of any of his kind. I have substantial grounds for believing that Marfa Petrovna, having had the misfortune to fall so deeply in love with him that she paid off his debts eight years ago, also assisted him in a different matter; and that it was only through her efforts and sacrifices that a criminal investigation was suppressed in its very earliest stages, involving a brutal and, if one might put it that way, fantastic homicide, for which he could most, most easily have ended up on a trip to Siberia. That is the sort of man he is, if you wish to know.'

'Oh, good God!' cried Pulkheria Alexandrovna. Raskolnikov was listening attentively.

'Is it true what you say—that you've got accurate information about this?' asked Dunia, sternly and impressively.

'All I am telling you is what I heard in person from the late Marfa Petrovna, in strict confidence. It must be pointed out that from the legal point of view this business is a very murky one. There used to live here, and I believe still does, a certain woman called Resslich, a foreigner and furthermore a small moneylender, who also has other business interests. And with this woman, Mr Svidrigailov has long been in some sort of extremely close and mysterious relationship. She used to have a distant female relative living with her, a niece as I believe, a deaf and dumb girl of some fifteen or even only fourteen years of age, for whom this Resslich nursed a violent hatred, grudging her every morsel she ate and even subjecting her to inhuman beatings. One day the girl was found hanged in the attic. The verdict was suicide. After the usual procedures, the case was closed, but later on a report was received that the child had been... cruelly ill-treated by Svidrigailov. It is true that all this was very mysterious, the denunciation had come from another woman, also a German, a woman of notorious character who inspired no confidence; indeed, in the event no report was actually submitted, thanks to the efforts and money of Marfa Petrovna. It all ended as no more than a rumour. However, that rumour was most significant. You, Avdotya Romanovna, when you were with them, will of course have heard the story of the servant Philip, who died of brutal ill treatment some six years ago, before serfdom was abolished.'

'No, what I heard was that this Philip had hanged himself.'

'That is so, but it was Mr Svidrigailov's ceaseless, systematic ill treatment and the punishments he inflicted that forced him, or I should rather say disposed him, to seek such a violent death.'

'I don't know about that,' replied Dunia shortly. 'All I heard was a very odd story about how this Philip was some sort of hypochondriac, a kind of home-grown philosopher—people said he had "read himself crazy"*—and that he hanged himself chiefly because Mr Svidrigailov made fun of him, not because he beat him. When I was there, Mr Svidrigailov treated his people well, and they actually liked him, although it's true that they did blame him for Philip's death.'

'I observe that you, Avdotya Romanovna, seem suddenly inclined to stand up for him,' remarked Luzhin, twisting his mouth into an enigmatic smile. 'It's true that he is a cunning man who fascinates women, and Marfa Petrovna who died so mysteriously serves as a lamentable instance of that. I merely wished to give you and your Mamasha the benefit of my advice, in view of the attempts he has recently made and will no doubt continue to make. For my part, I am firmly convinced that this man will undoubtedly disappear again into a debtor's prison. Marfa Petrovna never had the slightest intention of bequeathing anything to him, having her own children to think of; and even if she had left him something, it could only have been some bare essentials, something ephemeral and of little value, which could never have kept a man of his habits for a single year.'

'Piotr Petrovich, I beg you,' said Dunia, 'do let's stop talking about Mr Svidrigailov. I'm sick of it.'

'He's just been round to see me,' said Raskolnikov suddenly, breaking his silence for the first time.

There were exclamations of surprise on all sides, and everyone turned to look at him. Even Piotr Petrovich took notice.

'About an hour and a half ago, while I was asleep, he came in and woke me, and introduced himself,' Raskolnikov went on. 'He was quite relaxed and cheerful, and seemed perfectly confident that we'd make friends. Incidentally, he's very keen to have a meeting with you, Dunia, and asked me to mediate for him. He has a proposal to make to you, and he told me what it was. What's more, he told me for a fact that a week before her death, Marfa Petrovna had made a will leaving you, Dunia, three thousand roubles, and you can have that money very shortly.'

'Thank God!' cried Pulkheria Alexandrovna, crossing herself. 'Pray for her, Dunia, pray for her!'

'That's the very truth,' Luzhin burst out.

'Go on, go on, what else?' Dunechka asked urgently.

'Then he said that he himself wasn't rich, and the whole estate goes to his children, who are with their aunt now. Then he said he was staying somewhere not far from me—but where, I don't know, I didn't ask him.'

'But what is it, what is it that he wants to propose to Dunechka?' asked Pulkheria Alexandrovna in alarm. 'Did he tell you?'

'Yes, he did.'

'So what is it?'

'I'll tell you later.' Raskolnikov said no more, and picked up his tea.

Piotr Petrovich drew out his watch and looked at it.

'I am obliged to leave: I have something to attend to, so I shall not be in your way,' he said, looking rather piqued, and made to rise from his chair.

'Do stay, Piotr Petrovich,' said Dunia. 'You know you meant to spend the evening with us. And you yourself wrote to say that you had something to sort out with Mamenka.'

'That is so, Avdotya Romanovna,' said Piotr Petrovich majestically, sitting down on his chair again but keeping hold of his hat. 'I did indeed wish to have matters out with both you and your respected Mamasha—matters of considerable importance, in fact. But, just as your brother is unable to explain to you in my presence certain pro-posals of Mr Svidrigailov's, so I too do not wish, and am unable, to discuss... in the presence of other people... certain most, most important matters. Moreover, my overriding and most earnest request has not been complied with...'

Luzhin put on a bitter expression and fell into a dignified silence.

'It was I alone who insisted that we shouldn't carry out your request for my brother not to come to our meeting,' said Dunia. 'You wrote to say that he had insulted you; I think this has to be sorted out at once, and the two of you must make your peace. And if Rodia really did insult you, then he *must* and *shall* apologize to you.'

Piotr Petrovich instantly took heart.

'There are certain insults, Avdotya Romanovna, which with the best will in the world cannot be forgotten. There is always a line that is dan-gerous to cross, because once crossed it is impossible to turn back.'

'That isn't actually what I was talking about, Piotr Petrovich,' inter-rupted Dunia somewhat impatiently. 'You must realize that our whole future now depends on whether or not all this is cleared up and settled as quickly as possible. I want to make it clear right from the start that I can't look at this any differently, and if you care about me at all, then—difficult or not—this whole story has to be settled this very day. I repeat—if my brother is at fault, he shall ask your pardon.'

'I am surprised that you put the question in that way, Avdotya Romanovna,' said Luzhin, growing more and more irritated. 'While esteeming you, and so to speak adoring you, as I do, I am still most, most capable of disliking a member of your family. While I aspire to the happiness of your hand, at the same time I cannot take upon myself obligations that are incompatible...'

'Ah, stop being so touchy, Piotr Petrovich!' Dunia interrupted him vehemently. 'Be the intelligent and noble-hearted man I've always thought you were, and wanted you to be. I have promised you a great deal, I'm engaged to marry you: trust me in this affair, and be sure that I'll judge impartially between you. If I set myself up as a judge, that's as much of a surprise to my brother as it is to you. When I got your letter today, and asked him to be sure to come to our meeting, I didn't tell him anything of what I planned. Please understand that if the two of you don't make peace, then I shall have to choose between you two:

either you, or him. That's how matters stand, for him and for you. I don't want to make a wrong choice—I mustn't. For your sake I'd have to cast off my brother; for my brother's sake, cast you off. Now is my chance to find out for certain: is he a brother to me? And for you: am I dear to you, do you value me—are you a husband for me?'

'Avdotya Romanovna,' said Luzhin in some annoyance, 'your words are too loaded for me; indeed I would say they're offensive, in view of the position I have the honour to occupy in relation to you. I shall not say a single word about your extraordinary and offensive juxtaposition, on an equal footing, of myself and... an impertinent youth; but in the words you use, you admit of the possibility that a promise made to me may be broken. You say: "either you, or him"; thereby indicating to me how little I mean to you... That is something that I cannot tolerate, in view of the relations and... obligations that obtain between us.'

'What!' exploded Dunia. 'I place your own interests side by side with everything that I have treasured in my life, everything that has made up my *whole* life so far, and all of a sudden you're offended because I set *too little* store by you!'

Raskolnikov smiled an acid smile and said nothing; Razumikhin was trembling with emotion. But Piotr Petrovich did not accept the reproof, becoming more persistent and more irritable with every word that was spoken, as if he were getting a taste for the quarrel.

'Love for the future companion of one's life, for one's husband, must exceed love for a brother,' he pronounced sententiously; 'and in any case I cannot stand on an equal footing with... Although I did insist, earlier on, that in the presence of your brother I would not and could not explain everything that I came to say, nonetheless I intend to address myself immediately to your respected Mamasha for a vital explanation of a certain matter of capital importance, and a painful one for me. Your son,' he went on, turning to Pulkheria Alexandrovna, 'yesterday, in the presence of Mr Rassudkin (or... I believe that is right? Forgive me, I do not recall your surname)'—with a courteous bow to Razumikhin*— 'insulted me by distorting an idea of mine, which I had expressed to you in a private conversation over coffee; namely that marriage with a poor girl who has already suffered life's afflictions is in my view preferable in conjugal terms to marriage with one who has known prosperity, because the former case is more conducive to morality. Your son wilfully exaggerated the sense of my words to an absurd degree, accusing me of evil intentions and, in my view, basing his accusations on your own correspondence. I shall count myself happy if you, Pulkheria Alexandrovna, are able to persuade me to the contrary—that would greatly reassure me. Would you kindly let me know in precisely what terms you conveyed my words in your letter to Rodion Romanovich?'

'I don't remember,' said Pulkheria Alexandrovna, somewhat flustered. 'I conveyed them as I understood them myself. I don't know how Rodia expressed himself to you... I suppose it's possible he may have exaggerated something.'

'He could not have exaggerated without prompting from you.'

'Piotr Petrovich,' Pulkheria Alexandrovna spoke out with dignity, 'the proof that Dunia and I did not put a very bad construction on your words is the fact that we are *here*.'

'Well said, Mamenka!' said Dunia approvingly.

'In other words, I am in the wrong again!' said Luzhin in injured tones.

'Well, Piotr Petrovich, you keep blaming Rodion, but in your letter recently you yourself wrote something untrue about him,' added Pulkheria Alexandrovna, taking heart.

'I do not recall writing anything untrue, madam.'

'You wrote', said Raskolnikov sharply, without turning to Luzhin, 'that yesterday I didn't hand over the money to the widow of the man who was killed, as I actually did, but to his daughter (whom I had never met before yesterday). You wrote that, so as to provoke a quarrel between me and my family, and for the same reason you added something, in vile terms, about the conduct of a girl you don't know. All that is nothing but despicable gossip.'

'Pardon me, sir,' answered Luzhin, trembling with fury. 'When I expressed my opinion of your qualities and actions in my letter, I did so purely in fulfilment of your sister's and your mother's request to describe to them how I had found you, and what impression you had made on me. And as for the matter alluded to in my letter, pray find me a single line that is unjust—can you say that you did not waste the money, or that that family, unfortunate though it may be, does not contain unworthy persons?'

'In my opinion you, for all your worthiness, are not worth the little finger of that unfortunate girl at whom you are casting a stone.'

'In other words, you could even contemplate introducing her into the company of your mother and sister?'

'I've already done so, if you want to know. I had her sit down today next to Mama and Dunia.'

'Rodia!' cried out Pulkheria Alexandrovna.

Dunechka blushed; Razumikhin frowned. Luzhin smiled a spiteful, haughty smile.

'You can see for yourself, Avdotya Romanovna,' said he, 'whether any reconciliation is possible here. I may now hope that this matter is concluded and cleared up, once and for all. I shall now withdraw, so as not to interfere any further with this pleasant family gathering and the sharing of secrets.' He rose from his chair and picked up his hat. 'But in leaving, allow me to say that I hope in future to be spared such encounters of a compromising nature, if I may so put it. I make an especial request to you, most respected Pulkheria Alexandrovna, in this matter, most particularly as my letter was addressed to you and no one else.'

Pulkheria Alexandrovna was rather offended.

'It looks as though you're taking us over completely, Piotr Petrovich. Dunia has told you the reason why your request wasn't carried out; she meant well. And the way you write to me—it's as if you were giving me orders. Do we really have to treat every wish of yours as a command? Let me tell you, on the contrary, that you ought now to be treating *us* with particular delicacy and consideration, because we have given up everything to come here, trusting in you, so that we're almost entirely at your mercy already.'

'That is not quite fair, Pulkheria Alexandrovna, especially at this precise time when you have just had news of Marfa Petrovna's bequest of three thousand roubles, which would appear to be most timely, judging from the new tone you're adopting towards me now,' he added caustically.

'From what you've just said, it really looks as if you'd been counting on our helplessness,' observed Dunechka irritably.

'But now, at all events, I cannot count on anything of the sort, and am particularly reluctant to interfere with the communication of secret proposals from Arkady Ivanovich Svidrigailov, which he entrusted to your young brother, and which, I see, are of capital importance to all of you, and perhaps most welcome too.'

'Oh my God!' cried Pulkheria Alexandrovna.

Razumikhin was itching to get up.

'And aren't you ashamed now, sister?' asked Raskolnikov.

'Yes, I am ashamed, Rodia,' said Dunia. 'Piotr Petrovich, get out!' she added, turning to face him, pale with fury.

Piotr Petrovich seemed not at all to have expected this turn of events. He was too sure of himself, his power, and the helplessness of his victims. Nor could he believe it was happening now. He turned pale, and his lips quivered.

'Avdotya Romanovna, if I walk out through that door now, with those words of yours to send me on my way, then you can be quite sure—I shall never return. Think well! I mean what I say.'

'What insolence!' cried Dunia, rising quickly from her seat. 'I don't in the least want you to come back!'

'What? So tha-a-at's how the matter stands, madam!' cried Luzhin. He had never until this moment believed that things would turn out this way, and now he was utterly at a loss. 'So that's how it is! But do you know, Avdotya Romanovna, that I could have grounds for complaint here?'

'What right have you to talk to her in that way?' intervened Pulkheria Alexandrovna heatedly. 'What is it that you can complain of? What rights are you talking about? Would I give my Dunia to a man like you? Get away, leave us in peace! It's our own fault for planning something that was wrong—and my fault most of all...'

'Nevertheless, Pulkheria Alexandrovna,' said Luzhin, now in a blind fury, 'you bound me by giving your promise, which you are now going back on... and in any case... in any case, I have been, so to speak, involved in some outgoings...'

This last grievance was so much in Piotr Petrovich's character that Raskolnikov, who had grown pale with rage and with his efforts to restrain it, could suddenly control himself no longer—and burst out laughing. But Pulkheria Alexandrovna exploded in fury:

'Outgoings? What outgoings would that be? You wouldn't be referring to our trunk, would you? But the train conductor took it for you free of charge. Good God, so we bound you, did we? Pull yourself together, Piotr Petrovich, it was you who bound us, hand and foot—not we who bound you!'

'That's enough, Mamenka, please, stop!' Avdotya Romanovna begged her. 'Piotr Petrovich, do us a favour—go away!'

'Yes, madam, I will go away—but I have one last word to say!' he pronounced, almost completely losing control of himself. 'Your Mamasha, it seems, has altogether forgotten that I decided to take you, so to speak, after the neighbourhood gossip over your reputation had spread throughout the district. For your sake, I disregarded public opinion and restored your reputation, and in return I might most, most justifiably have hoped for some return, and could even demand some gratitude from you... But now at last my eyes are opened! Now I can see for myself that I may have acted most, most rashly in disregarding the voice of society...'

'Is he asking to have his head smashed in, or what?' yelled Razumikhin, jumping up from his chair and preparing to set about him.

'Despicable, wicked man!' said Dunia.

'Nobody speak! Nobody move!' cried Raskolnikov, restraining

Razumikhin. Then he walked right up to confront Luzhin. 'Kindly get out!' he said quietly and distinctly. 'And not another word, or else...'

Piotr Petrovich stared at him for a few seconds, his face pale and twisted with rage. Then he turned and walked out. Rarely if ever had anyone carried away so much venomous hatred in his heart as this man nursed against Raskolnikov. He blamed him, and him alone, for everything. Remarkably enough, even on his way downstairs, he continued to imagine that his cause might perhaps not be entirely lost, and that if it depended only on the ladies, things might 'most, most possibly' still be put right.

CHAPTER III

THE main thing was that up to the very last minute he had not at all expected things to end this way. He had maintained his overbearing manner without letting up, never believing it possible that two poor and defenceless women might escape from his clutches. That conviction was greatly furthered both by his vanity and by that degree of self-confidence that one might best call self-adoration. Piotr Petrovich, having fought his way up from nowhere, had become morbidly fond of admiring himself, and had a high opinion of his own intelligence and abilities; sometimes, when alone, he even used to gaze in admiration at his face in the mirror. But what he loved and treasured most of all in the world was his money, accumulated by hard work and every other means he could command. Money raised him to the level of everything that used to be above him.

Just now, when he had bitterly reminded Dunia of how he had resolved to take her despite the bad rumours surrounding her, Piotr Petrovich had been speaking quite sincerely, and even feeling profound indignation at her 'black ingratitude'. And yet when he had begun courting her, he had already been quite convinced of the absurdity of all that gossip, publicly refuted by Marfa Petrovna herself and long ago dismissed by everyone in town, who by now all hotly defended Dunia. He himself would never have denied that he had known all that at the time. And yet he set a high value on his determination to raise Dunia to his own level, and regarded it as something heroic. When he had said all this to Dunia during their meeting, he had been voicing a secret and cherished idea of his, which he had repeatedly admired in himself, and he could not understand how others could fail to be impressed by such a noble deed. When he had gone round to visit Raskolnikov, he had entered his room feeling like a benefactor about to reap the fruits of his generosity and to hear the most flattering expressions of gratitude. And now, of course, as he descended the stairs, he saw himself as having been roundly insulted, and his merits completely ignored.

As for Dunia, he simply could not do without her. To give her up was unthinkable. A long time ago, several years earlier, he had begun indulging in voluptuous dreams of marriage; but meanwhile he had piled up more and more money, and waited. In the deepest secrecy, he would summon up delectable thoughts of some virtuous girl, who was poor (she had to be poor), very young, very pretty, of good birth and education, a timid girl who had suffered great misfortunes and would be utterly humbled before him, regarding him for all her life as her saviour, worshipping him, obeying him, and marvelling at him—only him. How many scenes, how many delicious episodes had he created in his imagination on this seductive and playful theme, during his quiet breaks from business! And now the dream of all those years had almost come true; he had been impressed by Avdotya Romanovna's beauty and education, and her helpless situation had been irresistibly alluring. In fact she represented even more than he had dreamed of: she had turned out to be a proud, spirited, and virtuous girl, whose breeding and education exceeded his own (he felt that); and yet such a creature was to be slavishly grateful to him for his great exploit, all her life long; prostrating herself reverently before him, while he wielded absolute and unbounded power over her!... Providentially, he had recently come to a firm decision, after much consideration and hesitation—to make a clean break in his career, take on wider responsibilities, and at the same time gradually penetrate a higher class of society—an alluring dream he had long cherished. In brief, he had resolved to have a try at St Petersburg. He knew that a woman could be 'most, most useful' in advancing him. The charm of a beautiful, virtuous, and well-bred woman could have made his path an astonishingly pleasant one, drawing people's attention to him, creating a radiance about him... and now it was all ruined! This sudden and horrible rupture had fallen on him like a thunderbolt. It must be some monstrous joke, an absurdity! He had only been the least bit overbearing, he hadn't even had time to say what he wanted, he hadn't really meant what he said, had been just a bit carried away—and it had all ended so seriously! And after all, in his own way he did already love Dunia, he was already lording it over her in his dreams—and then suddenly this!... No! Tomorrow, no later than tomorrow, he must restore everything, heal the wound, put everything right, and most important of all—he must destroy this conceited milksop, this young lout who was behind everything. Almost in spite of himself, and with painful feelings, he recalled Razumikhin... but soon reassured himself on that score. 'How could one ever set someone like him on the same level as me!' Yet there was one man he was seriously afraid of, and that was Svidrigailov... In short, he foresaw a great deal of trouble to come.

'No, it's my fault, mine, more than anyone's!' said Dunechka, hugging and kissing her mother. 'I was tempted by his money, but I swear, brother—I never imagined he was such an unworthy person. If I'd seen through him earlier, I'd never have been tempted! Don't think badly of me, brother!'

'God has delivered us! God has delivered us!' muttered Pulkheria Alexandrovna, seemingly in some confusion, as though she hadn't yet quite taken in all that had happened.

They were all very happy, and five minutes later they were actually laughing. But from time to time Dunechka would turn pale and knit her brows, as she remembered what had just passed. Pulkheria Alexandrovna couldn't have imagined that she too would have been happy: that very morning, a break with Luzhin had seemed an utter catastrophe to her. But Razumikhin was delighted. He still dared not give free rein to his feelings, but he was trembling feverishly all over, as if a great weight had just rolled off his heart. Now he had the right to devote his whole life to them, to serve them... And who knew what might yet happen! Yet he was even more anxiously banishing any further thoughts on the subject, scared of his own imagination. Only Raskolnikov was still sitting in the same place, almost gloomy and even indifferent. He, who had been the most insistent on getting rid of Luzhin, now seemed less interested than anyone in what had passed. Dunia couldn't help thinking that he was still very cross with her; while Pulkheria Alexandrovna kept looking apprehensively at him.

'So what did Svidrigailov say to you?' said Dunia, coming over to him.

'Oh, yes, yes!' cried Pulkheria Alexandrovna.

Raskolnikov looked up. 'He's insisting on making you a present of ten thousand roubles, and at the same time he's expressed a wish to see you once, in my presence.'

'To see her! Not for anything in the world!' cried Pulkheria Alexandrovna. 'And how dare he offer her money!'

So Raskolnikov recounted, fairly shortly, his conversation with Svidrigailov, leaving out all about Marfa Petrovna's ghost so as not to be drawn into irrelevancies, and feeling distaste at saying anything beyond what was most essential.

'What did you say to him?' asked Dunia.

'First I said that I wouldn't take any messages to you. Then he announced that he would use every means in his power to get a meeting with you. He insisted that his passion for you had been a mere passing whim, and that he no longer felt anything for you... He doesn't want you to marry Luzhin... But his talk was generally quite confused.'

'What do you think of him yourself, Rodia? How did he seem to you?'

'I must confess, I don't really understand what's going on. Here he is, offering you ten thousand roubles, and yet he himself said that he wasn't rich. Next he declares that he wants to go away somewhere, and ten minutes later he forgets he said it. And he suddenly announces that he wants to marry, and that a wife has already been found for him... Of course he has his own plans, and most likely they're bad ones. But then again, it's hard to imagine him taking such a stupid line if he had wicked intentions towards you... Needless to say, I refused his money once and for all, on your behalf. But all in all he struck me as very strange, and... even... that he showed possible signs of madness. But I could be wrong; he may just have been playing a part. Marfa Petrovna's death seems to have affected him...'

'God rest her soul!' cried Pulkheria Alexandrovna; 'I'll pray to God for her, all my life long! Where should we have been by now, Dunia, without those three thousand roubles? Lord, they were a gift from heaven! This morning, Rodia, all we had left in the world was three roubles, and Dunechka and I were just wondering how we could quickly find somewhere to pawn her watch, so as not to take any money from that man until he offered some himself.'

Dunia seemed profoundly shaken by Svidrigailov's offer. She was still standing sunk in thought.

'He has some terrible plan!' she whispered to herself, and shuddered.

Raskolnikov had observed her extreme alarm.

'I expect I'll have to see him again, and more than once,' he said to Dunia.

'We'll watch him! I'll hunt him down!' cried Razumikhin enthusiastically. 'I won't let him out of my sight! Rodia has allowed me to. Just a while ago, he said to me: "Look after my sister." So will you let me, Avdotya Romanovna?'

Dunia smiled and held out her hand, but her anxious expression did not change. Pulkheria Alexandrovna was looking fearfully at her. However, she was evidently reassured by the three thousand roubles.

A quarter of an hour later they were deep in lively conversation.

Even Raskolnikov listened carefully for a while, though without saying anything. Razumikhin was holding forth.

'And why, why should you leave here?' he declaimed fervently, quite carried away. 'What can you do in your little town? The main thing is that you're all together here, and you all need each other, you really do—believe me! I mean, for a while at least... Let me be your friend, and your partner, and I promise you that we'll set up a splendid business. Listen, I'll explain it all in detail to you, the whole plan! It came into my head this very morning, before anything had happened... It's like this: I have an uncle (I'll introduce you—he's a very nice, very respectable little old man!), and he's got a capital of a thousand roubles, which he doesn't need because he lives on his pension. For the last two years he's been begging me to take those thousand roubles on loan, and just pay him six per cent on them. I can see what he's thinking: he just wants to help me. Last year I had no use for the money; but this year I decided to accept it, and I've just been waiting for him to get here. Then you can let me have another thousand out of your three, and that's all we need to start off with; we'll go into partnership. And what are we going to do?'

Here Razumikhin set about expounding his plan, talking at length about how little our booksellers and publishers understand their business, and that makes them bad publishers, while good-quality books generally sell well and yield a profit, sometimes a considerable one. It was publishing that Razumikhin had been thinking about. He had worked for other publishers for two years and had a fair knowledge of three European languages, despite having told Raskolnikov some six days ago that his German was *schwach*.* He had said that because he was trying to persuade him to take on half the translating work and accept an advance of three roubles; but it had been a fib, and Raskolnikov had known it.

'Why ever should we miss such a chance, when we've suddenly got hold of one of the main necessities—our own money?' insisted Razumikhin. 'Of course it'll be hard work, but we'll work at it—you, Avdotya Romanovna, and I, and Rodion... some publications these days are amazingly profitable! And the main strength of our business will be the fact that we'll know exactly what needs to be translated. We'll be translating, and publishing, and learning, all at once. Right now I can be useful because I've had some experience. I've been nosing around the publishing houses for almost two years now, and I know all their ins and outs; it doesn't take a saint to bake clay pots, believe me! Why on earth shouldn't we leap at the chance! And then, I know of two or three works that I'm keeping quiet about; just the idea of translating and publishing them is worth a hundred roubles for each book, in fact the idea for one of them is something I wouldn't pass on for five hundred. Just think—if I did tell anyone, they might even have second thoughts about publishing them, they're such blockheads! As for all the business of publishing, the printers, paper, sales—leave all that to me! I know all the tricks of the trade! We'll start off in a small way, and then grow bigger. At least we'll have something to live on; and we'll always get our money back.'

Dunia's eyes were shining.

'I very much like what you're saying, Dmitry Prokofich,' she said.

'Well, of course I don't know anything about all this,' said Pulkheria Alexandrovna. 'Maybe it's a good idea, but then again, God alone knows! It all seems new and strange to me. Of course we have to stay here, for a while at least...'

She looked at Rodia.

'What do you think, brother?' asked Dunia.

'I think that's a very good idea of his,' he replied. 'Naturally there's no point in thinking about having our own firm at this stage, but it's true that there are five or six books that could be published and would certainly be successful. And I know of one work myself that's bound to do well. As for his ability to run the business, there's not the slightest doubt: he knows all about it... Anyway, you'll have plenty of time to arrange things.'

'Hurrah!' cried Razumikhin. 'And now listen, there's a flat here, in this same building, with the same landlords. It's a separate flat, divided off, it doesn't communicate with these rooms, it's furnished and the rent's reasonable. Three rooms. Take it for the time being. I'll pawn the watch for you tomorrow and bring you the money, and then it can all be sorted out. And the main thing is, you can all three live there together, Rodia and you two... Where are you off to now, Rodia?'

'What is it, Rodia, are you going already?' asked Pulkheria Alexandrovna in dismay.

'At a moment like this!' cried Razumikhin.

Dunia was watching her brother, mistrustful and astonished. He was holding his cap in his hands and preparing to leave the room.

'You sound as if you were burying me, or saying farewell for ever,' he said in an odd voice.

He seemed to smile, but it didn't seem to be a real smile.

'And who knows, perhaps we really are meeting for the last time,' he added unexpectedly. It appeared to have been a private thought, which had escaped him of its own accord.

'What's wrong with you?' cried his mother.

'Where are you going, Rodia?' asked Dunia in a strange voice.

'Yes, well, I really have to go,' he replied vaguely, as if unsure of what he meant to say. But his pallid face showed crisp determination.

'I was meaning to say... on my way here... I wanted to tell you, Mamenka... and you, Dunia, that it's best if we part company for a while. I'm not feeling well, I'm uneasy... I'll come later, I'll come of my own accord, when... when it's possible. I'll think of you, and I love you... Let me be! Leave me alone! That's what I decided, even before... That was my firm decision... Whatever happens to me, whether I perish or not, I want to be alone. Forget all about me... That's best... Don't make enquiries about me. When it's necessary, I'll come myself, or... I'll send for you. Perhaps everything will turn out all right!... But now, if you love me, give up on me... Otherwise I'll hate you, I can feel that I shall... Goodbye!'

'Oh God!' exclaimed Pulkheria Alexandrovna.

Mother and sister were both terribly frightened, and so was Razumikhin.

'Rodia, Rodia! Let's make it up again, let's be as we were before!' wailed his poor mother.

Slowly he turned round towards the door and slowly went out. Dunia caught him up.

'Brother! What are you doing to Mother!' she whispered, looking at him in burning indignation.

He gave her a sad look.

'Never mind, I'll come back, I'll keep coming,' he muttered under his breath, as if not fully aware of what he wanted to say; and left the room.

'Callous, wicked egoist!' cried Dunia.

'He's i-n-sane, not callous! He's mad! Can't you see that, really? That makes you the heartless one!...' Razumikhin whispered hotly in her ear, and squeezed her hand tight.

'I'll come straight back!' he called out to Pulkheria Alexandrovna, as she stood there horror-struck; and he rushed out of the room.

Raskolnikov was waiting for him at the end of the corridor.

'I knew you'd rush out,' he said. 'Get back to them, and stay with them... Come and see them tomorrow, and... always. I... may come, perhaps... if I can. Goodbye!'

And he left him without holding out his hand.

'But where are you off to? What's up? What's happened to you? How can you!...' stammered Razumikhin, utterly bewildered.

Raskolnikov paused again.

'Once and for all: don't ever ask me about anything. I've no answers to give you... Don't come to me. Perhaps I really will come here... Leave me... but *don't leave them*. Do you understand me?'

The corridor was dark; they were standing by a lamp. For a minute they stared at one another in silence. Razumikhin remembered that minute all his life. Raskolnikov's intense, burning gaze seemed to grow more intense moment by moment, penetrating into his very soul and consciousness. Suddenly Razumikhin shuddered. Something strange seemed to have passed from one to the other... Some idea, some hint had flashed between them, something terrible, monstrous, suddenly understood on both sides... Razumikhin grew pale as a corpse.

'You understand now?...' Raskolnikov suddenly asked, his face distorted with pain. 'Go back, get back to them,' he added, then quickly turned his back and left the building...

I shall not attempt to describe what happened that evening in Pulkheria Alexandrovna's room: how Razumikhin returned to them, how he reassured them, swore that Rodia had to be allowed to rest while he was ill, swore that Rodia would certainly come back, would come every day, that he was very, very disturbed, that he mustn't be irritated; and that he himself, Razumikhin, would watch over him, and get him a doctor, a good one, the best one, a whole faculty of doctors... In a word, from that evening on Razumikhin became their own son and brother.

CHAPTER IV

RASKOLNIKOV, meanwhile, went straight to the house on the canal where Sonia lived. It was an old three-storey house painted green. He sought out the porter, who gave him vague directions to the tailor Kapernaumov's lodging. In a corner of the yard he found the door to a dark, narrow stairway, and went up to the second floor; here he came out onto a gallery that went round the whole floor on the courtyard side. As he was wandering about in the dark, wondering where the entrance to Kapernaumov's flat might be, a door suddenly opened three paces away. Instinctively he took hold of it.

'Who's there?' asked a frightened female voice.

'It's me... I've come to see you,' replied Raskolnikov, and stepped into the narrow hallway. Here, on a chair with a broken seat, stood a candle in a battered copper candlestick.

'It's you! Oh God!' cried Sonia faintly, standing rooted to the spot.
'Where's your door? This one?'

And Raskolnikov, trying not to look at her, quickly entered her room.

A moment later Sonia came in with the candle, set it down and stood
before him, utterly bewildered, filled with inexpressible agitation,
and evidently frightened by his unexpected visit. Suddenly the colour
returned to her pale features, and her eyes filled with tears... She felt
sick, and ashamed, and happy... Raskolnikov quickly turned away and
sat down on a chair by the table. He cast a rapid glance over the room.

It was a large room but a very low one: the only room that the
Kapernaumovs rented out. The locked door to their own rooms was in
the left-hand wall. Opposite it, in the right-hand wall, was another door
that was fastened shut; beyond it was the separate neighbouring flat,
with a different number. Sonia's room looked rather like a shed. Its very
irregular four-sided construction made it appear misshapen. A wall
with three windows looking out onto the canal cut obliquely across the
room, making a terribly narrow corner that ran off into the depths of
the room, scarcely visible in a poor light; while another corner was so
excessively obtuse as to be ugly. The whole of this large room contained
almost no furniture. A bed stood in the corner on the right, and beside
it, closer to the door, was a chair. Against the same wall where the bed
was, right up against the door to the neighbouring flat, stood a plain
deal table covered with a little blue tablecloth, with two rush-bottomed
chairs beside it. By the opposite wall, near the narrow corner, stood
a small plain wooden chest of drawers that looked lost in that empty
space. That was all the furniture in the room. The yellowish, faded,
tattered wallpaper was blackened in every corner; evidently the room
was damp and smoky in wintertime. Its poverty was apparent; even the
bed had no curtains.

Sonia gazed silently at her guest who was so attentively and unceremoniously inspecting her room; eventually she actually began to shake
with fear, as if standing before a judge who would determine her fate.

'It's late... is it eleven yet?' he asked, still without looking up at her.

'Yes,' whispered Sonia. 'Oh yes, it is!' she went on hurriedly, as if
that was all that mattered to her. 'The landlord's clock has just struck...
I heard it myself. Yes, it is.'

'This is the last time I'll come to see you,' went on Raskolnikov
gloomily, though actually this was his first visit. 'I may never see you
again...'

'Are you... going away?'

'I don't know... It all depends on tomorrow...'

'So you won't come to Katerina Ivanovna's tomorrow?' asked Sonia tremulously.

'I don't know. It all depends on tomorrow morning... That's not the point. I wanted to say something to you...'

He gave her a thoughtful look, and suddenly realized that he was sitting down while she was still on her feet in front of him.

'What are you standing for? Do sit down,' he said quickly in a changed voice, now quiet and gentle.

She sat down. He gave her a long, kind, almost compassionate look.

'How thin you are! Look at that hand! It's quite transparent. Your fingers are like a dead woman's.'

He took her hand. Sonia gave a faint smile.

'I've always been like that,' she said.

'Even when you lived at home?'

'Yes.'

'Well, of course!' he said abruptly, and his expression and tone of voice suddenly changed again. He looked round once more.

'Are you renting this from Kapernaumov?'

'Yes.'

'Are they there, behind that door?'

'Yes... They've got a room just like this.'

'All in one room?'

'That's right.'

'If I were in your room, I'd be afraid at night,' he said morosely.

'They're very kind, very good to me,' replied Sonia, still seeming absent and bewildered. 'And all the furniture, and everything... it's all theirs. And they're very nice to me, and the children often come to see me...'

'They're the people with speech defects?'

'Yes... He stammers, and besides that he's lame. And his wife stammers too... Not exactly stammers, but she can't seem to get the words out. She's kind, very kind. He used to be a house servant. And there are seven children... and it's only the eldest one that stammers, the others are just ill... but they don't stammer... How do you know about them?' she added in some surprise.

'Your father told me all about them, that time. He told me all about you too... and how you went out at six in the evening, and came home after eight, and how Katerina Ivanovna knelt by your bed.'

Sonia was embarrassed.

'I thought I saw him today,' she whispered hesitantly.

'Who?'

'Father. I was walking along the street, near here, by the corner; it was after nine, and he seemed to be walking ahead of me. And it really seemed to be him. I was wanting to go round to Katerina Ivanovna's...'

'You were out walking?'

'Yes,' whispered Sonia abruptly, again lowering her eyes in confusion.

'But Katerina Ivanovna used to beat you, almost, didn't she, when you lived with your father?'

'Oh no! What do you mean, how can you say that? No!' exclaimed Sonia, looking at him with something like alarm.

'So you love her, then?'

'Love her? I should think I do!' said Sonia slowly, in a voice full of sadness and distress, clasping her hands together. 'Oh dear! You... if only you knew. She's really just like a child... She's almost out of her mind... with grief. And how intelligent she used to be... how generous... how kind! You don't know anything, anything at all... Oh dear!'

Sonia seemed to be near despair as she said this, wringing her hands in agitation and misery. Her pale cheeks were flushed once more, and her eyes were filled with anguish. She was evidently profoundly moved and desperately anxious to say something, to express herself, to plead for understanding. Every feature of her face was suddenly filled with a sort of *insatiable* compassion, if one can use such an expression.

'Beat me! What are you saying? Good heavens, beat me! And even if she did, so what? What of it? You don't know anything, anything at all... She's so unhappy, oh, how unhappy she is!... And sick too... She wants things to be fair... She's a pure person. She really believes there has to be fairness in life, and she wants it... Even if you tortured her, she'd never commit an injustice. She can't see how impossible it is for everything to be fair among people, and it makes her annoyed... She's like a child, really like a child! But she's a just person, she really is!'

'And what's going to happen to you?'

Sonia gave him a questioning look.

'They're all depending on you, aren't they? True enough, they all depended on you even before this, and your father himself used to come and beg you for money to buy drink. But what's going to happen now?'

'I don't know,' said Sonia sadly.

'Are they going to stay there?'

'I don't know; they're behind with the rent, and it seems the landlady was saying today that she wants to turn them out, and Katerina Ivanovna says she won't stay there a moment longer anyway.'

'What makes her so bold? Depending on you, is she?'

'Oh no, please don't talk like that!... She and I, we're all one and the same, we share everything'—and she suddenly became agitated and almost angry again, like a canary or any other little bird when it gets its feathers ruffled—'And what can she do? I ask you, what can she do?' she asked heatedly and anxiously. 'And how she cried today, how she cried! She's going out of her mind, haven't you noticed? Sometimes she worries like a little child, wanting to make sure that everything's right and proper for tomorrow, and there are snacks to eat, and all that... and then she'll wring her hands, and cough up blood, and weep, and suddenly start banging her head against the wall in despair. And then she calms down again, and puts all her hopes in you: she says you'll help her, and that she'll borrow a bit of money somewhere and go back to her home town, and take me with her, and set up a boarding school for young ladies, with me to oversee it, and we'll start a lovely new life; and she kisses and hugs me, and comforts me—and she really believes it! She believes all those impossible dreams! Well, how can I contradict her? And then she spent all today washing and cleaning and mending; she dragged the tub into the room herself, weak as she is, and got all out of breath and collapsed on the bed. And we'd been to the market* together in the morning to buy little boots for Polechka and Lena* because theirs have all fallen to pieces, but we didn't have enough money to pay for them, we were just a little bit short, and she'd chosen such dear little boots, because she's got good taste, you don't know her... And she burst into tears, right there in the shop, in front of the shopkeepers, because she didn't have enough... Oh dear, what a sad sight that was.'

'Well, after all that, I can understand why... you live the way you do,' said Raskolnikov with a bitter smile.

'Why, don't you feel sorry too? Don't you?' Sonia fired up again. 'You too—you gave away the last money you had, before you'd seen anything. And if you'd seen everything, oh Lord! And how many, many times I've driven her to tears! Only last week, too! Yes, I did! Only a week before he died. I was cruel to her! And how many times that happened! Oh dear, how painful it's been all day, remembering that!'

As she spoke, Sonia wrung her hands in distress at the memory.

'You, cruel? Are you saying that?'

'Yes, I am, I am! I'd come home that day,' she went on, weeping, 'and my father said "Read to me, Sonia, I've got a bit of a headache, please read to me... here's the book"—he had some book or other that he'd got from Andrei Semionich, Lebeziatnikov that is, who lives there; he was always buying such odd books. And I said "I have to go," I really didn't want to read; I'd gone there mainly to show Katerina Ivanovna some collars, because Lizaveta, the dealer, had let me have some collars and cuffs cheap, nice new ones, with a pattern. And Katerina Ivanovna liked them a lot, she tried them on and looked at herself in the mirror, and she really, really loved them. "Please, Sonia," she asked, "would you give them to me?" She said "please", and she wanted them so much. But how could she have worn them? It was just that they reminded her of how happy she used to be when she was young! Looks at herself in the mirror, and admires herself, but she hasn't got a single dress, nothing nice at all, and hasn't had for I don't know how long! But she'll never ask anyone for anything; she's proud, she'd sooner give away her last possessions herself; and here she was asking me—she liked those things so much! And I didn't want to give them away, "what do you need them for, Katerina Ivanovna?"—I really said that: "what for?" I never ought to have said that to her! She gave me such a look, and she was so dreadfully upset that I'd refused, I felt so sorry to see her... It wasn't the collars she minded, it was the fact that I'd refused her—I could see that. If only I could have it all back again, and do it differently, and take back what I said... Oh, I'm... What's the point?... You don't care, do you!'

'So you knew Lizaveta the dealer?'

'Yes... Why, did you know her too?' asked Sonia in some surprise.

'Katerina Ivanovna has consumption, very badly; she'll die soon,' said Raskolnikov after a silence, without answering the question.

'Oh, no, no, no!' And Sonia, with an unconscious gesture, seized him by both hands, as if begging for that not to happen.

'Why, it's better if she dies, isn't it?'

'No, it isn't better, it isn't, it's not better at all!' she repeated involuntarily, sounding frightened.

'What about the children, then? Where are they going to live, if not with you?'

'Oh dear, I really don't know!' cried Sonia almost in despair, clutching her head. It was clear that this thought had already occurred to her many, many times; all he had done was bring it out into the open again.

'Well, if you fall ill now, while Katerina Ivanovna is still alive, and you're taken off to hospital, what then?' he insisted pitilessly.

'Oh, how can you, really! That couldn't ever happen!' Sonia's face was contorted with fearful dread.

'Why couldn't it?' Raskolnikov continued with a harsh smile. 'You aren't insured, are you? So what'll happen to them? They'll be out on the streets, every one of them; and she'll be coughing, and begging, and beating her head against a wall somewhere, as she was today, and the children will be crying... And then she'll fall down, and they'll take her off to the police, and then the hospital, and she'll die, and the children...'

'Oh no!... God could never allow that!' The words finally burst from Sonia's anguished breast. As she listened, she had gazed imploringly at him, clasping her hands in dumb entreaty as if everything depended on him.

Raskolnikov rose and began pacing about the room. A minute or so passed. Sonia stood with bowed head and drooping arms, in utter misery.

'Can't you save up? Put something aside for a rainy day?' he asked, pausing suddenly in front of her.

'No,' whispered Sonia.

'No, of course you can't! Have you ever tried?' he added, with an almost mocking smile.

'Yes, I have.'

'And you didn't manage! Well, naturally! No need to ask!'

And he began pacing the room again. Another minute passed.

'You don't make money every day, do you?'

Sonia became even more embarrassed, and her cheeks flushed again.

'No,' she whispered with a painful effort.

'Polechka will probably go the same way,' he suddenly said.

'No! No! It can't be, no!' Sonia shrieked in desperation, as if she had been stabbed with a knife. 'God will never allow such a horror!'

'He lets it happen to others.'

'No, no! God will protect her, He will!...' she repeated, quite beside herself.

'But maybe God doesn't even exist,' replied Raskolnikov with malicious pleasure. Then he laughed and looked at her.

Sonia's face suddenly underwent a terrible change, and became contorted with spasms. She threw him a glance of inexpressible reproach and tried to speak, but couldn't bring out a single word. Instead she suddenly burst into bitter sobs, covering her face with her hands.

'You said that Katerina Ivanovna was going out of her mind; you're going out of your mind yourself,' he said after a silence.

Some five minutes passed. He kept pacing back and forth, without speaking or looking at her. Eventually he came up to her, his eyes blazing. He took her shoulders in both hands, and looked straight into her weeping face. His expression was hard, sharp, and burning, and his lips twitched violently... Suddenly he bent down, quickly sank to his knees on the floor, and kissed her foot. Sonia recoiled from him in horror, as though he were a madman. And he did look completely mad.

'What do you mean? What are you doing? To me!' she whispered. Her face paled, and her heart contracted painfully.

He stood up at once.

'I wasn't bowing down to you, I was bowing before all human suffering,' he said wildly, and walked away to the window. 'Listen,' he went on after a moment, turning back to her, 'I've just told one offensive lout that he wasn't worth your little finger... and that I was doing my sister an honour when I sat her down beside you today.'

'Oh, how could you say such a thing! And in front of her?' cried Sonia in alarm. 'Sitting down with me—an honour! When I'm... dishonoured... when I'm a wicked, wicked sinner! Oh, how could you say that?'

'I didn't say that about you because of your dishonour or your sin, but because of your great suffering. As for being a great sinner, so you are,' he added almost exultantly, 'but worst of all, you're a sinner because you've destroyed and betrayed yourself *to no purpose*. That really is a horror! What a horror it is, that you live in this filth you hate so much, and at the same time you know for yourself (if you just open your eyes) that you're not helping anyone by all that, you're not saving anyone from anything! Just tell me, for goodness' sake,' he said, almost in a frenzy, 'how can all this shame and foulness exist within you alongside all the other, opposite, sacred feelings? Surely it would be better, a hundred times better and wiser, to throw yourself headlong into the water and have done with it all!'

'But what would become of them?' asked Sonia faintly, with an anguished look at him. Yet she seemed not at all surprised at what he was suggesting. Raskolnikov looked at her with a strange expression.

In that one glance of hers, he had read everything. So she herself had already had that thought. Perhaps, in her despair, she had often seriously thought of putting an end to everything at once—so seriously that she was now hardly surprised by what he had suggested. She didn't even notice how cruel his words were (and of course she also hadn't noticed the sense of his reproaches, nor his particular view of her shame; he could see that too). But he fully realized how excruciating, how unbearably painful, the thought of her dishonour and shame had always been for her. What on earth, he wondered, could have still prevented her from resolving to end it all? And only now did he fully realize how much these poor little orphan children meant to her, and that pitiful, half-crazed Katerina Ivanovna, with her consumption, beating her head against the wall.

But he also clearly saw that Sonia, with her character and the way she had been brought up in spite of everything, couldn't possibly go on as she was. The question for him was still this: how had she managed to go on living as she had done, for so long, without going mad—since she didn't have the strength to throw herself into the water? Of course he understood that Sonia's situation in society was a matter of chance, though unfortunately far from a unique or exceptional one. But this very chance, this limited degree of upbringing she had received, and all her previous life, might have been expected to kill her at her very first step along that loathsome path. So what was it that sustained her? Not depravity, surely? For the shame of it seemed only to have touched her in a mechanical way; not one drop of corruption had yet found its way to her heart—he could see right through her.

'There are three ways she could go,' he thought. 'Throw herself into the canal, or end up in a madhouse, or... or end up by sinking into debauchery, which stupefies the mind and turns the heart to stone.' This last idea he found the most repulsive of all; but he was already a sceptic, he was young, had an abstract and therefore cruel outlook on life, and consequently he couldn't help believing that this last outcome—debauchery—was the likeliest.

'But can that really be true,' he protested to himself, 'can it be that even this creature, who still preserves her pure soul, will end up by being consciously drawn into that repulsive, reeking pit? Can it be that the attraction has already begun, and can it be that that's the only reason why she's been able to bear it so far—because vice no longer seems so repellent to her? No, no, it can't be!' he exclaimed, just as Sonia had exclaimed earlier. 'No, what has kept her out of the canal so far has been the thought of the sinfulness of it, and the thought of *them, those little ones*... If only she hasn't yet gone mad... But who says she hasn't gone mad yet? Is she in her right mind, then? Can one talk the way she does? Can a person in his right mind reason as she does? Can one really sit on top of the abyss, on the very edge of the reeking pit which is already drawing her in, and just wave aside the thought of it, blocking her ears when she's warned of the danger? Can it be that she's waiting for a miracle? That's probably it. And aren't all those things signs of madness?'

Obstinately he held on to that idea. In fact he preferred that conclusion to any other. He began examining her more closely.

'So, do you pray to God a lot, Sonia?' he asked.

Sonia said nothing. He stood beside her, waiting for her answer.

'Where would I be without God?' she whispered rapidly and firmly, casting him a quick look from her glistening eyes, and squeezing his hand tightly with her own.

'Well, there you are!' he thought.

'And what does God do for you in return?' he questioned her again.

Sonia remained silent, as if unable to answer. Her thin little chest heaved with agitation.

'Stop it! Don't ask me! You're not worthy!' she suddenly cried out, glaring at him sternly and angrily.

'So that's it! That's it!' he repeated insistently to himself.

'He does everything!' she whispered quickly, lowering her eyes.

'That's the answer then! That explains it!' he decided, watching her with avid curiosity.

He gazed with a strange, new, almost morbid feeling at that pale, thin, irregular, angular little face, those meek blue eyes that were capable of glittering with such fire, such austere energy; at that little body, still trembling with indignation and anger; and it all seemed stranger and stranger to him, in fact almost inconceivable. 'She's a Holy Fool! A Holy Fool!'* he repeated to himself.

There was a book of some kind lying on the chest of drawers. He had noticed it each time he passed it as he paced back and forth, and now he picked it up to look at it. It was the New Testament in Russian, in an old, worn leather binding.*

'Where did you get this?' he called to her across the room. She was still standing where she had been, a few steps from the table.

'Someone brought it to me,' she replied reluctantly, without looking up at him.

'Who brought it?'

'Lizaveta did—I asked her.'

'Lizaveta! Strange!' he thought. Everything about Sonia was becoming more and more peculiar and strange for him, minute by minute. He brought the book nearer to the candle and began leafing through it.

'Where does it tell about Lazarus?' he suddenly asked.

Sonia gazed stubbornly at the floor, without answering. She was standing slightly sideways to the table.

'The raising of Lazarus—where's that? Find it for me, Sonia.'

She gave him a sidelong glance.

'You're looking in the wrong place... it's in the fourth Gospel...' she whispered sternly, without moving towards him.

'Find it and read it to me,' he said, and sat down, leaned his elbows on the table, rested his head in his hand and stared gloomily to one side, preparing to listen.

'In three weeks' time or so, at the seventh verst;* you're cordially invited. I'll probably be there myself too, unless something even worse happens,' he muttered to himself.

Sonia came hesitantly up to the table, after listening mistrustfully to his strange request. But she picked up the book anyway.

'Haven't you read it, really not?' she asked, giving him a lowering look across the table. Her voice was growing more and more severe.

'A long time ago... at school. Read it!'

'Haven't you heard it in church?'

'No... I didn't go. Do you go often?'

'N-no,' whispered Sonia.

Raskolnikov smiled ironically.

'I understand... So you won't be going to your father's funeral tomorrow either?'

'Yes, I will. I went last week too... I had a requiem sung.'

'For whom?'

'For Lizaveta. She was killed with an axe.'

He was growing increasingly rattled. His head was beginning to swim.

'Were you friends with Lizaveta?'

'Yes... She was a good person... she used to come here... not often... she couldn't. We used to read together... and talk. She shall see God.'

Those last bookish words sounded strange to him. And here was something else new: secret meetings with Lizaveta, and both of them— holy fools.

'I'll turn into one myself here! It's catching!' he thought. 'Read!' he suddenly cried, insistently and irritably.

Sonia still hesitated. Her heart was pounding. For some reason she didn't dare read to him. He gazed at the 'poor mad girl' in a state of near-torment.

'What for? When you're not a believer?...' she whispered quietly, almost gasping.

'Read! I want you to!' he insisted. 'You read to Lizaveta, didn't you?'

Sonia opened the book and found the passage. Her hands trembled, her voice was failing her. Twice she tried to begin, but couldn't bring out a single syllable.

'Now a certain man was sick, named Lazarus, of Bethany...' she finally managed to say with an effort; but then, three words on, her voice wavered and broke like an overstretched violin-string. Her chest tightened and she couldn't get her breath.

Raskolnikov partly understood why Sonia couldn't bring herself to read to him, but the more he understood, the more roughly and irritably he insisted that she should. He could see all too well how hard it was for her now to expose and strip bare everything of *her own*. He realized that these feelings did indeed represent a real *secret* of hers, one that she had perhaps cherished for a long time, perhaps ever since she was a young girl, living with her family, alongside her wretched father and her stepmother crazed with grief, amongst the hungry children, the terrible shrieks and scolding. Yet at the same time he had now found out, and found out for certain, that although she had felt bad and terribly afraid when she began reading, at the same time she herself desperately wanted to read, despite all her bad feelings and fears: to read to *him*, for him to hear her, and to do it *now*—'whatever happens later on!'... He had read that in her eyes, and understood it from her excited agitation... She mastered herself, overcame the spasm in her throat that had cut off her voice at the beginning of the verse, and went on reading the eleventh chapter of the Gospel of St John. She reached verse 19: 'And many of the Jews came to Martha and Mary, to comfort them concerning their brother. Then Martha, as soon as she heard that Jesus was coming, went and met him: but Mary sat still in the house. Then said Martha unto Jesus, Lord, if thou hadst been here, my brother had not died. But I know, that even now, whatsoever thou wilt ask of God, God will give it thee.'

Here she stopped again, feeling with shame that her voice was about to quaver and break off once more...

'Jesus saith unto her, Thy brother shall rise again. Martha saith unto him, I know that he shall rise again in the resurrection at the last day. Jesus said unto her, I *am the resurrection*, and the life: he that believeth in me, though he were dead, yet shall he live: And whosoever liveth and believeth in me shall never die. Believest thou this? She saith unto him' (and drawing a painful breath, Sonia read in a clear, powerful voice, as though proclaiming her faith for all to hear), 'Yea, Lord: I believe that thou art the Christ, the Son of God, which should come into the world.'

She almost stopped, almost raised her eyes quickly to *him*, but controlled herself at once and went on reading. Raskolnikov sat motionless listening to her, without turning round, leaning his elbows on the table and looking away. They went on to verse 32:

'Then when Mary was come where Jesus was, and saw him, she fell down at his feet, saying unto him, Lord, if thou hadst been here, my brother had not died. When Jesus therefore saw her weeping, and the Jews also weeping which came with her, he groaned in the spirit, and was troubled. And said, Where have ye laid him? They said unto him, Lord, come and see. Jesus wept. Then said the Jews, Behold how he loved him! And some of them said, Could not this man, which opened the eyes of the blind, have caused that even this man should not have died?'

Raskolnikov turned to her and watched her anxiously. Yes, this was it! She was shaking all over now with real, genuine fever. This was what he had expected. She was approaching the account of the greatest, unheard-of miracle, and a feeling of great triumph had taken possession of her. Her voice took on an iron resonance, filled with the power of triumph and joy. The lines of print swam before her eyes, she could no longer see clearly, but she knew what she was reading by heart. At the last verse: 'Could not this man, which opened the eyes of the blind...' she dropped her voice, and with heat and passion conveyed the doubts, reproaches, and censure of the blind, unbelieving Jews, who would now, a minute later, fall down as if thunderstruck, sobbing and believing... 'And *he, he*—who is also blinded and unbelieving—he too shall hear now, and believe, yes, he shall! Now, this very moment,' she dreamed, and trembled with joyful expectation.

'Jesus therefore again groaning in himself cometh to the grave. It was a cave, and a stone lay upon it. Jesus said, Take ye away the stone. Martha, the sister of him that was dead, saith unto him, Lord, by this time he stinketh: for he hath been dead *four* days.'

She laid heavy stress on the word *four*.

'Jesus saith unto her, Said I not unto thee, that, if thou wouldest believe, thou shouldest see the glory of God? Then they took away the stone from the place where the dead was laid. And Jesus lifted up his eyes, and said, Father, I thank thee that thou hast heard me. And I knew that thou hearest me always: but because of the people which stand by I said it, that they may believe that thou hast sent me. And when he thus had spoken, he cried with a loud voice, Lazarus, come forth.

'*And he that was dead came forth*' (she read the words loudly and exultantly, chilled and trembling as though she had seen it with her own eyes), 'bound hand and foot with graveclothes: and his face was bound about with a napkin. Jesus saith unto them, Loose him, and let him go.

'*Then many of the Jews which came to Mary, and had seen the things which Jesus did, believed on him.*'

She did not and could not read any further, but closed the book and quickly got up from her chair.

'That's all about the raising of Lazarus,' she whispered sternly and abruptly, and stood motionless, her body turned away, not daring to raise her eyes to him, and almost ashamed to do so. Her feverish tremor continued. The candle stub in the crooked candlestick had been guttering for some time, casting a dim light through the poverty-stricken room, on the murderer and the harlot, who had so strangely come together to read the eternal book. Five minutes or longer went by.

'I came to tell you something,' Raskolnikov began brusquely in a loud voice, with a frown. He stood up and walked up to Sonia. She looked up at him silently. He looked particularly stern, with a kind of savage determination in his eyes.

'I walked out on my family today,' he said, 'my mother and sister. I shan't be going to them any more. I've broken with them completely.'

'Why?' asked Sonia in amazement. Her recent meeting with his mother and sister had left a strong impression on her, which she could not entirely understand. She heard the news of this rupture almost with horror.

'You're all I have now,' he went on. 'Let's go on together... I've come to you. We're both cursed; so let's go together!'

His eyes glittered. 'Like a madman!' Sonia thought in her turn.

'Go where?' she asked fearfully, taking an involuntary step backward.

'How do I know? All I know is that we'll follow the same road, and that I know for certain. That's all. We're both going the same way!'

She watched him, not understanding anything. All she understood was that he was dreadfully, endlessly unhappy.

'None of them will understand anything, if you talk to them,' he went on. 'But I've understood. I need you, and that's why I've come to you.'

'I don't understand...' whispered Sonia.

'You will. Haven't you done the same yourself? You've crossed the barrier too... you managed to cross it. You've laid hands on yourself, you've destroyed a life... *your own* life (but that makes no difference!). You might have lived by the spirit and by reason, instead of which you'll end up on the Haymarket... But you won't be able to stand it, and if you remain *alone* you'll go mad, like me. You're like a madwoman already; and so we have to go on together, along the same path. Let's go!'

'Why? Why are you saying all this?' said Sonia, strangely agitated and resistant to what he said.

'Why? Because you can't go on like this—that's why! Eventually you have to think things out honestly and seriously, instead of crying like a baby and yelling that God won't allow it! Just think what'll happen if you really are taken off to hospital tomorrow! She's crazy and consumptive, and she'll soon die, and what about the children? Won't Polechka be done for? Have you really not seen children hanging about the street corners here because their mothers have sent them out to beg? I've been finding out where and how those mothers live. It's impossible for children to remain children in those places—a seven-year-old is already depraved and a thief. And yet children are made in Christ's image: "Of such is the Kingdom of God."* He commanded that they should be honoured and loved, for they are the future of mankind...'

'But what's to be done? What's to be done?' repeated Sonia, weeping hysterically and wringing her hands.

'What's to be done? Smash what needs to be smashed, once and for all, that's what! And take the suffering on ourselves! What? You don't understand? You'll understand later on... Freedom and power, but the main thing is power! Over all the trembling creatures, the whole ant heap! That's the aim! Remember that! Those are my parting words to you! Perhaps this'll be the last time I talk with you. If I don't come tomorrow, you'll hear all about it yourself, and then remember what I've just said. And one day, later on, years later, perhaps a lifetime later, maybe you'll understand what it meant. But if I come tomorrow, I'll tell you who killed Lizaveta. Goodbye.'

Sonia shuddered in terror.

'Do you mean you know who killed her?' she asked, turning cold with horror and looking wildly at him.

'Yes, I know, and I'll tell you... You, and only you! I've chosen you. I shan't come begging you for forgiveness, I'll just tell you. I chose you long ago, because I wanted to tell you that—even when your father was talking about you, and Lizaveta was alive, I had that thought. Goodbye. Don't give me your hand. Tomorrow!'

He went out. Sonia looked at him as if he was mad; but she herself was half out of her mind, and felt that. Her head was spinning. 'Good God! How can he know who killed Lizaveta? What did he mean? How frightening!' But all the same, *the idea* never entered her mind. Never once! Never once! 'Oh, he must be dreadfully unhappy... He's abandoned his mother and sister. Why? What happened? And what was he planning to do? What was it he'd been saying to her? He had kissed her foot, and said... he had said (yes, he had said it quite clearly) that he couldn't live without her. Oh, God!'

Sonia passed a feverish and delirious night. Sometimes she would start up, weeping and wringing her hands, and then fall into a feverish sleep again, and dream of Polechka, Katerina Ivanovna, Lizaveta, the reading of the Gospel, and of him... him, with his pale face and burning eyes... He's kissing her feet, and weeping... Oh God!

Behind the door on the right, the one that separated Sonia's lodging from Gertruda Karlovna Resslich's flat, there was another room, which had long stood empty. It was part of Madame Resslich's flat, and was to let; there were little fliers to that effect on the gates, and notices stuck to the windowpanes looking out onto the canal. Sonia had long believed the room to be unoccupied. But all through this latest encounter, Mr Svidrigailov had been hiding in the empty room, standing by the door and eavesdropping. When Raskolnikov came out, he stood and thought for a little, then tiptoed back to his own room, next door to the empty one, got a chair and silently brought it right up against the door to Sonia's room. He had found the conversation fascinating and important, and had very much enjoyed it—so much so that he had brought over his chair, so that on the next occasion—perhaps tomorrow—he shouldn't be subjected to the unpleasant experience of standing on his feet for an hour on end, but could listen in greater comfort, thus obtaining complete satisfaction in every way.

CHAPTER V

WHEN, at precisely eleven next morning, Raskolnikov entered the building in the —— district that housed the offices of the chief criminal investigator,* and asked to be announced to Porfiry Petrovich, he was quite surprised at how long he was kept waiting—at least ten minutes passed before he was called in. He had been expecting to be pounced on at once. Meanwhile he stood in the waiting room, while the people passing back and forth didn't seem at all concerned about him. In the next room, which appeared to be an office, several clerks were sitting writing, and it was clear that none of them had the least idea of who or what Raskolnikov was. He looked around anxiously and suspiciously, trying to make out whether there was some guard there, some secret watcher posted to keep an eye on him and make sure he didn't leave. But there was nothing of the sort; all he could see was official faces engrossed in trivial business, and then some other people too, but no one who was in the least interested in him. He might just as well have walked off into the blue, without anyone minding. He was becoming ever more firmly convinced that if that mysterious man from yesterday, that phantom who had emerged from under the earth, really knew everything and had seen everything, they would never have allowed him, Raskolnikov, to stand here like this, calmly waiting. And would they really have waited for him here till eleven o'clock, when it finally suited him to put in an appearance? It looked as if that man either hadn't reported anything yet, or... or he simply didn't know anything either, and hadn't seen anything himself, with his own eyes (and how on earth could he have done?); and consequently all that, everything that had happened to him, Raskolnikov, on the previous day, was no more than a phantom magnified by his sick and overexcited imagination. Even yesterday, in the throes of his terror and despair, he had become more and more convinced that this was so. Thinking it all over now, as he prepared for this new battle, he suddenly felt himself trembling; and he began to boil with indignation at the thought that he was trembling with fear before the detested Porfiry Petrovich. Worse than anything, he dreaded meeting that man again; he had an endless, immeasurable loathing for him, and even feared that his hatred might somehow bring him to betray himself. So powerful was his indignation that it instantly stopped his trembling; he prepared to go in with a cold, insolent air, and promised himself to keep as silent as he could, to observe and listen to the man, and—no matter what happened, at least this time—to control his morbidly irritable nature. At that moment he was summoned by Porfiry Petrovich.

Porfiry Petrovich turned out to be alone in his office. The room was neither big nor small; it contained a large writing desk standing in front of a sofa covered in oilcloth, a bureau, a cupboard in the corner, and a number of chairs, all government issue, made of polished yellow wood. In the corner of the far wall, or rather partition, was a closed door; so presumably there must be other rooms beyond it. When Raskolnikov came in, Porfiry Petrovich at once shut the door behind him, and they were on their own. He welcomed his visitor with a seemingly genial and hospitable air, and it was not until a few minutes later that Raskolnikov noticed some signs that suggested he was rather flustered—as if he had suddenly been taken by surprise or caught out in some very secret and private activity.

'Ah, my dear fellow! So here you are... in our part of town...' began Porfiry, extending both hands to him. 'Well, do sit down, my friend! But perhaps you don't like being addressed as my dear fellow, and... my friend—*tout court*,* like that? Please don't mind my familiarity... Over here, sir, please, on my little sofa.'

Raskolnikov sat down without taking his eyes off him.

The words 'in our part of town', the apology for overfamiliarity, the French phrase '*tout court*', and so on and so forth—all that was typical of him. 'But just the same, he held out both hands to me without giving me either: he drew back in time,' he thought with a spark of suspicion. Each was watching the other, but as soon as their eyes met, they both looked away as quick as lightning.

'I've brought you this paper... about the watch, that is... here you are. Will it do, or must I write it out again?'

'What's that? A paper? Oh, yes... don't worry, that'll do perfectly,' said Porfiry Petrovich as if he were hurrying off somewhere; not until he had finished speaking did he take the paper and look at it. 'Yes, that's perfect. That's all we need,' he confirmed, talking just as hurriedly, and laid the paper on the table. A minute later, while already talking about something else, he picked it up off the table again and transferred it to his bureau.

'You said yesterday, I believe, that you wanted to question me... officially... about my acquaintance with that... woman who was killed?' Raskolnikov began; '(but why did I put in "I believe"?)' was his lightning thought. '(But why am I so bothered about the fact that I put in "I believe"?)'—another lightning thought instantly followed the first.

And he suddenly felt that his mere contact with Porfiry, a couple of words and a couple of glances, had been enough to magnify his distrust to monstrous proportions in an instant... and that this was terribly dangerous: his nerves were rattled, he was becoming increasingly agitated. 'This is dreadful, dreadful! I'll say too much again.'

'Yes, yes, yes! Don't worry! There's plenty of time, plenty of time,' murmured Porfiry Petrovich, wandering back and forth around the table, seemingly quite aimlessly; darting over to the window, then to the bureau, then to the table again, now avoiding Raskolnikov's suspicious gaze, now stopping still to stare straight at him. His plump, short, round little body produced a very strange effect all the while, like a ball rolling this way and that and bouncing back off all the walls and corners.

'We'll get round to it, we'll get round to it!... By the way, do you smoke? Have you got any? Here, have a cigarette,' he went on, offering one to his visitor. 'You know, I'm receiving you here, but my own flat is right here too, behind that partition... my official quarters; but I'm staying somewhere else for a time. I had to have some little improvements done here. It's almost ready... You know, an official flat* is a splendid thing, isn't it? What do you think?'

'Yes, a splendid thing,' replied Raskolnikov, looking at him almost mockingly.

'A splendid thing, a splendid thing...' repeated Porfiry Petrovich, as if suddenly sunk in thought about something quite different. 'Yes! a splendid thing!' he almost cried out at last, suddenly looking up at Raskolnikov and halting two steps away from him. This constant stupid repetition of the same banal phrase was strikingly out of keeping with the serious, reflective, and enigmatic look he now directed at his visitor.

But that only further aggravated Raskolnikov's venom, and by now he could no longer restrain himself from uttering a mocking and rather rash challenge.

'Do you know what?' he suddenly asked, looking almost insolently at Porfiry and evidently relishing his impertinence. 'Surely there exists a legal rule, some sort of accepted judicial practice—for any kind of investigator—which tells him to start off a long way from the actual point, and ask about trivial things, or even serious but quite irrelevant ones, so as to encourage the person under interrogation, as it were, or rather distract him; to lull his caution to sleep, before suddenly and unexpectedly flooring him with a blow straight to the head, with some dangerous, fatal question. Isn't that so? Isn't that enshrined like holy writ, to this day, in all your rules and codes of practice?'

'Yes, yes... were you thinking of my talk about an official flat... eh?' Having said which, Porfiry Petrovich screwed up his eyes and winked; a merry, sly expression passed over his face, the wrinkles on his brow smoothed out, his eyes narrowed, his features relaxed, and he suddenly burst into a long, nervous laugh; his whole body quivered and shook, and he looked Raskolnikov straight in the eyes. Raskolnikov began laughing too, with something of an effort; but when Porfiry saw him laughing, he exploded in such guffaws that he almost turned purple in the face. Raskolnikov's disgust at him now overcame all his caution: he stopped laughing, frowned, and directed a sustained look of loathing at Porfiry, keeping his eyes on him throughout his long, and seemingly deliberately extended, fit of laughter. A lack of caution, however, was evident in both of them. It looked as if Porfiry Petrovich was openly laughing at his visitor, who responded to his laughter with hatred; and obviously Porfiry was not particularly put out by that. This observation was very important to Raskolnikov. He realized that Porfiry Petrovich had probably not been at all embarrassed earlier on, but that he, Raskolnikov, had in fact fallen into a trap; that there was clearly something about all this, some sort of motive, which he knew nothing about; and that perhaps it had all been prepared in advance, and was about to declare itself and crush him any minute.

He came straight to the point, stood up and picked up his cap.

'Porfiry Petrovich,' he began resolutely, but in considerable agitation, 'yesterday you expressed a wish for me to come in for some kind of interrogation' (he laid particular stress on the word *interrogation*). 'I have come, and if you have any questions, then ask them; if not, then kindly allow me to leave. I don't have time to spare, I have an engagement... I have to attend the funeral of that same clerk who was trampled by horses, the man you... also know about...' he added, becoming instantly annoyed with himself for this addition, and consequently instantly more irritable. 'I'm fed up with all this, do you hear, and have been for some time... that was one of the things that made me ill... In short,' he almost shouted, sensing that the mention of his illness was even more out of place, 'in short, will you kindly either question me or let me go, right now... and if you're going to question me, then do it in the proper form or not at all! I won't have it any other way; and so goodbye for now, since there's nothing for the two of us to do at present.'

'Good Lord! What can you mean? What am I supposed to question you about, anyway?' clucked Porfiry Petrovich, at once taking on a new tone of voice and expression, and instantly cutting short his laughter. 'Please don't upset yourself,' he fussed, first darting this way and that again, and then ushering Raskolnikov to a seat. 'There's plenty of time, plenty of time, sir, and none of it's of any consequence. On the contrary—I'm so pleased that you've finally come to see us... I look on you as my guest. As for my wretched laughter—my dear Rodion Romanovich, please forgive me. Rodion Romanovich? I believe that's your name, after your papa, yes?... I'm all nerves, myself, and your comment was so witty I couldn't help laughing; honestly, there are times when I shake like a jelly for half an hour on end... I laugh easily. With my constitution, I'm actually afraid of having a paralytic stroke. Anyway, do sit down, why won't you?... Please do, my friend, or I'll think you're cross with me...'

Raskolnikov said nothing; he just watched and listened, still scowling angrily. He did sit down, however, though still keeping hold of his cap.

'I'll tell you one thing, my dear Rodion Romanovich, about myself, I mean, to explain my character,' Porfiry Petrovich went on, scurrying about the room and still apparently avoiding his visitor's eyes. 'I'm a bachelor, you know; I don't go out in society and don't know many people; what's more, I'm too old to change now, I'm set in my ways, I've gone to seed, and... and... have you ever noticed, Rodion Romanovich, that people here, I mean here in Russia, and particularly here in Petersburg circles, when two intelligent people who don't know each other too well, but, I mean, respect each other, as it might be you and me now, when they meet one another, they'll spend a whole half-hour not knowing what to talk about, sitting like stuffed dummies, getting embarrassed with each other. Everyone has something they can talk about; ladies, for instance... in society, for instance, among fashionable people, they always have a subject for conversation, *c'est de rigueur*, but middling people like us, thinking people I mean—we're all awkward and tongue-tied. Now why does that happen, my friend? Is it because we aren't interested in public affairs, or are we all too honest and don't want to deceive each other? I don't know. Eh? What do you think? But do put down your cap, sir, you look as if you were just on your way out, honestly, it makes me uncomfortable to look at you... When I'm so delighted...'

Raskolnikov laid down his cap, still saying nothing, and continued listening with a serious, frowning expression to Porfiry's vacuous, chaotic chatter. 'Can it really be that he's trying to distract my attention with his stupid rigmarole?'

'I can't offer you coffee, it wouldn't do here; but why not spend five minutes together as friends, enjoying each other's company?' Porfiry rattled on irrepressibly. 'And do you know, sir, all these official duties... but please don't mind if I keep walking back and forth like this; you must forgive me, my friend, I'm very scared of upsetting you, but I simply have to have this exercise. I'm always sitting down, and I'm so glad of the chance to walk about for five minutes... piles, you know... I keep meaning to see if gymnastics will help; they say State Councillors and Senior State Councillors, even Privy Councillors, can be found happily skipping over skipping ropes there; that's what science has brought us to, in this day and age... so it has, sir... And as for my duties here, interrogations and all those kinds of formalities... you were just talking about interrogations yourself, weren't you?—well, do you know, my dear Rodion Romanovich, it sometimes happens that those interrogations confuse the investigator even worse than the people he's questioning... You yourself have just made a most apt and witty comment on that subject.' (Raskolnikov had not made any such comment.) 'You get in a muddle! Honestly, you do! And going on and on about the same thing, like beating a drum! Now there are reforms on the way, and we'll at least be getting new titles,* heh-heh-heh! And as for our accepted judicial practices, as you so wittily put it, I'm absolutely in agreement with you. I mean, is there a single accused person, even the most ragged peasant, who doesn't know that people will start off by lulling him to sleep with irrelevant questions (to use your happy expression), before suddenly flooring him with a blow right on the head, from the butt of an axe, heh-heh-heh! Right on the crown of his head, as you put it so well! So you really thought that when I talked about my flat, I was trying... heh-heh! What an ironic fellow you are! Well, I won't go on. Ah, yes, by the way—one idea leads to another—you also said something about formalities, you know, regarding some little interrogation... But what's the sense of formalities! You know, formalities are often quite pointless. Sometimes it's better just to have a friendly little talk, and more useful too. The formalities won't go away, I promise you; and anyway, what do formalities actually mean, may I ask? You can't tie an investigator down with formalities at every step. His job, after all, is what you might call, in its own way, a liberal art, or something of the kind... heh–heh–heh!'

Porfiry Petrovich paused a moment to get his breath. He had been rattling on tirelessly, mostly pouring out empty phrases but suddenly letting slip a few enigmatic words, only to relapse back into his meaningless patter. By now he was almost running around the room, his podgy little legs going faster and faster, his eyes fixed on the ground, his right hand shoved behind his back while his left waved this way and that, making all sorts of gestures that were always astonishingly inappropriate to whatever he was saying. Raskolnikov suddenly noticed that as he ran about the room, it almost looked as if he had paused by the door a couple of times, just for an instant, and listened... 'Can he be expecting something?'

'But you're absolutely right about that,' Porfiry began again, with a cheerful and extraordinarily guileless look at Raskolnikov (which made him start, and instantly put him on his guard), 'truly, you're right to laugh so wittily at judicial formalities, heh–heh! Those profound psychological techniques of ours (some of them, I mean) really are extremely comic, and I dare say useless too, if they're overly constrained by the formalities. Yes... well, coming back to formalities: if I know, or rather suspect, that this, that, or the other person is a criminal, in some case that's been passed on to me... I believe you're training for the law, aren't you, Rodion Romanovich?'

'Yes, I was...'

'Well there you are then, an example for you for the future—please don't think I'm presuming to teach you; after all, just look at the articles you publish about crime! No, but let me just offer you a little factual example: supposing I suspect that this, that, or the other person is a criminal, well, I ask you, why should I trouble him before I need to, even if I have evidence against him? There might be one man I'd be obliged to arrest straight away; but another one could be quite a different sort of person, truly, so why not leave him free to gad about town a bit, heh–heh! No, I see you don't quite understand, so let me give you a clearer picture. If I were to lock him up too soon, say, then I'm actually giving him a kind of moral support, heh–heh! You're laughing?' (Raskolnikov wasn't dreaming of laughing: he was sitting tight-lipped, never shifting his burning gaze away from Porfiry Petrovich's eyes.) 'And yet that's just how it is, particularly with a certain sort of person, because everybody's different, and you can only be guided by experience. Now you were just talking about evidence; well, yes, evidence is all very well, but evidence, my boy, mostly points both ways; and I'm an investigator, which means I'm a weak man, I'm sorry to say; it would be nice to submit an investigation as a mathematical certainty, so to speak—it would be nice to have evidence that was as solid as twice two is four!* And looked like straight irrefutable proof! But if I lock him up before time—even if I'm certain that it's *him*—then I'll probably deprive myself of the chance to find further evidence against him. And why? Because I'll have put him in a definite position, so to speak; I'll have psychologically defined him and ended his suspense, and now he'll go and withdraw into his shell—he'll realize he's a prisoner. They say that out in Sebastopol, just after the battle of the Alma, the intelligent people were terribly scared that the enemy was about to mount a direct assault, and would take Sebastopol straight off. But as soon as they saw the enemy had opted for a regular siege, and started digging the first lines, well, the intelligent people were delighted and reassured, so they say: the thing would drag on for two months at least, before the town could be reduced by a siege!* You're laughing again, you still don't believe me? Well, of course, you're right there too. Yes, you are! Those are all special cases, I grant you; the example I just gave you is a special case, sir! But my dear Rodion Romanovich, this is what you need to realize: the general case, the very case on which all judicial formalities and regulations are based, the one for which they've been worked out and set down in the books—that general case doesn't exist, for the simple reason that every case, every crime for instance, as soon as it's actually been committed, immediately becomes an absolutely special case, sometimes a very special one indeed, like nothing that's ever happened before. You sometimes come across extremely comic cases like that. And if I leave some particular gentleman quite alone, without pulling him in or bothering him, but making sure he knows, or at least suspects, every minute of every day, that I know all about it, every last detail, and that I'm watching him day and night, never sleeping, following his every move, and if he's aware that he's under constant suspicion, and terrified of it, then he's bound to lose his head, he'll come to me of his own accord, and probably do something more which really does look like twice two, something with the appearance of a mathematical proof. Which is very nice. That can even happen with a lumbering peasant, while as for our own kind, intelligent modern people with some level of education—it's almost bound to! Because, my dear fellow, it's very important to understand where a man's education has brought him. And then his nerves, sir, his nerves—you'd quite forgotten about those! These days they're all sick, and worn down, and frazzled!... And all the bile they've stored up! Let me tell you, that can sometimes be a gold mine for us! And then, why should I worry if he's walking about the town, a free man? Let him do it, let him walk about for a while, I don't mind; I know very well that he's my quarry, and he won't get away from me. Where could he run away to? Abroad, perhaps? A Pole would escape abroad, but *he* won't; particularly since I'm watching him, and I've taken certain steps. Or run away into the depths of the country? But that's where peasants live, real, homespun Russian peasants; your educated man of today would sooner go to jail than live with foreigners like our own peasants, heh-heh! But all that's nonsense, it's all superficial stuff. What does "run away" mean? That's a formal matter, but it isn't the point. The reason he won't escape from me isn't just that there's nowhere to escape to: he can't escape from me *psychologically*, heh-heh! What a wonderful expression! The laws of nature will prevent him from escaping from me, even if there was somewhere to run to. Have you ever seen a moth near a flame? Well, he'll be constantly fluttering around me, all the time, like the moth by the flame; his freedom will grow stale on him, he'll start wondering, and get confused, and all tangled up in a web, and worry himself to death!... And not only that: he'll produce some kind of mathematical proof for me himself, something like twice two—so long as I leave him enough time. And he'll keep circling and circling around me, getting closer and closer every time,—until—snap! He'll fly straight into my jaws, and I'll swallow him down, and that's very nice indeed, heh-heh-heh! You don't believe me?'

Raskolnikov didn't reply. He was sitting pale and motionless, staring into Porfiry's face with unwavering intensity.

'A good lesson!' he thought with a shiver. 'This isn't yesterday's cat-and-mouse game. He's not showing off his power to me for nothing, and... throwing me hints: he's far too clever for that! He's got something else in mind, so what is it? No, brother, that won't do—you're wasting your time scaring me and being devious! You haven't got any evidence, and that man from yesterday doesn't exist! You're just trying to unnerve me, upset me in advance, and then when you've got me where you want me, you'll swat me down; but you can't, you'll get nowhere, nowhere at all! But why prompt me at such length?... Is he counting on my shaken nerves?... No, brother, you'll get nowhere, even if you've got something up your sleeve... Well, then, let's just see what it is.'

And he braced himself with all his might, ready for some unknown and dreadful catastrophe. There were moments when he longed to hurl himself at Porfiry and throttle him on the spot. Even when he was just arriving here, he'd been afraid of his own rage. He could feel his dry lips, his pounding heart, the foam around his mouth. But still he was determined to stay silent and not say a single word until the time came. He could see that this was the best tactic in his situation, since he'd not only avoid letting anything slip, he might even irritate his enemy by his silence, and the other might then let something slip himself. That, at least, was what he was hoping.

'No, I can see that you don't believe me, you still think I'm playing harmless pranks on you,' Porfiry began again, becoming increasingly merry and constantly giggling with pleasure, and starting to walk round the room again. 'And of course you're right: God himself created me with the sort of figure that only arouses comical thoughts in others. I'm a buffoon, sir; but let me tell you this, let me repeat it to you: you, my dear friend Rodion Romanovich (excuse an old man for saying so), you're still young; you're in your first youth, as it were, and consequently you rate the human intellect above anything else, as all young people do. You're seduced by playful wit and abstract arguments. And that's just like the late Austrian *Hofkriegsrat*, to take an example, as far as I can judge about military matters. Back there in his cabinet he'd done his sums and worked it all out brilliantly, and on paper he had Napoleon beaten and taken prisoner; and then lo and behold, General Mack goes and surrenders with all his army,* heh-heh-heh! Yes, I know, I know, my dear Rodion Romanovich, you're laughing at me, civilian that I am, constantly going to military history to find my little examples. Well, what can I do—it's a weakness of mine, I'm fond of military science, and I really love reading about all those military campaigns... truly, I've missed my vocation. I should have joined the army, I really should. Perhaps I might never have become a Napoleon—but I would have got to major, heh-heh-heh! Well then, my dear fellow, now I'm going to tell you the whole truth, in every detail, about that particular *special case*: actual fact and the human temperament, my dear sir, are very important things, and just see how they sometimes undermine the most penetrating calculations! Do listen to an old man, I'm talking seriously, Rodion Romanovich' (at this point the barely thirty-five-year-old Porfiry Petrovich really did seem to age suddenly; even his voice changed, and he became all hunched up), 'and besides, I'm a candid person... Am I candid or not? What do you think? I believe I really am; look at the things I'm telling you for nothing, not even looking for a reward, heh-heh! Well, then, to continue: wit, in my opinion, is a splendid thing; it's like an ornament of nature, and one of life's consolations, and what tricks it can play! Such tricks that your poor investigator hasn't a hope of seeing through them, especially when he's carried away by his own imagination, which is what always happens, because he's human too! But it's the individual's nature that saves the poor investigator, that's the trouble! That's what young people never think of, so carried away by their own wit, "striding over all obstacles" (as you so wittily and slyly put it). Let's suppose he tells a lie, this person I mean, this *special case*, this unknown quantity; and he'll tell an excellent lie, most cleverly; you'd think that would be his triumph, and he could start enjoying the fruits of his cleverness; but then—crash! right at the most interesting moment, the most fateful moment, he falls down in a faint! All right, I grant you he's ill, and sometimes those rooms can get stuffy, but all the same! All the same, he's given us the idea! He told brilliant lies, but he didn't allow for his temperament. You see where all that cunning gets you! Or again, he'll get carried away by his playful cleverness and start making a fool of whoever's suspecting him, he'll turn pale seemingly on purpose, seemingly as a prank, only his pallor is *all too natural*, it looks too much like the real thing, and once again he's given us the idea! He may fool the investigator at first, but that man will think it out overnight, if he isn't stupid. And the same thing happens every step of the way! And on top of that, your man starts coming round of his own accord, pushes in when nobody's asked him to, starts going on and on about things he ought to shut up about, and talking in all sorts of allegories, heh-heh! He comes round by himself and asks why he hasn't been arrested ages ago, heh-heh-heh! And all this could happen to the cleverest man, someone who knows all about psychology and literature! Temperament is a mirror, yes, a mirror, and a most transparent one! Look into it and admire yourself, that's what! But why have you turned so pale, Rodion Romanovich, is it too stuffy for you? Shouldn't we open a window?'

'Oh, please don't trouble yourself!' cried Raskolnikov, suddenly beginning to laugh. 'Don't trouble, please!'

Porfiry stopped in front of him, waited a moment, and suddenly burst out laughing himself. Raskolnikov rose from the sofa, abruptly cutting short his convulsive fit of laughter.

'Porfiry Petrovich!' he said loudly and distinctly, though his legs were trembling so much that he could barely stand up. 'It's become quite clear to me that you definitely suspect me of the murder of that old woman and her sister Lizaveta. Let me tell you for my part that I'm sick of this, and have been for ages. If you feel you've got the right to prosecute me, then prosecute me; if to arrest me, then arrest me. But I won't have you laughing at me to my face and tormenting me.'

Suddenly his lips trembled, his eyes blazed with rage, and his voice, which he had so far kept in check, rang out.

'I won't have it!' he shouted, thumping his fist on the table with all his strength. 'Do you hear, Porfiry Petrovich? I won't have it!'

'Oh Lord, what's all this again!' cried Porfiry Petrovich, looking thoroughly frightened. 'My boy! Rodion Romanovich! My good fellow! My dear friend! Whatever's up?'

'I won't have it!' Raskolnikov shouted once more.

'Not so loud, my dear man! People will hear, they'll come in! And what'll we say to them then? Just think about it!' whispered the horrified Porfiry Petrovich, bringing his face right up to Raskolnikov's.

'I won't have it, I won't have it!' Raskolnikov repeated mechanically, but now in a hushed whisper.

Porfiry quickly turned away and ran to open a window.

'We must let some air in, some fresh air! And you ought to have a drink of water, my boy—this is an attack you're having!' And he was going to run to the door and send for water, when he found a decanter conveniently standing in the corner.

'Have a drink, my boy,' he whispered, hurrying back to him with the decanter. 'You'll feel better...' Porfiry's fright and his sympathy seemed so natural that Raskolnikov fell silent and began watching him with wild curiosity. However, he didn't drink any of the water.

'Rodion Romanovich! My dear fellow! You'll drive yourself mad like this, honestly you will! Oh dear! Oh dear! Do drink something! Just a little, do!'

He managed to get Raskolnikov to take the glass of water in his hands. Raskolnikov almost raised it mechanically to his lips, but stopped himself and put it back on the table in disgust.

'Yes, sir, that was a little attack we had there. If you go on like that you'll be as ill as you were before,' clucked Porfiry Petrovich, full of friendly sympathy—but still looking somehow lost. 'Lord! Why don't you look after yourself better? There was Dmitry Prokofich, too, he came to see me yesterday—yes, I admit it, I admit it, I've got a nasty sarcastic character, but look what he made of that!... Good Lord! He came yesterday, after you, and we dined together, and he talked and talked, and all I could do was throw up my hands: oh my God,

I thought!... Was it you that sent him, then? Do sit down, my boy, for Christ's sake!'

'No, it wasn't! But I knew he'd gone to see you, and why he went,' replied Raskolnikov brusquely.

'You knew?'

'Yes, I did. But so what?'

'Just this, my friend, Rodion Romanovich: that's not the only one of your exploits that I know about—I know everything! Don't I know that you went to *rent that flat*, just at dusk, when night was falling, and began ringing the little bell, and asking about blood, and upset the workmen and porters? I understand your mental state at the time... but all the same, truly, you'll drive yourself crazy that way! You'll set your head spinning! You're absolutely seething with indignation, noble indignation, at the injuries you've suffered, first at the hands of fate and then from the police, and now you're flinging yourself this way and that, trying to get everyone to hurry up and talk, and then put a stop to the whole thing at once, because you're fed up with all this nonsense and all these suspicions. That's right, isn't it? Have I read your mood right?... But that way you'll make Razumikhin lose his head, as well as yourself; he's much too *good* a person for all this, you know that yourself. You're a sick man, but he's a virtuous one, and he'll get infected with your sickness... When you've calmed down, my lad, I'll tell you... but do sit down, for Christ's sake! Please take a rest, you're looking just terrible; do sit down, please.'

Raskolnikov sat down. His shivering was passing off and he was beginning to feel hot all over. He had been listening tensely, and in profound amazement, to Porfiry Petrovich, who seemed scared as he fussed over him with friendly solicitude. But Raskolnikov didn't trust a single word that he spoke, despite feeling a strange inclination to believe him. Porfiry's unexpected words about the flat had utterly disconcerted him. 'How can this be—so he knows about the flat, does he?' he suddenly thought, 'and he's telling me all about it himself!'

'Yes, there was another case almost exactly like this one, a psychological one, in our forensic practice, a pathological case,' Porfiry hurried on. 'This man had also confessed to a murder, and how convincing he made it: reeled out a whole hallucination, came up with all the facts and circumstantial details, he muddled everyone up, confused us all, and what for? He'd been the entirely unwitting cause, in part, of a killing— but only in part; and when he discovered that he'd given the murderers their chance, he got depressed, lost his head, started imagining things, and went right out of his mind; he persuaded himself that he was the actual murderer himself! But eventually the Senate sorted the affair out, and the wretched man was acquitted and put into care. Well done, the Senate! Well, well, oh dear, dear me! So what now, my dear lad? This is the way to get yourself into a high fever—feeling driven to tax your nerves like this, going round at night ringing bells and asking about blood! All that psychology, I've studied it on the job. That sort of thing sometimes gives people an urge to jump out of a window or off a bell tower, and it's such a tempting feeling. Doorbells, too... It's a sickness, Rodion Romanovich, a sickness! You're taking far too little care of your sickness. You ought to consult an experienced doctor—what's the use of that fat fellow of yours?... You're delirious! All this is delirium, no more nor less!'

For an instant Raskolnikov felt everything spinning about him.

'Can it really, really be', he thought, 'that he's lying even now? No, impossible, impossible!' He tried to banish the thought, already feeling that it might drive him to such a pitch of blind rage and fury that he would lose his mind.

'That wasn't delirium, I was well aware of what I was doing!' he cried, straining all his powers of reasoning to see through Porfiry's game. 'Aware, I say! Do you hear?'

'Yes, I understand, I hear you! Yesterday, too, you said that you weren't delirious—in fact you made a particular point of it, that you weren't delirious! I know everything you could possibly say to me! E-eh!... But listen to me, Rodion Romanovich, my very dear friend, just listen to this point. If you'd really and truly been a criminal, or been involved in this damned business in any way at all—well I ask you, would you yourself be insisting that you weren't doing all this in a state of delirium, but in full possession of your senses? And insisting so particularly, so very stubbornly, making such an issue of it? I mean, could that ever happen? I ask you, could it? Surely if you felt in the least guilty about something, you ought to have been insisting that everything had happened in a delirious state! Isn't that so? Aren't I right?'

Raskolnikov could feel something devious in the question. He recoiled from Porfiry, who was leaning over him, and moved to the far end of the divan, where he silently watched him with intense puzzlement.

'Or what about Mr Razumikhin, then, I mean about whether he came to see me of his own accord, or whether you put him up to it? You ought to have been saying that he came of his own accord, and hiding the fact that you put him up to it! And yet you're not hiding it at all! You're actually insisting it was you that got him to come!'

Raskolnikov had never insisted on that. A chill ran down his spine.

'You keep lying to me,' he said slowly and faintly, his lips twisted into a sickly smile. 'Once again, you're trying to show me that you can see through my whole game, and know all my answers in advance,' he went on, beginning to feel that he was no longer weighing up his words as he should; 'you're trying to intimidate me... or simply making fun of me...'

He went on staring at Porfiry as he spoke, and suddenly his eyes flashed with uncontrollable fury.

'You're still lying!' he shouted. 'You know perfectly well that a criminal's best policy is never to try to hide what he doesn't need to hide. I don't trust you!'

'What a slippery customer you are!' chuckled Porfiry. 'There's no getting past you, my friend; you've got some sort of obsession. So you don't trust me? Well, I'll tell you that you do trust me, you halfway trust me already, and I'll get you to trust me all the way, because I'm sincerely fond of you and wish you well.'

Raskolnikov's lips trembled.

'Yes, I really do, believe me,' Porfiry went on, gently pressing Raskolnikov's arm in a friendly way, just above the elbow. 'And my firm advice to you is: keep an eye on your illness. Here's your family come to visit you; think of them. You ought to be reassuring and cherishing them, and all you do is scare them...'

'What business is that of yours? How do you know? Why are you so interested? So you're keeping a watch on me, are you, and you want to make sure I know it?'

'Good heavens, boy! I heard all that from you yourself! You're so worked up, you don't even notice that you keep blurting everything out yourself, to me and everyone else. And I learned a lot of interesting details from Mr Razumikhin yesterday, too. No, sir, you interrupted me just then, but let me tell you that for all your sharp wits, you've such a suspicious nature that you can't see things straight. Just take one example, to come back to what we were talking about, this business with the bells: now there's a priceless thing, a fact (and it is a whole fact, isn't it!), and I've just made you a present of it myself—me, the investigator! And don't you make anything of that? If I were to suspect you even a little bit, would I be acting like that? I ought to have started by lulling your suspicions, without letting on that I knew about that fact already; I should have led you off in the opposite direction—and suddenly felled you with an axe blow to the head (to use your own expression): "and what, my good sir, were you doing in the murdered woman's flat at ten o'clock in the evening, if indeed it wasn't eleven? And why were you ringing at the doorbell? And why were you asking questions about blood? And why did you try to confuse the porters, and send them off to the police station to see the district superintendent?" That's how I ought to have acted, if I'd had the least suspicion of you. I ought to have taken a proper formal statement from you, and carried out a search, and probably arrested you too... So since I acted differently, it follows that I don't suspect you! But I'll tell you again, you're not viewing things rationally any more, in fact you can't see anything!'

Raskolnikov's whole body shuddered, as Porfiry Petrovich could see all too clearly.

'You keep lying to me!' he shouted. 'I don't know why, but you keep lying... You weren't talking that way just now, and I can't be wrong about that... You're lying!'

'Lying, am I?' retorted Porfiry, seemingly growing heated but maintaining his cheerful, ironic expression. He did not appear in the least concerned by what Raskolnikov thought of him. 'Lying?... What about the way I treated you a while ago (and I'm the investigator, remember), handing you hints and arguments in your defence, and giving you all that psychology: "It's the illness," I said, "and the delirium, and the insults; and melancholia, and the police officers," and all the rest of it? Eh? Heh-heh-heh! Although it's true, actually—while I'm on the subject—that all those psychological arguments in a person's favour, all those excuses and evasions, are very feeble ones, and what's more they cut both ways: "Illness, you say, and delirium, delusions, visions, I don't remember"—all that's very fine, but why, I'd like to know, do the illness and delirium throw up just those sorts of delusions, instead of different ones? There could have been different ones, couldn't there? Isn't that so? Heh-heh-heh-heh!'

Raskolnikov gave him a proud, scornful look.

'In short,' he said loudly and forcefully, rising from his chair and giving Porfiry a slight shove as he did so, 'in short, I want to know: do you regard me as definitely free from suspicion, *or not*? Tell me that, Porfiry Petrovich, tell me once and for all, now, at once!'

'My, what a fuss! What a fuss you're making!' cried Porfiry with an utterly cheerful, sly look, evidently not in the least alarmed. 'What do you need to know that for, why do you have to know such a lot, when nobody's even begun bothering you yet in the slightest! You're just like a child: "Let me have fire, I want to play with fire!" And what makes you so anxious? Why do you keep coming here of your own accord, what's the reason for that? Eh? Heh-heh-heh!'

'I repeat,' cried Raskolnikov in fury, 'I can't stand this any longer...'

'Stand what? The uncertainty?' interrupted Porfiry.

'Stop baiting me! I won't have it! I won't have it, I tell you!... I can't stand it and I won't have it! Listen to me! Listen!' he cried, thumping the table with his fist again.

'Do be quiet, please! They'll hear you! I'm warning you, seriously: take care of yourself. I'm not joking!' whispered Porfiry. But this time he no longer wore his previous expression of simple womanish good nature and alarm; on the contrary, now he was frankly *giving orders*, with a stern frown, apparently brushing aside in an instant all mystery and ambiguity. But that only lasted a moment. Raskolnikov, after a second's perplexity, fell into a towering rage; yet the strange thing was that he again obeyed the order to talk quietly, despite being in a perfect paroxysm of fury.

'I shan't let you torment me!' he said, suddenly dropping his voice to a whisper as before, and instantly realizing with a sense of anguish and hatred that he had no choice but to obey the order, which enraged him even more. 'Arrest me, search me, but be so good as to act in due form, and stop playing with me! Don't you dare...'

'Please don't worry about due form,' interrupted Porfiry, with the same sly grin, seemingly gloating over Raskolnikov. 'I invited you here quite informally today, my lad, absolutely as a friend!'

'I don't want any of your friendship, to hell with it! Do you hear? And now look: I'm picking up my cap and leaving. So what do you say to that, if you're planning to arrest me?'

He grabbed his cap and walked to the door.

'But wouldn't you like to see a little surprise?' chuckled Porfiry, again taking hold of his arm a little above the elbow and stopping him by the door. He was clearly growing ever more high-spirited and playful, and this was driving Raskolnikov into an utter frenzy.

'What little surprise? What's all this?' he asked, stopping dead and looking fearfully at Porfiry.

'It's a little surprise, right here, waiting behind this door, heh-heh-heh!' (And he pointed at the locked door in the partition wall, which led to his official quarters.) 'I've even locked it up, so it can't run away.'

'What is it? Where? What?'—Raskolnikov went over to the door and tried to open it, but it was locked.

'It's locked—here's the key!'

And indeed, he took a key from his pocket and showed it to him.

'You're still lying!' yelled Raskolnikov, losing all control. 'Lying, you damned clown!' And he hurled himself at Porfiry, who had backed off to the other door but wasn't in the least frightened.

'I see it all now, all of it!' cried Raskolnikov, rushing at him. 'You're lying and taunting me to get me to betray myself!'

'You couldn't possibly betray yourself any worse than you have already, my dear Rodion Romanich. Look at you, all in a frenzy. Stop shouting, or I'll call for assistance!'

'You're lying, nothing's going to happen! Call away! You knew I was ill and you wanted to upset me, drive me mad, get me to betray myself, that's what you're after. No, you kindly produce some facts! I see it all! You haven't got any facts, all you have is wretched rubbishy guesswork, Zametov's guesswork!... You knew my character and you wanted to drive me mad, and then knock me out with priests and deputies... Is it them you're waiting for? Eh? What are you waiting for? Where are they? Let's have them!'

'What deputies are you on about, my lad? What an imagination! How could one possibly act that way and still stick to due form, as you say—you don't know how things are done, my friend... But the due form won't go away, you'll see that for yourself!...' muttered Porfiry, listening at the door.

And indeed, some sort of noise could be heard from behind the door, in the next room.

'Aha, they're coming!' cried Raskolnikov, 'you've sent for them... You were waiting for them! You expected... Well, let's have them all in then, deputies, witnesses, anyone you like... let's have them! I'm ready for them! I'm ready for them!'

But at this point something strange occurred, something so unexpected in the ordinary course of events that, naturally, neither Raskolnikov nor Porfiry Petrovich could have anticipated any such development.

CHAPTER VI

LATER on, when he thought back to that moment, Raskolnikov recalled it like this:

The noise outside the door suddenly got much louder, and the door opened a fraction.

'What's going on?' cried Porfiry Petrovich in annoyance. 'I warned you...'

For a moment there was no reply, but it was clear that there were a number of people outside the door, and they seemed to be pushing someone away.

'What on earth is going on?' repeated Porfiry Petrovich anxiously.

'They've brought the prisoner, Nikolay,' said someone's voice.

'No, no! Get out! Wait till I say!... What's he doing here? Outrageous!' cried Porfiry Petrovich, hurrying over to the door.

'But he's...' the same voice began, and was suddenly cut short.

For a couple of seconds, no longer, there was a real fight, after which someone suddenly and violently shoved someone else aside, and a man, very pale in the face, strode straight into Porfiry Petrovich's office.

At first sight this was a man of an extremely strange appearance. He was staring straight ahead of him, but apparently without seeing anyone. His eyes shone with determination, but his face was shrouded in deathly pallor, as if he had just been brought to the scaffold. His white lips twitched faintly.

He was still very young, dressed like a simple workman, of average height, thin, with his hair cut in a round crop, and thin, parched-looking features. The man he had just pushed away was the first to follow him headlong into the room, and had managed to grab him by the shoulder; this was a warder. But Nikolay wrenched his arm away and pulled himself free again.

A number of curious onlookers had crowded round the doorway, and some of them were trying to get in. The whole thing had taken no more than a moment.

'Get out, you're too early! Wait till you're sent for! Why's he been brought here so soon?' grumbled Porfiry Petrovich to himself, highly annoyed and apparently very disconcerted. But suddenly Nikolay sank to his knees.

'What are you doing?' cried Porfiry in astonishment.

'I did it! I'm the sinner! I'm the murderer!' Nikolay suddenly announced, panting slightly but speaking quite loud.

For ten seconds or so there was a stunned silence; even the warder recoiled and made no further attempt to approach Nikolay, but mechanically backed away to the door and stood there motionless.

'What's going on?' demanded Porfiry Petrovich, shaking off his momentary stupefaction.

'I'm... the murderer...' repeated Nikolay after a momentary silence.

'What... do you... What?... Whom did you kill?'

Porfiry Petrovich was clearly at a loss.

Nikolay again stood silent for a moment.

'Aliona Ivanovna and her sister, Lizaveta Ivanovna. I... killed them... with an axe. Everything went black...' he added abruptly, and fell silent again, still kneeling.

Porfiry Petrovich stood and thought for a moment, but then suddenly shook himself and started waving away the uninvited spectators. They instantly vanished, and the door was pulled to. Then he glanced at Raskolnikov, who was standing in the corner gaping at Nikolay, and moved towards him, but stopped short, looked at him again, then at once turned to look at Nikolay, then at Raskolnikov again, then at Nikolay again, and suddenly, on an impulse, darted towards Nikolay.

'What are you doing, running ahead of yourself, talking about everything going black?' he shouted almost angrily at him. 'I never asked you about things going black... Just tell me: did you kill them?'

'Yes, I'm the murderer... I'm confessing...' said Nikolay.

'A-ah! What did you kill them with?'

'An axe. I'd got it ready.'

'Running ahead again! On your own?'

Nikolay didn't understand the question.

'Did you do the killing on your own?'

'Yes. And Mitka's innocent, he had nothing to do with it all.'

'Steady on with your Mitka! A-ah! So what did you... well, what were you doing running down the stairs just then? Didn't the porters meet you both?'

'I did it as a blind... just then... running off with Mitka,' replied Nikolay hurriedly, as if he had prepared his answer.

'Well there you are!' cried Porfiry furiously. 'Reciting what he's been told!' he muttered to himself, and again noticed Raskolnikov. He was evidently so taken up with Nikolay that he had forgotten all about Raskolnikov for a moment. But now he recollected himself, and actually felt embarrassed...

'Rodion Romanovich, my dear fellow! Do forgive me,' he said, hurrying over to him. 'This won't do; do you mind... you're not needed here... even I... you see, what a surprise!... would you mind?...'

He took him by the arm and motioned him to the door.

'You don't seem to have been expecting this?' asked Raskolnikov, who of course hadn't understood anything properly as yet, but nevertheless already felt greatly reassured.

'And neither were you. Look at your hand, trembling like that! Heh-heh!'

'You're trembling yourself, Porfiry Petrovich.'

'So I am, too. I wasn't expecting this!'

By now they were standing in the doorway. Porfiry was waiting impatiently for Raskolnikov to leave.

'So you're not going to show me your little surprise, then?' Raskolnikov asked suddenly.

'Listen to him—and his very teeth are still chattering, heh-heh! What a joker you are! Well, goodbye for now.'

'As far as I know, it's just *goodbye* and that's it!'

'Well, that's in God's hands, God's hands!' muttered Porfiry with a twisted grin.

As he passed through the office, Raskolnikov noticed many of the people there staring at him. Among the crowd in the entrance hall he picked out the two porters from *that* house, the ones he had invited to go with him to the district police office that night. They were standing waiting for something. But no sooner had he gone out onto the stairs than he heard Porfiry Petrovich's voice again behind him. He turned round and saw the man chasing after him, all out of breath.

'Just one word, Rodion Romanovich. As far as all that other business is concerned, that's in God's hands; but I'll have to ask you some questions about this and that, for form's sake; so we'll be meeting again, that's what I wanted to say.'

And Porfiry stopped in front of him and smiled.

'That's what I wanted to say,' he said again.

One might have thought he was wanting to add something further, but somehow couldn't get the words out.

'Well, Porfiry Petrovich, you must forgive me, too, for what I said just then... I got angry,' Raskolnikov began, now so self-assured that he couldn't resist the temptation to swagger a bit.

'That's all right, quite all right,' rejoined Porfiry, almost joyfully. 'I myself was... I have a venomous character, I'm sorry to say! Anyway, we'll meet again. We'll be seeing a great deal of one another, God willing!...'

'And get to know one another properly?' Raskolnikov took him up.

'And get to know one another properly,' nodded Porfiry Petrovich, screwing up his eyes and giving him a very serious look. 'So you're off to a party now?'

'A funeral, actually.'

'Oh yes, of course, a funeral. Well, look after your health; mind your health!'

'Well, for my part, I don't know what to wish you!' answered Raskolnikov as he started off down the stairs. But suddenly he turned back to Porfiry. 'I would wish you greater success, but you can see what a comical job you have!'

'Why comical?' Porfiry had also turned to leave, but instantly pricked up his ears.

'Well of course it is; there's that wretched Mikolka, you must have been teasing and tormenting him, psychologically, the way you do, until he confessed; you must have spent days and nights proving to him that "You're the murderer, you're the murderer"—and now that he has confessed, you'll start pulling him apart again, bone by bone, "Liar!" you'll say, "You're not the murderer! You couldn't be! You're just reciting what you've been told!" What could be more comical than all that?'

'Heh-heh-heh! So you did notice me telling Nikolay just now that he was "reciting what he'd been told"?'

'How could I help it?'

'Heh-heh! Very clever, very clever. You notice everything, you do! Quite sharp-witted! And you find the most comical string and pluck that one... heh-heh! It was Gogol, wasn't it, among our writers, who they say had that facility to the highest degree?'

'Yes, Gogol.'

'Yes indeed, Gogol. Goodbye, till our next delightful encounter.'

'Till our delightful encounter.'

Raskolnikov went straight home. He was so disconcerted and confused that once he had reached his room and flung himself down on the divan, he stayed there for about a quarter of an hour, simply resting and doing his best to gather his thoughts. He didn't even attempt to reason with himself about Nikolay, he felt so dumbfounded. It seemed to him that there was something so astonishing and inexplicable in Nikolay's confession that he had no hope of understanding it. But that confession of Nikolay's was an incontrovertible fact. He could at once see clearly what its consequences would be. The lie couldn't fail to be exposed, and then they'd come after him again. But at least he was free until that happened, and he simply had to do something for himself, because the danger to him would inevitably return.

But how much danger was there? The position was becoming clearer. Remembering, *roughly*, in broad outline, the whole of his recent meeting with Porfiry, he couldn't help once more shuddering with horror. Of course he still didn't know all Porfiry's intentions, and couldn't work out what had been in his mind just then. But he had shown a part of his hand, and of course no one could see better than himself how terrifying was this 'move' of Porfiry's. A little more, and he *could* have given himself away completely, facts and all. Porfiry knew his nervous temperament, and had read and understood him correctly at first glance; and Porfiry's strategy now, though overly decisive, was almost bound to succeed. There was no doubt about it—Raskolnikov had already succeeded in seriously compromising himself during that last encounter; but still, they had never got as far as *facts*; everything was still circumstantial. And yet—had he got it right, now? Quite right? Wasn't he making a mistake? What exactly had Porfiry been after today? Did he really have something up his sleeve? And just what was it? Had he really been waiting for something, or not? How exactly would they have parted today, if it hadn't been for the unexpected bombshell of Nikolay's arrival?

Porfiry had shown almost all his hand; despite the risk, he had shown it, and (Raskolnikov still believed), if Porfiry really had anything more, he would have shown that too. What had that 'surprise' been? A joke? Did it mean anything or not? Could it have been hiding anything remotely like factual evidence, or a definite accusation? And the man from yesterday? Where had he vanished to? Where had he been today? Because if Porfiry really possessed anything definite, it must be to do with the man from yesterday...

He was sitting on his divan, his head bowed, resting his elbows on his knees and hiding his face in his hands. His whole body still shook with a nervous tremor. Eventually he stood up, picked up his cap, thought for a moment, and walked to the door.

He had a kind of presentiment that for today at least, he could almost certainly consider himself safe. And suddenly his heart filled with what was almost happiness: he wanted to go to Katerina Ivanovna's at once. He had missed the funeral, of course, but he'd be in time for the wake, and there, in a moment, he'd see Sonia.

He stopped still and thought, with a sad smile on his lips.

'Today! Today!' he repeated to himself. 'Yes, this very day! It has to be...'

And he was on the point of opening the door, when it suddenly began opening on its own. He started back. The door opened slowly and quietly, and suddenly a figure appeared in the doorway—yesterday's man '*from under the ground*'.

The man stopped in the entrance, looked silently at Raskolnikov and took a step forwards into the room. He looked exactly as he had yesterday—the same figure, the same clothing—but there had been a profound change in his face and eyes. He was now looking rather mournful, and after a pause he sighed deeply. If he had only leaned his face sideways a little, resting his cheek in the palm of his hand, he would have looked exactly like a peasant woman.

'What do you want?' asked Raskolnikov in horror.

The man stood in silence, and suddenly bowed low before him, almost to the floor; at least, he touched the floor with one finger of his right hand.

'What's all this?'

'I've done wrong,' said the man quietly.

'How?'

'Evil thoughts.'

The two looked at one another.

'I got annoyed. When you went there that time, tipsy perhaps, and told the porters to come along to the police, and asked them about the blood—I got annoyed that everyone was letting you alone and just reckoned you were drunk. I was so annoyed I couldn't sleep. And since we remembered your address, we came here yesterday and asked about you...'

'Who came?' interrupted Raskolnikov, instantly beginning to remember.

'I did, I mean; I did you wrong.'

'So you come from that house?'

'I was right there, standing in the gateway with the others, have you forgotten? I've got my workshop there, have had for years. We're furriers, working people, we take in work there... And the worst of it was how annoyed I felt...'

Suddenly Raskolnikov clearly recalled the whole scene of two days earlier; he could see that apart from the porters, a few other people had been standing around, and some women too. He remembered one particular voice calling for him to be taken straight to the police. He couldn't remember the speaker's face, and didn't recognize him even now; but he did remember answering the man, and turning towards him...

So this, it turned out, was what yesterday's horror had all been about. The most terrible thing was his realization that he had almost been undone, had almost destroyed himself because of such an *insignificant* circumstance. For in fact, apart from the question of renting the flat and the talk about blood, there was nothing that this man could tell. And consequently Porfiry, too, had nothing, nothing at all except for this *delirium*, no facts apart from his *psychology*, which *cut both ways*— so nothing definite at all. And consequently so long as no new facts emerged (and they mustn't emerge, they mustn't, they mustn't!), then... what could they do to him? What could they definitely prove against him, even if they did arrest him? And this meant that Porfiry could only just have discovered about the flat, and hadn't known about it before.

'Was it you that told Porfiry today... about me coming there?' he cried, struck by a sudden idea.

'Who's Porfiry?'

'The chief investigator.'

'Yes, I told him. The porters didn't go, so I went.'

'Today?'

'I was there just a minute before you. And I heard it all, the way he was squeezing you.'

'Where? What? When?'

'Right there, behind his partition, I was sitting there the whole time.'

'What? So you were the surprise! But how could that have happened? Good heavens!'

'When I saw', began the man, 'that the porters didn't want to go when I told them, because they said it was too late, and maybe the policeman would be cross with them because they didn't come at once, I got annoyed, and I couldn't sleep, and I started asking questions. And I found it all out yesterday, and so I went today. First time I went, he wasn't there. So I waited an hour and came back, and he wouldn't see me; and then I went a third time, and he saw me. And I told him everything that had happened, and he started running around the room and hitting his chest with his fist: "You villains, what are you doing to me?" he said, "If I'd known about this, I'd have sent a squad of police to bring him in!" Then he ran out, sent for someone and started talking to him in the corner, and then he came back to me, and started asking me questions and telling me off. He scolded me a lot; but I told him everything, and I said that you hadn't dared answer me when I spoke to you yesterday. And then he started running around again, and kept hitting himself in the chest, and being furious, and running about, and then when they reported that you'd come—well, he says, get behind that partition and sit there, and don't move, no matter what you hear; and he brought a chair for me himself, and locked me in; perhaps, he says, I'll call you in. And when they brought Nikolay, he got me out again after you'd gone. I'll be sending for you again, he says, and asking you more questions...'

'And did he question Nikolay while you were there?'

'After he'd seen you out, he sent me off right away, and then he started questioning Nikolay.'

The man stopped speaking and suddenly bowed low again, touching his finger on the floor.

'Forgive me for slandering you, and being spiteful to you.'

'God will forgive you,' replied Raskolnikov, and as soon as he had pronounced the words, the man bowed to him, not to the floor this time but waist-high, and slowly turned and left the room. 'Everything cuts both ways, it all cuts both ways now,' repeated Raskolnikov, and walked out more confident than ever.

'Now we'll fight on,' he said with a malicious smile as he walked downstairs. But his malice was directed at himself: he was recalling his own 'cowardice' with shame and contempt.

PART FIVE

CHAPTER I

THE morning following Piotr Petrovich's fateful meeting with Dunechka and Pulkheria Alexandrovna exerted its sobering effect even on Piotr Petrovich. To his great displeasure, he was obliged little by little to accept as an accomplished and irreversible fact, what had yesterday still appeared to him as an almost fantastical event, something which, although it had actually happened, still seemed almost impossible to him. The black serpent of injured vanity had gnawed at his heart all night. As soon as he got up, Piotr Petrovich looked at himself in the mirror. He was afraid he might look bilious after that night. But so far all was well on that front, and when he saw his distinguished, pale features—a little plumper now than they used to be—Piotr Petrovich was almost reassured for a moment, and felt quite certain that he'd find himself another bride, very likely an even better one, somewhere else. But he quickly pulled himself together and spat vigorously to one side, provoking a silent but sarcastic smile from his young friend and fellow lodger Andrei Semionovich Lebeziatnikov. Piotr Petrovich noted that smile and at once mentally set it down against his young friend's account. He had recently had occasion to set a lot of things down on that account. And his anger redoubled when he realized that he ought never to have told Andrei Semionovich about what had happened the day before. That had been his second impulsive mistake that day, committed when annoyance had made him overconfiding... And all that morning, one unpleasantness had followed another, as though on purpose to vex him. Even in the Senate he had met with a setback in the case he was pursuing there. But he was particularly irritated by the landlord of the lodgings which he had taken with a view to an early marriage, and had decorated at his own expense. This landlord, a prosperous German tradesman, was resolutely refusing to cancel the contract they had just concluded, and insisting on the full penalties set down in that contract, despite the fact that Piotr Petrovich was handing him back the flat almost freshly redecorated. And the furniture shop, too, was flatly refusing to pay him back a single rouble of the deposit he had put down for furniture which he had bought but not yet had delivered to the flat. 'I won't get married just for the sake of the furniture!'

muttered Piotr Petrovich, grinding his teeth; and at the same moment the desperate hope once more flashed through his mind: 'But has it all really fallen through, is it really all over, is there no hope of recovery? Can I really not have another try?' The seductive thought of Dunechka once again shot a pang through his heart. It was a moment of torment for him; and if he could, just by wishing it, have killed Raskolnikov at that instant, then Piotr Petrovich would of course have wished it at once.

'And another mistake I made was never giving them any money,' he thought, walking despondently back to Lebeziatnikov's little room. 'Why did I have to be such a Jew, damn it? I hadn't begun to think it through! I'd been thinking I'd keep them on a pittance, and get them to see me as their Providence; and now look at them!... Phoo!... No, if I'd given them, say, fifteen hundred roubles over this period, for a dowry, and presents, and boxes of this and that, dressing cases, jewellery, fabrics, and all that trash from Knopp's and the English shop,* it would all have turned out easier and... surer! They wouldn't have been quite so keen to turn me down! They're the sort of people who would have felt duty-bound to hand back my presents, and my money, if they broke it off; and they'd have found that quite difficult and painful! And they'd have had a conscience about it, too: how could they suddenly send a man packing when he'd been so generous and delicate with them so far? Hmm! I played that badly!' And Piotr Petrovich ground his teeth again, and called himself a fool—only to himself, of course.

Having come to that conclusion, he arrived back home twice as venomous and irritable as when he left. The preparations for the wake in Katerina Ivanovna's room aroused his curiosity. He'd heard something about this event the day before; he even seemed to remember being invited himself; but he'd been so bound up in his own affairs that he'd paid no attention to anything else. He hastily made enquiries from Madame Lippewechsel, as she busied herself about the table in the absence of Katerina Ivanovna (who was at the cemetery), and found out that the wake was to be a grand affair, with almost all the tenants invited, including some who hadn't known the dead man; that even Andrei Semionovich Lebeziatnikov had been asked, in spite of his recent quarrel with Katerina Ivanovna; and finally, that he himself, Piotr Petrovich, was not only invited but eagerly awaited, as being almost the most important of all the lodgers to be asked. Amalia Ivanovna herself was also invited with great ceremony, notwithstanding all past unpleasantnesses, and was now taking charge and organizing everything, and almost taking pleasure in it; and though she wore mourning, she had on all her new black silk finery and was very proud of herself. All this news gave Piotr Petrovich an idea, and he went through to his room—Andrei Semionovich Lebeziatnikov's room, that is—rather thoughtfully. For he had also heard that one of the invited guests was to be Raskolnikov.

Andrei Semionovich had for some reason spent all that morning at home. The relations that Piotr Petrovich had established with this gentleman were rather strange, though natural in a way: he despised and hated him beyond measure, and had done from the day he arrived, yet at the same time he seemed rather afraid of him. He had come to lodge with him as soon as he arrived in Petersburg, not entirely out of miserly economy, though that had perhaps been his chief consideration. There was another reason too. Even back in the provinces he had heard that Andrei Semionovich, a former protégé of his, was now one of the foremost young progressives, and actually played a significant part in certain curious and legendary circles. That had greatly impressed Piotr Petrovich. These powerful, omniscient groups, who despised and denounced everyone else, had long filled Piotr Petrovich with a kind of ill-defined but profound fear. He himself could not of course have gained the least understanding, not even a rough idea, of *that sort of thing*—particularly while still in the provinces. Like everyone else, he had heard that there existed, especially in Petersburg, people called progressives, or nihilists, or denouncers,* or whatever; but like many others he had exaggerated and twisted the meaning and significance of those terms to an absurd degree. His worst fear, for some years now, had been of *denunciation*; and that was the chief cause of his constant, exaggerated uneasiness, especially when considering moving to work in Petersburg. He was *scared* in that way, as small children are sometimes *scared*. Several years back, when he was in the provinces and just embarking on his career, he had known of two quite highly placed people in his province, people to whom he had attached himself and who had patronized him, who had then been viciously denounced. One case had ended in a highly scandalous way for the man in question, while the other had almost led to serious trouble. And so Piotr Petrovich had resolved that as soon as he got to Petersburg, he'd immediately discover what was going on, and if necessary get ahead of the game by currying favour with 'our younger generations'. He was relying on Andrei Semionovich here, and had already learned, after a fashion, to mouth a few useful phrases he'd picked up, in case he found himself meeting people like, for example, Raskolnikov.

Of course he had quickly realized that Andrei Semionovich was an exceptionally ordinary, naïve man. But that had done nothing to reassure him or change his mind. Even if he had satisfied himself that all the progressives were just as stupid, that would still not have calmed his anxiety. None of the actual doctrines, ideas, and systems that Andrei Semionovich pestered him with, were of any interest to him; he had his own aims. All he needed was to find out, as quickly as possible— at once, in fact—what had gone on *here*, and how? Were *those people* in power or not? Did he personally have anything to fear, or not? Would he be denounced if he undertook some particular enterprise, or not? And if he was, what would it be for; what were people being denounced for these days? And not only that: wasn't there some way of getting round them and tricking them, if they really were so powerful? Should he do that, or shouldn't he? Might he not, for instance, use them to promote his career? In short, he had hundreds of questions to answer.

This Andrei Semionovich was a short, scrawny, scrofulous individual, a clerk in some department or other, with quite strangely pale-coloured hair and mutton-chop whiskers of which he was inordinately proud. On top of that, his eyes were almost permanently sore. He was quite soft-hearted, but his speech was very self-assured and occasionally downright overbearing—which, coming from such a little man, almost always made him look absurd. Amalia Ivanovna, however, regarded him as one of her better lodgers, since he didn't get drunk and kept up with his rent. Despite all these qualities, Andrei Semionovich was really rather stupid. He had joined up with the progressives and 'our younger generations' out of enthusiasm. He was one of that vast and varied crowd of mediocrities, lifeless stillborns, and stubborn-headed ignoramuses, who rush to embrace the latest fashionable craze and instantly vulgarize it, producing a ridiculous caricature of whatever they themselves may sometimes sincerely believe in.

Lebeziatnikov, as a matter of fact, despite his kind heart, was also beginning to find his housemate and former protector Piotr Petrovich rather hard to bear. This feeling, which was mutual, had come about almost unnoticed. However naïve Andrei Semionovich might be, he had gradually come to see that Piotr Petrovich was fooling him, secretly despised him, and 'wasn't at all the kind of man he had thought'. He had tried to explain Fourier's system and Darwin's theory* to him, but Piotr Petrovich had lately been listening to him with an altogether too sarcastic air, and most recently had actually begun being rude to him. The fact was, Piotr Petrovich was coming to the instinctive conclusion that Lebeziatnikov was not only a commonplace and rather stupid man, but might perhaps be a bit of a liar too, and didn't have any important connections even in his own circle, but had merely picked up odd ideas at third hand; indeed, he might not even know much about his own chosen task of *propaganda* either, since he got so confused about it; so how could he ever denounce anyone! It must be noted in passing that over the last week and a half Piotr Petrovich had— especially at first—willingly accepted some extremely odd praise from Andrei Semionovich; he had, for instance, raised no objection and said not a word when Andrei Semionovich credited him with willingness to promote the early establishment of a new '*commune*' somewhere in Meshchanskaya Street;* or to consent to Dunia's taking a lover if she chose to do so, even in the first month of her marriage; or not to have their future children baptized; and so on, along the same lines. Piotr Petrovich, as was his custom, made no objection when such qualities were ascribed to him, but allowed himself to be praised even in such terms—so fond was he of praise of any kind.

Piotr Petrovich had chanced to cash some five-per-cent bonds that morning, and was now sitting at a table counting out bundles of bank-notes. Andrei Semionovich, who almost never had any money, was walking about the room pretending to himself that he was quite indif-ferent to all those bundles, and even contemptuous of them. Piotr Petrovich would never have believed that Andrei Semionovich could really be indifferent to such a lot of money; while Andrei Semionovich in his turn was bitterly reflecting that Piotr Petrovich might indeed be capable of thinking that of him, and in fact was probably glad of the chance to tease and upset his young friend by laying out those bundles of banknotes and thereby reminding him of his own insignificance and the great difference between the two of them.

On this occasion he was finding Piotr Petrovich unbelievably, exas-peratingly inattentive, despite his own attempts to hold forth on his beloved topic of a new and special type of 'commune'. The curt objec-tions and comments that escaped from Piotr Petrovich in between the clicking of the beads on his abacus breathed the most blatantly rude, deliberate mockery. But Andrei Semionovich 'humanely' put Piotr Petrovich's mood down to the after-effects of his rupture with Dunechka on the previous day, and burned with a desire to address that question without delay. He had some words of progressive propaganda to con-tribute, which might console his respected friend and 'unquestionably' promote his further enlightenment.

'What sort of a funeral party is it they're preparing at that... at the widow's?' asked Piotr Petrovich suddenly, interrupting Andrei Semionovich at the most fascinating point.

'As if you didn't know already—I was talking to you about it only yesterday, and saying what I thought about all those ceremonies... And I heard she'd invited you too. You were talking to her yourself yesterday...'

'I never expected that fool of a beggarwoman to squander everything on a funeral party, all the money she got from that other fool... Raskolnikov. Actually I was astonished just now, as I walked past: the preparations that are going ahead, and all the drinks!... They've invited a lot of people—God knows what's going on!' said Piotr Petrovich, pressing on with the same subject as though he had some idea in his mind. 'What's that? Are you telling me I was invited too?' he added suddenly, looking up. 'When was that? I don't recall it. Anyway, I shan't go. What's the point? All I did was mention to her in passing that, as the destitute widow of a government clerk, she could get a one-off grant of a year's salary. I wonder if that's the reason she invited me! Heh-heh!'

'I don't mean to go either,' said Lebeziatnikov.

'I should think not! When you'd thrashed her with your own hands! No wonder you feel awkward, heh-heh-heh!'

'Who did? Thrashed whom?' exclaimed Lebeziatnikov hastily, and actually blushed.

'Why, you did, you thrashed Katerina Ivanovna, a month ago, didn't you! I heard all about it yesterday... So much for your political convictions!... And what price equality for women, then? Heh-heh-heh!'

As though reassured by that, Piotr Petrovich went back to clicking on his abacus.

'That's all slanderous rubbish!' Lebeziatnikov fired up; he always hated being reminded of that episode. 'And it wasn't like that at all! It was quite different... You've got the wrong story, it's all gossip! I was just defending myself. She started it, flinging herself at me and scratching me... Pulled out all my side whiskers... Anyone's entitled to defend himself, I hope. And I won't stand for violence from anyone... on principle. Because that practically amounts to tyranny. What was I supposed to do—just stand there and do nothing? All I did was push her away.'

'Heh-heh-heh!' Luzhin went on, with another malicious laugh.

'You're just getting at me because you're annoyed and angry yourself... And that's all rubbish and nothing whatever to do with the women's question. You've misunderstood it—I was actually thinking that if we accept that women are equal to men in everything, even physical strength (which they're now claiming), then there has to be equality here too. Of course I worked out later that a question like that shouldn't really exist at all, because conflict shouldn't exist, and in the society of the future any kind of fighting is unthinkable... and of course it's a strange idea to look for equality in a fight. I'm not all that stupid... although fights do actually still happen... I mean, later on they won't, but right now they still do... Oh hell! Damn it all! You get me all mixed up! It's not because of that unpleasantness that I shan't go to the wake. I'm just not going on principle, so as not to join in that sort of a revoltingly superstitious ritual, that's what! Actually, I might even have gone, just for a laugh... But it's a shame there won't be any priests. Otherwise I'd have gone for sure.'

'You mean you'd sit down to enjoy someone's hospitality, and then spit on it and those who invited you. Is that it?'

'Not spit on them at all, just protest. I only aim to be useful. I might indirectly be promoting education and propaganda. It's everyone's duty to promote enlightenment and propaganda, and perhaps the more harshly it's done, the better. I could be planting an idea, a seed:... And that seed will grow into something real.* How would I be offending them? They'd be offended at first, and then they'd see for themselves that I'd done them some good. Look, our people were criticizing Terebyeva (she's in the commune now), because when she left her family and... gave herself to a man, she wrote to her mother and father saying that she didn't want to live surrounded by old-fashioned prejudices, and was entering into a free marriage; and people said that writing like that was too rude, to her parents I mean, and she might have spared them pain by writing more gently. In my opinion that's all nonsense, and there's no need to be gentle, on the contrary, quite the opposite, that's the moment to make your protest. Look at Varents—she lived with her husband for seven years, then she left her children and broke it off with the husband, and wrote him a letter to say: "I've realized that I can't be happy with you. I'll never forgive you for deceiving me, and concealing from me that there's a different way of organizing society, in communes. I recently found that out from a great-hearted man, to whom I have given myself, and he and I are founding a commune. I'm talking straight to you, because I consider it dishonourable to deceive you. Carry on as you please. Don't hope to get me back, it's too late for that. I wish you happiness." That's how to write that sort of letter!'

'That Terebyeva, now, isn't that the same person who you once said was in her third free marriage?'*

'Only her second, strictly speaking! Anyway, even if it had been her fourth, or her fifteenth—that's neither here nor there! And if I've ever been sorry that my father and mother are dead, I'm sorry now! I've often dreamt of the protest I'd fling in their teeth, if only they were still alive! I'd have set the thing up on purpose... I'd show them what a "clean break" is, damn it! I'd make them take notice! Honestly, it's a shame there's nobody left!'

'Nobody to astonish? Heh–heh! Well, have it your own way,' interrupted Piotr Petrovich, 'but just tell me this, if you please: you must know the dead man's daughter, that sickly young girl. It's perfectly true, isn't it, what they say about her, eh?'

'And so what? What I say is—I mean, this is my personal conviction—that's the most normal situation for a woman. Why not? Well, I mean, *distinguons*.* In today's society, of course, it isn't quite normal, because it's forced on her; but in the society of the future it'll be perfectly normal, because it's free. And even today she had the right to do that: she was suffering, and that was her asset, her capital as it were, which she had every right to make use of. Naturally in the society of the future there won't be any need for assets; but a woman's role will be determined in a different way, harmoniously and rationally. As for Sofia Semionovna herself, at the present time I view her actions as a concrete and forceful protest against the social structure, and deeply respect her for it; indeed, I look on her with joy!'

'But they tell me it was you that got her evicted from these lodgings!'

Lebeziatnikov grew livid with rage.

'More gossip!' he yelled. 'It wasn't anything like that, at all! That's all lies! That was all Katerina Ivanovna's invention, because she hadn't understood anything! Katerina Ivanovna made it all up because she'd got it all wrong! And I never tried to make up to Sofia Semionovna! All I did was educate her, in a totally selfless way, trying to persuade her to protest... All I needed was a protest from her, and in any case Sofia Semionovna herself couldn't stay in these lodgings any longer!'

'Were you inviting her to join the commune, then?'

'You keep trying to make fun of me, and it won't wash, I'm telling you. You don't understand a thing! There's no such function in the commune. Communes are created so that such functions shouldn't exist. In a commune, that function will change its whole character; what's stupid here will become sensible there; what's unnatural here, in today's surroundings, will become entirely natural there. Everything depends on a person's surroundings and social environment. The environment is everything,* the person himself is nothing. And Sofia Semionovna and I are still on good terms, which proves to you that she never saw me as her enemy or thought I'd wronged her. Yes! I'm trying to attract her to join a commune, but on an absolutely, utterly different basis! What's so funny? We want to set up our own special commune, but on a broader foundation than the earlier ones. We've taken our principles further. We reject even more! If Dobroliubov were to rise from the grave, I'd have a bone to pick with him. As for Belinsky,* I'd make mincemeat of him! But for the time being I'm still educating Sofia Semionovna. She has a beautiful, beautiful nature!'

'And you're making the most of her beautiful nature, eh? Heh–heh!'

'No, no! Oh, no! Just the opposite!'

'Quite so, just the opposite! Heh–hch–heh! You've said it!'

'Oh, please believe me! Why would I ever want to hide that from you, I ask you? On the contrary—I find it strange myself, but with me she's very particularly, almost timidly, chaste and bashful!'

'And needless to say, you're educating her... heh–heh! proving to her that all this modesty is nonsense?...'

'Not at all! Not at all! Oh, how coarsely, how stupidly—excuse me—you're interpreting what I say about educating her! You d–d–don't understand a thing! Oh my God, how... how immature you still are! We're seeking women's emancipation, and all you can think about is... Leaving aside any question of chastity and feminine modesty, which are useless and utterly outdated ideas in themselves, I totally, totally accept that she's chaste with me, because that's to do with her liberty and her rights. Naturally, if she herself were to tell me "I want to have you", I'd count myself very fortunate, because I find the girl very attractive; but at the moment, for the time being at least, no one has ever treated her with greater courtesy and consideration than I do, or with more respect for her dignity... I wait in hope, that's all!'

'You'd better make her a present of some kind. I bet you've never even thought of that.'

'You don't understand a thing, I tell you! Of course you're right, she is in that sort of situation, but this is a different matter, quite a different one! You just despise her. You see a fact, which you wrongly think is despicable, and that makes you refuse to look at a human being in a human way. You don't know what kind of a person she is yet! My only great regret is that she's recently given up reading for some reason, and doesn't borrow my books any more. She used to do that. And it's a pity, too, that with all her vigour and determination to protest—as she's already proved—she still doesn't seem to have much self-reliance, independence I mean; not much of a spirit of denial that could help her set herself free from certain superstitions and... stupidities. But all the same, she has an excellent understanding of some issues. For instance she's brilliantly understood the hand-kissing question,* I mean the fact that a man insults a woman with her inferiority when he kisses her hand. We had debated that question, and I told her about that straight away. And she listened carefully when she was told about workers' associations in France. Now I'm teaching her about the question of entering rooms, in the society of the future.'

'What's all that about?'

'There's recently been some discussion about whether a member of a commune has the right to enter another member's room, a man's or a woman's, at all times... well, and the decision was that he does.'

'And supposing the man or woman is busy with a call of nature at the time? Heh-heh!'

Andrei Semionovich got quite cross.

'You keep going on and on about the same thing, these damned demands of nature!' he cried in a voice full of hatred. 'Ugh, I'm so furious and cross with myself for ever mentioning those wretched demands of nature to you, before I had to, when I was explaining the system to you! Damn it all! People like you invariably trip up over that, and the worst thing is that you all start making jokes about it before you understand any of it. And you think you've got it right! And you seem to be proud of yourselves! Phoo! I've often insisted that you can only explain that whole question to a novice at the very end, when he's already convinced of the system, when he's been educated and steered in the right direction. And anyway—what, would you kindly tell me, do you find so shameful and despicable in a cesspit, even? I myself would be the first to volunteer to clean out any cesspit you like! And there's no self-sacrifice to it either! It's just work, an honourable, socially beneficial activity, worthy of any other; and far superior, of course, to the doings of any Raphael or Pushkin, because it's more useful!'*

'And more honourable, more honourable too—heh-heh-heh!'

'What does "honourable" mean? I don't understand that sort of expression, as a way of defining human activity. "More honourable", "more generous"—all that's just absurd nonsense, outdated superstitions which I reject! Anything that's *useful* to humanity is honourable! There's only one word I understand, and that's *useful*! Snigger as much as you like, but that's a fact!'

Piotr Petrovich was laughing heartily. He had finished counting his money and had cleared it away, although some of it was still lying on the table for some reason. That 'cesspit question', for all its vulgarity, had several times served to set Piotr Petrovich and his young friend at loggerheads. The stupid thing was that Andrei Semionovich was genuinely angry; Luzhin himself was enjoying the spat, and just at that moment he particularly wanted to needle Lebeziatnikov.

'You're just getting so angry and spiteful because things went wrong for you yesterday,' Lebeziatnikov finally burst out. As a rule, in spite of all his 'independence' and his 'protests', he somehow never dared stand up to Piotr Petrovich, and generally continued to treat him with the same habitual deference he had had for him in years gone by.

'But you just tell me this, if you please,' interrupted Piotr Petrovich in a tone of haughty annoyance. 'Can you, sir... or rather, are you really on sufficiently friendly terms, and just how friendly, with the young person previously mentioned, to request her to come up now, for a moment, into this room? I believe they've all come back now, from the cemetery, I mean... I can hear people moving about... I need to see her, that young person.'

'What on earth do you want her for?' asked Lebeziatnikov in astonishment.

'I just need to see her, that's all. I'll be moving out of here any day now, and I should like to let her know... Actually, you might as well be here too, when I talk to her. That'll be better still. Otherwise you might be thinking goodness knows what.'

'I shan't be thinking anything at all... I just asked, and if you've got business with her, there's nothing easier than to ask her up. I'll go down straight away. And you can be sure I shan't get in your way.'

And indeed, some five minutes later Lebeziatnikov returned with Sonechka. She was utterly astonished, and as usual entered the room timidly. She was always scared in such situations, and very frightened by new faces and new acquaintances; she had been fearful ever since she was a child, and now was even more so. Piotr Petrovich greeted her in a 'courteous and friendly manner', though with a hint of good-humoured familiarity, appropriate in his opinion for a respectable gentle-man of such solid worth as himself, in the presence of such a young and in a certain sense *interesting* creature. He hastened to 'reassure' her, and sat her down opposite him at the table. Sonia sat down and looked round—at Lebeziatnikov, at the money on the table, and then suddenly back at Piotr Petrovich; after that she looked fixedly at him and never took her eyes off him. Lebeziatnikov moved towards the door, but Piotr Petrovich stood up, gestured to Sonia to stay seated, and stopped Lebeziatnikov in the doorway.

'Is that man Raskolnikov there? Has he come?' he whispered to him.

'Raskolnikov? Yes. Why? Yes, he's there... He's just come in, I saw him... But why?'

'Well then, I must earnestly beg you to stay here with us, and not to leave me alone with this... young person. It's a trivial matter, but heaven knows what people might read into it. I don't want Raskolnikov repeating things *down there*... Do you see what I'm talking about?'

'Oh, yes, I see, I see!' said Lebeziatnikov, suddenly realizing what he meant. 'Yes, you've a right to... In my personal opinion, of course, you're overdoing your scruples, but... all the same, that's your right. By all means, I'll stay here. I'll stand over by that window and not disturb you... I believe you've a right to that...'

Piotr Petrovich came back to the divan, sat down opposite Sonia, looked carefully at her, and suddenly put on a particularly dignified and quite stern expression, as if to say: 'Don't you get any ideas into your head, young lady.' That put the final touch to Sonia's confusion.

'First of all, Sofia Semionovna, please present my excuses to your very respected Mamasha... That's so, isn't it? Katerina Ivanovna stands as a mother to you?' Piotr Petrovich began in a very portentous but still quite gentle voice. He evidently had only the friendliest of intentions.

'That's right, sir, that's it, as a mother, sir,' answered Sonia hurriedly and fearfully.

'Well, then, please make her my excuses and say that I am prevented by circumstances beyond my control from attending your pancake-feast— your funeral dinner, I mean—despite your mother's kind invitation.'

'Yes indeed, sir; I'll tell her, sir, right away.' And Sonechka hurriedly got up from her chair.

'That's not *quite* all,' said Piotr Petrovich, detaining her and smiling at her naïve ignorance of social conventions. 'You can't know me very well, my dear Sofia Semionovna, if you think that such an unimportant matter, which concerns me alone, could have led me to trouble a person like yourself with a request to come and see me. I have something else in mind.'

Sonia hastily sat down. The grey and rainbow-coloured banknotes* that were still left on the table once more attracted her gaze, but she quickly turned away from them and looked up at Piotr Petrovich. It suddenly seemed dreadfully unseemly, especially for *her*, to be looking at someone else's money. She tried to fix her eyes on Piotr Petrovich's gold eyeglass which he held in his left hand, and at the same time on the massive and extremely fine ring with a yellow stone he wore on the middle finger of that hand—but suddenly looked away from that too, and no longer knowing where to look, ended by staring straight into Piotr Petrovich's eyes again. After an even more majestic pause than the last, he went on:

'I happened yesterday to exchange a couple of words in passing with poor Katerina Ivanovna. That sufficed to make it clear to me that she was in an... unnatural state, if I might use that expression...'

'Yes, sir... unnatural, sir,' Sonia hurriedly assented.

'Or, putting it more simply and clearly—ill.'

'Yes, sir, more simply and clear... yes, sir, ill, sir.'

'Quite so. So now, out of a sense of humanity and... and... as it were, compassion, I should wish, for my own part, to be useful to her in some way, in view of her sad but inevitable fate. I believe that this whole most destitute family now depends on you alone.'

'Could I ask you', began Sonia, suddenly standing up, 'what it was that you were good enough to tell her yesterday, about the chance of a pension? Because she told me yesterday that you'd offered to try and get a pension for her. Is that right, sir?'

'Not in the least; in fact that's quite an absurd idea. All I did was mention some temporary help for the widow of a clerk who dies on official service—so long as she has the right contacts; but I believe your late parent had not only not served out his time, but had not actually worked at all of late. In short, although there might have been some hope, it would have been a very ephemeral one, since she does not actually have any real right to assistance in her present situation, indeed quite the contrary... So she'd actually begun thinking of a pension, heh-heh-heh! A lady with ideas!'

'Yes, sir, about a pension... Because she's credulous and kind-hearted, and her kind heart makes her believe anything, and... and... and... her mind is like that... Yes, sir... excuse me, sir.' And Sonia rose again to leave the room.

'Just a minute, I hadn't finished.'

'Yes, sir, hadn't finished,' mumbled Sonia.

'Well then, sit down, do.'

Sonia got dreadfully flustered and sat down for the third time.

'In view of this situation of hers, with those unfortunate little children, I should like, as I said earlier, to be useful in some way, so far as lies in my power; lies in my power, as they say—no more than that. It would be possible, for instance, to get up a subscription on her behalf, or a lottery, as it were... or something of the sort—as is always done in such situations by a person's nearest and dearest, or even by unconnected persons, if they wish to help. That was what I intended to tell you. That might be done.'

'Yes, sir, very well, sir... God will reward you...' Sonia stammered, staring hard at Piotr Petrovich.

'It might be done, but... we'll come back to that later... I mean, one might begin this very day. We'll see each other this evening, decide what to do, and lay the foundations, as it were. Come and see me here

around seven or so. Andrei Semionovich will join in too, I hope... But...
There's a certain matter that needs to be mentioned and carefully considered beforehand. That was why I troubled you, Sofia Semionovna,
and asked you to come up here. The fact is that, in my view, it is inad-
visable and dangerous to give money for Katerina Ivanovna into her
own hands. The proof of that is this very funeral wake taking place
today. At a time when she hasn't a single crust of daily bread set aside
for tomorrow, nor... well, nor any shoes or the rest of it—she buys
Jamaica rum, and even Madeira I believe, and—and—and coffee. I saw
all that on my way past. And tomorrow everything will fall back onto
your shoulders, right down to the last bit of bread. That's ridiculous,
I tell you. So that any subscription, in my own personal opinion, would
have to be organized so that the unfortunate widow, so to speak, knew
nothing about the money, and only you, for instance, knew about it. Am
I right?'

'I don't know, sir. It was just today that she... it's only once in a lifetime... she was so anxious to have him remembered, to do him honour,
in his memory... but she's very sensible, sir. Anyway, it's as you like, sir,
and I'll be very, very, very... they'll all be... and God will reward... and
the little orphans, sir...'

Sonia broke off and burst into tears.

'Quite so. Well then, bear that in mind; and now be so good as to
accept, on behalf of your parent, for her immediate needs, what I personally can afford. It is my most pressing wish that my name should not
be mentioned in this connection. Here you are, then... having cares of
my own, so to speak, I can't rise to any more...'

And Piotr Petrovich held out to Sonia a ten-rouble note, after first
carefully unfolding it. Sonia took it, blushed, jumped up, murmured
something, and began hurriedly taking her leave. Piotr Petrovich majestically escorted her to the door. She finally escaped from the room, full
of anguished agitation, and returned to Katerina Ivanovna in a state of
extreme embarrassment.

Throughout this scene Andrei Semionovich was either standing by
the window or walking about the room, not wishing to interrupt the
conversation. But when Sonia left, he suddenly approached Piotr
Petrovich and solemnly offered his hand:

'I heard everything, and *saw* everything,' he said with particular
emphasis. 'That was noble of you, I mean to say, it was humane of you!
You didn't want her gratitude, I could see that! And I must admit that
although I don't approve of private charity on principle, because it not
only cannot radically abolish an evil—it actually promotes it; even so

I have to admit that I viewed your action with pleasure—yes, yes, I was pleased at it.'

'Oh, that's all rubbish!' muttered Piotr Petrovich in some agitation, giving Lebeziatnikov a curious look.

'No, it's not rubbish! A man who has been insulted and vexed as you have been by yesterday's events, and who is still capable of thinking of other people's misfortunes—such a man... although his actions constitute a social error—nevertheless... deserves respect! I had actually not expected that from you, Piotr Petrovich, particularly since your own ideas—Oh, how your ideas get in your way! How upset you are, for instance, by yesterday's setback!' exclaimed the kind-hearted Andrei Semionovich, once more feeling particularly well disposed towards Piotr Petrovich. 'And what on earth do you need that particular marriage for, that *legal* marriage, Piotr Petrovich, my most kind and honourable friend? What's the point of that *legality* in your marriage? Well, thrash me if you like, but I'm glad, I'm glad that it didn't come off, and that you're free, that you're not entirely lost to humanity: I'm glad... There, I've spoken my mind!'

'The point is that in your sort of free marriage, I don't wish to wear a pair of horns and bring up another man's children; that's why I require a legal marriage,' replied Luzhin, just to say something. He was particularly preoccupied and pensive.

'Children? You mentioned children?' Andrei Semionovich started like a warhorse at the sound of a trumpet. 'Children are a social question, and a question of the utmost importance, I agree; but the question of children will be solved in a different way. Some people in fact reject children altogether, as they reject any reference to the family. We can talk about children later, but for now let's deal with the horns! I must confess they're my weakness. That grubby expression, straight out of Pushkin and his hussars,* is unthinkable in the lexicon of the future. What do horns mean? Oh, what a false idea! What horns? Why horns? What nonsense! On the contrary, in a free marriage they won't exist! Horns are nothing but the natural consequence of any legal marriage, the correction of it, as it were—a protest; and in that sense they're not in the least humiliating... And if—to assume an absurd idea—I were ever to enter into a legal marriage, I should actually be glad to wear your wretched horns: I'd say to my wife: "My friend, up till now I have merely loved you, but now I respect you, because you have actually made a protest!" You're laughing? That's because you're incapable of shaking yourself free from your preconceived ideas! Damn it, I understand very well how unpleasant it is when you're deceived in a legal marriage; but that's no more than the sordid consequence of a sordid situation, degrading to both partners. When horns are bestowed openly, as in a free marriage, then they no longer exist, they're unthinkable, and they lose the name of horns. On the contrary, your wife will do no more than prove her respect for you, viewing you as incapable of standing in the way of her happiness, and as progressive enough not to take revenge on her for her new husband. Dash it, I sometimes dream that if I were given in marriage—tchah! if I were to take a wife, I mean (in a free or a legal marriage, it doesn't matter), I believe I should personally introduce her to a lover, if she was very slow to find one for herself. "My friend", I'd say to her, "I love you, but beyond that I also want you to respect me—here, take him!" Isn't that right, what I'm saying?'

Piotr Petrovich sniggered as he listened to this, but without any particular amusement. Indeed, he wasn't really listening. In point of fact he was thinking about something else, as even Lebeziatnikov eventually noticed. Piotr Petrovich was quite agitated, rubbing his hands and brooding. Later on, Andrei Semionovich remembered this and realized why...

CHAPTER II

IT would be hard to say exactly what had caused Katerina Ivanovna's disordered mind to settle on the notion of this pointless funeral wake. Almost ten roubles had been squandered on it out of the twenty-odd she had received from Raskolnikov for Marmeladov's actual funeral. Perhaps Katerina Ivanovna had felt herself duty-bound before her late husband to honour his memory 'properly', so that all the lodgers, and Amalia Ivanovna in particular, should know that he was 'not only no worse than them, but perhaps much better', and that none of them had the right to 'turn up their noses at him'. It may be that she was chiefly motivated by that particular *poor person's pride* which drives a great many poor people, faced with one of those social rituals that our way of life imposes on anyone and everyone, to use up their last ounce of energy and waste the last penny of their savings in trying to prove that they're 'no worse than other people', and to prevent those other people from somehow 'thinking the worse' of them. And it's also highly likely that Katerina Ivanovna had wanted, on this particular occasion and at this precise moment, when everyone in the world seemed to have abandoned her, to demonstrate to all those 'nasty, worthless lodgers' that she not only 'knew how to live properly and entertain people', but had been brought up for a different sort of life altogether, in 'the genteel, practically aristocratic, household of an army colonel', and had never been meant to sweep her own floors or scrub her children's rags every night. Even the poorest and most abject people are sometimes visited by such paroxysms of pride and vanity, and among such people these occasionally grow into a morbid and irresistible compulsion. But Katerina Ivanovna herself wasn't abject: she might be driven to her death by circumstances, but she couldn't be morally crushed, that is, intimidated or subjected to another person's will. Furthermore, Sonechka had quite rightly said of her that her mind was becoming deranged. This couldn't yet be said as a positive, definite fact; but it was true that in recent times, over the whole of the past year, her poor head had been so tormented that it couldn't have failed to suffer some harm. And the doctors tell us that advanced consumption also tends to impair one's mental faculties.*

There was no great quantity or variety of wines and spirits there, nor was there any madeira; that had been an exaggeration. But there were alcoholic drinks. There was vodka, and rum, and port, all of the poorest quality, but all in adequate amounts. Apart from the *kutya*,* there were three or four kinds of food (incidentally including pancakes), all from Amalia Ivanovna's kitchen, and in addition there were two samovars going at the same time, for the tea and punch to be served after dinner. Katerina Ivanovna had seen to all the shopping herself, with the help of one of the lodgers, a pathetic little Pole living at Madame Lippewechsel's, heaven knows why; he had immediately volunteered his services to Katerina Ivanovna and had been running back and forth at a breakneck pace all the previous day and all this morning, with his tongue hanging out—and apparently trying his hardest to make sure that everyone observed this last fact. He sought out Katerina Ivanovna in person for all his trivial queries, even running to find her at Gostiny Dvor,* and constantly addressing her as 'Madam *Pani* Lieutenant'.* Eventually she grew sick to death of him, although to start with she had said she would have been utterly lost without this 'obliging and generous-hearted' person. It was a trait of Katerina Ivanovna's character that she would instantly paint anyone she met in the brightest and most flattering colours, praising them to the skies in terms that some even found embarrassing, inventing all sorts of stories to their credit that had never really happened, and believing sincerely and wholeheartedly that all of it was true; then she would suddenly become disillusioned, and rudely and contemptuously repulse the person she had been literally idolizing only a few hours earlier. By nature she was a humorous, cheerful, and peaceable woman, but her endless misfortunes and setbacks had made her long so *passionately* for everyone to live in peace and harmony together, and *not dare* to live otherwise, that the slightest discord in her life, the least upset, at once drove her into a frenzy, and from indulging the brightest of hopes and fantasies she would instantly fall to cursing fate, ripping up and throwing about whatever came to hand, and banging her head against the wall. Amalia Ivanovna, too, had suddenly come to impress Katerina Ivanovna as enormously important and worthy of extraordinary respect, perhaps just because of this funeral wake, and because Amalia Ivanovna had thrown herself heart and soul into the preparations. She had undertaken to set the table, provide table linen, cutlery and the rest, and prepare the food in her own kitchen. Katerina Ivanovna left everything to her, while she herself set off for the cemetery. And indeed, the preparations had been a triumph: the table was set quite neatly, with plates, forks, knives, small and large glasses and cups—everything borrowed from different lodgers, all in different sizes and patterns, but all set out ready by the appointed time. Amalia Ivanovna, feeling that she had acquitted herself very well, proudly welcomed the returning guests in all her finery, wearing a black dress and new mourning ribbons in her cap. This pride of hers, though well deserved, for some reason displeased Katerina Ivanovna—'just think, as if but for Amalia Ivanovna we'd never have got the table laid!' Nor did she approve of the cap with its new ribbons—'can it be that that stupid German woman is actually proud because she's the mistress of the house, and she's consented to help her poor lodgers out of charity? Charity! I ask you! My Papa, who was a colonel and very nearly Governor, would sometimes have a table laid in his house for forty guests, and your Amalia Ivanovna, or rather Ludwigovna, wouldn't even have been allowed in his kitchen...' However, Katerina Ivanovna had decided not to give vent to her feelings for the time being, although she had resolved in her heart that Amalia Ivanovna must be given a snub this very day and be put firmly in her place, or else she'd get heaven knows what ideas about herself. But meanwhile she just treated her coldly. And another unpleasant fact had contributed to Katerina Ivanovna's annoyance: out of all the lodgers invited to attend the funeral, almost no one had turned up apart from the little Pole, who had just managed to run down to the cemetery; and yet all the most insignificant and impoverished lodgers had turned up to the wake, the meal that is—some of them not even sober; nothing but riff-raff in fact. The older and more solid lodgers seemed to have deliberately conspired to stay away. Piotr Petrovich Luzhin, for instance, perhaps the most solid of them all, hadn't turned up, although only last night Katerina

Ivanovna had made a point of telling anyone and everyone—that is, Amalia Ivanovna, Polechka, Sonia, and the little Pole—that he was a most noble and generous man, very well connected and possessed of a fortune, who had been a friend of her first husband, had been received in her father's home, and had promised to do everything possible to procure her a substantial pension. It should be noted at this point that even if Katerina Ivanovna did boast of a person's connections and fortune, that was completely disinterested and devoid of any ulterior motive, purely out of the altruistic fullness of her heart, for the simple pleasure of adding to the consequence of whatever individual she was praising to the skies. Luzhin wasn't the only one who hadn't turned up; 'that nasty wretch' Lebeziatnikov, probably 'following his lead', had never appeared either. 'Who does that man think he is anyway? He was only invited out of kindness, merely because he shares a room with Piotr Petrovich and is friendly with him, so it would have been awkward not to ask him.' Another person who failed to turn up was a genteel lady with her 'old maid of a daughter', who although they had only lived in Amalia Ivanovna's rooms for a few weeks, had several times already complained of the noise and shouting coming up from the Marmeladovs' room, particularly when the late Marmeladov came home drunk; Katerina Ivanovna had of course found this out from Amalia Ivanovna herself, when that lady, in the midst of a quarrel with Katerina Ivanovna during which she had threatened to evict her whole family, had yelled at the top of her voice that they were upsetting the 'respectable lodgers whose shoes they weren't fit to wipe'. Now Katerina Ivanovna had made a point of inviting this lady and her daughter, whose shoes she supposedly 'wasn't fit to wipe'—and who, furthermore, had been haughtily turning her back on her if they ever happened to meet; just to let that woman know that 'there were people here who were more high-minded and delicate, and would proffer an invitation without harbouring any hard feelings', and show them that Katerina Ivanovna herself hadn't been used to living like this. She was resolved to explain all this to them at table, and tell them how her late Papa had been a Governor, and obliquely hint at the same time that turning away when they met was both unnecessary and extraordinarily stupid. The fat lieutenant colonel (in fact a retired staff captain) hadn't appeared either; but it turned out that he had been 'laid up' ever since the previous morning. In short, the only ones to turn up were the little Pole, a weedy little spotty-faced clerk in a greasy frock coat who smelt bad and never said a word, and a deaf and nearly blind old man who had once worked in some post office and whom someone had been supporting at Amalia

Ivanovna's since time immemorial, nobody knew why. And then there was a drunken retired lieutenant (in point of fact a supply clerk), with an offensively loud guffaw, and, 'just imagine', without a waistcoat! Another visitor had sat straight down at table without even bowing to Katerina Ivanovna; and finally, one person who didn't even possess a decent outfit had tried to come along in his dressing gown; but that was so grossly improper that he was turned away by the combined exertions of Amalia Ivanovna and the little Pole. The little Pole, as a matter of fact, had brought along a couple of other little Poles as well, who had never even lived at Amalia Ivanovna's and had never been seen in the house before. All this utterly exasperated Katerina Ivanovna. 'If that's how it's turned out, then what was the use of going to all this trouble?' To save space, even the children hadn't been given places at the table, which anyway filled the whole room; instead, places had been laid for them on a trunk in the far corner, where the two little ones sat on a bench while Polechka, as their big sister, had to look after them, feed them, and wipe their noses 'like well-brought-up children'. Katerina Ivanovna was obliged, whether she liked it or not, to welcome everyone with an even more ceremonious, not to say haughty, manner. She gave some of the guests a particularly stern look, as she loftily invited them to take their places at table. For some reason she regarded Amalia Ivanovna as responsible for all those who failed to appear, and suddenly began treating her in an extremely offhand way; which Amalia Ivanovna immediately observed, and took great offence. Such a beginning didn't bode well for the ending. Eventually everyone was seated.

Raskolnikov entered almost at the very moment when everyone was coming in from the cemetery. Katerina Ivanovna was terribly glad to see him, firstly because he was the only 'educated guest' of the whole company, who 'as everyone knew, was going to be appointed to a professorial chair at this university in two years' time'; and secondly because he immediately tendered his respectful apologies to her for having been prevented from attending the funeral as he had wished. She simply pounced upon him, seated him on her left hand at table (with Amalia Ivanovna on her right), and despite her constant fussing and worrying about having the food served up properly and making sure there was some for everyone, and despite her agonizing cough which kept interrupting her and leaving her gasping for breath—and which seemed to have got much more stubborn over the last two days—she kept up a constant flow of comments to Raskolnikov, hurriedly pouring out all her pent-up emotions and righteous indignation at the fiasco of this wake. But her indignation regularly alternated with the merriest and most uncontrollable laughter at the assembled guests, and particularly at the landlady herself.

'It's all that she-cuckoo's fault. You know whom I mean—her, over here!' and Katerina Ivanovna nodded towards the landlady. 'Look at her—her eyes are popping out, she can tell we're talking about her, but she can't hear what we're saying, so she's just goggling. Oooh, what an owl! Ha-ha-ha! Khe-khe-khe! And what's she trying to prove, with that cap of hers? Khe-khe-khe! Have you noticed, she keeps wanting everybody to feel that she's patronizing us and honouring us by her presence. I'd asked her, as a decent soul, to invite some respectable people, and especially some who knew my husband; but look what she's brought in! A bunch of clowns! Scarecrows! Look at that one with the spotty face—a wet nose-rag on two legs! And those Polacks... ha-ha-ha! Khe-khe-khe! Nobody on earth has ever seen them here before, and nor have I; so what have they come for, I ask you? All sitting meekly side by side. Hey, *Pane*!' she suddenly called out to one of them. 'Have you had some pancakes? Have some more! And beer, have some beer! Or wouldn't you like some vodka?—Look at him, he's jumped up, and he's bowing in all directions, look, look! They must be famished, poor things! Never mind, let them eat. At least they're not making a noise; though... though honestly, I fear for the landlady's silver spoons!... Amalia Ivanovna!' she addressed her, almost out loud. 'If somebody happens to steal your spoons, I take no responsibility: you've been warned! Ha-ha-ha!' and she roared with laughter, turning back to Raskolnikov, nodding once again in the landlady's direction and enjoying her sally. 'She hasn't got it, she still hasn't got it! Sitting there with her mouth open, just look: a proper owl, a screech-owl in new ribbons, ha-ha-ha!'

At this point her laughter again gave way to a fit of unbearable coughing which went on for five minutes. There was some blood left on her handkerchief, and beads of sweat appeared on her brow. She silently showed Raskolnikov the blood, and as soon as she got her breath back she began whispering to him again with extraordinary animation, while the red spots came out on her cheeks:

'Look, I'd entrusted her with the most delicate task—inviting that lady and her daughter, you know who I mean? It was vital for her to be as tactful as she possibly could, and manage it really cleverly—but the way she went about it meant that that half-witted newcomer, that arrogant piece, that provincial nobody, just because she's the widow of some major or other and has come here to get herself a pension, fraying her skirts on government office floors, a woman of fifty-five who dyes her hair and covers herself in rouge and powder (everybody knows that)... and a creature like that not only didn't condescend to appear, she didn't even send an apology when she didn't turn up, though that would have been no more than common politeness! And I can't understand why Piotr Petrovich hasn't come either! But where's Sonia? Where's she got to? Oh, here she is at last! Well, Sonia, where have you been? Strange that you're so unpunctual, even for your father's funeral. Rodion Romanovich, make room for her next to you. There's your place, Sonechka... have whatever you like. Have some meat jelly, that's the best. They're just going to bring the pancakes. Have the children been served? Polechka, have you got everything there? Khe-khe-khe! Well, that's fine. Be a good girl, Lenia; and Kolia, don't swing your legs, sit properly like a well-bred little boy. What can you tell me, Sonechka?'

Sonia hastily passed on Piotr Petrovich's apology, trying to raise her voice so that everyone could hear, and using the most select and respectful expressions which she put into Piotr Petrovich's mouth and then embellished on her own account. She added that Piotr Petrovich had especially asked her to convey to her mother that he meant to come and see her without fail, just as soon as he could manage it, to discuss some *business* alone with her, and arrange what could be done for her and undertaken in the future, and so on.

Sonia knew that this would calm and reassure Katerina Ivanovna, that she'd feel flattered, and above all that her pride would be gratified. She had sat down next to Raskolnikov and made him a hurried bow, while giving him a fleeting and curious look; but otherwise she seemed to avoid looking at him or speaking to him. She looked almost absent-minded, although she kept watching Katerina Ivanovna's face to see if she could help her. Neither she nor Katerina Ivanovna was wearing mourning, since they possessed nothing suitable; Sonia was wearing dark brown, while Katerina Ivanovna was wearing the only dress she had, a dark-coloured striped cotton print. The news about Piotr Petrovich was very well received. Katerina listened with dignity to what Sonia told her, and enquired with no less dignity about Piotr Petrovich's health. Then she went straight on to whisper to Raskolnikov, almost aloud, that it would indeed have been a strange thing for such a respected and well-to-do man as Piotr Petrovich to find himself in such 'extraordinary company', for all his devotion to her family and his old friendship with her Papa.

'That's why I'm particularly grateful to you, Rodion Romanich, for not turning up your nose at my hospitality, even in such surroundings,' she added half-aloud; 'but I'm sure it was only your particular friendship with my poor late husband that induced you to keep your word.'

After which she again cast a proud, dignified glance over her guests, and suddenly and most solicitously called loudly across the table to the deaf old man to ask him whether 'he wouldn't like a little more of the roast, and had he been served with port?' The old man didn't reply, and for a long time couldn't understand what he was being asked, though his neighbours were amusing themselves by vigorously nudging him. He just stared about him open-mouthed, which made everyone laugh even more.

'What an oaf! Look, look at him! What did they bring him here for? But as for Piotr Petrovich, I always had every confidence in him,' Katerina Ivanovna went on to Raskolnikov, 'and of course he's nothing like...'—and here she startled Amalia Ivanovna by addressing her sharply and loudly, and putting on an extraordinarily severe expression, 'nothing like those tarted-up draggle-tails, who'd never even have been taken on as cooks in Papa's house, while my late husband, needless to say, would have been doing them an honour by receiving them, and that only because he was so endlessly good-natured.'

'Yes, he liked his drink, that he did, and he certainly drank!' cried the retired supply-clerk suddenly, draining his twelfth glass of vodka.

'My late husband did indeed have that weakness, as everyone knows,' said Katerina Ivanovna, turning on him sharply; 'but he was a kind and noble man who loved and respected his family; his only fault was that his kind heart led him to place too much trust in all sorts of dissolute people, and heaven only knows whom he didn't drink with—people who weren't fit to wipe his shoes! Imagine, Rodion Romanovich: they found a gingerbread cockerel in his pocket: he was walking about dead drunk, but he'd remembered the children.'

'A cock-er-el? Did you say a cock-er-el?' cried the supply clerk.

Katerina Ivanovna didn't deign to answer him, but sighed, lost in thought.

'Now I dare say you think, like everybody else, that I was too severe with him,' she went on to Raskolnikov. 'But that wasn't so! He respected me, he respected me very deeply! He was a good-hearted man! And he made one so sorry for him sometimes! He'd be sitting in the corner, looking at me, and I'd feel so sorry for him, and want to be nice to him, and then I'd think to myself: "if you're nice to him now, he'll just get drunk again". The only way to control him at all was to be strict with him.'

'Oh yes, he used to get his hair pulled, that happened time and again,' roared the supply clerk once again, tipping another glass of vodka down his throat.

'There are some fools that could do with more than hair-pulling— a thrashing with a broom handle would serve them right! And I don't mean my poor husband!' Katerina Ivanovna snapped back at him.

The red patches on her cheeks stood out more and more, and her chest heaved. Another minute and she'd have started a scene. Many of the guests were tittering and openly enjoying this. People were nudging the supply clerk and whispering something to him, evidently keen to get the two of them into a fight.

'And might I a-a-ask you just what you meant, madam,' began the supply clerk, 'that is, which... honourable individual... you had in mind just now... Oh well, never mind! It's nothing! A widow! Little widow! I forgive you... Forget it!' And he downed another shot of vodka.

Raskolnikov sat and listened in silent disgust. He ate very little, and only out of politeness, barely tasting the morsels that Katerina Ivanovna kept loading onto his plate, and just trying not to upset her. He looked intently at Sonia, who was growing ever more anxious and fearful. She, too, could feel that the wake wasn't going to end peacefully, and was watching in mounting alarm as Katerina Ivanovna grew more and more annoyed. She knew, incidentally, why the two lady newcomers had treated Katerina Ivanovna's invitation with such contempt: it was because of Sonia herself. She had heard from Amalia Ivanovna in person that the mother had actually taken offence at the invitation, and demanded 'how could she possibly have seated her daughter next to *that young person*?' Sonia had the feeling that Katerina Ivanovna had somehow already found out about this, and that the insult to her, Sonia, meant more to Katerina Ivanovna than an insult to herself, or her children, or her Papa; in fact it was a mortal insult, and Sonia knew that Katerina Ivanovna would never rest now 'until she had shown those two draggle-tails that they were both...' etc. etc. To make matters worse, someone at the other end of the table had passed along to Sonia a plate bearing two hearts pierced by an arrow, moulded out of black bread. Katerina Ivanovna flared up and instantly retorted down the table that the person responsible was obviously 'a drunken ass'. Amalia Ivanovna also had a premonition that something bad was going to happen, besides being wounded to the depths of her soul by Katerina Ivanovna's supercilious attitude; so she tried to dissipate the unpleasant atmosphere of the party and at the same time improve people's opinion of her by suddenly launching, apropos of nothing, into a story about some acquaintance of hers, 'Karl from the pharmacy', who was riding in a carriage one night when 'the coachman want to killing him, and Karl very, very much begging that he don't him kill, and crying, and clasping together hands, and frightening, and from fright his heart piercing'. Katerina Ivanovna did smile at this, but remarked straight away that Amalia Ivanovna had no business telling stories in Russian. Amalia Ivanovna took even greater offence at this and rejoined that her '*Vater aus Berlin* is being very, very important mans and always in pockets hands putting'. Katerina Ivanovna couldn't stop herself getting the giggles, at which Amalia Ivanovna came close to losing the last shreds of her patience and barely managed to control her temper.

'Look at that screech owl!' Katerina Ivanovna whispered merrily to Raskolnikov. 'She meant to say he went around with his hands in his pockets, but what came out was that he was always picking pockets, khe-khe! And Rodion Romanovich, have you noticed that it's always this way—all these foreigners in Petersburg, I mean, the Germans most of all, who come here from heaven knows where—they're all stupider than us! You must admit, how could anyone tell a story about "Karl from the pharmacy who from fright his heart piercing", and how he—what a drip!—instead of tying up his coachman, "is clasping together his hands, and crying, and very much begging"! What an ass! And you know, she thinks all that's very moving, and has no idea how stupid she is! I reckon that drunken supply clerk is far smarter than she is; at least you can see he's a soak who's drunk himself silly, while everybody else is so very prim and proper... Just look at her sitting there, with her eyes popping. She's so cross! So cross! Ha-ha-ha! Khe-khe-khe!'

Katerina Ivanovna had now cheered up, and launched straight away into a most detailed explanation of how she was going to use the pension that she was about to receive to set up a boarding school for young ladies in her home town of T——.* Raskolnikov had never heard of this boarding school from Katerina Ivanovna, and she instantly began expanding on all its most attractive details. Somehow or other she turned out to have in her hands that same 'certificate of merit' that Marmeladov himself had described to Raskolnikov, when they were in the drinking shop and he had told him how his wife Katerina Ivanovna, on leaving school, had danced the shawl dance 'in the presence of the Governor and other personages'. This certificate was evidently now intended to demonstrate Katerina Ivanovna's right to set up her own boarding school; but more importantly still, it had been kept in reserve as a final put-down to 'those two tarted-up draggle-tails', should they turn up to the wake, and as conclusive proof that Katerina Ivanovna came from 'the most honourable, one might even say aristocratic home,

that she was a colonel's daughter, and undoubtedly superior to certain
adventure-seekers of whom there were so many about these days'. The
certificate of merit was immediately passed round the drunken guests,
with Katerina Ivanovna doing nothing to prevent it, because it did
indeed state *en toutes lettres* that she was the daughter of a Court Councillor
with a civil decoration, and in consequence was really almost a colonel's
daughter.* Getting rather carried away, Katerina Ivanovna went on to
describe in full detail the fine and tranquil life she would lead at T——,
and mentioned the high-school teachers she would invite to give lessons at her establishment, and a certain respectable old Frenchman,
Monsieur Mangot, who had taught French to Katerina Ivanovna herself when she was a schoolgirl, and who was still living out his days in
T—— and would no doubt come and teach at her school at a most reasonable rate. Eventually her talk turned to Sonia too, 'who would accompany Katerina Ivanovna to T—— and assist her in every way'. But at
that someone snorted with laughter, and although Katerina Ivanovna
tried to pretend that she scorned to notice the mirth that erupted at the
far end of the table, she immediately raised her voice and started talking
enthusiastically about Sofia Semionovna's undoubted qualifications to
serve as her assistant, and how 'meek, long-suffering, selfless, noble and
well-educated' she was. And she patted Sonia on the cheek, and stood
up to give her a couple of affectionate kisses. Sonia flushed, and
Katerina Ivanovna suddenly burst into tears, telling herself that 'she
was a silly, nervous thing and much too upset, and it was time to finish;
and since the meal was over it was time to pour the tea'. At that very
moment Amalia Ivanovna, by now thoroughly offended at not having
had the slightest part in this whole conversation, nor even been listened
to, ventured on one last effort and allowed herself, despite secret misgivings, to risk imparting to Katerina Ivanovna a highly practical and
well-considered suggestion: that in her future boarding school she
would need to pay particular attention to the young ladies' linen (*die
Wäsche*) and 'is absolute necessary there is one very good lady (*die Dame*)
that is after the linen vell looking', and furthermore, 'that all young
ladies in night-time not secretly any novel reading'. Katerina Ivanovna,
who really was very tired and upset, and quite fed up with the wake by
this time, instantly cut Amalia Ivanovna short and retorted that she was
'talking a lot of rubbish' and didn't understand anything; that attending to *die Wäsche* was the housekeeper's business and not that of the
directress of a superior boarding school; and as for reading novels, the
whole idea was most improper and would she kindly hold her tongue.
Amalia Ivanovna fired up and venomously remarked that she 'only

wishing good', and 'always very much wishing good', but that she 'is for long time not paid *das Geld* for lodging'. Katerina Ivanovna instantly 'put her down' again, maintaining that her claim to be 'wishing good' was a lie, since only yesterday, with the dead man still laid out on the table, she had been badgering her for the rent. To this Amalia Ivanovna very logically replied that she 'inviting those ladies, but those ladies not coming because those ladies respectable ladies are, and to unrespectable lady not can come'. Katerina Ivanovna forcefully pointed out to her that since she was a slut she couldn't judge what true respectability meant. Amalia Ivanovna couldn't put up with this and instantly announced that her '*Vater aus Berlin* is very, very important person and with both hands in pockets walking, and all the time so speaking: Puff! Puff!' And in order to better portray her father, Amalia Ivanovna sprang up from her chair, shoved both hands in her pockets, blew out her cheeks, and began uttering indistinct noises that sounded like 'puff-puff'; all the lodgers laughed loudly at this and tried to egg her on, in the hopes of a fight. Katerina Ivanovna could stand this no longer, and rapped out in everyone's hearing that Amalia Ivanovna might well have never had a *Vater* at all, being nothing but a drunken Petersburg Finn who had very likely once served as someone's cook, if not worse. Amalia Ivanovna flushed red as a lobster and shrieked that it might be Katerina Ivanovna who 'is never at all a *Vater* having', but she herself had a '*Vater aus Berlin* who is such long frock-coat wearing and always making Puff! Puff! Puff!' Katerina Ivanovna replied contemptuously that her own origins were known to all and that this very same certificate of merit stated in print that her father was a colonel; but that Amalia Ivanovna's father (if indeed she had ever had one) had no doubt been some sort of Petersburg Finn and a milk merchant; even more likely, she had never had a father at all, since to this very day nobody knew what Amalia Ivanovna's patronymic was—was she Ivanovna or Ludwigovna?* Amalia Ivanovna, now wild with fury, thumped her fist on the table and shrieked that she was 'Amal-Ivan' and not Ludwigovna, and her *Vater* 'is Johann calling and he is *Bürgermeister*',* and that Katerina Ivanovna's *Vater* 'is quite never a *Bürgermeister* being'. Katerina Ivanovna rose from her chair and remarked in a stern but seemingly calm voice (though she had turned very pale and her chest was heaving) that if she ever again dared 'to mention her wretched little *Vater* in the same breath as her own Papenka, then she, Katerina Ivanovna, would tear off her cap and stamp on it'. On hearing this, Amalia Ivanovna began running about the room shouting at the top of her voice that she was the mistress of the house and that Katerina Ivanovna was 'in this minute from the flat leaving';

after which for some reason she rushed to retrieve her silver spoons from the table. Amid shouts and uproar, the children burst into tears. Sonia ran to try and restrain Katerina Ivanovna; but when Amalia Ivanovna suddenly yelled something about a yellow card, Katerina Ivanovna shoved Sonia aside and advanced on Amalia Ivanovna, meaning to carry out her threat about the cap on the spot. At that moment the door opened, and on the threshold appeared Piotr Petrovich Luzhin. He stood and surveyed the assembled company with a stern, piercing gaze. Katerina Ivanovna ran over to him.

CHAPTER III

'Piotr Petrovich!' she cried, 'you at least must stand up for me! Get this half-witted creature to see that she's not to dare treat a respectable lady like this, when she's struck down by misfortune. There are laws against it... I'll go to the Governor General myself... She'll have to answer for it... Remember my father's hospitality to you, and defend us orphans!'

'Allow me, madam... Allow me, please, allow me, madam,' said Piotr Petrovich, brushing her aside. 'As you are well aware, I never had the honour of knowing your Papa... Excuse me, madam!' (Someone guffawed loudly at this point.) 'And I don't mean to get involved in your everlasting squabbles with Amalia Ivanovna... I'm here for reasons of my own...and I should like to have a talk, straight away, with your stepdaughter Sofia... Ivanovna... isn't it? Kindly let me pass...'

And Piotr Petrovich edged past Katerina Ivanovna and advanced towards Sonia in the far corner.

Katerina Ivanovna stood frozen to the spot as if thunderstruck. She couldn't fathom how Piotr Petrovich could deny her Papa's hospitality. Having once invented it, she now devoutly believed in it herself. And she was shocked, too, by Piotr Petrovich's cold and businesslike tone of voice, sounding full of contempt and menace. Indeed, everyone had gradually fallen silent when he appeared. Not only was this 'businesslike and serious' person quite out of keeping with everyone else there—it was obvious, too, that he had come about something important; there must have been some extraordinary reason to bring him into this company, and consequently something must be about to happen. Raskolnikov, standing beside Sonia, stood aside to let him pass; Piotr Petrovich didn't seem to notice him at all. A minute later, Lebeziatnikov also appeared in the doorway; he didn't come into the room, but stood there with an air of extreme curiosity and almost astonishment. He listened to what was said, but for a long time seemed not to understand.

'Forgive me if I am intruding, but the matter is rather important,' began Piotr Petrovich, speaking to the assembled company without addressing anyone in particular. 'As a matter of fact, I am glad to have this audience. Amalia Ivanovna, may I entreat you, as mistress of the house, to pay attention to the conversation I am about to have with Sofia Ivanovna. Sofia Ivanovna,' he went on, now directly addressing her as she stood there, shocked and apprehensive about what was to come, 'on my table, in the room of my friend Andrei Semionovich Lebeziatnikov, I had a banknote to the value of one hundred roubles, and immediately after your visit to me that banknote had disappeared. If you know, in any way at all, where it is now, and you tell us, then I give you my word of honour, and call on everyone here to witness, that the matter will end there. If you do not, I shall be obliged to have recourse to very serious measures, and in that case, miss..., you will only have yourself to blame.'

The room fell completely silent. Even the children stopped crying. Sonia stood pale as death, staring at Luzhin and unable to say a word. She seemed not to have understood. A few seconds passed.

'Well, so what do you say?' demanded Luzhin, staring hard at her.

'I don't know... I don't know anything...' Sonia finally managed to answer in a faint voice.

'You don't? You don't know?' insisted Luzhin, and waited in silence a few seconds longer. 'Think, mademoiselle,' he said sternly, but still in a coaxing tone, 'think about it; I am willing to allow you time to reflect. You must understand—if I were not so certain, then obviously with my experience I should never risk directly accusing you like this; for I would, in a sense, have to answer for it if I made such a direct and public accusation and it was then found false, or even merely mistaken. I am aware of that. This morning I had occasion to cash a number of five-per-cent bonds with a nominal value of three thousand roubles. I made a note of the calculations in my pocketbook. On returning home, I proceeded to count this money, as Andrei Semionovich can witness; and having counted out two thousand three hundred roubles, I put that money away in my pocketbook, and placed the pocketbook in the side pocket of my overcoat. There remained on the table some five hundred roubles in banknotes, including three notes of one hundred roubles each. At that moment you arrived (at my invitation), and as long as you were with me you were in a state of extreme embarrassment, so much so that on three occasions, in the middle of our conversation, you rose and seemed for some reason in a hurry to leave, although our conversation was not yet over. Andrei Semionovich can testify to all this. You yourself, mademoiselle, will probably not refuse to confirm and declare that I sent for you, through Andrei Semionovich, for the sole purpose of discussing with you the destitute and helpless situation of your relative, Katerina Ivanovna (whose funeral dinner I was unable to attend), and the question of how best to set up something like a subscription, a lottery, or something of the sort, for her benefit. You thanked me, and were even in tears (I am relating everything just as it happened, firstly to remind you, and secondly to show you that not the slightest detail has escaped my memory). After that I picked up a ten-rouble note from the table and handed it to you, as a gift from myself, for the benefit of your relative, for her immediate needs. All this was observed by Andrei Semionovich. Then I saw you to the door—with you still in the same state of embarrassment—after which I remained alone with Andrei Semionovich and talked with him for ten minutes or so. Then he left, and I returned to my table with the money on it, intending to count it and then put it aside in a separate place, as I had already decided. To my surprise, I found that one of the hundred-rouble notes was missing. Now just consider: I cannot possibly suspect Andrei Semionovich—I'm embarrassed even to mention such a thing. Nor can I have made a mistake in the count, since one minute before your arrival I had finished the calculation and found the total to be correct. You must agree that—remembering your confusion, your haste to be gone, and the fact that for some time you had your hands on the table, and finally, considering your social situation and the habits associated with it—I was compelled, in horror, so to speak, and against my will, to harbour a suspicion which, while of course cruel, is justified! I would further add, once again, that despite all my *evident* certainty, I am aware that my present accusation carries a certain risk to myself. But as you see, I could not let the matter pass. I acted, and I shall tell you why: solely, miss, solely because of your blackest ingratitude! What? I invite you to come and see me in the interests of your destitute relative, and personally offer you such help as I can afford, that is, ten roubles; and instantly, on the spot, you repay me with such a deed! No, miss, that was very, very bad! You need to be taught a lesson. So think well: I am asking you, as your sincere friend (for at this time you could have no better friend than I): think carefully! Otherwise I shall be merciless! So, how is it to be?'

'I never took anything from you,' whispered Sonia in terror. 'You gave me ten roubles: here, take them.' Sonia pulled out her handkerchief, hunted for the little knot in it, untied it and took out a ten-rouble note, which she offered to Luzhin in her outstretched hand.

'And the other hundred roubles—you still deny any knowledge of them?' he pronounced insistently and reproachfully, without taking the note.

Sonia looked about her. Everyone was staring at her with such dreadful, stern, mocking, hateful faces. She glanced at Raskolnikov... who stood by the wall, arms folded, watching her with burning eyes.

'Oh God!' Sonia burst out.

'Amalia Ivanovna, the police will have to be informed, so meanwhile I respectfully request you to send for the porter,' said Luzhin quietly, even gently.

'*Gott der barmherzige!** I know all the time, she stealing!' exclaimed Amalia Ivanovna, throwing up her hands.

'You knew?' Luzhin took her up. 'So even before this, you had some grounds at least for suspecting that. If you please, most respected Amalia Ivanovna, remember your words, which in any event have been spoken before witnesses.'

Loud voices suddenly broke out all around them, and there was a general stir.

'Wha-a-at!' cried Katerina Ivanovna, suddenly recalling herself and launching herself at Luzhin. 'What! You're accusing her of stealing? Accusing Sonia? Oh, you villains, you villains!' And she ran over to Sonia and flung her withered arms around her, squeezing her in a vice-like grip.

'Sonia! How dared you take ten roubles from him? Oh, you foolish girl! Hand them over! Give me those ten roubles at once! Here they are!'

And snatching the note from Sonia, Katerina Ivanovna crumpled it in her hands and hurled it straight at Luzhin's face. The ball of paper hit him in the eye and fell to the ground. Amalia Ivanovna ran to pick the money up. Piotr Petrovich grew angry.

'Restrain that madwoman!' he shouted.

At that moment some new faces appeared beside Lebeziatnikov in the doorway, the two visiting ladies among them.

'What's that? Madwoman? I'm a madwoman, am I? Fool!' shrieked Katerina Ivanovna. 'Fool yourself, you courtroom rat, you disgusting brute! Sonia, Sonia, to take money off him! You think Sonia's a thief? Why, she'd give you her own money herself, you fool!' And Katerina Ivanovna burst into hysterical laughter. 'Ever seen such a fool?' she demanded, addressing everyone around her and pointing at Luzhin. 'What? You too?' she added, noticing her landlady. 'So you're in it too, you German sausage-merchant, claiming that "she stealing", you worthless Prussian chicken-leg dressed up in crinolines! Oh, you people! You people! She's never even been out of this room—as soon as she came back from you, you villain, she sat right down here beside Rodion Romanovich!... Search her! She's never gone anywhere, so the money still has to be on her! So find it, look for it, look for it! Only, if you don't find it, then I'm sorry, my dear man, but you'll answer for it! I'll go straight to the Emperor, the Emperor himself, I'll run to the Tsar in person, the merciful Tsar, and throw myself at his feet—I'll do it right now, this very day! I'm a poor orphan! They'll let me pass! You think they won't? Lies, I'll get there! I'll get there, I will! You banked on her being so meek and mild, did you? Was that your idea? Well, I'm not meek, my friend! You'll come unstuck! So hunt for it! Go on, go on, I tell you, go on, find it!'

And Katerina Ivanovna shook Luzhin in a fury and tried to drag him towards Sonia.

'I'm prepared to do that, and I'll take the responsibility... but calm down, madam, calm down. I'm all too well aware that you're not meek!... But... but... what's to be done?' Luzhin mumbled, 'This ought to be done with the police here... although actually, there are more than enough witnesses here anyway... I'm ready... But in any case it's not right for a man... because of his sex... If we could have the assistance of Amalia Ivanovna... although actually that's not how it ought to be... What's to be done?'

'Anyone you like! Anyone who wants to search her, go right ahead and search her!' cried Katerina Ivanovna. 'Sonia, turn out your pockets for them! Here, here! Look, you monster, here's an empty one, there was a handkerchief here, the pocket's empty, see! And here's another pocket, here, here! Look, look!'

And Katerina Ivanovna didn't so much turn out the pockets as yank them out, one after the other. But out of the second pocket, on the right, a piece of paper suddenly flipped out, described a parabola through the air, and fell at Luzhin's feet. Everyone saw it, and many cried out. Piotr Petrovich bent down, picked the paper up from the floor between two fingers, lifted it high so that everyone could see, and unfolded it. It was a hundred-rouble banknote, folded in eight. Piotr Petrovich waved his arm around in a circle to show the note to everyone.

'Thief! Out from the house! Police, police!' howled Amalia Ivanovna. 'They must sending to Siberia! Out!'

People were exclaiming on all sides. Raskolnikov said nothing, but kept his eyes fixed on Sonia, only switching his gaze briefly to Luzhin from time to time. Sonia still stood where she had been, looking utterly dazed—she was barely even surprised. Suddenly the colour flooded back to her face, she cried out and covered it with her hands.

'No, it wasn't me! I didn't take it! I don't know anything!' she cried with a heart-rending shriek, and ran over to Katerina Ivanovna, who caught her up and pressed her close, trying to shield her with her own body against everyone around.

'Sonia! Sonia! I don't believe it! You can see I don't believe it!' she cried, in the face of all the evidence. And she rocked her in her arms like a little child, giving her endless kisses, catching up her hands and fervently kissing them too. 'The idea that you could have taken it! What stupid people they are! Oh Lord! You're all stupid, stupid!' she cried, addressing everyone present. 'You don't know anything, you don't know what a heart she has, what sort of a girl she is! For her to steal, her of all people! When she'd give up her last garment and sell it, and go barefoot, and give you everything, if you needed it, that's what she's like! And she only took the yellow card because my own children were starving to death, she's sold herself for us!... Oh, my poor husband, my husband! Oh, my husband, my husband! Do you see? Do you see? What a funeral wake for you! Good God! Well, go on, defend her, what are you all standing there for? Rodion Romanovich! How come you don't speak up for her? Do you believe it too? You're not worth her little finger, any of you, not one, not one! Oh God! Save her now!'

The wails of poor, consumptive, bereaved Katerina Ivanovna seemed to have a powerful effect on the company. There was so much anguish, so much suffering in that face, distorted with pain and wasted with disease, in those parched lips flecked with dried blood, in those hoarse screams, those sobbing cries like the cries of a weeping child, that everyone appeared to feel pity for the wretched woman. At all events, Piotr Petrovich *took pity* on her at once.

'Madam! Madam!' he exclaimed in impressive tones. 'All this does not touch you! No one would dare to accuse you of planning or consenting to such a thing, particularly since it was you who found it out, when you turned out her pockets—evidently you had suspected nothing. I am most, most ready to be compassionate if it was, so to speak, destitution that motivated Sofia Semionovna too—but why, mademoiselle, would you not confess? Scared of the disgrace? The first step? Lost your head, perhaps? Understandable, most understandable... But how could you let yourself go down that path? Gentlemen!'—and he turned to the assembled company, 'Gentlemen! I regret and, so to speak, sympathize, and am even ready to forgive, even now, despite the personal insults heaped on me. But,' turning to Sonia, 'may your present shame, mademoiselle, serve as a lesson to you for the future. And now I shall leave it at that—so be it, the matter is closed. Enough!'

Piotr Petrovich cast a sidelong glance at Raskolnikov, and their eyes met. Raskolnikov's burning look could have shrivelled him to ashes. Katerina Ivanovna, meanwhile, seemed deaf to everything now, hugging and kissing Sonia like a crazed woman. The children had also flung their little arms around Sonia, while Polechka—who didn't entirely understand what was going on—was drowning in tears, shaking with sobs, and hiding her pretty little face, all swollen with crying, on Sonia's shoulder.

'How shabby!' proclaimed a loud voice from the doorway.

Piotr Petrovich looked round quickly.

'What a low trick!' repeated Lebeziatnikov, glaring straight in his face.

Piotr Petrovich gave a start. Everyone noticed. (Later on, people remembered it.) Lebeziatnikov strode into the room.

'And you dared to call me as a witness?' he demanded, coming up to Piotr Petrovich.

'What is the meaning of this, Andrei Semionovich? What is it you're talking about?' muttered Luzhin.

'What it means is that you're a... slanderer. That's what my words mean!' declared Lebeziatnikov vehemently, looking sternly at him out of his short-sighted little eyes. He was frightfully angry. Raskolnikov was devouring him with his eyes, as though seizing and weighing up every word. Another silence fell. Piotr Petrovich seemed at a loss, particularly at first.

'If it's me you mean...' he stammered, 'what's up with you? Are you in your right mind?'

'I'm in my right mind, but as for you... you're a swindler! Oh, how vile that was! I was listening to everything, I kept waiting to try and make it all out, because I have to admit that even now it doesn't quite make sense... But why you did all that, I just can't comprehend.'

'But what is it that I've done? Will you stop talking in these stupid riddles! Or perhaps you're drunk?'

'You may be a drinker, you scum, but I'm not! I never even touch vodka—it's against my principles! Would you believe it—he was the one, he himself, who gave Sofia Semionovna that hundred-rouble note, with his own hands—I saw it, I'll bear witness to it, I'll take an oath on it! It was him, him!' repeated Lebeziatnikov, addressing each and every person in the room.

'Are you raving mad, you imbecile?' bellowed Luzhin. 'She's just confirmed, right here in front of you, confirmed in everybody's presence, just now, that apart from ten roubles she received nothing from me. So in that case, how could I possibly have given it her?'

'I saw it, I saw it!' Lebeziatnikov shouted insistently. 'And even if it's against my principles, I'm prepared to swear whatever oath you like, before a court, right now, because I saw you slipping it to her on the sly! Only, like a fool, I thought that you'd done that out of generosity! When you were seeing her out of the door, and she turned round and you shook her hand with one of yours, your other hand, the left one, was secretly sliding the note into her pocket. I saw you! I did!'

Luzhin turned pale.

'What nonsense!' he snapped. 'Anyway, how could you have made out the banknote, when you were standing over by the window? With your short sight, you simply imagined it. You're raving!'

'No, I didn't imagine it! And although I was standing quite a way off, I saw it all, all of it, and I grant it would have been difficult to make out a banknote from the window—you're quite right there—but there was a particular reason why I knew it was a hundred-rouble note, because when you were giving Sofia Semionovna the ten-rouble note—I saw this myself—you took a hundred-rouble note off the table at the same time (I saw that because I was standing nearby just then, and since a particular idea occurred to me at once, I didn't forget that you were holding the note). You folded it and kept it hidden in your hand from then on. After that I almost forgot about it again, but when you got up, you shifted it from your right hand to your left, and almost dropped it; and then I remembered once more, because the same idea occurred to me again, which was that you wanted to do her a kindness without my seeing it. You can imagine how closely I watched you after that—and so I saw you manage to slip it into her pocket. I saw it, I saw it, and I'll swear on oath I did!'

Lebeziatnikov was gasping for breath. Exclamations could be heard on every side, mostly surprised ones—but some sounded menacing. People crowded round Piotr Petrovich. Katerina Ivanovna rushed over to Lebeziatnikov.

'Andrei Semionovich! I was wrong about you! Please defend her! You're the only one on her side! She's an orphan, God has sent you to her! Andrei Semionovich, our dear friend and protector!'

And Katerina Ivanovna, scarcely aware of what she was doing, fell to her knees before him.

'That's a pack of lies!' roared Luzhin, in a blind rage. 'Nothing but a pack of lies, sir. "I forgot, I remembered, I forgot"—what's the meaning of all that? So I slipped it to her on purpose, did I? What for? What was I thinking of? What have I got in common with that...'

'What for? Now that's something I can't understand myself; but that I'm telling the honest truth, that's a fact! I'm so sure of myself, you loathsome criminal, that I remember asking myself that question straight away, just as I was thanking you and shaking your hand. Why exactly did you put it into her pocket on the sly? I mean, why do it stealthily? Could it really have been just so as to keep it from me, because you knew that my principles are the opposite of yours, and that I don't believe in private charity because it never really solves the problem? Well, I did decide that you were embarrassed to let me see you giving such a large sum; and besides, I thought, perhaps he wants to give her a surprise—wants her to be so astonished when she finds a whole hundred roubles in her pocket. (Because some do-gooders like to disguise their good deeds that way, I know.) And then it occurred to me that you might be wanting to test her, to see if she'd come and thank you when she found the money. Or else that you wanted to avoid her gratitude, so that, how do they put it—so that the right hand shouldn't know...* or whatever it is; anyway, something like that... Well, a whole lot of ideas passed through my mind at the time, so I decided to think it all through later, but I still thought it would be indelicate of me to let you see that I knew your secret. However, another problem occurred to me straight away: that Sofia Semionovna might accidentally lose the money before ever noticing it; that was why I decided to come here, ask for her and let her know that a hundred roubles had been put in her pocket. And on my way I dropped in to the Kobyliatnikovs' room to take them *A General Deduction from the Positive Method*, and especially to recommend Piderit's article (and Wagner's too, actually);* then I got here, and what a scene I found! Now could I ever, ever have had all those thoughts and ideas if I hadn't really seen you putting a hundred roubles into her pocket?'

When Andrei Semionovich had finished his long-winded argument, with such a logical conclusion at the end of it, he was dreadfully tired, and the sweat was running down his face. Unfortunately he couldn't even express himself properly in Russian (though he knew no other language), so he had suddenly grown utterly exhausted and even seemed to have become thinner after this feat of advocacy. He'd been talking so vehemently and with such conviction that everyone clearly believed him. Piotr Petrovich could feel that things were turning nasty.

'What's it to do with me, if you had all sorts of stupid questions going through your head?' he shouted. 'That's no proof! You could have dreamt the whole thing, that's all! And I tell you that you're lying, sir! Lying and slandering me out of spite, just because you're furious with me for not going along with your godless, freethinking social theories, that's what!'

But this ruse did Piotr Petrovich no good at all; angry murmurs were heard all around.

'Oh, so that's your line!' cried Lebeziatnikov. 'Liar! Send for the police, and I'll take an oath! There's only one thing I don't understand—why he risked doing something so vile! You mean, nasty wretch!'

'I can explain why he risked doing something so vile, and if need be I'll take an oath on it myself!' Raskolnikov finally announced in a firm voice; and he stepped forward.

He appeared calm and resolute. Just from looking at him, everyone felt convinced that he really did know what was going on, and the mystery was about to be cleared up.

'Now I see it all perfectly clearly,' Raskolnikov went on, directly addressing Lebeziatnikov. 'Right from the start, I'd been suspecting some sort of foul trick; I'd become suspicious because of certain facts which only I knew about, but now I'll tell you all about them. They explain everything! And you, Andrei Semionovich, with your invaluable account, you've made everything completely clear to me. Please listen carefully, all of you. This gentleman' (pointing to Luzhin) 'recently proposed to a certain young lady—my sister, Avdotya Romanovna Raskolnikova. But two days ago, after he'd arrived in Petersburg, he quarrelled with me at our first meeting, and I threw him out; there are two witnesses to that. This man is very angry now... The day before yesterday I didn't yet know that he was staying at your lodgings, Andrei Semionovich, which meant that on the very day of our quarrel two days ago, he'd observed me, as a friend of the late Mr Marmeladov, giving some money to his widow Katerina Ivanovna towards the funeral expenses. He at once wrote a note to my mother, telling her that I'd given away all my money, not to Katerina Ivanovna, but to Sofia Semionovna, referring in the most infamous terms to... to Sofia Semionovna's character; I mean, he made insinuations about my relations with Sofia Semionovna. All this, you understand, was aimed at making mischief between me and my mother and sister, by suggesting that it was for my own depraved purposes that I'd squandered the last of the money they had sent to help me. Yesterday evening, in the presence of my mother and sister and of that man, I established the true facts, proving that I'd handed the money to Katerina Ivanovna for the funeral, and not to Sofia Semionovna; and that two days ago I didn't even know Sofia Semionovna, in fact I'd never set eyes on her. And I added that he, Piotr Petrovich Luzhin, for all his virtues, wasn't worth the little finger of that same Sofia Semionovna whom he spoke so ill of. And when he asked me whether I'd have allowed Sofia Semionovna to sit down with my sister, I replied that I'd already done so, that very day. He got cross with my mother and sister for not falling out with me in spite of his insinuations, and as the conversation went on he began making unforgivably impertinent remarks to them. It ended in a terminal row, and he was thrown out of the house. All this happened last night. And now I want you to pay careful attention. Suppose that, just now, he'd managed to show that Sofia Semionovna was a thief. In the first place, he'd have proved to my sister and my mother that he'd been almost right in his suspicions, and had been justly angry with me for setting Sofia Semionovna on a level with my sister; so that he'd have been right to attack me by way of defending the honour of my sister, his betrothed bride. In short, all that could have helped him stir up a quarrel between me and my family, while he himself, of course, was hoping to get back into their good graces. And on top of that, he'd have scored a personal revenge against me, since he had reason to suppose that Sofia Semionovna's honour and happiness were very dear to me. There's what he was counting on! That's how I see this business! That's the whole explanation, and there can't be any other!'

That, more or less, was how Raskolnikov ended his speech, which had been repeatedly interrupted by exclamations from his otherwise very attentive audience. But through all the interruptions he had gone on speaking crisply, calmly, precisely, clearly, and firmly. His incisive voice, his tone of conviction, and his stern expression had produced an extraordinary effect on everybody.

'That's it, that's it, quite right!' Lebeziatnikov agreed enthusiastically. 'That's how it must have been, because as soon as Sofia Semionovna came into his room, he actually asked me whether you were here, and whether I'd seen you among Katerina Ivanovna's guests. He beckoned me over to the window, to ask me without being overheard. So he absolutely needed you to be here! That's right, all of it!'

Luzhin remained silent, with a scornful smile on his face. But he was very pale. He seemed to be wondering how to get out of this. He might perhaps have happily let it all drop and gone away, but at the moment that was almost impossible—it would have meant openly admitting that the accusations against him were true, and that he really had slandered Sofia Semionovna. Besides, the guests (who had had a fair amount to drink) were too restive. The supply clerk, though he hadn't understood it all, was shouting louder than anyone, and suggesting various steps that would be very unpleasant for Luzhin. But there were some who weren't drunk, for people had gathered there from all the rooms. All the three little Poles were getting terribly excited and kept shouting at him '*Pan lajdak!*',* and muttering all sorts of other threats in Polish. Sonia was listening tensely, but also seemed not to understand everything, as though just coming round from a swoon. She, too, never moved her eyes from Raskolnikov, feeling that he was her only protector. Katerina Ivanovna was gasping hoarsely, and looked utterly exhausted. Amalia Ivanovna cut the stupidest figure of all; she stood there with her mouth hanging open and had no idea what was going on. All she could see was that Piotr Petrovich had somehow got the worst of it. Raskolnikov tried to add something more, but wasn't allowed to finish; everyone was crowding round Luzhin and shouting oaths and threats. But Piotr Petrovich wasn't daunted. He could see that his accusation against Sonia had utterly failed, so he went straight for brazen effrontery.

'By your leave, ladies and gentlemen, by your leave, no crowding, let me pass!' he said, shoving his way through the crowd. 'Do me a favour, please, and stop threatening me; I assure you, that won't get you anywhere, it won't wash, I'm not scared; it's you, gentlemen, who'll have to answer for covering up a criminal offence. The thief has been worse than unmasked; and I'll be taking the matter further. The courts aren't as blind as you, nor... as drunk, and they won't give credence to these two shameless atheists, agitators, and freethinkers who are accusing me out of personal spite, which they're stupid enough to acknowledge... Yes, sir, let me pass please!'

'Will you clear out of my room at once; get yourself gone, and everything is over between us! When I think of the efforts I've made to explain... two whole weeks!...'

'I told you myself, Andrei Semionovich, just the other day, that I'd be moving out, while you were trying to talk me out of it. All I would add now is that you're a fool. I hope you manage to cure your sick brain and your half-blind eyes. Come on, gentlemen, let me through, will you!'

He forced his way through, but the supply clerk didn't want to let him off so easily, with mere verbal abuse; he seized a glass from the table, took a swing, and flung it at Piotr Petrovich. But the glass scored a direct hit on Amalia Ivanovna. She screamed, and the supply clerk lost his balance from his swing and fell heavily under the table. Piotr Petrovich went off to his room, and half an hour later was gone from the house. Sonia, timid by nature, had always known that she could be ruined more easily than anyone, and that everyone was free to insult her with impunity. And yet, up till this moment, she had felt that there was some way of avoiding disaster—by being cautious, meek, and humble before anyone and everyone. This present disillusionment was too much for her. Of course she could bear anything, patiently and uncomplainingly—even this. But despite the fact that she had been triumphantly vindicated—once her initial numb terror had passed and she could see everything clearly—a sense of hurt and helplessness still wrung her heart. She fell into hysterics. Finally, unable to bear it any longer, she rushed out of the room and ran home. That happened almost straight after Luzhin's departure. Amalia Ivanovna, when the glass hit her and everyone burst out laughing, couldn't bear to be the victim of someone else's misfortune either. Screaming like a crazed woman, she rushed at Katerina Ivanovna, whom she blamed for everything.

'Out from flat! Right now! *Marsch!*' And she set about grabbing all of Katerina Ivanovna's belongings that she could lay hold of, and flinging everything to the floor. Katerina Ivanovna, utterly worn out, pale, gasping, almost fainting, jumped up from the bed onto which she had collapsed almost senseless, and hurled herself at Amalia Ivanovna. But the struggle was too unequal; Amalia Ivanovna brushed her aside like a feather.

'What! Not only a godless slander—but then this creature starts attacking me too! What! Thrown out of my home on the very day of my husband's funeral, after all my hospitality to her, out on the street, with my orphans! Where can I go!' wailed the poor woman, gasping and sobbing. 'O Lord!' she suddenly shrieked, her eyes glittering, 'is there no justice in the world? Whom will you protect, if not us, poor orphans! Ah, now we'll see! There is truth and justice in the world, there is, and I'll find it! Straight away, just you wait, you godless creature! Polechka, stay with the children, I'll be back. Wait for me—in the street, if you have to! We'll see if there's justice in the world!'

And throwing over her head that same green shawl of drap-de-dames that the late Marmeladov had described in his story, Katerina Ivanovna squeezed through the disorderly crowd of drunken lodgers who still filled the room, and ran shrieking and sobbing out into the street, with the vague idea of finding justice, somewhere, right now, without delay, at any cost. Polechka huddled in terror on the trunk with the children, hugged the two little ones, and waited trembling for her mother to come back. Amalia Ivanovna was rushing round the room, screaming and wailing, throwing onto the floor anything that came her way, and creating havoc. The lodgers were all shouting nineteen to the dozen, some telling anything they knew about what had happened, others quarrelling and swearing, yet others singing songs...

'And now it's time for me to go too,' thought Raskolnikov. 'Well, Sofia Semionovna, let's see what you have to say now!'

And he set off for Sonia's lodgings.

CHAPTER IV

RASKOLNIKOV had defended Sonia vigorously and effectively against Luzhin, despite carrying so much horror and suffering in his own heart. But having endured such anguish that morning, he was almost glad of the chance to escape his own worries, which were becoming unbearable; besides, he had his own heartfelt personal reasons for his eagerness to stand up for Sonia. He was anxious, too, and at some moments terrified, at his forthcoming meeting with Sonia. He *had to* tell her who had killed Lizaveta; he could already foresee the dreadful torment he would have to endure, and seemed to be trying to push it away. And then, when he was leaving Katerina Ivanovna's lodgings and exclaiming 'Well, Sofia Semionovna, let's see what you have to say now!', he had evidently still been full of excitement and outward confidence, relishing his challenge to Luzhin and the victory he had just scored. But now something strange occurred. When he reached Kapernaumov's flat, his strength suddenly deserted him and he felt afraid. He stopped at the door, pondering the strange question: 'Do I have to tell her that I killed Lizaveta?' It was a strange question, because he had suddenly felt, at the same instant, that not only was there no escape from telling her—he couldn't delay the moment either, not even for a short time. He still didn't know why that was impossible; he merely *felt* it, and was crushed by the agonizing awareness of how helpless he was in the face of what had to be. To spare himself the torment of thinking it all through, he quickly opened the door; standing in the doorway, he looked at Sonia. She was sitting with her elbows on the little table, hiding her face in her hands, but when she saw Raskolnikov she quickly stood up and came over to meet him, as if she had been expecting him.

'Whatever would have become of me, if you hadn't been there!' she said quickly, when they met in the middle of the room. Evidently she had been in a hurry to say just this one thing to him. Then she waited.

Raskolnikov walked up to the table and sat down on the chair she had just left. She stood two paces in front of him, just like the day before.

'Well, Sonia?' he said, and suddenly felt his voice trembling. 'So, the whole thing rested on your "social situation and the habits associated with it". Did you realize that, just now?'

Her face was full of distress.

'Only don't talk to me the way you did yesterday!' she interrupted him. 'Please, don't start. There's enough suffering as it is...'

She gave a quick smile, afraid that he might have taken offence at her rebuke.

'It was stupid of me to come away. What's going on there now? I was just wanting to go back, but I kept thinking that... you'd come here.'

He told her that Amalia Ivanovna was evicting them from their lodging and that Katerina Ivanovna had run off somewhere 'to find justice'.

'Oh, my God!' exclaimed Sonia. 'Let's go there at once...'

And she snatched up her cape.

'It's always the same!' cried Raskolnikov in exasperation. 'All you think about is them! Stay with me a bit.'

'But... what about Katerina Ivanovna?'

'Katerina Ivanovna, for sure, won't fail to find you—she'll come here herself, if she's left the house,' he added petulantly. 'And then if she doesn't find you here, it'll be your fault, won't it?...'

In an agony of indecision, Sonia sat down on a chair. Raskolnikov said nothing, but stared at the floor, pondering something.

'Let's suppose that Luzhin didn't want you arrested right now,' he began without looking at Sonia.—'Well, but if he had wanted that, or if it was part of his plan—he'd have got you locked up, wouldn't he, if Lebeziatnikov and I hadn't turned up? Eh?'

'Yes,' she said faintly. 'Yes!' she repeated absently, in a frightened voice.

'But I might easily not have been there! And Lebeziatnikov—he was only there by pure chance.'

Sonia said nothing.

'And so, if you'd been locked up, what then? Remember what I was saying yesterday?'

She still said nothing. Raskolnikov waited.

'I thought you'd cry out again, "Oh, don't say that, stop!"' laughed Raskolnikov, in a rather strained voice. 'So—nothing to say, yet again?' he asked after a minute. 'But we do have to talk about something, don't we? Now, I'd be interested to hear how you've resolved one particular "problem", as Lebeziatnikov calls it.' (He seemed to be getting a bit muddled.) 'No, really, I mean it. Just imagine, Sonia—suppose you'd known all about Luzhin's plans beforehand—that you'd known (for certain, I mean), that they would have meant utter ruin for Katerina Ivanovna, and the children; and for you too, into the bargain (I put it like that because you regard yourself as of no importance; so "into the bargain"). And Polechka too... because she'll be going the same way. Well then: supposing all this had been left for you to decide: does he, or do they, carry on living on this earth—I mean, is Luzhin to live on and commit vile deeds, or does Katerina Ivanovna have to die? So, how would you decide? Which of them is to die? That's what I'm asking you.'

Sonia looked at him anxiously. She sensed that there was something important behind this vague, roundabout approach.

'I had a feeling that you'd ask something like that,' she said with an enquiring look at him.

'I dare say you did; but how's the question to be answered?'

'How can you ask about something that's impossible?' said Sonia with revulsion.

'Then it's better for Luzhin to live and do vile things! Didn't you even have the courage to say that?'

'But I can't know God's providence... And why are you asking things that can't be asked? What's the point of such empty questions? How could it ever depend on my decision? And who has appointed me a judge here, to say who's to live and who's not to?'

'Oh well, once God's providence gets mixed up in it, there's nothing more to be said,' muttered Raskolnikov sulkily.

'Why don't you talk straight and say what you mean?' Sonia cried unhappily. 'You're leading up to something again... Did you really only come here to torment me?'

Suddenly she could stand it no longer, and burst into bitter tears. He gazed at her in profound misery. Some five minutes passed.

'You know, you're right, Sonia,' he said quietly at last. His voice had suddenly altered; he had dropped his tone of pretended insolence and hopeless defiance. Even his voice had become quieter. 'Yesterday I told you myself that I wouldn't be coming to ask for forgiveness, and yet today I almost started by doing just that... What I said about Luzhin and Providence, I said for myself... I was asking for forgiveness, Sonia...'

He tried to smile, but there was something helpless and unfinished in that pale smile. He bowed his head and covered his face in his hands.

Suddenly and unexpectedly, a strange sensation of almost bitter hatred towards Sonia passed through his heart. Surprised and quite startled by this feeling, he raised his head and stared at her, and met her own look of troubled, anguished concern. There was love in it; and his hatred vanished like a phantom. This wasn't what he had thought: he had mistaken one emotion for another. All it meant was that *that moment* had arrived.

Once more he bowed his head and covered his face with his hands. Then he suddenly grew pale, stood up from his chair, looked at Sonia, and without saying anything moved mechanically over to her bed and sat down there.

That moment felt dreadfully similar, to him, to the one when he had stood behind the old woman, having already taken the axe out of its sling, and felt that 'there wasn't another instant to lose'.

'What is it?' asked Sonia fearfully.

He couldn't get a word out. This wasn't at all, at all, how he had meant to *tell it*, and he couldn't understand what was happening to him now. She came gently up to him, sat down next to him on the bed, and waited with her eyes fixed on him. Her heart was pounding and stumbling. It was more than he could bear; he turned his deathly pale face towards her; his contorted lips moved helplessly, straining to say something. A feeling of horror passed through Sonia's heart.

'What is it?' she asked again, moving a little away from him.

'It's nothing, Sonia. Don't be frightened... It's nonsense! Truly, if you think about it, it's nonsense,' he muttered, like a delirious man half-unconscious of himself. 'But why did I come to torment you, of all people?' he suddenly added, looking at her. 'Honestly, what for? I keep asking myself that, Sonia...'

Perhaps he really had been asking himself that question a quarter of an hour ago, but now he was speaking in a state of utter helplessness, barely aware of himself, and trembling all over his body.

'Oh, how you're torturing yourself!' she said in an anguished voice, staring intently at him.

'It's all nonsense! Look here, Sonia' (and he suddenly smiled for some reason, a pale, helpless sort of smile that lasted a couple of seconds), 'remember what I wanted to tell you yesterday?'

Sonia waited anxiously.

'When I left, I told you that I might be saying goodbye for ever, but that if I came back today, I'd tell you... who killed Lizaveta.'

A sudden shudder shook her whole body.

'Well, there you are, that's what I've come to tell you.'

'So you really meant that, yesterday...' she managed to whisper. 'But how do you know?' she asked quickly, as if suddenly recollecting herself.

She was having difficulty breathing now, and her face grew paler and paler.

'I do know.'

She said nothing for a minute.

'So have they found *him*?' she asked timidly.

'No, they haven't.'

'Then how can you know about *that*?' she asked, barely audibly again, after another minute's silence.

He turned to her and looked steadily, very steadily, at her.

'Guess,' he said, with the same twisted, helpless smile as before.

A convulsive shudder shook her body.

'But you... you're... why are you... frightening me like this?' she said, with a childish smile.

'I must be a great friend of *his*... if I know,' Raskolnikov went on, continuing to stare at her face as if he no longer had the strength to look away. 'That Lizaveta... he didn't mean to kill her... He... killed her by accident... He wanted to kill the old woman... when she was alone... so he went there... And then Lizaveta came in... so he... killed her too.'

Another dreadful minute went by. Each was still staring at the other.

'Can't you guess, then?' he suddenly asked, feeling as if he was throwing himself off the top of a church tower.*

'N-no,' whispered Sonia; her voice could scarcely be heard.

'Take a good look.'

And as soon as he had spoken, an old, familiar feeling spread an icy chill through his soul. He was looking at her, and in her face he suddenly seemed to see the face of Lizaveta. He had a vivid memory of Lizaveta's expression on that day, as he advanced towards her with the axe in his hand, and she backed away from him towards the wall, stretching out her arm in front of her, with a look of childish fear on her face, just exactly like little children when they are suddenly scared of something, and stare fixedly and anxiously at the terrifying object, and back away from it, stretching out their little hands, on the point of bursting into tears. Almost the same thing happened to Sonia now: she watched him just as helplessly, just as fearfully, for a time, and then suddenly stretched out her left arm, pressing her fingers ever so lightly against his chest, and slowly began to get up from the bed, edging further and further away from him, with her eyes ever more firmly fixed on his face. Her horror suddenly spread to him too, and his face took on the same frightened expression; he began looking at her in just the same way, with almost the same *childish* smile.

'Guessed?' he whispered at last.

'Oh God!' A terrible wail burst from her chest, and she sank helplessly onto the bed, burying her face in the pillows. But a moment later she quickly raised herself, quickly moved closer to him, seized both his hands, and squeezing them vice-tight in her thin fingers, gazed motionless at his face again, as though her eyes were glued to it. With this last, despairing look, she was trying to find and seize hold of any last, faint hope for herself. But hope there was none; no doubt at all remained; it was all *true*! Even later on, when she recalled that minute, it seemed strange and puzzling to her—why had she realized so *immediately*, at the time, that there was no longer any doubt? For she couldn't have said, for example, that she'd had a premonition of something of the kind, could she? But now, as soon as he'd spoken, she suddenly felt as if she had been expecting exactly *that*.

'Stop it, Sonia, that's enough! Don't torment me!' he begged her miserably.

He hadn't at all expected to tell her like this; but *this* was how it had turned out.

She leapt up, scarcely knowing what she was doing, and moved to the middle of the room, wringing her hands; but quickly turned and came back to sit down next to him, almost touching him, shoulder to shoulder. All of a sudden, as though she had been stabbed, she recoiled, cried out, and sank down on her knees before him, without knowing why.

'Whatever have you done to yourself, whatever have you done?' she said despairingly; then she jumped up from her knees, fell on his neck, embraced him, and hugged him tightly in her arms.

Raskolnikov drew back and looked at her with a sad smile.

'How odd you are, Sonia—hugging and kissing me when I've just told you about *that*. You don't know what you're doing.'

'No, there's no one unhappier than you in the whole world!' she cried frantically, without hearing what he said; and suddenly burst into hysterical sobs.

A long-forgotten feeling suddenly flooded into his heart and softened it on the instant. He did nothing to fight it. Two tears welled up from his eyes and hung on his lashes.

'So you won't leave me, Sonia?' he asked her, with something like hope in his eyes.

'No, no, never and nowhere!' cried Sonia. 'I'll follow you, wherever you go! Oh, God!... Poor wretched me!... And why, why didn't I know you before! Why didn't you come to me before? Oh, God!'

'Here I am now.'

'Yes, now! Oh, what's to be done now?... Together, together!' she repeated half-unconsciously, hugging him again. 'I'll go to the prison camp with you!' He seemed to wince with revulsion, and his earlier smile, almost arrogant and full of hatred, returned to his lips.

'But Sonia, perhaps I don't want to go to a prison camp yet,' said he.

Sonia looked quickly at him.

After her first, passionate, anguished impulse of sympathy for this unfortunate man, she was once again overcome by the dreadful idea of the murder. In his altered tone of voice she could suddenly hear the murderer speaking. She stared at him in astonishment. She still didn't know anything about the event—not why it had happened, nor how, nor what for. All these questions suddenly burst in on her. And once again she couldn't believe it: 'Him, a murderer? Him? How can that be possible?'

'What is all this? Where am I?' she asked in utter bewilderment, as if she still hadn't collected her thoughts. 'How ever could you, a man like you... make up your mind to that?... What does it mean?'

'Well, yes, it was to rob her. Stop it, Sonia!' he answered wearily, almost in annoyance.

Sonia stood seemingly dumbfounded, but suddenly cried out:

'You were hungry! You... it was to help your mother? Was it?'

'No, Sonia, no,' he muttered, turning away and hanging his head. 'I wasn't all that hungry... it's true, I did want to help my mother, but... even that isn't quite right... Don't torture me, Sonia!'

Sonia threw up her hands.

'But can this all really, really be true? Oh God, how can it be true? Who could ever believe it?... And how could you, how could you yourself have given away all the money you had, and then killed somebody to rob her? Oh!...' she cried suddenly, 'that money you gave to Katerina Ivanovna... even that money... oh God, could that money really have been...'

'No, Sonia,' he interrupted her hastily, 'that money wasn't it, keep calm! That was the money my mother had sent me, through some merchant, and it reached me when I was ill, on the same day I gave it away... Razumikhin saw... it was he that received it for me... that was my money, my very own, truly mine.'

Sonia was listening to him in bewilderment, trying her hardest to understand anything at all.

'But *the other* money... as a matter of fact I don't even know whether there was any money there at all,' he added quietly and rather thoughtfully, 'I took a purse from round her neck, a chamois leather one... a full, plump sort of purse... but I didn't look inside; I can't have had time... But the things, some sort of studs and little chains—I buried them all, and the purse, under a stone in someone's courtyard on V—— Prospekt, the very next morning. It's all still there now.'

Sonia listened intently to all he said.

'Well then, why... how could you say you did it to rob someone, seeing you took nothing for yourself?' she asked quickly, clutching at a straw.

'I don't know... I hadn't yet decided whether I'd take that money or not,' he said, seeming lost in thought once more; then he suddenly recollected himself and smiled a brief, hasty smile. 'Oh, what nonsense I'm talking here, aren't I!'

'Could he have gone mad?' The thought flashed through Sonia's head. But straight away she changed her mind. No, this was something different. She couldn't understand anything, anything at all, of all this!

'You know what, Sonia,' he said suddenly, with a sort of inspiration, 'listen to what I'm telling you. If I'd just cut her throat because I was hungry,' he went on, emphasizing every word and giving her a sincere but enigmatic look, 'then I'd be... *happy* now! Be sure of that!'

'And what's it to you, what's it to you,' he cried a moment later, in something like despair, 'what good would it do you, even if I confessed now that I'd done wrong? What good would it do you to score such a stupid triumph over me? Oh, Sonia, was it for this I came to see you?'

Sonia was about to say something again, but stayed silent.

'That was why I asked you to join me, yesterday—because you're all I have left.'

'Join you where?' asked Sonia timidly.

'Not in robbing and murdering, don't worry, it wasn't that,' he said with a bitter smile. 'We're different sorts of people... And do you know, Sonia, I've only just realized, just now, *where* I was asking you to come with me. Yesterday, when I asked you, I myself didn't realize where I meant. I asked you for just one thing—I only came for one reason: so that you shouldn't leave me. You won't leave me, will you, Sonia?'

She squeezed his hand.

'And why, why did I ever tell her? Why did I let it all out?' he cried in desperation a minute later, looking at her in endless anguish. 'There you are, Sonia, waiting for me to explain, I can see you, sitting and waiting—but what can I tell you? You won't understand anything about it, you'll just suffer endless misery... because of me! Look at you, crying and hugging me again—and whatever are you hugging me for? For not being able to bear it all myself, so that I've come to dump it all on someone else: "you suffer too, that'll make it easier for me!" How can you love a villain like that?'

'But aren't you tormented as well?' cried Sonia.

Once again, that same feeling flooded into his soul, and once again it softened him for a second.

'Sonia, I have an evil heart, don't forget that; it explains a lot. I only came here because I'm evil. There are some people who wouldn't have come. But I'm a coward, and... a villain! Anyway... never mind that! That's not the point. We need to talk now, but I can't manage to begin...'

He stopped and became thoughtful.

'A-ah, what different people we are!' he cried at last. 'We don't fit together. And why, why ever did I come? I'll never forgive myself for that!'

'No, no, it was good that you came!' exclaimed Sonia. 'It's better for me to know. Much better!'—He looked unhappily at her.

'Well, perhaps you could even be right,' he said after some consideration. 'Because that's how it really was! Look here: I wanted to make myself into a Napoleon, and that was why I killed her... So, can you understand now?'

'N-no,' whispered Sonia innocently and timidly, 'but... do go on, please go on! I'll understand it, I'll understand it in my inside!' she begged him.

'You will? Very well, let's see!'

He paused and thought for a long time.

'Here's what it's about. I once asked myself the following question: supposing, say, Napoleon had happened to be in my shoes, and he didn't have Toulon behind him to launch his career, nor Egypt, nor the crossing of Mont Blanc,* and instead of all those fine, grandiose things, all he'd had was some absurd old woman, some clerk's widow, whom he'd have to kill so as to get the money out of her strongbox (for his career, you understand?); well, could he have made up his mind to do it, if there was no other way? Wouldn't he have been too squeamish, because the thing was so far from grandiose... in fact, so sinful? Well, I tell you, I agonized over that "question" for a dreadfully long time, and got dreadfully ashamed, until I finally realized (it happened all of a sudden) that he not only wouldn't have been too squeamish—it wouldn't even have ever occurred to him that it wasn't grandiose... he wouldn't have understood what exactly there was to be squeamish about. And if he'd really had no other choice, then he'd have throttled her before she could give a squeak, and never given it a second thought!... Well, so I... stopped wondering about it... and throttled her... following the master's example... And that's just exactly how it happened! You think it's funny? Yes, Sonia, and the funniest thing of all is that it may have happened just like that...'

Sonia didn't find it in the least funny.

'You'd better explain it to me straight... without any examples,' she begged him even more timidly, almost too quietly to be heard.

He turned to her, gave her a sorrowful look and took her by the hands.

'You're right again, Sonia. It really is all nonsense, nothing but empty words! Look: you know that my mother hardly has any money at all. My sister has had an education, one way or another, and now she's reduced to trailing around working as a governess. All their hopes were on me. I studied, but I couldn't keep myself at university, and I had to leave it for a while. Even if things had gone on like that, then some ten or twelve years later (provided everything turned out well), I could have hoped to become a teacher of some kind, or a government official, on a thousand roubles a year...' (He seemed to be reciting a learned lesson.) 'And by that time my mother would have died of worry and grief, and I wouldn't have been able to comfort her, while my sister... well, things might have turned out even worse for her!... And what would be the point of spending my whole life walking past everything and looking away, forgetting about my mother, and humbly accepting the injuries that my sister would suffer? What for? Just so that, once I'd buried my family, I could get myself a new one—a wife and children, whom I'd leave penniless and starving in their turn? So... so then I decided that I'd take the old woman's money and use it to keep going for the first few years, without bothering my mother; to pay for myself at university and for my first steps after that;—and to do all that properly and comfortably, organize a whole new career for myself, and start out on a new and independent path... Well... well, that's it, really... Well, of course, I did kill the old woman, and that was bad of me... but, well, that's enough of that!'

He struggled exhaustedly to finish his speech, and bowed his head.

'Oh, that's not it, not it at all!' cried Sonia in anguish. 'And how can you... no, it wasn't like that, it wasn't!'

'You can see yourself that it wasn't! But I was telling the truth—that was the truth!'

'How could that be the truth? Oh God!'

'All I did was kill a louse, Sonia, a useless, nasty, wicked louse.'

'That louse was a human being!'

'I know she wasn't a louse,' he replied, giving her a strange look. 'Actually I'm wrong, Sonia,' he added, 'I've been telling it wrong all the way... That wasn't it, you're quite right. I had quite, quite, quite different reasons!... I haven't talked to anyone for ages, Sonia... My head aches dreadfully now.'

His eyes burned with a feverish fire. He was on the verge of delirium; a restless smile played over his lips. Terrible exhaustion showed through his excited agitation. Sonia could see his anguish. Her own head was beginning to swim. And how strangely he was talking: as if there was something that could be understood, but... 'But how could it be? How could it? Oh God!' She wrung her hands in despair.

'No, Sonia, that's not right!' he began again, suddenly raising his head as if struck by a new line of thought, which had aroused him once more. 'That's not it! Or rather... Suppose (yes! this really is better!), suppose that I'm vain, and jealous, and evil, and nasty, and vindictive, well... and even inclined to madness. (Let's have it all at once! People have been talking about madness before this, I've noticed it!) I've just told you that I couldn't keep myself at university. But do you realize that actually I might have done? My mother would have sent me enough for the fees, and I could probably have earned what I needed for boots and clothes and food. I'm sure I could! I was getting lessons, and they were offering me half a rouble. After all, Razumikhin works! But I got furious, and I refused. Yes, *furious*—that's the right word for it! So then I scuttled back into my corner, like a spider. You've been to that hole, you've seen it... But do you know, Sonia, that low ceilings and cramped rooms oppress one's heart and soul? Oh, how I loathed that kennel! And yet I didn't want to leave it. I stayed there on purpose! I spent days without going out, and I wouldn't work, and wouldn't eat, and all I did was lie there.* If Nastasia brought me something, I might eat it, and if she didn't, well, the day would pass like that, and I was too angry to ask for anything! And I had no light at night, I'd lie there in darkness, but I didn't want to earn money to buy candles. I ought to have studied, but I'd sold all my books; and the notebooks and papers on my table are an inch deep in dust to this day. I preferred to lie and think. And I went on thinking... And I kept having such dreams, all sorts of strange dreams, I can't tell you! Only then I began imagining that... No, that's wrong too! I'm telling it wrong again! You see, then I kept asking myself—why am I so stupid that if other people are stupid and I know for certain that they are, I still don't want to be cleverer? And then I realized, Sonia, that if I waited for everyone to become clever, that would take far too long... And I realized, too, that that'll never happen, people never will change, and there's no one to make them different, and there's no point trying! Yes, that's how it is! That's the law of their nature... The law, Sonia! That's how it is!... And I know now, Sonia, that the man who is firm and strong in mind and spirit is master over them! The man who dares much, is right in their eyes. The one who cares least about anything, he'll make their laws; and the one who dares most, is the most right for them! That's how things have always been, and always will be! You'd have to be blind not to see it!'

Although Raskolnikov was still looking at Sonia while he said all this, he no longer cared whether she understood him or not. He was wholly under the sway of his fever, in a sort of gloomy ecstasy. (It was true, he had spent far too long speaking to no one!) Sonia realized that this sombre creed had become his faith and his law.

'I understood then, Sonia,' he went on fervently, 'that power is only granted to the man who dares to stoop and pick it up. There's only one condition, just one: all you have to do is dare! And at that time I worked out an idea, for the first time in my life, which nobody had ever thought of before me! Nobody! I suddenly saw as clear as daylight: how could it be that not a single person had ever dared, nor dared now, when faced with this completely absurd situation, to take the whole thing by the tail and hurl it to perdition! I... I wanted to *have that courage*, and so I killed... I just wanted to have the courage, Sonia, that's all it was!'

'Oh, stop, stop!' cried Sonia, throwing up her hands. 'You've abandoned God, and God has struck you down, and delivered you to the devil!'

'So, Sonia, when I was lying there in the darkness and imagining all those things, that was the devil leading me on, was it?'

'Stop it! Don't mock, you blasphemer! You don't understand anything, anything at all! Oh, God! He'll never understand anything, anything!'

'Be quiet, Sonia, I'm not mocking at all, I know perfectly well myself that it was the devil tempting me. Be quiet, Sonia, shut up!' he repeated gloomily and insistently. 'I know it all. I've already thought it all through, and whispered it to myself, lying there in the darkness... I've argued it all out with myself, down to the very last detail, and I know it all, all of it! And I was so, so sick of all that talk! I wanted to forget it all and start again, Sonia, and have done with all the talk! Can you really imagine that I just went into it headlong, like an idiot? No, I went for it like a sensible man, and that was what did for me! Do you really think that I couldn't even see the simple fact that if I'd started asking and questioning myself about whether I had the right to assume power—that in itself meant that I didn't have that right? Or that once I asked myself the question, whether this was a louse or a human being, that meant that this human being wasn't a louse *for me*, though it was still a louse for the man who wouldn't waste a thought on all that, but would do the deed without asking any questions... And if I spent so many days torturing myself over whether Napoleon would have done it or not, then I must have clearly felt that I was no Napoleon... I endured all the agony of that endless talk, Sonia, and I wanted to shake it off; I wanted to kill without all the casuistry, Sonia, to kill for myself, myself alone!

I didn't want to tell lies about it, even to myself! It wasn't to help my mother that I did the killing—that's rubbish! And I didn't do it in order to get money and power, so as to become the benefactor of the human race. All rubbish! I simply killed, I killed for myself, for myself alone; and whether I became somebody's benefactor after that, or spent the rest of my life lurking like a spider, enticing everyone else into my web and sucking the lifeblood out of them—I oughtn't to have cared about any of that, at that moment!... And the main thing is—it wasn't money I needed, when I killed; Sonia, it wasn't money so much as something else... I can see all that now... Please understand me: perhaps if I'd gone on along the same path, I might never have done another murder. It was something else I needed to discover, something else that drove me on: I needed to discover, straight away, whether I was a louse like everyone else, or a human being. Would I manage to overstep the boundary or not? Would I dare to stoop down and pick up what I wanted, or not? Am I a tremulous little creature, or do I have the *right*...?'

'To kill? Whether you have the right to kill?' Sonia threw up her hands.

'Oh, Sonia!' he cried irritably. He was about to make some objection, but remained contemptuously silent. 'Don't interrupt me, Sonia! I just wanted to prove one thing to you: that the devil drove me on, at the time, and afterwards he explained to me that I had no right to go there then, because I'm exactly the same sort of louse as everyone else! He mocked at me, and that's why I've come to you now! So welcome your guest! If I hadn't been a louse, would I have come to you? Listen: when I went to the old woman's, that day, I was just going to *try it out*... Be sure of that!'

'But you killed her! You did!'

'Yes, but how did I kill her? Is that the way people kill? Do they go to commit a murder as I went that day? One day I'll tell you how I went there... Was it the old woman I killed? It was myself I killed, not the old woman! Finished myself off on the spot, once and for all!... That old woman, it was the devil murdered her, not me... That'll do, that's enough, Sonia, that's enough! Leave me alone!' he cried out in sudden anguish. 'Leave me alone!'

He bent forward with his elbows on his knees, squeezing his head in a pincer-like grip.

'How you're suffering!' Sonia burst out in an agonized wail.

'So, what's to be done now? You tell me!' he demanded, raising his head and staring at her, his face contorted in a dreadful expression of despair.

'What's to be done?!' she exclaimed, leaping up; and her eyes, hitherto full of tears, suddenly glittered. 'Get up!' She seized him by his shoulder, and he rose, looking at her in some astonishment. 'Go straight away, this very minute, and stand at the crossroads; bow down and first kiss the earth which you've defiled,* and then bow to the whole world, all four corners of the earth, and proclaim aloud to everybody: "I have killed!" Then God will send you life again. Will you go? Will you?' she demanded, trembling convulsively, as she seized him by both hands and squeezed them between her own with a burning look.

He was impressed and utterly amazed by her sudden ecstasy.

'Is this all about prison camps, Sonia? Do I have to hand myself in, then?' he asked morosely.

'You have to accept suffering, and redeem yourself through it, that's what you must do.'

'No! I shan't go there, Sonia.'

'Then how are you going to live? What will you live by?' exclaimed Sonia. 'Is it possible any more? And how can you talk to your mother? (Oh, what on earth, what on earth will happen to them, now?) But what am I saying? You've already abandoned your mother and your sister, abandoned them completely, you have. Oh God!' she cried, 'but he knows all that himself already! How can you, how can you go on living without another human soul? Whatever will happen to you now?'

'Don't be such a child, Sonia,' said he quietly. 'How am I guilty before all of them? Why should I go? What can I tell them? All that's just a fairy tale. Those people destroy folk in their millions, and they're proud of themselves for doing it. They're villains and scoundrels, Sonia!... No, I won't go. And what can I say: that I did a murder, but I didn't dare take the money, so I hid it under a stone?' he added with a bitter smile. 'That'll just make them laugh at me; they'll say: "What a fool, not to take the money!" A coward and a fool! They won't understand a thing, Sonia, not a thing, and they're not fit to understand. Why should I go? No, I shan't go. Don't be a child, Sonia.'

'You'll destroy yourself with suffering!' she repeated, stretching out her hands to him in a desperate plea.

'Maybe I've not been fair to myself even now,' he remarked darkly, seeming lost in thought. 'Maybe I'm a human being after all, not a louse, and I was too quick to condemn myself... I'll fight on.'

His lips curled in an arrogant smile.

'What a burden of suffering to bear! Your whole life long, your whole life!'

'I'll get used to it...' he replied grimly and pensively. 'Listen,' he went on a minute later, 'that's enough crying, let's talk seriously. I came to tell you that they're after me now, they're looking for me...'

'Oh no!' cried Sonia in alarm.

'What are you shrieking for? You wanted me to go to a prison camp, and now you're scared? Only here's what: I shan't let them get me. I'll have another fight with them, and they won't do anything. They don't have any real evidence. Yesterday I was in great danger, and I thought I was done for; but today it's all right again. All their evidence points both ways; I mean to say, I can turn their accusations to my own advantage, understand? And I shall, because by now I've learned how to... But they'll send me to prison, that's for sure. If it hadn't been for one particular thing, they might even have locked me up today; in fact they'll probably still do that... But that doesn't matter, Sonia: I'll do a bit of time, and then they'll let me out... because they haven't got a single piece of solid evidence against me, and they never will, I promise you. And what they've got isn't enough to convict anyone. Anyway, enough of that... I'm just telling you, so that you know... As for my sister and mother, I'll try and arrange things to reassure them and not scare them... Well, my sister actually seems to be sorted out now... which means my mother is too... Well, that's it. But be careful. Will you come and visit me in prison, when they lock me up?'

'Oh yes, yes, I will!'

The two of them sat side by side, weary and dejected, like storm-tossed castaways on a barren shore. He looked at Sonia and felt how much love she had for him, and strangely enough he found it oppressive and painful to be so much loved. Yes, that was a strange and terrible feeling. On his way to see Sonia, he had felt that she was his only hope, his only rescue; he had thought that he could lay at least some of his suffering on her shoulders; and now, when all her heart was turned towards him, he suddenly realized that he was immeasurably more unhappy than before.

'Sonia,' he said, 'actually you'd better not come and visit me in prison.'

Sonia said nothing. She was weeping. A few minutes passed.

'Have you a cross on you?' she asked suddenly and unexpectedly, as if she had just remembered.

He didn't understand her question at first.

'No, you haven't, have you? Here, take this one, it's cypress wood.* I've got another one, a brass one, Lizaveta's. Lizaveta and I exchanged crosses—she gave me hers, and I gave her my little icon. I'll wear Lizaveta's now, and this one's for you. Take it—it's mine! It's my own!'

she begged him. 'We'll be going off to suffer together, and we'll carry our crosses together!'

'Give it to me!' said Raskolnikov, not wishing to upset her. But then he instantly withdrew his hand, which he had stretched out to take the cross.

'Not now, Sonia. Better do it later,' he added to reassure her.

'Yes, yes, that'll be better, so it will,' she agreed with feeling . 'When you go for your punishment, that's when you'll put it on. You'll come to me, and I'll put it on you, and we'll pray, and set off.'

At that moment someone gave three knocks on the door.

'Sofia Semionovna, can I come in?' asked a polite and very familiar voice.

Sonia ran to the door in alarm. The fair-haired face of Mr Lebeziatnikov looked in.

CHAPTER V

LEBEZIATNIKOV was looking anxious.

'I've come to see you, Sofia Semionovna. Excuse me... I thought I'd find you here,' he said, suddenly addressing Raskolnikov. 'I mean, I wasn't thinking anything... of that sort... but I did think... Back home, Katerina Ivanovna has gone crazy!' he suddenly blurted out to Sonia, no longer addressing Raskolnikov.

Sonia gave a little scream.

'Well, that's what it looks like, anyway. Though actually... We've no idea what to do about it, that's the trouble! She came back—I think she'd been turned away from somewhere, and maybe they'd knocked her about... at least that's what it looks like... She'd run off to see Semion Zakharich's old chief, but he wasn't at home, he was having dinner with some other general... So just imagine, she rushed off to where they were having dinner... to that other general's house, and believe it or not, she managed to get to see Semion Zakharich's chief, I think she even called him away from his table. You can guess what happened then. They threw her out, of course; and she says she shouted at him, and flung something at him. You can even picture her doing that... how she got away without being arrested, I've no idea! Now she's telling everyone about it, even Amalia Ivanovna, but it's hard to make out what she's saying, she's screaming and flinging herself about so much. Oh yes: she's telling everyone, and yelling about it, that every-one's abandoned her now, so she's going to take the children and go out

on the streets with a barrel organ, and the children are going to sing and
dance, and she will too, and beg for money, and she's going to go and
stand under the general's window every day... "Just let him see the
respectable children of a man in his service, wandering the streets like
beggars!" And she's been beating the children and making them cry.
She's teaching Lenia to sing "My Little Farmstead",* and the boy to
dance, and Polina Mikhailovna too; and she's ripped their clothes, and
made them all little cap things, like actors. And she's going to carry
a bowl around, to beat on it, instead of music... She won't listen to
anyone... Think of it—what on earth's she up to? This can't go on!'

Lebeziatnikov would have continued, but Sonia, who had been listening breathlessly to him, suddenly snatched up her cloak and hat and
rushed out of the room, pulling them on as she ran. Raskolnikov followed her out, with Lebeziatnikov coming after him.

'She's gone mad, no doubt of it!' he said to Raskolnikov as they
emerged into the street; 'I didn't want to frighten Sofia Semionovna,
so I said that was what it looked like; but there's no question about
it. They say that in consumption, there are lumps of some kind that
develop on your brain—it's a pity I don't know any medicine. I tried to
talk her out of it, but she wouldn't listen.'

'Were you telling her about the lumps?'

'Well, not exactly. Not that she would have understood anything. But
what I wanted to say is this: if you prove logically to someone that
there's really nothing to cry about, then they'll stop crying. That's
obvious. Or are you really sure they won't?'

'That would make life far too simple,' replied Raskolnikov.

'No, but listen, listen: obviously it's quite hard for Katerina Ivanovna
to understand; but did you know that in Paris they've already done
serious experiments on trying to cure insanity by using nothing but
logical arguments?* There was one professor there, he's just recently
died, a serious scientist who thought of treating patients that way. His
basic idea was that there's no actual organic disorder in someone who's
insane; that insanity is a sort of logical error, an error of judgement,
a mistaken view of things. He would gradually refute the patient's mistakes, and would you believe it, he got results! But as he was using
showers at the same time, the results of his treatment are still doubtful,
of course... At least, that's how it looks...'

Raskolnikov had given up listening long before this. As they reached
his own house, he nodded to Lebeziatnikov and turned into the gateway.
Lebeziatnikov pulled himself together, looked about him and ran on.

Raskolnikov went up to his garret and stopped in the middle of the room. Why had he come back here? He glanced around at the tattered yellowing wallpaper, and the dust, and his divan... From outside came an incessant noise of repeated sharp knocking; someone was probably hammering in a nail or something... He went to the window, raised himself on tiptoe and spent a long time looking out at the courtyard, seeming intensely interested in what was going on. But the yard was empty and he couldn't see anyone hammering. There were some open windows in the building on the left, and window boxes with drooping geraniums on the windowsills. Clothes were hanging out of the windows to dry... He knew all that by heart. Turning away, he sat down on the divan.

Never, never had he felt so dreadfully lonely!

Yes, once again he could feel that he might really come to hate Sonia: now of all times, when he had made her even more unhappy. Why had he gone to beg her to weep for him? Why did he have such a need to poison her life? Oh, how vile of him!

'I'll stay alone!' he said suddenly and resolutely. 'She's not to go visiting the prison!'

Five minutes or so later he raised his head and smiled a strange smile. An odd thought had suddenly occurred to him: 'Perhaps it'll really be better than this in the prison camp!'

He had no idea how long he went on sitting in his room, with all sorts of vague thoughts crowding his head. Suddenly the door opened and Avdotya Romanovna came in. First she stopped in the doorway to look at him, as he had looked at Sonia earlier; then she came right in and sat down on a chair opposite him, where she had sat the day before. He gazed vacantly at her and said nothing.

'Don't be angry with me, brother, I've just come for a minute,' said Dunia. Her expression was thoughtful but not stern; her eyes were clear and calm. He could see that she, too, had come to him with love in her heart.

'My brother, I know everything now, *everything*. Dmitry Prokofich has told me everything and explained it all. You're being persecuted and tormented on account of a foul and stupid suspicion... Dmitry Prokofich tells me that there's no danger, and you've no need to be so terrified by it all. I don't agree; I *completely understand* what a state you're in, and that you may be permanently affected by your indignation. That's what I'm afraid of. I don't blame you, I daren't blame you, for leaving us; so please forgive me for reproaching you about it earlier. I know that if I'd suffered as much as you have, I'd have turned my back on everyone too. I shan't tell Mother about *that*, but I'll keep telling her about you, and I'll tell her from you that you're going to come and see her very soon. Don't distress yourself about her—I'll make it all right with her; but don't distress her either. Come and see her, at least once—remember she's your mother! And now, all I've come to say' (and Dunia began to get up from her chair) 'is that if by any chance you ever need me, or if you need... my whole life, or anything... just call me and I'll come. Goodbye!'

She turned away abruptly and walked to the door.

'Dunia!' cried Raskolnikov, calling her back. He stood up and went over to her. 'That Razumikhin—Dmitry Prokofich—he's a very good man.'

Dunia blushed faintly.

'Well?' she asked after a pause.

'He's a serious person, hard-working and honest, and capable of loving someone deeply. Goodbye, Dunia.'

Dunia flushed red; then she suddenly became anxious.

'What's all this, brother—are we really parting for good, or why are you... pronouncing such solemn last words to me?'

'Never mind... Goodbye.'

He turned and walked away to the window. She stood watching him anxiously for a little, and then uneasily left the room.

No, he hadn't treated her coldly. There had been a moment (the very last one) when he had terribly wanted to hug her tight and *say farewell* to her, and even *tell her*; but he hadn't even been able to give her his hand.

'Just supposing she shudders, later on, when she remembers me hugging her, and says that I stole her kiss!'

'And will *she* be able to stand it, or not?' he went on to himself a few moments later. 'No, she won't—that sort never does! People like her never can!'

And he thought of Sonia.

A cool draught blew in through the window. The sunlight in the courtyard was less intense than before. Suddenly he picked up his cap and went out.

Of course he was incapable of worrying about his own morbid state; nor did he want to. But all the endless worry, and all this spiritual terror, couldn't fail to leave their mark on him. And if he hadn't yet been actually laid low with fever, that might be just because of this constant inner alarm that was still keeping him awake and on his feet; but it all felt somehow artificial and temporary.

He wandered along aimlessly. The sun was setting. A special sort of misery had begun to weigh on him lately. There was nothing particularly poignant or burning about it; but it breathed an air of permanence, of eternity; a foretaste of hopeless years of this cold, deathly misery, an everlasting 'one square yard of space'. Towards evening this feeling generally came to oppress him even more heavily.

'If I have such totally idiotic attacks of pure physical weakness, brought on by no more than a sunset or something, how am I to prevent myself from doing something stupid! Never mind going to Sonia, you'll be going off to Dunia next!' he muttered viciously.

Someone called him by name. He looked round and saw Lebeziatnikov racing towards him.

'Just imagine! I've been to your place, looking for you. Just imagine— she's done what she said, and gone off with the children! Sofia Semionovna and I had a job finding them. She's beating on a frying pan and making the children sing and dance. The children are crying. They stop at crossroads and in front of shops, and there's a crowd of idiots running after them. Come along!'

'What about Sonia?...' asked Raskolnikov anxiously as he hurried after Lebeziatnikov.

'Simply frantic. I mean, it's not Sofia Semionovna who's frantic, but Katerina Ivanovna. Actually, Sofia Semionovna's frantic too. But Katerina Ivanovna is absolutely frantic. I'm telling you, she's gone right out of her mind. They'll take her off to the police. You can imagine the effect that'll have... They're by the canal now, next to —— Bridge, very close to Sofia Semionovna's place. It's near here.'

Beside the canal, not very far from the bridge and just a couple of buildings short of the one where Sonia lived, a small crowd had gathered—mostly little street urchins and girls. The hoarse, strained voice of Katerina Ivanovna could be heard all the way from the bridge. It was indeed a strange sight, and one that was bound to attract a street crowd. Katerina Ivanovna was wearing her old dress, the drap-de-dames shawl and a tattered straw hat crushed into a grotesque lump on one side of her head. She really was in an absolute frenzy, exhausted and panting for breath. Her tormented, consumptive face was filled with even more suffering than ever (besides which, a consumptive person always looks more wasted and sick outdoors in the sunshine than at home). But her excitement hadn't flagged, and she was growing more agitated every minute. She would dash at the children, shout at them, implore them, instruct them how to dance and what to sing, right there in front of the crowd, and start explaining to them why this had to be done, and fall into despair when they didn't understand, and start beating them... And then, before she'd finished, she would run towards the onlookers, and if she noticed anyone the least bit well dressed who had paused to have a look, she would instantly launch into an explanation: 'See what the children of a genteel, indeed aristocratic family, are reduced to!' If she heard any laughter or jeering from the crowd, she would hurl herself at the impertinent culprits and start brawling with them. Some people did indeed laugh; others shook their heads; but everyone was curious to take a look at this madwoman with her terrified children. There was no sign of the frying pan mentioned by Lebeziatnikov, or at least Raskolnikov didn't see it. Instead of banging on a frying pan, Katerina Ivanovna would begin beating time by clapping her withered hands whenever she made Polechka sing and Lenia and Kolia dance; she even tried to join in the singing herself, but was always forced by her racking cough to give up after the first note; this cast her back into despair, and she would curse her cough and actually weep. What infuriated her most was the tears and terror of Kolia and Lenia. She really had done her best to dress the children up in the sort of costumes that street singers wear. The boy had on a turban made of something red and white, to make him look like a Turk. There hadn't been any costume that Lenia could use; all she had was a red worsted cap on her head (more precisely, a nightcap) that had belonged to the late Semion Zakharich, with a broken bit of white ostrich feather stuck into it— a feather which had once belonged to Katerina Ivanovna's grandmother, and had been preserved in a trunk as a precious family relic. Polechka was in her everyday dress. She was watching her mother in timid bewilderment, not moving from her side, hiding her tears, realizing that her mother was insane, and looking anxiously around her. She was dreadfully frightened of the street and the crowd. Sonia was following Katerina Ivanovna wherever she went, weeping and begging her every minute to come back home. But Katerina Ivanovna was inexorable.

'Stop it, Sonia, stop it!' she cried in hurried tones, gasping and coughing. 'You don't know what you're saying—just like a child! I've told you, I'm not going back to that drunken German woman. Let them all see, let the whole of Petersburg see a gentleman's children begging for alms—when their father spent his whole life in faithful and honourable service, and as one might say, died in harness.' (Katerina Ivanovna had already concocted this fanciful account and now believed it blindly.) 'I only hope that worthless scum of a general sees them. And you're silly, Sonia: what are we to eat now, tell me that? We've tormented you long enough; I won't have any more of it! Oh, Rodion Romanich, it's you!' she cried, seeing Raskolnikov and running over to him. 'Could you kindly explain to this silly girl that this is the most sensible thing we can do! Even organ grinders make a living; and everyone can see straight away that we're different—poor orphans from a good family, reduced to beggary—and as for that wretched little general, he'll be sacked, you'll see! We'll go and stand under his windows every day, and if the Tsar drives past, I'll get down on my knees and have these little ones stand in front of me, and I'll point to them and say "Our Father, defend us!" He's a father to the orphans, he's merciful, he'll defend them, you'll see, and as for that wretched little general... Lenia! *Tenez-vous droite!* Kolia, you're to dance again now. What are you snivelling for? snivelling again! Whatever are you afraid of, you little silly? Lord, what am I to do with them, Rodion Romanich? If you only knew how hopeless they are! Whatever am I to do with children like that!'

And although she was near tears herself (which didn't prevent her from rattling on irrepressibly and unstoppably), she pointed out her whimpering children to him. Raskolnikov began trying to persuade her to go home, and even—hoping to work on her vanity—said that it was unseemly for her to walk the streets like an organ grinder, when she was preparing to become the principal of a boarding school for young ladies...

'A boarding school, ha-ha-ha! That'll be the day!' cried Katerina Ivanovna, laughing and instantly bursting into a volley of coughs. 'No, Rodion Romanich, that dream's all over! Everyone has abandoned us! And that wretched little general... You know, Rodion Romanich, I threw an inkwell at him—there happened to be one on the table in the lobby, next to the register that people had to sign, so I signed, and threw it at him, and ran away. Oh, the villains, the villains! But to hell with them—I'll be feeding the children myself now, I won't be beholden to anybody! We've been a burden to her long enough!' (And she pointed at Sonia.) 'Polechka, how much have we collected? Show me. What? Only two kopeks? Oh, the horrible people! They don't give you anything, they just run after us and stick out their tongues at us! Well, what's that blockhead laughing at?' (pointing at someone in the crowd). 'It's all because Kolka here is so clueless, he wears me out! What is it, Polechka? Speak French to me, *parlez-moi français*. I taught you, remember—you must know a few sentences!... Or else how can we show them that you come from a genteel family, you're well brought up, nothing like those organ grinders; we're not putting on some kind of street Punch and Judy show here, we'll be singing a proper song... Oh yes! so what shall we sing them? You keep interrupting me, but we've... you see, Rodion Romanich, we've just stopped here to choose something to sing— something that even Kolia could dance to... because as you can imagine, all of this is unrehearsed; we have to settle what to perform, so we can rehearse it all properly and then we'll go off to Nevsky Prospekt, where there are far more upper-class people and we'll be noticed straight away. Lenia knows "My Little Farmstead"... Only we keep singing "My Little Farmstead" again and again, and everybody sings that! We have to sing something much more genteel... Well, what have you thought up, Polia? You at least might help your mother! My memory's quite, quite gone, or I should have thought of something! After all, we can't sing "The Hussar leaned on his sword",* can we! Oh, let's sing "*Cinq sous*" in French—I taught you that, you know I did. And the main thing is, it's in French, so they'll see straight away that you're upper-class children, and that'll make it much more moving... Or we could even do "*Malbrouck s'en va-t-en guerre*", because that's a real children's song and it's used as a lullaby in all the aristocratic households.

> *Malbrouck s'en va-t-en guerre,*
> *Ne sait quand reviendra...'**

she began... 'No, let's do "*Cinq sous*" instead! Now, Kolia, hands on hips, quickly, and Lenia, you turn around too, but in the opposite direction, and Polenka and I will sing and clap our hands!

> *Cinq sous, cinq sous,*
> *Pour monter notre ménage...**

Khe-khe-khe!' She burst into a fit of coughing. 'Straighten your dress, Polechka, the shoulders are slipping,' she pointed out between coughs when she got her breath back. 'Now, you simply must behave nice and properly, so everyone can see that you're well-born children. I said at the time that the bodice had to be cut longer, and made up of two pieces. But along you came, Sonia, with your advice—"make it shorter, make it shorter", so now the girl looks an absolute fright... Now you're all crying again! What's the point of that, you sillies! Come on, Kolia, get started, quick, quick, quick—oh, what an impossible child he is!

> *Cinq sous, cinq sous...*

Here's another soldier! Whatever do you want?'

And indeed, a policeman was pushing his way through the crowd. But at the same moment a gentleman in a greatcoat and civilian uniform, a well-to-do official in his fifties with a decoration round his neck (which was a very welcome sight for Katerina Ivanovna, and impressed the policeman) approached and silently handed her a green three-rouble note. His face wore an expression of sincere compassion. Katerina Ivanovna took it and bowed politely, even ceremoniously, to him.

'Thank you, kind sir,' she began condescendingly. 'The reasons that forced us... take the money, Polechka, you see, there are noble and generous-hearted people in the world who are ready on the instant to come to the aid of a poor gentlewoman fallen on hard times. You see before you, kind sir, these well-born orphans, with the most aristocratic connections, as you might say... But that wretched little general, sitting munching his grouse... stamping his feet because I disturbed him... "Your Excellency," said I, "protect those orphans, well acquainted as you are", said I, "with the late Semion Zakharich, whose very own daughter was slandered on the day of his death by the most villainous of scoundrels..." That soldier again! Protect us!' she cried out to the official. 'What's that soldier pestering me for? We've only just escaped from another one on Meshchanskaya,* and come here... what do you want with us, you fool?'

'That there's not allowed in the streets. Kindly stop being disorderly.'

'Disorderly yourself! I could just as well have been walking about with a barrel organ, and what business is it of yours?'

'You need a licence for a barrel organ, but you're just going around causing a disturbance. Where do you live?'

'What do you mean, a licence? I've only just buried my husband today, and he's talking about a licence!'

'Lady, lady, calm down,' began the official, 'come along now, I'll see you home... it's not right, carrying on like this in front of the crowd... you're not well...'

'My kind sir, kind sir, you don't know anything!' cried Katerina Ivanovna. 'We're on our way to Nevsky Prospekt... Sonia, Sonia! Wherever has she got to? She's crying too! What's wrong with you all?... Kolia, Lenia, where are you off to?' she suddenly screamed in alarm. 'Oh, you stupid children! Kolia, Lenia, wherever are they going?'

What had happened was that Kolia and Lenia, already frightened out of their wits by the street crowd and their mother's mad behaviour, and now catching sight of this soldier who wanted to catch them and take them away somewhere, had instantly got the same idea, grabbed each other by the hand and run away. Weeping and screaming, poor Katerina Ivanovna set off after them. It was a pitiful and horrible sight to see her running along, weeping and gasping. Sonia and Polechka rushed after her.

'Get them back, Sonia, get them back! Oh, the stupid, ungrateful children!... Polia! Catch them! I was doing it all for you, and...'

She tripped over, running at full tilt, and fell to the ground.

'She's hurt herself! She's bleeding! Oh God!' screamed Sonia as she bent over her.

Everyone caught up with her and crowded round her. Raskolnikov and Lebeziatnikov were among the first; the official joined them, and the policeman too, muttering 'Oh, Lord!' with a gesture of annoyance, suspecting that there'd be a lot of bother now.

'Get along now! Get along!' he said, trying to disperse the people crowding round.

'She's dying!' someone cried.

'She's crazy!' said someone else.

'Lord help them!' said a woman, crossing herself. 'Did they catch that girlie, and the little lad? Oh, there they are, someone's bringing them back, the big girl caught up with them... Look at the wild little things!'

But a closer look at Katerina Ivanovna showed that she wasn't bleeding from her fall on the stones, as Sonia had thought. The blood staining the pavement crimson had gushed out of her chest and throat.

'I know about this, I've seen it before,' muttered the official to Raskolnikov and Lebeziatnikov. 'It's consumption—the blood pours out like that and chokes them. I've seen it happen to a relative of mine, I was with her, not long ago—a cupful and a half, and it poured out all of a sudden. But what can we do now—she's dying!'

'Bring her in here, in here, to my place!' begged Sonia. 'I live right here!... That house there, two doors along... Get her to my place, quickly, quickly!...' she went on, running from one person to the next. 'Send for a doctor!... Oh God!'

With the official's help they brought Katerina Ivanovna indoors; even the policeman helped carry her. They brought her to Sonia's room more dead than alive, and laid her on the bed. The bleeding was continuing, but she seemed to be coming to herself. Sonia, Raskolnikov, and Lebeziatnikov came in, with the official and the policeman, once he had chased the crowd away; people had followed them all the way to the door. Polechka came in holding Kolia and Lenia by the hand; they were trembling and crying. Some people from the Kapernaumovs' flat came in too; there was the tailor himself, an odd-looking man, lame and hunchbacked, with side whiskers and bushy hair standing on end; his wife, who looked permanently scared; and several of their children, whose open-mouthed faces were set in expressions of constant surprise. And in the midst of all this crowd, Svidrigailov also turned up. Raskolnikov looked at him in amazement, not understanding where he had sprung from, since he didn't remember seeing him in the street crowd.

There was talk of a doctor, and a priest. The official whispered to

Raskolnikov that it seemed too late for a doctor, but still arranged for one to be sent for. Kapernaumov went himself.

Meanwhile Katerina Ivanovna had got her breath back. The bleeding had stopped for the moment. Her sick eyes were staring, fixed and intent, at Sonia who stood pale and trembling, wiping the drops of sweat from her brow. Eventually she asked to be raised, and they sat her up on the bed, supporting her on both sides.

'Where are the children?' she asked in a faint voice. 'Did you bring them, Polia? Oh you sillies!... Whatever did you run off for?... Oh!'

Her parched lips were still covered with blood. She looked around, and said:

'So this is how you live, Sonia! I'd never once been to your place... and now here I am...'

She looked miserably at her.

'We sucked you dry, Sonia... Polia, Lenia, Kolia, come over here... Well, here they are, Sonia, all of them; you take them now... from my hands to yours... I've had enough!... The ball is over! Kha! Let me down, at least let me die in peace...'

They laid her back on the pillow.

'What's that? A priest?... Don't bother... Where are you going to find a spare rouble?... I've no sins on me!... God will have to forgive me without that... He knows how I've suffered!... And if he won't forgive me, too bad!...'

She was growing ever more restless and delirious. Sometimes she would give a shudder, turn her eyes this way and that, and recognize everyone for a moment; but then her consciousness would fade away into delirium again. Her breathing was hoarse and laboured; there seemed to be a rattle in her throat.

'I told him: "Your Excellency!..."' she cried out, gasping after every word. 'That Amalia Ludwigovna... ah! Lenia, Kolia! Hands on hips, quickly, quickly, *glissé-glissé, pas-de-basque*!* Stamp your feet... Gracefully, child!

> *Du hast Diamanten und Perlen...*

How does it go on, though? That's what we ought to sing...

> *Du hast die schönsten Augen,*
> *Mädchen, was willst du mehr?**

I mean, I ask you! *Was willst du mehr*—what's he thinking of, the idiot!... Oh yes, here's another one:

> In the noonday heat, in the vale of Dagestan...*

Oh, how I loved it!... I used to simply adore that song, Polechka!... do you know, your father... used to sing it when we were courting... Oh, happy days!... Now, we ought to sing it now! But how, how does it go... no, I've forgotten it... Do remind me, how does it go?'

She was in a state of terrible agitation, struggling to lift herself up. Finally, in a dreadful, hoarse, broken voice, she began singing, crying out and gasping on every word, with an expression of mounting terror on her face:

> 'In the noonday heat!... In the vale!... of Dagestan!...
> A lead bullet in my breast!...

Your Excellency!' she shrieked suddenly with a heart-rending cry, and burst into tears. 'Protect the orphans! Remember the hospitality you had from the late Semion Zakharich!... One might even say aristocratic!... Kha!' And she gave a sudden shudder, coming back to her senses and looking around at everyone in horror; but at once she recognized Sonia. 'Sonia, Sonia!' she pronounced gently and tenderly, as though surprised to see her there. 'Sonia, my darling, are you here too?'

They sat her up again.

'That's enough!... My time's up!... Farewell, wretched thing!... The poor nag's been driven to death!... I'm done for!' she cried out, full of despair and loathing, and collapsed with her head on the pillow.

Once again she lost consciousness, but this time it was not for long. Her wasted, pale yellow face fell back, her mouth opened, and her legs straightened convulsively. She drew a deep, deep sigh and died.

Sonia fell onto her body, flung her arms around her and lay motionless, her head on the dead woman's emaciated breast. Polechka fell at her mother's feet, kissing them and sobbing her heart out. Kolia and Lenia hadn't yet realized what had happened, but felt that it must be something terrible; they put their arms round each other's shoulders, stared at one another, and suddenly, in unison, opened their mouths and started screaming. They were still wearing their costumes—one in his turban, the other in her nightcap with the ostrich feather.

And how did that 'certificate of merit' come to be on the bed by Katerina Ivanovna's side? There it lay, next to her pillow. Raskolnikov saw it.

He went over to the window. Lebeziatnikov hurried to join him there. 'Dead!' said Lebeziatnikov.

'Rodion Romanovich, I have to say a couple of things to you,' said Svidrigailov, coming up to join them. Lebeziatnikov at once yielded his place and tactfully stood to one side. Svidrigailov led the astonished Raskolnikov further away into the corner.

'This whole business, I mean the funeral and all that, I'll deal with it all. You know, all it takes is money, and I told you before that I've got money to spare. Those two little fledglings and Polechka, I'll find a good orphanage to take them, and settle fifteen hundred roubles on each of them for when they come of age, so Sofia Semionovna can be quite easy about them. And I'll get her out of the swamp too, because she's a good girl, isn't she! Well then, you go and tell Avdotya Romanovna from me, that's how I used the ten thousand I meant for her.'

'What's the idea of all this lavish generosity?' asked Raskolnikov.

'A-ah! What a suspicious fellow you are!' laughed Svidrigailov. 'Didn't I tell you I had money I didn't need? Anyway, can't you accept a simple act of humanity? She was no "louse", was she?' (And he pointed his finger towards the corner where the dead woman lay.) 'Not like some old pawnbroking woman. Well, wouldn't you agree—"Is Luzhin really to go on living and doing vile things, or does she have to die?" And if I don't help, then, as you know, "Polechka, for one, will go the same way..."'

All this he spoke with an air of *winking*, roguish merriment, without taking his eyes off Raskolnikov. Raskolnikov grew pale and a shiver passed through him when he heard the expressions he himself had used to Sonia. He recoiled and looked wildly at Svidrigailov.

'How... do you know all that?' he whispered breathlessly.

'I live right here, you know, just behind that wall, at Madame Resslich's. Kapernaumov's this side, and Madam Resslich through there, and she's an old and devoted friend of mine. So I'm a neighbour.'

'You?'

'Yes, me,' Svidrigailov went on, shaking with mirth. 'And I can honestly assure you, my very dear Rodion Romanovich, that you interest me strangely. I did say we'd get to know one another, I promised you that would happen; and now we have. And you'll see how easy-going I am. You'll see how well we can get on together.'

PART SIX

CHAPTER I

A STRANGE time began for Raskolnikov: it was as if a sudden mist had descended before him, enclosing him in miserable solitude from which there was no escape. When, long afterwards, he thought back to this period, he could see that his mind was clouded from time to time, and that this state of his continued, with a few breaks, right up to the final catastrophe. He was firmly convinced that many of his ideas had been wrong then, for instance about the length and timing of certain events. At least, when trying later on to remember things and clarify what he could remember, he found out a great deal about himself from information he got from other people. He would confuse one event with a different one, or regard another one as a consequence of something which had actually only happened in his imagination. Sometimes he fell prey to morbid, agonizing anxiety, which might grow into sheer panic. But he also remembered that there were some minutes, hours, even perhaps whole days, filled with apathy that took hold of him as though in reaction against his earlier terror; apathy that resembled the pathological indifference of some dying men. All in all, he himself had recently seemed to be trying to avoid understanding his situation fully and clearly. There were certain facts demanding immediate attention, which weighed on him particularly heavily. How glad he would have been to get out of having to face some of his worries, though neglecting them in his present situation would have meant risking total, unavoidable disaster.

He was particularly alarmed about Svidrigailov; one might even say he was obsessed with him. Ever since Svidrigailov had pronounced those all too ominous and explicit words in Sonia's room, at the moment of Katerina Ivanovna's death, the normal train of his thoughts had been disrupted. But although Raskolnikov was intensely preoccupied by this new development, he somehow seemed in no hurry to explain it. Sometimes, finding himself unexpectedly far away in a deserted part of town, sitting alone at a table in some wretched drinking den, brooding to himself and barely aware of how he had ended up there, he would suddenly think of Svidrigailov; he would become all too clearly and uneasily aware that he had to come to terms with that man, as quickly as he could, and if possible settle things once and for all. Once, he had found himself somewhere beyond the city limits and had actually been under the impression that he was expecting Svidrigailov to be there, and that they had an appointment to meet. Another time he woke before dawn to find himself lying on the ground among some bushes, with almost no idea how he had got there. He had in fact met Svidrigailov two or three times after Katerina Ivanovna's death, generally at Sonia's, where he had dropped in for no particular reason; but it had only been for a minute or two. They had merely exchanged a few words, never mentioning the crucial matter, as though bound by some unspoken agreement to say nothing about all that for the time being. Katerina Ivanovna's body was still lying in its coffin. Svidrigailov was busying himself about the funeral. Sonia, too, was very busy. At their last meeting, Svidrigailov had explained to Raskolnikov that he had managed to make final arrangements for Katerina Ivanovna's children, and very satisfactory ones. Through some of his connections, he had found certain persons with whose help all three orphans could immediately be placed in highly suitable institutions; and the money settled on them had also been very helpful, since it was much easier to place orphans who had some capital than those who were destitute. He had said something about Sonia too, promising to drop in on Raskolnikov one of these days, and mentioning that he'd 'like to consult him, they really needed to talk, there were certain matters to discuss...' That conversation had taken place on the landing, by the staircase. Svidrigailov had looked Raskolnikov straight in the eyes, and then, after a silence, suddenly lowered his voice to ask:

'What's up, Rodion Romanich, you seem quite out of sorts! Honestly! You're looking and listening, but you don't seem to take anything in. You ought to cheer up. Let's have a little chat: the pity is that I have to attend to a lot of other people's business, as well as my own... Ah, Rodion Romanich,' he suddenly went on, 'every human being needs air, air, yes, air... More than anything!'

Suddenly he stood aside to make way for a priest and server who were coming up the stairs. They had arrived to say a requiem mass. Svidrigailov had arranged for masses to be said punctually twice a day. Now he went on his way; Raskolnikov stood and thought for a minute, then followed the priest into Sonia's room.

He stopped in the doorway. The service began—quiet, dignified, and sad. Ever since he was a child, he had always found something oppressive, something mystically dreadful, in the awareness and presence of death; and it was a long time since he had heard a mass for the dead. But here was something else too, something terrible and disturbing.

He looked at the children. They were all kneeling by the coffin; Polechka was in tears. Behind them was Sonia, weeping quietly, almost shyly, as she prayed. 'Over these last few days she hasn't once looked at me, nor said anything to me,' Raskolnikov suddenly thought. The sun shone brightly into the room; the incense smoke billowed up in the air; the priest was reciting 'Lord, grant her peace'. Raskolnikov remained for the entire service. As the priest blessed the mourners and took his leave, he looked around him in rather an odd way. After the service, Raskolnikov went up to Sonia. She suddenly took him by both hands and laid her head on his shoulder. This slight gesture astonished Raskolnikov. He really found it strange. What, not the least revulsion, not the least loathing for him, not the faintest trembling of her hands? It was something like an act of infinite self-abnegation. At least that was how he saw it. Sonia said nothing. Raskolnikov pressed her hand and went out. He suddenly felt dreadfully miserable. If he had been able to get away somewhere at that moment, to be quite alone, even for the rest of his life, he would have counted himself lucky. But the fact was that although he had indeed been alone almost all the time recently, he never felt that he was on his own. He might find himself walking out of the city, along a main road, even on one occasion walking into a little wood somewhere; but the more solitary the place was, the more power-fully aware he was of some disturbing presence close by; not that it was exactly frightening, but rather extremely annoying, so that he would walk quickly back into the city, mix with the crowds, enter some tavern or drinking den, or make his way to the flea market* or the Haymarket. Somehow he felt easier there, and even more solitary. In one restaurant, towards evening, people were singing songs: he stayed there listening for a whole hour, and remembered actually enjoying it. But by the end he suddenly began feeling anxious again; it was as if he were suddenly overcome by pangs of conscience. 'Here I am,' he found himself think-ing, 'sitting here listening to songs—but is that really what I'm sup-posed to be doing?' But he realized straight away that that wasn't the only reason for his anxiety. There was something else that must be set-tled immediately, but he could neither get it clear in his mind nor find words for it. It all got somehow tangled up in a ball. 'No, some sort of fight would be better! Better have Porfiry... or Svidrigailov... Some sort of challenge, some attack, and quickly!... Yes! Yes!' he thought. And he left the restaurant and almost broke into a run. The thought of Dunia and their mother threw him into a state of near-panic. It was that same night, in the small hours, that he had awoken in the bushes on Krestovsky Island, shaking with fever. He went home, arriving in the early morning. After several hours' sleep his fever had settled, but when he awoke it was already late—two o'clock in the afternoon.

He remembered that Katerina Ivanovna's funeral had been arranged for that day, and was glad that he hadn't gone. Nastasia brought him something to eat, and he ate and drank with a good appetite, in fact almost greedily. His head was clearer, and he himself felt calmer, than he had for the last three days. He even felt a moment's surprise at his earlier attacks of terrified panic. The door opened and Razumikhin came in.

'Aha! He's eating—that proves he's not ill!' said Razumikhin, getting a chair and sitting down at the table opposite Raskolnikov. He was agitated, and made no attempt to hide the fact. He spoke in evident annoyance, but without hurrying or particularly raising his voice. One might have thought he had some very special fixed purpose.

'Listen,' he began firmly, 'I don't care a damn about any of you, but it's obvious, as far as I can see, that I don't understand a thing about what's going on. Please don't imagine that I'm here to question you. I don't care a bit! I don't want to know! If you were to tell me everything now, all your secrets, I might not even listen to you; I'd just say to hell with you, and walk out. All I've come for is to find out for myself, once and for all, whether it's actually true that you're mad. You see, there's a belief in certain quarters (well, some people out there) that you're either mad or very liable to become so. I admit that I felt very much like agreeing with them myself, partly because of your own stupid and sometimes revolting behaviour (which nothing could justify), and partly because of the way you've been treating your mother and sister. Only a villain and a monster, or else a madman, could have treated them the way you did; so you've got to be mad...'

'How long is it since you last saw them?'

'Just now. Haven't you seen them since that last time? Where have you been traipsing about, would you kindly tell me? I've come round to see you three times. Your mother has been seriously ill since yesterday. She managed to get herself to your place; Avdotya Romanovna tried to stop her, but she wouldn't listen. 'If he's ill,' she says, 'if his mind's disturbed, then who's to help him but his mother?' So we all came here—obviously we couldn't leave her to come on her own. All the way right up to your door, we were begging her to calm down. In we came, and you weren't here; and she sat down right here. Sat and waited ten minutes, while we stood over her, not saying anything. Then she got up and said: 'If he's left the house, that means he's well, and he's forgotten about his mother. And in that case, it's shameful and degrading for his mother to stand by his door begging for the favour of some kindness from him.' So she went back home and took to her bed; now she's in a fever. 'I see', she says, 'he's got time for *his own* woman.' She reckons that '*your own*' woman is Sofia Semionovna, your fiancée, or mistress, or whatever she is. So, brother, I went straight round to Sofia Semionovna's, because I wanted to find out exactly what was going on. In I came, and looked, and there was the coffin, and the children crying. Sofia Semionovna was measuring up mourning clothes for them. No sign of you. So I looked, and apologized, and left, and told it all to Avdotya Romanovna. That meant that the whole story was nonsense, and you didn't have a woman of *your own*, so the most likely thing was that you'd gone mad. And now, here you are, sitting there gorging yourself on boiled beef as though you hadn't eaten for three days. Well, naturally, madmen have to eat too; but although you haven't said a single word to me, you're... not mad! I'll take my oath on that. Whatever else, you're not mad. So you can go to hell, all of you, because there's some mystery here, some secret or other; and I don't mean to crack my brains over your secrets. Well, I just dropped in to give you a piece of my mind,' he concluded, standing up; 'I wanted to get it off my chest; but now I know what I've got to do!'

'So what do you want to do now?'

'What business is it of yours what I want to do now?'

'Watch out—you're going to get drunk!'

'How... how can you tell that?'

'What else?'

Razumikhin said nothing for a minute or so.

'You've always been a very rational person, and you've never, ever, been mad,' he burst out heatedly. 'You're right: I'm going to get drunk! Goodbye!' And he got up to leave.

'I talked about you to my sister, Razumikhin—a couple of days ago, I think it was.'

'About me! But... wherever could you have seen her a couple of days ago?' Razumikhin stopped short and turned rather pale. He looked as if his heart was throbbing slowly and heavily in his chest.

'She came here on her own; she was sitting here talking to me.'

'She did!'

'Yes, she did.'

'What did you say... I mean, about me?'

'I told her that you were a very good, honest, industrious man. I didn't tell her you loved her, because she knows that herself.'

'Knows it herself?'

'Of course she does! Wherever I may end up, whatever happens to me—you'll stay and look after them. I'm handing them over to you, Razumikhin, in a manner of speaking. I'm telling you this because I know perfectly well that you love her, and I believe you've a pure heart. And I know, too, that she's capable of loving you, and perhaps she actually does already. So now—decide for yourself whether or not you ought to go and get drunk.'

'Rodia... Look... Well... Oh, damn it! But where are you planning to go off to? Look, if it's all a secret, then never mind! But I... I'll find out the secret... And I'm certain that it's all some sort of nonsense that doesn't even matter, and you've dreamed it all up yourself. Anyway, you're a terrific fellow! A terrific fellow!...'

'And I was just going to add, when you interrupted me, that you were quite right to say just now that you wouldn't try to discover any of those mysteries and secrets. Leave them alone for now, don't worry about them. You'll find out all about them in due course, just when you need to know. Someone said to me yesterday that air is what a human being needs, air and air! I want to go round to see him now and ask him what he means.'

Razumikhin remained thoughtful and anxious, thinking something out.

'He's a political conspirator!* Has to be! And he's just about to do something decisive—that's how it must be! There can't be any other explanation, and... and Dunia knows...' Razumikhin suddenly thought to himself. 'So Avdotya Romanovna came to see you,' he said in slow and measured tones, 'and you yourself want to meet up with some man who says that people need more air, more air, and... and that means that this letter, too... it's to do with the same business,' he concluded, apparently to himself.

'What letter?'

'She got a letter today which upset her very much. Very much indeed. Too much. I began talking about you, and she asked me to stop. Then... then she said that we might perhaps be parting very soon; then she started thanking me warmly for something; and then she went and locked herself in her room.'

'So she got a letter?' asked Raskolnikov thoughtfully.

'Yes, she did. Didn't you know? Hmm.'

They both fell silent for a while.

'Goodbye, Rodion. Brother, I... there was a time when... Anyway, goodbye; you see, there was a time... Well, goodbye! It's time for me to go too. I shan't get drunk. There's no point now... you got it wrong!'

He was in a hurry; but even as he was leaving, and had almost shut the door behind him, he suddenly opened it again, and said without looking at Raskolnikov:

'By the way! Remember that murder, I mean, Porfiry and all that—that old woman? Well, you know what? The murderer's been found, he's confessed and produced all the evidence. He's one of those same workmen, the house painters, remember, can you believe it? And there I was standing up for them! Would you believe it, all that performance with the fighting and laughing on the staircase, with his friend, while the others were coming upstairs, the porter and the two witnesses—he set up all that on purpose, just to divert suspicion. That little dog! Wasn't he crafty! What quick thinking! You'd hardly believe it—but he explained everything, and made a full confession! What a fool I made of myself! Well, I reckon he's just brilliant at making up stories, and brilliant at confusing the lawyers—so there's nothing particularly surprising about it all. People like that must exist, mustn't they? And then the fact that he couldn't keep it up, and confessed—that makes me all the more inclined to believe him. It's more plausible... But what about me—what a fool I made of myself! Falling over myself to defend them!'

'Would you mind telling me where you heard all this, and why you're so interested?' asked Raskolnikov with evident unease.

'Get along with you! Why I'm so interested! What a question!... I heard it from Porfiry, among others. Actually I heard almost all of it from him.'

'From Porfiry?'

'Yes, Porfiry.'

'What did he... what did he mean?'

'He explained the whole thing. Gave me a psychological explanation, as he does.'

'Explained it all? Explained it all to you himself?'

'Yes, yes, himself! I'll tell you more later, but now I've got things to do. There... there was a time when I thought... Never mind, I'll tell you later!... What's the point of getting drunk now? You've got me drunk yourself, without any drink! Because I am drunk, Rodka! Drunk without drinking, I am now, and so goodbye. I'll look in again, very soon.'

And he left.

'That man—he's a political conspirator, he has to be, has to be!' Razumikhin decided firmly as he went slowly downstairs. 'And he's involved the sister too—that's very, very possible, given Avdotya

Romanovna's character. And they've started meeting one another... She dropped hints to me too. A lot of the things she said... and half-spoke... and her hints—all point to the same thing! How else to explain this whole muddle? Hmm! And there was I thinking... Oh Lord, what was I thinking! Yes, I really was deluded, and I owe him an apology! It was when we were standing in the corridor by the lamp, that was when he got me deluded. Phoo! What a wicked, coarse, vile idea I had! Well done, Mikolka, for confessing... And everything that happened before—how it all falls into place now! That illness of his just then, and all his peculiar behaviour, even earlier, before that, while he was still at university—the way he was always gloomy and morose... But what can that letter mean, now? That must mean something too, I expect. Who's it from? I suspect... Hmm. No, I'm going to find out all about it.'

Then he remembered everything that had been said about Dunechka, and realized what it meant, and his heart froze. He suddenly broke into a run.

As soon as Razumikhin left him, Raskolnikov got up, turned towards the window, bumped into one corner and then another as if he had forgotten how cramped his garret was, and... sat back down on the divan. He felt quite renewed. Another battle for him to fight—so there was a way out!

Yes, that meant there was a way out! Everything had become so constricted and closed in, it was torture trying to push his way through, a kind of stupefaction would take him over. Ever since the scene with Mikolka at Porfiry's office, he had started to feel shut in, stifled, with no means of escape. After Mikolka, the same day, there had been his meeting with Sonia; the way he had behaved, and how he'd ended it, hadn't gone in the least as he might have expected... so he must have gone all to pieces, all in an instant! All at once! And after all, he'd agreed with Sonia at the time, agreed in his heart and mind, that he couldn't manage to survive on his own, with that thing on his conscience! What about Svidrigailov? Svidrigailov was a riddle... Svidrigailov preoccupied him, that was true, but somehow it wasn't in that way. Perhaps he had a battle ahead of him with Svidrigailov too. Perhaps Svidrigailov himself was another means of escape; but Porfiry was a different matter.

So, Porfiry himself had explained things to Razumikhin—explained them *psychologically*! Yet again, he'd begun bringing in his damned psychology! Porfiry? Him? The very idea that Porfiry might believe, even for a moment, that Mikolka was guilty, after what had passed between the two of them at the time—their tête-à-tête, before Mikolka arrived: a conversation which could only possibly be interpreted *that way*... (During the past few days, Raskolnikov had several times recalled scraps and fragments of that scene with Porfiry, though he couldn't bear to remember the whole of it.) Words had passed between them then, and movements, and gestures, and such looks had been exchanged, and things pronounced in such tones, and they had taken the matter to such a point, that after that no Mikolka (whom Porfiry had seen through, right from his very first word and gesture), no Mikolka was going to succeed in shaking the very foundations of what Porfiry firmly believed.

Besides—even Razumikhin had almost begun to suspect! That scene in the corridor, by the lamp, had meant something too. And then he'd rushed off to Porfiry... But why ever had Porfiry started lying to him like that? What was his idea, throwing dust in Razumikhin's eyes with his talk of Mikolka? He must certainly have been planning something; all of that had been deliberate, but why? True, a lot of time had passed since that morning—far, far too much time—without any further sight or sound of Porfiry. Well, of course, that was a bad sign... Raskolnikov picked up his cap and left the room, deep in thought. This was the first day for some time when he had at least felt normally rational. 'I have to finish with Svidrigailov,' he thought, 'and as quickly as possible, whatever happens. I suppose he's waiting for me to seek him out myself.' And at that moment his exhausted heart suddenly overflowed with such hatred that he might even have been capable of murdering one or other of them—Svidrigailov or Porfiry. At the very least he felt that he'd be capable of doing it, if not now, then later on. 'We shall see, we shall see,' he repeated to himself.

But as soon as he opened the door to the landing, he unexpectedly ran into Porfiry himself. The man was on his way to see him. Raskolnikov stood there stunned for a moment. Oddly enough, he wasn't all that surprised to see Porfiry, nor particularly scared. He merely gave a shudder, and then quickly, instantly, prepared himself. 'Perhaps this is the end of it all! But how ever could he have got here so silently, like a cat, so that I never heard anything! Can he have been listening at the door?'

'You weren't expecting a visitor, Rodion Romanich!' laughed Porfiry Petrovich. 'I've been meaning to drop in for some time, and I was just passing, so I thought—why not come up and see you for five minutes or so. Were you just off somewhere? I shan't keep you. Just time for one cigarette, if you'll allow me.'

'Come and sit down, Porfiry Petrovich, do,' urged Raskolnikov with such apparent pleasure and affability that he would have been quite surprised if he could have seen himself. The last drops, the very dregs were now to be drained! Just so, a man may endure half an hour of mortal terror in the hands of a robber, and yet when the knife is actually pressed against his throat, he loses all his fear. Raskolnikov sat down in front of Porfiry and stared unflinchingly at him. Porfiry screwed up his eyes and lit a cigarette.

'Well, come on then, say something,'—the words were almost bursting from Raskolnikov's heart. 'Go on, go on, why don't you say anything?'

CHAPTER II

'Oh, these cigarettes!' Porfiry Petrovich finally began, after lighting up and inhaling. 'They're bad for you, really bad, but I can't give them up! I cough, and my throat tickles, and I get breathless. You know, I'm such a coward, I recently went to see Doctor B——n,* who examines each of his patients for at least half an hour. He actually laughed at me; tapped me and listened to me, and said "Tobacco's no good for you—your lungs are dilated." But how can I give it up? What's to take its place? I don't drink, that's the mischief, heh-heh-heh! That's the trouble, I don't drink! It's all relative, Rodion Romanich, it's all relative!'

'What's all this, is he getting into that old routine of his again?' thought Raskolnikov in disgust. He suddenly recalled the whole of their last meeting, and the same feelings overwhelmed him again.

'Yes, I came round to see you the day before yesterday evening—didn't you know?' went on Porfiry Petrovich, casting an eye over the room. 'I came into your room, this very room. It was just like today—I was going past and I thought, "why don't I return his call?" So I came up, and found the door ajar; I looked round, and waited a bit, but I didn't announce myself to your maid—I just left again. Don't you lock up?'

Raskolnikov's expression grew darker and darker. Porfiry seemed to be reading his thoughts.

'I've come to explain myself, my dear Rodion Romanich. Yes, to explain myself. I owe you an explanation, and must give you one,' he went on, smiling and even lightly patting Raskolnikov's knee. But almost at the same instant, his face suddenly took on a serious, worried look; to Raskolnikov's surprise, there was even a shadow of sadness in it. Raskolnikov had never seen him looking like that, nor suspected him capable of it. 'That was a strange scene between us last time, Rodion Romanich. Well, our first meeting was a strange one too, of course; but that time... Anyway, now it all boils down to the same thing. Look here:

it seems I may have treated you very badly; I feel that. The way we parted then, do you remember?—your nerves were jangling, your knees were shaking, and my nerves were jangling and my knees shaking too. And you know, it all ended up quite wrongly between us at the time—it was quite ungentlemanly. And yet we are gentlemen—at least, we're gentlemen first and foremost, and that needs to be understood. But you remember, things got to such a point... it was really quite embarrassing.'

'What's he up to? What does he take me for?' Raskolnikov wondered in amazement, lifting his head and staring straight at Porfiry.

'I've decided that it's best for us to be frank and open with each other,' Porfiry Petrovich went on, leaning his head back a little and lowering his eyes, as if not wishing to further upset his former victim by looking at him, and seeming now to have given up his earlier strategies and subterfuges. 'Yes, we can't have suspicions and scenes of that sort going on. Mikolka saved us then, or I don't know what we'd have come to. That damned little tradesman was sitting hidden behind my office partition, can you believe it? Of course, you know that already; and I know, too, that he came to see you after that; but what you supposed, hadn't happened at all. I hadn't sent for anyone, nor made any sort of arrangements. You might ask, why hadn't I? Well, what can I say— I was absolutely knocked sideways by it all. In fact I hardly got round to sending for the porters. (I dare say you noticed the porters as you passed.) I had a thought at the time, a lightning thought: you see, Rodion Romanich, at that time I was firmly convinced I was right. So I thought, even if I let one thing slip for the moment, I'll grab the other by the tail—at least I won't let my own man escape me. You're very irritable, Rodion Romanich, by nature; too irr-it-able, in fact, in spite of all the other essential qualities of your character and your heart, which I flatter myself I've partly come to understand. Well, naturally enough, even then I realized that you can't always rely on a man standing up and blurting out all the details for you. That may happen, especially when you've driven him out of all patience; but it doesn't happen often. Even I could see that. No, I thought, all I need is one little fact! Even the tiniest little fact, just one, but something I could get hold of in my hands, some actual thing, rather than nothing but all that psychology. Because, I thought, if a man's guilty, then you can at least expect to get something meaningful out of him; you might even hope for some surprising new twist. I was relying on your character then, Rodion Romanich; on your character more than anything! I was hoping for great things from you.'

'So what are you... what are you talking like this for, now?' Raskolnikov finally mumbled, not even quite clear what he was asking. 'What's he talking about?' he wondered hopelessly. 'Can he really believe that I'm innocent now?'

'Why am I talking like this? Because I've come to explain myself, so to speak; I see that as my sacred duty. I want to explain it all to you, every last detail, the way it all happened—the whole story of that mis-understanding, as you might say. I've put you through a lot of suffering, Rodion Romanich. I'm not a monster. Even I can understand what it's like, for a man who's worn down by circumstances, but who's proud, arrogant, and impatient—above all impatient—to have to go through all that. At all events, I regard you as a most honourable man, with something even magnanimous about you, although I don't hold with all your opinions: I see it as my duty to let you know that in advance, frankly and sincerely, because the most important thing for me is not to trick you. The moment I met you, I felt drawn to you. Perhaps you'll laugh at me for saying that? That's your privilege, sir. I know that you took a dislike to me as soon as you'd met me, and indeed there's nothing to like about me. But you can think what you please—what I want for myself now is to do everything I can to smooth over the impression I've made on you, and prove that I'm a man with a heart and a conscience. I'm being quite sincere.'

Porfiry Petrovich paused in dignified silence. Raskolnikov felt a new wave of terror take hold of him. He was suddenly scared by the thought that Porfiry regarded him as innocent.

'I scarcely need to tell the whole story in order, the way it suddenly started,' Porfiry Petrovich went on; 'I don't think that's necessary. In fact I doubt I'd be able to. How could one explain it all, step by step? First there were rumours. What sort of rumours they were, and who started them, and when... and how exactly your name was brought in—I think that's best passed over as well. But for me personally, it all began with a chance event, something completely accidental, which might easily never have happened, but it did. And what was that? Hmm, I think there's no point going into that either. All that, all those rumours and chance happenings came together and gave me a particular idea. I admit quite openly—because if I'm confessing, I have to make a clean breast of it—I was the first one to point the finger at you. All those notes and things the old woman wrote on her pledges, and all that—none of that amounted to anything. You could find a hundred bits of evi-dence like that. And I happened just then to hear all the details of the scene in the local police office—that was by chance too, but it wasn't

merely in passing—I was told it by a particular man, an excellent witness, who brought the whole scene amazingly to life, without even realizing it. So it was one thing after another, one after another, my dear
Rodion Romanich! How could I avoid letting my thoughts run in one
particular direction? A hundred rabbits will never make a horse,* and
a hundred suspicions will never make a proof, as the English proverb
says; but that's just rational talk, and yet passions come into it too, and
you have to deal with them, because even an investigator is a human
being. I remembered your article too, the one in that magazine, remember, you were telling me about it in detail at your very first visit. I laughed
at you, but that was just to lead you on. I tell you again, Rodion
Romanich, you're a very impatient man, and a very sick man. You're
daring, and arrogant, and earnest, and you feel things, and feel them
deeply—I'd known that about you all along. I'm familiar with all those
feelings, and I read your little paper with a sense of familiarity. It was
thought up during sleepless nights, when you were carried away, your
heart pounding with excitement, full of suppressed enthusiasm. But
there's a danger in that suppressed, proud enthusiasm when you're
young! I made fun of you at the time, but now I'll tell you that I really
like, I mean I admire, those first passionate literary outpourings of
youth. There's smoke, and mist, and there's a chord vibrating in the
mist.* Your article was absurd and fanciful, but there's such sincerity
shining through it, it's so full of incorruptible youthful pride, and the
courage of despair; it's a gloomy article, but that's good. I read it, and
then put it aside, and... when I put it aside, I thought: "Well, this man
won't stop there!" Well, would you tell me—after such a beginning,
how could I fail to be intrigued by what followed! Oh, my Lord! Am
I saying anything here? Am I affirming anything now? It was just
a thought that struck me then. "What's going on here?" I wondered?
Nothing, absolutely nothing, perhaps nothing whatsoever, at all. So it
was quite wrong of me, as an investigator, to get so carried away; there
I was with Mikolka on my hands, and hard facts against him too—for,
say what you like, they're hard facts! And there's his psychology too;
that has to be taken into account, because this is a matter of life and
death. Why am I explaining all this to you? So that you know it, and
so that with your intelligence and understanding, you don't blame me
for behaving aggressively towards you then. It wasn't aggression,
honestly, I promise you, heh-heh! What do you think—do you think
I never came round to search your place? Oh yes I did, I did, heh-heh,
I came when you were lying here sick in your bed. Not officially, and
not myself in person, but we came. Every last strand of hair in your

lodgings was examined, when the traces would still have been fresh; but—*umsonst!** I thought to myself—"now this man will come to me, of his own accord, and he'll come soon; if he's guilty, he's bound to come. Another man wouldn't, but this one will." And do you remember how Mr Razumikhin began to let things out? We'd arranged that to get you anxious—we intentionally started a rumour, so that he'd blab about it to you; and Mr Razumikhin is the sort of man who can't control his indignation. The first thing that struck Mr Zametov was your anger and your open daring; well, how could one suddenly blurt out "I've done a murder!", right in the middle of a tavern! That's too daring, too provocative—"if this man's guilty," I thought, "he's a real fighter!" That was exactly what I thought then. And I waited! I waited for you on tenterhooks; but you just crushed Zametov that time, and... well, the trouble is that all this damned psychology cuts both ways! So there I was, waiting for you, and lo and behold, God sent you along—in you came! My heart really gave a thump. Hey! What made you turn up right then? You were laughing, do you remember, laughing as you came in; it was as if I could guess it all from the other side of the glass; and yet if I hadn't been so particularly expecting you, I wouldn't have thought anything of your laughter. That's the thing about being in the right frame of mind. And Mr Razumikhin that day—ah! that stone, that stone, the one you buried the things under, remember? I can just seem to see it somewhere out there, in a kitchen garden—you did say a kitchen garden, talking to Zametov then, didn't you—and then again to me? And the way we got to talking through that article of yours, and you began explaining it—every word you spoke could be understood in two ways, as if there was another meaning hidden behind it! Well then, Rodion Romanich, that was how I got to the very end of the question, and banged my head against a post, and came to myself. "No," said I, "what am I up to? Because if one wanted to, one could interpret everything," I said to myself, "right up to the very end, in a different way, and it would come out even more natural." I was at my wits' end! "No," thought I, "I really need to find a little fact of some kind!..." So when I heard about those doorbells, just then, I simply froze, I was trembling all over. "Well," I thought, "there's my little fact then! That's the one!" And I didn't even think it out just then, I just didn't want to. I'd have given a thousand roubles at that moment, of my own money, just to have seen you *with my own eyes*, the way you walked a hundred steps side by side with that tradesman, after he'd accused you to your face of being a murderer, and for all those hundred steps you never dared ask him a thing!... What about that chill up your spine then? And ringing those doorbells, when you were ill and half delirious? So how can you be surprised after all that, Rodion Romanich, at my playing those tricks on you? And what made you turn up of your own accord, that very minute? Someone must have prodded you to do it, I swear; and if Mikolka hadn't distracted us... do you remember Mikolka just then? Remember it all clearly? What a thunderbolt that was! A bolt from a thundercloud, a real stroke of lightning! And how did I take it? I didn't believe a word of it, as you could see yourself! How could I? And afterwards, when you'd gone, and he started answering all kinds of questions very coherently indeed, enough to surprise me myself, even then I didn't believe a thing! That's what it means to have an unshakeable belief. "No," I thought, "tell me another! Mikolka, indeed!"'

'Razumikhin has just been telling me you're still accusing Nikolay. He says you told him so, quite emphatically...'

He caught his breath, and couldn't finish his sentence. He was in a state of indescribable agitation, listening to this man who had seen right through him, and who was now going back on what he had just said. He was afraid to believe him, and didn't believe him. In those double-edged words, he searched desperately to find anything more precise and definite.

'Oh, that Mr Razumikhin!' cried Porfiry Petrovich, apparently delighted that Raskolnikov, obstinately silent so far, had come up with a question. 'Heh-heh-heh! Mr Razumikhin—I simply needed to put him off. Two's company, three's a crowd. Mr Razumikhin doesn't come into it at all, for all that he came running to see me, white as a sheet... Well, bless the man, why mix him up in all this? But as for Mikolka, do you want to know what sort of a man he is, I mean, as I see him? First of all, he's still a child, he's never grown up; not exactly a coward, but some sort of an artist, in my view. Honestly, don't laugh at me for putting it like that. He's an innocent soul, very impressionable. He has a good heart, but he lets his imagination run away with him. He'll sing for you, and dance for you, and tell stories—such stories that folk will come a long way just to hear them. He's been to school, and he'll giggle himself silly over a rude sign, and drink himself unconscious, not because he's a vicious character but just because someone plies him with drink; just like a child, as I said. He committed a theft, that time, but he never realized it, because he thought, "If I found it lying on the ground, what kind of theft is that?" And do you realize, he's a schismatic, well, not exactly a schismatic, but a sectarian; some of his family once joined the "Runaways", and he himself, quite recently, spent a whole two years in the provinces as a disciple of some *starets* or other.* I found all that out from Mikolka himself and his people from Zaraysk. Honestly! He was actually wanting to run away into the wilderness! He had an urge of that sort, praying to God every night, reading himself silly out of old books, seeking for the "truth". Petersburg had a powerful effect on him, particularly the women, and the vodka too, of course. But he's impressionable; he forgot about the *starets* and everything else. I happen to know that there was a painter here who took a liking to him, and Mikolka used to go and see him; and then this business happened! Well, he took fright—wanted to hang himself! To run away! What's to be done, when people have notions like that about our legal system? I mean, some people are terrified of the word "trial". Whose fault is that? The new courts may change things a bit. I hope to God they do! Well, when he was in prison he apparently remembered that honest *starets*; and the Bible reappeared again. Do you know, Rodion Romanich, what the idea of "suffering" means to some of those people? It doesn't mean suffering on someone else's behalf; it's just the idea that "one has to suffer"; you have to accept suffering, and if it comes from the authorities, so much the better. In my time there was one very meek convict who served a whole year in prison, and every night he'd lie on the stove reading the Bible, and read and read so much that one day, out of the blue, he pulled out a brick and threw it at the governor, without the slightest provocation. And the way he threw it—a whole yard wide, on purpose, to be sure of not hurting him. Well, you know what happens to a convict who commits an armed assault on an officer; so there it was, he "accepted his suffering". Well then— I suspect now that Mikolka wants to "accept suffering", or something like that. I'm certain of it, there are facts that prove I'm right. Only he himself doesn't know that I know. Why, surely you'd agree that this class of people throws up men with weird ideas? They're everywhere! That *starets* has begun to weigh on Mikolka again, especially after he tried to hang himself. But he'll come to me of his own accord and tell me everything. Do you think he'll be able to hold out? Just you wait, he'll recant all right! I'm expecting him hour by hour to come and take back his confession. I've taken a liking to this Mikolka, and I'm going to investigate him thoroughly. And what do you think? Heh-heh! He gave me the most convincing answers to some points—he'd obviously got hold of the information he needed, and made up a good story; and then on other points he fell flat on his face, didn't know the first thing; not only he didn't know anything, but he didn't even realize that he didn't know! No, my dear old Rodion Romanich, this isn't about Mikolka! This is a fantastic, murky business, a modern affair, a sign of our times, of the darkness of the human heart; when people quote the idea that blood "refreshes";* when life is supposed to be all about comfort. These are dreams got up out of books; hearts troubled by theories. You see a man resolving to take a first step, but his resolution is of a special kind—he resolves to do it, and then it's as if he'd fallen off a cliff or thrown himself off a steeple,* and he goes off to commit his crime without knowing what he's doing. He forgets to close the door behind him; but he's committed a murder, two murders, all because of a theory. He committed murder, but didn't manage to pick up the money; and what he did pick up, he went and hid under a stone. And as if the agony he went through wasn't enough for him, hiding behind the door while they were hammering at it and ringing the bell—no, he had to go back to that empty flat, half-delirious, to remind himself about that bell; he needed to get that chill down his spine all over again... Very well, he was ill when he did that; but what about this: he's committed a murder, but he still regards himself as an honest man, despises other people, walks around like a pale angel... no, what's this got to do with Mikolka, my dear Rodion Romanich? There's no Mikolka in all this!'

These last words, after everything that had gone before, which had sounded like a retraction—all this was completely unexpected. Raskolnikov gave a shudder, as if he had been stabbed.

'So... who was it... that did the murder?' he asked in a choking voice, unable to bear it any longer. Porfiry Petrovich flung himself backwards against the chair-back, as if he too were amazed by the unexpected question.

'What do you mean, who's the murderer?...' he repeated, as if he couldn't believe his ears. 'Why, it was *you*, Rodion Romanich! You did the murder...' he added almost in a whisper, in a voice of total conviction.

Raskolnikov sprang up from the divan, stood there for a few seconds, and sank down again without uttering a word. His whole face suddenly twitched convulsively.

'Your lip's trembling again, just as it did then,' murmured Porfiry Petrovich, almost sympathetically. 'I believe you hadn't understood me quite right, Rodion Romanich,' he added after a brief silence, 'and that's why you were so astonished. This was just why I came here—to tell you everything, and get it all out in the open.'

'It wasn't me that killed them,' Raskolnikov whispered, like a frightened little child caught red-handed.

'Oh, yes it was, Rodion Romanich, it was you; it couldn't have been anyone else,' whispered Porfiry with stern certainty.

Then they were both silent, and their silence lasted a strangely long time—quite ten minutes. Raskolnikov leaned his elbows on the table and ran his fingers through his hair, saying nothing. Porfiry Petrovich sat calmly waiting. Suddenly Raskolnikov looked scornfully at Porfiry.

'Up to your old tricks again, Porfiry Petrovich! Same old games as before. How come you aren't sick of them by now?'

'Oh, give over now, what do I need tricks for any more? If there were witnesses here, now, it'd be a different matter; but we're whispering to each other on our own here. You can see for yourself—I didn't come here to hunt you down and catch you like some hare. You can confess or not—right now I don't care. For my part, I'm sure of myself, whatever you say.'

'And if that's so, what have you come for?' Raskolnikov demanded angrily. 'I'll ask you the same thing as before: if you reckon I'm guilty, why aren't you taking me to prison?'

'Well now, that's the question! I'll answer you point by point. Firstly, arresting you straight away wouldn't do me any good.'

'What do you mean, any good? If you're convinced, then you have to...'

'Who says I'm so convinced? That's just a dream of mine, for now. And why should I lock you up in there *in peace*? You know that's what it would mean, since you're asking me to do it yourself. Supposing I bring that tradesman along to accuse you, and you say to him "Were you drunk, or what? Who saw me with you? I just took you for a drunk, and so you were"—well, how could I answer that, particularly since your story will be more plausible than his, because there's nothing but psychology to back up his evidence—which doesn't look at all good, with a mug like his—while what you say will be spot on, because he does drink, the villain, he drinks like a fish and he's well known for it. Moreover, I've admitted to you quite frankly, more than once, that all this psychology cuts both ways, and the opposite interpretation will carry much more weight and conviction. Besides which, I don't have anything against you right now. And even if I am actually going to arrest you, and though I've come along myself (against all the rules) to warn you in advance, even so I'm telling you frankly (also against the rules) that it won't do me any good. Well, and secondly, I came to see you...'

'Yes, and secondly?' (Raskolnikov's voice was still choked.)

'As I've just told you, I consider I owe you an explanation. I don't want you to regard me as a monster, particularly as I sincerely wish you well, whether you believe me or not. And thirdly, that's why I've come to you with a straight, open proposal: come in and confess of your own accord. That'll be infinitely better for you, and for me too, because it'll be a weight off my shoulders. So, now, is that plain speaking from me or isn't it?'

Raskolnikov thought for a minute.

'Listen, Porfiry Petrovich—you said yourself that this was all about psychology, yet now you've launched into mathematics. But what if you're making a mistake here yourself?'

'No, Rodion Romanich, I'm not. I've got a particular piece of evidence. A piece of evidence I'd already found before, you know—the Lord sent it my way!'

'What piece of evidence?'

'I shan't tell you what it is, Rodion Romanich. In any case, I've no right to put things off any longer: I am going to arrest you. So work it out for yourself—*right now* I don't care any more, this is all just for your benefit. Honestly, it'll be better, Rodion Romanich!'

Raskolnikov smiled a venomous smile.

'All this isn't merely ridiculous, it's downright shameless. Even supposing I'm guilty (which I don't for a second admit), why ever should I come and volunteer a confession, when you've just said yourself that once you lock me up, I'll be *at peace*?'

'Oh, Rodion Romanich, don't believe everything you're told. Maybe you won't be entirely *at peace*! That was just a theory, and merely one of my own; what kind of an authority am I for you? I may be hiding something from you even now. I can't go revealing everything just like that, heh-heh! And then again, how can you ask what good it'll do you? Don't you know how much they'd knock off your sentence? Look at when you'd be presenting yourself, look at the timing of it! Just think about it! When someone else has already confessed to the crime, and confused the whole issue! And I swear to you before God, I'll arrange it all *back there* to make your confession seem completely unexpected. We'll get rid of all that psychological stuff, I'll wipe out all our suspicions of you, so that your crime looks like some kind of brainstorm, because quite frankly, that's what it was. I'm an honest man, Rodion Romanich, and I'll keep my word.'

Raskolnikov remained in dejected silence and hung his head. He thought for a long time, and eventually smiled once more, but this time his smile was meek and sad.

'Oh, what's the point!' he said, apparently now addressing Porfiry quite openly. 'It's no good! I don't need your remission of sentence!'

'Well, that's just what I was afraid of!' exclaimed Porfiry heatedly, almost despite himself. 'That's what I was afraid of—that you wouldn't need our remission of sentence.'

Raskolnikov gave him a sad, solemn look.

'Hey, don't write off your life!' Porfiry went on. 'There's a lot of it ahead of you. How can you not need a remission—whatever do you mean? What an impatient man you are!'

'There's a lot of what, ahead of me?'

'Your life! You're not a prophet, are you—what do you know? Seek and ye shall find. Perhaps God has just been waiting to find you here. Those shackles aren't for ever, you know...'

'No, there'll be a remission...' laughed Raskolnikov.

'Well, are you scared of the disgrace, scared of what respectable people will think? Perhaps you really are, and don't realize it yourself— you're so young! But you, of all people, shouldn't be afraid or ashamed of making a voluntary confession.'

'A-ah, who cares!' whispered Raskolnikov, full of scorn and revulsion, as if he didn't even want to talk about it. He started to get up, as though he meant to go out somewhere, but sat down again in evident despair.

'Who cares, indeed! You've lost your beliefs and think I'm telling you barefaced lies—but have you had much of a life so far? Do you understand a lot? You thought up a theory, and now you're ashamed that it didn't work out—and it all ended up looking very unoriginal! Yes, it did turn out disgracefully, that's the truth, but even so you're not a hopeless villain. Not at all that sort of villain! At least you didn't go deceiving yourself for long—you went straight to the very limit. What do you think I take you for? I take you for the sort of person who—even if he's being disembowelled alive—will stand there smiling at his torturers—so long as he finds a faith or a God. So—find yourself one, and you'll live. First off, you've needed a change of air for some time. And suffering is no bad thing either. Go and suffer a bit. Perhaps that Mikolka is right to seek for suffering. I know you don't believe me—but don't try to be too clever; give yourself up to life, straight off, don't think about it; and don't worry, it'll cast you up on the shore and set you on your feet. Which shore? How can I know? All I believe is that you still have a lot of living to do. I know you think that what I'm telling you is nothing but a sermon I've learnt by heart; but perhaps you'll remember it one day, and it'll stand you in good stead. That's why I'm talking to you. And another good thing is that you only killed an old woman. If you'd thought up a different theory, you might have done something a hundred million times more wicked! Perhaps you ought to be giving thanks to God; for all you know, he may be saving you just for that! Be of good heart, and don't be so fearful. Are you frightened by the great ordeal ahead of you? No, it's shameful to be frightened of it now. Once you've taken a step like that, you have to stand firm. That's only fair. Now you must do what fairness demands. I know you don't believe me; but I swear to God, life will carry you through. And you'll be glad of it later on. All you need now is air, air, air!'

Raskolnikov gave a start.

'Who are you, anyway?' he cried. 'Some kind of prophet? Making these all-knowing pronouncements from your sublime pinnacle of serenity?'

'Who am I? I'm a man who's gone as far as he ever will, that's all. A man capable of feeling and empathy, perhaps, and one who knows a fair amount, perhaps, but one who's going no further. But you—you're different. God has a life prepared for you (although who knows, maybe your life, too, will just drift by like a puff of smoke and never come to anything). So what does it matter if you join a different class of people? It's not comfort you'll miss, is it—you with your great heart? So what if you're not seen for a very long time? It's not a question of time, but of you yourself. If you become a shining sun, everyone will see you. The first duty of the sun is to be the sun. What are you smiling at again? Because I sound like Schiller? And I bet you anything you think I'm flattering you now! And do you know, perhaps I really am, heh-heh-heh! Don't you believe everything I say, Rodion Romanich; in fact, don't ever believe in me completely; that's just the sort of person I am, I grant you. But here's what I'll add: how much of a scoundrel I am and how much of an honest man, that's something you can judge for yourself!'

'When are you thinking of arresting me?'

'Well, I can let you run around another day and a half, or two days. Think about it, dear boy, and say a prayer to God. It'll be better, I swear. Better for you.'

'And supposing I run away?' asked Raskolnikov, with a strange grin.

'No, you won't run away. A peasant would run away; a young sectarian would run away—the lackey of some other person's ideas—because that kind of person, if you just show him the tip of your finger, he'll believe whatever you want him to, like that Midshipman Hole,* for the rest of his life. But you don't even believe in your own theory any more; so why would you run away? What would be the use? A runaway's life is difficult and horrible; while what you need most of all is a life, and a definite situation, and enough air. When you run away, is the air your own? You'd run away and come back of your own accord. *You can't do without us.** If I were to lock you up in jail, you might stick it for a month, or two, or three, and then suddenly, mark my words, you'd come forward and confess—and what's more, you'd do it without even having realized you were going to. An hour before, you wouldn't even know you were about to confess. In fact I'm certain you'll "resolve to accept your suffering"; right now you don't believe what I'm saying, but you'll come to the same conclusion yourself. And then, Rodion Romanich, suffering is a great thing; don't look at how fat I've grown, that's not the point—but I do know this: don't laugh, but suffering has a point. Mikolka's right. No, Rodion Romanich, you won't run away.'

Raskolnikov stood up and picked up his cap. Porfiry Petrovich rose too.

'Going out for a walk? It looks like a fine evening, so long as the thunder holds off. Although that might be even better, if it got cooler...'

And he picked up his own cap.

'Porfiry Petrovich, don't get any ideas, please,' announced Raskolnikov sternly and insistently. 'Don't imagine I've confessed to you today. You're an odd fellow, and I've been listening to you out of pure curiosity. But I haven't confessed to anything... Just remember that.'

'Yes, of course, I'll remember that.—Look at him, actually trembling. Don't you fret, dear boy, have it your own way. Do take a little walk—but you mustn't go too far. I've another little request for you, just in case,' he added, lowering his voice; 'a bit of a ticklish one, but it's important. If, I mean just in case the question arises (which I don't believe it will, and it's something I consider you quite incapable of): if it should by any chance come about—well, I mean, just in case—if you were to find yourself inclined, during the next forty or fifty hours, to put an end to this business in some different way, in some fantastic manner—by laying hands on yourself (an absurd suggestion, do please forgive me for it), then would you please leave a brief explanatory note? No more than a couple of lines, just two short lines, and mention the stone; that would be most kind of you. Well, goodbye for now... Happy thoughts and good beginnings!'

Porfiry left, stooping and, it seemed, avoiding looking at Raskolnikov. Raskolnikov went over to the window and waited with tense impatience until he calculated that Porfiry must have come out into the street and walked off. Then he hurriedly left the room himself.

CHAPTER III

HE was hurrying to Svidrigailov's. What he hoped for from that man, he had no idea himself. But the man had some hidden hold over him. Once he realized this, he could have no peace; and now the moment had come.

On his way there, he was tormented by one particular question. Had Svidrigailov been to see Porfiry?

As far as he could see—and indeed he'd have taken an oath on it—the answer was no. He thought it over and over, recalling the whole of Porfiry's visit, and decided: no, Svidrigailov hadn't gone there.

But if he hadn't gone yet—would he or wouldn't he go to Porfiry?

For the moment, he felt that he wouldn't go. Why not? He couldn't even explain; but if he had an explanation, he wouldn't have been racking his brains for it now. All this worried him, and yet at the same time, in a way, he couldn't be bothered with it. It was a strange fact, which might seem unbelievable; but his present, immediate fate was something that only vaguely and distantly troubled him. What tormented him was something different, something far more important, something extraordinary—something that concerned him and him alone, but it was something different, and something of the greatest importance. At the same time he was overcome by a boundless moral fatigue, although his reasoning powers were functioning better this morning than they ever had over the past few days.

But was there any point in trying, now, after everything that had happened, to overcome all these new and trivial complications? Was there any point, for instance, in plotting and planning to stop Svidrigailov from going to see Porfiry; in puzzling things out, and asking around, and wasting his time, all for some wretched Svidrigailov?

Oh, how fed up he was with it all!

And yet, meanwhile, he was still hurrying to Svidrigailov's. Might he even be expecting something *new* from him—information of some kind, or a way out? People grasp at straws, don't they? Was it their destiny, or some instinct, that drew the two of them together? Perhaps it was only his exhaustion and despair; perhaps it wasn't Svidrigailov he needed but someone else, but Svidrigailov had happened to turn up. Sonia? But why should he go to Sonia now? To beg for her tears again? Besides, he was scared of Sonia. Sonia represented an inexorable sentence, an unchangeable decision. Before him there lay either her path, or his own. At this moment above all, he lacked the strength to meet her. No, wouldn't it be better to try Svidrigailov, and find out what all that was about? And he couldn't avoid admitting to himself that for some reason, he'd needed that man for a long time.

But what could the two of them have in common? Even their wrong-doing couldn't have been the same. What was more, the man was extremely unpleasant, evidently depraved through and through, undoubtedly sly and dishonest, and perhaps very spiteful. There were all sorts of rumours about him. True, he had done a lot for Katerina Ivanovna's children; but who knew why, or what it all meant? He was a man of endless schemes and designs.

There was another thought that kept running through Raskolnikov's mind, and worried him dreadfully, although he did his best to shut it out because it was so unbearable. He found himself thinking that Svidrigailov had always hung around him, and was still doing so. Svidrigailov had found out his secret; Svidrigailov had had his eye on Dunia. Supposing he still did? Almost certainly the answer was yes. So what if, now that he'd found out Raskolnikov's secret and got him in his power, he decided to use his power as a weapon against Dunia?

This idea had tormented him from time to time, even in his dreams; but it had never entered his conscious mind so clearly as now, when he was on his way to Svidrigailov's. The very thought drove him into a state of morose rage. In the first place, that would change everything at once, even his own personal situation. He would have to tell Dunechka his secret. Perhaps he would have to give himself up, just to save Dunechka from taking some rash step. A letter? This morning Dunia had received some letter, and who could be sending her letters, here in Petersburg? (Unless it was Luzhin?) Of course, Razumikhin was on guard there; but Razumikhin knew nothing. Perhaps he should tell Razumikhin everything? Raskolnikov recoiled from the very thought.

'Whatever happens, I have to see Svidrigailov as soon as I can,' he decided firmly. 'I needn't really trouble with the details here, thank goodness, only with the essence of it all; but if, if he's actually capable, if Svidrigailov is plotting something against Dunia,—then...'

Raskolnikov had grown so exhausted over this time, over this whole month, that he could only think of one way to solve this sort of problem. 'Then I'll kill him,' he thought in cold desperation. His heart was suddenly weighed down; he stopped in the middle of the road and looked around him, wondering which street he was on and how he had got there. He was on ——sky Prospekt, thirty or forty yards from the Haymarket, which he had just crossed.* The whole second floor of the house on his left had been taken over as a tavern. All the windows were wide open, and judging from the figures moving about by the windows, the place was full to bursting. There were sounds of singing, a clarinet and a fiddle playing, and the boom of a Turkish drum. He could hear women squealing. He made to turn back, wondering why he had come onto ——sky Prospekt; but suddenly he noticed Svidrigailov, sitting at a tea-table right next to one of the wide-open end windows, and holding a pipe between his teeth. This sight astonished and horrified him. Svidrigailov was silently watching and examining him, and another thing that instantly struck Raskolnikov was that Svidrigailov seemed to be intending to get up and slip silently away before he was noticed. Raskolnikov immediately pretended not to have noticed him either, and affected to be looking thoughtfully away to one side, while still watching Svidrigailov out of the corner of his eye. His heart was pounding with anxiety. He was right: Svidrigailov evidently didn't want to be seen. He had taken the pipe out of his mouth and was already on the point of disappearing; but after standing up and pushing his chair aside, he seemed to suddenly realize that Raskolnikov could see him and was watching him. What passed between them now was rather like their first meeting in Raskolnikov's lodgings, when Svidrigailov had come while Raskolnikov was asleep. A mischievous grin appeared on Svidrigailov's face, and grew gradually wider. Each of them knew that he could see the other, and was watching him. Eventually Svidrigailov burst into a loud guffaw.

'Come on then! Come on in if you like—I'm here!' he called down from the window.

Raskolnikov went upstairs to the tavern.

He found him in a very small back room with a single window, adjoining the saloon where merchants, clerks, and all kinds of other people were sitting drinking tea at about twenty little tables, to the wild din of a chorus of singers. From somewhere else came the click of billiard balls. On Svidrigailov's table stood an open bottle of champagne and a half-full glass. There was a boy in the room, too, with a little hand organ, and a healthy-looking red-cheeked girl of eighteen, a singer, wearing a tucked-in striped skirt and a Tyrolean hat with ribbons on it. Ignoring the noise from the chorus next door, she was singing a servants' song in a rather hoarse contralto voice, to the accompaniment of the barrel organ.

'Stop, that'll do!' Svidrigailov interrupted her as Raskolnikov came in.

The girl broke off at once and stood waiting respectfully. Indeed, she had had a rather serious and respectful look on her face, even as she sang her rhyming ballad.

'Hey, Filipp, a glass!' called Svidrigailov.

'I won't have any wine,' said Raskolnikov.

'Just as you like, I didn't mean you. Drink up, Katya! Run along now, I shan't be needing you any more today.' He poured her a full glass of champagne and put a yellow banknote* on the table. Katya drained the whole glass, drinking her wine the way women do, taking twenty gulps straight off without drawing breath; then she picked up the money, kissed Svidrigailov's hand which he solemnly let her take, and left the room, the little boy trailing behind her with his barrel organ. They had both been brought in off the street. Svidrigailov hadn't been in Petersburg a week before he had organized everything around him as though he were some sort of patriarch. Filipp the tavern waiter had already become his 'old friend' and grovelled obsequiously to him. The door to the saloon would be locked for him; Svidrigailov treated this room as his home and might spend the whole day there. The tavern was mean and dirty and worse than third-rate.

'I was on my way to your place, to find you,' began Raskolnikov; 'but why on earth did I turn onto ——sky Prospekt from the Haymarket? I never turn this way, never come along here. I always take a right turn from the Haymarket. And this isn't the way to yours. But the moment I turned the corner, there you were! Very odd!'

'Why don't you say straight out: it's a miracle!'

'Because it may have just happened by chance.'

'All you lot are just the same!' laughed Svidrigailov. 'Even if you believe in miracles in your heart, you won't admit it! You yourself just said that "it may have" simply happened by chance. And what cowards people are about admitting what they really think, you wouldn't believe, Rodion Romanich! I'm not talking about you. You have your own opinions, and aren't afraid to have them. That was just what made me curious about you.'

'Nothing else?'

'That was enough, wasn't it?'

Svidrigailov was evidently exhilarated, but only slightly so—he hadn't drunk more than half a glass of wine.

'I believe you came to see me before you'd even found out that I'm capable of having my own opinions, as you call them,' remarked Raskolnikov.

'Oh, then, that was different. Everyone looks to his own concerns. But as for miracles, let me tell you that you seem to have slept through these last two or three days. I told you about this tavern myself, and there was no miracle about your coming straight here—I told you where this place was and how to get here, and what time you could expect to find me here. Remember?'

'No, I'd forgotten,' replied Raskolnikov in surprise.

'I'm sure you had. Twice, I told you. The address got fixed mechanically in your memory. And you turned this way mechanically too, and came straight to the right address, without even being aware of it yourself. Even when I told you about it then, I didn't actually believe you'd understood me. You do give yourself away a lot, Rodion Romanich. And another thing: I'm sure there are many people in Petersburg who walk about talking to themselves. This is a city of semi-lunatics. If only we had any science, doctors and lawyers and philosophers could have done very valuable research on Petersburg, each in his own line. There aren't many places where the human soul is subject to so many gloomy, violent, and strange influences as here in Petersburg. The climate alone is bad enough! And at the same time, this is the administrative centre for the whole of Russia, and everything's bound to reflect its character. But that's not the point just now—the point is that I've watched you a few times. When you leave the house, you hold your head high. But twenty paces on, you hang your head and clasp your hands behind you. Your eyes are open, but you're quite obviously not seeing anything ahead of you, or on either side. Eventually you start moving your lips, talking to yourself, and sometimes you raise your arm and start declaiming; and finally you stop still in the middle of the road and stand there for a long time. That's not good at all. Somebody besides me might notice you, and that'll do you no good. Personally I don't actually care, and I'll never cure you—but of course you understand me.'

'Do you know that I'm being followed?' asked Raskolnikov, looking inquisitively at him.

'No, I know nothing about that,' replied Svidrigailov in some surprise.

'Well then, let's say no more about me.'

'All right, let's say no more about you.'

'I'd rather you told me this: if you come here to drink, and twice instructed me to come and find you here, then why, when I looked up at your window from the street, did you hide and try to get away? I saw that quite clearly.'

'Heh-heh! And why, when I was standing in your doorway that day, did you lie there on your sofa with your eyes shut and pretend to be asleep, when you weren't asleep at all? I saw that quite clearly.'

'I might have had... my reasons... you know that yourself.'

'And I might have had my reasons too, though you won't ever know them.'

Raskolnikov leaned his right elbow on the table, rested his chin on the fingers of his right hand, and stared intently at Svidrigailov. For about a minute he examined his face, which had always intrigued him. It was an odd face, almost like a mask—part pale, part pink, with ruddy crimson lips, a light-coloured beard, and fair hair that was still quite thick. His eyes were somehow too blue, and their look somehow too heavy and unmoving. There was something terribly unattractive about that handsome face, so extraordinarily young for his years.* He was wearing stylish lightweight summer clothes, and his linen was particularly elegant. One finger bore a huge ring with a precious stone.

'Do I really have to bother myself with you too?' Raskolnikov demanded abruptly, coming straight to the point in a burst of impatience. 'You may be the most dangerous man around, if you feel like doing me an injury; but I simply don't want to trouble myself with you any longer. And now I'm going to show you that I don't hold myself as dear as you probably think I do. Listen to this: I've come to tell you straight out that if your intentions towards my sister are the same as before, and if you're thinking of making use of anything that's recently come to light, so as to get your own way, then I'll kill you before you can get me locked up. I'll keep my word: you know I can. And secondly: if there's anything you want to tell me (for I've always had the feeling that you wanted to tell me something), then do it quickly, because time's precious, and very soon it may be too late.'

'What on earth's the hurry?' asked Svidrigailov, giving him a curious look.

'Everyone attends to his own business,' replied Raskolnikov darkly and impatiently.

'Right now you were insisting that we had to be open with one another, and the very first time I ask you a question you won't answer,' remarked Svidrigailov with a smile. 'You keep imagining I've got some kind of interest of my own, and that makes you wary of me. Well, of course that's quite understandable in your situation. But however much I'd like to become your friend, I'm not going to put myself out just to convince you you're wrong. Honestly, the game isn't worth the candle, and in any case I never planned to talk to you about anything so very special.'

'Then what did you need me for? It was you who came hanging round me, wasn't it?'

'Only because you were a curious subject for observation. I was attracted to you by the fantastic situation you were in, that's what!

Besides which, you're the brother of a person who used to interest me very much; and lastly, at one time I used to hear a great deal about you from that same person, which led me to conclude that you had a lot of influence over her. Isn't that enough? Heh-heh-heh! Actually, I admit that your question is a very complicated one for me, and I find it hard to answer you. Well now, for instance, you've come to see me today for some particular purpose, but you're also wanting something nice and new, aren't you? Isn't that so? Isn't it?' Svidrigailov insisted with a roguish grin. 'Well then, just imagine that I too, when I was sitting in the railway carriage on my way here, was counting on you to tell me something *nice and new* in return; and hoping I'd get to borrow something from you that way. See how rich we are!'

'Borrow what?'

'What can I say? How should I know? See what a low dive I spend my time in, and yet I love it—well, not that I actually love it, but one has to sit somewhere. Think of that poor Katya—did you see her? If I'd been a great glutton, some sort of club gourmet... but you see the kind of food I'll settle for!' (He jerked his finger at a little table in the corner, where a tin dish held the remnants of a dreadful steak and some potatoes.) 'Incidentally, have you had anything to eat? I've already eaten, I don't want any more. Wine, for instance—I don't drink it. No wine at all, except for champagne; but a single glass would last me the whole evening, and even that would give me a headache. I only ordered it just now to set myself up, because I'm off somewhere, and you find me in a very particular frame of mind. That was why I hid from you like a schoolboy just then—because I thought you'd get in my way; but it looks' (taking out his watch) 'as if I can spend an hour with you: it's half past four now. Would you believe it—if only I'd been something—well, a landowner for instance, or a father, or an Uhlan,* a photographer, a journalist... but I never was any good at anything! It actually gets boring sometimes. I really thought you'd have something nice and new to tell me.'

'But what sort of a man are you, and why did you come here?'

'What I am? You know what I am—a gentleman, spent two years in a cavalry regiment, then hung about here in Petersburg, then I married Marfa Petrovna and lived in the country. That's the story of my life!'

'You're a gambler, I believe?'

'No, I'm no gambler. A card sharp, not a gambler.'

'So you've been a card sharp?'

'Yes, I've been a card sharp.'

'And got beaten up, I suppose?'

'Yes, on occasion. Why?'

'Well, so you might have been challenged to a duel... That sort of thing adds spice to your life.'

'I wouldn't disagree with you; but I'm no great expert at philosophizing. I must admit I mainly came here for the women.'

'When you'd only just buried Marfa Petrovna?'

'Why, yes.' Svidrigailov smiled with disarming frankness. 'But so what? You seem to object to the way I talk about women?'

'You mean, do I object to debauchery?'

'Debauchery! So that's what you're on about! Well, first things first, let me answer you about women in general. You know, I feel like a chat. So tell me, why should I restrain myself? Why should I give up women, when I'm so fond of them? At least they keep one busy.'

'So all you're after here is debauchery?'

'All right then, if you like—yes, debauchery! How you do go on about it! But at least I like your straightforward question. That sort of debauchery at least makes some sense, it's rooted in our nature and not subject to fanciful whims; it's a constant glowing ember in our blood, something that everlastingly fires you up, and perhaps even the passing years won't be in too much of a hurry to quench it. It's a sort of occupation in its way, wouldn't you agree?'

'What are you so pleased about? It's a sickness, and a dangerous one.'

'So that's what you're after! I agree it's a sickness, like anything else done to excess—and you absolutely have to do it to excess; but firstly, one man does this way, and another one that way; and secondly, of course, people ought to do everything in moderation, that's the best policy, though it's a mean sort of one, but what's a man to do? If all that didn't exist, he'd probably have to shoot himself. I agree that any decent man is condemned to boredom, but really, I mean...'

'And would you be capable of shooting yourself?'

'Well there you go!' Svidrigailov brushed the question aside with disgust. 'Do me a favour, don't talk about that,' he added hastily, without the bombast that had coloured all he had said so far. Even his expression seemed to have changed. 'I admit I'm unpardonably weak, but what am I to do? I'm afraid of dying, and I don't like having it talked about. Did you know that I'm a bit of a mystic?'

'Aha! Those apparitions of Marfa Petrovna! So, do they still come and visit you?'

'Don't talk about them, please! There haven't been any in Petersburg, so far; but to hell with them anyway!' he cried irritably. 'No, let's talk about the... although... Hmm! No, there isn't much time, I can't stay here with you for long, but it's a pity! I would have had something to tell you.'

'Why, are you meeting a woman?'

'Yes, a woman, something came up by chance... but that's not what I wanted to say.'

'And your whole repulsive way of life here—doesn't that weigh on you any more? Have you lost the strength to stop yourself?'

'So you claim to have strength, too? Heh-heh-heh! You've just surprised me, Rodion Romanich, though I could see how it was going to be. There you are, talking to me about debauchery and aesthetics! You're a Schiller,* an idealist! Of course that's how it all has to be, and it'd be surprising if it was any different; but even so, the fact that it's that way is a bit odd... Oh, what a pity there's so little time; because you yourself are a most intriguing subject. Incidentally, do you like Schiller? I simply love him.'

'Honestly, what a big mouth you are!' said Raskolnikov in disgust.

'No, really I'm not!' replied Svidrigailov with a laugh. 'Or—all right, I won't argue, perhaps I am; but why shouldn't one talk big, if it does no harm? I spent seven years living with Marfa Petrovna in the country, so now, when I come across an intelligent man like you—an intelligent and most extremely intriguing man—I'm simply glad to have a chat. Besides which I've just had that half-glass of wine, and it's gone to my head a bit. But the main thing is that there's one particular circumstance which has really got me going... but I'm not going to say anything about it. Where are you off to?' Svidrigailov suddenly asked in alarm.

Raskolnikov was making to rise. He had begun to feel oppressed and stifled, and somehow uncomfortable at having come here. He was now convinced that Svidrigailov was the most worthless and petty scoundrel in the world.

'Hey! Sit down again, wait a bit,' Svidrigailov begged him. 'Order yourself some tea, at least. Do stay a bit longer, and I won't talk nonsense, not about myself, I mean. Let me tell you something. Well, would you like me to tell you about a woman who was trying—as you'd put it—to "save" me? That would actually be an answer to your first question, because the woman I'm talking about is your sister. Can I tell you the story? It'll kill time, too.'

'All right then, tell me, but I hope you...'

'Oh, don't worry! In any case, Avdotya Romanovna can only inspire the most profound respect, even in a vicious and worthless person like me.'

CHAPTER IV

'You may know—in fact I told you myself—', began Svidrigailov, 'that I was in the debtors' prison* here, for an enormous debt which I hadn't the faintest chance of paying. There's no point going into detail about how Marfa Petrovna bought me out at the time; do you realize how half-witted a woman can become when she's in love? She was an honest woman, and not at all stupid (though completely uneducated). Just imagine this same honest and jealous woman, after a number of dreadful, furious, reproachful outbursts, demeaning herself to agree to a sort of contract with me, which she honoured for the whole of our married life. The point is that she was much older than me; besides which she was always sucking at a clove or something in her mouth. I was enough of a swine by nature, and in a way honest enough too, to warn her straight out that I wouldn't manage to be entirely faithful to her. My admission made her furious, and yet I believe my brutal frankness rather appealed to her too. "That must mean", she'll have thought, "that he doesn't mean to deceive me, seeing that he's warning me about it beforehand"—well, that's what matters most to a jealous woman. And after a lot of tears, we came to this sort of unwritten contract: firstly, I'd never leave Marfa Petrovna, and I'd stay her husband for ever; secondly, I'd never go off anywhere without her permission; thirdly, I'd never take a permanent mistress; fourthly, in return for that, Marfa Petrovna would let me cast an eye on the maidservants from time to time, but only provided she secretly knew about it; fifthly, heaven preserve me from ever falling in love with a woman of our own class; and sixthly, if ever, God forbid, I was overcome by some great and serious passion, I must confess it to Marfa Petrovna. As to that last point, Marfa Petrovna could actually be fairly easy the whole time; she was an intelligent woman, so she could never see me as anything but a debauched lecher, incapable of genuinely loving anybody. But an intelligent woman and a jealous woman are two different things, and that was the trouble. Actually, if you want to judge certain types of people impartially, you have to start by shaking off some preconceived ideas and accepted notions about the usual sorts of people and things we see around us. Your own judgement, more than anyone else's, is something I've a right to rely on. You may have heard people say a lot of comical and ridiculous things about Marfa Petrovna, and it's true that she did have some very ridiculous ways; but let me tell you honestly that I'm truly sorry for the endless times I made her unhappy. Well, I think that's enough for a very honourable *oraison funèbre* to the most tender wife of a most tender husband. When we quarrelled, I generally held my peace and didn't get annoyed, and my gentlemanly behaviour almost always got away with it. It influenced her, and she actually liked it; sometimes she was even proud of me. Even so, your sister was someone she couldn't stand. How on earth did she come to risk importing such a raving beauty into her home as a governess? My own explanation is that Marfa Petrovna was an ardent, impressionable woman and she quite simply fell in love, literally in love, with your sister. And what about Avdotya Romanovna herself! I saw quite clearly, at first glance, that she was bad news; and—what do you think?—I resolved I wouldn't even look at her. But she was the one who took the first step—can you believe that? And what's more, believe it or not, in the beginning Marfa Petrovna actually used to be angry with me for never saying a word about your sister—for always being so indifferent to her own endless, rapturous praises of Avdotya Romanovna! I simply don't understand what she was about! And of course, Marfa Petrovna told Avdotya Romanovna all there was to know about me. She had this unfortunate habit of telling all our family secrets to everyone around, constantly complaining about me to everybody: so how could she pass up such a wonderful new friend? I don't suppose they ever talked about anything but me; and there's no doubt at all that Avdotya Romanovna came to know all those dark and mysterious tales that get told about me... I bet you've heard something of the kind yourself, haven't you?'

'Yes, I have. Luzhin even accused you of being responsible for some child's death. Was that true?'

'Do me a favour, forget all those vulgar tales,' Svidrigailov protested with disgust and revulsion. 'If you really insist on hearing about all that rubbish, I'll tell you sometime; but right now...'

'And there was some talk about a servant of yours in the country—apparently you were responsible for something there too.'

'For goodness' sake, that's enough!' Svidrigailov interrupted with obvious impatience.

'Wasn't that the same servant who came to fill your pipe after he was dead... you told me the story yourself?' demanded Raskolnikov with mounting irritation.

Svidrigailov looked hard at Raskolnikov, who seemed to see in his eyes a lightning flash of spiteful mockery; but Svidrigailov controlled himself and answered very politely:

'Yes, that was the same man. I can see you're very interested in all that yourself, and I'll do my best to satisfy your curiosity on every point, at the first convenient moment. Good Lord, I can see that I might really seem like a romantic figure to certain people. So you can see for yourself how much I have the late Marfa Petrovna to thank for telling your sister so many curious and mysterious stories about me. I can't judge what impression they made on her; but in any event it did me some good. For all her natural disgust at me, and in spite of my always looking gloomy and forbidding, she eventually came to feel sorry for me—sorry for a lost soul. And of course, when a young girl's heart feels *pity*, that's the most dangerous thing of all for her. That means she's bound to want to "save" the person, and bring him to his senses, and raise him up, and get him to live and act in a new way—we all know the sort of fine dreams a girl can have along those lines. I saw straight away that the little bird was flying straight into my net of its own accord, so I made some preparations myself. You seem to be frowning, Rodion Romanich? Don't worry, it all came to nothing, as you know. (My God, what a lot of wine I'm drinking!) You know, I've always been sorry, right from the start, that your sister wasn't fated to be born in the second or third century AD, as the daughter of a powerful princeling somewhere, or some governor or proconsul in Asia Minor. She'd undoubtedly have ended up suffering martyrdom, and of course she'd have been smiling as they branded her breast with red-hot pincers.* She'd have embraced her fate of her own free will. Or in the fourth or fifth century, she'd have gone out into the Egyptian desert and lived there for thirty years on roots and ecstasies and visions. The one thing she hungers and thirsts for is to suffer some kind of torment, on someone's behalf, as soon as may be, and if she isn't granted that torment I dare say she'll jump out of a window. I've heard something about a Mr Razumikhin. They say he's a sensible young man (his very surname confirms it: he must be a theology student); well, let him take care of your sister. In short, I believe I've understood her, and I'm proud of that. But at the time, I mean when I first met her—well, you know yourself that one's somehow more careless and stupid then, one gets a wrong view of things, one doesn't see straight. Confound her, why does she have to be so pretty? It's not my fault! So, anyway, it all started for me with an explosion of uncontrollable lust. Avdotya Romanovna is terribly, unbelievably, unimaginably virginal. (Please note: what I'm telling you about your sister is a fact. She's chaste, maybe morbidly so, for all her profound intelligence; and that'll do her no good.) We happened to have a particular girl in the house, Parasha, black-eyed Parasha,* who'd just been brought in from another village, a serving maid whom I'd never seen before. She was extremely pretty, but stupid beyond belief— burst into floods of tears, howled the place down, and it all ended in a scandal. One day, after dinner, Avdotya Romanovna made a point of seeking me out on my own in an avenue in the garden, and with glittering eyes, *ordered* me to leave poor Parasha in peace. That was practically the first private conversation we'd ever had. Naturally I saw it as an honour to obey her orders; I tried to appear put out, embarrassed—in a word, I acted my part quite creditably. And that was the beginning of our meetings together—secret conversations, moral lessons, sermons, entreaties, supplications, even tears—would you believe it, even tears! See how far some young girls will go, if they're passionate about converting someone! For my part, I blamed everything on my destiny, pretended to be hungering and thirsting after enlightenment, and finally called up the greatest and most irresistible weapon for conquering a female heart, a weapon that'll never let anyone down, and works on every last one of them, with no exception. Everyone knows it—it's flattery. Nothing in the world is harder than straight talking, and nothing is easier than flattery. If there's a hundredth part of a false note in your straight talk, it creates an instant discord, and that leads to trouble. But even if every last note in your flattery is a false one, it's still agreeable and can be listened to with pleasure; a crude sort of pleasure perhaps, but still pleasure. And however crude the flattery may be, at least half of it sounds true, every time. That goes for every level of education and every class of society. Never mind ordinary people—even a vestal virgin can be seduced by flattery. I can never remember without a laugh how I once seduced a certain young lady who was devoted to her husband, her children, and her own virtues. What a treat it was, and how easy! Yet the young lady really was virtuous, at least by her own lights. My whole strategy consisted simply in being everlastingly crushed and prostrated by her chastity. I flattered her shamelessly: no sooner had I succeeded, say, in pressing her hand, or even meeting her eyes, than I'd reproach myself at having forced it on her, implying that she'd resisted me, resisted me so hard that I could probably never have won anything from her, if I hadn't been so depraved myself; that she, in her innocence, hadn't detected my cunning, and had yielded without meaning to, without knowing what she was doing, taken unawares, and so on and so forth. In short, I got all I wanted, while my young lady remained utterly convinced that she was innocent and chaste, and had honoured all her duties and obligations, and had only succumbed by the purest accident. And how furious she was with me, when I finally declared to her that in my honest opinion she'd been out for enjoyment just as much as I had. Poor Marfa Petrovna, too, was terribly susceptible to flattery, and if I'd only wanted, I could have got her to make over her whole property to me even while she was alive. (But I'm drinking far too much wine, and talking too much.) I hope you won't be cross if I mention at this point that the very same effect was beginning to work on Avdotya Romanovna too. But I was too stupid and impatient, and spoiled everything. On a number of occasions before that, and one time in particular, Avdotya Romanovna had taken great exception to the look in my eyes, would you believe? There was a sort of fire that burned up in them, stronger and more unguarded as time went on, which scared her and which she eventually came to hate. No need to go into all the details, but we parted. And then I made another stupid mistake. I began poking fun at all her sermons and entreaties, in the coarsest possible way; Parasha came up again, and not just her—and it all ended in a violent scene. Oh, Rodion Romanich, if you could ever, just once in your life, have seen how your sister's eyes can flash sometimes! Never mind that I'm tipsy now, never mind that I've drunk a whole glass of wine already—I'm telling the truth; I assure you, I used to see that look of hers in my dreams. By the end I couldn't even bear to hear the rustle of her dress. I honestly thought I was going to have an attack of the falling sickness*—I never imagined I could get so frantic. Anyway, we absolutely had to make peace; but that wasn't possible any more. And what do you think I did then? What idiotic behaviour a man can be driven to by an insane passion! Never undertake anything in an insane passion, Rodion Romanich. I calculated that Avdotya Romanovna was actually a beggar (oh, pardon me, I didn't mean... but does it matter, so long as the meaning comes across?). Anyway, that she had to work for a living, and keep both her mother and yourself (oh God, you're scowling again...); and I decided to offer her all my money (I could have raised as much as thirty thousand, even then), if she'd run away with me, even just here to Petersburg. Naturally I'd have sworn her eternal love, and blissful happiness, and all that sort of thing. Can you believe it, I was so far gone that if she'd said to me: "Cut Marfa Petrovna's throat, or poison her, and marry me," I would have done that on the spot! But as you know already, it all ended in disaster; and you can judge for yourself how livid I was when I discovered that Marfa Petrovna had got hold of that villainous pen-pusher Luzhin, and almost rigged up a marriage with him—which would have been pretty much the same as what I was offering her myself. Isn't that so? Isn't it? It is, right? I see you've begun listening very attentively... what an interesting young man you are...'

Svidrigailov impatiently thumped the table with his fist. He had gone red in the face. Raskolnikov could see quite well that the glass or two of champagne he had drunk, sipping it discreetly drop by drop, had had a bad effect on him; and decided to make the most of it. He was very suspicious of Svidrigailov.

'Well, after all that, I'm quite convinced that you only came here because you had designs on my sister,' he said bluntly and openly to Svidrigailov, meaning to irritate him still more.

'Oh, drop it,' said Svidrigailov, as if suddenly recollecting himself. 'I've already told you... and anyway, your sister can't stand me.'

'I quite agree with you there, she can't, but that's not the point.'

'Are you really so convinced that she can't stand me?' (Svidrigailov screwed up his eyes with a mocking smile.) 'You're right, she doesn't love me; but don't ever be too certain about what goes on between a husband and wife, or a lover and his mistress. There's always a little corner which no one in the world knows about, except for the two of them. Would you swear that Avdotya Romanovna finds me repulsive?'

'You dropped some hints when you were telling your story which made me see that you still have your own ideas about Dunia, and you're plotting something against her, something vicious of course, which won't wait.'

'What? Have I been dropping words and hints like that?' asked Svidrigailov in naïve alarm, taking no notice whatever of the adjective used to describe his plans.

'You're still dropping them even now. What are you so frightened of, for instance? Why were you suddenly so alarmed just now?'

'Me, frightened and alarmed? Frightened of you? It's you who ought to be frightened of me, *cher ami*. But what a lot of nonsense... Anyway, I'm tipsy, I can see that: I almost said too much just then. Damn the wine! Hey, let's have some water!'

He seized the wine bottle and flung it unceremoniously out of the window. Filipp brought some water.

'That's all nonsense,' said Svidrigailov, moistening a cloth and pressing it against his forehead. 'I can confound you with a single word, and explode all your suspicions. Do you know, for one thing, that I'm getting married?'

'Yes, you've already told me that.'

'Have I? I'd forgotten. But at that time I couldn't be definite about it—I hadn't seen my fiancée yet. That was no more than my plan. Now I've actually got a fiancée, and the whole thing is settled, and if only I didn't have urgent business to see to, I should certainly have taken you along with me right now to meet them all—because I want to ask your advice. Oh, damn it! I've only got ten more minutes. See, look at the clock; but still, I'll tell you about it, because it's an interesting business, my marriage I mean, in its own way—but where are you off to? On your way again?'

'No, I shan't be going away now.'

'What, not ever? We'll see about that! I'll take you there, sure enough, and let you see my bride, but not now; and now you're soon going to have to leave. You'll go off to the right, and I'll go to the left. Do you know that Resslich woman? That same Resslich whose place I'm living in now—eh? D'you hear me? So, what do you think—that same one who, they say... about a little girl, in the water, in wintertime—do you hear me? Do you? Well, it was she that cooked all this up for me; your life's boring, living the way you do, she says, why not have a little fun for a while? Now I'm a gloomy, morose sort of a fellow. Did you think I was a cheerful type? No, I'm gloomy; I do no one any harm, I just sit in a corner, sometimes I don't say a word to anyone for three days on end. But that Resslich is a sly creature, let me tell you; this is what's in her mind: I'll get bored, leave my wife and go away, and she'll get the wife and put her in circulation, among our sort of people I mean, or even higher-class than that. There's an invalid father, she says, a retired official, who spends all his time sitting in his armchair and hasn't been able to move his legs for over two years. And there's a mother too, she says; a sensible sort of woman, that mother is. Their son has a post somewhere in the provinces; he gives them no help. And their daughter's married and doesn't visit them. They've got two little nephews on their hands (as if their own children weren't enough), and they've taken their youngest daughter out of school before she finished her education. She'll turn sixteen in a month, and then they can marry her off. To me, that is. We drove out to see them. What a comic situation it was. I introduced myself: a landowner, a widower with a well-known name, and all kinds of connections, and some capital—so what does it matter if I'm fifty and she's not yet sixteen? Who takes any notice of that? Tempting, isn't it? Well, it is tempting, ha-ha! You should have seen me chatting up Papa and Mama! It would have been worth paying just to watch me at it. Out she comes, makes a curtsey, can you imagine, still in a short frock, a rosebud not yet in flower. She blushes, pink as the dawn (she'd been told, of course). I don't know how you feel about female faces, but as far as I'm concerned, a sixteen-year-old, still with childlike eyes, all timid and tearful with shyness—I find that even better than beauty; and besides, she's a picture to look at. Light-coloured hair, in tight ringlets like a little lamb's fleece, plump lips, all rosy, and her little feet—just delightful!... Well, we met, and then I said I had to hurry off about some domestic affairs, and the very next day—the day before yesterday, that was—we were betrothed and blessed. Since then, every time I turn up, I sit her on my knee at once, and won't let her go... So, she blushes like the dawn, and I keep giving her kisses; her Mama, naturally, always tells her that this is your husband, and this is how it has to be—what a peach she is! And this present state of affairs, as a betrothed husband-to-be, may really be better than actual marriage. It's what they call *la nature et la vérité*!* Ha-ha! I've had a couple of conversations with her—a very sensible little girl. Sometimes she'll give me one of those furtive looks—they burn right through me. And you know, her little face is like a Raphael Madonna. The Sistine Madonna, now, has a fantastic face, the grieving face of a religious maniac*—hasn't that ever struck you? Well, hers is like that. As soon as they'd blessed our engagement, the very next day I brought along fifteen hundred roubles' worth of presents: a set of diamond jewellery, and a pearl set, and a silver dressing case this big, with all sorts of other stuff; so that even my Madonna's face went all pink with pleasure. Yesterday I sat her on my lap, very unceremoniously I dare say, and she blushed crimson, and tears started from her eyes, but she didn't want to give herself away, though she was burning hot. Everyone had left the room for a moment, so she and I were left all alone; suddenly she flung herself on my neck (the first time she'd done that of her own accord), and put both her little arms round me, and kissed me, and swore that she'd be an obedient, faithful and loving wife, and she'd make me happy, and devote her whole life, every minute of her life, to me, and sacrifice everything else to me, absolutely everything, and all she wanted in return was *just my respect*, and she didn't want anything beyond that, she said, nothing at all, no presents! You must admit—hearing that sort of confession, when we're all by ourselves, from a little sixteen-year-old angel like her in a muslin frock, with all those little curls, blushing with maidenly shame and with tears of enthusiasm in her eyes—you must admit, that's quite tempting. It is, isn't it? It's something worth having, isn't it? Well, isn't it? Well then... well then, listen to me... let's go and see my bride... only not just now!'

'In other words, this monstrous difference in your age and experience is what arouses your sensual appetite! And are you really going to get married on the strength of that?'

'Why not? Absolutely. Each of us looks after himself, and the happiest man of all is the one who manages to deceive himself best of all. Ha-ha! But why are you so desperately keen on virtue? Have pity on me, old man, I'm a sinful soul, heh-heh-heh!'

'And yet—you looked after Katerina Ivanovna's children. Although... although you had your own reasons for that... Now I understand it all.'

'Children—I'm very fond of them. I like children very much,' laughed Svidrigailov. 'As far as that goes, I could tell you about one very curious episode—one that isn't over yet. The very first day after I arrived here, I went to visit a few low dives—in fact, after seven long years I made straight for them. You've probably noticed that I'm in no hurry to take up with my own set, my old friends and acquaintances. And I'll keep out of their way as long as I possibly can. You know, when I was living in the country with Marfa Petrovna, I was maddened by the memory of all those secret, mysterious dens and dives where a man who knows his way around can find all sorts of things. Damn it! Common folk get roaring drunk, educated young people with nothing to do burn themselves up in impossible dreams and fancies and grotesque theories; the Jews have moved in from somewhere and they're piling money away, and everyone else gets debauched. As soon as I got here, I could feel the familiar reek of the town's breath on my face. I landed up at what was supposed to be a dance—it was in a dreadful den (and I like my dens to be a little bit grubby); well, obviously, they had a cancan that you'd never see anywhere else, the kind that didn't even exist in my day. Yes, sir, that's progress. And suddenly I noticed a little girl of thirteen or so, very sweetly dressed, dancing with a pro, and another one opposite them. And her mother sitting on a chair by the wall. Well, you can just imagine what sort of a cancan that was! The little girl was embarrassed, and blushed, and in the end she felt insulted and started to cry. The pro picked her up and started twirling her round and showing her off, everyone around was roaring with laughter, and (I love our audiences at moments like that, even our cancan audiences) they all laughed and yelled "That's the stuff! Serves them right! Shouldn't bring children here!" Well, what did I care, and anyway it was none of my business; whether or not it made any sense, they were there to have fun! I could see straight away what I had to do: I sat down next to the mother and started telling her that I was a newcomer there myself, and what ignorant louts all these other people were, and how they couldn't recognize real worth or give it due respect; and mentioned that I had lots of money, and offered to take them home in my own carriage; and I did take them home, and got acquainted with them. They were living in a poky room sublet by tenants somewhere—they'd only just arrived. The mother declared that both she and her daughter could only regard their acquaintance with me as an honour. I discovered that they didn't possess a stick or stone of their own, they'd come to town to hand in a petition at some ministry or other. I offered to help, I offered them money; the mother said that coming to that dance had all been a mistake, she'd thought there were going to be proper dancing lessons; I offered to help educate the young lady myself, and teach her French and dancing. That was enthusiastically accepted, taken as a great honour, and I'm still friendly with them... We can go and see them if you like... but not just now.'

'Shut up, stop telling me your nasty revolting stories, you debauched, vile, lecherous man!'

'Look at our Schiller, our very own Schiller! *Où va-t-elle la vertu se nicher?** You know, I'm going to go on telling you things like that on purpose, just for the pleasure of hearing you yell at me!'

'Well naturally—don't I seem absurd even to myself right now?' muttered Raskolnikov furiously.

Svidrigailov was laughing his head off. Eventually he called Filipp, paid the bill, and got up.

'How drunk I am, though! *Assez causé!** he said. 'That was just delightful!'

'How could you fail to be delighted?' cried Raskolnikov, standing up in his turn. 'A seedy old libertine recounting all his past exploits—and even now plotting something monstrous of the same sort—how could that not be delightful, particularly in your present situation, and faced with someone like me... It must get you fired up!'

'Well, if that's how you take it,' replied Svidrigailov in some surprise, looking at Raskolnikov, 'if so, you're a pretty fair cynic yourself. At least, you have all the makings of a terrific one. You can take in a lot of things... well, and you can achieve a lot too. Anyway, enough of that. I'm truly sorry we haven't managed to have much of a chat; but I'm not going to lose touch... Only wait a bit...'

Svidrigailov left the tavern. Raskolnikov followed him. Svidrigailov was not in fact particularly tipsy; the wine had gone to his head for a moment, but its effects were wearing off minute by minute. Something was troubling him a great deal, something extremely important, and he was frowning. He was evidently expecting something, and this was making him anxious and agitated. His attitude towards Raskolnikov had suddenly changed in the last few minutes; he was becoming more and more mocking and rude. Raskolnikov was aware of all this and was anxious himself. He had become very suspicious of Svidrigailov, and resolved to follow him.

They came out into the street.

'Now you're off to the right, and I'm going to the left; no, it's the other way about. Anyway, *adieu, mon plaisir*—until our next happy meeting!'

He turned right and went towards the Haymarket.

CHAPTER V

RASKOLNIKOV followed him.

'What's the meaning of this?' cried Svidrigailov, turning back. 'I thought I told you...'

'What it means is that I'm not letting you out of my sight.'

'Wha-a-at?'

They both stopped still and stared at one another, as if taking each other's measure.

'All your half-drunken tales', Raskolnikov snapped, 'have made it absolutely clear to me, not only that you haven't given up your repulsive designs on my sister, but that you're busier than ever about them. I know that my sister got some sort of letter this morning. And you've been twitching with impatience all this time... All right, so you may have managed to dig up some kind of wife for yourself, but that doesn't mean a thing. I want to see for myself...'

Raskolnikov would hardly have been able to say what exactly he wanted just then, and quite what he wanted to see for himself.

'So that's how it is! Do you want me to call the police?'

'Go ahead!'

They stood facing one another for perhaps a minute. Eventually Svidrigailov's expression changed. Seeing that Raskolnikov wasn't frightened by his threat, he suddenly put on a very cheerful, friendly air.

'Just look at you! I deliberately said nothing to you about your own affair, though naturally I'm dying to hear about it. What a fantastic business! I'd have put it off to another time, but really, you'd drive even a dead man wild... All right, then, let's go, but let me warn you that I'm just going home for one minute, to pick up some money; then I'll lock up my lodgings, take a cab, and spend the whole evening on the Islands. What's the point of you following me?'

'I'll just drop in at the flat, but not at your place—I'll go to Sofia Semionovna's, to apologize for missing the funeral.'

'Just as you like, only Sofia Semionovna isn't at home. She's taken all the children off to a lady, an aristocratic old lady whom I used to know a long time ago, who's involved in running some orphanages. She was enchanted with me when I made a contribution on behalf of

Katerina Ivanovna's three little fledglings, and gave some extra money to the orphanages too; what was more, I told her Sofia Semionovna's whole story, sparing none of the details. The effect of my story was indescribable. That's why Sofia Semionovna was instructed to turn up today at the —— Hotel, where my lady is staying while she's up from the country.'

'Never mind, I'll drop in anyway.'

'Whatever you like, but I shan't come with you. But what do I care? Here we are, almost at my home. Tell me—I'm sure you're so suspicious of me because I've been tactful so far, and haven't bothered you with questions... you understand me? You must have thought that extraordinary—I bet you did! So you see how far one gets by being tactful!'

'And eavesdropping in doorways!'

'Oh, so that's what you're after!' laughed Svidrigailov. 'Yes, I'd have been surprised if you hadn't mentioned that, after all that's happened. Ha! ha! I could actually make out a bit of what you'd been getting up to... and were telling Sofia Semionovna about—but what does it all add up to anyway? I may be quite out of date, and quite incapable of understanding anything. Do explain it to me, my dear fellow, for goodness' sake! Bring me up to date with modern thinking.'

'It's all lies, you couldn't have heard anything!'

'No, that's not what I'm talking about, not at all (though actually, I did hear a bit). No, what I mean is the way you keep sighing and moaning! The Schiller in you is up in arms the whole time. And now you say it's wrong to listen at doors. If that's the case, why don't you go straight to the authorities and declare that such and such a thing happened to you, and your theory turned out a little bit wrong. Or if you're convinced that people mustn't listen at doorways, but it's all right to crack old women's heads open whenever the fancy takes you, then hurry up and go off to America* somewhere! Run away, young man! There may still be time. I mean it. Or haven't you got any money? I'll pay for your trip.'

'I wouldn't dream of it,' Raskolnikov interrupted in disgust.

'I understand (but you needn't trouble yourself to say much about it, if you don't want to); I understand what's on your mind—moral questions, aren't they? The duties of a citizen and a human being? Forget all that—why should any of it matter now? Heh-heh! Because you're still a citizen and a human being? Well, if you are, you shouldn't have got into such a scrape; you've no call to take up something you're not fit for. You could shoot yourself now—or perhaps you don't feel like it?'

'I believe you're purposely trying to infuriate me, just to make me leave you alone...'

'What an odd fellow you are—here we are already, do come upstairs with me. Look, here's Sofia Semionovna's door: see, there's no one there! You don't believe me? Ask Kapernaumov, she leaves her key with them. And look, it's Madame de Kapernaumov herself, isn't it? Well (she's a bit deaf), has she gone out? Where? So, did you hear that? She's not here, and she may not be back till late tonight. And now let's go along to my place. You did want to go to my place too, didn't you? Well, here we are. Madame Resslich is out. That woman is always busy about something, but she's a good woman, I assure you... perhaps she might have been useful to you, if you'd been a bit cleverer. Well now, have a look: I'm taking this five-per-cent bond out of my desk (see how many I've still got left!); this one's on its way to the money changer's today. So, did you see all that? Now I don't need to waste any more time. I lock the desk, I lock the flat, and here we are on the stairs again. And now, if you like, we'll take a cab. You know I'm on my way to the Islands. Wouldn't you like a little drive? And here I am, taking this carriage to Elagin Island,* eh? You don't want to come? Can't stand any more? Come on, we'll have a little ride. It looks a bit like rain, but never mind, we'll put the hood up...'

Svidrigailov was already sitting in the carriage. Raskolnikov concluded that his suspicions, at least for the time being, were unjustified. Without saying a word, he turned away and walked back towards the Haymarket. If he had once looked back, he would have had time to see Svidrigailov paying off the cab before they had driven so much as a hundred yards, and stepping down onto the pavement again. But he saw nothing, and by now had already turned the corner. A feeling of profound revulsion drove him away from Svidrigailov. 'And how could I ever, for a single moment, have hoped for anything from that coarse ruffian, that debauched, villainous lecher!' he couldn't help exclaiming. But it must be said that this judgement of Raskolnikov's was overhasty and ill-considered. There was something about Svidrigailov's whole being which at least lent him an air of originality, if not of mystery. As for the part played by his sister in this business, Raskolnikov was still firmly convinced that Svidrigailov wouldn't leave her in peace. But it was becoming unbearably painful for him to keep turning all that over and over in his mind. Once he was alone and had walked on twenty yards or so, he fell into deep thought, as he usually did. Coming onto the bridge, he stopped by the parapet and looked down at the water. And there, all the time, standing close by him, was Avdotya Romanovna.

He had passed her as he walked onto the bridge, but had walked straight past without noticing her. Dunechka had never seen him on the street in this state before, and was quite frightened at the sight. She stood still, not knowing whether to call out to him or not. Suddenly she saw Svidrigailov hurrying towards her from the direction of the Haymarket.

But he seemed to be approaching her cautiously and furtively. He didn't come onto the bridge, but stopped to one side of it, on the pavement, trying his very best not to let Raskolnikov see him. He had noticed Dunia some time before, and was making signs to her. She thought he was trying to tell her not to speak to her brother, but let him be, and come over to him.

So she did as he asked, quietly stepping behind her brother's back and going over to Svidrigailov.

'Quick, come along,' whispered Svidrigailov. 'I don't want Rodion Romanich to know that we're meeting. I must warn you that I've been sitting with him in a tavern not far away; he came to find me there himself, and I've had trouble getting rid of him. Somehow or other he's found out about my letter to you, and he suspects something. It couldn't have been you that told him about the letter, could it? But if it wasn't you, who could it have been?'

'Here we are now, round the corner; my brother won't see us now. I must tell you that I shan't go any further with you. Tell me everything right here—it can all be told in the street.'

'First of all, it can't possibly be told in the street; and secondly, you have to hear what Sofia Semionovna has to say; and thirdly, there are some documents I'm going to show you... Well, and finally, if you don't agree to come to my lodgings, I refuse to enter into any further discussions and I'll walk away right now. What's more, please don't forget that there's a very curious secret concerning your beloved brother which is entirely in my hands.'

Dunia paused irresolutely, casting a penetrating glance at Svidrigailov.

'What are you afraid of?' he remarked coolly. 'This is the city, not the countryside. And even in the countryside, you did me more harm than I ever did you; while here...'

'Has Sofia Semionovna been warned?'

'No, I haven't said a word to her; in fact I'm not entirely sure if she's at home now. Although she probably is. She buried her relative today; it's not the sort of day to go visiting. I don't want to tell anybody about all this for the time being, in fact I'm a bit sorry that I told you. The least bit of carelessness here would amount to denouncing him. I live right here, in this building we're coming up to. Here's the house porter; he knows me very well, look, he's bowing to me; he can see that I'm walking with a lady, and of course he's had time to notice your face; that'll be useful for you, if you're very afraid and suspicious of me. I'm sorry to be putting it all so crudely. I'm living in a room sublet by tenants here. Sofia Semionovna lives in the next-door room, she's renting from tenants too. The whole floor is rented out. What is there to be so frightened of, as if you were a child? Am I really all that terrifying?'

Svidrigailov twisted his face into a condescending smile; but he was no longer in any mood for smiling. His heart was pounding and he could hardly breathe. He began talking louder to hide his growing agitation; but Dunia didn't particularly notice it. She was too annoyed by his comment about her being as afraid of him as a child, and finding him so terrifying.

'Although I know that you're a man... without honour, I'm not in the least afraid of you. Go on ahead,' she said, apparently coolly, though her face had grown very pale.

Svidrigailov stopped outside Sonia's flat.

'Let me just find out whether she's at home. No, she isn't. What a pity! But I know she may be back very shortly. If she's gone out, it can only be to visit a certain lady, about her orphans. Their mother's just died. I got involved in that too, and made some arrangements. If Sofia Semionovna isn't back in ten minutes, I'll send her along to see you, if you like, this very day. So, and here's my lodging. These are my two rooms. Behind that door is my landlady, Madame Resslich. Now have a look in here, I'll show you my most important documents; this door here leads from my bedroom to two completely empty rooms, which are up for rent. Here they are... now you have to take a closer look at this...'

Svidrigailov occupied two quite spacious furnished rooms. Dunechka looked around mistrustfully, but noticed nothing special about either the furnishings or the arrangement of the rooms, although there might have been something worth noticing; for instance that Svidrigailov's apartment was located between two practically uninhabited ones. The way in to his apartment was not directly off the corridor, but through two rooms of his landlady's, which were almost empty. Once in his bedroom, Svidrigailov opened a locked door and showed Dunechka another room, also empty and up for rent. Dunechka paused in the doorway, not understanding why she was being invited to look at it, but Svidrigailov hurried to explain:

'Now, just look in here, see this other large room. Note this door, which is locked shut. There's a chair beside the door, and it's the only chair in either of the rooms. I brought it here from my own flat, so as to make it easier to listen. Right behind that door is Sofia Semionovna's table; she was sitting there talking with Rodion Romanich. And I sat here on that chair and listened in, two evenings running, for a couple of hours at a time; so naturally I managed to find something out, what do you think?'

'You were eavesdropping?'

'Yes, eavesdropping. Now let's go to my place—there isn't even anywhere to sit here.'

He led Avdotya Romanovna back to his first room, which served as his living room, and invited her to sit down on a chair. He himself sat down at the opposite end of the table, at least seven feet from her; but his eyes were probably gleaming with the same fire that had once so frightened Dunechka. She shuddered and again looked round uneasily. It was an instinctive movement; evidently she didn't want to betray her suspicion. But she had suddenly been struck by the isolated situation of Svidrigailov's apartment. She wanted to ask him whether his landlady, at least, was at home; but she didn't ask... out of pride. And besides, her heart was filled with anguish of a different sort, infinitely worse than any fear for her own safety. She was in unbearable distress.

'Here's your letter,' she began, laying it on the table. 'Can the things you wrote possibly be true? You said something about a crime that my brother is supposed to have committed. Your hints were too clear for you to dare to back out now. But let me tell you that I'd heard that stupid tale before you ever mentioned it, and I don't believe a word of it. Such a suspicion is revolting and absurd. I know the story, and I know how and why it was made up. You can't possibly have any proof. You promised to prove it to me—so go on then! But I'm telling you right now, I don't believe you! I don't believe you!'

Dunechka spoke fast and hurriedly, and her face flushed for an instant.

'If you hadn't believed me, how could you possibly have risked coming to see me on your own? What have you come for? Mere curiosity?'

'Don't torture me, tell me, tell me!'

'Well, I can't deny that you're a brave girl. I honestly thought you'd ask Mr Razumikhin to come with you. But he wasn't with you, nor anywhere about, for I took a good look. That was courageous of you—it means you must have wanted to spare Rodion Romanich. But then, everything about you is divine... As for your brother, what can I tell you? You've just seen him yourself. What do you think of him?'

'Surely that can't be the only evidence for your story?'

'No, not that, but his own words. He came here to see Sofia Semionovna, two evenings running. I showed you where they were sitting. He made a full confession to her. He's a murderer. He murdered an old woman, an official's widow, who was a pawnbroker; he had pawned things with her himself. And he killed her sister, a pedlar called Lizaveta, who happened to come in while he was killing her sister. He killed them both with an axe which he'd brought with him. He killed them to rob them, and he did rob them: he took money and various objects... He said all that, word for word, to Sofia Semionovna, who's the only person that knows his secret; but she had no part in the murders, by word or deed; far from it, she was just as horrified as you are now. Don't worry, she won't betray him.'

'That can't be true!' gasped Dunechka, her lips deathly pale. 'It can't be true, there wasn't the least, the faintest reason, no motive whatever... It's a lie! A lie!'

'He robbed her, that was his whole reason. He took money, and some objects too. It's true that, as he himself admits, he didn't make any use of the money or the objects, but just took them and buried them under a stone, where they still are. But that's because he didn't dare make use of them.'

'But is it likely that he'd steal, that he'd rob someone? Or even think of such a thing?' cried Dunia, jumping up from her chair. 'You know him, don't you? You've seen him? How could he be a thief?'

She was almost imploring Svidrigailov. She had forgotten all her fear of him.

'Avdotya Romanovna, there are thousands and millions of combinations and chances here. A thief may steal, and yet he may know himself to be a villain; and I once heard of a gentleman who robbed the mail; who knows, perhaps he truly believed that he was doing right! Obviously I wouldn't have believed it myself, any more than you do, if I'd just heard the story from someone else. But I did believe my own ears. And he explained all his reasons to Sofia Semionovna too; and at first she didn't believe her own ears, but in the end she did believe her eyes, her very own eyes. Because he was telling it all to her himself.'

'But what possible... reasons?'

'It's a long story, Avdotya Romanovna. There was, how can I put it, a kind of theory behind it—just as I would consider, for instance, that a single wicked deed can be allowed if the main motive for it is good. A single evil deed and a hundred good ones! And then, of course, it's galling for a young man of good qualities and overwhelming self-esteem to know that if he only had, say, an extra three thousand roubles, then his whole career, and the whole course of his future life, would be transformed—but he just hasn't got those three thousand roubles. Add to that the stress of hunger, his tiny room, his ragged clothing, and his vivid awareness of his good social position; plus the situation of his sister and his mother. More than anything else, it's a matter of vanity—pride and vanity; and perhaps, God knows, with the best of intentions... For I'm not blaming him, please don't think that I am; in any case it's not my business. A special little theory of his own came into it too, a kind of theory—according to which the human race is divided, if you follow me, into the common herd and extraordinary individuals, that is, the sort of people who, because of their exalted position, aren't subject to laws; in fact they're the ones who write the laws for the rest of humanity, the common herd, the rubbish heap. It'll do, it's a theory of a sort, *une théorie comme une autre*. He was very much carried away by Napoleon; or rather, he was carried away by the idea that a great many people of genius took no account of individual evil deeds, they strode over them without a thought. And I believe he imagined that he was a man of genius; I mean, he was convinced of that for a time. He suffered a great deal, and still suffers, from the thought that although he was capable of formulating his theory, he wasn't capable of striding over those obstacles without a thought—which meant that he wasn't a man of genius. Well, and that's humiliating for a young man with great self-esteem, particularly in this day and age...'

'But what about his conscience? Are you denying that he possesses any moral sense? Is he really that sort of man?'

'Oh, Avdotya Romanovna, everything has got so muddled by now—not that it was ever very organized. The Russians in general are people with grandiose ideas, as grandiose as their land, and they're very much drawn towards everything that's fanciful and chaotic; but having grandiose ideas without any particular genius leads to disaster. Do you remember how often the two of us used to talk along those lines, on this very topic, sitting together on the garden terrace in the evenings after dinner? You used to reproach me for just that sort of grandiose thinking. Who knows, perhaps we were having those conversations just at the same time that he was lying here dreaming up his own ideas. After all, there aren't any particularly sacred traditions in our educated society these days,* Avdotya Romanovna; unless someone concocts something for himself out of some book or other... or fishes something out of an ancient chronicle. But people like that are mostly scholars, and you know, just bookworms in their way, so it would be embarrassing for a society person to behave like that. Anyway, you know my general outlook on life; I don't blame anyone at all. I'm an idle fellow myself, and I stand by that. We've discussed that together several times. I've even had the good fortune to interest you in my views... You're very pale, Avdotya Romanovna!'

'I know that theory of his. I've read his article in the journal, about people to whom everything is permitted... Razumikhin brought it to me...'

'Mr Razumikhin? An article by your brother? In a journal? Is there such an article? I didn't know that. Well, that must be fascinating. But where are you off to, Avdotya Romanovna?'

'I want to see Sofia Semionovna,' replied Dunechka faintly. 'How do I get to her room? She may have come in. I absolutely have to see her, straight away. She has to...'

Avdotya Romanovna couldn't finish. Her breath literally failed her.

'Sofia Semionovna won't be back before tonight. I believe she won't. She should have come back very quickly, and if she hasn't, she'll be very late...'

'Ah, so you're lying! I see... you were lying... everything you said was lies!... I don't believe you! I don't believe you!' cried Dunechka in a real rage, completely losing her head.

Almost fainting, she collapsed onto a chair which Svidrigailov had hurriedly brought her.

'Avdotya Romanovna, what's wrong with you? Wake up! Here's some water—just take a sip...'

He splashed some water over her. Dunechka awoke with a shudder.

'That had a powerful effect!' Svidrigailov muttered with a frown. 'Avdotya Romanovna, calm down! Remember that he's got friends. We'll save him. We'll rescue him. Do you want me to take him abroad? I have money—I can get him a ticket in three days. As for the fact that he has killed—he'll go on to do a great many good deeds, so it'll all be smoothed over. Don't worry. He may yet end up a great man. But what's wrong with you? How do you feel now?'

'Wicked man! Making fun of me too! Let me out!...'

'Where are you off to? Where are you going?'

'To him. Where is he? Do you know? Why is this door locked? We came in through this door, and now it's locked. When did you manage to lock it?'

'We couldn't have you yelling through all the rooms about what we were talking about here. I'm not playing tricks on you at all; I was just fed up with talking in that tone of voice. Where do you think you're going in that state? Or do you want to betray him? You'll drive him insane, and he'll betray himself. You should know that they're following him already, they're on his track. All you'll do is give him away. Wait a bit: I've just seen him and spoken to him. We can still save him. Wait a bit, sit down and we'll think it over. That was why I sent for you—to talk it over on our own, and think it all through properly. But sit down, do!'

'How can you ever save him? Is that even possible?'

Dunia sat down. Svidrigailov took a seat next to her.

'That all depends on you, you alone,' he began. His eyes were glittering, and he spoke in a whisper, stuttering with agitation and almost failing to get some of his words out.

Dunia recoiled from him in alarm. He was trembling all over.

'You... one word from you, and he's saved! I... I can save him. I have money and friends. I'll send him away right now, while I arrange a passport—two passports. One for him and one for me. I've got friends—I know people who can fix things... Shall I? I'll get a passport for you too... and your mother... what do you need Razumikhin for? I love you too... I love you beyond measure. Let me kiss the hem of your dress, let me! Let me! I can't bear to hear it rustling. Tell me to do whatever you like, and I'll do it! I'll do anything, I'll do the impossible. Whatever you believe in, I'll believe it too. I'll do anything, anything! Don't look at me like that! Please don't! Do you know that you're killing me?...'

He was almost raving. Something had suddenly happened, as though he'd had a rush of blood to the head. Dunechka leapt up and ran to the door.

'Open up! Open up!' she shouted through the door, rattling it with her hands and calling for help. 'Please, open the door! Is nobody there?'

Svidrigailov recollected himself and stood up. An angry, mocking smile forced its way onto his still trembling lips.

'There's no one at home here,' he announced quietly and deliberately. 'The landlady's gone out, and you're wasting your time screaming like that. You'll only upset yourself to no purpose.'

'Where's the key? Open the door at once, immediately, you foul man!'

'I've lost the key, I can't find it anywhere.'

'Aha! So this is a rape!' cried Dunia, pale as death. She ran over to the corner and quickly barricaded herself in with a little table that happened to be there. She didn't scream, but fixed her eyes on her tormentor and intently followed his every movement. Svidrigailov, too, made no move, but stood facing her at the opposite end of the room. He had actually taken himself in hand, at least outwardly. But his face was as pale as ever, and he still wore his mocking smile.

'You cried "rape" just now, Avdotya Romanovna. If it's a rape, you'll realize that I've taken my precautions. Sofia Semionovna's not at home; and it's a long way to the Kapernaumovs, five locked rooms away. And I'm at least twice as strong as you are; besides which I've nothing to fear, because you won't ever be able to complain. After all, you won't really want to betray your brother, will you? And no one will believe you: whatever would a young girl be doing, visiting a solitary man alone in his apartment? So even if you do sacrifice your brother, you still won't prove anything. Rape is very difficult to prove, Avdotya Romanovna.'

'You foul monster!' whispered Dunia in outrage.

'Just as you like; but don't forget that I've only been talking hypothetically so far. In my own personal opinion you're absolutely right—rape is a foul thing. The only point I was making was that you'll have absolutely nothing on your conscience even if... even if you wanted to save your brother of your own free will, in the way I'm suggesting. That'll just mean that you gave in to circumstances... well, to force, then, if we can't do without that word. Think about it: the fate of your brother and your mother is in your own hands. And I'll be your slave... all my life... Now I'll wait right here...'

Svidrigailov sat down on the couch, about eight steps away from Dunia. She was no longer in the slightest doubt of his firm resolution. Besides, she knew him...

Suddenly she drew a revolver from her pocket, cocked it, and rested her hand on the table, holding the revolver. Svidrigailov leapt up from his seat.

'Aha! That's the way it is!' he cried out in surprise, with a vicious smile. 'Well, that changes everything. You've made things infinitely simpler for me yourself, Avdotya Romanovna! But wherever did you get that revolver? It wasn't Mr Razumikhin, was it? Hey! But that's my own revolver! An old friend! And there was I, searching for it, back then!... Those shooting lessons I had the honour to give you out in the country—they haven't gone to waste!'

'It's not your revolver but Marfa Petrovna's, whom you killed, you scoundrel! You didn't own a single thing in her house. I took it when I began to suspect what you were capable of. If you dare move a single step, I swear to you, I'll kill you!'

Dunia was beside herself with fury, holding the revolver ready.

'Well, and your brother? I'm asking out of curiosity,' said Svidrigailov, still standing where he had been.

'Denounce him if you want! Not a move! One step, and I'll fire! You poisoned your wife, I know—you're a murderer yourself!...'

'Are you really so sure that I poisoned Marfa Petrovna?'

'It was you! You dropped hints yourself—you talked to me about poison... I know you went to get some... you had it ready... It must have been you... you villain!'

'Even if that were true, it was all for your sake... you were still the cause of it.'

'That's a lie! I've always hated you, always...'

'Hey, Avdotya Romanovna! You seem to have forgotten how you were softening and melting towards me, when I was pressing you so hard... I could see it in your lovely eyes—do you remember that evening, with the moon shining, and the nightingale singing?'

'Lies!' Dunia's eyes glittered with rage. 'All lies, you slanderer!'

'Lying, am I? Very well then, I'm lying. I made it up. Women should never be reminded of that sort of thing.' He grinned. 'I know you'll fire, you pretty little beast. Go on then, shoot!'

Dunia raised the revolver. She was deathly pale; her lower lip was white and trembling, her big dark eyes glittered like fire. She stared at him, with her mind made up, measuring the distance and awaiting his first movement. Never in his life had he seen her so beautiful. The fire darting from her eyes as she raised the revolver seemed to burn him up; his heart felt a pang of anguish. He took a step, and the shot rang out. The bullet skimmed his hair and buried itself in the wall behind him. He stopped still and laughed quietly:

'A wasp sting! And she aimed straight at my head... What's this? Blood!'—He drew out a handkerchief to wipe away the blood that ran in a thin trickle down his right temple. The bullet must have just grazed his scalp. Dunia lowered the revolver and stared at Svidrigailov, not so much in alarm as in a kind of wild amazement. She seemed no longer to understand what she had done, nor what was happening now.

'Well, you missed—so what! Fire again, I'll wait,' said Svidrigailov quietly, still smiling, but now with a gloomy smile. 'Otherwise I'll have time to grab hold of you before you can cock the gun!'

Dunechka shuddered, quickly cocked the revolver and raised it once more.

'Let me alone!' she said in desperation. 'I swear, I'll fire again... I'll... kill you!...'

'Yes indeed, at three paces you can't fail to kill me. Or supposing you don't... then...' His eyes sparkled and he took another two steps forward.

Dunechka pressed the trigger, but the revolver misfired.

'You didn't load it right. Never mind! You've got another percussion cap there. Load it properly, I'll wait.'

He was standing two steps away from her, waiting and watching her with wild determination; a dark, feverish passion was in his eyes. Dunia realized that he would sooner die than let her go. And of course, she'd kill him now, at two paces!

Suddenly she flung the revolver away from her.

'Dropped it!' said Svidrigailov in surprise, and drew a deep breath. Something seemed suddenly to have fallen away from his heart, and perhaps it wasn't just the burden of mortal fear. Indeed, that was probably not what he was feeling at that moment. It was a release from some other, darker and more painful emotion, which he himself couldn't have defined in all its power.

He went up to Dunia and put his arm gently round her waist. She made no resistance, but trembled like a leaf and looked at him with imploring eyes. He tried to say something, but could only move his lips without uttering a sound.

'Please let me go!' Dunia begged him.

Svidrigailov started. The tone of her voice was no longer the same as before.

'So you don't love me?' he asked quietly.

She shook her head.

'And... you can't?... Not ever?' he whispered in despair.

'No, never!' Dunia whispered.

For a moment, a dreadful, wordless struggle raged in Svidrigailov's heart. He looked at her with inexpressible emotion. Then he suddenly withdrew his arm, turned away, quickly moved over to the window and stood facing it.

Another moment passed.

'Here's the key!' He took it out of the left-hand pocket of his coat and laid it on the table behind him, without looking at Dunia or turning towards her. 'Take it. Go away, quickly!...'

He stared fixedly out of the window.

Dunia came to the table and picked up the key.

'Quick! Quick!' repeated Svidrigailov, still without moving or turning round. But there was a note of terrible significance in that word 'Quick!'

Dunia understood it, seized hold of the key, and ran to the door. Quickly she unlocked it and ran out of the room. One minute later she rushed out onto the canal side like a demented person, not knowing where she was going, and ran off in the direction of —— Bridge.

Svidrigailov continued standing by the window for another three minutes or so. Then he slowly turned round, looked about him, and quietly passed his hand over his brow. His face was twisted into a strange smile—a sorry, mournful, feeble smile, a smile of despair. The almost-dry blood stained his palm. He looked crossly at it, then moistened a towel and dabbed his temple clean. His eye was suddenly caught by the revolver which Dunia had thrown down, and which had fallen by the door. He picked it up and examined it. It was a little triple-barrelled pocket revolver of old-fashioned design, with two bullets and one percussion cap still left in it. It could be fired one more time. He thought for a while, then put the revolver in his pocket, picked up his hat, and went out.

CHAPTER VI

THE whole of that evening until ten o'clock he spent in a succession of taverns and dives, moving on from one to the next. Somewhere or other Katia turned up, singing another servants' song about how some 'villain and tyrant' had 'started kissing Katia'.

Svidrigailov bought drinks for Katia, and the organ grinder, and the singers, and the servants, and a couple of little clerks. He had actually taken up with the two little clerks because they each had a crooked nose: one of them had a nose bent over to the right, and the other one to the left. Svidrigailov had been struck by that. They eventually persuaded him to accompany them to a pleasure garden, where he paid their entrance tickets and treated them. The garden contained a single lanky three-year-old fir tree and three little shrubs. There was also a 'Vauxhall',* in other words a bar, where you could get tea as well; and a number of little green tables and chairs. The public was being entertained by a chorus of bad singers and a German from Munich who was got up as a red-nosed clown, and for some reason was particularly mournful. The little clerks had a quarrel with some other little clerks, and almost got into a fight with them. They appointed Svidrigailov to judge between them. He'd been hearing their case for a whole quarter of an hour, but they were shouting so much that there wasn't the faintest hope of making anything out. Most likely one of them had stolen something and actually managed to sell it to some Jew who happened by; but having sold it, he hadn't wanted to go halves with his friend. Eventually it turned out that the stolen item was a teaspoon belonging to the Vauxhall. It had already been missed there, and things were turning awkward. Svidrigailov paid for the spoon, got up, and left the garden. It was about ten o'clock. He hadn't drunk a drop of wine all evening; he had just ordered some tea at the Vauxhall, and that more for the sake of appearances. The evening was sultry and dark. By ten o'clock, great clouds had rolled in from everywhere; now there was a rumble of thunder and the rain cascaded down, splashing onto the ground not in drops but whole torrents. The lightning flashed incessantly, each flash lasting a count of five. He reached his home soaked to the skin, locked the door, opened his bureau, took out all his money, and tore up two or three papers. Then he shoved the money into his pocket and was about to change his clothes; but looking out of the window and listening to the thunder and rain, he gave up the idea, took his hat, and went out without locking the flat. He went straight to Sonia's. She was at home.

She wasn't alone. She had Kapernaumov's four little children with her, and was giving them tea. She greeted Svidrigailov silently and respectfully, gave his sodden clothing a surprised look but said nothing. All the children fled at once in unspeakable terror.

Svidrigailov sat down at the table and invited Sonia to sit down beside him. Timidly she prepared to listen to him.

'Sofia Semionovna, I may be going to America,' said Svidrigailov, 'and since this is probably the last time we'll see each other, I've come to make some arrangements. Well now, did you see that lady today? I know what she'll have told you, there's no need to repeat it to me.' (Sonia had blushed and made a slight movement.) 'Those people have their own way of doing things. As for your sisters and your brother, they really will be looked after, and I've paid over the money meant for each one of them to the appropriate trustworthy people, and been given a receipt. Actually, you might as well have those receipts yourself, just in case. Here they are, take them! So now that's all settled. Here are three five-per-cent bonds, amounting to three thousand roubles altogether. They're for you, for your own; take them, and let that be between ourselves; nobody else needs to know about it, whatever you may hear people say. You'll need the money, Sofia Semionovna, because it's not right to live the way you did before, and you've no need to do it any more.'

'I'm so indebted to you, sir, and the orphans, and my poor stepmother,' Sonia said hurriedly, 'and if I haven't thanked you enough for it all... please don't think...'

'Well, that'll do, that'll do.'

'But this money, Arkady Ivanovich—I'm very grateful to you, but I really don't need it now. I'll always manage to keep myself, please don't think I'm ungrateful; but if you're so generous, that money...'

'It's for you, for you, Sofia Semionovna, and please don't go on about it, I haven't time. And you'll need it. Rodion Romanovich has one of two ways to go—either a bullet through his head, or off along the Vladimirka.'* (Sonia gaped at him and began trembling.) 'Don't worry, I know all about it, from his own lips, and I'm not a chatterbox; I shan't tell anyone. You were quite right when you told him to hand himself in and confess. That'll be much better for him. So, and when they send him out along the Vladimirka—he'll go, and you'll follow, won't you? Surely you will, won't you? Well then, if you do, you'll need that money. You'll need it for him, understand? By giving it to you, I'm as good as giving it to him. Besides, you promised to pay Amalia Ivanovna what she's owed; I heard you. How can you take on all those commitments and obligations, Sofia Semionovna, without thinking them through? After all, it was Katerina Ivanovna, not you, who was in debt to that German woman; so you could have let her go hang. You won't survive long like that. Now, if anyone ever asks you—say, tomorrow or the next day—about me or anything to do with me (and they will ask you), you mustn't mention that I came round to you today, and don't show the money to anyone, and don't tell anyone about it, anyone at all. There, and now goodbye.' He rose from his chair. 'My regards to Rodion Romanich. Incidentally: you ought to hand over that money for safe keeping, to Mr Razumikhin, say, for the time being. You know Mr Razumikhin? Of course you do. He's all right, that young man. Take it to him tomorrow or... when the time comes. And till then, hide it away.'

Sonia herself had also leapt up from her chair and was looking at him in fright. She very much wanted to say something, or ask something, but at first she didn't dare to, nor indeed did she know how to begin.

'But how can you... how can you go off now, in all this rain?'

'Well, no point setting off for America and being scared of the rain, heh-heh! Goodbye, Sofia Semionovna, my dear! I wish you a long life, you'll be needed by other people. By the way... would you tell Mr Razumikhin that I sent him my greetings. Just like that: Arkady Ivanovich Svidrigailov, you'll say, sends you his greetings. Make sure you do that.'

He went out, leaving Sonia full of amazement and alarm, and with a feeling of vague, troubled suspicion.

It later turned out that on that same evening, after eleven o'clock, he had made yet another highly eccentric and unexpected visit. It was still raining. At twenty past eleven he arrived, wet through, at the tiny flat occupied by the parents of his fiancée on Vasilievsky Island, at the corner of the Third Line and Maly Prospekt.* He knocked and knocked and eventually was let in, causing great embarrassment at first. But Arkady Ivanovich could behave with delightful manners when he chose, so that he quickly dispelled the sensible parents' initial supposition— quite a perceptive one too—that he'd managed to drink himself so silly that he had no idea what he was doing. The bride's kind-hearted and sensible mother wheeled out her enfeebled husband in his armchair to greet Arkady Ivanovich, and then, as was her way, started making conversation about all kinds of irrelevant topics. (This woman would never ask a question directly, but always started by smiling and rubbing her hands, and then, supposing she needed a firm and definite answer—for instance about the date which Arkady Ivanovich would like for the wedding—she would launch into curious and eager questions about Paris and court life there, before eventually going on to mention the Third Line and Vasilievsky Island.) On another occasion, all of this would of course have inspired great respect, but this time Arkady Ivanovich turned out to be somehow particularly impatient, and abruptly demanded to see his fiancée, although he had been told as soon as he arrived that she'd already gone to bed. Needless to say, the bride made her appearance. Arkady Ivanovich told her straight out that he had to leave Petersburg for a while on some very important business, and had therefore brought her various banknotes to the value of fifteen thousand silver roubles, which he requested her to accept from him as a gift, since he had long intended to give her this trifling present before their wedding. Of course these explanations failed to demonstrate any particular logical connection between the gift and his imminent departure, nor any absolute need for him to turn up in the pouring rain in the middle of the night in order to give it; nevertheless, everything passed off very smoothly. Even the unavoidable oohs and aahs, questions and expressions of amazement, somehow turned out unusually modest and restrained; but there were the most ardent expressions of gratitude, supported by actual tears from the very sensible mother. Arkady Ivanovich stood up, laughed, kissed his bride, patted her cheek, and promised to come back soon. Then, noticing that her eyes held not only childish curiosity but also a very serious, silent enquiry, he reflected a bit and kissed her again, feeling a sincere and heartfelt regret that his gift would immediately end up locked away for safety by that most sensible of mothers. He went out, leaving them all in a state of extraordinary excitement. The kind-hearted Mama immediately resolved some of their most pressing problems, explaining in a hurried half-whisper that Arkady Ivanovich was a great man, a man of affairs with important connections, and very rich; God knew what was in his mind; he had simply taken it into his head to go away; and simply taken it into his head to give away his money; so there was nothing to wonder at. Of course it was odd that he was wet through; but the English were even more eccentric, and all those high-class folk didn't care what people said about them, and didn't stand on ceremony. Perhaps he went around like that on purpose to show that he wasn't afraid of anybody. The main thing was not to say anything to anyone about all that, because God knew what would happen next, and the money had best be locked up straight away, and of course the best of it was that Fedosia had stayed in the kitchen all this time, and the most important thing of all was not to say a word, not one word, not a single word, to that old cat Madame Resslich, and so on and so on. They sat up whispering to each other until two in the morning. But the bride went to bed long before this, puzzled and rather sad.

Meanwhile, on the stroke of midnight, Svidrigailov crossed —— Bridge to the Petersburg Side. The rain had stopped, but there was still a howling wind. He was beginning to shiver; for a minute he stood staring with particular interest, indeed with a question in his mind, at the dark waters of the Little Neva. But soon he decided that it was too cold to stand staring at the water; he turned back and walked along the —— Prospekt.* He walked on along the endless avenue for a very long time, almost half an hour, stumbling here and there on the wooden pavement in the dark, and constantly searching for something along the right-hand side of the road. Somewhere towards the far end of the avenue, he had recently noticed while driving past that there was a large hotel, built of wood, which he seemed to remember was called something like Adrianople.* He was quite right—that hotel, in this derelict part of town, was such a conspicuous landmark that there was no fear of missing it even in the dark. It was a long wooden structure, black with age, and despite the late hour there were still lights burning and signs of life inside. He entered, and meeting a ragged waiter in the corridor, asked him for a room. The man cast an eye over Svidrigailov, pulled himself together and immediately led him to a tiny, stuffy little room somewhere far away at the end of the corridor, in a corner under a staircase. There was no choice; all the other rooms were taken. The ragged man looked enquiringly at him.

'Got any tea?' asked Svidrigailov.

'Yes, sir.'

'What else have you got?'

'Veal, vodka, snacks, sir.'

'Bring me some veal and some tea.'

'Won't you be wanting anything else?' asked the ragged man in some surprise.

'No, nothing!'

The ragged man went away, deeply disappointed.

'This must be a fine place,' thought Svidrigailov, 'how is it I've never discovered it before? As for me, I probably look like someone on his way back from a *café-chantant*,* who's already had an adventure on the way. But I wonder what sort of people stop and spend the night here?'

He lit a candle and took a closer look at his room. It was a poky little place, scarcely big enough to stand up in. There was one window. A very dirty bed, a plain painted table, and a chair took up almost all the floor. The walls, which seemed to have been knocked together out of planks, were covered with tattered wallpaper, so dusty and worn that though one could still guess at its original (yellow) colour, it was impossible to make out any pattern. Part of one wall was cut off at a slant under the sloping ceiling, in the usual way for an attic room, but here the slope was formed by a staircase above it. Svidrigailov put down the candle, sat on the bed, and fell into thought. But eventually his attention was attracted by a strange, continuous whispered conversation, sometimes rising almost to shouts, in the tiny next-door room. The whispering had been going on ever since he came in. He listened: someone was abusing and almost tearfully scolding his room-mate, but only one voice could be heard. Svidrigailov stood up and shaded the candle with his hand; at once he could see the glint of a crack in the wall. He stood close by it and peered through. There were two people in the next room, which was a bit larger than his own. One of them, in his shirtsleeves, had a remarkably curly head and a red, inflamed face; he was standing in an oratorical pose, legs apart to keep his balance, and striking his chest with his hand as he emotionally reproached the other for being a beggar, with no social position; he had dragged him up out of the dirt, could send him packing at will, and only the finger of the Lord saw it all. The friend and butt of these reproaches was sitting on a chair and looking like someone who is desperate to sneeze but can't manage it. From time to time he glanced at the orator with dull, sheeplike eyes, but clearly hadn't the faintest idea what the lecture was about and probably wasn't hearing any of it either. A candle was burning itself out on the table, beside an almost empty decanter of vodka, spirit-glasses, bread, tumblers, some gherkins, and the remains of the tea they'd been drinking earlier on. Svidrigailov inspected the tableau with interest, then turned indifferently away from the crack in the wall and sat down on his bed again.

When the ragged waiter returned with tea and veal, he couldn't resist asking yet again: 'Won't you be wanting anything else?' On receiving a negative reply once more, he went away for good. Svidrigailov flung himself on the tea, to warm himself up, and drank a glass of it; but couldn't eat a single bite, having lost all his appetite. He was evidently starting a fever. He took off his coat and jacket, wrapped himself up in a blanket and lay down on the bed. He was annoyed. 'Right now I'd rather have been well,' he thought with a wry smile. The room was stuffy, the candle gave a dim light, the wind howled in the yard outside, a mouse scrabbled in a corner somewhere; in fact the whole room seemed to smell of mice and some kind of leather. He lay there in a dreamlike state, one thought driving out another. He wished he could fix his thoughts on one particular thing. 'There must be a sort of garden outside my window,' he thought, 'there are trees rustling; how I hate the sound of the wind in the trees, on a dark and stormy night—it gives you a nasty feeling!' And he remembered how, as he walked past Petrovsky Park a while ago, he had actually thought of it with loathing. Then he thought about the —— Bridge too, and the Little Neva, and once again he felt a chill, as he had done earlier while standing looking down into the water. 'I've never in my life liked water, not even in a landscape painting,' he remembered; and again he laughed at the strange thought that occurred to him. Right now, he felt, he oughtn't to care for any of those ideas of aesthetics or comfort, and yet right now he had become very particular, like an animal intent on choosing the right place... in a situation like this. 'I really ought to have gone into Petrovsky Park back then! But I expect it looked very dark and cold, heh-heh! Almost as though I'd been looking for pleasant sensations!... Incidentally, why don't I put out my candle?'—He blew it out. 'They've gone to bed next door,' he thought, seeing no light through the crack in the wall. 'Now, Marfa Petrovna, this is just the time for you to pay me a visit: it's dark, and the place is right, and the moment an original one. But right now I know you won't come...'

For some reason he suddenly remembered that a little while back, an hour before making his attempt on Dunechka, he had recommended Raskolnikov to entrust her to Razumikhin's care. 'Actually I said that mostly to tease myself, as Raskolnikov guessed. But what a rascal that Raskolnikov is! He's brought a lot on himself. He could grow into a great scoundrel with time, when he gets all the nonsense out of him; but at the moment he's too keen to stay alive! People like him are all cowards in that way. Anyway, to hell with him, let him do what he likes, what do I care?'

He still couldn't fall asleep. Little by little, the image of Dunechka arose before him, as he had just seen her; and suddenly a shiver ran over his body. 'No, I really have to stop this,' he thought, coming to himself; 'I must think of something different. How strange and absurd: I've never particularly hated anyone, never even especially wanted revenge—but that's a bad sign, yes, a bad sign! I never enjoyed quarrelling either, and never got heated—another bad sign! What a lot I promised her then—oh, the devil! But I bet she'd have reformed me somehow...' He stopped again, clenching his teeth: once again the image of Dunechka appeared before him, exactly as she had been when she fired the first shot and, overcome with fright, lowered the revolver and stared dazedly at him; he would have had more than enough time to seize hold of her without her lifting a finger in her defence, if he hadn't prompted her himself. He remembered actually feeling sorry for her at that moment; remembered a sort of anguish in his heart... 'Oh the devil! These thoughts again—I have to stop all this! I must stop it!'

He was beginning to drift off; his feverish tremor was abating; but suddenly he felt something run along his arm and leg under the blanket. He started. 'What the devil—that might even be a mouse!' he thought. 'That comes of leaving the veal on the table...' He felt terribly reluctant to take off the blanket, get up, and freeze, but suddenly something brushed unpleasantly against his leg again. He whipped off the blanket and lit his candle. Shivering with the feverish chill, he bent down to look at the bed. There was nothing there. He shook the blanket, and suddenly a mouse hopped out onto the sheet. He leapt forward to catch it; the mouse didn't run off the bed, but started zigzagging about in all directions, slipping from between his fingers, running along his arm, and then suddenly darted away under the pillow. He threw off the pillow, and instantly felt something jump inside his shirt and scrabble around his body, and now it was there on his back, inside his shirt. He shuddered with disgust, and awoke. The room was dark, he was lying on his bed, wrapped up in the blanket as before, and the wind was gusting outside the window. He felt annoyed. 'How revolting!' he thought.

He got up and sat on the edge of the bed, with his back to the window. 'Better not sleep at all,' he decided. Cold, damp air was blowing in through the window. Without standing up, he pulled the blanket round him and wrapped himself up in it. He didn't light the candle. He wasn't thinking about anything, nor did he want to; but images rose before him, one after another, and scraps of ideas with no beginning or end or connection between them. He seemed to be dropping into a half-doze.

It might have been the cold, or the darkness, or the damp, or the wind howling outside the window and rocking the trees—something was filling him with an imperious, fanciful longing, and in his imagination he kept seeing flowers. He imagined a charming landscape, on a fine bright day, warm, almost hot, a festival day, Pentecost Sunday.*A wealthy, luxurious country cottage in the English style, all overgrown with sweet-smelling flowers; flower beds surrounding the house; the porch twined about with creepers and planted about with rose bushes; a bright, cool stairway, richly carpeted, and decorated with rare flowers in Chinese vases. He particularly noticed the vases full of water on the windowsills, filled with delicate white daffodils that bent forwards on their long, sturdy, bright green stems and gave off a heavy scent. He was reluctant to move away, but climbed the stairs and entered a tall, spacious hall, and once again there were flowers here, flowers everywhere, by the windows, by the open doors to the terrace, and on the terrace itself. The floors were strewn with fragrant newly-cut grass; the windows were open, and a light, fresh, cool breeze wafted into the room; birds were twittering by the windows; and in the middle of the hall, on a pair of tables shrouded in white satin, there lay a coffin. The coffin was lined with heavy white silk, with a rich white frilled border. Garlands of flowers surrounded it on every side. Lying inside it, with flowers all around her, was a young girl in a white tulle dress. Her hands, which seemed carved out of marble, were pressed together against her breast. But her unloosed hair, her pretty fair hair, was wet. Round her head was a wreath of roses. Her stern and already rigid profile, too, seemed carved out of marble, but the smile on her pale lips was filled with unchildish, boundless sorrow and deepest grief. Svidrigailov knew the girl. There was no holy icon, nor any lighted candles beside the coffin; no prayers could be heard. The girl was a suicide. She had drowned herself. She was only fourteen years old, but her heart was broken, and she had destroyed herself, crushed by an assault that had astonished and horrified her young, childlike mind, had defiled her pure, angelic soul with undeserved shame, and torn from her a last cry of despair. That cry had gone unheard, brutally cut off in the midst of a black night, in the darkness, the cold, the damp of a spring thaw, with the wind howling around her...

Svidrigailov came to himself, arose from his bed, and stepped over to the window. He felt for the bolt and opened the casement. The wind tore wildly into his narrow room, blowing icy hoar-frost against his face and against his chest, covered by only a shirt. There must indeed be a sort of garden outside his window, probably another pleasure garden;

probably there would be singers out there in the daytime, and little tables where tea was served. But now, raindrops flew in through his window off the trees and bushes, and it was as dark as a cellar, so that nothing could be made out but dim patches where something was standing. Svidrigailov leaned his elbows on the windowsill and spent a full five minutes staring out at the blackness, unable to tear himself away. Through the dark night came the boom of a cannon,* and then another.

'Aha! The signal! The water is rising,' he thought, 'by morning it'll have poured along the streets in the low-lying parts of town, flooding the basements and cellars; the cellar rats will swim out, and the people will come out in the rain and wind, all soaked and cursing, to drag their rubbishy stuff upstairs... But what time is it, I wonder?' As soon as the thought occurred to him, a wall clock somewhere nearby, ticking away in a desperate hurry, struck three. 'Hey, in another hour dawn will be breaking! What am I waiting for? I'll get out right away, straight to Petrovsky Park;* and I'll find a tall shrub somewhere, all wet with the rain, so that if I just brush it with my shoulder, millions of droplets will shower onto my head...' He stepped back from the window, locked it, lit his candle, pulled on his waistcoat and overcoat, put on his hat and went out into the corridor with his candle to find the ragged waiter, no doubt sleeping in a tiny chamber somewhere surrounded by all sorts of trash and candle ends; he'd pay him for his room and leave the hotel. 'This is the very best moment, one couldn't choose a better!'

He spent a long time pacing the long, narrow corridor, without finding anyone. He was about to shout for someone when he caught sight of a strange shape, something that seemed to be alive, in a dark corner between an old wardrobe and a door. He bent down with his candle and saw a child—a girl aged no more than five, wearing a little frock soaked through like a wet dishrag. She was shivering and crying. She didn't seem frightened of Svidrigailov, but just stared at him in dull surprise, with her big dark eyes, uttering a sob from time to time, as a child does when it has been crying for a long time but has stopped and even calmed down, and yet may suddenly start sobbing again any minute. Her little face was pale and exhausted, and she was stiff with cold. 'How ever did she get here? She must have hidden here and slept through the whole night!' He began asking her questions. The girl livened up and lisped something in a hurried, childish voice. There was something about 'Mamasya', and how 'Mamasya will tlash me', and something else about a cup which the little girl had 'bwoken'. She chattered on without stopping; it appeared from her tales that she was an unloved child, whom her mother, some sort of a cook who was permanently drunk, and probably worked in this very hotel, had beaten and terrified; the girl had broken Mamasha's cup and had been so frightened that she'd run away early in the evening; no doubt she'd spent ages hiding somewhere out in the yard, in the rain, and eventually crept in here and hidden behind the cupboard, where she'd crouched in the corner all night, crying, shivering from the damp and the darkness and her terror of being cruelly beaten for what she'd done. He lifted her in his arms and carried her back to his room, sat her on the bed and undressed her. The torn little shoes on her bare feet were as wet as if they'd been lying in a puddle all night. When she was undressed, he laid her on the bed, covered her up, and wrapped her from head to toe in the blanket. She fell asleep straight away. When all was done, he fell into gloomy thoughts again.

'Now look what I've got myself mixed up in!' he suddenly thought, full of heaviness and anger. 'How stupid!' In his irritation he picked up the candle, feeling that whatever happened he had to go and find the ragged waiter, and get out of here as quick as he could. 'Oh, but the wretched girl!' he remembered with a curse, just as he was opening his door. He came back to take another look at her, to see whether she was asleep, and how she was sleeping. He carefully lifted the blanket. The girl was sleeping soundly and blissfully. She had warmed up under the blanket, and the colour had returned to her pale cheeks. But the strange thing was that her colour seemed deeper and more marked than the ordinary pinkness of a child's skin. 'That's a feverish flush,' thought Svidrigailov. 'That looks just like the flush you get from wine—as if she'd been given a whole glass to drink. Her crimson lips seem to be glowing, burning—but what's this?' Suddenly her long black eyelashes seemed to flutter and blink, her eyelids lifted, and out from under them peeped a sharp, sly little eye which gave him a far from childish wink, as though the girl wasn't sleeping at all, just pretending. Yes, so it was: her lips parted in a smile, and quivered as though she was trying to control them. But now she'd given up any attempt to control herself, she was laughing, openly laughing; there was something impudent and provocative that shone from her utterly unchildlike face. This was depravity; this was the face of a courtesan, the impudent face of a mercenary French harlot. And now, with no attempt at concealment, both her eyes opened, and scanned him with a fiery, shameless look, leading him on, laughing... There was something infinitely hideous and offensive about that laugh, and those eyes, and all that nastiness, in a child's face. 'What! A five-year-old!...' whispered Svidrigailov in genuine horror. 'It's... What on earth is going on?' And now she had turned fully towards him, her little face burning; she stretched out her arms to him... 'Aah! Accursed creature!' cried Svidrigailov in horror, raising his arm to strike her... But at that very moment he awoke.

He was lying on the very same bed, himself wrapped up in the blanket; the candle wasn't lit, but broad daylight was coming through the window.

'Nothing but nightmares all night!' Full of annoyance, he raised himself. He felt shattered; all his bones were aching. There was a thick mist outside, and nothing could be made out. It was nearly five o'clock: he'd overslept! He got up and put on his jacket and coat, which were still damp. He felt for the revolver in his pocket, took it out, and adjusted the percussion cap; then he sat down, took a notebook from his pocket, and wrote a few lines in large letters on the front page, where they were most sure to be seen. He read them through and sat a while in thought, leaning his elbows on the table. The revolver and the notebook lay side by side, near his elbow. Some flies had woken up and were settling on the untouched portion of veal which still lay on the table. He gazed at them for a long while, and finally began trying to catch one of them with his free right hand. He wore himself out trying, but didn't manage to catch it. Finally he came to his senses, abandoned this interesting activity, gave a shudder, stood up, and walked firmly out of the room. A minute later he was in the street.

A thick, milk-white mist lay over the city. Svidrigailov walked along the dirty, slippery wooden pavement towards the Little Neva. In his mind's eye he saw the waters of the Little Neva, risen in flood during the night, and Petrovsky Island, and the wet paths, the wet grass, the wet trees and bushes, and finally that very same bush... He looked in annoyance at the houses he was passing, so as to think of something different. He didn't meet a single passer-by or cab on the avenue. The wooden houses, painted bright yellow, their shutters locked, looked dirty and miserable. Cold and damp penetrated his whole body; he began to shiver. Every now and then he came across a sign over a shop or vegetable stall, and read each one carefully. Now he had reached the end of the wooden pavement. He was standing outside a large stone building. A dirty, shivering little dog ran across his path, its tail between its legs. A man in a greatcoat, blind drunk, lay face down across the pavement. Svidrigailov looked at him and walked on. To his left he could make out a tall watchtower. 'Bah!' he thought. 'Here will do, why go to Petrovsky? At least I'll have an official witness...' He almost sniggered at this new idea, and turned into —— Street. This was where the

tall building and the watchtower stood.* Outside the big locked gates of
the building stood a little man, leaning his shoulder against the gates,
wrapped in a soldier's grey greatcoat and with a brass Achilles helmet*
on his head. He cast a cold, sleepy sidelong glance at Svidrigailov when
he approached him. The man's face bore that timeless look of distaste
and dejection which has etched its acid mark on the face of every last
member of the Jewish race. The two of them, Svidrigailov and Achilles,
stared silently at one another for a while. Achilles eventually decided
that it was wrong for a man who wasn't drunk to be standing three paces
away from him and staring at him without a word.

'Vell, vat you vanting here, hey?' he asked, still without moving from
the spot or altering his stance.

'Oh, nothing, my man; how do you do?'

'Move along zen!'

'I'm on my way to foreign parts, my man.'

'Foreign parts?'

'America.'

'America?'

Svidrigailov took out the revolver and cocked it. Achilles raised his
eyebrows.

'Vot's all zis? You can't play zese games here!'

'Why not here?'

'Because here you can't.'

'Well, my man, never mind about that. Here's a good place. If anyone
asks you, just tell them: the man said he was off to America.'

He raised the revolver to his right temple.

'No, not do zat here, here is not place!' protested Achilles, getting
agitated. His eyes grew wider and wider.

Svidrigailov pressed the trigger.

CHAPTER VII

ON that same day, but towards seven in the evening, Raskolnikov was
walking towards the apartment where his mother and sister were staying—that same apartment in Bakaleyev's house where Razumikhin had
settled them in. The entrance to their staircase was directly on the
street. As he approached, Raskolnikov slowed his pace and seemed to
be wondering whether to go in or not. But nothing would have made
him turn back—he had already taken his decision. 'And it doesn't matter anyway—they don't know anything yet,' he thought, 'and they're

used to finding me eccentric...' His clothing was dreadful—everything was ragged and torn, and dirty from a whole night spent in the rain. His face was almost disfigured by fatigue, exposure to the elements, physical exhaustion, and his battle with himself, which had lasted almost a night and a day. He had spent the whole night on his own, heaven knows where. But at least he had made up his mind.

He knocked at the door, and his mother let him in. Dunechka wasn't at home. It so happened that the maid wasn't there either. At first Pulkheria Alexandrovna was dumbfounded, astonished, and overjoyed; then she seized him by the hand and pulled him into the room.

'So here you are too!' she began, stammering with joy. 'Don't be cross with me, Rodia, for welcoming you so stupidly, all in tears— I'm not crying, I'm laughing. Did you think I was crying? No, I'm simply thrilled, but I've got this stupid habit of bursting into tears. It started when your father died—everything makes me cry. Sit down, my darling, you must be tired—I can see you are. Goodness, how muddy you are!'

'I was out in the rain yesterday, Mamasha...' began Raskolnikov.

'No, please, no!' Pulkheria Alexandrovna interrupted him vehemently. 'You thought I was going to start questioning you, just like an old woman, as I used to do; but don't worry. I understand now, I understand it all, I've learned how things are done here, and, truly, I can see for myself that it's more sensible this way. I've thought it through, once and for all: how can I understand what's in your mind, or insist on your explaining yourself to me? God knows what's on your mind, or what you're planning; you may have all sorts of ideas running through your head; so how can I go prodding you to tell me what you're thinking? I've just... Oh Lord, why am I running on in this distracted way, as if I was crazy? I've just been reading your article in the magazine, Rodia, for the third time—Dmitry Prokofich brought it for me. I just gasped when I read it: you fool, I thought to myself, just see what he's busy with—it explains everything! He may have new ideas in his head just now; he's thinking them over, and here am I nagging him and getting in the way. I read it, my dear, and of course I didn't understand much of it; but I suppose that's how it has to be—how could I ever understand it?'

'Show me, Mamasha.'

Raskolnikov took the paper and cast a glance at his article. However out of keeping it was with his present situation and mood, he still experienced that strange, bitter-sweet feeling that a writer feels when he first sees himself in print. Besides, he was only twenty-three, and that made a difference too. His reaction only lasted a moment. Once he had read a few lines he frowned, and a terrible anguish gripped his heart. All his spiritual struggles of the past few months came back to him in an instant. Angry and disgusted, he tossed the article on the table.

'Only, Rodia, I may be stupid, but I can still see that very soon you'll be one of the leading figures, if not at the very top, in the world of Russian thinking. How dared they think that you were mad! Ha-ha-ha! You don't know—but that's what they were thinking! Oh, what miserable worms they are—but how could they ever understand what intelligence means! Even Dunechka almost believed it—what do you say to that? Your poor father twice sent things he'd written to a magazine—the first time it was poetry (I still have the notebook, I'll show it to you sometime), and the next it was a proper story (I made him let me copy it out): and how we both prayed for those things to be accepted—but they weren't! Rodia, six or seven days ago I was dreadfully upset to see what you were wearing, and how you live, and what you eat and what you go out in. But now I see that was silly of me too, because with your brains and talents, as soon as you want anything, you can get it all for yourself. So it means that for the time being you don't want to do that, because you're busy with far more important things...'

'Is Dunia out, Mama?'

'Yes, she's out, Rodia. Very often I don't see her here, she leaves me on my own. Thank goodness Dmitry Prokofich drops in and sits with me, and he keeps talking about you. He loves and respects you, my dear. As for your sister, I'm not saying she doesn't respect me much. I don't complain, you know. She has her own character, and I have mine. She's got secrets of her own now; but I don't have any secrets from either of you. Of course I'm absolutely sure that Dunia is too intelligent, as well as loving both you and me... but I don't know how everything will end up. You've made me so happy now, Rodia, coming to visit me; but she's not here to see you. When she comes in, I'll tell her: your brother came by while you were out, so where did you choose to pass your time? Rodia, you mustn't spoil me too much: if you can, then drop in, and if you can't, never mind; I'll wait. Because I'll still know that you love me, and that's enough for me. I'll read your articles, and hear about you from everybody else, and then one day you'll come yourself, to see how I am—what more could I want? I mean, here you are, you've come along today to comfort your mother, I can see that...'

Pulkheria Alexandrovna suddenly burst into tears.

'Here I go again! Don't look at me—how silly I am! Oh Lord, what am I doing, sitting here!' she cried, jumping up, 'there's coffee, and

I haven't offered you anything. You see how selfish an old woman can be. Just wait a second!'

'Mamenka, never mind all that, I'm just leaving. That wasn't what I came for. Please, just listen to me.'

Timidly Pulkheria Alexandrovna moved closer to him.

'Mamenka, whatever happens, whatever you may hear about me, whatever people tell you about me—will you always love me as much as you do now?' he suddenly asked out of a full heart, not considering or weighing up his words.

'Rodia, Rodia, what's wrong? How can you ask me that? Whoever is going to tell me things about you? I won't even believe them, whoever they are—I'll send them packing!'

'I've come to promise you that I've always loved you, and now I'm glad we're alone—I'm even glad Dunechka isn't here,' he added just as impulsively; 'I've come to tell you straight out that you're going to be unhappy, but you still have to know that your son loves you now, better than he loves himself, and that everything you've been thinking about me, about how I'm cruel and don't love you—all that was untrue. I shall never stop loving you... There, that's enough; I thought I had to do that, I had to begin this way...'

Pulkheria Alexandrovna was silently hugging him, pressing him to her breast, and quietly weeping.

'Rodia, I don't know what's up with you,' she finally said. 'All this time I've thought that you were simply fed up with us; but now I can see from all this that there's some sort of great grief ahead of you, and that's why you're unhappy. I've seen it coming for ages, Rodia. Forgive me for talking about it, but I keep thinking about it and it keeps me awake at night. Your sister spent the whole of last night talking in her sleep, and she kept mentioning you. I heard a bit of it, but I couldn't understand a thing. All this morning I felt as if I were walking to my execution—expecting something, feeling something in the air, and now here we are! Rodia, Rodia, where are you off to? Are you going away somewhere?'

'Yes, I'm going away.'

'That's what I thought! But you know, I can travel with you, if you need me. And Dunia too—she loves you, she loves you very much; and Sofia Semionovna could come with us as well, if you like; you see, I'll be happy to take her along as if she was my own daughter. Dmitry Prokofich will help us get ready... but... where is it... that you're going?'

'Farewell, Mamenka.'

'What! This very day!' she cried out, as if she were losing him for ever.

'I can't stay, it's time, I really have to...'

'And I can't come with you?'

'No. But you must get down on your knees and pray to God for me. Your prayers might even get through.'

'Let me make the sign of the cross over you, and give you my blessing! There, there we are. Oh God, what are we doing?'

Yes, he was glad, very glad, that there was no one else, that he was alone with his mother. For the first time, after all those terrible days, his heart suddenly melted. He fell down before her, kissing her feet; then the two of them embraced each other and wept. And this time she showed no surprise, and asked no questions. She had long realized that something dreadful was happening to her son, and now the terrible moment had arrived.

'Rodia, my darling, my firstborn child,' she said through her sobs, 'you're just the same now as you were when you were a child; you used to come to me just like this, and hug me and kiss me; when your father was still with us, and we had all those troubles, you'd comfort us just by being there with us; and after I buried your father—how many times did we hug each other just as we're doing now, and weep over his dear grave! I've been weeping a long time now, because this mother's heart of mine could feel a misfortune coming. The very first time I saw you here, that evening, remember, as soon as we'd got here, I guessed it all just from the look on your face, and my heart gave a shudder; and today when I opened the door for you, and looked at you—well, I thought, the fateful hour has come. Rodia, Rodia, you're not leaving straight away, are you?'

'No.'

'Will you come back here?'

'Yes. Yes, I will.'

'Rodia, don't be cross—I don't even dare ask you anything. I know I daren't, but just tell me, in two words—are you going a long way away?'

'Yes, a very long way.'

'What is it—some sort of service, a career for you?'

'Whatever God sends... Only pray for me...'

Raskolnikov walked to the door, but she seized hold of him and looked despairingly into his eyes. Her face was contorted with dread.

'That's enough, Mamenka,' said Raskolnikov, deeply regretting that he had thought of coming.

'It's not for ever? Not for ever, yet, is it? You'll come back, won't you—you'll come back tomorrow?'

'Yes, I'll come; goodbye.'

He finally tore himself away.

It was a fresh, warm, bright evening. The weather had been clearing ever since morning. Raskolnikov was on his way to his lodgings, and walking in a hurry. He wanted to have done with everything before sundown. Until then, he didn't want to meet anyone. On the way up to his room, he noticed that Nastasia had turned away from the samovar and was staring at him, watching him go up. 'Could there be someone in my room?' he wondered. With a sense of disgust, he imagined Porfiry there. But when he reached his room and opened the door, he saw Dunechka. She was sitting there all by herself, deep in thought; she looked as if she had been waiting for him a long time. He stopped in the doorway. She rose from the divan in alarm and straightened herself up in front of him. She looked fixedly and intently at him, her eyes filled with horror and inconsolable grief. Her look alone told him at once that she knew everything.

'Shall I come in, or go away?' he asked uncertainly.

'I've spent the whole day sitting at Sofia Semionovna's—we were waiting for you together. We thought you'd be sure to go there.'

Raskolnikov came into the room and sank down exhausted onto a chair.

'I'm a bit weak, Dunia; I'm very tired now. But just at this moment, at least, I'd like to be in proper control of myself.'

He looked warily up at her.

'Where were you all night?' she asked.

'I don't remember very well. You see, sister, I wanted to come to a final decision, and I kept going back to walk by the Neva; that much I remember. I wanted to put an end to it all there, but... I couldn't make up my mind to it...' he whispered, glancing uncertainly at Dunia once more.

'Thank God! How frightened we were of just that, Sofia Semionovna and I! That means you still believe in life—thank God! Thank God!'

Raskolnikov smiled a bitter smile.

'I'm not a believer, but just now when I was with Mother, we hugged each other and wept; I'm not a believer, but I asked her to pray for me. God knows what all that means, Dunechka—I don't understand a thing.'

'You've been to see Mother? You must have told her then?' Dunia cried in horror. 'How could you bring yourself to do that?'

'No, I didn't tell her... not in words; but she's understood a lot. She heard you talking in your sleep last night. I'm sure she understands half of it already. Maybe I was wrong to go and see her. I don't even know why I went. I'm no good, Dunia.'

'No good—but you're ready to go and accept your suffering! You are going, aren't you?'

'Yes, I am. Right now. Yes, it was to escape the disgrace of it that I wanted to drown myself, Dunia. But even as I stood and looked into the water, I thought that if I'd regarded myself as a strong person up till then, I oughtn't to be scared of the disgrace either,' he said, hurrying on. 'Was that pride, Dunia?'

'Yes, pride, Rodia.'

Something like fire flashed in his dull eyes. He seemed to find pleasure in the fact that he still had his pride.

'And you don't think, sister, that I was simply afraid of the water?' he asked with a twisted grin, looking into her face.

'Oh, Rodia, stop it!' Dunia exclaimed bitterly.

For a couple of minutes they remained silent. He sat there hanging his head and staring at the floor; Dunechka stood at the opposite end of the table and watched him in anguish. Suddenly he stood up.

'It's late—time to go. I'm off now to give myself up. But I don't know what I'm doing it for.'

Big tears ran down her cheeks.

'You're crying, my sister—but can you bring yourself to give me your hand?'

'Did you ever doubt that?'

And she hugged him tight.

'Don't you wash away half your crime, when you go off to accept your suffering?' she exclaimed, smothering him in an embrace and kissing him.

'Crime? What crime?' he suddenly cried, in a sudden outburst of fury. 'That I killed a foul, malignant louse, an old pawnbroker-woman of no use to anybody—just killing her, you'd atone for forty other sins—a woman who sucked the blood of the poor—and that's a crime? I don't think about it, and I've no thought of washing it away. Why does everyone go on at me like that—"a crime, a crime!" It's only now that I see clearly how absurd it was of me to be such a coward—now, when I've already made up my mind to accept that pointless disgrace! I only made up my mind because I'm despicable and incompetent—and perhaps because it'll do me some good too, as that... Porfiry suggested!...'

'Brother, brother, what are you saying! You've spilled blood!' cried Dunia in desperation.

'Blood that everybody spills,' he retorted in a rage; 'blood that's shed and always has been shed, in torrents, all over the world—blood that's poured out like champagne, blood that gets you crowned with a laurel wreath in the Capitol and called a benefactor of the human race.* Just look a little closer and see what you see! I wanted to do good to people myself; I would have done hundreds, thousands of good deeds, instead of that one act of stupidity—not even stupidity, just clumsiness, for that whole idea of mine wasn't at all as stupid as it looks now, just because it failed... (Anything looks stupid if it fails!) All I wanted from that stupid act was to make myself independent, to take the first step, to get the resources I needed; after that everything would have been put right by an immeasurably greater good, in comparison... But I didn't even manage the very first step, because I'm contemptible! That's what it all boils down to! Even so, I'm not going to look at things the way you do: if I'd succeeded, I'd have been crowned with glory, but as it is, I'm caught in the trap!'

'But that's not how it is—not at all! Brother, what on earth are you saying?'

'Oh, so that's not the right formula, the aesthetically correct formula! But I don't begin to understand: why is the formula more respectable if you chuck bombs at people in a regular siege?* Fear of aesthetics is the first sign of weakness!... I've never, ever seen all this more clearly than now; less than ever do I understand what my crime was! Never, never have I been stronger or more convinced than I am now!..'

The colour flooded into his pale, exhausted face. But as he pronounced his final exclamation, his eyes happened to meet Dunia's; and there was so much anguish for him in that look of hers that he involuntarily stopped short. He could feel that he had brought misery to those two unfortunate women. In the end, it was his fault...

'Dunia, my dear one! If I'm at fault, forgive me (though I can't be forgiven, if I'm at fault). Farewell! Let's not quarrel! It's time, high time. Don't follow me, I beg you, I still have to go and see... But you go now, straight away, and sit down with our mother. Do that, I beg you! That's the last and greatest thing I'm asking of you. Don't keep going away from her; I left her in such dread, she'll hardly be able to stand it: she'll either die of it, or go mad. Do stay with her! Razumikhin will be there too; I've told him... Don't weep for me: I'll try to be brave, and honest, all my life, even though I'm a murderer. Maybe you'll hear my name mentioned one day. I shan't disgrace you, you'll see: I'll finally prove... but for now, goodbye,' he hastily concluded, once again noticing a strange expression in Dunia's eyes at his final words and promises. 'Why are you crying like that? Don't cry, don't cry; we're not parting for ever!... Oh, yes! Wait a minute, I'd forgotten!...'

He went to the table and picked up a thick, dusty book, unwrapped it, and took out from between its pages a little portrait, painted in watercolours on ivory. It was a portrait of his landlady's daughter, to whom he had once been engaged, and who had died of a fever; that same strange girl who had wanted to enter a nunnery. For a minute or so he gazed at her expressive, suffering face; then he kissed the portrait and handed it to Dunechka.

'She was someone I often talked to, about all that, too—to her alone,' he said thoughtfully; 'I confided to her heart much of what later turned out so horribly. Don't worry,' he added to Dunia, 'she didn't agree with me, any more than you do, and I'm glad she's not here any more. The main thing, the main thing is that everything is going to turn out differently now.—My life will be snapped in two!' he suddenly cried out in fresh despair. 'Everything, everything—but am I ready for that? Is that what I want, myself? They say that's necessary for my suffering! What's the point, what on earth is the point of all these useless tribulations? What purpose do they serve? Shall I be better able to understand things then, when I'm crushed by suffering and idiocy, when I'm a helpless old man, after twenty years in a labour camp, than I understand them now? So what's the point of living, then? Why am I consenting to live like that now? Oh, I knew I was a miserable wretch, when I stood on the banks of the Neva at dawn this morning!'

At last they both went out. It was hard for Dunia, but she loved him! She walked on, but after some fifty paces she turned round to look at him again. He was still within sight. On reaching the corner he too turned round; their eyes met one last time; but when he saw her watching him, he made an impatient, even irritable gesture to tell her to walk on, and himself abruptly turned the corner.

'I'm being unkind, I can see that myself,' he thought a minute later, feeling ashamed of his gesture of annoyance to Dunia. 'But why do they love me so much, if I don't deserve it? Oh, if only I were alone, and no one loved me, and I had never loved anyone! *None of this would have happened!* I wonder—will my spirit really be so broken over the next fifteen or twenty years that I'll come to other people whimpering with adoration, and call myself a robber every time I open my mouth? Yes, that's it, exactly! That's what they're exiling me for now, that's just what they want... Here they all are, scurrying through the streets this way and that, and yet every one of them is a robber and a villain just by his very nature—and worse still, an idiot! And yet, try letting me off my exile and they'll all go wild with righteous indignation! O, how I hate them all!'

He fell to thinking hard about this question: what process could ever finally and completely reconcile him to his fate, without reservation, out of genuine conviction, in the face of all those other people? 'But no, why ever not? Of course, that's how it has to be. Won't twenty years of unrelenting oppression end up by crushing me? Water wears away a stone. And if that's so, what on earth is the point of living, why am I going there now, when I know myself that's exactly how it's going to be, all according to the book, and no other way!'

It might have been the hundredth time since last evening that he had asked himself the same question. But still he walked on.

CHAPTER VIII

DUSK was falling when he reached Sonia's room. She had been waiting for him all day, in a state of dreadful anxiety. Dunia had been with her: she had come in the morning, remembering Svidrigailov's words of the day before, that 'Sonia knows it all'. We will not go into all the details of the women's conversation, and their tears, and what close friends they became. Dunia came away from that conversation with one consolation at least: that her brother wouldn't be alone. Sonia had been the first person he had come to with his confession; when he needed another person, and looked for one, he came to her; and now she'd go with him wherever his destiny took him. Dunia didn't even ask about this—she knew it would be so. She even regarded Sonia with something like reverence, and rather embarrassed her by treating her with such profound respect. Sonia almost burst into tears at this, feeling herself unworthy even to look at Dunia. The lovely image of Dunia when she bowed to her so graciously and respectfully at their first meeting in Raskolnikov's lodgings had lived in her heart ever since, as one of the most beautiful and unattainable visions of her life.

Dunechka eventually lost patience; leaving Sonia, she went to wait for her brother in his own room; she had always imagined that he would go there first. As soon as Sonia was left alone, she at once fell into a torment of dread at the thought that he really might commit suicide. Dunia had feared the same thing. But the two of them had spent the whole day persuading one another that it could never happen, for all sorts of reasons; and as long as they were together, they were calmer. Now that they had parted, each of them could think of nothing else. Sonia remembered Svidrigailov telling her, the day before, that Raskolnikov had two paths open to him—the Vladimirka highway, or... Besides, she knew how vain, arrogant, and proud he was, and how lacking in faith. 'Is it possible that nothing but faint-heartedness and the fear of death will keep him alive?' she finally thought in desperation. Meanwhile the sun was already setting. She stood sadly by the window, staring fixedly out of it—but all that could be seen there was the blank, unpainted wall of the next building. Eventually, when she had quite convinced herself that the unhappy man was dead—he came into the room.

A cry of joy burst from her. But then she looked hard at his face, and suddenly turned pale.

'Yes, yes!' laughed Raskolnikov, 'I've come for your crosses, Sonia. It was you yourself who sent me off to the crossroads; have you lost heart, now that it's come to that?'

Sonia stared at him in astonishment. She found his tone of voice strange, and a cold shiver ran over her; but a moment later she realized that both his tone of voice and his actual words had all been assumed. Even as he spoke to her, he seemed to be staring into the corner of the room, so as not to look her in the face.

'You see, Sonia, I've worked out that it'll actually be better for me this way. There's a particular issue... Well, it's a long story, no point going into it. You know what's the one thing that makes me angry? I'm annoyed that all those stupid, bestial faces are going to be crowding round me, gawping at me, and asking stupid questions which I'll have to answer—pointing their fingers at me... Phoo! You know, I'm not going to Porfiry, I'm sick of him. I'm going to see my friend Gunpowder; and won't he be amazed, won't I cause a sensation—of a sort! But I ought to be cooler about it; I've been too irritable lately. Would you believe it— I've just practically shaken my fist at my sister, simply because she turned round to take a last look at me. What a swine! What a state I'm in! Look what I've come to! Now then, where are those crosses?'

He seemed not to be in control of himself: he couldn't stand still for a minute, nor focus his mind on a single thing. His thoughts tumbled over one another, he talked incoherently, and his hands trembled slightly.

Silently Sonia took two crosses out of a case—one of cypress wood and one of copper. She made the sign of the cross over herself and then him, and hung the little cypress-wood cross on his breast.

'So this is the symbol of me taking up my cross, heh-heh! True enough—as though I hadn't suffered much yet! The cypress-wood one, that's the peasant one; the copper one was Lizaveta's, you're taking that for yourself—will you show it to me? So she was wearing it... at that moment, was she? I know another pair of crosses like these, a silver one and a little icon. I tossed them onto the old woman's breast that day. Actually I ought to be wearing those ones now... Anyway, I keep talking nonsense—I'm missing the point, I'm so absent-minded!... You see, Sonia, I've actually come specially to tell you, to let you know... That's all. That was all I came for. (Hmm—I really thought I'd be telling you more than that.) It was you that wanted me to go, wasn't it? So now I'll be locked up in prison, and you'll get your wish—so why are you crying? You too? Do stop, that's enough! Oh, how I hate all this!'

But his feelings were aroused; his heart ached at the sight of her. 'But why's she so upset, this one as well?' he thought to himself. 'What am I to her? What's she crying for, why's she preparing me for it all, as though she were my mother, or Dunia? She'll turn into my nursemaid!'

'Cross yourself. Say a prayer, just one,' Sonia begged him in a timorous, trembling voice.

'Oh, that, by all means, all you want! With all my heart, Sonia. With all my heart...'

But in fact he had wanted to say something different.

He crossed himself several times over. Sonia picked up her shawl and put it on her head. It was a green drap-de-dames shawl, probably the very same one that Marmeladov had once talked about, the 'family shawl'. The thought crossed Raskolnikov's mind, but he didn't ask. He was beginning to be aware that he really was terribly distracted, and quite grotesquely agitated. It frightened him. What was more, he was suddenly put out by the thought that Sonia meant to go with him.

'What are you doing? Where are you off to? Stay here, stay here! I'm going on my own,' he cried in petty annoyance, and walked to the door almost in a fury. 'What do I need a whole procession for?' he muttered on his way out.

Sonia was left standing in the middle of the room. He hadn't even said goodbye; he had forgotten about her already; a single bitter, mutinous doubt boiled up in his soul.

'Is this really how it has to be—like this?' he thought once more on his way down. 'Can't I really stop and put it all right again... and not go there?'

But still he went on. He suddenly had the definite feeling that there was no point asking himself questions. As he came out into the street, he remembered that he hadn't said goodbye to Sonia, and that he'd left her standing in the middle of the room, in her green shawl, not daring to move after he'd shouted at her. And he paused for a moment. At that same instant another thought flashed through his mind—as though it had been lying in wait to strike him down.

'Why did I go and see her now—what for? I said I had a purpose in coming; so what was the purpose? I never had any purpose! To tell her I was going—so what? What did I need to do that for? Do I love her, or something? I don't, do I? Since I've just driven her away like a dog? Was it really the crosses that I needed to get from her? Oh, how low I've sunk! No, what I needed was her tears; I needed to see her terror, see her heart aching and suffering! I needed something, anything, to clutch hold of, to delay things, to see another human being! How dared I have such confidence in myself, such dreams about what I'd achieve, worthless beggar that I am, villain, villain!'

He was walking along the canal bank, and didn't have far to go now. But when he reached the bridge he paused, and suddenly turned aside, crossed the bridge and walked towards the Haymarket.

He looked hungrily to right and left, peering intently at everything he passed, without managing to concentrate on anything; it was all slipping away from him. 'In a week now, or a month, I'll be driven off somewhere in one of those prison carts, and I'll cross this bridge; so how will I look at this canal then? Should I remember this?' That was the thought that crossed his mind. 'That sign over there—how will I read those same letters then? Here's the word "Campany"—well, I ought to remember that "a", that letter "a", and look at it in a month's time, that same letter "a"; how shall I be looking at it then? What'll I be feeling and thinking then?... God, how petty all this must be, all these... preoccupations of mine right now! Of course, all this must be very curious... in its way... (ha-ha-ha! whatever am I thinking of!)—I'm turning into a child, showing off to my own self; why am I making such a fool of myself? Bah, how people jostle you! Look at that fat... German, he must be—who shoved me aside; well, does he know whom he was shoving? There's a peasant woman with a baby, begging; how odd that she thinks I'm happier than she is. Why don't I give her something, just for curiosity's sake? Look, I've still got a five-kopek piece in my pocket, wherever from? Here you are then... take it, little mother!'

'God save you!' came the beggarwoman's plaintive voice.

He came out onto the Haymarket. He found it unpleasant, very unpleasant being jostled by the passers-by; but he went straight for where the crowd was thickest. He'd have given anything in the world to be alone; yet he felt that he couldn't spend a single minute more on his own. A drunk was making a fool of himself in the crowd; he kept trying to dance, but couldn't help toppling over. People were pressing round him. Raskolnikov forced his way through, watched the drunk for a few minutes, and suddenly gave a short, abrupt laugh. A minute later he'd forgotten the man; he didn't even see him, though he was still looking at him. Eventually he walked away, not even remembering where he was; but when he reached the middle of the square, he was overcome by a sudden impulse, filled with a rush of feeling that took him over body and soul.

He suddenly remembered Sonia's words: 'Go to the crossroads, bow down before the people, and kiss the earth, because you've sinned against that too; and proclaim out loud to the whole world: "I am a murderer!"' His whole body trembled at the memory. He was so weighed down by the hopeless anguish and anxiety of all the past days, and particularly the past few hours, that he simply flung himself at the possibility of this new, unalloyed, complete sensation. It came over him like a sort of convulsion; a spark burned up in his soul, consuming his whole being like a fire. Everything inside him melted, and the tears poured down his cheeks. Not moving from where he stood, he fell to his knees...

Kneeling in the middle of the square, he bowed down to the ground and kissed the filthy earth with joy and bliss. Then he rose to his feet and bowed once more.

'Got a skinful, he has,' commented a young man nearby.

People laughed.

'He's off to Jerusalem, fellows, he's saying goodbye to his children and his country; he's bowing to the whole world, and kissing the ground of our capital city of St Petersburg,' added another tipsy tradesman.

'Quite a young lad too!' put in a third.

'And respectable!' someone remarked in a pompous voice.

'There's no telling who's respectable and who isn't, these days.'

All these exclamations and comments held Raskolnikov back, and the words 'I have killed', which he might have been preparing to utter, died on his lips. But he bore all the outcry patiently, and then without looking back walked straight across the street towards the police office. On his way there he caught sight of something which didn't actually surprise him—he had a premonition that this was bound to happen. When he bowed down to the ground the second time, on the Haymarket, and looked to his left, he saw Sonia some fifty yards away. She was hiding from him, behind one of the wooden booths that stood on the square. So she had followed him on his whole sorrowful walk! At that moment Raskolnikov felt and understood, once and for all, that Sonia would remain with him for evermore, that she would follow him to the ends of the earth, wherever his fate led him. His heart turned over within him... but now he had already reached the fateful spot...

He entered the courtyard quite briskly. He had to go up to the third floor. 'I'll just go up, anyway,' he thought. It felt as if the fateful minute was still a long way off, there was still plenty of time, he could still think it all over.

Once again the same litter, the same eggshells lying about on the winding staircase, once again the doors to the apartments standing wide open, the same kitchens with their reek of smoke. Raskolnikov had never been back since that last time. His legs felt weak and numb, but they carried him on. He stopped for a moment to catch his breath and pull himself together, so that he could enter *like a man*. 'But what for? Why?' he suddenly thought, realizing what he was doing. 'If I really have to drink this cup, then what does it all matter? The more revolting the better.' In his mind's eye he suddenly saw the figure of Ilya Petrovich Gunpowder. 'Am I really going to him? Can't I go to someone else? Why not Nikodim Fomich? Turn back now and go to the superintendent himself, at his home? At least it'd all happen privately, then... No, no! I'm going to Gunpowder, to Gunpowder! If I'm to drink it, let me drain it all off at once!...'

With his blood running cold, barely aware of what he was doing, he opened the door to the office. This time there weren't many people about: a porter and a peasant. The doorman didn't even look out of his cubbyhole. Raskolnikov went through to the next room. 'Perhaps I won't have to tell anyone anything,' he suddenly thought. Here was one of the clerks, in a civilian frock coat, just sitting down to write something at a desk. Another clerk was settling himself in a corner. Zametov wasn't there. Nor was Nikodim Fomich, naturally.

'Nobody here?' asked Raskolnikov, addressing the man at the desk.

'Who did you want?'

'Aha! Not a sight nor sound of you, but here breathes the breath of Russia... how does that fairy tale go?...* I've forgotten! My r-r-respects, sir!' came a familiar voice.

Raskolnikov jumped. There in front of him stood Gunpowder, just emerged from the third office. 'This is Fate itself!' thought Raskolnikov. 'Why's he here?'

'You here to see us? What's it about?' exclaimed Ilya Petrovich. (He was evidently in an excellent mood, even a little exhilarated.) 'If it's business, you're early. I just happened to be here... Anyway, I'll do what I can for you. I must confess... what was your name again? I'm so sorry...'

'Raskolnikov.'

'Of course you're Raskolnikov! How could you think I'd forget! Please don't take me for such a... Rodion Ro... Ro... Rodionich, wasn't that it?'

'Rodion Romanich.'

'Yes-yes, of course! Rodion Romanich, Rodion Romanich! It was on the tip of my tongue. I've been asking about you a lot. I must confess, I was sincerely sorry after that last time, when we treated you so... they explained it to me afterwards—I heard you were a young writer, in fact a scholar... and as it were, your first steps... Oh Lord! Where's the writer or scholar who hasn't been a bit eccentric, at the start! My wife and I—we both admire literature, and as for my wife, she's just passionate about it!... Literature and art! So long as a man's a gentleman, all he needs is talent, knowledge, reason, genius, in order to get on! A hat, now—what does a hat signify? A hat's a pancake, I can buy one at Zimmermann's*—but what's stored underneath that hat, what that hat covers: that's something I can't buy!... I must admit, I was going to go round to see you and explain, but then I thought you might... However, I haven't even asked you: do you actually want anything here? I believe your family's visiting you?'

'Yes, my mother and sister.'

'I've actually had the honour and the pleasure of meeting your sister—what a charming and cultured lady! I must say I felt sorry that you and I got so heated with each other that day. How odd that was! And then, when you fainted, I looked at you in a particular way—well, that was all explained afterwards, most brilliantly! Bigotry and fanaticism! I can understand your getting so annoyed. Perhaps you're moving to new lodgings, now your family's here?'

'N-no, I just... I came in to ask... I thought I'd find Zametov here.'

'Ah, yes! You're friends now, I heard about that. Well, Zametov isn't here—you've missed him. Yes, we've lost our Alexander Grigorievich! He's not been here since yesterday; he's been transferred... and when he left, he had a shouting match with everyone. Quite rude, actually... He's an excitable young lad, that's all; in fact he even showed some promise; but what can you do with them all, these brilliant young men of ours? Apparently he wanted to sit some exam or other—but over here, all you have to do is spout something and show off a bit, and that's your exam done. It's nothing like you, for instance, or your friend Mr Razumikhin there! You've gone for a learned career, and setbacks won't stop you! All the beauty of life, you might say—so far as you're concerned, *nihil est*, you're an ascetic, a monk, a hermit!... A book in your hands, a pen behind your ear, scientific research—that's what makes your spirit take flight! I myself have, to some extent... have you happened to read Livingstone's journals?'*

'No.'

'Well, I have. These days, of course, there are a great many nihilists around; well, that's understandable; look at the times we live in, I ask you! Anyway, you and I... but of course you're not a nihilist! Give me an honest answer, an honest one, do!'

'N–no...'

'No, please, you can talk straight to me, don't hold back—talk as if you were alone and talking to yourself. Duty is one thing, but... you thought I was going to say "*friendship* is another"—no, you guessed wrong! It's not friendship, but the sentiment of a citizen and a human being; a feeling of humanity and love of the Almighty. I may be an official personage, and hold an official post, but I always have to remember that inside I'm a man and a citizen,* and I must be answerable to that... Now you mentioned Zametov. Well, Zametov, he'll blow up a scandal in the French way, in some low dive, over a glass of champagne or Russian wine—that's Zametov for you! Whereas I've burned myself up, so to speak, with devotion to duty and lofty sentiments, besides which there's my consequence, my rank, my position in society! I'm a married man with a family. I carry out the duties of a man and a citizen, but what's that, I ask you? I'm addressing you as a man who's ennobled by his education. And then there are these countless numbers of midwives cropping up all over the place.'

Raskolnikov raised his eyebrows enquiringly. Ilya Petrovich had evidently come straight from his table, and the words that poured and tumbled out of his mouth seemed for the most part to be mere empty sounds. But some of them Raskolnikov managed to understand; and now he looked questioningly at the speaker and wondered what all this was leading to.

'I'm talking about those crop-haired girls,'* went on Ilya Petrovich garrulously; 'midwives is what I call them myself, and I think it's a very good name. Heh-heh! They scramble into the Academy and learn anatomy: well, I ask you—if I fall ill, am I going to send for a lass to treat me? Heh-heh!'

Ilya Petrovich chortled, very pleased with his own wit.

'I grant you, a man may have an insatiable thirst for enlightenment; but now he's enlightened, and that's enough. Why abuse the fact? Why insult respectable people, as that scoundrel Zametov did? Why should he insult me, may I ask? Look at all these suicides happening everywhere—you can't imagine. All that rabble, they eat up the last of their money and then they kill themselves. Boys, girls, old men... Just this morning there was a story about some gentleman who'd recently arrived here. Nil Pavlich! Hey, Nil Pavlich! What was his name, that gentleman we've just been told about, the one who they say has just shot himself?'

'Svidrigailov,' replied someone from next door, in a hoarse and indifferent voice.

Raskolnikov jumped.

'Svidrigailov! Svidrigailov has shot himself?' he cried.

'Why, do you know Svidrigailov?'

'Yes... yes, I do... he hadn't been here long...'

'That's right, he arrived a short while ago, he'd lost his wife; a man of disreputable conduct, and he suddenly shot himself, in such a shocking way, you can't imagine... and he left a short message in his notebook to say that he was dying in possession of his faculties, and please not to blame anyone for his death. Had a lot of money, that one, they say. So, how did you know him?'

'I... knew him... my sister used to be their governess...'

'Well, well, well... In that case, you could tell us something about him. Didn't you suspect anything yourself?'

'I saw him yesterday... He was... drinking wine... I didn't know anything.'

Raskolnikov felt as if a heavy weight had fallen on him and was crushing him.

'You've gone all pale again. It's so stuffy in here...'

'Yes, I have to go now,' muttered Raskolnikov. 'Excuse me for disturbing you...'

'Oh, not at all, whenever you like! It was a pleasure to see you, and I'm happy to say so...'

Ilya Petrovich even offered him his hand.

'I just wanted... I came to see Zametov...'

'I understand, I understand; it's been good to see you.'

'I'm... very glad... goodbye now...' said Raskolnikov with a smile.

He left. He swayed as he walked. His head was spinning. He couldn't feel the ground beneath his feet. He began walking downstairs, steadying himself with his right hand against the wall. He had the impression that a porter carrying a book had jostled him on his way upstairs to the office; and that there was a dog barking its head off somewhere downstairs; and that a woman had yelled and thrown a rolling pin at it. He reached the bottom of the stairs and came out into the yard. There, not far from the gate, stood Sonia, pale as death. She gave him a wild, desperate look. He stopped in front of her. Her eyes were full of pain, torment, and despair. She threw up her hands. His lips twisted in a hideous, lost smile. He stood there a moment, grinned and turned back upstairs to the office.

Ilya Petrovich had sat down and was rummaging through some papers.

Before him stood the same peasant who had just jostled Raskolnikov on his way up.

'A-a-ah? Back again? Forgotten something?... What's up?'

Raskolnikov's lips were white, his eyes fixed, as he slowly advanced towards Ilya Petrovich. He came right up to the table, leaned his hand on it, and tried vainly to say something; but all that came out was inarticulate sounds.

'You're not well! Get a chair, someone! There, sit down on the chair. Sit down! Water!'

Raskolnikov sank down onto the chair, but never took his eyes off Ilya Petrovich's face, now full of disagreeable surprise. For a minute each stared at the other and they both waited. Someone brought water.

'It was I...' began Raskolnikov.

'Drink some water.'

Raskolnikov waved the water aside and spoke quietly, slowly and distinctly:

'It was I who killed the old pawnbroker-woman and her sister Lizaveta with an axe, and robbed them.'

Ilya Petrovich gaped. People came running from all sides.

Raskolnikov repeated his statement...

EPILOGUE

CHAPTER I

SIBERIA. On the banks of a wide, desolate river stands a town, one of the administrative centres of Russia. In the town there is a fortress, and in the fortress a prison.* In that prison, Rodion Raskolnikov, second-category exiled convict,* has been held for nine months now. Almost a year and a half has passed since the day of his crime.

His trial had passed off without any particular difficulties. The criminal had maintained his confession firmly, precisely, and clearly, without confusing any of the circumstances nor softening them in his favour; he neither misrepresented the facts, nor forgot the smallest particular. He described in the fullest detail exactly how the murder had been done; he explained the mystery of his pledge (the little wooden board with the metal strip) which had been found in the dead woman's hands; he gave a detailed account of taking the keys from his victim, describing the keys and the trunk and its contents; he even named some of the items in it. He cleared up the puzzle of Lizaveta's murder, and described how Koch had come and knocked at the door, and the student after him; he reported everything they had said to one another; then he described how he, the criminal, had run downstairs and heard the yells from Mikolka and Mitka; and how he had hidden in the empty apartment, and then gone home; and he ended by pointing out the stone in the gateway of the courtyard off Voznesensky Prospekt, under which the purse and the other things were found. In short, everything turned out to be quite clear. The investigators and judges were very surprised, incidentally, that he'd hidden the purse and other items under the stone, without making any use of them; and most surprised of all that he not only didn't remember the details of all the objects he had actually stolen, but had actually got the number of them wrong. It seemed incredible that he'd never once opened the purse, and didn't even know just how much money it contained (it turned out to be three hundred and seventeen silver roubles and three twenty-kopek pieces; some of the biggest notes at the top of the pile had almost rotted away from lying so long under the stone). The investigators spent a long time trying to discover why the accused was lying about this single question, while voluntarily and truthfully confessing everything else.

Eventually some of them (particularly the psychologists) actually conceded that he might really have never looked inside the purse, and consequently hadn't known what was in it, and had buried it under the stone without finding out; but they concluded from this that the crime couldn't have been committed other than in a state of temporary insanity, driven by a morbid fixation on murder and robbery with no ulterior motive or hope of gain. This fitted in neatly with the latest modish theories of temporary insanity,* which people tend to try to apply to criminals nowadays. Moreover, a number of witnesses testified in detail to the state of hypochondria that Raskolnikov had been suffering for some time; they included Dr Zosimov, Raskolnikov's former companions, his landlady, and the servant. All this strongly reinforced the conclusion that Raskolnikov wasn't quite like an ordinary murderer, robber, and thief; that there was something different about this case. To the great annoyance of the proponents of this view, the prisoner himself made almost no attempt to excuse himself; when he was asked outright what exactly had motivated him to commit murder and to rob, he answered quite clearly and with the most brutal frankness that it had all resulted from his wretched situation, his helplessness and poverty, and his hope of furthering the first steps in his career with the help of the three thousand roubles at least that he had counted on getting from his victim. He had been driven to commit the murder by his shallow and cowardly nature, further exacerbated by privation and failure. And when he was asked what had induced him to go and confess, he answered straight out that it was sincere repentance. All of this was said almost rudely...

The sentence, however, turned out more lenient than might have been expected from the nature of the crime; perhaps this was precisely because the criminal not only made no attempt to justify himself, but in fact seemed to want to incriminate himself still further. All the strange and special features of the affair were taken into account. There wasn't the faintest doubt that before he committed the crime, the accused had been in a sick and impoverished condition. The fact that he hadn't made use of the stolen property was credited partly to the effects of his awakening repentance and partly to his impaired mental state at the time the crime was committed. The unplanned killing of Lizaveta in fact served as an example in support of the latter idea: here's a man who commits two murders and yet at the same time forgets that the door is unlocked! And finally, his voluntary confession, at a time when the affair had become extraordinarily confused on account of the false confession made by the melancholic and fanatical Nikolay, and when there was not only no clear evidence against the true culprit, but not even any real suspicion of him (Porfiry Petrovich had faithfully kept his word)—everything ultimately combined to soften the defendant's sentence.

There were, too, other quite unexpected facts which greatly helped the accused. The ex-student Razumikhin somehow unearthed the information, which he then presented with proofs, that the criminal Raskolnikov, while a student at the university, had spent the last of his money helping a poor, consumptive fellow student, supporting him almost single-handedly for six months. When the student died, Raskolnikov had taken on the care of his surviving father, an old and ailing man (whom his son had maintained and fed by his own exertions ever since he was thirteen or so); eventually Raskolnikov had found a place for the old man in a hospital, and when the old man died he had buried him.* All this information had a favourable effect on Raskolnikov's fate. His own landlady, the widow Zarnitsyna, mother of Raskolnikov's late fiancée, also testified that while they were living in their former home near Five Corners, the house had caught fire one night and Raskolnikov had rescued two little children out of one of the burning apartments, suffering burns in the process himself. This story was carefully investigated and quite convincingly confirmed by numerous witnesses. In short, it all ended with the criminal being sentenced to penal servitude of the second category for a term of only eight years, in consideration of his voluntary confession and a number of extenuating circumstances.

At the very beginning of the trial, Raskolnikov's mother fell ill. Dunia and Razumikhin managed to move her out of Petersburg for the whole duration of the trial. Razumikhin chose a town on the railway line, not far from Petersburg, so that he could follow every step of the trial and yet see Avdotya Romanovna as often as possible. Pulkheria Alexandrovna's illness was a strange sort of nervous disorder, accompanied by what looked like at least partial, if not complete, mental derangement. Dunia, on returning from her latest visit to her brother, found her mother seriously ill, feverish and delirious. That same evening she and Razumikhin agreed on what to tell her mother when she asked about her son; together they concocted a whole story for her about how Raskolnikov had left for somewhere far away on the Russian frontier, on a private mission which would eventually earn him fame and fortune. But they were much struck by the fact that Pulkheria Alexandrovna herself never asked them any questions about all this, neither at the time nor later on. Instead, she herself came up with a whole story about her son's sudden departure, telling with tears in her eyes how he had come to take his leave of her, and dropping hints that there were many very important and secret facts known to her alone, and that Rodia had many very powerful enemies, so that he was obliged to hide away. As for his future career, she too apparently saw it as secure and brilliantly successful, once he had overcome some adverse circumstances; she assured Razumikhin that her son would in time actually become a statesman, as proved by his magazine article and his outstanding literary talent. She was constantly reading that article; sometimes she even read it aloud; she almost took it to bed with her; and yet she almost never asked where exactly Rodia was now, despite the fact that people clearly avoided talking to her about that—something that might itself have aroused her suspicions. Eventually they became anxious about Pulkheria Alexandrovna's silence on certain matters. For instance, she never complained that no letters came from him, although when she had been living in her little town earlier on, the hope and expectation of soon getting a letter from her adored Rodia had been all she lived for. This last fact was too inexplicable, and greatly worried Dunia; she came to think that her mother had a presentiment of something terrible happening to her son, and was afraid to ask questions for fear of hearing something even more dreadful. At all events, Dunia could clearly see that Pulkheria Alexandrovna was not in her right mind.

On a couple of occasions her mother herself led the conversation round in a way that made it impossible to answer her without mentioning where exactly Rodia was now. When all the answers she got turned out to be unsatisfactory and suspicious, she became very sad, gloomy, and silent, and stayed so for a very long time. Eventually Dunia realized that it was hard to keep lying and inventing things, and made up her mind that on certain matters it was best to say nothing at all. But it became increasingly obvious that her poor mother suspected something terrible. She remembered hearing her brother say that their mother had overheard her talking in her sleep, the night before that last fateful day, after her scene with Svidrigailov. Could she have heard something then? It would often happen that after several days or even weeks of morose, gloomy silence and wordless tears, the sick woman would become hysterically cheerful and suddenly take to talking out loud, almost without stopping, about her son, her hopes, their future... Her fantasies were sometimes very strange. The others humoured her, agreeing with everything she said; perhaps she realized clearly enough that she was just being humoured, yet still she talked on...

Five months after the criminal's confession, sentence was passed. Razumikhin visited him in prison whenever he was allowed to. So did Sonia. And at last came the partings. Dunia vowed to her brother that this parting wasn't for ever; Razumikhin vowed the same. The youthful, hot-headed Razumikhin had firmly resolved to spend the next three or four years laying the foundations of his future fortune, saving whatever money he could, and then emigrating to Siberia, where the land was rich in every way, while workers, inhabitants, and capital were all scarce. He would settle in the same town where Rodia was, and... they would all start a new life together. Everyone was in tears when they parted. Raskolnikov had spent the last few days in a very thoughtful state, asking a lot of questions about his mother and worrying endlessly about her. In fact the thought of her tormented him a great deal, and that in turn worried Dunia. When he found out the details of her unhealthy state of mind, he became very depressed. All this time he was for some reason very uncommunicative with Sonia. With the help of the money left her by Svidrigailov, Sonia had long ago made all the necessary preparations to follow the party of convicts that Raskolnikov would be joining. Neither she nor he ever said a word to each other about this; but they both knew that it was going to happen. At their final parting, he smiled oddly at his sister's and Razumikhin's ardent assurances of a happy future once he was released from prison, and predicted that his mother's sickness would soon come to an unhappy end. At last he and Sonia set off.

Two months later Dunechka and Razumikhin were married. It was a quiet, sad wedding. The guests included Porfiry Petrovich and Zosimov. Throughout this time, Razumikhin had looked like a man who had taken a firm decision. Dunia was in no doubt at all that he would carry out everything he planned—she couldn't fail to believe that, for his iron will was plain to see. At the same time he had again started attending university lectures, so as to complete his course. The two of them were endlessly planning their future together, and both were confidently counting on emigrating to Siberia in five years' time. Until then, they placed their trust in Sonia out there...

Pulkheria Alexandrovna happily gave her daughter her blessing when she married Razumikhin; but after the wedding she seemed even sadder and more troubled. To give her a moment of pleasure, Razumikhin told her the story about the student and his ailing father, and also about how Rodia had got burned and actually fallen ill after saving the lives of two little children last year. Both these stories brought Pulkheria Alexandrovna's already disordered mind to a state of near-ecstasy. She talked incessantly about these events, even buttonholing people in the street (though Dunia accompanied her wherever she went). Whenever she got hold of someone who would listen to her, in a public carriage or a shop, she would bring up the subject of her son, and his article, and how he had helped a student, and got himself burned in a house fire, and so on. Dunechka couldn't think how to control her. Quite apart from the dangers of such a morbidly exalted frame of mind, there was the dreadful risk that someone might mention Raskolnikov's name in connection with the recent trial, and bring that into the conversation. Pulkheria Alexandrovna even found out the address of the mother of the two rescued children, and made up her mind to go and visit her. Her agitation eventually reached fever pitch. Sometimes she would suddenly burst into tears; often she fell ill and became fevered and delirious. One morning she roundly declared that according to her calculations Rodia was soon due back; she remembered that on parting with her, he had told her to expect him in nine months. So she set about tidying up the whole flat and making ready to receive him, doing up her own room for him, cleaning the furniture, washing and hanging new curtains, and so forth. Though alarmed, Dunia said nothing; in fact she even helped her prepare the room for her brother. After an anxious day filled with endless fantasies, blissful visions, and tears, she fell ill that night, and by morning was feverish and delirious. Her fever worsened, and in two weeks she was dead. In her ravings some words escaped her which showed that she knew a great deal more about her son's dreadful plight than anyone had thought.

Raskolnikov didn't hear of his mother's death for a long time, although a correspondence with Petersburg was set up as soon as he arrived in Siberia. It was kept up by Sonia, who wrote to Razumikhin in Petersburg regularly every month, and just as regularly received monthly replies from there. Sonia's letters at first struck Dunia and Razumikhin as somehow dry and unsatisfactory; but in the end they both concluded that it wasn't possible to write any better, and that these letters gave them the fullest and clearest possible idea of their unfortunate brother's life. Sonia's letters were filled with the most commonplace factual accounts, and the simplest and clearest descriptions of every detail of Raskolnikov's life as a convict. They said nothing about any personal hopes of hers, nor speculation about the future, nor accounts of her own feelings. Instead of trying to describe his mental state or say anything about his inner life, she wrote nothing but facts, quoting his own words, giving detailed accounts of his health, what he had asked for on this or that visit of hers, what he had wanted to know, what commissions he had entrusted her with, and so forth. All this she passed on in meticulous detail. A picture of their unfortunate brother eventually emerged of its own accord, clear and precise; there could be no mistake about it, since it consisted of nothing but true facts.

But there was little cheer for Dunia and her husband in these accounts, at least to start with. Sonia repeatedly wrote that he was constantly sullen, uncommunicative, and almost indifferent to the news she passed on to him every time she received a letter; that he sometimes asked about his mother; and when she eventually saw that he already suspected the truth, and told him his mother had died, she was surprised that even this news didn't particularly affect him, at least so far as she could see. She also wrote that although he seemed so immersed in his own thoughts, and closed off from everybody else, he accepted his own new way of life in a very direct and simple way, clearly understanding his situation, expecting no improvement any time soon, cherishing no frivolous hopes (so characteristic for people in his situation), and showing almost no surprise at anything about his new life, so unlike anything he had ever known.

Sonia said that his health was satisfactory. He carried out his work, not shirking it nor seeking more. He was almost indifferent to his food, though it was so bad (except on Sundays and feast days) that in the end he willingly accepted a little money from Sonia to pay for some tea every day; for the rest, he asked her not to trouble herself, and insisted to her that all her concern for him was merely annoying him. Sonia also wrote that he was in shared accommodation with all the other convicts; she hadn't seen the inside of the barracks, but understood that they were crowded, dirty, and unhealthy; he slept on a piece of felt stretched over a wooden bunk, and wasn't interested in improving the arrangement. But she said that his poor, rough conditions weren't in any way deliberate on his part; it was just that he didn't notice them and clearly didn't care about them. Sonia said quite openly that especially at the beginning of his imprisonment, he had not only taken no interest in her visits, but had even been almost irritable with her, uncommunicative and rude, but that in the end these visits had become a habit for him, indeed almost a necessity, so that he really missed her badly when she fell ill and was unable to visit him for several days. On holidays she would see him either by the prison gates or in the guardhouse, where he would be summoned to see her for a few minutes; on working days she would visit him at his outside work, or in a workshop, or the brickworks, or a warehouse on the banks of the Irtysh. For herself, Sonia wrote that she had managed to make some acquaintances and find some protectors in the town; that she occupied herself with sewing, and since there was no proper dressmaker in the town, she had made herself indispensable in several households. What she didn't mention was that she had managed to get some favours from the authorities for Raskolnikov too, so that he was given easier work and the like. Eventually there came the news (Dunia herself had sensed from her latest letters that she was very anxious and alarmed) that he had started shunning everybody, his fellow prisoners had taken a dislike to him, he might spend days on end without saying a word, and he had grown very pale. And all of a sudden, in her last letter, Sonia wrote to say that he had fallen gravely ill and been moved to the hospital's prison ward...

CHAPTER II

HE had been ill for a long time. But it wasn't the horrors of prison life, the hard labour, the food, his shaved head,* or the rags he wore that had broken his spirit. Oh, what did he care about all those trials and hardships! On the contrary, he was glad to have to work; physically exhausted by it, he at least earned a few hours of peaceful sleep. And what did the food matter to him—that watery cabbage soup with cockroaches in it? As a student, in his previous life, he often didn't even have that. His clothes were warm and right for the life he was leading. He didn't even feel the fetters he wore. Was he to feel ashamed of his shaved head and particoloured coat? Ashamed before whom? Sonia? Sonia was frightened of him, and was he supposed to be ashamed before her?

And yet... he was indeed ashamed of himself before Sonia too, so he punished her by rough, contemptuous treatment. But it wasn't his shaved head or the fetters that made him ashamed: it was his pride that was deeply hurt. And it was his hurt pride that made him ill. Oh, how happy he would have been if he could have blamed himself! Then he could have borne everything, even this shame and disgrace. But he had rigorously examined himself, and in all conscience he could find no particularly terrible guilt in his past, nothing beyond a simple *blunder*, which could have happened to anyone. What made him ashamed was the fact that he, Raskolnikov, had come to grief so blindly, hopelessly, obtusely, stupidly, through some decree of blind fate; and now, if he wanted to find any peace whatsoever, he must reconcile himself to the 'absurdity' of that decree, and humble himself before it.

Empty, meaningless anxiety in the present, and endless sacrifice in the future—sacrifice that would get him nowhere. That was what awaited him in the world. And what good was it to him if in eight years he would only be thirty-two years old, and could start his life again? What was the point of living? What should he aim for? What should he strive for? Just to live, so as to exist? But even before this, he had been ready a thousand times over to sacrifice his existence to an idea, a hope, or simply a fantasy. Mere existence wasn't enough for him—he would always need something more. Perhaps it had only ever been the intensity of his desires that had led him to feel that he was a man to whom more was allowed than to others.

If only fate had granted him remorse—burning remorse, that would crush his heart, and drive away sleep; remorse whose dreadful torments would make him long for the noose, or death in deep waters. Oh, how he would have welcomed that! Torments and tears—they, too, meant life. But he didn't repent of his crime.

At least he might have gone on raging at his stupidity, as he had raged in the past at those monstrously stupid actions of his that had brought him to prison. But now that he was here, in prison, and *free*, he considered and reviewed all his past actions, and couldn't find them by any means so monstrously stupid as they had seemed to him in those fateful days of the past.

'Why, why,' he asked himself, 'should my idea have been any stupider than all the other ideas and theories that have swarmed and jostled one another in this world, for as long as the world has existed? All you need is to take a broad, completely unbiased view of the matter, free from everyday considerations, and then, of course, my idea turns out not to be so... strange, at all. Oh, you sceptics, you twopenny sages, why did you stop halfway?'

'What is it that makes my action seem so monstrous to them? The fact that it's an evil deed? What do those words mean—"an evil deed"? My conscience is clear. Of course I've committed a crime; of course I've infringed the letter of the law, and spilt blood—so I'll pay for the letter of the law with my own head, and let that be enough! In that case, of course, many benefactors of the human race who never inherited power, but seized it for themselves, ought to have been executed right from the start. But those men succeeded in doing what they did, and consequently *they were right*; whereas I didn't succeed, and therefore I never had the right to let myself take that step.'

That was the only way in which he could accept that he had committed a crime: nothing but the fact that he hadn't succeeded, but instead had given himself up and confessed.

Another thought also made him suffer. Why hadn't he killed himself that day? Why had he stood looking down at the water, and then chosen to give himself up instead? Was his desire to live really so powerful, so hard to overcome? Had Svidrigailov, with his fear of death, been the winner?

He tormented himself with that question, unable to see that even then, standing and looking down into the river, he might perhaps have already sensed how deeply wrong he and his convictions were. He couldn't see that this sensation might foreshadow a profound change in his life, a future resurrection, and a new view of life to come.

He was more inclined to accept that this was no more than the force of instinct, which he could never break, and which he was unable to over-step (because he was too weak and insignificant). He looked at his fellow convicts and wondered at them: how much they all loved life, how dearly they treasured it! Indeed, it seemed to him that people loved, valued, and treasured their lives here in prison even more than where they were free. What horrible pain and suffering some of them had endured—the vagrants,* for instance! How could a man find so much meaning in a sin-gle ray of sunlight, a deep forest, a cool spring somewhere in the trackless wilderness, which he had once seen two years ago and which he now yearned for as though it was a lovers' tryst, dreaming about it and the green grass around it, with a bird singing in the bushes? As he went on thinking about this, he found examples that were even more inexplicable.

There was much in his prison and in the world around him that he didn't notice, nor wish to notice. It was as though he lived with eyes downcast: looking about him was unbearably repugnant. But eventu-ally he found much that surprised him; almost despite himself, he began noticing things he had never suspected before. What came to astonish him more than anything else was the dreadful, impassable gulf between him and all these people. He felt as if he and they belonged to different nations.* He and they regarded one another with distrust and hostility. He recognized and understood the broad reasons for this dif-ference; but he had never before believed that those reasons could be so deep and powerful. Some of the convicts here were exiled Polish polit-ical prisoners.* They simply regarded everyone else as ignorant yokels, and looked down on them with contempt. But Raskolnikov couldn't share their attitude; he clearly saw that these ignorant folk were in some ways far wiser than the Poles themselves. There were some Russians here, too—a former officer and two seminarians—who despised the convicts; but Raskolnikov saw their error too.

He himself was disliked and avoided by everyone; eventually they actually came to hate him. Why? He had no idea. People who had com-mitted far worse crimes than him despised him, laughed at him, and mocked his crime.

'You're gentry!' they'd say. 'You'd no business going around with an axe. That's not what gentry do.'

During the second week of Lent it was his turn to fast, along with the rest of his hut. He went to church to pray with the others. One day a quarrel broke out, he didn't know why; and they all turned on him with savage jibes.

'You're an unbeliever! You don't believe in God!' they shouted at him. 'We ought to kill you!'

He had never talked to them about God or religion, but they wanted to kill him as an unbeliever. He remained silent, without arguing. One convict flung himself at him in a blind rage; Raskolnikov stood waiting for him, calmly and silently, not even raising an eyebrow; not a muscle of his face moved. A guard just managed to get between him and his would-be killer, or blood would have been spilt.

There was another question he still hadn't found an answer to. Why did they all love Sonia so? She never tried to win their affection; they rarely came across her; sometimes it only happened during work, when she'd come along for a minute to see him. And yet everybody knew her; they knew that she had followed him here, and knew how and where she lived. She never gave them money, nor did anything particular for them. Except once, at Christmas-time, when she brought pies and loaves as a treat for the whole prison. But bit by bit a closer friendship grew up between them and Sonia. She wrote letters for them, and posted them to their families. When their relatives came to the town, the prisoners would tell them to leave their presents, and even money, in Sonia's care. The wives and sweethearts knew her and came to see her. And when she went to visit Raskolnikov at his workplace, or met a party of convicts on their way to work, they would all take off their caps, and bow to her. '*Matushka*, Sofia Semionovna, you're a mother to us, so gentle and kind!' That was how those coarse, branded convicts* would address this slight, thin creature. And she would smile and return their bow, and they all loved it when she smiled at them. They liked the way she walked, and would turn round to follow her with their eyes, and say nice things about her; they even praised her for being so small—in fact there was nothing about her they didn't praise. Some even came to her to have their illnesses treated.

He remained in the hospital for the rest of Lent and Holy Week. During his recovery he remembered the dreams he had had while lying in a feverish delirium. In his sickness he had seemed to see the whole world on the point of being overrun by a dreadful, unheard-of pestilence advancing out of deepest Asia into Europe. Everyone was doomed, save for a very few chosen individuals. A new strain of parasitic worms had emerged, microscopic creatures that invaded human bodies. But these organisms were spirits, endowed with a mind and a will. The people they invaded went mad at once, as though possessed.* Never before had people regarded themselves as so wise, or been so impregnable in their view of the truth, as these infected people were. Never had people been more unshakeably confident in their decisions, their scientific deductions, their moral convictions and beliefs. Whole villages, towns, and nations became infected and went mad. Everyone was afraid; people no longer understood one another, they all believed that they alone knew the truth, and suffered dreadfully at the sight of everyone else, and beat their breasts, weeping and wringing their hands. Nobody knew who should be judged, nor how; nobody knew how to tell evil from good. Nobody knew who should be found guilty and who acquitted. People killed one another in senseless fury. Whole armies assembled to fight one another, but even as an army advanced, its soldiers suddenly began fighting among themselves, breaking ranks and falling on one another, stabbing and slashing and biting and devouring each other. In the towns, alarm bells rang all day, summoning all the people to gather together; but who was summoning them, and why, nobody knew. Everyone was afraid. The most everyday trades were abandoned, because everyone put forward his own ideas and improvements, and no one could agree. Agriculture came to a halt. Here and there people would gather in groups, decide on something amongst themselves, and swear never to separate; but then they would immediately undertake something quite different from what they had just proposed, and begin to accuse one another, fighting and stabbing one another. Fires and famine broke out. Everyone and everything was perishing. The pestilence grew and spread ever further. Only a few people in the whole world could save themselves. They were the chosen few—pure souls destined to found a new race of men and a new life, to renew and purify the earth. But no one had seen those people anywhere, nor heard their words or their voices.

Raskolnikov was distressed by the fact that this senseless fantasy had cast such a dark shadow on his memory, and that the impression of this feverish dream remained with him for such a long time. By now it was the second week after Easter, and the weather was warm, fine, and springlike. The windows of the prison ward were open (barred windows, with a sentry patrolling below). Through all his illness, Sonia had only been able to visit him in the ward on two occasions: she had to apply for permission each time, and that was difficult. But she would often come into the hospital courtyard beneath his window, especially in the evenings; sometimes she would simply stand there a minute or two, so as to catch just a glimpse of the windows of his ward in the distance. One evening, when he was almost well again, Raskolnikov fell asleep, and on awakening he happened to go over to the window. Suddenly he caught sight of Sonia in the distance, standing by the hospital gates and apparently waiting for something. At that moment something seemed to pierce his heart. He shuddered and quickly walked away from the window. Next day Sonia didn't come, nor the day after; and he realized that he was waiting anxiously for her. Finally he was discharged. When he returned to the prison, the other convicts told him that Sofia Semionovna had fallen ill; she was in bed and not going out anywhere.

He was very worried, and sent to ask about her. Soon he heard that her illness wasn't serious. When she in her turn heard that he was missing her and worrying about her, Sonia sent him a pencilled note to say that she was feeling much better, that all she had was a slight cold, and that she'd come again very, very soon to see him at his work. As he read the note, his heart pounded painfully.

It was another fine, warm day. Early in the morning, about six o'clock, he went out to work on the riverbank, where there was a shed with a kiln for heating the alabaster they beat there. Just three workers had been sent to work there. One of the convicts had gone back to the fortress with the guard to fetch some tool; the second one set about chopping wood and putting it into the kiln. Raskolnikov went out of the shed onto the riverbank, sat down on the pile of logs beside the shed, and gazed at the wide, desolate river. The bank was high, with a distant view all round. Far away on the opposite bank, he could just make out the sound of singing. There, on the wide stretches of the steppe, bathed in sunlight, the nomads' yurts showed as barely visible dots. There was freedom out there, and different people, nothing like the people back here; out there, time seemed to have stopped, as if the age of Abraham and his flocks had never passed away. Raskolnikov sat without moving and looked out without shifting his gaze; his thoughts turned into daydreams and reflections; he wasn't thinking of anything particular, but his mind was troubled and distressed.

Suddenly Sonia was at his side. She had come up almost noiselessly, and now sat down next to him. It was still very early; the morning chill hadn't yet dissipated. She was wearing her shabby old cloak and the green shawl. Her face still bore the marks of her illness: it was thinner, paler, more gaunt. She gave him a happy, welcoming smile, but, as usual, timidly offered him her hand.

She always used to hold out her hand to him timidly, and sometimes she didn't offer it at all, as though afraid that he'd push it aside. He always took her hand with seeming repugnance, always greeted her with apparent irritation; sometimes he would stay stubbornly silent for her whole visit. There had been times when she had trembled before him and gone away deeply distressed. But now their hands didn't part. He glanced quickly and fleetingly at her, said nothing, and looked down at the ground. They were alone; no one could see them. The guard had turned away.

How it happened he didn't know, but suddenly something seemed to seize him and throw him down at her feet. He was weeping and clasping her knees. For an instant she was dreadfully frightened; her face turned deathly pale. She jumped up and looked down at him, trembling. But in that moment she understood it all. Her eyes lit up with endless happiness. She had understood, and now no longer doubted, that he loved her, loved her for ever, and that the moment had finally come...

They tried to speak, but couldn't. Their eyes were full of tears. Both of them were pale and thin; but those pale, sick faces of theirs were already shining with the dawn of a new future, a perfect resurrection into a new life. It was love that had raised them; the heart of each of them held endless springs of life for the other's heart.

They resolved to wait and be patient. There were still seven years ahead of them; how much unbearable suffering and how much endless happiness would fill those years! But he had risen again, and he knew it; he could feel it with all his being, now newly reborn; and she—she lived only through him!

That same evening, when the huts were locked up for the night, Raskolnikov lay on his bunk and thought about her. It had seemed to him that day that all the other convicts, all his old enemies, were looking at him differently. He had even spoken to some of them, and they had answered him kindly. He remembered that now; but of course that was how it had to be. Didn't everything have to change now?

He thought about her. He remembered how he always used to torment her and wound her heart; he remembered her poor, thin little face; but now these memories no longer distressed him. He knew that his endless love would atone for all her sufferings now.

And what were they, then—all those sufferings of the past? Everything, even his crime, even his sentence and exile, now appeared to him, in this first flush of emotion, as something external, something strange, something that hadn't happened to him in person. But that evening he wasn't capable of thinking long and coherently about anything, nor concentrating his thoughts; in fact he wouldn't have wanted any conscious thoughts; all he could do was feel. The dialectic had given place to life, and now something entirely different had to work itself out in his consciousness.

Under his pillow lay the New Testament. He picked it up mechanically. The book belonged to her—the same copy from which she had read him the story of the raising of Lazarus. At the beginning of his sentence he had been expecting her to pester him with religion, keep talking about the New Testament and press books on him. But to his great surprise, she never once raised the subject; never once even offered him the New Testament. He had asked her for it himself, and she had brought it to him without a word. He had never opened it before.

Nor did he open it now. But one thought flashed through his mind. 'Is it possible that her beliefs can fail, now, to be my beliefs too? Her feelings, her aspirations, at least...'

She too had spent the whole of that day full of agitation, and that night she fell ill again. But she was so happy, she felt almost afraid of her happiness. Seven years, *only* seven years! At the beginning of their happiness, there were moments when they were both ready to look on those seven years as if they were seven days. He wasn't even aware that this new life would not be his for nothing: he was going to have to pay dearly for it, to redeem it by some great exploit in the future...

But here begins a new story, the story of the gradual renewal of a man, of his gradual rebirth, his gradual transition from one world to another, as he learns to know a new reality, one which had so far escaped him. That might be the subject of a new tale; but our present one is ended.

LIST OF PRINCIPAL CHARACTERS

Russians have three names: a given name; a patronymic, formed from their father's name with the masculine ending -ovich, -evich or -ich, and the feminine ending -ovna or -evna; and a surname, which also has masculine (ending in a consonant or -y) and feminine versions (usually ending in -a or -ya). Given name and patronymic are used for polite address, while among close friends and family the norm is to use a diminutive of the first name. Some patronymics also have shortened forms for familiar or colloquial usage. Diminutives and other variants are given in brackets. The stressed syllable is marked with an acute accent; stressed 'e's (as in Zamétov) are pronounced like 'yo' in 'beyond'.

In order of appearance:

Ródion (Ródia, Ródka) Románovich (Románich) Raskólnikov, *a former student*

Alióna Ivánovna, *a moneylender and widow to a Collegiate Registrar*

Semión Zakhárovich (Zakhárich) Marmeládov, *a low-grade civil servant and alcoholic*

Katerína Ivánovna Marmeládova, *his wife*

Pólia (Pólenka), Léna (Lénia; called Lída or Lídochka in Part 2), Kólia, *their children*

Amália Ivánovna (also called Fédorovna and Ludwígovna) Líppewechsel, *the Marmeladovs' landlady*

Nastásia (Nastásyushka, Nástenka) Petróva, *servant to Raskolnikov's landlady*

Praskóvia (Páshenka) Pávlovna Zarnítsyna, *Raskolnikov's landlady*

Lizavéta, *Aliona Ivanovna's half-sister, a dealer in old clothes*

Nikoláy (Mikoláy, Mikólka) Deméntyev, *a house painter and religious sectarian*

Dmítry (Mítry, Mítia, Mítka), *a house painter*

Alexánder Grigórievich Zamétov, *chief clerk at the police station*

Ilyá Petróvich (nicknamed Gunpowder), *a police official*

Nikodím Fómich, *the chief of police*

Dmítry Prokófich Razumíkhin, *Raskolnikov's friend*

Zosímov, *a doctor and friend of Razumikhin's*

Piótr Petróvich Lúzhin, *businessman and lawyer, Raskolnikov's prospective brother-in-law*

Sófia (Sónia, Sónechka) Semiónovna Marmeládova, *Marmeladov's eldest daughter, a prostitute*

Pulkhéria Alexándrovna Raskólnikova, *Raskolnikov's mother*

Avdótya (Dúnia, Dúnechka) Románovna Raskólnikova, *his sister*

Pórfiry Petróvich, *an examining magistrate*

Arkády Ivánovich Svidrigáilov, *a landowner*

Márfa Petróvna Svidrigáilova, *his wife*

Andréi Semiónovich Lebeziátnikov, *a young radical employed in the civil service*

EXPLANATORY NOTES

Two sources have been used extensively in compiling the following notes. B. N. Tikhomirov, *'Lazar! Griadi Von'. Roman F. M. Dostoevskogo 'Prestuplenie i nakazanie' v sovremennom prochtenii: Kniga-kommentarii* (St Petersburg: Serebriannyi vek, 2005) is the most recent and extensive commentary of *Crime and Punishment*. Volume vii of the standard complete works contains the author's notebooks for the novel, textual variants, and commentary: F. M. Dostoevskii, *Polnoe sobranie sochinenii v tridtsati tomakh* (Moscow and Leningrad: Nauka, 1972–90).

3 *hot weather*: the novel is set in 1865, the year in which Dostoevsky began work on it. Some artistic licence has been taken with descriptions of the hot weather, but details about the heatwave and Marmeladov's last receipt of his salary allow us to date the opening of the novel to 7 July 1865.

S—— Lane... K——n bridge: Stolyarny Lane, on the north side of the Ekaterininsky (now Griboyedov) Canal, and Kokushkin Bridge, which crosses the canal and leads to the Haymarket and other scenes of the novel's action. Dostoevsky lived in a flat on Stolyarny Lane whilst writing the novel. The location already had strong literary connections, as the home of one of the talking, letter-writing dogs in Nikolay Gogol's 'Diary of a Madman' (1835) and of the hero of Mikhail Lermontov's story 'Shtoss' (1841).

4 *Jack and the Beanstalk*: the Russian is *tsar Gorokh*, literally 'Tsar-Pea', a colloquial expression for 'time immemorial'.

dacha out of town: a summer house or allotment in the suburbs.

common in that part of town: Stolyarny Lane was infamous for having eighteen taverns in its sixteen buildings.

Haymarket: established in 1737 as a market for hay, firewood, and cattle, the Haymarket Square in St Petersburg was the first port of call for peasants arriving in the city and became a byword for poverty and vice.

5 *Zimmermann's*: a hat shop on Nevsky Prospekt, opposite the Gostiny Dvor arcade.

—— Street: the moneylender's house has been identified through the reference to its unusual arrangement with two courtyards. As a result it has two addresses: 104 Griboyedov Embankment and 15/25 Srednyaya [Middle] Podyacheskaya Street.

yardkeepers: responsible for the maintenance and security of the courtyards of tenement buildings.

6 *Raskolnikov*: the surname indicates 'schismatic' or 'dissenter', referring to his internal divisions, but also alluding to a more profound spiritual basis for Raskolnikov's crisis, as it echoes the Russian religious sectarians who split off from the Orthodox Church following Patriarch Nikon's reforms

in the seventeenth century (known as *raskolniki*). The painter Mikolka is a *raskolnik*.

9 *drinking den*: this cannot be on the Haymarket, as many critics have claimed, as it is so close to the moneylender's flat. The most likely location is the corner of Bolshaya [Great] Podyacheskaya Street and Rimsky-Korsakov Prospekt.

wench and an accordion: the first reference to the novel's recurring motif of street music.

shopkeeper: *meshchanin*, literally 'townsman', referring to the lower order of urban tradesmen and craftsmen, often with connotations of philistinism and pettiness. Russian society was divided into estates (*sosloviia*): the nobility, the clergy, urban dwellers (including merchants, tradesmen, and artisans), and rural dwellers (the peasantry and non-Orthodox native peoples). Membership of these estates was essentially hereditary, although it was possible to move up or down between categories through marriage, accumulation (or loss) of wealth, or service to the state.

Off I went down Scrivener's Row: Dostoevsky changes the words of this popular song to refer to Scrivener's Row (Podyacheskaya, from *podiachii*, scribe) instead of Nevsky Prospekt. The three parallel Podyacheskaya streets are home not only to the moneylender Aliona Ivanovna, but also to the Marmeladov family.

11 *Titular Councillor*: the 'poor clerks' or 'little men' of Russian literature, oppressed by the inhuman Petersburg bureaucracy, habitually hold the rank of Titular Councillor. The most famous examples include Gogol's Popryshchin in 'Diary of a Madman' and Akaky Akakievich in 'The Overcoat' (1845), as well as Mr Goliadkin in Dostoevsky's *The Double* (1846). See Note on the Table of Ranks, p. xxvi.

13 *modern ideas...political economy*: Lebeziatnikov represents, in mildly caricatured fashion, the progressive youth of St Petersburg, inspired by the study of empirical science, denial of the existence of the human soul and dualism (and, implicitly, of God), and promotion of 'rational egoism', a form of utilitarianism that claimed human beings would soon be able to identify their own best interests and act accordingly, for the benefit of all. Developed by the radical author and critic Nikolay Chernyshevsky, in his philosophical tract 'The Anthropological Principle in Philosophy' (1860) and his highly influential novel of 'new people', *What is to be Done?* (1863), these ideas were the main target of the narrator's polemic in part I of Dostoevsky's *Notes from Underground* (1864).

yellow ticket: the registration system to regulate and monitor prostitutes was established in 1843, ostensibly to combat an epidemic of sexually transmitted diseases. Registered women were subjected to a strict regime of medical checks, and carried a 'yellow ticket' that replaced other identification documents. This prevented them taking other employment and restricted their ability to find accommodation, hence Sonia having to take lodgings away from the rest of her family.

14 *the corner we live in is cold*: although the family's lodgings turn out to more closely resemble a corridor, and are used as a thoroughfare by other lodgers, the term 'corner' was generally used to refer to any very poor lodging or portion of a room rented separately. This very common practice amongst the poor was a consequence of the serious overcrowding that afflicted this part of the city in the second half of the nineteenth century.

shawl dance: a privilege granted to the best students graduating from educational establishments for young ladies. The practice began when Persian shawls were in fashion in the early nineteenth century.

16 *Cyrus of Persia*: Cyrus II, or Cyrus the Great (*c*.600–530 BC), founded the Achaemenid Empire and conquered territories from the Mediterranean Sea to the Indus River.

Lewes's Physiology: George Henry Lewes's *Physiology of Common Life* (1859) popularized scientific positivism and Darwinism. A Russian translation by S. A. Rachinsky and Ya. A. Borzenkov, published in Moscow in 1861, was widely read among young progressive Russians.

Holland shirts: shirts made from a linen fabric known as Holland cloth, originally produced in the province of Holland in the Netherlands.

17 *drap-de-dames*: soft woven woollen cloth, first made in France, usually black and worn by women in mourning.

Kapernaumov the tailor: the name derives from the biblical town of Capernaum, home of several of Christ's Apostles and scene of one of the first miracles in the New Testament, when Jesus heals a man possessed by an unclean spirit (Mark 1:21–8; Luke 4:33–6). Dostoevsky used the version of the story from Luke's Gospel as the epigraph to his 1871–2 novel *Devils*.

18 *'My Little Farmstead'*: a popular song from 1840 with words by A. V. Koltsov and music by E. Klimovsky.

20 *Egyptian Bridge*: decorated with sphinxes, columns, and hieroglyphs, and crossing the Fontanka River at Lomonosov Street (then joining Mogilevskaya Street and Zagorodny Prospekt).

21 *crucified on a cross... our Judge*: this passage, and Marmeladov's monologue more generally, contains multiple allusions to the New Testament.

22 *Kozel's house... two or three hundred yards to go*: near Sadovaya (Garden) Street, on Bolshaya Podyacheskaya Street, running parallel to the street on which the moneylender's flat is located. Many Petersburg buildings were named after their owners; 'Kozel' is an invented name, meaning 'goat'.

no real nightfall... time of year: the action of the novel takes place shortly after the 'white nights' when, due to the city's northern latitude, the sun does not sink far enough below the horizon for true darkness to descend. Dostoevsky's early short story 'White Nights' (1848) depicts the romantic atmosphere of the city at this time of year as reflecting the inner life of the 'dreamer' protagonist.

26 *student's overcoat*: until 1861 students in imperial Russia wore uniforms.

27 *R—— Province*: Ryazan Province, around 190 km (120 miles) south-east of Moscow.

30 *verst*: an old Russian unit of measurement, equivalent to 1.06 km (0.66 miles).

32 *'convictions…generations'*: an allusion to the nihilism and 'rational egoism' of Chernyshevsky and his followers. See note to p. 13.

34 *the Senate*: the legislative and executive arm of the Russian monarchy, established under Peter the Great. In the nineteenth century it became the highest judicial body in Russia.

35 *Assumption*: celebrating the resurrection of Mary, mother of Jesus, on 15 August, the Assumption, known in the Orthodox tradition as the Dormition of the Virgin, is preceded by a two-week fast in the Orthodox Church during which marriage would not be possible.

36 *Vasilievsky Island, along V—— Prospekt*: Vasilievsky Island, on the north side of the River Neva, is home to some of the city's oldest institutions, including the university, stock exchange (the Bourse), Imperial Academy of Sciences, and Kunstkamera (Peter the Great Museum of Anthropology and Ethnography). Peter the Great initially envisaged the centre of the city being located on this island. Voznesensky (Ascension) Prospekt is the westernmost of three major thoroughfares radiating out from the Admiralty building south of the Neva.

37 *Our Lady of Kazan*: an icon of the Virgin Mary as protector of the city of Kazan, 800 km (500 miles) east of Moscow, and one of the most important holy images in the Russian Orthodox Church. Raskolnikov receives his mother's letter on 8 July, the anniversary of the day on which the discovery of the icon in 1579 was celebrated.

Golgotha: the site of Jesus' crucifixion, just outside Jerusalem's city walls.

39 *Schiller*: the German poet, playwright, and philosopher Johann Christoph Friedrich von Schiller (1759–1805) was a significant influence on Dostoevsky's youth. The first original work he wrote (now lost) was a play titled *Maria Stuart*, after Schiller's play, and Dostoevsky and his brother Mikhail embarked on a project to translate Schiller into Russian; Dostoevsky contributed to the translation of *The Robbers* and Mikhail went on to translate *Don Carlos*. Dostoevsky's view became more critical after his arrest and imprisonment, and in his mature works Schiller is consistently associated with youthful, sentimental idealism, although the connections made between Dmitry Karamazov and Schiller's poetry in *The Karamazov Brothers* emphasizes the continued importance of the 'sublime and beautiful' to the author's world view.

Anna in his buttonhole: the Order of St Anna was an imperial order of chivalry awarded for distinguished service in state bureaucracy or for military valour. Anton Chekhov's 1895 story 'Anna on the Neck' depicts another, similarly pompous, civil recipient of the honour.

39 *Schleswig-Holstein*: the Schleswig-Holstein question was a complex set of diplomatic and constitutional problems over whether the duchies of Schleswig and Holstein belonged to the Danish crown or the German Federation. The Second Schleswig War took place in 1864 following Danish attempts to reintegrate the duchy in 1863.

40 *casuistry…Jesuits*: the Society of Jesus, expelled from Russia in 1820 in part due to fears that too many upper-class Russians were converting to Catholicism under its influence, became a byword for political and moral intrigue. Dostoevsky frequently refers to the ethics of the Jesuits as being derived from false reasoning. His anti-Catholicism stemmed not only from a conviction that Catholicism was a deviation from the true, Orthodox faith, but also from his own family history. His father descended from Uniate priests, belonging to a branch of the Eastern Rite Catholic Church that had broken away from Orthodoxy and recognized the Pope.

42 *K—— Boulevard*: Konnogvardeisky (Horse Guards) Boulevard.

43 *Svidrigailov*: the name Svidrigailov would have been familiar to Dostoevsky's readers from a satirical feuilleton on provincial morals published in the journal *Iskra* (*The Spark*), 14 July 1861, where he is described as 'a man of obscure origins, with a dirty past, a repulsive personality that's disgusting to any fresh, honest gaze, who insinuates and creeps into your soul […]. And this low, crawling, eternally creepy personality, who insults the dignity of every human being, thrives: building house by house, acquiring horses and carriages, throwing toxic dust into the eyes of society at whose expense he flourishes.'

48 *the Islands*: Krestovsky (Cross), Petrovsky, Elagin, and Kamenny (Stone) Islands in the northern Neva delta were, and remain, important areas for leisure and summer excursions in St Petersburg.

49 *Pushkin…Turgenev*: the poet, playwright, and prose writer Alexander Pushkin (1799–1837) is often considered the founder of a distinctive Russian voice in literature, a view that Dostoevsky's speech at the inauguration of the Pushkin memorial in Moscow in 1880 was influential in establishing. The realist novelist Ivan Turgenev (1818–83) had a Western outlook, and although Dostoevsky admired his literary style, the men were bitter rivals. The character of the writer Karmazinov in *Devils* is a vicious lampoon of Turgenev.

50 *sugary rice…cross*: kutya, a sweet grain pudding traditionally served at Orthodox funerals.

51 *lash those horses…almost cries*: on the journey from Moscow to his school in Petersburg, Dostoevsky witnessed a horse being cruelly whipped by a peasant, who in turn was being beaten by a government courier. 'This disgusting scene has stayed in my memory all my life', he later commented in his *Writer's Diary*.

54 *T—— Bridge*: Tuchkov Bridge, crossing the Lesser Neva, connecting Petrovsky Island to Vasilievsky Island.

55 *K—— Alley*: Konny (horse) Alley, now Grivtsov Alley, leading on to the Haymarket.

59 *N—— Province*: the initial *N* was used frequently in nineteenth- and twentieth-century Russian literature to indicate a remote, provincial back-water, as in Gogol's *Dead Souls* (1842) and *The Government Inspector* (1836).

60 *A hundred, a thousand good deeds... arithmetic*: the conversation Raskolnikov hears about the moneylender introduces one possible motive for his crime, the altruistic idea that her death can benefit society, underpinned by utilitarian reasoning of sacrificing one for the good of all. The fact that this conversation is overheard is significant not only because Raskolnikov sees the coincidence of it mirroring his own thoughts as justification for the crime, but also because it confirms that such ideas were common currency at the time, among the '"unfinished" ideas that are floating around in the air'.

66 *Yusupov Park... Summer Gardens... Field of Mars... Mikhailovsky Palace Gardens*: Yusupov Park is situated between Sadovaya Street and the Fontanka River, to the south-west of the Haymarket. The Summer Gardens, Field of Mars, and Mikhailovsky Palace Gardens are all to the north of Nevsky Prospekt and west of the Fontanka. Raskolnikov's day-dream of redesigning the city has echoes of both contemporary ideas for the reorganization of society (see note to p. 119) and Baron Haussmann's reconstruction of Paris under Emperor Napoleon III. Napoleon III's 1865 *History of Julius Caesar*, especially the introduction which seeks to justify not only Caesar but also Napoleon and the author, was known to Dostoevsky, and was influential in formulating the idea of the Great Man who stands outside the law and morality.

67 *a man being led to his execution... on his way*: the idea of impending execution leading to heightened perception was inspired by Dostoevsky's own experience of awaiting execution for his participation in the Petrashevsky circle (see Introduction, p. x), and by his reading of Victor Hugo's 1829 novella *The Last Day of a Condemned Man*. Dostoevsky developed this theme particularly in *The Idiot*, where the hero Prince Myshkin's epileptic seizures give him insight into altered perceptions of time that he equates to the moments before execution, the biblical phrase 'There should be time no longer' (Revelation 10:6), and the 'second in which the epileptic Mahomet's overturned water-jug failed to spill a drop while he contrived to behold all the mansions of Allah'.

75 *Gambrinus*: a beer hall on Vasilievsky Island.

76 *examining magistrate*: the detective Porfiry Petrovich is also an examining magistrate. The appearance of this incidental character in a similar role indicates the importance of institutions and representatives of the law to the novel, following Alexander II's reforms of the judicial system from the late 1850s.

85 *office... new building*: either the Kazan district police station, at 67 Ekaterininsky Canal, or the Spassky district station, at 35 Bolshaya Podyacheskaya Street.

87 *lieutenant...inspector's assistant*: equivalent to the twelfth grade in the Table of Ranks.

92 —— *Province*: Ryazan Province (see note to p. 27).

97 *V—— Prospekt...blank walls*: the yard where Raskolnikov buries the purse and other items he stole is located at 3–5 Voznesensky Prospekt. This is one of the places Anna Dostoevskaya recorded being shown by her husband.

101 *flea market*: Tolkuchy Market in Apraksin Dvor arcade, off Sadovaya Street.

natural science...whether a woman is a human being or not: the study of natural sciences, and ideas of female emancipation and equality, generally referred to as the 'woman question', were central preoccupations of contemporary radical thought.

Rousseau is a sort of Radishchev: Alexander Radishchev (1749–1802) was a Russian author who rose to prominence as an early radical following the 1790 publication, and subsequent banning, of his *A Journey from St Petersburg to Moscow*. Radishchev was sentenced to death for writing this indictment of Russian social conditions, the absence of personal freedoms, and, in particular, the enserfment of the peasantry. Following an appeal to Catherine the Great, his sentence was commuted to Siberian exile, where he remained until 1797. After his return to European Russia he worked briefly on Russian legal reform for Alexander I, but he committed suicide in 1802. *A Journey from St Petersburg to Moscow* was not published again in Russia until 1905. A significant aspect of Dostoevsky's interest in Rousseau relates to the latter's *Confessions*, in particular the episode in which Rousseau commits a petty theft and stands by as a maid is blamed for it, a motif which undergoes several transformations in Dostoevsky's work.

schwach: weak (German).

102 *First Line*: in the grid system that characterizes the main residential area of Vasilievsky Island, opposite sides of the streets perpendicular to the Neva Embankment—originally intended to be canals—are designated by numbered 'lines'. The First Line is also known today as Kadetskaya (Cadet) Line.

Nikolaevsky Bridge: Nikolaevsky (now Blagoveshchensky) Bridge was the first permanent bridge built over the Neva connecting Vasilievsky Island to the central part of St Petersburg.

103 *palace...cathedral dome*: from his position on Nikolaevsky Bridge, Raskolnikov has a view of the Winter Palace and St Isaac's Cathedral. However, this description is also notable for what is not mentioned: Étienne Falconet's statue of the Bronze Horseman, which is also clearly visible from this spot.

deaf and mute spirit: an allusion to the spirit Jesus casts out of the child in Mark 9:25.

107 *Vrazumikhin...not Razumikhin*: Razumikhin comes from *razum*, meaning 'reason' while *vrazumet´* has connotations of 'to enlighten', 'make see
reason'. His name may associate Razumikhin with the reasoning 'new
people' of Chernyshevsky's novel *What is to be Done?*, as may his previous
appearance, which emphasizes his positive attitude, but this attractive,
boisterous, and frequently tipsy character otherwise seems a far cry from
Chernyshevsky's dull, rationalist figures. His playful change of name
introduces a motif of misnaming that runs throughout the novel.

110 *Five Corners*: a five-way junction in the centre of the city, to the south of
Nevsky Prospekt and east of the Fontanka River. The Cathedral of the
Vladimir Icon of the Mother of God is located at this junction. Dostoevsky,
who particularly after his return from exile liked to live within sight of
a church, lived at several addresses close to Five Corners, including at 5
Kuznechny Lane, now home to the St Petersburg Dostoevsky Literary-
Memorial Museum.

111 *registered there*: when arriving in St Petersburg or moving house, all residents had to register at the address bureau, located at 49 Sadovaya Street.

113 *Countess*: an allusion to Pushkin's short story 'The Queen of Spades'
(1833), in which the young officer Germann tries to wrest the secret of the
three cards from the elderly countess.

116 *Palmerston*: Henry John Temple, third Viscount Palmerston, twice served
as British prime minister in the mid-nineteenth century. Palmerston's
Russophobic pronouncements in the early 1860s led to the appearance of
caricatures of the statesman in the Russian press, where he was frequently
depicted wearing a rounded hat.

118 *Scharmer*: an exclusive and expensive tailor, as its address near the Winter
Palace and the General Staff headquarters, at 5 Bolshaya Morskaya Street,
suggests.

119 *Palais de Cristal*: the Crystal Palace was built in Hyde Park for the Great
Exhibition of 1851, then reconstructed on Sydenham Hill in south London,
where it stood until it was destroyed by a fire in 1936. In Chernyshevsky's
What is to be Done?, the heroine Vera Pavlovna dreams of the Crystal Palace
as the rational future utopia of equality, harmony, and useful labour.
Dostoevsky's narrator in *Notes from Underground* rails against this vision
as he asserts the irrational side of human nature. Various leisure establishments in Petersburg were named after the Crystal Palace, but Razumikhin's
reference to the Yusupov Park identifies it as a hotel on the corner of
Sadovaya Street and Voznesensky Prospekt. The location close to the Yusupov
Park also connects Raskolnikov's dream of reconstructing the city (see
note to p. 66) to the radicals' ideas of social reorganization.

122 *Zaraysk .. around Ryazan*: an ancient town 130 km (90 miles) south-east
of Moscow and 75 km (46 miles) north-west of Ryazan (see note to p. 27).
In 1831 Dostoevsky's father purchased an estate just outside Zaraysk.

123 *the Sands, with Kolomna folk*: the Sands (Peski) is an area of central
Petersburg between the River Neva, Nevsky Prospekt, and Ligovsky

Prospekt. Kolomna is an ancient town 114 km (70 miles) to the south-east of Moscow.

123 —— *toll gate*: toll gates controlled the entrances to St Petersburg and marked the city's boundaries until 1858, after which their names remained in use as toponyms. The reference is most likely to the Moskovsky toll gate, to the south of the city at the junction of Moskovsky Prospekt and Ligovsky Prospekt.

131 *Jouvins*: a famous high-quality glove manufacturer founded in Paris in the 1830s.

Bakaleyev's house ... Voznesensky Prospekt: located at the corner of Voznesensky Prospekt and Bolshaya Meshchanskaya (now Kazanskaya) Street.

133 *self-interest*: Luzhin's characterization of these 'new ideas' indicates his protégé Lebeziatnikov's adherence to the doctrine of 'rational egoism'. See note to p. 13.

135 *former student robbing ... financial reason*: criminal cases from 1865. Dostoevsky frequently made use of events that were reported in the press while he was writing his novels, augmenting their contemporary feel.

139 *organ grinder*: the recurring motif of street musicians relates Dostoevsky's depiction of the city to the sympathetic treatment of the poor and oppressed in literature by the 'natural school' that was popular in the 1840s and to which Dostoevsky's first novel *Poor Folk* belonged. Street musicians feature in a famous 'natural school' sketch by Dostoevsky's school friend Dmitry Grigorovich, 'The Petersburg Organ Grinders', which appeared in Nekrasov's collection *Petersburg: The Physiology of a City* in 1845. Dostoevsky and Grigorovich shared a flat at the beginning of both men's literary careers.

140 *Zaraysk*: see note to p. 122.

princesses: a euphemism for the prostitutes who populated the area.

towards V—— ... alley: Voznesensky Prospekt, and Tairov (now Brinko) Alley, which bends round the side of the Haymarket, joining Moskovsky Prospekt to Sadovaya Street.

142 *condemned to death ... die at once*: see note to p. 67.

143 *Aztecs ... Bartola—Massimo ... Izler*: Izler's Pleasure Garden and Spa was on the northern bank of the Bolshaya Nevka, opposite Kamenny Island. The dwarves Bartola and Massimo, supposedly descended from the Aztecs, were exhibited in Petersburg in 1865 by the entrepreneur Moris.

fire on Peterburgskaya: the north bank of the River Neva, now called the Petrograd Side. An epidemic of arson attacks in the 1860s in St Petersburg was blamed on radical students.

148 *Assez causé!*: 'That's enough talk!' (French). A favourite expression of Dostoevsky's, used by Vautrin, Balzac's escaped convict, who first appeared in *Le Père Goriot* (1834–5).

151 —— *Bridge*: Voznesensky Bridge, over the Ekaterininsky Canal.

157 *drunk . . . candle*: one of the phrases from Dostoevsky's *Siberian Notebooks*, in which he collected sayings he heard among the peasant convicts in the prison camp in Siberia.

159 *Gentleman of the Bedchamber*: an honorary court rank, generally granted to young noblemen.

he danced the mazurka with me: the mazurka, originally a Polish folk dance, was generally reserved for a favoured suitor at Russian balls. In Tolstoy's *Anna Karenina* (1875–7), Kitty turns down other invitations as she assumes Alexei Vronsky will partner her for the mazurka. When he dances with Anna herself, it marks the beginning of their affair.

185 *Rubinstein*: Anton Rubinstein (1829–94), composer, conductor, and pianist who founded the St Petersburg Conservatory in 1862.

195 *'That queen . . . processions'*: the reference is to Marie Antoinette (1755–93), the Austrian-born wife of the French king Louis XVI, guillotined during the French Revolution. A period of imprisonment preceded her execution during which she showed dignity and courage in the face of deprivation and humiliation.

201 *"Crevez, chiens, si vous n'êtes pas contents!"*: 'Die, dogs, if you're not happy!' (French). A near quotation from Victor Hugo's novel *Les Misérables* (1862).

210 *Mitrofanievsky cemetery*: founded in 1831 in the south of St Petersburg as a burial ground for cholera victims, Mitrofanievsky became one of the largest Orthodox cemeteries in the city. It was closed in 1927, and its three churches destroyed, although it was used for burials during the siege of Leningrad.

216 *canal bank . . . her flat*: the building where Sonia lives is located by the Ekaterininsky Canal at one end or other of Malaya [Little] Meshchanskaya (now Kaznacheiskaya) Street.

218 *sing Lazarus*: a reference to the Lazarus Song, based on the parable of the rich man and the beggar Lazarus in Luke 16:19–31 that has become a phrase meaning 'to tell a hard-luck story'. This reference to the other Lazarus of the New Testament complements *Crime and Punishment*'s use of the more celebrated story of Lazarus of Bethany (see note to p. 231) to bring together the themes of charity and resurrection.

220 *costing the State money*: a reference to Gogol's play *The Government Inspector*.

227 *"corrupted by their environment"*: in an article on *Crime and Punishment*, radical critic Dmitry Pisarev (1840–68) claimed that 'the root of Raskolnikov's illness was not in the brain but in the pocket'. This was typical of the progressive tendency to blame crime on the perpetrator's environment. Dostoevsky rejected this argument in his article 'Environment' in *A Writer's Diary*.

social system . . . living pathway: Chernyshevsky's article 'The Anthropological Principle in Philosophy' claimed that ultimately all human actions would be calculable by science, enabling everyone to act in their own and others' best interests. This idea was the basis for the social reorganization he depicted in the novel *What is to be Done?*.

227 *phalanstery*: a self-contained utopian community designed by the pioneering French utopian socialist Charles Fourier (1772–1837), whose ideas were popular in Russia in the 1840s, when Dostoevsky was beginning his literary career.

violates a girl of ten: child abuse, as the ultimate crime against innocence that challenges the notion of God's justice, is a recurrent theme in Dostoevsky's novels. The allusion recalls the alleged crimes of Svidrigailov, the landowner pursuing Raskolnikov's sister.

228 *tower of Ivan the Great... tall*: Ivan the Great Bell Tower, at a height of 81 metres (266 feet), is the tallest tower in the Moscow Kremlin. It was built in 1508 for the Assumption, Annunciation, and Archangel Russian Orthodox cathedrals in Cathedral Square.

229 *people are somehow all subdivided... extraordinary*: the narrator of *Notes from Underground* refers to social reorganization as an 'anthill'. However, Raskolnikov's idea of the 'great man' represents the first full elaboration of Dostoevsky's 'anthill theory' of slavery for the masses and freedom for the chosen few. Further conceptions of the 'anthill' are found in Shigalev's theory of ultimate slavery and social levelling in *Devils* and in Ivan Karamazov's 'poem' 'The Grand Inquisitor', in which the eponymous inquisitor replaces the misery of free will with 'miracle, mystery, and authority' to endow enslaved mankind with happiness.

230 *Kepler's and Newton's discoveries*: Johannes Kepler (1571–1630), German mathematician who developed the laws of planetary motion and founded the modern sciences of physics and astronomy. Isaac Newton (1542–1726/7) furthered Kepler's work, defining the laws of gravitation and motion that dominated science until the beginning of the twentieth century.

Lycurgus, Solon: Lycurgus of Sparta (*c*.800–730 BC) was the legendary lawmaker who reformed Spartan society. Solon (*c*.638–558 BC) was an Athenian lawmaker and statesman.

231 *vive la guerre éternelle!*: 'long live eternal war!' (French). A slightly rephrased citation from the French anarchist Pierre-Joseph Proudhon's *La Guerre et la Paix* (War and Peace, 1861).

New Jerusalem: in the New Testament, the New Jerusalem will be founded with the second coming of Christ (Revelation 21:2).

raising of Lazarus: appearing only in John's Gospel, the raising of Lazarus of Bethany by Jesus four days after his burial prefigures the death and resurrection of Christ (John 11:1–44).

233 *law of nature... be discovered*: see note to p. 227.

235 *which of us Russians... a Napoleon these days*: an allusion to lines from Pushkin's poem *Eugene Onegin* (1825–32), chapter 2, verse 15.

238 *thirty degrees Réaumur*: 37.5 degrees Celsius. On the Réaumur scale the freezing and boiling point of water are 0 and 80 degrees respectively.

242 *V—— church*: Voznesensky church, on the corner of Voznesensky Prospekt and the Ekaterininsky Canal, built in 1769 and destroyed in 1936.

243 *A real master… pun at Vilna*: references to Napoleon's campaigns.

everything is permitted: in *The Karamazov Brothers*, the idea that if there is no immortality then everything is permitted is ascribed to Ivan Karamazov.

aren't flesh and blood… they're bronze: an allusion to Falconet's statue of the Bronze Horseman in St Petersburg, which connects the figure of Peter the Great, who generally remains the hidden subtext of Raskolnikov's 'great man' theory, to that of Napoleon.

aesthetic sense: compare this to Stavrogin's confession to the rape of a young girl, and her subsequent suicide, in the suppressed chapter of *Devils*, 'At Tikhon's'. Bishop Tikhon, having read the confession, states that the 'ugliness' of the crime makes Stavrogin appear ridiculous and will prevent him repenting.

little brick… common good: a further reference to Fourier's Phalanstery, rephrasing the words of the French utopian socialist and popularizer of Fourier's ideas, Victor Considerant (1808–93), from *La Destinée sociale* (Social Destiny, 1834).

absolute justice, by weight and measure: an allusion to the third horse of the Apocalypse: 'and he that sat on him had a pair of balances in his hand. And I heard a voice in the midst of the four beasts say, A measure of wheat for a penny, and three measures of barley for a penny' (Revelation 6:5–6).

244 *Oh, how I understand the "Prophet"… "tremble and obey"*: an allusion to the first poem in Alexander Pushkin's 1824 cycle 'Imitations of the Koran'.

248 *et nihil humanum*: a misquotation from the Roman poet Terentius' *The Self-Tormentor* (*Heauton Timorumenos*): 'Homo sum: humani nihil a me alienum puto' (I am human, and I reckon nothing which is human is alien to me).

249 *la bonne guerre*: fair game (French).

250 *"disgraceful act of The Century"*: the performance by a provincial official's wife of verses about Cleopatra's lovers from Pushkin's unfinished *Egyptian Nights* was denounced in an article in the Petersburg weekly *The Century* as an immoral act that revealed the true aims of the women's emancipation movement. 'The Disgraceful Act of *The Century*' was the title of an attack on *The Century*'s article and defence of emancipation published in the *St Petersburg Gazette* on 3 March 1861.

251 *peasant reforms*: the emancipation of the serfs, in 1861.

those Dussauts, those Pointes: Dussaut's restaurant was on the corner of Bolshaya Morskaya Street and Kirpichny Lane, near Nevsky Prospekt. The Pointe Fete Ground was on the spit of Elagin Island.

252 *North Pole… vin mauvais*: in 1865 the Petersburg press reported on plans by the Royal Geographical Society of Great Britain for an expedition to the North Pole. *Avoir le vin mauvais* is a French idiom meaning 'to get nasty after a few drinks'.

252 *Berg's... Yusupov Park on Sunday*: Wilhelm Berg, proprietor of various leisure and entertainment attractions in Petersburg, organized a number of hot-air balloon rides from Yusupov Park in the mid-1860s.

253 *Malaya Vishera station*: in Novgorod region, around 200 km (125 miles) south-east of St Petersburg.

259 *Raphael's Madonna*: also known as the Sistine Madonna, this was Dostoevsky's favourite painting, perhaps an unexpected choice given his Orthodox faith.

Vyazemsky's house on the Haymarket: a notorious dosshouse on Obukhovsky (now Moskovsky) Prospekt to the south of the Haymarket, Vyazemsky's house was the subject of the author Vsevolod Krestovsky's sensationalist bestseller *The Slums of Petersburg* (1864–6). Krestovsky moved in the same circles as Dostoevsky in the early 1860s, but a rift occurred between them after Dmitry Averkiev, in a review in Dostoevsky's journal *The Epoch*, criticized Krestovsky's novel for its pornographic tendencies and compared the author to the Marquis de Sade.

264 *"read himself crazy"*: from Makar Devushkin's horrified response to his reading of Gogol's 'The Overcoat' in *Poor Folk*, which he takes to be a lampoon of himself, and the 'dreamers' of short stories such as 'White Nights' and 'The Landlady' for whom books are a means of evading real life, reading plays a central role in Dostoevsky's works. In *The Idiot*, the characters' reading informs their response to others, as when Aglaia compares Prince Myshkin to the 'Poor Knight', Pushkin's version of Don Quixote.

267 *Mr Rassudkin... Razumikhin*: although both *rassudok* and *razum*, the roots of these surnames, have similar meanings, they have slightly different connotations: *rassudok* is rationality in the literal sense, while *razum* refers to a higher form of reason. *Vernunft* and *Verstand* are the German equivalents, from which the Russian distinction derives. Luzhin's apparent courtesy notwithstanding, changing Razumikhin's surname to Rassudkin is therefore an implicitly derogatory act that associates the character with the lower form of reason.

275 *schwach*: see note to p. 101.

282 *market*: the Riady arcade, on Nevsky Prospekt.

Lena: one of Dostoevsky's occasional inconsistencies: the younger daughter is named Lida, not Lena, in Part Two of the novel.

287 *Holy Fool*: holy foolishness, or foolishness for Christ's sake (*iurodstvo*), is a form of religious asceticism particularly associated with the Eastern Orthodox Church. Often characterized by true or feigned madness, the outrageous and provocative behaviour of holy fools challenged the norms of society. Prince Myshkin in *The Idiot* is also described as a holy fool.

New Testament... leather binding: based on Dostoevsky's own copy of the New Testament, given to him by wives of the Decembrist revolutionaries in Tobolsk when he was on his way to his sentence of penal servitude in

Omsk, and which he kept with him for the rest of his life. The only book permitted in the prison camp, Dostoevsky marked important passages with his fingernail.

288 *seventh verst*: an allusion to the psychiatric hospital built to the south of the city on the road to Peterhof. The original institution was in fact located 11, rather than 7, versts from the centre of Petersburg.

292 *"Of such is the Kingdom of God"*: a quotation from Mark 10:14.

293 —— *district... offices of the chief criminal investigator*: as distinct from the police stations (see note to p. 85), this could refer to the Kazan district office at 28 Ofitserskaya Street or the Spasskaya district office at 60 Sadovaya Street, on the corner of Bolshaya Podyacheskaya Street.

294 *tout court*: simply (French).

295 *official flat*: the Russian phrase *kazennaia kvartira* has a second, colloquial meaning of prison.

298 *reforms... new titles*: the judicial reforms announced in 1864 aimed to separate the justice system from the civil service, but a lack of new qualified examining magistrates meant that older officials like Porfiry simply continued their jobs under different titles.

300 *mathematical certainty... twice two is four*: in *Notes from Underground*, Dostoevsky's narrator declares that while 'twice two's four is a marvellous thing, [...] twice two is five can also be a very nice little thing'.

     Sebastopol... siege: following the battle of the Alma on 20 September 1854, the defeated Russian troops retreated to Sebastopol, which was then besieged for almost a year by the Allies, with enormous casualties, as depicted in Tolstoy's *Sebastopol Sketches* (1855). Defeat in the Crimean War had a profound effect on Russia and was a major catalyst for reform after Alexander II's accession to the throne.

302 *Austrian Hofkriegsrat... General Mack... all his army*: the *Hofkriegsrat* was the court war council of the Habsburg monarchy. General Karl Mack von Leiberich was the commander who surrendered the entire Austrian army to Napoleon in the battle of Ulm in October 1805, before the latter's victory over the Russian army at Austerlitz in December 1805. General Mack appears briefly in the first volume of *War and Peace*, which was serialized alongside *Crime and Punishment* in the *Russian Messenger*.

320 *Knopp's and the English shop*: Knopp's fancy goods shop was at 14 Nevsky Prospekt, and Nichols and Plincker's English shop was at 16 Nevsky Prospekt.

321 *progressives, or nihilists, or denouncers*: the term 'nihilist' was embraced by the young progressives of Petersburg, following Turgenev's use of the word in 1862 to describe his radical hero Evgeny Bazarov.

322 *Fourier's system and Darwin's theory*: on Fourier, see note to p. 227. Charles Darwin's evolutionary theory was widely discussed in the Russian press in the 1860s, including an article by N. N. Strakhov in the Dostoevsky brothers' journal *Time* (*Vremia*, 1 (1862)). Dostoevsky himself addressed

the social and ethical consequences of Darwinism in articles in *A Writer's Diary*.

323 *new 'commune' somewhere in Meshchanskaya Street*: Chernyshevsky's *What is to be Done?* inspired numerous young people to experiment with communal models of living in Petersburg, particularly in pursuit of women's emancipation. Dmitry Karakozov, a student acting on behalf of a small revolutionary society who made the first attempt on the life of Alexander II in April 1866, was associated with a commune on Srednyaya Meshchanskaya Street, but Dostoevsky's absence from Petersburg from mid-June of that year makes it unlikely that he knew about this at the time of writing.

325 *seed will grow into something real*: the seed bringing new life is a recurring symbol in Dostoevsky's work, notably in his use of the metaphor from John's Gospel 12:24 as the epigraph for *The Karamazov Brothers*: 'Verily, verily, I say unto you, Except a corn of wheat fall into the ground and die, it abideth alone: but if it die, it bringeth forth much fruit.'

Terebyeva... Varents... free marriage: Luzhin's reference to free marriage ('civil marriage' in the original) is euphemistic, as no such legal institution existed in Russia at the time. The cases of Terebyeva and Varents that Lebeziatnikov mentions are similar to the plot of Chernyshevsky's *What is to be Done?*

326 *distinguons*: let us draw a distinction (French).

environment is everything: see note to p. 227.

327 *Dobroliubov... Belinsky*: Nikolay Dobroliubov (1836–61) was a radical literary critic who worked on the journal *The Contemporary*. He was most famous for his highly influential essay on Ivan Goncharov's 1859 novel *Oblomov* ('What is Oblomovitis?'), that defined the hero as a 'superfluous man'. Vissarion Belinsky (1811–48) was the most influential literary critic of the 1830s and 1840s.

hand-kissing question: a further reference to *What is to be Done?*, where the heroine Vera Petrovna rejects the practice as offensive to women. Lebeziatnikov's repeated regurgitation of motifs from Chernyshevsky's novel emphasizes his limited and unoriginal nature.

328 *Raphael or Pushkin, because it's more useful*: an allusion to radical critic Dmitry Pisarev's notorious rejection of art as useless. Bazarov in *Fathers and Sons* states that 'a good chemist's twenty times more useful than a poet'.

330 *grey and rainbow-coloured banknotes*: notes of fifty and one hundred roubles respectively.

333 *grubby expression... Pushkin and his hussars*: a reference to Pushkin's *Eugene Onegin*, chapter 1, verse 12. A poem attributed to the schoolboy Pushkin had been published in *The Contemporary* in 1863, containing the lines, 'But hussars are not to blame | If husbands have long horns'.

335 *advanced consumption... mental faculties*: Maria Isaeva, Dostoevsky's first wife, who suffered from tuberculosis, also experienced psychiatric symptoms towards the end of her life.

kutya: see note to p. 50.

Gostiny Dvor: the merchants' arcade on Nevsky Prospekt.

'Madam Pani Lieutenant': *Pan* and *Pani* are honorific Polish titles corresponding to Sir and Madam, or Mr and Mrs.

343 *home town of T——*: Taganrog, in southern Russia, where Dostoevsky's first wife was born.

344 *daughter of a Court Councillor…almost a colonel's daughter*: Court Councillor is equivalent to Lieutenant Colonel, but Katerina Ivanovna promotes him to Colonel and therefore Collegiate Councillor. See Note on the Table of Ranks, p. xxvi.

345 *Ivanovna or Ludwigovna*: a further confusion of names, Katerina Ivanovna's questioning of the landlady's patronymic implies the impossibility of comparing their fathers' social status or ethnicity, as Ivan is the name of the Russian everyman.

Bürgermeister: Mayor.

349 *Gott der barmherzige!*: Merciful God (German).

354 *the right hand shouldn't know…*: reference to Matthew's Gospel 6:3–4: 'But when thou doest alms, let not thy left hand know what thy right hand doeth: that thine alms may be in secret: and thy Father which seeth in secret himself shall reward thee openly.'

A General Deduction…Piderit's article…Wagner's too, actually: a collection of articles translated from German and French and published in 1866. The German doctor Theodor Piderit's article was titled 'The Brain and its Activity: A Sketch in Physiological Psychology for all Thinking People'. The German economist Adolph Wagner's contribution was 'Necessity in Apparently Voluntary Human Actions from the Statistical Point of View'.

357 *'Pan lajdak!'*: 'The scoundrel!' (Polish).

363 *church tower*: allusion to Christ's second temptation in the wilderness (Matthew 4:5–7).

367 *Toulon…Mont Blanc*: further references to Napoleon's campaigns.

369 *I spent days…all I did was lie there*: Tolstoy, in his essay 'Why do Men Stupefy Themselves?' (1890), identifies the changes that took place in Raskolnikov and led to his crimes as happening while he was lying on his bed thinking quite unrelated thoughts.

372 *bow down…defiled*: the injunction to kiss the earth as an act of atonement is associated with Ivan Shatov in *Devils*, who tells Stavrogin, 'Kiss the earth, bathe it in tears, beg forgiveness!', and in particular, with the Elder Zosima in *The Karamazov Brothers*: 'When you are left on your own, pray. Be ready to throw yourself on the ground and smother it with kisses. Kiss the ground, … Flood the earth with tears of joy, and love those tears.' This type of earth worship is not part of mainstream Orthodoxy, but its emphasis on the sanctity of the *Russian* earth connects it with Dostoevsky's own belief in the 'God-bearing' Russian people.

373 *cypress wood*: the True Cross in the Orthodox tradition was made of cedar, pine, and cypress wood.

375 *"My Little Farmstead"*: the same song sung by the child street performer when Raskolnikov arrives at the tavern where he meets Marmeladov in Part One, Chapter II (see note to p. 18).

   in Paris... logical arguments: an absurd distortion of the work of the pioneering French psychiatrist Jean-Baptiste-Maximien Parchappe de Vinay (1800–60).

381 *"The Hussar leaned on his sword"*: a popular song with words from Konstantin Batiushkov's poem 'Parting' and music by M. Vielgorsky, it is sung by prostitutes in Krestovsky's *The Slums of Petersburg*.

   Malbrouck... reviendra: 'Marlborough has gone to war | Nobody knows when he'll return.' A French ditty loved by Louis XVI and Marie Antoinette that became popular in Russia after the Napoleonic invasion of 1812.

   Cinq sous... notre ménage: 'Five pence, five pence, | For setting up our house.' A song from the melodrama *God's Grace* (Grâce de Dieu) that was part of the repertoire of the French troupe at the Mikhailovsky Theatre in Petersburg from 1842.

382 *Meshchanskaya*: the three Meshchanskaya streets (now Kazanskaya, Grazhdanskaya, and Kaznacheiskaya) crossed Stolyarny Lane, where Raskolnikov lives. According to Dmitry Grigorovich in 'The St Petersburg Organ Grinders', these streets, alongside the Podyacheskaya streets where the moneylender Aliona Ivanovna and the Marmeladovs lived, were traditionally where Italian organ grinders set up home in the city.

384 *glissé, pas-de-basque*: ballet steps.

   Du hast Diamanten... willst du mehr?: 'You have diamonds and pearls... | You have the most beautiful eyes, | Girl, what more could you want?' From a Heinrich Heine poem, with the original 'Mein Liebchen' (my darling) changed to 'Girl'.

   In the noonday... vale of Dagestan: the opening line of Mikhail Lermontov's poem 'The Dream' (1841).

389 *flea market*: see note to p. 101.

392 *political conspirator*: in the face of the failure of the Tsar's programme of reforms, young radicals like Dmitry Karakozov were increasingly beginning to consider terrorism as the only means of instigating change in Russia. The reference is a further example of Dostoevsky's habit of incorporating contemporary events and reports from the press in his works.

396 *Doctor B——n*: Dr Sergei Botkin, court physician and well-known clinician who made significant advances in Russian medical science and education. Dostoevsky consulted him in 1862 and 1865, whilst working on *Crime and Punishment*.

399 *A hundred rabbits... horse*: this supposed English proverb is actually made up.

There's smoke... in the mist: an inexact quotation from Gogol's 'Diary of a Madman'.

400 *umsonst!*: In vain! (German).

401 *schismatic... some starets or other*: on schismatics, see note to p. 6. The Runaways, founded in the eighteenth century, were a radical Old Believer sect whose members sought to flee the secular world they saw as being in the service of the Antichrist. A *starets* or elder is a spiritual mentor within the Orthodox tradition, a venerated holy figure standing outside the Church establishment. The most famous depiction of a *starets* in Russian literature is Zosima in Dostoevsky's *The Karamazov Brothers*.

403 *blood "refreshes"*: an allusion to Proudhon's *La Guerre et la Paix* (see note to p. 231).

thrown himself off a steeple: see note to p. 363.

407 *Midshipman Hole*: Hole (Dyrka) is warrant officer in Gogol's *The Marriage* (1842), here confused with another character from the play, Petukhov.

You can't do without us: in *Notes from Underground*, the narrator's attempts to live without other people prove ironically futile, as he continues to need their affirmation of the fact that he is rejecting them. The concept of dialogue, developed by the theorist Mikhail Bakhtin initially in relation to Dostoevsky's works, posits a mutual interdependence of self and other on the level of language, as every utterance contains either a response to or an anticipation of the other's words. Dostoevsky's characters similarly emerge fully only in their continuing interaction with others, although many—from Goliadkin in *The Double* to Raskolnikov and Ivan Karamazov—desire to separate themselves from this interrelationship and prove their independence of the other.

410 ——*sky Prospekt... crossed*: Obukhovsky Prospekt, in the vicinity of Vyazemsky's house (see note to p. 259).

412 *yellow banknote*: a one-rouble note. The Russian term for a banknote was *kreditnyi bilet*, *kreditka* or *bilet* for short. The colloquial term used here, *zheltyi bilet*, literally 'yellow ticket', is the same term used for the prostitutes' registration card that Sonia carries (see note to p. 13).

414 *like a mask... young for his years*: some of Dostoevsky's most sinister and amoral characters, including Stavrogin in *Devils*, are referred to as having faces like masks. The uncanny effect of Svidrigailov's 'extraordinarily young', 'terribly unattractive' face with its eyes that are 'too blue' suggests something demonic about his character.

415 *Uhlan*: a soldier in a light cavalry regiment.

417 *Schiller*: see note to p. 39.

418 *debtors' prison*: known as Tarasov's house, the debtors' prison was located in the First Company of the Izmailovsky Regiment, no. 3 (now 1st Krasnoarmeiskaya Street). In 1865 Dostoevsky's younger brother Nikolay was incarcerated in the prison for a debt of 120 roubles, which the author paid off, and Dostoevsky himself was threatened with imprisonment for debts whilst working on *Crime and Punishment*.

420 *martyrdom... red-hot pincers*: the voluntary acceptance of suffering is associated in the Orthodox tradition with Sts Boris and Gleb, venerated as martyrs for their non-resistance to evil. A major theme in Dostoevsky's works, while this type of innocent suffering often denotes pure Christian virtue related to humility, it can also appear as an expression of egoism.

black-eyed Parasha: reworks the first line of the 1798 poem 'Parasha' by Enlightenment poet Gavriil Derzhavin (1743–1816), which begins 'Blonde-haired Parash'.

422 *falling sickness*: epilepsy. See also note to p. 67.

425 *la nature et la vérité*: the French philosopher Rousseau's conception of man living in a state of nature and truth acquires a sinister meaning when uttered by Svidrigailov.

Raphael Madonna... religious maniac: see note to p. 259.

427 *Où va-t-elle la vertu se nicher?*: 'Where will virtue find its nest?' (French). According to Voltaire's *Life of Molière*, the French playwright said these words when a beggar to whom he had given a gold coin gave him the money back, assuming it was a mistake.

Assez causé!: see note to p. 148.

429 *America*: in Chernyshevsky's *What is to be Done?* the hero Lopukhov fakes his own suicide and emigrates to America to free the heroine Vera Pavlovna from their marriage of convenience so she can be with Kirsanov, with whom she has fallen in love. Far from being a land of opportunity, America in Dostoevsky's novels gains negative connotations. In *Devils*, Kirillov and Shatov's attempt to make their own way in America results in them being beaten and cheated, while in *The Karamazov Brothers*, escape to America is associated with the evasion of guilt.

430 *Elagin Island*: see note to p. 48.

435 *sacred traditions... these days*: an allusion to Piotr Chaadaev's 'First Philosophical Letter' (1829; published 1836), in which the author states that in Russia, 'No charming memories and no gracious images live in our memory, no forceful lessons in our national tradition.' Chaadaev's letter was banned shortly after publication. The editor of the journal in which it appeared, *The Telescope*, was exiled to Siberia, and Chaadaev was placed under house arrest and declared insane. His critique of Russia became the basis for the debate between the Slavophiles and Westernizers over Russia's past and future in the 1830s and 1840s.

441 *'Vauxhall'*: the Vauxhall pleasure gardens in south London gave their name to similar establishments in Russia, and because the first railway line in Russia extended south from St Petersburg via Tsarskoe selo to Pavlovsk, home of Tsar Paul I's palace and an extensive pleasure garden, the word *vokzal* came to mean 'mainline railway station' in Russian.

443 *Vladimirka*: popular name for the highway leading east from Moscow, part of the Great Siberian Road, and the route commonly taken by convicts and exiles to Siberia.

444 *Vasilievsky... Maly Prospekt*: the flat Svidrigailov visits is very close to Razumikhin's room, where Raskolnikov visited; Svidrigailov's subsequent journey on foot parallels Raskolnikov's walk to the islands before he commits the murder.

445 —— *Prospekt*: Bolshoi Prospekt, the main thoroughfare on the Petersburg (Petrograd) Side.

Adrianople: no such hotel existed, but wooden buildings predominated in the area.

446 *café-chantant*: a type of entertainment establishment, based on a French model, that became popular in St Petersburg and Moscow in the 1860s. The Russian version was more likely to feature magicians, acrobatic displays, and the cancan than singing.

449 *Pentecost Sunday*: celebrated fifty days after Easter, Pentecost is one of the most important festivals in the Orthodox calendar.

450 *boom of a cannon*: a cannon is fired at noon every day in St Petersburg. At any other time, it denotes a flood warning.

Petrovsky Park: the park where Raskolnikov dreamed of the horse being beaten.

453 —— *Street... watchtower stood*: the police house and fire watchtower at the corner of Sezhinskaya Street and Bolshoi Prospekt.

brass Achilles helmet: firefighters' helmets were of a similar design to that worn by Achilles in classical depictions.

459 *crowned... benefactor of the human race*: an allusion to Julius Caesar.

460 *regular siege*: a further allusion to Napoleon and the siege of Toulon.

467 *Not a sight... fairy tale go*: a saying used upon the arrival of an unexpected guest, taken from the folk tales collected and published by Alexander Afanasiev.

468 *Zimmermann's*: see note to p. 5.

Livingstone's journals: the explorer David Livingstone's *Narrative of an Expedition to the Zambesi [sic] and Its Tributaries* (1865) had just been translated into Russian and was due for publication in December 1866, the same month in which the current chapter appeared in the *Russian Messenger*. Reference to it in the summer of 1865 is therefore anachronistic, but is used to indicate the very latest literary sensation.

469 *a man and a citizen*: an allusion to the 'civic poet' and publisher Nikolay Nekrasov (editor of *Petersburg: The Physiology of a City*), but also a general formula used in the nineteenth century that had its origins during Catherine the Great's reign, in a translated work by the German pedagogue Johan Ignaz von Felbiger.

crop-haired girls: female nihilists frequently cut their hair short for practical reasons.

472 *prison*: based on the penal fortress in Omsk where Dostoevsky himself was incarcerated, as the subsequent reference to the River Irtysh makes clear.

472 *second-category exiled convict*: convicts of the second category were sentenced to perform forced labour in a fortress (the first category entailed work in mines, and the third in factories, especially in distilleries and salt production). Dostoevsky was also a second-category convict.

473 *temporary insanity*: a popular theory around Europe in the 1860s, temporary insanity appears frequently in Dostoevsky's fiction as a dubious legal solution that enables questions of motivation to be sidelined.

474 *poor, consumptive ... buried him*: this episode echoes plots from the socially aware 'natural school' literature of the 1840s, including Dostoevsky's *Poor Folk*.

479 *shaved head*: convicts had half their head shaved, enabling easy identification in case of escape.

481 *vagrants*: the large number of vagrants (*brodiagi*) was one result of the Russian policy of colonizing Siberia through exile; they formed a significant proportion of the Russian convict population.

impassable gulf ... different nations: the separation of the peasant convicts from upper-class prisoners is one of the major themes of Dostoevsky's *Memoirs from the House of the Dead* (1861).

Polish political prisoners: a large number of Poles who participated in the armed November uprising against the Russian Empire and subsequent Polish–Russian War (1830–1) served long sentences of hard labour in Siberia.

482 *branded convicts*: the facial branding of convicts, first with hot irons and later with tattooed letters denoting the crimes of which they were convicted, began in the seventeenth century and was abolished in 1863.

483 *unheard-of pestilence ... as though possessed*: Dostoevsky's novel *Devils* depicts contemporary Russian society under the sway of a similar type of demonic possession. The author later reworked the central idea of Raskolnikov's dream in the short story 'The Dream of a Ridiculous Man' (1877).